Bracken was born on an April night in a warm dark burrow deep in the historic system of Duncton Wood, six years after Rebecca. This is the story of their love, and their epic struggle to find it . . .

DUNCTON WOOD

"A MODERN MASTERPIECE . . . Classic themes of conflict are here, good and evil, love and hate, the clash of traditional and modern values."
Houston Chronicle

"A PASSIONATE, LYRICAL, APPEALING TALE . . . Consistently absorbing . . . Enchanting."
Cosmopolitan

(Please turn the page for more rave reviews of
DUNCTON WOOD)

DUNCTON WOOD

A NOVEL
William Horwood

BALLANTINE BOOKS • NEW YORK

For Leslie
with my love

Library of Congress Catalog Card Number: 79-23235

ISBN 0-345-29113-1

This edition published by arrangement with
McGraw-Hill Book Company

Manufactured in the United States of America

First Ballantine Books Edition: February 1981

Acknowledgments

My thanks to the Scottish University Press for permission to quote, and translate into mole language, passages of the graces and invocations in Alexander Carmichael's *Carmina Gadelica;* and to the University of California Press for extracts from Patrick K. Ford's translation *The Poetry of Llywarch Hen.*

The verse on page 385 is by the sixteenth-century poet William Dunbar, quoted in *Medieval English Lyrics,* edited by R. T. Davis, Faber and Faber, London.

Special acknowledgment to the authors of the two standard British works on moles—G. Godfrey and P. Crowcroft, *The Life of the Mole* (Collins, London), and K. Mellanby, *The Mole* (Collins, London)—whose work is as loving as it is scholarly. Each of these authors will know where I have used artistic license, and any exaggerations or errors are entirely my own.

I am grateful to Valerie Gilmore of Oxford and London, to whom I owe much of my knowledge of healing; to Lowri Gwilym, of Trefenter, Wales, for the translations into Welsh; to my father, Chesney Horwood, Emeritus Fellow of St. Catherine's College, Oxford, for help with Middle English; to the Trustees of Wytham Wood near Oxford for permission to carry out research on their land; and to Marjorie Edwards for typing a difficult manuscript.

Special thanks to Sheri Safran, my literary agent, and Beverly Jane Loo, my editor at McGraw-Hill, who between them made the passage from idea to finished book a continued pleasure.

Finally, no words can repay the debt I owe my former wife Janet, whose consistent loyalty and support made the writing so much easier.

CONTENTS

Bracken was born on an April night in a warm dark burrow deep in the historic system of Duncton Wood, six moleyears after Rebecca. This is the story of their love, and their epic struggle to find it.

It is a true story drawn from many sources, and the fact that it can be told at all is as great a miracle as the history it relates. But without one other mole, the Blessed Boswell of Uffington, Bracken and Rebecca would have died the death of legend, their tale declining into the darknesses of time as a simple story of love. It was much more than that, as the records kept by Boswell show, and it is these that form the bulk of the material on which this history is based.

There are other sources, some in the libraries of the Holy Burrows, others hewn in solitary stone or carried still in the legends of each system whose tunnels life made these three moles enter. But these are mere shadows when set against the work of Boswell himself.

But for his love and enterprise there would be no Bracken now. Yet without Bracken, Boswell could never have found his great task.

And without Rebecca there would be nothing at all to tell.

So link their three names together in a blessing on their memory, and on the troubled time in which they had to make their lives. . . .

I

DUNCTON WOOD

1

SEPTEMBER. A great gray storm swept its pelting rain up the pastures of Duncton Hill and then on into the depths of the oaks and beeches of Duncton Wood itself. At first the wind lashed the trees, which swayed and whipped each other in the wet. But then the wind died and solid rain poured down, running in rivulets down the tree trunks and turning the leaf mold of the wood into a sodden carpet, cold and wet.

And the noise! The endless random drumming of the rain drowning every other sound—not a scurrying fox or a scampering rabbit or a scuffling mole could be heard above the noise. Until, when all had found their burrow, the wood was as still in the endless eternal rain as a lost and forgotten tunnel.

All the moles but one were deep in the ground, hiding themselves from the wet and noise: safe and sound in the warmth of their dark burrows.

Only solitary Bracken stayed out, crouching up on top of the hill among the great beeches that had swayed in the wind and at the coming of the rain and now stood in sullen surrender to it, dripping and gray.

He had left the fighting and the talons of the tunnels far behind below the hill and found himself now in the shadow of the great Stone, the curious isolated standing stone that stood silent and huge at the highest point of the wood. It was tens of millions of years old and it looked its age—hard, gnarled and gray. There were others like it scattered across the Downs of southern England, remnants of the mass that once covered all the chalk. As heartstones of the old mass they retained its rhythm, and this gave them a life and mystery that every creature sensed. Until some, like the moles, learned to turn to them at times of thanksgiving or wonder, suffering or pain. Or change, as Bracken did now.

He had been there since the early afternoon when the shifting September sky, now blue and clear, now white and cloudy, had given way to the deep mauve-grays of stormclouds. He had crouched enthralled, sensing the rain lash the country far away in great sweeps of wet, and in

3

awe of the white lightning whose bright flashes his eyes only dimly saw, and the strong shakings of the thunder that entered his body. He felt the storm coming closer and closer, looming toward and above him, and then finally all around, the wind ruffling his fur before the rain turned it shiny black.

Now he was absolutely lost in it, his paws seeming part of the ancient ground on which they rested, his fur seeming the sky itself, his face the wind and rain. Bracken was lost, no longer conscious of what he thought he was. Not a mole, but a part of everything. As the rain beat down upon him it finally washed away a hopeless desire he had long struggled with—to be a mole like so many of the others with talons flashing, fighting, rough and tough and eating worms with a hungry crunch.

When he laughed they didn't laugh, but in the rain it no longer mattered. When he lay still as surface roots they fought and strove, and as the rain ran off his shining black fur into the leaves, he knew it would always be like that. When he made for a shaft of sun among the fern they pointed, nervous, to the owl heights above, and always would. He had lived three moleyears alone and in silence struggling with his desire to run down and back to try to start again with them, but now that desire was being washed away forever in a storm. There was no mole, not in the Duncton system at least or that he knew of, to share his love of the sun and his hatred of talons.

Above him the Stone was running with rain, leaning away from the beech tree whose roots entwined its base, toward the farthest hills and vales his weak eyes could never see. Toward the west where Uffington lay. But he could feel the world beyond like sun upon his face and it was greater, far greater, than the system in which he was born and which, in a storm, he now shed.

He crouched surrendered like this for a long time before he became even dimly aware that another mole was near him, watching him from a clump of green sanicle. He didn't move; he wasn't afraid. Indeed, after he realized that somemole was there, he started thinking of something different—how strange it was that as evening fell the sky grew lighter. Perhaps it had something to do with the softening rhythm of the rain. . . .

He was right, for high above the hill the swirling masses of the stormclouds gave way to cliffs of whiter cloud and the rain's noise became a patter as the irregular drip of individual droplets from the trees that surrounded the clearing around the Stone could be heard once more.

Then, as the mantle of rain dropped from him, he turned to face the watching mole with no fear and little interest. The mole was a little older than he, and a female. From the great distance he felt himself to be in, he sensed rather than watched her, feeling her to be perplexed, anxious, lost. To his surprise he sensed no aggression at all toward him, none whatsoever, though she was as big as he was. Almost an adult, but not quite. Finally she came forward into the open by the Stone.

"I'm lost. How do I get back into the system?" she asked. He didn't answer immediately, so she added, "I'm a Duncton mole, you know."

He knew all right; he could tell by the way she was, the woody scent. His silence was not suspicion, as she seemed to think, but pleasant surprise—no mole had ever asked him a favor like this in the days when he had lived in the main system.

"It's easy," he said. "very easy." She seemed happy at this, relaxing in his calm as she rubbed her head with one of her paws and waited. Suddenly he scurried past her down the hill, by a track she had crossed a dozen times in her journey up the hill: one of the ancient forgotten tracks up to the Stone.

"Come on," he called. "I'll show you." They twisted and turned down the wet track, the great evening clouds swirling between the treetops high above, while the wet fronds of the undergrowth tumbled rainwater on their fur. He darted this way and that, down and down the hill, until she was quite out of breath following him. Suddenly, by a fallen oak branch, he stopped at an entrance she knew, dark, warm and inviting.

"There you are," he said. "I told you it was easy. You know where you are now, don't you?" Yes, yes she did and she nodded, but she was thinking of him, looking right into him it seemed. He remembered no other mole ever looking at him like this: curious, compassionate, friendly. Suddenly she came forward and touched him with her paw, or rather caressed him on his shoulder, for a second that he remembered a lifetime.

"What's your name?" she asked.

"I'm Bracken," he said after a moment, and then sud-

denly turned and scurried off up the track and into the
evening light. And light dawned on her. She gasped and
reached out after him and started to run back the way he
had gone. Bracken! So he was Bracken! So hunched, so
small, so defenseless. "I'm Rebecca," she called. "My
name is Rebecca." But he was gone long before the words
were out. Then she stopped and turned back to the tunnel he had led her to and ran with relief back into the
depths of the main system.

At the spot by the entrance to the tunnel where she
had touched him so briefly the air was very still and quiet,
with just the drip, drip, drip of the last of the rain from
the trees, while far away the heart of the storm moved on
across country, leaving Duncton Wood to the silence of
the evening and its higher deserted part to the silence of
the Stone.

⤙ 2 ⤚

THE entrance down which Rebecca ran so thankfully was the highest of those leading into the main Duncton system. Above it the wood narrowed to the summit of the hill, flanked on one side, the southeast, by the steep, rough face of the chalk escarpment and to the west by rolling pastures that fell gently away to clay vales in the distance.

Up there the chalk reached nearly to the surface of the ground, yielding only a thin, worm-scarce soil, but supporting tall gray beech trees whose fall of leaves formed a dry, brown rustling carpet in the wood. The roots of the trees twisted like torn flank muscles among the leaves, while here and there a patch of shiny chalk reflected the sky.

There was always a windsound there, if only just a murmur among the leaves. But sometimes the strong gray branches of the trees whipped and cut the wind into whines and whispers; or a tearing screech of winter gales raced headlong up from the slopes below, exploding into the trees on top of the hill before rushing on over the sheer scarp face, carrying a last falling leaf or tumbling a dry and broken twig out and down to the chalkfall below.

This highest and most desolate part of Duncton Wood is also the most venerable, for beneath its rustling surface is the site of the ancient mole system of Duncton, long deserted and lost.

Here too stands the great Stone, at the highest point of the hill where the beeches thin out, bare to all the winds —north, south, east and west. And from here a mole might see, or rather might sense, the stretching triangle of Duncton Wood, spreading out below to the escarpment to the east, the pastures to the west, with the marsh, where no mole goes, beyond the northern end.

At the time Bracken and Rebecca first met, and for many generations before, the system lay on the lower slopes of the hill where the wood was wide and rich. There the beeches gave way to oaks and ashes and thick fern banks, and pockets of sun in the summer. Down there, birds sang or flittered, while badgers padded and barked

7

at night. Down there, life ran rich and good with a worm-full soil black with mold, moist with change. There the wind was slowed and softened by the trees.

No mole, not a solitary one, lived now up in the Ancient System. Slowly they had migrated down from the desolate heights, rolling down through the generations as a pink mole pup rolls blindly down a slope too steep for its grip. First its stomach rolling over its weak front paws, then its soft talons scrabbling uselessly at the soil, then its rump and back paws arching over, until at last it lies still again. So, bit by bit, the generations had come down to the lower system where the wood lay rich and welcoming. They migrated still, but only from one side of the wood to the other, as each new generation left its home burrows in the middle of summer to make burrows for itself or reoccupy deserted ones.

In Bracken's time the strongest group in the system were the westsiders, whose burrows flanked the edge of the wood next to the pastures. The soil there was rich and much desired, so only the toughest moles could win a place and defend it. With the dangerous pasture moles nearby as well, westsiders needed an extra measure of aggression to survive. Naturally they tended to be big and physical, inclined to attack a stranger first and ask questions after. They laughed at physical weakness and worried if their youngsters didn't fight the moment they were weaned. Gentler moles like Bracken, whose father, Burrhead, was one of the strongest of the westsider males, had a tough time of it. They were ridiculed and bullied for not wanting to fight and only the most wily learned quickly enough that to survive they needed to be masters of compromise, cajolery and the art of disappearance at times of trouble.

Eastsiders were less aggressive. They lived on a drier, harder soil, which made for fewer of them. They were small and stocky and superb burrowers. Independent, not to say eccentric, eastsiders were rarely seen and hard to find, for their tunnels spread far in their worm-poor soil. Their territory was bounded to the east by the steep drop of the chalk scarp and to the south by the rising slopes of the hill.

Northward lay the marsh, where the air hung heavy and damp with strange rush grasses clicking scarily above a mole's head. Although the Duncton moles called it marsh, it was in fact a range of poorly drained fields, permanently wet from the two streams that started near the edge of the wood where clay overlay the tilted chalk. Because the marsh was always waterlogged, it couldn't be burrowed, which made it dangerous ground for moles. The smell was wrong, the vegetation different, the noises of birds and other creatures strange and terrifying. The marsh assumed vast proportions in their minds, a place of dark, dank danger never to go near.

The northern stretch of the wood next to it was called the Marsh End and the moles who lived there—the marsh-enders—were feared and reviled, as if they carried a curse from the dangerous place they lived so near. They were felt to be a treacherous lot, known to attack outsiders in twos or threes, something the westsiders would never do. They were unhealthy, too, for if disease came to the system, it always seemed to start in the Marsh End. Their females were coarse and mocking, inclined to spur on their mates with encouraging shouts or mock them the moment they suffered defeat, switching their loyalties at the fall of a talon.

No one group lived on the slopes above the main system below the top of the hill. Just a few older, hardy moles, who liked to tell stories of the old days and who eked out a scraggy living in the poorer chalky soil there. Many went mateless in the spring, and few pup cries were heard there in the April weeks.

No mole knew the whole system—it was too large—but all knew and loved its center: Barrow Vale. Here the elder burrows lay, and in early spring white anemones glistened between the trees before the bluebell carpet came, mirroring a clear spring sky.

At Barrow Vale a pocket of gravelly soil caused the oaks to thin out, creating a natural open space warmed by the sun in summer, white and silent in the snow of deep winter, always the last place of light in the wood at nightfall. Being worm-scarce because of the poor soil, its tunnels were communal and everymole went there without fear. It was a place of gossip and chatter, where young moles met to play and venture out, often for their first time, onto the surface. It was relatively safe from predators, too, for the tunnels that radiated from it to all parts of the system made for early warning of an approaching danger long before it arrived.

As for owls, the most fearsome enemies of the moles, they rarely came there, preferring the wood's edge where they could wait in the trees and dive down on their prey clear of the branches. So, for a Duncton mole, Barrow Vale was a place of security to go back to from time to time.

Yet it had also become something of a trap as well. For long, long before when the system had been smaller, up on top of the hill, with the Stone as the natural center, the lie of the land made them outward-looking, seeking new places, eager to follow their snouts into the distance. But lower Duncton Wood was worm-rich and safe, so it was foolishness to want to go outside it.

Inevitably there were dark stories of those who had tried and always, so it seemed, met a terrible end. Some had actually been seen to be torn in the talons of an owl almost the moment they set paw onto the pastures; some had died of sadness, others had suffocated in the mud of the marsh.

But generally, few moles concerned themselves with these places or such fears: they kept their snouts clean, fought for their own patch, found and ate their worms, slept in their dark burrows, and pulled themselves through the long moleyears of winter until, blinking but aggressive, they came out in spring for the mating time.

Each full moon represented the passing of another moleyear with the Longest Day at Midsummer the happiest time and the Longest Night—at the end of the third week of December—the darkest and most treacherous: a time to placate the Stone with prayers and to celebrate the safe passage into the start of the new cycle of seasons in the snug safety of a warm home burrow. A time to tell stories of fights gone by, and worms and mates to come. A time to survive.

A place to survive! By the time Rebecca and Bracken were born, that was all the once-proud Duncton system had become. Its pride was all in the past when, setting out from the shadow of the great Stone, many a young adult male ventured forth from Duncton Wood carrying its name far off to other systems. Inspired by the talk of scribemoles, many of them headed for the Holy Burrows of Uffington, others simply wanted to show that they could live for a while alone, or in other systems, and then come back with their experience and wisdom to

their home system. And how exciting it was when one
returned! Word would go round the chalky tunnels of the
Ancient System and many would gather about him and
give him worms for encouragement as he told his stories.
Of fights and strange places and different .customs. A
very few were able to tell how at Uffington they had had
the honor to see, perhaps even to touch, one of the legendary White Moles said to live there.

But that was past. Even the oldest mole in the
system, Hulver the elder, could not remember a time when
a mole had left the system and returned, or a time
when the system had been visited by a friendly mole.
Hulver himself rarely talked of the past—he tried but
had found that the ears of the new generations seemed
increasingly deaf and he had given up. He preferred to
mutter and sing to himself, picking out his hard life as one
of the isolated moles who lived in the worm-poor slopes
below the hilltop.

Once in a while he would talk, though, and the moles
around would listen out of respect for his age (or rather
for his ability to survive). Indeed, after the last elder
meeting before the Longest Night preceding Bracken's
birth, when everymole was in a mellow mood, he had
told a group of chattering moles in Barrow Vale: "I can
remember my father telling me that the system used to be
visited each Midsummer year by a scribe from the Holy
Burrows" (and old Hulver inclined his head to the west
where Uffington lay). "He would crouch with the elders
by the Great Stone, for that was the center of things then,
and question them about the state of the system.

"But even when I was young, it was a long time since a
scribemole had been. They said then, and I believe it
now, that something happened to stop the scribes coming
and that no scribe could ever come again. If I had known
that to be so when I was young—when I was *your* age,"
he added, looking especially at the younger moles about
him, "I think I would have gone forth as my father's father did, even if it meant that, like him, I never came
back." But Hulver was old and they dismissed this last
comment as old age talking, a foolish dream that may
have crossed each of their minds at one time or another,
but which none with sense should listen to.

Yet Hulver was right; something had happened. The
system, the Ancient System of Duncton—a system whose

glorious past was written up by the scribes in some of the most venerable histories in Uffington—had been cut off.

It was isolated, anyway, by the sheer chalk escarpment, and the marsh to the north. And then, in Hulver's grandfather's time, the road that had always been a hazard far off to the north and west had been developed so that it was uncrossable for moles, or hedgehogs or almost any creature.

Scribemoles charged with the fearful task of visiting Duncton had tried and failed. Some were killed on the road by what the moles who lived near it called "the roaring owls," some never had the courage, or the faith, to venture onto it at all.

So Duncton had been left unvisited, safe enough in its isolation but declining in spirit through the years for want of the kind of stimulus new moles, especially scribes, could give. Many of its traditions died, only the most important, like the trek of the elders to the Stone at Midsummer—and on the Longest Night—surviving. Its legends and stories were passed down but in an increasingly romantic or simple form, for few of the new moles had the love of language or spiritual strength that taletellers of the Ancient System had had.

Yet had they been able to know what was happening in other systems, the Duncton moles might have drawn a small consolation from the fact that their own decline merely echoed a decline in the spirit and energy of moles in general. Even the scribes were not quite what they were, for in the past a scribe *would* have made his way to Duncton Wood, reveling in the trial to his soul that the new dangers created; and once there he would have left no doubt about what he thought of the fat, sleek, complacent mole the Duncton mole seemed often to have become.

But would the Duncton moles have cared? Certainly most of the seven elders of Bracken's youth would have been unimpressed by a scribe's comments, for they were of the new breed, born with the inward-looking attitude of the lower system. Elders like his own father, Burrhead, for example, simply would not have understood a scribe-mole's comments about the lack of spirit at Duncton: "Haven't we got worms, don't we defend the system, aren't there plenty of youngsters coming out?" That's what he would have said.

Rune was another elder, originally from the westside as well, though to be near the center of things he had moved his burrow nearer to Barrow Vale. He was a menacing mole who wove warning into his words, which were usually as dark and dank as the Marsh End soil. What he lacked in terms of Burrhead's size and muscle he more than made up for in cunning and deviousness. His ear was tuned to disaster, for he knew when the bad weather was coming or when a tree might fall. He knew when the owls were hungry (and was capable then of leading his opponents to a place where they might become owlprey) or where disease might be found.

He was always the clever one, was Rune, always so clever. But you didn't stay long with him without sadness creeping into you and a desire for clean air in your fur. You didn't meddle with Rune either, because a terrible thing would happen to moles who did: they seemed to die.

His voice was cold as ice, dry as dead bark and covered with the red velvet of a dangerous sky. No mole liked to fight him, no mole ever came forward who ever saw him kill. Yet each mating time he would kill for a mate, luring his rival somewhere dark and treacherous. Rune was a shadow on life, and much feared.

"He's the clever one, he is," moles were inclined to whisper about him. "He'll know when his opportunity comes. He'll take over the system one day with his cunning ways and warning words."

Two elders came from the south of the system, Mekkins and Dogwood. Mekkins was the nearest the system ever got to having a marshender as an elder, for his mother was from there, though he was raised in the neutral territory south of Barrow Vale. He spoke in the quick snouty way marshenders used, and enjoyed combining direct talk with a mocking turn of phrase.

"Yer not going to tell me yer serious about that daft idea, Burrhead me old lad?" he'd say to one of the westsider's more ponderous ideas. "You'll not get anymole *I* know ter go along with it. I'll tell you that right now."

His contacts with the marshenders made him a useful elder, while his contacts with the other elders made him useful to the marshenders. He was tough and quick, and likely to flare up for no reason at all, as it seemed to the victims of his temper. Dogwood, the other elder from the

south, was his close friend and, as close friends often are,
a complete contrast. He was plump and perennially
cheerful. He had the reputation, envied throughout the
system, of being the best wormfinder in Duncton Wood.
"He'd find a worm in a snowflake if he had to" was how
Mekkins once put it.

The oldest of the elders was Hulver, who had seen six
Longest Nights through—six!—and it made many a
Duncton mole gasp to think of it. But he was old now,
very old, and had not mated last spring. But he was still
cheerful and sprightly, with a way of laughing at the end
of a sentence that made a mole think that nothing he said
was more than a joke. But wiser moles knew better, and
listened well to what he had to say. In his lifetime he had
seen the system decline and had often said so. He was
one of the few who remembered the old rituals and sayings and he talked of the Stone as if it were a friend at
his flank.

"The less that he do say, the more then he do mean,"
his confidant, colleague, fellow elder and hearty protago-
nist, Bindle, was fond of saying. Bindle himself had seen
four Longest Nights through and though he fought little
and was one of the eccentrics who lived over on the poor
eastside near the chalk escarpment, he was never short of
a mate.

He and Hulver would often meet and chatter in the
wood, old moletalk about worms and past summers, and
mates and litters the like of which you never see today.
No, sir! The females just aren't what they used to be!

Between them, Hulver and Bindle had taken over the
duties of conducting the rituals, principally the two treks
up to the Stone at Midsummer and Longest Night. Only
Hulver knew all the rituals, and he worried that no other
mole knew them as he did. But somehow, Bindle himself
never wanted to learn them, not the important parts, the
parts that mattered. And the truth was that Hulver didn't
want to teach them to him. For to speak the rituals you
had to know that power of life was in the Stone, and outside it, too. And you had to see that an acorn, a worm,
an anemone in Barrow Vale, and even a swooping owl
were finally the same, and that a mole's strivings were
nothing but the crack of an acorn husk in a deserted
wood.

Hulver tried to explain to Bindle, but the words

couldn't come right: and Bindle, who loved old Hulver as if he were his own father, could only smile and nod as he tried to explain, and wish he could please his old friend by understanding. But both knew he did not.

So there they were, six out of the seven elders; Burrhead, Rune, Mekkins, Dogwood, Bindle and Hulver. An unimpressive bunch when set against the elders of the past who had fought and bred in pride when the system was on top of the hill in every sense of the word. None of them, with the exception perhaps of gentle Hulver, remains even a whisper in the tunnels of memory.

But there was one more, the seventh. A mole whose shadow had the smell of evil, whose very name still seems a curse on the mole who utters it.

Many a mother has tried to still the tongues of youngster moles who ask in an excited, unknowing whisper "Who was Mandrake? Tell us about *him!*" Many a father has cuffed a son as he pretended to be "as strong as Mandrake was." They felt his name was better left unsaid, his memory much better scratched with talons from the recesses of the mind.

But that is not the way to fight evil. Let its name be called. Let the fire of the sun do battle with its form until it lies dried out ond colorless in the evening shade; no more than a dead beetle's wing to be carried off on the midnight wind.

But there *are* books in Uffington that tell his tale and this must do the same. For he is the shadow against which the light of the love of Bracken and Rebecca should be set. But let compassion and burning love be in the heart of any that thinks, or speaks, or dreams or reads the name of Mandrake.

৵§ 3 §৵

HE came to the system over the open fields, unopposed by owl or pasture mole, a thunderstorm that rained down blood. He cast his shadow on the wood long before he reached it, for the adult males shuddered and shook in advance of his coming, gathering first at Barrow Vale and then going in twos and threes down the tunnels to the westside, where the pastures are.

They saw him in the setting sun one spring evening, his silhouette growing bigger and more threatening as the sun set. They scuffed and stamped in the tunnels, running this way and that, crying out in fear and upset, half attacking each other before turning to face a mole whose very size made their muscles grow weak.

Saying nothing, he slowly advanced on them all, his great head hunched forward, his snout like a huge talon, his shoulders like yew trunks.

The first that came to him he hardly seemed to touch, yet down he fell, not only dead but torn to death; the second died of a talon thrust so powerful that it seemed to start at his snout and end at his tail; the third turned to run even before he attacked, but too late. A mighty lunge from Mandrake caught him too, and he lay screaming, his black fur savaged open, red blood glistening. And as Mandrake passed by, he coldly crushed his snout and left him there arced out in a bloody, searing, ruthless death. Then they backed before him this way and that, chattering in fear, running away, taking to surface routes in their fright.

So Mandrake entered the Duncton westside, resistance by the toughest moles in the system crushed, and made straight for Barrow Vale. There, he roared and smote the walls so that all the system would know from the shuddering vibrations that he had come. "My name is Mandrake," he roared, "Mandrake! Let anymole that opposes me come forward now." But the three bravest were dead and not one single mole more stirred. Then he cried out in a strange, harsh tongue, the language of Siabod, which lay far to the northwest and was a system of which no Duncton mole had ever even heard at that time.

"Mandrake Siabod wyf i, a wynebodd Arthur Helgi Cwmoerddrws a'i anwybyddu. Wynebais Gerrig Castell y Gwynt a'u gwatwar. Ga dewch i unrhyw wadd a feddylio nad yw'n f'ofni wynebu'm crafangau nawr." Whatever it meant its intent was clear. It was a threat, and one no Duncton mole dared answer.

He had come at mating time, a full cycle of seasons before Rebecca's maturing and Bracken's birth, and he traveled to all parts of the system killing male after male to take their females. Even the males that refused to fight, or tried to run clear, he killed. Fighting is one thing, killing another, and no mating time in Duncton was ever so overcast as that. And when it was over and the warmer days of May came on, he brooded here and there —now over to the westside, now down to the Marsh End. He said barely a word throughout this terrible time, a brooding, silent curse upon anymole whose territory he moved into. Many were the empty burrows that he found, still warm from the moles who had left in haste to avoid facing him. Only mothers with young remained, watching terrified as he stared at them from a burrow entrance, his head massive and his eyes as black as night, staring at their children. But these, at least, he didn't harm.

He became an elder without asking or being asked, after killing an elder in a mating fight and taking his place.

He said nothing at the first elder meeting he attended, merely staring at the others, who conducted the business in a hurried hush with furtive glances in his direction. Only two males showed any reaction other than fear at the meeting: Hulver greeted him formally and then ignored him, refusing to be hurried or harried by the others into doing *his* part of the business any faster, while Rune, ever conscious of where he might find advancement, made ingratiating comments like "We would all agree that it would be a privilege if he that is new, and welcome, among us might give us his view." To which Mandrake said absolutely nothing.

In May he attended his second elder meeting, again saying not a word. But at his third, in June, when plans for the Midsummer trek to the Stone were being debated, he made his first move.

There were now grave doubts among some of the younger elders as to whether the Midsummer trek was

worthwhile; Burrhead, in particular, argued that the
known presence of more owls up on the hill, combined
with the scarcity of worms that year and the many
changes that had come over the system (they all knew
that he was referring to the many deaths that had overtaken them following Mandrake's arrival) were all factors
that made the Midsummer trek of doubtful value. Rune
agreed, adding that the trek was merely a sentimental
throwback to the past when "aims were different than
they are now and there was a greater need to keep the
system together by a show of unity such as the trek represented."

"We've grown beyond that now, and many of us," and
Rune glanced slowly round at them all in turn, his dark
gaze settling finally on Hulver, "no longer accept the kind
of invocations and nonsense that the Midsummer ritual
involved."

This was too much for old Hulver, who found that a
combination of anger and fear ran through him as he
listened to Rune's words: "I am the oldest here," he
started, sensing immediately that it was just the wrong
thing to say, "and I tell you that our ancestors would
shudder if they thought that the Midsummer trek, the
happiest celebration in the system, was talked of as a
sentimental tradition. It is a part of the system, a celebration of the fact that, individually, we are nothing"—and
he looked at all of them in turn as Rune had done, including Mandrake, who sat brooding at the end of the
burrow—"but that we acknowledge in the Stone the
presence of something beside which we may feel we are
nothing but without which, I tell you all, we truly are
nothing, however strong we may think we are."

His words, especially the last ones, hung ominously
over the meeting for a while as everymole there expected
Mandrake to react to them. But he stayed still, listening.
Then Hulver came forward into the center of the burrow
so that he was in their midst, his aging, wrinkled snout
and graying fur contrasting with the younger, glossy fur
all about him. "Something has happened in our system,"
he said quietly, "something more difficult to fight than
owls, or wormless soil, or a gang of pasture moles. I wish
I had the words to explain to those who do not understand how bold and true Duncton moles once were. They
were warriors, not fighters; believers, not arguers. And

that is how they still could be and how, deep down and with the right leadership from us elders, they still are."

He paused for a moment, sensing that of them all only Bindle was truly listening and even he, for all his love, could not understand.

His snout wearily touched the burrow floor for a moment, despair seeping through his body, for he had not the strength or the words to say what he meant. He wanted to wrench out the feeling that was so strong in his heart and show it to them and say "Look, *now* can you see it, now can you see what we must do?"

But he could only wish he could conjure up before these young tradition-killing moles what it was once *like,* when fighting and worms and territory weren't everything. But finally all he had strength to say, and then really only to himself, was "We must go on the Midsummer trek to the Stone and speak the ritual as our fathers have, as their fathers did, as we always have. This is not a thing to talk about but do!" Then, looking at each in turn, an upright pride replacing the despair in his stance, he added: "Let anymole who doubts my word go up to the Stone now and crouch in its shadow and feel its strength. Feel, as you crouch there, that far beyond this stricken system, as I believe it has now become, there are other systems—wiser and better than ours. Feel, if you have the strength to do so that . . ."

But not a single elder, including Bindle, was listening any more, for as Hulver spoke these words Mandrake stirred; as Hulver's wise old voice carried the pride of his challenge to go to the Stone, the massive form of Mandrake loomed forward and up, until it seemed to hover above old Hulver like an owl above its prey. Each mole there crouched in frozen fear, snouts still and almost senseless, for they felt the power of Mandrake like owls' talons on them. Each seemed to feel an anger and terrible rage emanating from him directed at them personally. Hulver stopped in midsentence and looked round, then up at Mandrake. And Hulver backed away, his words seeming suddenly nothing but dry beech leaves in the wind. "There will be no trek to the Stone," said Mandrake in a voice they were to get used to as time went on, a voice that made a mole absolutely certain that what it said would be *would be.* A voice that shriveled opposition in the bud. A voice whose impulse seemed evil itself.

"No mole will go, not one. If any try, I shall crush them against the Stone itself. Their blood will dry on the Stone as a warning to any others who might try, in their foolishness, to do what some of you already realize has no purpose. The Midsummer trek will not be." Then he raised his talons massively above old Hulver as if about to strike him dead. The silence in the elder burrow at that moment was broken only by a gasp of horror from Bindle, while Rune gazed with pleasure at the scene.

But Mandrake only spread his poised talons wide in what suddenly seemed to be a blessing on them all, a friendly gesture, and he chuckled deeply as if the whole thing were but a minor difference between friends. "Come now, Hulver," he said, his talons resting hugely for a moment on the old mole's shoulder, "let us not argue any more. All here respect you, most of all myself. But times change and traditions must go, and I think all of us but you now agree that the Midsummer trek should be held no more, for good and honorable reasons."

He looked round at them all and they nodded, though it would have been a brave mole indeed who shook his head at that moment. "Good! Then let us talk of this no more and proceed to other things." With that the argument was over and the other elders sighed with relief. Some even laughed or chuckled as Mandrake had done, so great was their sense of release.

Hulver returned to his place next to Rune, muttering and miserable, the only one there without a smile in his voice. No younger mole was going to jolly *him* into accepting something he disagreed with and which seemed like a death in the system. But he had no more strength to argue. Bindle, too, was unhappy, but not so much because of the loss of the Midsummer trek as that, in some way, he felt he had let his friend down. "Times change," he kept saying to himself, but his eyes stayed clear of Hulver's. The others chattered, carried along by Mandrake's dark will and their own weakness, and phrases like "Of course he's right" and "The soil *is* very worm-scarce, as Burrhead says" and "The trek was always a bore, anyway" filled the burrow. Even Bindle began to think this, adding as his own particular justification "If we are going to build up the system we've got to create *new* rituals, haven't we?"

Of them all only one, Rune, saw Mandrake's intervention for what it truly was: a demonstration of power rather than persuasion. He welcomed it, for here at last was a mole strong enough to bring the kind of trouble to the system that he would need himself to gain the power he had always wanted. Rune knew that what they had just seen was the end of Hulver as a force in the system, and it was done without a talon scratch. As the other elders chattered together in their relief that the crisis seemed over, Rune took his opportunity to leave his place next to Hulver, where, many meetings ago, he had stationed himself, and crouched down next to Mandrake, in whose shadow he now began to thrive; an evil coupling of moles whose power and ruthlessness now began to spread through the system like black ivy on a dying elm.

So Mandrake came to power in the system. By the time Bracken was born the following spring, his power was absolute and unquestioned. Inevitably other, weaker moles clustered to his support, enjoying the prestige and power that allegiance to him gave. Moles like Burrhead, who under a strong, true leader might have been a force for good, now became one of Mandrake's toughest hench-moles. His dominance on the westside made him especially useful to Mandrake, who flattered him with words, asked his advice (or seemed to) and even visited him in his burrow; Dogwood willingly gave his support, too, telling Mekkins pragmatically, "If you can't beat 'em, join 'em."

Bindle never became a Mandrake henchmole but slipped away from the elder burrow and relinquished his rights as an elder, deliberately making his peace with Mandrake so that he would be left alone. "I'm getting old now," he told Mandrake, "and you need younger moles as elders these days." Bindle went back to the eastside and kept out of everymole's way. He felt ashamed and had neither the courage nor the heart to go and see his friend Hulver. So it was through weakness that Mandrake's evil spread, souring even the love between two old and harmless moles.

As for Hulver, Mandrake let him live. He may have lost power at the June elder meeting, but Mandrake knew that many still loved and respected him and there was no virtue in killing him yet. Better to wait and choose a time when Hulver's death would be seen as a natural end to the Ancient System and its ways, whose end seemed to be Mandrake's main intent. They even let Hulver say the Midsummer Blessing that June, though he said it alone, for no other mole joined him—except Rune, who watched secretly from the shadows.

Rune stayed outside the Stone clearing—being too near the Stone disturbed him—but near enough to watch Hulver, solitary and old, go through the ancient celebration of Midsummer Night. He whispered its magic words for the Stone to hear, raising his paws so that the strength of the Stone could come into him for another year.

A soft wind ran among the trees, shaking the beech leaves so that their shiniest side caught the moon's light like rippling water in the sky. The moon shone, too, on Hulver's fur, which seemed new and smooth in the light. But where Rune crouched in the twisting crook of a huge gray beech-tree root that ran like a thick snake into the chalk soil, there was thick, black shadow, which only thickened when he stirred. His talons dug into the beech root as he watched Hulver, for he itched to kill him there and then.

Somewhere in the moonlit trees high above them, a tawny owl called, and Rune shivered. But Hulver, safe in the circle of trees around the Stone, seemed not to notice and carried on his chant. Midnight passed as Hulver raised his paws in a final supplication to the Stone, saying with happiness the last words of the Midsummer ritual.

He was relieved that for another twelve moleyears, at least, its words had been spoken.

But Hulver had not quite finished. He turned from the Stone and faced the west toward the Holy Burrows of Uffington. He might never go there himself, he might never have had the courage to try, but he hoped his prayers might reach that holy place. So now, with the Stone behind him to give him strength, he added a final petitionary prayer to the ritual, whispering it urgently into the night over the tops of the westside trees and out over the pastures beyond: "Send us a scribe," he prayed, "for somewhere in this lost system he will find moles who will honor him. So send us a scribe, for now we need one. Send us the strength to fight this Mandrake and Rune, whose evil I fear."

Rune heard the prayer, and also heard the owl calling again, uncertain if it was the prayer or the owl that upset him. He wished again that he could kill Hulver, sensing that he was in some way more dangerous to them than he or Mandrake realized.

Still, prayer or no, Mandrake extended his power by threats, intimidation and, occasionally, by exercises in black charm. Even the independent eastsiders fell easily under his spell, for none of them—including Bindle—gave him any trouble.

Occasionally he would provoke a fight somewhere and savagely kill his opponent as a reminder of what he was capable of. More often he would encourage henchmoles to kill each other, watching the slaughter with ghastly satisfaction.

So, by the time Bracken was born, Mandrake's power was total, and every new young Duncton mole soon shuddered at his name and knew that no mole was more powerful. In Bracken's case rather more than most, since his father, Burrhead, was one of Mandrake's most important henchmoles.

Yet Rebecca had far more to fear than Bracken, far more. For Mandrake was her father.

4

THE system under Mandrake changed as a wood changes when dirty fog invades it; the trees are still there, the flowers still have color, but everything looks different and *feels* sinister.

So it was in Duncton Wood. The westsiders still fought and struggled in the usual way; the young moles went to Barrow Vale to go onto the surface as they always had; Dogwood carried on finding worms where no other mole could; owl talons still cut through the evening air to kill the careless young and weakening old; and the wood itself still swayed and stilled to the passing of the days.

But under Mandrake's thrall, the tunnels seemed darker and burrows far less safe. Males felt threatened even in their own home burrows, while the females became dissatisfied and bitchy, wondering what mole it was that could so terrify their mates. Moles had to watch what they said, too, because Mandrake's henchmoles seemed everywhere. Sadly, the one way of getting any security and the freedom to travel in the system was to do what Rune and Burrhead had been the first to do—declare yourself a supporter of Mandrake and do his bidding.

Not that his bidding was very specific, which was one reason there was so much doubt and suspicion in the system, even among the henchmoles. No mole ever quite knew what Mandrake wanted. He did, at least, make clear that there were certain things he did *not* want. He did not like moles who went too far from their home territory, for example, because "it makes for confusion and uneasiness." So a henchmole who found an adult wandering too far from his home burrow felt he had Mandrake's sanction to ask the reason why, and if he wasn't satisfied, to fight and, if necessary, kill. In this way each area in the system became more insular and suspicious of outsiders, ready to drive away a wanderer by force with the righteous confidence that they had official sanction to do so.

What was worse, as his first winter in Duncton approached, Mandrake let it be known that he did not like a mole to go onto the surface unless it was for a good reason. "Too many of us are being taken by owls and badgers, so this is in the interest of everymole and the strength of the system" was the way he put it to Rune, who was beginning to act as his main agent.

But it happened that a great many moles went onto the surface for no other reason than that they liked the sun on their fur, or the sound of wind in the trees, or to get a breath of fresh air outside the oppressive atmosphere that the tunnels seemed increasingly to possess.

Now moles had to be going somewhere specific or grub-hunting for food or seeking a herb for some ailment or other. And if they *did* just crouch in the wood, their snouts warmed by the sun, or watching the texture of moss by an exposed root, their enjoyment was marred by having to be ever ready with an excuse in case an inquisitive henchmole happened by.

Mandrake also let it be known that he did not want any contact with the marshenders: "They bring disease to the system and have never contributed very much" was the way Rune explained it to the others. Adding, with distant menace, "The day may well come when they must be driven out of Duncton altogether, for they have no rightful place here."

This put Mekkins, half marshender himself and an elder, into something of a difficulty, but he got round it with characteristic cunning by pretending to become Mandrake's spy in the Marsh End camp and offering to bring back news of their doings—while still convincing them that he was their only hope with Mandrake and the other elders. But the position made him unhappy.

Mandrake's decision to isolate the marshenders was carefully thought out. He sensed early on that if there was going to be any opposition to him from any quarter, it would be from their grubby, muddy, dank little part of the wood—as he thought of it. As time went on, he could blame things on them—a spread of disease here, a shortage of worms there—and isolate them further.

He was right, for marshenders, though frightened of Mandrake, were not as generally struck dumb by him as other moles were. It was true that the males had been too frightened to attack him when he visited them, but it was equally true that one of the females at the time had commented "Bloody load of cowards you lot were," which spoke of a spirit of resistance that did not live elsewhere.

One thing that made Mandrake even more unpopular was that he liked to keep his mates as his own. Not that he created a harem for himself, a string of females ready to do his bidding. Instead, having found a mate, he would fight and kill any male he found trying to consort with her, watching over each he had taken until their litters were born.

The curious thing about it all was that the females he had mated with did not seem to mind. Long years after, they would remember the time they had lain in the power of Mandrake, the cruel, evil Mandrake, and a light would come to their spirits and a terrible excitement to their souls. For they knew (which others who never came near him never did) that beneath the murderous bloodlust of his mating lay a passion and love that cried out to be cherished.

It seemed to possess him for only a moment when they mated, but it was of such tenderness that they could never forget it. For a moment in the wild darkness of a burrow filled with Mandrake's menacing presence and massive body, the same paw that maimed or killed a rival could caress as gently as a June wind and pass on the passion of a heart that ached to be loved. And sometimes in such moments Mandrake spoke out in Siabod, his own language, words of love that seemed addressed less to his mate than to all the creatures he had ever harmed.

Yet he did not like his mates themselves to try to caress him or whisper back comfort. For then his love would be gone in an instant, replaced by contempt or terrible anger.

What he *did* like, he told a group of henchmoles once when he was tired and nearing sleep and his stomach was full of food, "is the kind of female who has a spark of life in her and makes you feel proud to be a male. They make you want to kill and make life at the same time."

Sarah must have been one of those females with the spark of life in her that made Mandrake feel a male, for he guarded her for himself more than any other mate, and she was loyal to him. Her fur was fairer than most, in some lights almost a gentle gray, and though bigger than most females, she was graceful and slim. She came from an old respected mole family that held territory next to Barrow Vale itself and who, as one of the leading families in the system, had often produced elders in the past. Mandrake knew all this—his henchmole Rune told him everything—but it was not what attracted him to Sarah one summer's day after his arrival in the system. It was the fact that she was one of the very few females still able to mate at the end of summer. He could tell it, as could other males, and he wanted her.

Some say he killed the males in her home burrow to get her, others that Sarah prevented any slaughter by approaching Mandrake directly herself. But perhaps it was as simple as the fact that she was one of the finest females of her generation and he the strongest male.

However it was, they mated and she stayed with him through the long, evil years of his sway over the Duncton system. It is from her, or rather from what she told close friends whose memories are recorded in the libraries of Uffington, that we know something of the gentler side of Mandrake and the terrible tragedy of his struggle with Rebecca.

For many it is a mystery that Sarah stayed loyal to Mandrake and yet never seemed corrupted by him—always preserving her grace and goodness, as a snowdrop does in the bitterest weather. The answer may lie in one word: compassion. None can ever know if she knew the terrible origin of Mandrake in the grim system of Siabod in North Wales, but if she did not know its details, perhaps she guessed that something like it had happened. No poet could make a verse of Mandrake's birth, no singer sing it as a song, no taleteller add it to his stories without his listeners covering their ears for horror. Only one account of it remains, written down as it was told directly to Boswell, the blessed scribemole, by an inhabitant of Siabod. Let his words tell the tale:

"Mandrake was born and survived in conditions beyond even the nightmares of the toughest Siabod moles. At the time of his birth—May—conditions around the mountain of Siabod were severe. A mild February and March had been followed by the coldest April any Siabod mole could remember, and that's saying something! When you're as high and exposed as we are, you get used to the cold. A lot of lowland moles would die just being here. Anyway, by mid-May, there were still many patches of ice and snow on Siabod's sides. In such conditions most moles keep below ground, securing themselves in a snug burrow with a worm supply that would survive the cold, or be driven down into the lower winter tunnels they had dug.

"No doubt Mandrake's mother had prepared a nest, yet for some reason that will never be known, she was out on the surface when her litter started—maybe seeking nesting material. It coincided with yet another sudden terrible change in the weather, which switched from pure clear cold to a terrifying blizzard that swept over from the heights of Snowdon, the Glyders and Cnicht to dash against the flanks and falls of Siabod. Perhaps the sudden weather change upset her rhythms and brought on the birth sooner than she expected.

"Whatever it was, she was on the surface when a blizzard started and naturally she tried to get back to her nest. She must have dragged herself through the storm over the ice-covered Siabod rock plateaus, paws and talons tearing at the snow and scanty vegetation to try to reach warmth and safety before the first was born.

"But we think she was on the wrong side of the slope and had to battle a little way uphill before she could reach back down to a tunnel into the system. She could no doubt have found a burrow or made one long before she became too exhausted to continue, but females with young like to return to the nest they have prepared.

"We can only imagine what happened. Overcome by exhaustion and cold, unable to battle further against the wind and icy snow, she settled down in the blizzard on what was little more than bare rock to give birth to her litter. She must have felt a terrible horror and loneliness out there on the side of Siabod, the sky obscured by snowclouds, the wind ripping at her fur trying to tear away each tiny mole pup as it was born. We do not know how many there were—four or five, probably. She must have watched their blind struggle desperately as the warmth from her womb was dashed and scurried away from them by the blizzard wind. Perhaps she tried to burrow into the snow to protect her young, but the wind was too strong for any more than an inch or two of snow to settle.

"Into this icy chaos Mandrake was born, struggling from birth to hang on to life, fighting with his siblings from the very start to find a place of warmth among his mother's teats. She no doubt set her back to the wind, taking the brunt of it herself, to give her young the warmth of her stomach and flanks. For days she fought the cold and wind, never resting for a moment lest one of her young slip out of the protection of her paws into the teeth of the blizzard. The storm continued for nearly eight days, the most vital time in any mole's life. Blind, furless, vulnerable, how Mandrake must have struggled to keep his place at her teats, unknowingly pushing his siblings out of the way, dashing their heads and snouts with his feeble paws, fighting to suck.

"At some point his mother must have realized that without food her milk would dry up, and yet known that if she left her litter for a second, it would mean certain death for all of them.

"It is hard to imagine that she deliberately decided to sacrifice one of the litter after another in the hope that one at least might survive. But everymole knows that, faced by acute danger, a littering mother will kill and sometimes eat her young. Perhaps what happened was that the weakest of the litter died from lack of milk and exposure and rather than let it lie there to be lost for nothing in the cold, she ate it, hoping that it might give her the nourishment she and the rest of the litter needed. One by one her litter died, exposed in the worst Siabod blizzard in mole memory. One by one she must have eaten them, their blood mingling with the snow and ice. One by one her nipples and teats dried up as the nourishment from the food stored in her body, and from the cannibalism of her own young, gave out.

"Until at last only Mandrake remained, struggling among her cold teats to find one that would yield milk to his desperate suckling. By now his eyes were open, but all he could have seen was the dark of his mother's fur, the pink of her teats, and the racing, gray blizzard all around. So, from the start, his world was one of extremes. How he must have struggled to keep his place! Not for him the peace and comfort of safe suckling; never for him the unremembered memory of a relaxed mother holding him warm and close. Fighting for life from the very start.

"Did his mother wonder if he must be sacrificed for her own survival? Or did she leave it to the elements, herself finally falling asleep, the freezing wind at her back taking a seeping hold on her body, her last memory being Mandrake trying to suckle her cold teats?

"If that was her last memory, then his first sight might

well have been the discovery that his mother was dead.
And though he would never know it, she had died to give
Mandrake the chance to live, to fight, and to mate. But
for him then, there was nothing left but the wind, and the
freezing flank of his dead mother. He was too young to
think. But think what he must have felt: desolate loneliness, loss, abandonment.

"It was almost certainly on the eighth day of the storm
that this moment came, for shortly after, it began to clear,
and it is unthinkable that Mandrake could have survived
these conditions for more than a few hours. The freak
weather conditions that had nearly killed him now re-
versed to save him. The sun broke out through the storm-
cast sky and the freezing wet was replaced by thawing
warmth. Steam began to rise from the rocks and peat as
it does sometimes after a storm in summer. Creature after
creature came out from shelter, stretching into the warm,
moist air and feeling themselves back into the light. Here
a mole, there a vole, above the larks tilting into the
breeze with their song hanging again above the flanks of
Siabod. And buzzards and ravens.

"Mandrake could easily have died then, taken by one
of the predators whose eyes now searched the mountain's
sides again. But perhaps his mother's instinct to return
home when the blizzard broke had been right, for where
she had finally lain to litter was not so far from one of
the outlying entrances to the Siabod system. And the wind
was in the right direction to carry his cries to a mole by
the entrance, and a female at that. She was very young
and yet she climbed across the slope toward the cries and
found Mandrake crying and nestling into the cold body
of his mother, surrounded by the pathetic remains of the
rest of the litter. She comforted him, warmed him and
nudged him down the wet slope into the system. Anymole
who saw him that day or in the days following will not
forget the sight; eyes open, fur barely grown, head big,
paws scrabbling and flailing—lost and untrusting and wild.
So he always remained, wild and aggressive.

"As he grew, he took to roaming Siabod's sides for
food. I have seen him myself, the great, fierce Mandrake,
silent and evil, leaving the system to search on the surface, fearless of weather or birds. One day he left like
that and he has never come back."

Such is the record in Uffington as told to Boswell himself so long ago. No more is said about how Mandrake came to leave Siabod and make his way to Duncton Wood. Perhaps he thought he might find something he had once lost in a storm. Who can say?

Nor can we say how much of this Sarah knew. But if she had but a tiny fraction of the compassion that her daughter Rebecca was to have—and where else would Rebecca have found it?—then in the mating burrow with Mandrake she must have felt his loss and tried to cherish him as, in other circumstances, he might have been cherished at birth: to help him escape the world of blackness into which he was born and in which he believed he lived.

At any rate, what *is* known is that Mandrake chose Sarah for a mate; that he watched her grow big with her litter; that he stayed nearby at the birth; and that he waited brooding, turning, twisting, scratching his face with his talons, never comfortable, in the tunnel outside until the litter showed.

He came to the burrow entrance—Sarah allowed him no farther—and looked at the litter. Three males and a female. He watched her croon to them and they, pink, comfortable and safe in her nest, her body warmly encircling their snouts and still-pale whiskers wet with her milk. But he seemed interested only in the female, who struggled, paws bending and flexing weakly, questing for milk as the others did. His eyes were on her alone.

"Call her Sarah, after yourself," he ordered. "It's a fine, strong name."

But Sarah looked up from her litter and straight at him with the same mixture of compassion and strength that the tiny female pup now suckling her was to have in her face when she looked on Bracken at their first meeting many moleyears later.

"Her name will be Rebecca," she said.

Mandrake looked at the tiny, struggling female and back at Sarah, and then back at his daughter again: he who had killed so many moles had once been as helpless as this, but he didn't think of that; he, who had taken so many females, had given them pups like this, but he didn't think of that either; nor did he think that he, whose talons ached with killing and whose shoulders hung huge and heavy on his body, now craved to lean into the burrow and touch his daughter.

But though he was not able to think these things and

say them to himself, they twisted and turned and racked his heart as he crouched in the tunnel unable to say anything. Mandrake, huge and menacing, unable to cut through the whirling darkness of his mind: impotent.

Rebecca, tiny, pink and suckling. Alive!

"Call her Rebecca, then," he said finally, finding himself unaccountably gasping and breathless and wanting to run away from the burrow. "Call her Rebecca!" he said more loudly, turning back into the tunnel clumsily, feeling more than ever the huge, cumbersome weight of himself on himself and wanting to shake and rip it off.

"Call her Rebecca!" he shouted, gasping for air, running down the tunnel and out of the nearest entrance onto the surface in Barrow Vale. "Rebecca!" he roared, as if he could not escape the name, slashing the base of an oak tree with his talons as he charged blindly into it.

Sarah heard him, licking her young, curling them into her and sighing in satisfaction. "Rebecca," she whispered, "Rebecca," as gently in the darkness of the burrow as, for the briefest of hidden moments, Mandrake had once whispered to her "Sarah."

From the first, Rebecca held a strange fascination for Mandrake, who would often stare at her from the tunnel by the burrow where Sarah nursed her litter. Sarah would sometimes waken and find him there, or see his black shadow move away down the tunnel as if, seeing her beginning to awaken, he didn't want to be seen simply watching over his daughter.

Yet as the days and molemonths went by, no one would have guessed, least of all Mandrake himself, that he loved Rebecca with a passion as strong as a gale across a moor. For he treated her harshly, disciplining her unmercifully to try, it seemed, to break her down to a mole of obedience. At first it was easy, for she was but a tiny pup who quailed and backed away from his deep-voiced commands. Her paws would fall over themselves in their anxiety to escape from her great father as she ran desperately back for the protection of her mother's flanks.

Sarah would hold her and say "She's only a pup, only a young thing." But this made little impact on Mandrake.

"A pup will do what I say, as I want," he would roar, glowering darkly at the cowering Rebecca. But never once did he try to wrest her from Sarah, or hit her when she was young.

Such threats had their effect and for a long time Rebecca did Mandrake's will, frightened of him not only when he was there, but also when he was out in the system with Rune or other henchmoles doing system business.

She grew quickly, so that by late autumn she was already nearing adult size. Not as big as moles born the preceding spring, but not so small that she could not put up a fair fight if necessary, though the youngsters still fought for fun rather than for real. The real fighting came only with the mating season or when one mole was trying to wrest away another mole's territory. She stayed in her home burrow longer than spring litters, who could take advantage of the good summer weather to leave their mother and find their own territory. Rebecca stayed at home, close by Sarah and Mandrake, kept innocent, childlike and cowed by Mandrake's continual aggression toward her.

Through the following January and early February, when the wood was at its bleakest, it seemed to her almost *everything* was bleak, for she could never please her father. It was then there occurred an incident about which she never told another mole until years, lifetimes, later and that deepened forever her relationship with Mandrake.

In mid-February the weather turned suddenly bitterly cold and hoarfrost delicately picked out the stalks and veins of the decaying leaves on the wood's floor. While other moles slept and kept warm, or grumbled at the cold as they hurried to find food, Rebecca snouted about on the surface, awed by the chill beauty of the frostbound wood. Then the lightest of snowflakes began to fall, feathering down through the leafless black branches from a gray sky, settling for a second on the back of her paw before melting with her warmth. As she tried to catch them falling about her she seemed to dance with delight in the silent wood.

"Like it, do you girl? Think it's fun?"

It was Mandrake on the surface behind her, interrupting her reverie, angry. She had done something wrong again but she had no idea what. He came closer, his heavy paws destroying the delicate patterns of frost on an oak leaf she had looked at moments before.

"Think it's pretty, don't you?"

His voice was getting louder and she wanted to get away. "You think this snow's just here for your special pleasure? Well, come with me . . ."

She wanted to run from him, to get away from his anger and his voice that was getting louder. She wanted the safety of Sarah. But looking up at his angry gaze she could not move a paw but in the direction in which he pointed—toward the pastures. But she didn't want to go there.

"Please can I go back to the home burrow?"

Mandrake cuffed her not once or twice but several times, so that her head stung and she found herself running tearfully before him toward the pastures, through a wood in which the snow that had once fallen delicate and light was beginning to swirl and whose trees were starting to strain before a blizzard.

She was cold and Mandrake was wild; her teeth chattered in fear. If she opened her mouth as she ran, to gain breath as Mandrake rushed her through the wood, the bitter wind seemed to want to blow her apart.

Then she was at the wood's edge and forced by Mandrake to gaze out onto the pastures whose grass was gray with a thin layer of snow over which more snow whined with the blizzard.

"Still think it's pretty, still think it's something to dance to?" roared Mandrake above the wind.

Then he pushed her out from the protection of the wood into the killer wind and her screams and sobs lost themselves in its wild bitterness, and her tears were part of the stinging blizzard snow. Until she was so far out from the wood that it was lost behind her in the storm and the only solid thing she could see was the dark shape of Mandrake himself, crouched like a black rock against the wind, snow swirling around him.

Mandrake seemed no longer interested in her, turning his attention instead to the blizzard and raising a paw against it as if searching for something beyond it that was threatening him and which he hated and would defy.

"Thought you could kill me, you bastard; thought Mandrake would yield. Siabod, you're nothing, your Stones are a nothing, Arthur is nothing, you . . ." and then he began to roar and rage at the blizzard, his language changing into the harsh tongue of Siabod whose words were like talon thrusts. He was no longer immobile rock but a moving mass of dark shadow and anger raging at the bitter wind and ignoring the harsh snow that flailed against his snout and mouth. But his roars began to get more high-pitched and wilted before the wind into what seemed the bleatings and mewings of a creature lost, and Rebecca's fear was gone.

She wanted to reach out and take him to her, tell him he was safe and so she shouted *Mandrake! Mandrake!* into the deafening wind. He turned to her and she saw that in his eyes, so menacing before, there was a terrible fear and a loss so great that she could only reach out to it. . . .

He hit her as she came to him, the look of loss replaced again by anger, and then he turned her to the wind and snow and shouted into her above the sound of the blizzard "This is what I faced, this is the force you face, and you Rebecca will never yield to it because you are part of me who knew Siabod once and defied its death . . ." and she wanted to cry no no no this isn't it, it isn't it isn't, but she was too young to know the words and the words only cried inside her and so she sobbed and struggled to get free. But she never forgot what she was unable to say, just as she never forgot the power of his grip as he forced her to face the blizzard wind. Nor could she forget the strangest thing—how safe she felt as he held her there.

That was what happened to Rebecca with Mandrake in mid-February, and what mole can doubt that in those wild half-remembered moments her love for him grew deep? Had he not shown her something of himself?

Yet what a shuddering memory it soon became, and how much more afraid of him she grew.

Still, through that bleak winter there were some comforts. Sarah would sit with her and tell stories about her family. She would play with her brothers when Mandrake was not about (he preferred to keep her separate when he was there), usually leading them in the games they played, for she had a good imagination and could always think of something to do.

As yet she had none of the grace of her mother, Sarah, every movement betraying an anxiousness to please Mandrake, even when he was not there. It unsettled her, too, that other moles' approach to her was unpredictable, because of who she was: some were overly nice to her, thinking it might pay dividends with Mandrake. Others, especially the females, were inclined to be bitchy, making remarks about "certain moles who think a lot of themselves and have it easy." Or, as one of them put it to a friend in Barrow Vale, loud enough for Rebecca to hear: "She's got all the worst qualities of both of them: stuck up as her mother and as heavy-pawed as Mandrake."

Faced by such comments, Rebecca at first cried and hid herself away, taking minor tunnels to avoid meeting adult moles if she went out. But as February advanced she grew brasher, though no less sensitive, and would walk boldly past the gossips, affecting total indifference to them.

But toward the third week of February, everything began to change as the earliest spring began and there was much less of the chatter and idleness that characterized the winter years. Rebecca began to go out onto the surface more, cheered by the growing lightness of the spring days.

From her very first venturing onto the surface, she loved the smell and color of trees and plants. At first it had been the acorns cracking down to the ground, the rustle of the last falling leaves, autumn fruit and the surprise of bright holly berries thrown in a red huddle by an entrance after a storm.

As February advanced, the slow growth of shoots and new leaves enthralled her, and she would run up into the wood day after day sniffing the cold air, to see what new delights she could find. One day it was the yellow delicacy of winter aconite rising among sodden leaves and stem bottoms as pale as the spring sunlight. Another day she crouched for hours before a cluster of snowdrops, their white petals dancing in the cold wind, the black leafless branches of a great oak hanging starkly above them.

Then she was amazed at the speed with which shoots of dog's mercury rose up into the spring light, but quickly learned to take paths avoiding them because of their rank smell. If she had to go through a patch of them, she would run and hold her breath as she did so, emerging gasping and laughing, often with a brother or two in tow.

As spring advanced, she found the flowers grew more scented and would bring them, wild and sweet-smelling, down to a place near the entrance to the home burrow so that their scent met anymole who entered. Her mother would tell her the names, and Rebecca would repeat them over and over, mingling them into verses with names of other flowers Sarah told her about, but which were not yet in bloom.

Adults got quite used to young Rebecca dancing with her brothers, singing flower songs, leading them in a game of her own invention, whose verse might run:

> *Vervain and yellowflag*
> *Feverfew and Rue;*
> *Some for my mother*
> *Plenty left for you.*

And they would tumble about laughing, mock-fighting and rolling on the wood's floor.

Now Mandrake found it harder to control her. It was not that *she*, Rebecca, was disobedient in any way, but her spirit was and that seemed something neither of them could control. It was almost as if her life, and love of it, thrived on his malevolence. Not that, for a moment, she ever enjoyed annoying him or being the subject of his anger. But each time he knocked her down, sometimes literally, up she would get to run off somewhere and, despite every good intention on her part, do something else that displeased him.

"You're not to play so roughly with your brother," he would say, but she would.

"It's dangerous up on the surface now by the edge of the wood," but there she would be found.

"You're to stay in the home burrow today because there are things to do," but she wouldn't.

She managed to do terrible things without even trying. Just before the April elder meeting, for example, she couldn't resist having a peek about the elder burrow, somewhere she had never seen and which, since everymole was always talking about it, she thought she would have a look at. So she did, and very impressive she found it. After she left it to wander off around Barrow Vale, a terrible cry went up: "The worms, the elders' worms! They've been eaten. Somemole has been into the elder burrow and eaten all the worms!"

She heard it, and it was true, dreadfully true! She had

eaten them! Well, she had seen them in a pile in the
corner of the burrow, squirming about in a delightful
way and, yes, she had had *one*, but she had hardly
thought about it because, well, she was looking around
the burrow and yes, then she *did* have another one; no, it
wasn't intentional; yes, she did eat it, the burrow was so
interesting you see and, she was hardly thinking, and . . .
Oh dear, *another* one, were there really five missing? She
couldn't possibly have eaten five perhaps another mole
came in . . . No? Well, she could always . . .

Only old Hulvar laughed when he heard about it. It
was a sign of the times, he thought, that everymole
took the whole thing so seriously. Mandrake attacked
Rebecca viciously and also hurt Sarah, who was trying
to protect Rebecca; the elder meeting was held in an
atmosphere of acrimony, though it was no mole's fault
among the elders.

If that had been the only incident it might not have
mattered, but despite her sincere good intentions, Rebecca did other things as bad. One day, for example, she
managed to lose not one of her brothers in the wood, but
all three. One of them nearly got killed by an owl and
the other two were gone for two days and were only
brought back to the home burrow by, of all moles, a
Marsh End female. "It was Rebecca's fault," they wailed,
though they were by now nearly adults.

Rebecca tried to explain to Mandrake: "It was only a
game of hide and seek and I thought it would be fun to
go a bit farther than usual in the tunnels and perhaps for
a moment or two onto the surface I'm terrible sorry *I*
didn't know where we were but it wasn't *hard* to find
the way back I don't understand how they got lost
for two days and there weren't any owls about I'm sure
please . . . ," but Mandrake was furious. Indeed, so furious was he that few moles have ever seen him like that
and survived. His anger with her on these occasions was
always out of proportion to the crime, if crime it was.
Yet still her spirit seemed to thrive on it.

But while she grew big and headstrong like Mandrake
himself, she also became smiling and graceful like her
mother. She loved to touch things and to dance or find
some quiet spot in the spring sun and lie softly, with the
ecstasy of it on her snout. She would chase her brothers
like a growing male yet comfort them when they were
hurt as the kindest female did.

There was a fine lightness of spirit, of life, about her and perhaps it was this that Mandrake, in his black anger, would try vainly to catch and crush. As she grew older, Mandrake's only recourse was to increasing violence toward her, and as the spring advanced, she found it best to keep her snout down, and well out of the way.

There came a time in April when suddenly there was wild blood in the air, and Rebecca found it exciting. Mating time was starting. She knew she shouldn't go onto the surface, but Mandrake himself seemed to be gone more these days and her mother was losing interest in the autumn litter because it was almost full-grown now. So though Rebecca felt tied still to her home burrow and was still not really an adult, she was drawn by the life in the air up into the busy wood.

Busy *and* noisy. Birds darted and flitted about the trees, which were now heavy with bud. Anemones, celandine, daffodils were almost everywhere. Some days, it was true, the sky would be gray and dark with the air around the trees and undergrowth heavy and still. But only some days. Increasingly she would poke her snout out of a tunnel entrance early in the morning and see a magical, light, swirling mist running through the wood, white and pink as the sun broke through it. The buds and flowers about her seemed to be opening, reaching up through the light mist to the sun beyond.

"Oh!" she sighed. "How beautiful!" Near her a cluster of celandine, yellow petals half open, reached up softly to the sky. The mist thinned before her eyes until it was almost gone, and she ran across the surface among the trees feeling she was part of the spring excitement of the wood. From afar off to the eastside, the soft caw-caws of rooks carried to her, long and slow compared with the trilling of the blackbirds and thrush that darted in and out among the trees as excited as she was. She ran to the center of Barrow Vale to watch the wood wake up as the last of the thin wisps of mist swirled away into the sunshine. A warm, moist, nutty smell had replaced the rotting smell of winter, which she now saw, for the first time, was unpleasant and hung about the tunnels still.

Duncton Wood spread away all around her—over to the westside and the east, down to the south where her brothers had gotten lost, and up toward the slopes leading to the top of Duncton Hill. Oh, she wanted to sing and

dance and call everymole together and celebrate! Duncton
Wood! The name was magical in the sunlight. The
winter's years have gone! She laughed, or rather smiled
aloud, her joy shaking among the yellow petals of the
celandine which were now open, and echoed in the constant calls and whistles of the birds. The great oaks,
round and solid at their bases, rose high about the edge
of Barrow Vale, and somewhere among their branches a
woodpecker drummed its territorial rights from a tree
and then flew direct to another oak to drum again.

"It's my wood," she whispered to herself, joyfully. "My
wood!"

"And mine too," said a voice behind her, the voice of
Rune. She turned round, startled, but as usual found it
hard to see him immediately, so good was he at hiding
in impenetrable shadows, even on a sunny day.

"You shouldn't be here, you know," he said coldly,
but with a smile to his voice that only seemed to underline the threat it carried.

To Rebecca, Rune, who still smelled of winter, spoiled
everything she was enjoying about the morning, and so
she ran off without a word, across Barrow Vale. Rune
followed urgently, easily keeping up with her but hanging
behind two or three paws' distance. Rune wanted Rebecca, he wanted to mate with her. His desire was not
lust, for Rune did not give way to simple lust, the lust he
felt for any female in mid-March, but a kind of sick
sensuality based on the fact that she was Mandrake's
daughter. He felt, in some way, that his position in the
system gave him the right to take her and also that it
would make him equal with Mandrake.

Sensing at least some of this, Rebecca's joy in the
morning died within her and she ran anxiously down into
the tunnels toward her home burrow, trying not to appear too disturbed by Rune's presence. He followed behind her, the sound of his paws on the tunnel floor liquid
and smooth. Her breath became irregular; she could smell
Rune behind her and hear his chill voice calling after
her "Rebecca, Rebecca, I was only joking about you not
being allowed out on Barrow Vale. Stay and talk."

Rebecca scurried on, ready now to turn with her talons
on Rune and draw his blood if she had to. Imperceptibly
the scamper along the tunnels turned into a chase, until
they were traveling at speed, and Rebecca had to think

very fast to twist and turn in the right direction. Sometimes Rune would disappear down a turn in the tunnel, only to reappear ahead or to the side of her, so she had to turn away from the direction of her home burrow to keep clear of him. Sometimes he would laugh or call after her "It's all right, Rebecca, I won't hurt you." She was out of breath with running and becoming confused as to which way to turn, everything rolling round in her mind as her chest heaved and panted with the effort of the chase. "I want you, Rebecca. I want you," Rune called, his voice seeming to echo darkly from all directions, as if there was a Rune down every turn in the tunnels.

Finally she could stand it no more and stopped in her tracks and turned round with talons raised but shaky to face him. He eyed her calmly and, inching forward very slowly, got bigger and bigger. He smelled of the dead of winter and she felt as if she was falling back into a pit, her talons soft and useless, scrabbling ever more weakly above her head as she fell back and back. Somewhere, far, far away, she thought she could hear the urgent drumming of the woodpecker on the oak's side, but it was only the pounding of her heart, which no longer seemed to be part of her. Rune came nearer, smoothly nearer, looking down at her, petrified before him, lusting in his power before her.

But the moment was suddenly broken by the terrible shout of "Rebecca!" It was Mandrake, suddenly Mandrake, and now she *did* hear her heart thump, thump, thumping, and she felt terribly frightened as the two male moles she most feared in the system loomed above her.

"This is not the time to leave the home burrow," said Mandrake, adding with threatening force, "How many times must you be told?"

"Just what I've been telling her, Mandrake, my very words," purred Rune, turning with a black smile to Mandrake. "It's not true," she said. "He wanted . . ."

But Mandrake ignored Rebecca, going straight to her and striking her so hard that she fell back and hit her snout against the tunnel wall, and it brought tears to her eyes. She ran crying from them both, back to her home burrow.

Mandrake turned to Rune: "She will not mate this

spring, Rune, not this spring. She is not ready, and I will
kill anymole that tries. Whichever mole he might be."

Then Rune ran off down the tunnel, as ever awed by
Mandrake, who, it seemed, was impossible to fool. However, he promised himself, a cold laugh in his voice, "I'll
have her yet."

So April ran on toward May and most Duncton
females grew big with young so that when the burrows
started to warm up, they were ready for their litters. Rebecca, who had seen the males grow aggressive and her
father angry with bloodlust, and Sarah grow excited and
running, sighing, nervous, taken in the burrow by Mandrake, and Rebecca near to hear the deep softness in
his voice and wonder about the world in a whirl about
her, and thinking of Rune chasing her not knowing where
to turn, watching the males who dared not come near
thinking of Mandrake and Sarah, Mandrake so powerful
on Sarah, she wanted to run to them. Oh Oh Oh she
would sigh alone, drifting into adulthood.

She heard the cries of littered pups and wanted to go
near and croon over them as she did flowers and the
sunlight, but she never dared go near for fear of attack.
She steered clear of males after her father found her
with Rune, for though he never said anything to her directly, she knew he would kill anymole who came near.
So, when males did come near, she would discourage
them, though often they were young like her and sweet,
so sweet, that she wanted to dance with them, and laugh
as they did to match her desire and run, her spirit rising
and diving like larks did over the pastures beyond the
edge of the wood.

As summer started, she felt miserable and isolated, for
even her brothers went off for long periods searching for
mates across the wood. Sometimes, though, they would
return to the home burrow, for they were still youngsters
at heart. If they had been beaten in a fight, as they always
were by the older, more experienced males, she would
delight in comforting them and making them laugh again.
But they had changed, becoming more aggressive toward
her, and sometimes she sensed in them the same urgent
demand that had been in Rune's voice in the tunnel
when he chased her, and she would turn away from them,
unhappy.

5

BRACKEN was raised on the westside, where fear was a dirty word and blood (provided it was somemole else's) was a thing to celebrate. Westsiders were tough and Burrhead was the toughest. That meant his mate's children had a lot to put up with in the way of fighting, bullying, being surprise-attacked, and generally being knocked about, as mole youngsters learned the arts of self-protection and aggression in the toughest school in the Duncton system.

Bracken's mother, Aspen, came from the eastside, Burrhead having fought and killed for her after the February elder meeting. Apart from Mandrake, who killed other moles automatically in mating fights, few of the moles actually killed opponents in fights. One or other retreated before they were hurt. So Burrhead's performance made him feared.

He was, in fact, unusually aggressive, and in a system without Mandrake might well have emerged as the toughest mole of all. He was, however, brutish-tough rather than cunning-tough, and moles like Rune or Mekkins had more native wit about them than he did.

It is unlikely that they, for example, would have put up with a mate as untidy as Aspen. Her burrow was always in a mess, littered with uncleared droppings, grubby, dried worm bits festering in the burrow's recesses, and vegetation brought in by the youngsters.

Aspen chose the names, as traditionally the females did—the strongest, Bracken's brother, being called Root for obvious reasons; the female was called Wheatear because there was a very slight discoloration over her right ear—as there was over Aspen's. And she gave Bracken a name traditionally given to the weakest of a litter of three.

Burrhead was never impressed by Bracken—in fact, he wasn't much impressed by the litter as a whole, since it only produced one useful male. Still, as he watched the three pink pups struggling at each other and their mother's teats, he got some satisfaction from the fact that the strongest, Root, seemed very strong indeed. A conclusion which was well justified, as Root developed into just the kind of bullying, aggressive mole Burrhead hoped for in a son.

Bracken had an unpleasant childhood. He was always struggling for food and losing, ending up with scraps. As a result, he was slow to grow, which perpetuated the situation, making him the skinny runt in the family, always ill and whining when very young, frightened and crying when older. However, he was at least intelligent ("cunning," Burrhead called him) and quickly learned to avoid being attacked when danger threatened or his bigger brother was feeling aggressive. He found that there was no point in fighting back, because he always got beaten, so he took to hunching up into a defensive stance so that he was always ready for the blows and scratches that came to him from all sides. He adopted a low snout, keeping eyes averted and playing the fool so that Root and Wheatear were bored with him.

His task of survival was easier because his two siblings, like their father, had a complete lack of imagination, which meant that he could usually work out well ahead of them what they would do and then take appropriate avoiding action.

At the same time, he had enough sense to work out what would please them—worms, new places to play, new tunnels to explore—and put it their way, which meant that they relied on him, grudgingly, for ideas. That didn't stop them thumping him quite a lot and ignoring him a great deal, but that was better than out-and-out assault. Still, he did often end up in tears, and it was then that Aspen came, for a rare moment, into her own. For along with her untidiness went a certain romantic whimsiness which meant she loved telling stories. And when Bracken was upset, she would comfort him with mole legends and tales, simple stories of honored, brave moles, or tales of fine males fighting for their mates.

Many were traditional mole legends of which every system had its version; others were peculiar to Duncton and were usually set in the long-distant past, when the moles lived in the Ancient System up on top of the hill. She entered into the spirit of these tales to such an extent that she would often moan and weep as she told them, and Bracken, his head against her flank, would feel her breathing getting heavier and faster as she neared a climactic end, and for a while he would forget his tears and the bullying in the drama of the tale.

He would enter into them as she did, his eyes perhaps half closed or affixed to some distant place beyond the walls of the burrow and soon he would be there, fighting to the death, weaving magic with his talons, facing the most dreadful dangers. Aspen loved to paint in the rich colors of her own whimsy the scene when the hero mole returns from his quest across the wood to fight owls, or outfox foxes, or find worms to save the system. This would move Bracken deeply, for he wished he might return home one day as his heroes did, to a snug burrow, warm with love, friendly and wormful. Wanted, not an outcast.

It was from these beginnings that Bracken's fascination with the Ancient System grew, and when he ventured onto the surface, he would often stop and stare dimly up in the direction of the top of Duncton Hill far beyond his sight and hopes and wonder if he might ever climb there himself. One day Aspen told him about the Stone that was said to stand there, "though it's a long time since anymole but the elders went up there, and then only at Midsummer and Longest Night. It's probably just legend, but a nice one, don't you think?"

The idea of the Stone fascinated him so much that he gathered his courage and dared ask Burrhead about it one day when he seemed in a mellow mood. To his surprise, Burrhead was very ready to give an answer: "Aye, the Stone's up there right enough. I've seen it myself, though I don't suppose that'll happen much more because, if I have my way, we'll stop the Midsummer trek."

"Why?" asked Bracken tentatively.

"Owls and worms, two words you should get into your head, my boy. Owls is dangerous up there and worms is scarce. No point risking ourselves for some ancient ritual which no one but old stick-in-the-muds like Hulver can remember."

"What's the Stone like?" demanded Bracken, encouraged by his father's unusual willingness to talk. And noticing that Aspen was listening too.

"It's nothing, really," said Burrhead, "just a stone. Well, a big stone. Tall as a tree, shoots straight up into the sky. It's gray. It turns dark blue as night falls and then pitch black, blacker than night itself, except where the moon catches it and it's silvery gray."

So there were moments of stillness for Bracken in his burrow, when Aspen would talk to him and even

Burrhead would tell him things, and he was unmolested.

But as May advanced and Root and Wheatear gained in strength, such moments became rarer, and he had to use all his ingenuity to avoid being hurt in their rough-and-tumble fighting, which always had him as the butt.

There came a time, at the end of May, when Root would seek him out and deliberately intimidate him, try-ing to make Bracken raise his talons so that he would have an excuse to fight him.

"He started it," Root would tell a despairing Aspen, faced once more by a bewildered, hurt Bracken.

As the days wore on, Bracken began more and more to spend time by himself, exploring away from his home burrow, finding he had farther and farther to come home again for sleep or worms. In this way he made his way to Barrow Vale one day, but found it too full of other moles, curious about who he was, as he turned away and tried other directions. Another day he went right to the edge of the wood and looked out for the first time onto the pastures, frightened by the open space and massive sky beyond the trees, terrified of the cows who hooved and pulled at grass beyond the fence.

But Burrhead did not call him cunning for nothing. Bracken quickly realized that his timid appearance and obvious youth allowed him to cross the tunnels of moles who might otherwise be hostile to him. He developed various ways of approaching them, finding that even if they started hostile, he would usually disarm them by asking a simple question which established his inferiority and their importance.

"I'm lost," he might say. "Can you tell me where the Barrow Vale is from here?"

Or, if he knew their names (which he would try to find out from the preceding mole he had encountered), "I was looking for Buckbean because he knows an awful lot about the system," and Buckbean suddenly did, in-deed, feel he knew an "awful lot" about the system, and would feel flattered and retract his talons—though still standing his ground until quite certain this youngster was safe.

Bracken was to use this approach later and more effec-tively with the eastsiders, who were more willing to pass the time of day talking than the westsiders. But even so, many westsiders yielded to Bracken's combination of youthful vulnerability, innocence and flattery to answer his sometimes spurious questions and let him continue his explorations.

The more so because, as Mandrake's power had increased, he had let it be known that he preferred moles to stay in their territory and not wander around without reason, so a safe stranger like Bracken was welcome for the interest he could bring. It was true, in fact—though the Duncton moles didn't know it, since they kept to themselves—that there was traditionally more mixing and visiting in Duncton than, for example, out on the pastures.

Mandrake himself came from a desolate system where individuals kept themselves to themselves, but his reasons for encouraging isolation in Duncton were not nostalgic: he knew that the more isolated each Duncton mole was, the better could he control them. And he seemed to have a peculiarly deep-rooted aversion to the Stone.

This all being so, a visiting youngster was more welcome than he once might have been. He could pass on a bit of gossip, he was safe, and Mandrake's rule didn't apply to youngsters.

In this way, Bracken was able to learn a great deal about the westside and something about the system, too. He would hear gossip about the elders, news of the havoc and deaths caused by Mandrake's henchmoles, among whom his own father was a leading member, and stories of Mandrake himself.

Of all things that he heard, it was these that made the biggest impression on him, for there seemed no end to Mandrake's strength and power:

"He's so strong he's been known to destroy an oak root thick as a mole to make a tunnel."

"He's the best fighter the system's ever seen and ever likely to see, if you ask me. Do you know, my boy, when he first came to Duncton he killed twelve of the strongest adults before he even set paw in a tunnel? Twelve! Mind you, I wasn't there myself."

"They say the first time he went down the Marsh End he stopped a group of marshenders from attacking him by just pointing his huge snout at them and staring. Didn't say a word; just crouched ready and stared. They backed away, tearing at each other to escape. *That's* how powerful Mandrake is."

Mole after mole, females and males, came out with stories like this, so that soon Mandrake assumed terrifying proportions in his mind.

Indeed, Mandrake might well have taken on the mantle of powerful protector of Duncton and its moles in Bracken's mind had it not been for the fact that his own bullying father was one of Mandrake's henchmoles and forever going on about the fact. So Mandrake took on a dark and sinister role in Bracken's imagination rather than a benevolent one.

It was for this reason that Bracken was both surprised and fascinated when, one day toward the end of May, he heard a westside female say, with the indirectness of a gossip who deliberately invites a follow-up question by the mystery of what she says: "Mind you, there's one mole who can stand up to Mandrake and there's nothing, I tell you, absolutely nothing, he can do about it. Not a single solitary thing."

"Who's that?" asked Bracken, amazed.

But she continued her train of thought, piling on the mystery for her own delight: "Yes, he can huff and puff all he likes, but I don't think he can do a thing."

"But who *is* it?" asked Bracken, eaten up with curiosity.

"Why, Miss Stuck-up-Rebecca, that's who. His darling daughter. Twists him round her talons *she* does. Mind you dear," his confidante placed her snout close to his ear and affected to look down the communal tunnel in the direction of Barrow Vale, "mind you, all that won't last much longer, if you know what I mean," digging him in the ribs.

Bracken didn't know what she meant and wanted very much to know. "Do you mean . . ." He hesitated encouragingly, and she obligingly continued.

"Yes, you know I do. We all know she was an autumn-litter mole, which means she'll be nearly ready to leave her home burrow by now. What's more, it wouldn't surprise anymole if Sarah, Mandrake's socalled mate, had another litter this summer. Mandrake's not one to hang about, is he? And Sarah isn't going to want Rebecca round with another litter of her own to bring up."

So, piece by piece, Bracken built up a picture of the system and its leading moles. He learned about Rune— "cunning as a stoat"; he heard about Bindle—"sulking over on the eastside now"; he delighted in the stories about Dogwood and Mekkins; they told him about Hulver, about how the owls were most dangerous on the edge of the wood, and about how dangerous the pasture moles were.

He often heard about Rebecca as well, especially from the males, who reveled in the scrapes she got herself into, causing Mandrake to tear a strip off her again and again, so they said.

She was, so he was variously told, wild, nearly as big as a male of her age, an autumn mole (which meant that she was tough), obstinate, always laughing, inclined to dance about Barrow Vale *on the surface*, the bane of her brothers' lives, and frequently punished by Mandrake.

Bracken, who naturally grew increasingly curious about Rebecca, might have been tempted to go and find her had she been any other mole's daughter and had he himself been more sociable. But despite his ability to wheedle his way into other mole tunnels and occasionally even their burrows, he was rather shy of his own generation. Talking with adults was one thing, consorting with his peers was another, and much more difficult. Still, for a while he looked out for her in the communal tunnels and ventured once or twice onto the surface at Barrow Vale thinking he might see Rebecca there, but nothing ever came of it.

Soon, other things about the system caught his interest. The stories Aspen had told him about the Ancient System and the occasional mentions it got as a long-unvisited place fascinated him. Also, there was something about the way moles talked about the Duncton Stone, and the mystery of why they mentioned as something separate from it, "The Stone," which was powerful and held all moles' lives in its power. Was there, then, a Stone a mole could never see?

"Where *is* it?" he would ask, "What is it?" But no mole gave him an answer. He thought he might find it if he went to the Ancient System, but as yet he didn't actually want to try to go there—it was far too dangerous—but he did want to meet a mole, apart from Burrhead, who had been there.

It was this interest and the fact that he had exhausted the exploration possibilities of westside and Barrow Vale that led him to strike out toward the slopes one day.

6

THERE were far fewer moles there, and after several visits, getting higher each time, he began to see that he would have to explore in a different way. For one thing, the higher he got, the more he found the mixed oaks and elms and safe undergrowth he had been used to giving way to open beech wood with its disconcerting layer of rustling beech leaves, which gave away every movement if a mole wanted to travel fast. The burrows and tunnels in this borderland had a curious, derelict air that, at first, Bracken found depressing. Tunnel after tunnel would be abandoned and dusty, or taken over by weasels or voles, though only for a short way past their entrances. Or he would find a system that had recently been lived in, for scraps of worms remained, or the entrances weren't grown over, or he could smell the demarcation marks left by their occupants, faint but discernible. But rarely any moles.

Then there were large areas where no mole seemed to have burrowed, though quite why, he couldn't work out. When he was there, he began to feel he would never see anymole here at all, and even found himself talking to himself on occasion, almost as if he missed company.

All this meant that he found the slopes wearing and at first could only take a short while of them, scampering back to the westside as quickly as he could—running down communal tunnels where they helped him and over the surface if a tunnel route meant a confrontation he preferred to avoid. It was so tiring placating moles!

May slid into June and he was no longer a pup. Root and Wheatear were nearly adult in size and tried more and more to behave like them, too, which meant they would ignore him totally, attack him, or push him out of the way. If he found worms when they had none, for example, they would simply take them from him, talons raised above his vulnerable snout as a warning that they meant business.

He sensed his time in the burrow was running out, so to try to extend it he exaggerated yet further his juvenile pose, going about in the defensive stance of a timid, placatory mole. Burrhead began to call him "young Bracken," as a way of differentiating him from Root and Wheatear, who seemed in his terms to be growing up normally. Bracken, he was beginning to think, was in some way backward and hardly worth getting into a lather about any more. He obviously wasn't going to last long once the summer came and the new generation started its search for territory.

"He won't stand a chance against this spring's lot," Burrhead told Aspen one day at the end of May. "But every litter has its wrongun's." Aspen nodded, but she was not so sure. Bracken was a disappointment and yet, well, "He's not so stupid as he sometimes seems, you know—he knows much more about the system than either of the other two—in fact he knows more than I do." But this was just a disguise for her true feelings about Bracken, which were those of many a female for the weakest of her litter: compassion mixed with hope that they might turn out better in the end. And he did like her stories, which was more than she could say for Root and Wheatear, for all their stolid, moleworthy qualities.

But she didn't say any of this to Burrhead because it just wasn't worth it, and she was losing interest in them all. The litter would be gone soon and they had the summer to get through, when she'd be on her own much more, and she was looking forward to it. Sensing these things, Bracken spent more and more time away from the home burrow and began to consider carefully where he might go when he finally left it. He had no desire to compete with the likes of Root for a place in the westside. He wasn't crazy!

Nor did he know enough about the north or the east-side yet to make plans in that direction. So increasingly he began to think the slopes were a possibility—they might be worm-scarce but they were also mole-scarce, which was a major attraction. He had seen enough to think he might make a living there, giving himself breathing space to consider what to do next.

With these ideas in his mind, he decided to make a trek to the slopes one day and explore them further, perhaps staying away from his home burrow for a day or two. He slipped away one quiet June morning, when everymole was asleep or preoccupied, and took a mainly surface route up toward the slopes. He didn't know it, but he was never to live in the westside again.

It took him until late in the morning before he reached his first beech tree, at a point he already knew where he could find some worms. Then he pressed on along what he called the beech-oak borderland until at last he was into new territory. And then on and on eastward, progressing along a contour line for a while, and then up for a bit.

He saw a lot of life—birds, a couple of voles, several squirrels, a possible fox—but no moles. By the early afternoon he was tired and stopped for food. He had never been so far in one day and knew he would be spending the night in a strange burrow, or perhaps one he must make for himself.

In search of worms he found an old, disused tunnel and went down it, snout aquiver, but not a whiff or sign of a mole. So he blocked one end of it to make a temporary burrow and, putting his back against it, crouched facing the entrance above and the continuation of the tunnel beyond. Safe, snug and just the place to crunch the worms he had found. He closed his eyes and settled down, heart thumping from the day's journey. But he was not asleep, and when there was a scratching at the earth block he had made and a warning vibration along the tunnel wall, he was awake and ready, still as a root. Moles feel safe in their own tunnels and make quite a lot of noise, and this one was no exception. Indeed, he was chatting to himself in a busy kind of way, interspersing it with snatches of a familiar worming song:

> *Now we dig and we scratch and we wedge and we*
> * pull*
> *Now we wedge and we dig and . . .*

Mmm. This shouldn't have happened, not in my tunnel. Mind you, its a long time since I was here. Too long. I'm hungry. Worms, that's what I want.

> *Worms, worms, worms*
> *Lots of lovely worms.*

Bracken relaxed when he heard all this, for the mole sounded old and good-humored and unlikely to cause him harm. Still, feeling it is better to be safe than sorry, he took advantage of the noise the mole was making to sneak out quietly onto the surface again to wait and see who would come.

The muttering and humming continued and an occasional heavy breathing of exertion, as the mole burrowed his way through Bracken's block, until finally a snout appeared at the entrance, sniffing about the warm evening air.

"Somemole's here," he said loudly. "I can smell it." At which the snout disappeared back into the tunnel and there fell a deep silence. Bracken held his breath, waited for several minutes, and finally could stand it no longer. "Hello. I'm here," he said as cheerfully as he could muster, "a youngster from the westside." Silence.

"I got lost." Silence. "I'm very sorry, really I am, but I thought your tunnel was deserted." Snuffling. Finally the mole spoke out from the dark tunnel.

"It *was* deserted. I've not had time to come here for months. It's merest chance" (at this point the snout poked out of the tunnel again) "that I happened along at this particular moment."

The mole's head appeared—the head of the oldest mole Bracken had ever seen. "At least I think it was merest chance. I'm not sure that chance exists any more."

The mole emerged completely from the entrance and stood on spindly paws peering in Bracken's direction. "By which I mean that I'm not *any more* sure . . . if you see what I mean. Haven't got a worm or two, have you?" he asked abruptly, settling down with slow dignity and not saying another word.

Bracken, half hidden behind a fallen branch, came out a little and crouched down himself. The old mole evidently gave up hope of a worm from Bracken and asked the questions moles traditionally ask of others on their territory: "Who are you and where do you come from?" He asked it in a singsong, almost as if he wasn't thinking about what it meant or expecting a reply. But he got one, all the same. "I'm Bracken from the westside, exploring." "Mmm, exploring! Very good." He dropped his voice a little and in a stage whisper that Bracken thought might be sarcastic, said "Haven't explored out any of my worms, have you?"

"Well, I . . . ," Bracken stuttered, because he didn't like to admit he had done just that, yet didn't want to tell a lie somehow. "Well, I could find you some worms in no time, I expect," he offered at last.

The old mole said nothing, but chomped his jaws together appreciatively and started to hum again. Bracken ran off busily to look for worms, pleased without knowing it to be doing something for another mole, even if the impulse was born of the fact that he had stolen some of the old mole's worms. He rummaged happily under fallen branches and down an old tunnel he had seen, half dug and abandoned. He sensed that the other mole was not aggressive; indeed, he seemed positively friendly, and obviously wanted to have a chat. And that would be nice, thought Bracken: he might know something about the slopes that he wants to tell me. And the Stone.

Soon he had got six or seven worms together, enough for them both. He deposited four by the old mole and, as a mark of respect, bit their heads off so they could not escape, and sat down again. The old mole thanked him and crouched in silence, looking at the worms as if he was pondering something. Then he said:

> *"Be with us Stone at the start of our feast*
> *Be with us Stone at the close of our meal*
> *Let no mole adown our bodies*
> *That may hurt our sorrowing souls*
> *Oh no mole adown our bodies*
> *That may hurt our sorrowing souls."*

The simple grace was over almost before it began and it so awed Bracken, so filled him with wonder, that he was shaken with silence. He had never heard a prayer before. He had never heard the Stone spoken to as if he were a friend at a mole's side.

The evening fell about them and they ate their worms in silence, in great peace with each other. When the mole had finished the four worms, which he ate with slow relish, he stopped and cleaned his face and licked his paws.

"That's better. I *am* grateful," he said. "My name's Hulver, by the way, and if I'm not much mistaken, your father is Burrhead from the westside."

"Yes, that's right. How did you know?" asked Bracken.

"He's an elder, like me," explained Hulver, "and he's

mentioned you once or twice." Hulver leaned forward like a fellow conspirator and whispered, "He's not pleased with your progress. You're not nasty enough!" Hulver laughed and Bracken decided he rather liked him, but still didn't know what to say. He was in the presence of an elder he had heard of as the wisest in the system, so what *could* he say? Hulver fell into silence again, snout quivering in the blue evening light, slowly lowering down onto outstretched paws, contemplating the fall of night.

Bracken's mind was in a whirl—the prayer had left him feeling very strange and, as far as he was concerned, it hung magically in the air about them, making everything beyond it seem dim and unclear. He felt lost in his thoughts, literally lost, for he couldn't find where among them he actually was. The old mole crouched before him as if he were one of the trees, or a plant growing or the soil, part of the whole thing that seemed around him contained in the prayer. He was finally dragged— that's what it felt like—out of these thoughts by Hulver, who asked him in a gentle voice, "Why have you come over to the slopes, can you tell me that?" Bracken started to tell him, explaining how he was interested in the system, liked exploring and . . . and soon he was telling Hulver everything.

Talking on and on into the night, telling Hulver things he hardly knew about himself, complaining bitterly about his life, criticizing Burrhead, saying finally that he hated him, expressing his contempt for Root, telling about Aspen's stories, admitting his fear about leaving the home burrow to find his own territory. Now and again Hulver would nod encouragingly, but never said more than two or three words or passed a judgment, making Bracken freer to say what he felt.

He was stopped finally by an ominous owl hoot somewhere high above and the sudden realization, as he looked up and saw the shining crescent of a moon dimmed by clouds, that it was late, and getting later. He was tired, and felt he had never talked so much in his life. Hulver yawned, looked about him, and said "Time for the burrow, my lad, time for sleep."

"Now you are welcome to use this tunnel, though perhaps I should say *continue* to use it. But I'm going down to my burrow, which is a little way off, because it's so much quieter." And with that he ran off into the night,

Bracken following his course by sound until he went
down an entrance and his sound was lost.

For a while Bracken crouched in the night alone, wondering about Hulver and enjoying the unusual calm and
peace he felt. A snatch of the grace Hulver had spoken
came back to him and he let its words run through his
tired mind like the sound of the breeze in the long grass
by the edge of the wood:

> Let no mole adown our bodies
> That may hurt our sorrowing souls.

He changed the "our" to "my" the second time round,
not knowing that Hulver, in his graciousness, had himself
modified the words to take account of Bracken's presence, for it was a prayer he often said for himself over
his solitary meals. Bracken couldn't remember all the
words and promised himself that he would ask Hulver to
repeat them so he could learn it; then he climbed down
into the tunnel, carefully reblocked it again, and fell into
a deep sleep.

But Hulver, resting his old snout on his graying paws,
did not fall asleep immediately, thinking about the
strange young mole now sleeping in one of his tunnels.
For all the youngster's confusion and bitterness, and his
youthful carping at the westside ways, there was something about him that pleased Hulver. He had a nice quick
way with words; his damning criticism of some of the
westside moles, including Burrhead, was on target, while
his obvious courage in exploring the system so far was
impressive in one so young.

Hulver was excited, too, that he seemed to have a
curiosity about the old system and something of the spirit
for exploration that too few moles had. He paused in his
thoughts, scratching his forehead with his left paw, trying
to catch the words to express the effect Bracken had on
him. "Never was much good with words," he muttered to
himself, shifting into something nearer a sleep position.
"But I like the youngster, there's something about him,
even if he doesn't look as if he could fight a flea."

He thought about the impulse that had taken him to
the part of his tunnels where he had found Bracken. The
same warm impulse he had felt in recent weeks lifting
him out of the long moleyears of pain and desolation

that had followed the preceding Midsummer Night when
he had been sure Rune had been listening in the shadows. Only with the new spring had the load lightened
and something of his old love of life returned. And now,
this Bracken had turned up on his territory, bold as a
brash young pup.

"Well," he told himself, drifting into a happy sleep,
"I'll teach him something about the Ancient System and
its ways. What I know of them. I might even mention
something of the rituals to him, some of these youngsters
ought to know about them."

So began the first friendship that Bracken ever knew
and the last that Hulver ever enjoyed. A strange association of the oldest mole in the system, who had long lost
his political power, and one of the weakest, who had
no power at all.

In the June days that followed Hulver told him a
great deal, and Bracken listened well, taking an active
part in his imagination in all the adventures and journeys,
fights and rituals that Hulver talked about.

He soon asked Hulver to take him up to the Ancient
System, but Hulver always refused, one excuse following
the other: "I'm too tired today for such a climb . . . it's
worm-scarce up there at the moment, better wait a while
. . . there's nothing much to see that I can't describe . . .
too many owls now because moles have been gone too
long." But all this didn't put off Bracken, who only became more determined to go.

But there were other things to talk about as well. It
was from Hulver that he first learned of Uffington, where
the Holy Burrows were, and where mysterious White
Moles were said to roam.

"It's far off, far to the west. I've never met a mole
who's been there, though I talked to some when I was
your age who claimed to have met moles who had."

"What do they do there?" Bracken wanted to know.
"What moles live with the White Moles? Do you know
anything about *scribe*moles, like Aspen mentioned in
her stories?"

The questions tumbled from him in a flow that sometimes made Hulver feel old and helpless, for there
were so many questions he didn't know the answers to

and, what was worse, had never *thought* of finding the
answers to.

"I don't know. I've never known," he would say. "The
scribes came from there, I know that!"

"Yes, but what do scribemoles *do?*" Bracken would
persist.

"They write the stories that moles want to remember
and the prayers and blessings that true moles love. They
go out from Uffington to remind us of the Stone."

"Have they ever been here?" asked Bracken tirelessly,
and Hulver told him what he knew of that.

So Bracken learned much from what Hulver talked
about, but more without knowing it from the gentle way
the old mole lived, seeking worms, openly seeking the
Stone's help, pausing sometimes to tell Bracken to listen
to the sound of "this beloved wood." Often just crouching and making Bracken do the same, even though he
found it irksome crouching in silence when he could be
doing something or talking.

"Which is why I make you do it," Hulver would tell
him mysteriously.

One day Hulver shocked Bracken by announcing that
it was time for the June elder meeting and he would be
gone for five or six days—"even though they don't listen
to what I say with Mandrake hard upon them."

Just before he left, he spoke to Bracken very seriously.
"Stay here quietly, live in my burrow silently as I have
been teaching you to do, for though being Midsummer
this should be a time of great happiness, I fear there is
much danger about. I can smell it, so take care."

A chill came over Bracken's heart at this, for the sudden prospect of being alone again made him recognize
the joy he had been living with in the last few days with
Hulver, who, seeing fear cross his face, softly touched
his shoulder with his paw and said, "There *is* danger,
but you are strong enough to face it. You will never
face an evil you have not the strength to master. When
I come back there will be a lot to do and you will have
much to learn," Hulver told him finally. "I am going to
take you up to the Ancient System. Meanwhile, do not
be lulled by the June sun. There is danger in the system
and I fear you may suffer in its coming, so be careful."

Hulver turned and ran a little way down the slope before disappearing down a tunnel leading to far-off Bar-

row Vale. He hated to leave Bracken, for he had rejoiced
in their friendship too.

Bracken watched him go, and with an enormous sense
of loss turned back down into Hulver's tunnels and along
to his burrow, where he crouched, shaken and desolate.
A terrible dark fear began to seep into him and he shivered, despite the June warmth. He had never felt so
alone. In the darkness he tried to find words to comfort
himself, the fear swirling about him, but they had gone.
Then the fear took him over until it felt like a black
cloud that would burst and explode inside him, and he
found himself crying and desolate, repeating between his
sobs lines from the first grace he had heard Hulver
speak:

> Let no mole adown my body
> That may hurt my sorrowing soul.

And though he did not know it, it was the first prayer to
the Stone that he ever spoke. Slowly it calmed him until
he was able to think of Hulver again and not himself. He
changed the "my" to "his" and said the grace again, hoping it might go down through the tunnels with Hulver to
the elder meeting at Barrow Vale, where it might protect
him.

But Hulver met another mole and had a conversation
with her, before he joined the elder meeting—a meeting
that affected him very much and caused him to think
that Bracken was a more special mole than he might
otherwise have thought.

The mole he met was Rebecca, and it would be the
first time that Rebecca ever heard the name of Bracken
spoken, for her now legendary first meeting with him by
the Stone did not take place until the following September. She had known that an elder meeting was taking
place in June and, as ever, her curiosity getting the better
of her fear of Mandrake, she had dared wait in Barrow
Vale to see the elders arrive for the meeting.

Other moles did the same. That was the nice thing
about the communal tunnels beneath Barrow Vale. The
moment she saw the old mole coming down through the
tunnels that led from the slopes, his snout wrinkled and
low, his fur ragged and graying, she knew who it was.

She ran up to him in the old friendly way she hadn't dared adopt with anymole during April and May, breathless and smiling. "Are you Hulver?" she asked. He stopped and looked up at her, for she stood more upright and young than he did, and he was so nice. Oh! he was wise and radiated love!

"I'm Hulver, I can't deny it," he said cheerfully. "Anyway, no mole else is as old as I am now, so it wasn't hard to guess. Who are you, my dear?"

She hesitated to say from habit, for moles tended to back away when they found she was Mandrake's Rebecca. But with Hulver she sensed it didn't matter. "Rebecca," she said.

"Sarah's daughter!" he said. "And Mandrake's. You're a fine-looking female, I must say, though I suppose you're an adult now, but you all look so young to me. Be the same for you, one day," he laughed.

"Would you tell me about the old times?" she asked eagerly. "Because they say you're the only one who remembers now, the only one who's left." She dropped her voice a little as she said these last words, because she felt an unaccountable desire to go close to Hulver, to press herself to him, to hold him.

"It would take a lifetime to tell you even a small part of it," he said, "and unfortunately I'm in a hurry for the elder meeting."

"Oh," sighed Rebecca, disappointed. There was so much she wanted to know about things and she felt Hulver could tell her. Indeed, she felt he could answer questions she didn't even know how to ask. She crouched down near him sadly.

Hulver, too, was affected by their meeting. She seemed so, so . . . so alive! Eager, and sighing, standing and crouching, sad, loving. Elder meetings never start on time, anyway, he thought to himself, settling down comfortably by her as a sign that he would talk for a little at least. "I'll tell you about Rebecca, your namesake, if you like, Rebecca the Healer of the Ancient System."

Rebecca changed mood again, now sighing contentedly, smiling, peaceful, and closing her eyes as she used to do when Sarah began to tell her a story.

"Mind you, I expect you know all about Rebecca; you can hardly fail to in Duncton, since she's the only claim to fame we seem to have and at least they haven't forgotten her, though they've forgotten everything else that matters." Rebecca nodded happily; she had heard all about Rebecca but she didn't mind hearing it again, not from Hulver.

But Hulver himself didn't know what he was going to say, since it all came into his mind and out as words without him seeming to have too much to do with it. He felt very peaceful. "Most of the stories you've heard are nonsense, I'm sure; harmless nonsense, of course. It's just that we all like a good tale and if there seems to be a gap in the telling of it, we fill it up with something we like to think might have been—and who knows, it *might* have been!" Hulver felt as if his words were exploring a tunnel down which he himself had never been.

"Do you know what I think?" He asked the question as much to himself as to Rebecca, but she shook her head and crouched even closer to Hulver, whose presence she found she loved, because there was something about his great age and goodness which seemed to grow out of the ground itself and make her feel safe and loved. "I believe she did stay here in Duncton for quite a time. I believe that in those days Duncton was a system where a mole like her would *want* to stay. I believe she loved Duncton Wood as you or I might love Barrow Vale in the spring.

"Now, what you are going to ask me, in fact, what I ask myself, is *why* I believe all that. Well, I'll tell you, my dear, because even if you don't understand now, one day you will, I'm sure.

"Twelve moleyears ago, before you were born, there was an elder meeting. It was the June meeting like the one about to be held. Much was said at it, though you needn't worry about that. But during it, your father became the leading elder and his real sway over the system began. There were threats, dark talk, much sadness over the system for some of us, as there still is. For a time I felt full of despair and wanted to die. I saw that your father would destroy the system and there was nothing I could do about it. I went back to my burrow and sat in silence. I would have liked to have talked to another mole, but even my dearest friend, Bindle, was too afraid to talk to me. Now he no longer attends the elder meetings. Anyway, I was alone. Everything

seemed bleak, although outside the June wind was warm,
the worms were plentiful and the youngsters were growing fast down in the main system. But I didn't eat. I
crouched alone and silent.

"The only thing that kept me alive was the knowledge
that I alone knew the full Midsummer ritual and although Mandrake said he would kill me"—here Rebecca gasped lightly, and Hulver put a paw on her
shoulder for a moment—"if I went through with it, yet I
knew I had to.

"Then one of the old legends came to me; you know
it, I'm sure—Groundsel the Owlkiller. You remember
how he saw that it was better to die than to live in the
thrall of fear? I began to feel the same. I went out onto
the surface and looked up at the great trees above me,
listening to the wood all around and waiting for first
light. June! What a time! How happy I suddenly was as
the light overtook the dark wood, cutting away its darkest
patches, turning black into gray and then gray into
the color of summer! When night came around again,
I climbed the hill to celebrate Midsummer. The fear that
had been hanging about seemed to have gone and, of
course, I wasn't killed by Mandrake. As I set off I *knew*
I wouldn't be killed, even though I was followed from
the moment I left my burrow. I'm not sure by whom, but
seeing how things have gone since in the system, and
who is Mandrake's most active henchmole, I think it
must have been Rune. He probably thought I didn't
know he was there, but you don't live as long as I have
without knowing what or who is nearby—especially something as unpleasant as Rune!"

Here Rebecca sighed and nodded. She knew what he
meant.

"Anyway, I went through the ritual carefully, not missing out one bit. I also said a special prayer and I said it
in the direction of Uffington—I asked that Duncton
might be visited once more by a scribemole. There was
something funny about that prayer, something powerful
that made me know that the Stone *does* listen. One day
you'll understand what I mean."

As he said this, Hulver looked full on Rebecca and into her eyes, which were alight with life and love, and
for a moment it was as if his old body had stopped and
was hung suspended in a place of wonder, for he knew

that this mole, this female, was special and that in some mysterious way the Stone was speaking to her through him. And that thought caused him to think of Bracken, who had looked so frightened when he left him up on the slopes, and made him see that there was a connection between the two. He felt as if he were crouched between them and that there was a power, a force, an enormous, troubled strength that was coursing unknown between them and taking its path through him! He shook himself and continued his story.

"When I had finished making this prayer, I turned back to my burrows on the slopes, feeling, I must admit, somewhat cast down. I felt Rune's evil presence near me and this time I couldn't resist it in the way I had when I went up the hill. Perhaps the ritual had drained me; such things are very tiring, you know. I could feel his evil coming into me as fear, as aching, as aging.

"Now what has all this got to do with Rebecca the Healer? Listen carefully. As the days went on, I felt sure that Rune had put some kind of curse on me, or left something of himself about my tunnels. Yet, though I felt tired and ill, my old head began to see things more clearly than before. What did I see? I can't possibly *explain* it all—I forgot things that ran so clearly before me almost as soon as I saw them. But the most important thing I saw, or rather felt, was that Rebecca the Healer was in the system; she *was* here. Now that's different from hearing a tale told, and enjoying it, about a mole who once stayed in the Ancient System. I *knew* she was here. What's more, I could *feel* she was still here—I should say *is* still here. I lived totally by myself for molemonths on end, or perhaps it was moleyears—I'm not quite sure, but I wasn't alone. Rebecca was there as she is with you, her namesake, or up there," he waved his paw in the direction of the slopes, "with . . . with Bracken!"

Before Rebecca could ask who Bracken was, which she was about to do, Hulver interrupted her and himself by touching the side of her head with his paw and saying "I don't think I will see you again, my dear, so remember what I say, however strange it seems." He was conscious again that the elder meeting was going to start soon, also that time was running out and he was sorry, so sorry, that he had not met Rebecca before.

"You see, my dear," he said urgently, "Rebecca the Healer was up on the slopes with me, or rather her love was, which is more or less the same thing. Often in the silence of my burrow, or crouching still on the surface, I would hear her in the wind or see her in a beech leaf or a root, and my old pains and aches would be gone. I'm an old mole and have had many mates, but I've never felt such a love as Rebecca seemed to fill me with. She loved Duncton Wood once, or the moles in it, and left her love here always. You only have to reach out a paw to touch it."

He stopped suddenly. He had to go. He wanted to get the elder meeting over and done with, because there was so little time. "Does any of that make sense to you?" he asked Rebecca gently. He knew it didn't matter whether she answered or not but, in fact, she was so involved with what he was saying that she said nothing at all. It didn't make much sense to him, come to think of it, so quite what he could expect Rebecca to say he didn't know. But after all this time away from friendly moles—his only appearance at Barrow Vale in the last few moleyears had been at elder meetings—it was a pleasure to be talking to a mole who listened to him with affection. So young, so much to live through that he couldn't—or wouldn't—be able to help with. He thought of Bracken again suddenly, up there in his burrow waiting for his return. He remembered the sad fear in the youngster's face as he left him there.

"Do you know a mole called Bracken, from the west-side?" he asked Rebecca. She shook her head. "A strange thing," he went on, half to himself. "I was drawn over to a part of my tunnels which I had more or less abandoned by . . . well . . . a feeling. A 'Rebecca kind of feeling,' as I call them. And there was a mole, bold as you please. A youngster looking as if he was hardly weaned. Not much to look at, inclined to complain about his home burrow, also inclined to steal other moles' worms. Be that as it may. Since Rebecca seemed to have led me to him, it seemed the least I could do was talk to him, which I did, though I was tired."

Hulver did not elaborate. It occurred to him that the fewer who knew Bracken was still in his burrow, the better.

"Please, Hulver, did you tell him the story about Rebecca, I mean *your* story?"

"No, no, he wouldn't understand. He was more interested in adventure and fighting and exploring the Ancient System. Oh, and in scribemoles, though I couldn't tell him much about those!"

"Well, *I* want to know about the Ancient System, too," said Rebecca, pretending for a moment to be just a youngster who has to be humored. "And about scribemoles as well."

Hulver ignored the sudden childishness in her voice and continued to speak to her as he had already—as if she were an adult.

"This Bracken," he said. "There's something about him . . . I don't know what. Perhaps I'm getting old. I wish I was young again so I could help him . . ." He stopped, his snout lowered, and Rebecca wanted him to go on. He was trying to say something to her, but he didn't know the words.

She looked at his old face and watched the struggle for words go across it and understood suddenly, in the way that often comes to youngsters, a truth they are still too young to articulate. She understood that a mole, even a wise one, may often not know what it is he is trying to say and that one who is listening to him must help, by being silent, and by listening to the silence between the sometimes stumbling words.

"This Bracken, he's a strange mole. He has given me hope, but I don't know why. He really isn't much to look at at all and certainly doesn't look as if he could defend himself. And yet . . . well . . . Rebecca . . ." He looked at her again, struggling for the words, caught between these two youngsters, unable to express the power and relief they unwittingly gave him. "Rebecca, sometimes you'll find there are moles you can help who don't seem worth the trouble. You wonder why you tried. They may be weak, or selfish, or stupid, or lazy. But you'll find that if you give such a mole your help, or in other words your love, they will often repay you in ways you could never have dreamed of. That's how the Stone works, do you see? That's it. These moles will pop up years later and suddenly the mystery of why they crossed your tunnel, and came briefly into your life, is solved. And then you know that there are powers beyond your-

self over which you have no control and before which a
mole should feel awe. That's something many moles have
forgotten. Don't you forget it. Never forget it!"

· He looked at her intently and she was wide-eyed before
him and wanted, oh how she wanted . . . and she did!
She went up to him and nuzzled him and held him for an
instant, her young glossy fur mixing with his own. Oh,
she felt such love for him, such awe for his wisdom and
the simple way he held his old body. "Oh, Hulver," she
whispered, oh oh oh.

A great sweetness came into Hulver, who had not
been touched by another mole for moleyears, and never
with such love. Never, ever. Why, she was beautiful—
had it taken him so long to see that the only beauty is
love? And then, once again, an image of Bracken came
into his mind and he found himself saying—or rather
whispering, because she was so very close—"You keep an
eye out for Bracken. There's more to him than a mole
might think when they meet him. Much more. He may
need your help, Rebecca."

He broke away from her and they smiled into each
other.

"Perhaps you'll need his help," said Hulver, "because
that's how the Stone works, you see. All of us need
what you can give, especially you yourself."

And with this last mysterious comment, Hulver left
her, and she found herself full of the strangest love and
joy. Oh, she sighed, oh.

BRACKEN stayed fast in Hulver's burrow for two days after he had gone. There was a good supply of worms, and Hulver's warning had frightened him enough to stay where he was. Indeed, it had put such a fear in him that for those two days Bracken expected some terrible danger to manifest itself at any moment, even in the burrow itself. So he started at every sound and worried at every silence.

By the third day the worms were running out and, anyway, he was getting restless. Even fear can be overtaken by boredom. He could feel that the weather was warm and June-like on the surface, so he went there, never straying far from the tunnel entrance. The entrance nearest Hulver's burrow was among the beech trees themselves; only below it did they disappear into the oaks and mixed wood that formed the level part of Duncton Wood.

Among the beeches the wood felt different, and he wasn't sure if he liked it so much. They were lighter and cleaner then oaks and no vegetation grew under them or cluttering hazel, hawthorn and holly about them. There was a purity in the air and a lack of distracting vegetation on the ground that made a mole think. If the top of the hill is like this, Bracken thought, then no wonder the ancient moles were different from us. He explored Hulver's tunnels in all directions and found, as he had suspected, that the system was too large for the old mole to maintain and in places was falling into disrepair.

He noticed that on the east side of Hulver's system the tunnels were older-looking, less straight and not in such good condition. He deduced from this that Hulver had tied his own tunnels onto another long-abandoned series of tunnels he had found a little higher up the slopes. Bracken was intrigued by this and sought the central home burrow this older system must have had, but he couldn't find it. Here and there, where tunnels rose up the slopes, he found they were blocked—and blocked a very long time ago, for the barriers looked like tunnel ends rather than mere walls of soil, but by tapping them

with his talons he could tell there were more tunnels beyond. He was tempted to burrow a way through, but this
would have been discourteous to Hulver.

As his explorations continued (and they spread over
several days because he still spent a lot of time in silence
in Hulver's home burrow) a gradual reorientation about
the shape of the whole Duncton system took place in his
mind. He had, of course, not yet been to some key areas
—the Ancient System, the eastside and the Marsh End.
But he became much more aware of them and their
relationship to each other than he had before. As a mole
pup sees his own home burrow in a different way once
he has been outside it into the tunnels, and those differently when he has been onto the surface, so Bracken
now saw that the westside was only a part of the system,
and a peripheral part at that.

These thoughts struck him with particular force one
morning, the seventh day of Hulver's absence, as he
crouched up on the surface again enjoying the June sun.
He had found a few worms, and having eaten them was
"listening to the wood" as Hulver himself often did. The
wood was exciting and very alive. Much more sound
came from the lower part, where the oak trees started
and there were more birds. Up here on the slopes the
air seemed clearer than he had ever known, and everything seemed possible. *Everything.* Bracken crouched facing south toward Barrow Vale far below, his back to the
Ancient System above.

The sun shone through the shimmering young beech
leaves from the east to his right, while down to his left
lay the westside and Aspen and Root going about . . .
and Burrhead must be straight ahead down there at the
elder meeting, talking, talking . . . and above was the
sky bigger than everything, arching away, far beyond even
the Marsh End. Bracken saw then, for the first time, how
the Duncton system was just a system, not the world.
One day he could go beyond it like the sky did, for
everything was possible.

He felt a surging pull above and behind him from
the Ancient System, whose edge he was on. He felt for
a moment like one of the ancients, looking down on the
new system. He saw that Hulver's system was superbly
placed in the system as a whole, poised as it was on
the edge of the ancient and the modern, the eastside

and the west. Bracken's heart raced as he felt an urge to run off through the wood, all over the wood, for everything *was* possible and must be explored.

He might well have done so had not a familiar scurrying sound warned him that a mole was coming up from the oak wood below. Bracken knew it was not Hulver when the sounds veered off to the west and disappeared belowground. Hulver would never enter his own system so stealthily. At this point Bracken was wary rather than frightened, and ran back down into the tunnels, crouching quietly in a side tunnel near the home burrow from where he would hear everything and be able to escape in several different directions. He knew the system well enough to be able to elude any alien mole if necessary.

The mole moved about here and there in the system but finally went up to the surface again, searching back and forth until he found the main entrance. This was only a few moleyards from where Bracken crouched and he waited tensely.

It was a strange position to be in—defending a system not his own. Suddenly the mole came boldly and resolutely into the system and stopped still as death in the main tunnel. Bracken shuffled about a little to establish his presence, for he had no intention of either waiting to be found or running off and leaving Hulver's burrow to the care of a stranger.

"Who is there, and what are you doing here?" the alien mole called in a commanding voice that took Bracken by surprise. He might have expected to ask the same question himself but had neither the presence of mind nor, perhaps, the courage, to do so. The mole was obviously tough and mature, and Bracken quickly persuaded himself that there was no possibility of fighting him successfully, even if he had wanted to, which he didn't.

He had no sooner poked his snout out of the side tunnel than the stranger was coming toward him—bold, calm, dominant.

"My name's Rune," said the mole, "and you had better tell me what you are doing here." He advanced the last few steps menacingly. For the first time in his life Bracken was faced by a mole he knew, with absolute certainty, would kill him if he felt like it. There was such indifferent power in Rune's gaze that what little courage Bracken felt inside him shriveled up, to be replaced by a desperate clutching in blackness that simply wanted to escape. Rune seemed huge and all-powerful and, for all Bracken knew, might continue his menacing walk right over him, leaving him like a squashed moth that has happened into a hurrying mole's path.

"Oh, Rune, sir, my name's Bracken and I came too far from the westside," he whined, his voice high from the tightness and constriction that, in his fear, had invaded his throat. He looked at the terrifying Rune, waiting to do his bidding. If Rune had said "Turn on your back and scratch the ceiling," Bracken would have done it without question. But Rune said nothing, simply gazing searingly at Bracken who, had he had sufficient wits about him to consider the matter, might have concluded that it would be better if he *had* been asked to scratch the ceiling. Instead, he chose to fill the silence with another catchphrase from his stock of "little mole lost" excuses for being in the wrong place at the wrong time. "I also ran out of worms and this burrow was deserted so I stayed here."

Rune knew perfectly well that Bracken was Burrhead's son, and though the lad was by all accounts an idiot (a good reason for killing him there and then) he had no wish to aggravate Burrhead and the westside needlessly. The time was not yet ripe. Though as he watched the stuttering youngster making his excuses, Rune was inclined to think he would be doing Burrhead a favor to get rid of him.

"Well, it's not deserted, because I'm here now and I suggest you return to the westside *fast*," he said slowly. "Moles shouldn't leave their territories and it's only because you're a youngster that I'm making allowances. If you get stopped on your way back to the westside you can tell them that I sent you back. But don't try this kind of exploration again; it's not safe. Now get going."

"Yes, Rune, sir, thank you, sir," said Bracken, adding with the effusiveness of a mole who has been let off the talon, "thank you, sir, I will go straight back now. Thank you, sir." And he dashed away, up into the fresh air.

There he found himself shaking and sweating and running all at the same time, desperate to get away from Rune, who put the fear of diseased darkness into his

soul. He had never been so frightened in his life, not by
Root, not by the wildest noises on the surface out of
reach of a tunnel entrance, not even by Burrhead.

Only when he was down below the slopes again and
well into the oaks did he pause to think. He couldn't go
back to the westside, because he would almost certainly
be killed by Burrhead or Root; he couldn't hang about
around Hulver's tunnels. So he didn't know where to go.
Having reached this cul-de-sac he moved on to thinking
about Hulver.

If Rune was here and Rune was an elder, the elder
meeting must be over. Which meant that Hulver must
also be on his way back. Hulver would be able to tell him
what to do or where to go, so he turned away from the
route back to the westside, cutting off toward the eastside, contouring round the slopes. He would try to locate
the main tunnel Hulver had headed down when he had
gone to Barrow Vale and which, presumably, Rune had
come up. With luck he might reach it before Hulver
passed by on up to his burrow—and Rune. Rune! It occurred to Bracken only then, after running so far and
fearing so much, that Rune was the danger Hulver must
have sensed would come. Rune had come to kill Hulver.

An urgency now came to his progress through the
wood, for he speeded up, not bothering to run from cover
to cover and shadow to shadow as any sensible creature
normally does. No time. Not bothering to avoid the dry
leaves because of the noise they made. No time. Dashing,
running, scampering along the contour. Against time. His
fear of Rune was replaced by an urgent desire to reach
Hulver and warn him.

Strangely, as he ran through the wood, aware of direction, aware of scent, feeling the dangers, head clear as
air after rainfall, an excitement he had never felt before
crept over him. He felt more in control of himself than
he had ever felt. All the skills he had added to his basic
gift for orientation and exploration were now working together, taking him toward the tunnel he knew must be
there to find. Probably no other Duncton mole but Rune
and one or two of the marshenders could have found
their way across the system to the communal tunnel with
the concentration and skill that Bracken, still a youngster,
was able to do. He *knew* where he was going. And he
found the tunnel as surely as a wasp finds its nest or an

owl its prey. He knew it by temperature change, by smell, and by location; he knew it by instinct. He lay above the tunnel for a moment or two and then ran up it toward the slopes, realizing that if he went down toward Barrow Vale it was just possible that Hulver might pass him. So he ran back up toward Hulver's burrow and the danger of Rune until he found an old, barely discernible entrance, and went down it. He crouched low and silent. There was no vibration in the tunnel at all, not a mole for miles. If Hulver had passed by, he was now far on and there was no chance of catching him. So he waited, snout on his paws, just as Hulver sometimes lay in the wood, eyes closed. Above, on the surface, the midday sun shone down poised for its downward arc to the west.

Not long afterward Bracken felt vibrations and the briefest rush of air as a mole approached. He waited trembling, for if it wasn't Hulver he would have to do some fast talking. He decided to claim that Rune had sent him down this way on his way back to westside. As the mole approached, Bracken decided to save time by announcing himself.

"Hello! I'm Bracken!"

The mole stopped, and Bracken heard a gentle laugh.

"Are you, indeed! Always finding your way into tunnels you shouldn't be in!" It *was* Hulver, and Bracken felt relief rush over him. "There's little time, Bracken, very little," said Hulver quickly, "and there is a great deal to do. I assume that Rune found you in my burrow and sent you packing?"

Bracken nodded. "Whether he has gone there to kill me or simply to warn me for a final (and fruitless) time, I cannot say," said Hulver. "But I'm not going to risk going back now that you are safe here with me. There are nine days left before Midsummer Night. We cannot return to my tunnels and so must hide somewhere else. I think the best thing is to head up toward the Stone and rely on its shadow to hide us for the days that remain. You have much to learn, more than you can know."

Bracken felt, or thought he felt, alien vibrations far down in the tunnel. Hard to say, but he wanted to get away as fast as possible.

"There may be other moles coming," he whispered. "I can hear something, or rather feel it." Hulver looked at the youngster who crouched still before him, his head and snout on one side, body tense and ready: feeling fear for him. For himself he felt nothing; he had little time left now. But this youngster had so much to do, so much, and Hulver trembled for him.

"We *must* go," said Bracken urgently. "*Please* may we go?" Hulver nodded and turned up to the entrance and out onto the surface into the afternoon sun.

Hulver led the way, taking the circular route below his own tunnels that Bracken had taken, then up toward the beech trees. At last the beech wood lay directly ahead of them, familiar to Hulver but as terrifying to Bracken in its tall silence as it had been when he had been alone by Hulver's burrow. Each step they took left the friendly oak wood farther behind, with its bird chatter and song, its scurrying blackbirds searching the leaves, its squirrels starting and champing among the oak branches.

"We had better stop for a while," said Bracken, his natural tracking instinct giving him a sense of command he had not felt before. "We'll wait for the evening wind to give us noise cover before we climb on."

Hulver smiled to himself. Just what he would have done—had he thought of it. Bracken certainly seemed to know his way about the wood. Yet, at the same time, the youngster was very nervous, jumping at every shadow and making Hulver himself start more than once. It *was* time to stop.

He let Bracken dig a temporary burrow, watching him tunnel away at the mold. The youngster looked vulnerable against the massive oak root that plunged into the ground beyond him.

He had a strong feeling that his long wait since the previous Midsummer, a wait that had often driven him to despair and doubt, had not been in vain.

Often on a dark night he had tossed and turned over in his mind why he, of all his generation, was still alive after six Longest Nights. Six! He shuddered at the number. When the long moleyears of winter had given way finally to the earliest stirrings of spring, the worst time came when the air was chill as ice and he knew he would not mate. Often, then, he would go to sleep in his burrow and wish that he might not wake up. He wanted never again to rise to the aches and pains, fears and doubts that had come upon him in old age. But as spring

advanced, the feeling that Rebecca the Healer was there
had come over him and gradually a tiny hope had come
back that something might happen. *Something might happen.* He had remembered the stories about her which they
had told him as a child when he was sure she was real
and walked the tunnels when no mole was there. Now he
saw she *was* real after all, but had gone away for most of
his life, only to come back at the end. "Old foolish mole,"
he scolded himself. "Living in the past."

"The burrow's ready, Hulver," Bracken said, breaking
into his thoughts. "Best go down it until the wind rises."
Hulver did, meek as an old mole. What could he give the
youngster in the time he had left?

Well, he could tell him the old stories and instruct him
in the rituals to pass on the heritage that is everymole's,
though so few want to honor it.

Seeing that Bracken was jumpy with waiting for nightfall, Hulver decided to start his education there and then
by recounting the tale of Merton, chosen mole of Uffington, just as it had been told to him by his father, and to
him by the very last scribemole ever to visit Duncton
Wood.

It was a tale that recalled the mole whose task in life
had turned out to be to save the secret song of Uffington,
which only chosen moles sing and then only once in a
cycle of seasons. How Bracken shuddered to hear of the
plague that wiped out most of the scribemoles back in
the distant past when Merton had lived. Now his heart
stirred to hear of Merton's escape from Uffington, and his
survival, and his remembrance of the sacred song he had
learned in secret and never forgotten. Then of his return,
when his days were nearly over, so that he could pass on
the song for other younger moles to sing so that it might
be known to future generations and perhaps, if the Stone
permitted it, finally be sung by all moles and not just a
chosen few.

"Will that ever happen?" asked Bracken, breaking the
silence that followed the ending of Hulver's long tale.
"And do they still sing the secret song in Uffington?"

Hulver shrugged, for how could he know if the song
still lived? Had not most of the rituals in his own system
died, and that within living memory?

"Perhaps, perhaps," he said, "but I remember one
thing my father told me, though blessed if I can make

much sense of it. He said there was a special Stone nearing Uffington—the Blowing Stone, I think he called it—
which sounds in the wind sometimes. He told me that
the scribemole said that when that Stone sounded seven
times *then* the secret song would be sung by all moles."

It was just the sort of story to stir a youngster's heart
and Bracken asked the question any youngster would
have asked: "What's the song about?"

Hulver stayed silent; he had often pondered the question himself. He had asked it of his father, and got no
clear answer. He could only answer it in terms of Duncton Wood, where he had spent his entire life, and think
that perhaps there were times when belief in the Stone
and celebration of its life becomes a hidden secret thing,
carried forward to new generations by those few who are
foolhardy enough, or brave enough, to trust in a power
they cannot see, and belief that it is worth far far more
than the comforts of food and shelter that a system like
Duncton offers.

He was confused about it, so how could he ever hope
to pass on anything useful to this youngster? All he could
do was to try, and to believe that tales like this one carry
truth forward in their own way.

This was the story a long-forgotten scribemole brought
to Duncton Wood. It was handed down through the generations as the song it is about was handed down. Until
one fraught day it was Hulver's task to hand it on to
young Bracken to carry it in his heart all his life,
as Hulver carried the song.

Although Bracken appeared half asleep as Hulver finished the tale, he had never been so awake. The tale
had the effect of carrying him far beyond Duncton Wood
and to make him see again, as he had seen before, that
Duncton was just one system, one place, one corner of
the world. He wondered where his task lay, for he supposed he had one.

Above them, on the surface, the wind stirred and a
beech leaf tumbled noisily against their temporary burrow entrance. It settled for a moment and then scurried
off a moleyard or two before eddying to a stop against
a beech-tree trunk, joining the others already there.

The evening wind had come and the light was beginning to lose its shine as the sun settled down toward the
distant hills no Duncton mole could ever see.

"It's time to go," said Bracken. "Show me the direction, but let me go first, for I'm used to sensing danger and can find my way very quickly."

They trekked up to the southwest, away from Hulver's burrow and the danger of Rune. Bracken had imagined his first climb up into the Ancient System, thinking that the sun would be high in the sky and he would walk boldly upward. Instead, here he was with very real danger about, skulking his way through the twilight. But there was something sweeter than his most delightful imaginings in having as a guide and friend this old mole for whom he was beginning to feel such deep affection and reverence.

It got darker as they rose higher, yet the farther they went, the stronger did Bracken feel the pull from the top. He felt it as a good wormhunter feels his prey. They scurried from tree to tree, from root to root, always seeking the darkest shadow. Here and there they came across a bare patch of chalk, white in the evening gloom, and they avoided it for fear that their movement might be seen against it by any predators that lurked in the trees above. Once they passed by a massive tangle of roots rising starkly into the air, the bowl of a tree that had toppled over in some storm. They steered well clear of its long trunk and shattered branches on the ground—what mole could tell what might be nesting there.

As they rose higher, Hulver suddenly stopped and put his paw on Bracken's shoulder, bringing him to a halt. "We are on the Ancient System," he whispered. "From here it runs upward and across the hill."

But Bracken knew it already, for he had sensed they were crossing old forgotten tunnels lost deep beneath the mold and debris of ages. His heart was beating with excitement for he felt as if, after a very long time, he was coming home. He knew the Ancient System was around him, he could *feel* it. It lay beneath them waiting, as it had waited for generations. And he could feel more than ever the great Stone which they were getting nearer and nearer.

"We'll go right to the Stone, now," he said quietly to Hulver, "and from there we'll know what to do."

It was at that moment in the evening when an eye-blink separates day from night. In the moment that a mole might wonder if it is still day, the question is answered by a sudden pall of purple in the sky. Bracken's snout pointed up through the wood directly toward the Stone, although he had never been there. "There is no mole here," he told Hulver, certain of himself, "and there is none on the Ancient System. Can't you feel it?"

Hulver couldn't feel it, didn't like it, and couldn't understand Bracken's certainty; but he followed after him, for as he watched Bracken's flanks disappearing upward into the dark and looked about him at the black tree-shapes with the wide open spaces in between, nothing else seemed as safe. He could feel that Bracken was gaining strength with each moment that passed. There was a power about him that swept Hulver along and he had the feeling that through this mole the Stone was revealing to him a tiny part of its pattern, the whole of which he could not see or feel, although he knew it to be there.

With this feeling, a slow calm fell over him that was never to leave him again. In some way he was watching a battle start, an enormous battle, a terribly dangerous time. It would happen, whatever happened, and his own part in it, if part he had, was best played by him being at peace with himself and the world about him.

"Hulver!" The whispered urgency of Bracken's voice struck Hulver as comic, but with compassion for the youngster he restrained himself from laughing happily. Instead he watched with love as Bracken ran back toward him, to hurry him up, no doubt.

To Bracken, Hulver looked so gentle in the soft night, he expressed such peace and love, that his nerves were suddenly calmed within themselves and his fear and nervousness became as easy to brush away as dust on his fur. "Come on," said Bracken softly, "come on, Hulver!" But there was no need, for Hulver was already starting up the hill again, and for some reason was chuckling quietly to himself.

As the hill leveled off and they reached its summit, Bracken slowed, almost afraid to advance, for he knew they were now very near the Stone. The windnoise in the trees was high and strong, swinging back from one side above them to the other as the wind billowed from one group of trees to another. It was a mass of great, invisible waves rolling across the top of the wood and way beyond it. "There!" said Hulver, pointing a talon forward into a clearing ahead of them. "There is the Stone."

And it was, huge and massive, towering upward, solid in the windy night. Ten or twelve moleyards from it stood an ancient beech tree, its roots plunging along and into the ground, across the clearing's floor to the Stone itself. From where Bracken crouched, the roots appeared solid waves that had rolled and heaved against the Stone, so that it tilted a little away from the tree away toward Uffington.

There was no other tree near it, for the clearing was quite wide, and as they ran across toward the Stone, the windnoise above them fell quieter, staying with the trees at its edge and Bracken had the impression that he had come into somewhere very quiet and still. But he felt the thunder of the generations and knew that all around him and beyond the clearing the Ancient System stretched forth, its lost tunnels hidden beneath the ages of leaf mold on the spare surface of the hill. He was at the heart of the Ancient System but more than that; he was home, at the center, at the true center of the system into which he had been born.

Hulver crouched down before the Stone and Bracken followed him. Up here the wood defined itself by windnoise. Off to the west lay the pastures, the wind running up off them and then through the massive branches above them. To the east was the escarpment where upward eddies of air met the wind in the trees and the wind tumbled above on the edge of the void. Below them were softer noises of the main wood itself, quieter then this, deeper. By the Stone there was silence, and a calm Bracken had never known anywhere in the wood.

He looked all around, got up and ran to the edge of the clearing in the direction toward which the Stone tilted: "How far is Uffington, Hulver?" he asked.

Hulver came to his side, both their snouts pointing out through the trees toward the west. Hulver was still breathing heavily from the long climb up from the slopes. "A long way, a very long way, but not so far if you have the Stone behind you."

"No, it's not so far, not too far," said Bracken to himself, for he could feel Uffington pulling him. "It's not that far, Hulver," he said quietly, "I can *feel* it."

When Hulver used the words "not so far if you have the Stone behind you," he was giving the standard reply senior moles used to give to youngsters who asked the once-inevitable question about Uffington. But as Bracken crouched there, Hulver saw it in a different way than he had before: perhaps it meant exactly what it said: perhaps Uffington *was* in some way nearer if you kept the Stone always directly behind you as you progressed toward it. Well, it made sense, didn't it? And he had been struck by the way in which Bracken had run exactly to the point on the edge of the clearing that lay nearest Uffington, without having been told.

"How do you know where Uffington is?" asked Hulver curiously. Bracken interested him more and more. "I can *feel* it. If you stand with the Stone behind you," said Bracken, "you can feel it pulling. Well, *you* know . . ."

But Hulver didn't, though he understood what Bracken was saying better than Bracken himself.

He would have stayed there all night if Hulver had not at last said "Come on, Bracken, we must hide ourselves now. We must find worms to eat and we must rest. There is much for you to learn tomorrow."

They finally hid themselves among the surface roots of the old beech in the clearing by the Stone. The soil was hard there, but there was mold and leaves to burrow under and the nearer the Stone they were, the safer they felt themselves from the danger of Rune.

Bracken was never sure afterward whether he slept right through until the sun rose or whether he kept waking up and looking at the Stone. But dream or reality, he later remembered a changing vision of the Stone, first deep black in the night, later mellowing to purple, suddenly very dark gray, gradually lightening to a dull gray before lighting to pink and soft gray and yellow as the sun broke through the beeches behind them with the dawn.

When he finally woke up, there was the Stone rising protectively above him, the soft gray and greens of the beech trees in June behind, and the sky beyond that. A shaking of leaves off his fur, two or three steps forward, and he was able, at last, to reach out with his paw and touch the Stone in the morning light.

THE threat from Mandrake against Hulver and Bracken over the performance of the Midsummer ritual was very real. At the previous Midsummer, Mandrake had not felt secure enough to order Rune to kill Hulver at the Stone. But now he had the system so cowed that he felt strong enough to kill off its old traditions and anymole who stood by them.

At the June elder meeting, which Hulver had left Bracken to attend, Mandrake left no doubt about his intentions. The Midsummer ritual must not be spoken, he told the elders, and no mole must go up to the Stone. This was an absolute ruling for which he now expected each elder publicly to signal his support. If it should be disobeyed, he stressed, then that would result in the death of the disobedient.

Before he asked each elder to show his support, Mandrake made himself very clear a final time: "I understand that a certain mole here among us performed the ritual last Midsummer Night, despite our agreement that it should be abandoned. I was prepared then to give him the benefit of my tolerance . . ." Mandrake looked about him with avuncular concern. "But no mole should depend on it again." He paused to let the message sink home, fixing Hulver with his gaze. "Now do we agree that the ritual must not be performed?"

One by one the elders signaled agreement. Except for Hulver, who stayed silent and motionless, snout on his paws and his eyes half closed. Very peaceful.

Mandrake affected to ignore him. "We have made our decision, then, and will see that it is carried out," he said with a heavy menace that amounted to a command to them all: he did not actually say that they must all take part in what looked to most of them like the inevitable slaughter of Hulver up by the Stone, but anymole there who refused to be involved, and take responsibility, had better watch out!

But Hulver was not the only mole there to disagree with Mandrake. Mekkins, the half-marshender, had no intention of adding his talons to those who might strike

Hulver down on Midsummer Night. True, he had signaled agreement, and he would go along with Mandrake's suggestion that they all take part in any punishment meted out to the "disobedient"—but Mekkins was good at appearing to do something and doing something else. He might not be a very moral mole—how could he be while he acted for Mandrake and the marshenders at the same time?—but he had never yet killed a youngster or a mole too old to defend himself and he wasn't going to start now. He would fight anymole that got in his way, but he didn't set out to kill them because they did something to which he was utterly indifferent, like the Midsummer Night ritual.

Soon after the decision on the ritual, the elder meeting fizzled out. Rune left early, muttering something about an important job as Mandrake gave him a nod of approving dismissal. Hulver was suspicious, and on his way out with the others, he stopped one of the youngsters hanging about Barrow Vale and asked if he had seen Rune pass by. The answer was as he had feared: "Yes, sir, he went up by the tunnel to the slopes. Not so long ago, so you might catch him."

So Hulver set off back to the slopes, regretting now that he had left Bracken so exposed. But he had found him and now, here they were, up on the ancient system, waiting for the days to pass to Midsummer Night.

The Midsummer ritual Mandrake, Rune and Burrhead made so much trouble about was a thanksgiving for the blessing of the new generation of youngsters born in the spring. Midsummer fell at about the time they left (or were pushed out of) their home burrows to find their own territory. It was the beginning of a more solitary life and a time in which many would be caught by a tawny owl or starve as they searched for new territory. As well as being a thanksgiving, the ritual was also a petition to the Stone that these youngsters might be safe from talon and beak.

As they began the first of many sessions of explanation and story-telling in the nine-day wait before Midsummer Night, Hulver explained to Bracken that in ancient times every youngster in the system made the trek to the Stone and witnessed the ritual. It helped give youngsters the courage they would need in the trials that lay immediately ahead of them. Indeed, after it, many never returned to

their home burrows—the ritual was the moment of departure and their home burrows were left for their mothers to
occupy by themselves again.

In ancient times, a scribemole would make the long
trek from Uffington to attend the Duncton ritual, for the
presence of the Stone gave it a special status among mole
systems generally. By Hulver's youth, of course, no
scribemole came, or had come, for a long time and the
ritual was beginning to decline in importance. Fewer
youngsters attended, perhaps initially because, as they
migrated down the slopes, the journey became too dangerous.

"Perhaps Mandrake's ban on the ritual is the inevitable
conclusion to what has been coming for generations," explained Hulver, "though why an outsider should be the
instrument of it, I do not know. It *may* be ending, but I
will not let it end as long as I am able. They think I'm
old and traditional down at Barrow Vale, and perhaps I
am, but unless you honor something, you honor nothing.
There's more to being a mole than burrows, worms, fighting and mating—much more. I hope you'll have the sense
to see that one day."

"Did you go to the ritual when you were young?"
asked Bracken.

"Yes, I went. I was one of the few—but then my mother
came from the slopes and insisted. It was the first time I
saw the elders together in the shadow of the Stone and
with the chanting and the words it was very awe-inspiring.
I remember afterward I felt I could do anything. *Anything!* It gave me the courage to face the fact that I could
never return to my home burrow, and after it, I never
did."

Bracken nodded with understanding. He remembered
his own feelings of fear and desolation when he was alone
in Hulver's burrow.

"What's a chanting song?" Bracken wanted to know
next.

"Oh!" Hulver was surprised, but then youngsters these
days didn't seem to know anything. "Why, they're ritual
songs, songs of courage, hope and prophecy. One mole
sings a verse and then the others join in."

Hulver began to sing one of the songs in his old voice,
but Bracken wasn't impressed and finally Hulver stopped

singing. "Well, you need a lot of moles singing it together. Hear that once and you never forget it!"

They stayed entirely on the surface for the first two or three days, because although Bracken was at first inclined to search for an entrance into the Ancient System, Hulver refused to let him. "No living mole has been down into the Ancient System and I'm certainly not going down now, after all these moleyears. There's something about it that makes it wrong. It's not ready yet."

Bracken, despite his desire to explore everything, understood. He could feel the Ancient System around him, apparently more than Hulver could, but he felt the Duncton moles had lost it and were not yet ready to find it again. He hadn't even seen an entrance to it since he had been up on the hill, because everything was so blocked up by mold and debris. But the tunnels were there, their secrets intact.

After two or three days of staying near the Stone, the two set off across the hill to the south end of the wood. On one side of it the chalk escarpment fell away sharply, the wind rushing up and blowing your snout into the air if you tried to peer over. On the other side, the pastures began—or ended, depending on your point of view—all rough and scrubby with billowing clumps of gorse whose bright yellow flowers attracted Bracken, though he didn't dare break cover from the last of the wood to take a closer look.

There was a no-mole's land of rough grass and stunted hawthorn between the wood and the pasture where they petered out into each other and it was here that they spent the last five days of their wait for Midsummer Night. Each made a burrow for himself, grubbing about in the wood itself for food. Bracken didn't like them to go back into the wood proper for fear that Rune or some other henchmoles might find them, but none ever did, nor did they see anymole. In fact, the only life they saw was rabbits, which Bracken had often heard about but never seen close. They scampered about, squatted still feeding, and shot their ears up with a start if Bracken so much as poked his snout out of a tunnel near them.

Until now Bracken had tended to sleep long and irregularly. Now he fell in with Hulver's habits, which consisted of three sleep periods every day. Hulver liked to check the burrows and tunnels in the afternoon, but as these were temporary and not extensive, there wasn't much to check, and Hulver got into the habit of using the afternoon period to tell Bracken scraps of history about Duncton, something about the great elders of the past, and of the famous fights and the notorious worm-poor years. He told of the coming of Mandrake and other tyrant moles of the past—"though none I've heard of was ever as malevolent as him." Bracken had to ask what malevolent meant, and when Hulver told him, he thought to himself that it sounded as if Rune was malevolent as well.

It was from Hulver that he first learned of Rose, the healer mole who occasionally came in from the pastures to work her magic on sick or diseased moles. "You've probably never seen her, because she tends to go only to the Marsh End, where they believe in her more than most other Duncton moles. Anyway, she comes mainly in the autumn and spring—one of which you haven't experienced and the other which you won't remember."

"She's a *pasture* mole?" Bracken was surprised, because all pasture moles he had ever heard of were treacherous and aggressive and if they ever tried to visit Duncton, they would surely be attacked.

"Ah, yes. But Rose is a healer and that's very different. Healers live by their own rhythms and ways. Anyway, Rose wouldn't hurt a flea and no mole would want to hurt *her*. Mind you, I've only seen her a few times myself and only in passing. She's never laid a paw on me!"

"How many Longest Nights has she seen?" asked Bracken.

"Mmm, well . . . she's certainly not *young*, and yet she's like a youngster all the time. She sings, you know, and dances, too, on occasion. She tells stories to the youngsters, if they can persuade her to."

"When does she come?"

"Ah, now, that's a good question. It's a bit of a mystery, because no mole ever knows when she's going to come, even the ones she comes to heal. In fact, some of them don't even know there's anything wrong with them. You see, as she lives somewhere out in the pastures, no Duncton mole ever goes and gets her, and yet, when she's needed, she suddenly appears, as if by magic. Of course, she doesn't come for every hurt and illness, otherwise she'd be here all the time."

A day or two after this, Hulver let forth another scrap of information about Rose. They were talking about aches and pains, and Hulver was explaining that he found it helpful to chew various plants like the seeds of dog rose ("Excellent when you're run down; you'll find them over on the westside edge of the wood if you want to risk it") and sanicle ("Good for wounds after a fight—and plenty about in Duncton"), and Hulver got to telling Bracken about how he loved the smell of some of the plants and herbs in the wood, especially the sunnier clearings and then said, "And you know that Rose I mentioned, the healer, well *she* always has the sweetest smell of herbs about her that I've ever come across. Makes you feel good just being near her! Mekkins is the one to talk to about Rose. He knows her best of all the elders, coming as he does from the Marsh End."

Hulver sighed. He often felt when he was talking to Bracken that his words didn't say what he wanted them to. He wanted to tell the youngster so much. He became irritated with himself because he seemed to know so little and there was so much for a youngster to face.

At such times, Bracken imagined that he was tiring Hulver, or annoying him. So much of what Hulver said he found hard to understand and when he tailed off in the middle of something after trying to explain it two or three different ways, he felt the loss as much as Hulver felt the irritation. But then Bracken was beginning to love the old mole so much that it didn't much matter what he said. He would have listened with reverence anyway.

Since they had moved to the farthest point of the wood, indeed almost out of it, they felt much safer and the days passed by peacefully.

As Midsummer Night drew near, Hulver became more specific about the ritual. He had explained something about its meaning and purpose in the first few days; now he began to repeat the ritual itself. He would quote sections of the words, explaining what they meant and how they should be said. But he made no attempt to teach them formally to Bracken.

"Words change in the speaking," he explained, "so I want you to know what they mean rather than what they are. Listen to the spirit that lies behind them, that's what you most need to remember. Should the day come when you have to say the ritual yourself, then you'll remember

enough of what I've taught you. Most of the words are
known by my friend Bindle, so he'll tell them to you if
you need to know. But he doesn't know the final blessing,
the most important part of all. I tried to teach him but
he wouldn't listen; he said he couldn't learn them because
they were just words to him. It's too late now—he didn't
come to the last Midsummer Night—frightened off by
Mandrake, if you ask me. I haven't seen him for moleyears now, literally moleyears. But he's my oldest friend,
is Bindle."

Bracken sensed sadness in Hulver as he talked of his
friend, the only time in their days together up on the hill
that Hulver ever showed sadness.

But there was one part of the ritual Hulver did make
Bracken learn—so much so that Bracken almost became
sick of its constant repetition. By the end, the words had
no meaning whatsoever, blurring themselves into the
same meaningless syllables as the two lines from the food
blessing had done when he repeated them too much.
They were lines of the final blessing—the words that
Bindle refused to learn. And he learned them by hearing
Hulver gently repeat them again and again:

> We bathe their paws in showers of dew
> We free their fur with wind from the west,
> We bring them choice soil
> Sunlight in life.
>
> We ask they be blessed
> With a sevenfold blessing:
> The grace of form
> The grace of goodness
> The grace of suffering
> The grace of wisdom
> The grace of true words
> The grace of trust
> The grace of whole-souled loveliness.
>
> We bathe their paws in showers of light
> We free their souls with the talons of love
> We ask that they hear the silent Stone.

"Repeat, repeat," Hulver would command Bracken.
"The rest you can learn when the time is ripe, but these
words I want to hear you say until they are part of you.

You need not understand them yet—indeed, they will change their meaning with the passage of time—but you must know them." So Bracken repeated them, whispering as the sun rose, saying them into the wind from the void, whispering them into sleep.

Though he grew tired of repeating them, he learned to love the words he was taught, and he wondered where the moles who had first made them had gone. Why had they left the system?

They heard molesounds only once, carried on the wind and in vibration in the soil from the direction of the Stone. They waited silently for the sounds to come nearer, but they never did and they were left again in trembling peace.

Only when Midsummer Day itself came did Hulver tell Bracken his plan. "There is only one way to complete the ritual, and even that is risky and I have my doubts that it will work. It will demand great courage from you. It depends on my belief that they do not think I will come with another mole. If this is so, then, if you advance from the direction of the slopes, they will mistake you for me. You will come toward the clearing so that you are seen, run off and draw them away, so that I can move into the clearing from another direction. Then, with the Stone's help, I can repeat the ritual."

The old mole stopped, for that was his plan, all of it. Bracken didn't like it—too simple, too much to go wrong. Supposing they didn't all chase him; supposing they caught him? But though he racked his brain for a better plan, he could not find one: there were too many imponderables whichever course they took. So in the end, Hulver's simple plan seemed the best.

As the afternoon fell away into evening, Bracken grew restless and hungry. Hulver had calmly fallen asleep, but Bracken was too nervous to do anything but toss and turn. Finally he went in search of worms and found six. He woke Hulver as dusk fell and laid his worms before him.

They wound and wriggled on the ground, extending their heads into a thin questing point to escape. Bracken made to stop them but Hulver said quietly, "Let them go. Eat yours, but let mine go."

Then he blessed them gently and, snout on paws, watched his three worms make their slow escape.

It was too much for Bracken. "They took a long time to find," he complained. "If you don't want them I'll eat them."

"Ah, I do want them," said Hulver, "but it is no longer important. I would rather those worms lived with my blessing than died without it."

"But I've only got three," said Bracken, "and there's a lot to face up to this evening." He hated to see the worms he had worked hard to get disappearing before his eyes.

"If it troubles you, imagine that I *have* eaten them. If you would be less hungry for my having eaten them than for my not eating them, then your hunger is in your head and not your stomach. So satisfy your head. Meanwhile, let the worms go off and find their own supper; I hope with your blessings as well."

It seemed to Bracken that there was something illogical in Hulver's reasoning, but he could not work it out. The whole thing left him irritated, the first time he had felt like that since he had been with Hulver. By the time the three worms had finally disappeared, Hulver had dozed off again, while Bracken had worked himself up to the point where he had to get going.

Eventually the late afternoon light lost the last of its luster and Hulver stirred. It was time to set off for the Stone. With a final look back at the great bushes of gorse on the edge of the pasture, whose flowers looked like yellow lights in the evening, they turned down into the darkness of the wood.

The night was clear and warm but Bracken felt shivery. He was afraid, and as he followed behind Hulver he felt as if they were both walking to their death. He had the sinking heart of a mole committed to a course of action that may result in disaster but with no option other than to go through with it. Every leafcrackle made him jump, every dark shadow hid a dozen moles, each rustle of wind behind him heralded a rush of talons through the air.

Yet each step forward found them safe and unharmed until they approached to within a few molefeet of the Stone clearing, where they stopped to listen for moles. They had approached in a wide arc, bringing them on the far side from the slopes, for they both suspected that Mandrake and his henchmoles would wait by the slope side for Hulver to arrive.

Now they were still and silent Bracken felt a little safer, for they could not be surprised where they crouched. At the same time some of Hulver's calm came through to him and his heartbeat slowed and his breathing grew quieter.

Beyond the trees and lower than the top of the Stone, the moon began to shine. Bland and white at first, it gained in brightness as it rose higher, casting the soft light that Bracken loved. The only part of Hulver it caught was his snout, which moved occasionally by his paws as he eased his position. The wind was very gentle in the beech-tree leaves high above them and there was no birdsound at all. Somewhere far below them they heard an untidy rustle, indifferent to being heard—probably a hedgehog.

Not until the moon was on a level with the top of the Stone did Hulver suddenly touch Bracken's shoulder and, bringing his head closer, pointed his talon to the slopes side of the clearing. At first Bracken could sense nothing but then, among the shadows, a darker shadow moved, and he could feel its vibration. Silence. Rune. Or probably Rune. Whichmole else could move so silently?

The mole snouted about the clearing, padding about its perimeter and peering beyond into the wood. At one point it appeared to look in their direction and Bracken froze, even though he knew the mole could not possibly sense them. He sniffed and snouted about the clearing, coming at one point to within fifteen molefeet of where they crouched. The moonlight was full on him, making him lighter than the Stone behind, and Bracken watched as his form moved across the Stone and then back again, toward the slope's side. Then they heard a scuffling and two noisier moles came chattering into the moonlit clearing.

"Ssh!" said the mole they had been watching.

"Sorry, Rune," said one of the others.

"That's Dogwood," whispered Hulver. "That must mean that Mandrake is keeping them to their word and so they'll all be here to . . . to see what happens." He stopped himself from saying "kill me" because he didn't want to alarm Bracken, who was going to need all his courage.

"There's no mole here, that's for sure," said one of the other moles.

"It's Burrhead," gasped Bracken, suddenly very frightened.

"Yes, I'm afraid it is," said Hulver softly.

". . . And there won't be anymole here at all if you carry on scuffling," said Rune. "Have none of you learned how to move *silently?* Remember, movement carries farther than words."

That did the trick, and they crouched down in the clearing quite still, right by the Stone where they could clearly be seen.

"I must have been right," whispered Hulver. "They wouldn't stay in that position if they weren't pretty certain that anymole coming from the slopes was going to be intercepted. Mandrake and the rest must be down there."

This was soon confirmed by Rune, who whispered: "Now, remember what Mandrake said—if he slips through here before Mandrake gets him, he must be kept alive. Is that clear?"

Horrified at this exchange, Bracken glanced at Hulver, but only his snout was visible in the moonlight. Even his form merged into the blackness of the beech leaves and stems of the wood ivy in which they were crouched. But to Hulver it was as if they were talking about someone else, and he was very peaceful—he knew that what he had to do had the blessing of the Stone. There was nothing anymole could do to stop him performing the ritual with all the love and dignity he could muster.

However, he could sense Bracken's fear. "Wait a little longer yet," he whispered, "for if you start now it will be too early for the ritual to be said. It needs to be said at midnight, or near it."

To fill in the time and to take Bracken's mind off his task, Hulver told him to repeat to himself the words he had taught him and to *think* about their meaning as he did so.

This was so effective that Bracken was surprised when Hulver nudged him gently in the dark and told him it was time. Now Bracken felt cold and frightened. The wood seemed suddenly a very dangerous place. Surely it was somemole else who was slowly rising to his paws so near the three dangerous moles in the clearing. Some other mole who stole away into the night, forgetting to say a word of good luck, or goodbye to Hulver as he left? Not *this* mole who was utterly alone in the wood, moving through the silent night, afraid of stirring even a beech leaf!

So Bracken began his long, nerve-wracking trek round the clearing, down toward the slopes and then turning back again by the route they had originally taken to get to the Stone when they first came up to the Ancient System. He crept from shadow to shadow; he held his breath at each tiny noise he made; and he dearly wished, every inch of the way, that he had been allowed to explore the Ancient System that lay somewhere beneath his paws, so that he might exploit its tunnels now to bring him safely underground to the point on the slopes where he must materialize and start his impersonation of Hulver. Behind him, Hulver watched the three moles by the Stone. The clearest thing about them was the spot of moonlight on their snouts, and from this he saw them occasionally move restlessly in the dark.

Meanwhile, far below, Bracken finally reached a point on the slopes where he could cut across with the contour of the hill and begin his more ostentatious climb up.

He was acutely aware of all the reference points of location about him. As he turned up toward the Stone, the pastures lay some distance away to his right. Far to his left was the void of the chalk escarpment, running right up into the pastures which swung around beyond the clearing. There were a couple of fallen beeches in the wood to his left which he had passed on his way down, and these were useful points to remember. Apart from that, all was the wood, the silence, and his progress up the hill into danger.

Now that he was committed to the task, he found he was icy cool in his thinking. He was nervous, sweating a little, but his mind had never felt more clear.

He proceeded up the hill toward the Stone, as he imagined Mandrake and his henchmoles would have expected Hulver to proceed, with care, slowly, and keeping well hidden. This suited him, because if he was seen even for a moment in the moonlight by one of them, then surely they would realize he was not Hulver. He stopped to listen frequently as Hulver—as anymole—would have done. He kept to the dark patches and slightly off the communal surface pathway—as Hulver would have done.

He made just enough noise to be detected, but not too much to be taken for a fool.

At last, off to his right, he sensed what he had taken to be part of a root move. It was only fractional, but roots don't move even fractionally, not on the surface, anyway. After this, he carried on, now totally committed, because a henchmole was now behind him. It made him proceed a little faster because he wanted to get as near to the clearing as possible before he was challenged. That way he would be able to draw off Dogwood, Burrhead and Rune as well as the others. By a movement, the slightest of vibrations, he detected a second mole off to his left, this one lurking in what must be a temporary burrow.

Somewhere, far off below them all, a creature moved heavily in the wood. A badger, a fox, perhaps only a hedgehog. He was getting nearer to the clearing—indeed, he could see the top of the Stone caught beyond two trees ahead of him in the moonlight, just as Burrhead himself had once described it to him. Any moment now, he knew, he would be attacked or stopped. He had to make his move ahead of the challenge. That would give him surprise and a split second's advantage in time.

Ahead of him lay the two beeches and beyond them, the clearing. There must be one other mole at least by the trees, probably lying among the roots between them, waiting for him to come into sight. He thought he detected a movement behind him, perhaps one of the moles he had passed closing in.

He was beginning to move to the right round the tree ahead, expecting any moment for the third mole to come forward and challenge him and then—and then he made his move. Realizing he was heading into unavoidable moonlight, he swung back sharply to the left, giving him an advantage on anymole who might be waiting for him by the tree and throwing whatever mole was behind him off balance. With a mighty thrust, he pushed narrowly past the beech tree, with the clearing and the Stone to his right, scattering beech leaves behind him.

The uneasy silence of the night suddenly shattered. As he passed the tree, he caught the briefest glimpse of the biggest mole he had ever seen, in the moonlight. His talons were swinging round in the air, his body was arching round as if he had been facing the wrong way, but his snout was already round toward Bracken, huge and horrible. Mandrake!

Bracken deliberately ran close to the clearing before swinging off into the wood, to draw Rune and the others away from Hulver, who was on the far side. It worked. He heard Rune call, some shouts, and then there was a rush of moles from the clearing adding to the noise of Mandrake and the others following behind and on his left. Then he swung away into the wood, taking them all with him and leaving the clearing free for Hulver. He felt alive and full of energy and ran at great speed through the wood, weaving in and out, listening to the confused shouts of the rushing moles behind him. His instinct was to burrow to safety and again he regretted that he had not found a way into the Ancient System. But there were so many moles chasing him that he felt a safety in their confusion. The wood was dark, for the moonlight could not penetrate the thick canopy of beech leaves above them, and there was so much noise that no mole seemed to know where he was going. But Bracken did. He started on a long arc toward the slopes, much the same route he had taken so nervously before.

Behind him, beyond the clearing, old Hulver rose slowly to his paws as the noise of the fleeing Bracken and his pursuers died off into the wood. He approached to the very shadow of the Stone. There he crouched still for a moment or two, for a mole must be calm to say a ritual properly. Then, as if there was all the time in the world, Hulver began the ritual of Midsummer.

Bracken ran on through the night, twisting and weaving among the trees, working his way toward the fallen beech that he had passed on his way up from the slopes with Hulver. He knew the moles about him were confused— indeed, one of them had called forward to *him*, thinking he was Dogwood, and told him to cut off to the left, which he had obligingly done. He heard Mandrake shouting from time to time, and Rune; and he realized that no mole knew exactly where he was.

It was then that he saw the great dead beech ahead of him and hid in the shadows among its dry branches, his chest heaving with the effort of running. The chase continued around and about him until, one by one, they came to rest in a group on the ground not far from where he lay hidden in the fallen tree.

It was some moments before any of them had caught breath sufficiently to speak, and then it was Rune. "He has escaped, Mandrake, and gone down to the slopes where he lives. At least he cannot do the ritual now."

They were gathered in a spot dappled with moonlight filtering through the gap in the canopy by the fallen tree where Bracken lay hidden. Bracken peered down to look at Mandrake. His presence was huge—he was massive, more like two moles than one. He seemed blacker than the night itself and Bracken could see that he held his head forward and low, as if about to attack the whole world.

"You say he has escaped? But *who* has escaped?" demanded Mandrake. "I do not believe that the oldest mole in the system, who appeared to be hardly alive at the last elder meeting, could run through the wood like a youngster and elude the"—he looked around him sarcastically, as if he was not one of them—"the toughest moles in the system. That was *not* Hulver."

At this, they followed his gaze down to the slopes. Then, quick as a flash, as they looked back up toward the distant Stone lost somewhere above them in the night, the realization came to all of them that they might have been fooled. They all started back for the Stone as one, and as fast as they could—Mandrake at their head.

Bracken decided that he must follow them. It would be easy enough to avoid them now, and they were making sufficient noise to cover his sounds.

One makes faster progress than six, and so it was that Bracken arrived on the far side of the clearing when Mandrake came to it from the slope side.

Hulver was there, clear in the moonlight, back to the Stone and paws raised toward Uffington. He was in the final stages of the ritual, his figure commanding in its calm, his voice awe-inspiring in its aged strength. Behind him the Stone towered up into the sky.

He seemed oblivious of the arrival of Mandrake and his henchmoles, who stopped for a moment in awe at the sight of him.

But there was one other mole there whose presence was unknown to any of the others, including Hulver. He was hidden among the roots of the great beech by the Stone where Hulver and Bracken had slept their first night in the clearing.

He had left his burrow on the eastside and come slowly and reluctantly through the wood to the Stone. He had not wanted to come, for he had heard the talk that Mandrake's henchmoles would be out, yet he knew he must, and he arrived as Bracken drew the others away, in time to watch Hulver start the ritual. He might have joined in, but he felt unworthy to do so, as if he had no right to be there. But he mouthed the words with Hulver, urging the old mole through each one and intending to see Hulver through to the end of the ritual. Then he would go quietly back, back to the eastside, so that none might ever know that he had watched over the ritual.

But now he saw that Hulver would be cut down before the end and he knew, as perhaps he had known all the time, what he must do. Perhaps he could stop them—he must at least try. In the moment Mandrake hesitated with the others at the clearing's edge he came from among the roots behind the Stone and stood with his back to Hulver, his talons raised toward Mandrake, ready to do his best to stop him while Hulver finished the ritual. Bracken did not recognize him—he was an older, sturdy mole whom he had never seen in his travels around the westside and Barrow Vale. But Rune knew him, and so did the others.

"Bindle!" hissed Rune. "It's Bindle come to be brave."

"Bindle!" roared Mandrake.

But Bindle stood firm as they advanced slowly toward him and holding his talons ready began to join in with Hulver:

> *By the shadow of the Stone,*
> *In the shade of the night . . .*

Mandrake began to speed his approach.

> *As they leave their burrows*
> *On your Midsummer Night . . .*

Mandrake's breath came out rasping and angry, black and dangerous against the gentle combination of the voices of Hulver and Bindle as they continued toward the final part of the ritual:

We the moles of Duncton Stone
See our young with blessing sown . . .

While Bracken watched in horror from outside the clearing, Mandrake reared his talons up high above Bindle.
And then they came crashing down with a terrible force,
plunging through Bindle's own upraised paws and ripping
deep into his body. He fell down and back, torn and
crippled, as Mandrake rushed past him toward Hulver,
while Rune and Burrhead cut at him as they too ran on
toward Hulver.

Bracken crouched in the shadows, frozen with fear,
unable to move, watching Hulver in anguish as the three
strongest moles in Duncton, one of them his own father,
bore down upon him with raised talons and ugly snouts.
They were shouting or screaming at him, it was hard to
tell which, and yet through it Bracken could hear Hulver
begin the very final part of the blessing, the part he himself had learned:

We bathe their paws in showers of dew
We free their fur with . . .

But old Hulver got no further. He half-turned at the final
moment to face his attackers and Bracken saw that his
talons were not raised at all—rather, his paws were outstretched as if he were blessing them. Just as he had
blessed the worms at the very first meal they had taken
together:

Let no mole adown my body
That may hurt my sorrowing soul . . .

And then frail Hulver was gone, lost beneath their stabbing, vicious, thrusting, tearing talons, any sound he made
drowned by the noise of their screams of anger and the
panting of their murderous effort. Torn down where he
stood in the shadow of the Stone, at the very heart of the
system he loved, uttering the blessing on the youngsters
in whose future he believed. Bracken was rooted to the
spot, his heart screaming out at the agony of watching
the mole he had so quickly grown to love, slaughtered
before him. Yet he could not move. He did not have the

courage, or the foolishness, to run out into the clearing and face Hulver's killers.

Then, in a moment, it was over. Mandrake stood back and the others fell away, and without a word to each other, they turned round like a pack of rats in the night and scampered out of the clearing. As they passed Bindle, lying stretched out on the ground, he stirred and moaned, but Mandrake said, "Leave him, let him be living owl-fodder."

They were barely gone before Bracken found his strength again and was able to run out into the clearing to Hulver.

But Hulver was dead, and all he could see was the body of a time-worn old mole terribly torn, small and crumpled in the moonlight, the left paw catching its light and curled softly like a young pup's. There was the shiny blackness of blood on him, from his snout to his rump.

With a terrible sob, Bracken ran over to Bindle, who was moaning and whispering, trying to raise himself on a shattered paw, the paw sliding out uselessly from under his weight. Bracken bent low over him and heard him whisper, "Bindle, my name is Bindle. I came back to say the ritual with my oldest friend. We almost finished it, didn't we?"

His breath came rasping and painful, and Bracken's heart ached to hear it. "We almost finished it. And in the end I knew the words. He never thought I knew them all, but I did. When they came at the end I remembered the words."

Bindle tried to say more but he rasped and coughed, and gasped in his terrible pain. Bracken pressed against him, supporting his torn body, blood on his fur. Bindle started to speak again, each word a massive effort: "Listen, youngster, and try to remember them: We . . . bathe . . . their . . . paws . . . in. . . ."

Bracken looked up at the Stone and across to the body of Hulver, whose wisdom he now began to see. And then, at first very softly, but with increasing strength, he joined his voice to the dying Bindle's:

> *We bathe their paws in showers of dew*
> *We free their fur with wind from the west*
> *We bring them choice soil*
> *Sunlight in life*

We ask they be blessed
With a sevenfold blessing . . .

Bracken spoke the words now with power, with the voice of an adult. They filled the clearing and carried on beyond it loud and clear, until they stopped Mandrake and his moles in their tracks.

The grace of form
The grace of goodness . . .

A wild storm of racing blood and blizzard cold swept through Mandrake's head and body; he seemed possessed by rushing darkness. With a mighty roar he turned back, thrashing back up toward the clearing, tormented by the powerful voice that carried words that agonized his soul.

The grace of suffering
The grace of wisdom
The grace of true words
The grace of trust
The grace of whole-souled loveliness.

Bracken had moved to the Stone and now stood in its dark shadow turned toward Uffington, aware of everything about him: the dead Hulver, the dying Bindle and the agonized rushing of Mandrake fast approaching him, but he ignored it all.

It seemed to Mandrake, as he arrived back at the clearing and saw at first only two moles lying on the ground, that the Stone itself was speaking:

We bathe their paws in showers of light
We free their souls with talons of love
We ask that they hear the silent Stone.

It was only with these very last words of the ritual that Mandrake saw Bracken in the shadow, and with a roar as agonized as it was angry, charged upon him.

Bracken stepped forward for a moment into the moonlight, where Mandrake saw him clearly for the first time, and then ran behind the Stone, beyond the great beech tree, and into the wood in the direction of the chalk escarpment.

As Mandrake followed after him, Bindle moved for the last time, stretching a paw toward his friend Hulver, his snout turned toward the Stone into whose silence and light he felt himself flowing, away from the rasping breathing that was no longer his and the numbing cold that had been spreading from his paws and flanks toward his heart, and thinking that the youngster somehow knew the words as well, and that was how it should be.

On Bracken ran, his strength failing rapidly. He could no longer think clearly and his breath was coming in pants and rasps as Bindle's had done. Behind him he could hear Mandrake getting nearer, carried forward as he was by an indescribable rage and malevolence, beech leaves and leaf mold scattering in his wake.

To his left, Bracken could hear other moles running toward him through the undergrowth, Rune, Dogwood and the others. To his right, the hill rose toward its final height, where he and Hulver had lain in secret before tonight. But he knew he had no strength left to climb up and away from Mandrake. So he ran straight on, straight toward the void of the chalk escarpment, his heart pounding in pain and each breath harder and harder to grasp hold of. Mandrake could see him now, just ahead, paws scrabbling over themselves, back almost within talon range. With a final push forward Mandrake reared up to try to bring his talons down on the failing Bracken.

Sensing what Mandrake was about to do, Bracken turned in midflight to make a valiant effort to ward off Mandrake's blows. But as he raised his own talons to defend himself, he felt his back paws continue forward into nothing, sliding downward through loose soil and vegetation, attempting, it seemed, to keep hold of nothing. As Mandrake's talons crashed down toward his upturned snout he felt the nothingness of the void swallowing him, pulling him down into blackness as his front paws flailed desperately at the cliff face slipping past his snout, felt loose vegetation and flints scratching at his face.

Above him he heard a mighty roar of triumph from Mandrake. But then, hardly realizing what was happening, he felt his front paws fall suddenly forward into an emptiness in the cliff face and caught hold of a surface. And he was flailing again, pulling himself forward, back paws again in contact with the cliff face, pulling, heaving, shoving himself up until he finally lay on the smooth, flat floor of a tunnel exposed by some winter cliff fall, whose ancient dark depth echoed back his gulps for air and life. From above him came the thumping of paws and more paws, as Rune and Mekkins, Dogwood and Burrhead joined Mandrake at the cliff's edge, and looked over into the blackness of its void.

"He has gone, gone to his death," screamed Mandrake. "I caught him with my talon before he went and ripped his flesh." And then Mandrake laughed terribly into the darkness beyond.

"Which mole was it?" asked Mekkins, wondering at the courage and strength of the three moles they had killed that night.

"It was Bracken," hissed Rune into the darkness beyond them. "The mole I found in Hulver's tunnels. I should have killed him then but I did not wish to warn Hulver that something was wrong. I should have killed him painfully then."

"It was Bracken, was it!" exclaimed Burrhead, trying to sound angry. But there was a hint of surprise in his voice, mingled with a touch of pride. He could not believe that it was his own strange son, who he had thought had been killed after leaving the home burrow without a word, who had given Mandrake so much trouble before his end. Best say no more, Burrhead thought.

Bracken heard them move off across the floor of the wood, back toward the slopes. Painfully he raised himself up, his left shoulder now stiff and almost lame, and pointed his snout forward into the Ancient System, which, after so many generations, had at last opened its tunnels to a mole again.

☙ 9 ❧

REBECCA'S bleak mateless spring had become an early summer of delights. When Sarah's litter by Mandrake arrived in April, Rebecca had the excuse she wanted to leave the home burrow to scrape a living for herself in her own tunnels. She had wondered whether to leave Barrow Vale altogether, to get away from Mandrake, but when it came to that, she had no real desire to do so. Perhaps she sensed that beneath his brutal hostility to her he loved her, the very viciousness of his assaults a sign of how deep his feelings ran.

Certainly she was pleased when he gruffly took her aside at the end of April to say "You'll be leaving the home burrow now, but you'll not go far, Rebecca— I want to keep an eye on you. There's a burrow not far from here which I'll show you . . ."

She was surprised that one should be so conveniently free, and only long afterward found out that Mandrake had driven away the mole who occupied it—an older female called Rue—threatening her with death if she tried to win it back. Not knowing this and flattered by Mandrake's sudden interest in her wellbeing, she settled down happily to wait for summer. She cleared out the runs and burrows in her new tunnels, replacing the nesting material with sweet-smelling grasses and leaves she found on the wood's floor. She opened up a new entrance which caught the morning sun, and another which threw light and fresh, cool air into her burrows toward the end of day.

All this occupied her so much that she hardly missed not seeing Sarah during May and early June, by which time Sarah's second litter was beginning to roam, and the two became friends again. They would talk of flowers and trees, and Sarah would tell her the ways of shrews and voles, laughing at their fights and antics. She warned of weasels and owls.

The flowers that had carpeted the wood's floor in spring died away as the trees above began to leaf, blocking the sun so that a heavier, duller undergrowth took their place. Rebecca, growing bolder as each summer

day advanced, took to seeking out flowers and sunlight
on the pasture edge, and in one or two more open places
toward the Marsh End. She would have liked to explore
deeper into the Marsh End itself, among the danker
darkness of its trees, but there was a musty smell about
the place, which she did not like on a summer's day,
created by the moss and fungi that grew about the one
or two rotting trees and many fallen branches.

But these herbal forays were interspersed by long
periods of simply sitting still in her own tunnels or at
their entrances, learning about the wood nearest to her.
Its summer noises were less frenetic than the spring's,
but fuller and richer. Very near one of her tunnel entrances were a couple of small oaks with patches of bramble and ground ivy nearby, and here, just before she
herself arrived, a pair of nightingales settled to breed and
raise their young. As the summer moved into July, she
grew to love their ferreting busyness as they grubbed
among the undergrowth for spiders and worms, an activity often followed by the rich *jug-jug-chooc-chooc* of
song, ascending to a powerful crescendo *pioo-pioo* which
she could hear in her deepest burrow. A night was blessed
that began with their song.

Often "her" nightingales joined the chorus that woke
with her at dawn as a colorful medley from a blackbird
or two joined the sounds of nuthatch and wren, tit and
the soft, distant cooing of a wood pigeon over on the
wood's edge. The birds scurried about the dead leaves
on the wood's floor or flittered among living leaves above.
And the smells of fresh growth! She loved that best of
all as she and the woods grew into the season together.

In this summer period she grew used to sounds that
had frightened her at first—the scurrying of a hedgehog,
often blindly running right past her snout, or the sudden
buzz in her face of a flying beetle or searching wasp.

One reason she tended to keep near her own tunnels
was that if she was caught too far away by hunger or
tiredness, she had to make a temporary burrow in a
place whose noises were strange and threatening. It was
a long time before she revisited the eastside, for example,
because when she stayed *there* overnight, she happened
on a mating fight between a couple of badgers who
sounded, in their thumping rushes and shrill, eerie
screams, as if they were about to fall through the burrow

roof onto her. They were, in fact, many moleyards away in the slopes of a bank where they had dug their own massive burrows, but how was she to know, never having heard them before? Worse than their terrible sounds was their rank smell, which wafted sickeningly into the tiny burrow and made her tremble and sweat with fear in the darkness.

But far, far worse were the chilling sounds of tawny owls hooting at night. They cast a terrible fear into her. She knew little of them beyond that they were the mole's most terrible enemy in Duncton in summer and were the taloned death that came with silent suddenness out of the darkness above. There were one or two moles in Duncton —and Rebecca had heard one of them tell his tale—who had been caught by an owl but by some freak chance escaped, talon-torn but alive. Some of the older moles said that to touch such a mole brought you luck, but Rebecca had been too shy to seek that privilege.

Mandrake came to visit her two or three times in June and July. He always claimed to be just passing and pretended to have no interest in her doings. He sat about for a while, asked her a few monosyllabic questions, cast his glowering glance about her system, and was off as suddenly as he had come. She sensed that in his own gruff way he was keeping an eye on her, and that gave her pleasure as well.

One hot July evening, when every insect in the wood seemed busy, Mekkins passed her way and she heard for the first time of the deaths of Hulver and Bindle. On Mandrake's orders the story had been kept dark for weeks past, but the idle summer months are a time for gossip and chatter and such a tale must eventually come out.

Mekkins, who felt the whole sorry story to be a shadow on Duncton, would have preferred to keep silent about it with Rebecca. She was so young, so innocent, so full of the joy of the season, that telling her seemed as shameful as trampling on a wood anemone. But she was so overjoyed to see him, though he knew her only passingly, and fixed him with such an open gaze that he found it impossible to tell a lie when she suddenly asked "Where can I find Hulver, the elder?"

He hesitated to answer, playing for time with "Why?"

She told him how Hulver had talked to her before the
June elder meeting and told him the legend of Rebecca
the Healer, and about a mole called Bracken who was
somewhere up on the slopes. Hulver had told her about
Bracken with such a curious passion that she had taken
to heart his odd suggestion that she should make sure that
Bracken was all right.

As Mekkins looked at her, free from the threat of
Mandrake—with whom she had been the last time he saw
her—he felt he had never seen such light radiance in a female before. He tried to say that he didn't know about
Hulver or Bracken, that perhaps they were up on the
slopes, that he was old now and . . . but one by one the
lies dried up before her simple gaze. Mekkins was clever,
a survivor, one well used to telling half truths to get his
way. But, well, there are times when a mole wearies of
the effort of not telling the truth, and he admired
the stand Hulver had made too much to want to tell any
lies about him. And he remembered the strong adult
voice of that strange mole, Bracken, whom none of them
had ever quite seen, who had cried out from the clearing
those ritual words of the Midsummer blessing, words that
had often come back to him:

> *The grace of whole-souled loveliness . . .*

and now, before the radiant Rebecca he could tell nothing but the truth. As she gazed happily at him, with joy
in her movements and life radiating from her, Mekkins
felt a poverty in his own spirit about the murders by the
Stone, and his snout lowered as his gaze fell to the wood's
floor.

Slowly, and with a low voice, he told her exactly what
had happened on Midsummer Night—as far as he understood it. He ended finally with a description of the shock
that had run through the elders when, en route back to
Barrow Vale, they were stopped short by the voice of an
unknown mole uttering the sevenfold blessing loud and
clear through the wood after them. "The grace . . . the
grace . . ." He could hear the words now.

"Whatmole said them?" asked Rebecca, who crouched
by him, listening, still and somber.

"Bracken, Burrhead's son, we think it must have been
him." Rebecca's heart seemed to stop when he said

Bracken's name, and every word Mekkins spoke seemed to be of great importance. Mekkins described the chase Bracken had led them on, describing the bravery of one so young as if it were a legend and not something that had happened only a short time before.

"Who is he?" whispered Rebecca, almost to herself. "Who is he?"

Mekkins repeated that he was Burrhead's son, one of Aspen's spring litter: but that was not what Rebecca meant. She explained that Hulver had said of Bracken that Rebecca the Healer had led them to one another. Now here he was again, the only mole in Duncton, so it seemed, who could lead Mandrake on a chase and get away with it.

"Oh, but 'e didn't!" exclaimed Mekkins. " 'E was killed. He ran clean over the chalk cliff edge trying to escape from Mandrake."

The hot July sun was suddenly cold. Every insect in the wood froze to its spot. The evening breeze ceased. The air was loud with anger.

Rebecca had listened in silence to Mekkins' miserable tale. She had heard him out in peace as he described the hunt for the most venerable mole in the system and his subsequent murder with Bindle. But now, with the news of Bracken's death in her ears, she reared up in terrible anger and for the first time attacked, really attacked, another mole, and her talons descended on Mekkins. She tore at him as if he were evil itself. And as she did so, she began to weep, striking out blindly through her tears.

Mekkins fell back before her assault, unable to strike Rebecca, even though he was bigger and more powerful and could almost have killed her with one blow. Instead, he warded off her blows, or dodged the wilder ones, until her rage was spent and she was stooped and sobbing before him.

"So much killing in the system," she cried. "He hates every mole and every living thing. I tried . . . to show him how much I love him, but he can't hear me . . ." She sighed deeply and looked out into the evening.

Then, to Mekkins' amazement, for he was just beginning to think he felt the depths of her sudden grief, she laughed in a tearful way: "Of course," she said, "this mole Bracken's not dead. He couldn't be, you see. He couldn't be."

She turned to Mekkins inquisitorially and said, "Did you *see* him dead?" And Mekkins, who could not keep up with Rebecca's changes of mood or understand them, had to admit that he hadn't. But then, how could you see if a mole who had gone over a cliff was dead?

"No, no," said Rebecca, "he's not dead. Or *if* he is, he's not."

With this mysterious comment Rebecca fell silent, and Mekkins fell to thinking that the Duncton system was going mad.

"Bloody 'ell," he thought to himself, "*I'm* going mad."

He told himself this because he felt a peculiar sense of escape coming over him that his commonsense character could do nothing at all to hold back. It was as if after weeks of misery his body could again feel the space and trees about him, and his paws feel the firm soil he loved so much. And just as Rebecca had asked "Who is he?" of Bracken, he now found himself asking "Who is *she?*" of Rebecca.

For, faced by Rebecca's absolute conviction that Bracken was alive, Mekkins found himself delightfully able to believe that this impossibility was, in fact, true. At the same time, in the space of this short conversation, Mekkins had shed, like last year's winter, whatever loyalty he may have had left to Mandrake. Duncton Wood could go and jump over the cliff as far as he was concerned. He was a marshender first, foremost and forever, and that was all he wanted to be.

"Maybe you're right after all," he said finally, getting up and playfully pushing her with his shoulder. Rebecca laughed with him and the July evening was warm again, the insects hurrying and busy with their life.

"Take care, Mekkins," she called after him as he left her for the Marsh End, as if she knew he had changed and made a decision about himself that would cause him trouble if he was to honor it. Mekkins found in going that he hated to leave her.

The end of July and the beginning of August turned out to be a time of delicious chatter and idleness. The females who had littered in spring were well clear of their young, who had gone off to find their own burrows and tunnels, while the males had lost their aggressiveness. Moles rarely came right to the center of Rebecca's system, as Mekkins had done, but out on its periphery, or on the edge of other moles' systems, Rebecca spent a lot of time with them, talking and learning new lore of the wood.

Her springtime fascination with plants continued and she was especially interested in what the older females had to say about how herbs could heal all kinds of ills and aches, if only a mole knew how to use them. Again and again the name that cropped up was Rose the Healer's, who was said, though no mole was certain, to live *on the pastures!* This was always whispered in a hush and gave Rose a special air of mystery that resulted in Rebecca regarding her with a great deal of awe.

"What's she like?" Rebecca would ask, but no mole seemed to express him- or herself the same way about her.

"She's the most understanding creature I do know," one would say.

"Commonsensical—that's the word *I'd* use," another would pronounce.

"Rose? Ah, well, Rebecca, if you want to know Rose, you get her to tell you a story. She's good at that."

Rose appeared to possess, for each mole that talked to her, the one characteristic *they* liked in another mole best of all. Rebecca wanted to meet her for lots of reasons, but most of all because of what she might be able to tell her about herbs.

However, Rose's appearances and disappearances were as mysterious and unpredictable as everything else about her. You didn't arrange to meet Rose—she just appeared.

It was at the beginning of August that Rebecca heard a snatch of an old rhyme that so intrigued her that she decided to make another herbal journey down toward the Marsh End. The snippet she heard was this:

> *When white stars have shone*
> *When their petals have gone*
> *Then pick thy ramson.*

Ramson was the old word for wild garlic and everymole knew how good that was in times of trouble. Hearing that it grew in the darker and moister parts of the Marsh End, she was at first put off trying to find it, but then one old female claimed to have seen it in a bit of a damp patch

over where the Marsh End butted on to the pastures and
so, hoping to avoid the dark places she did not like by
keeping to the wood's edge, Rebecca set off one dawn to
find it.

But it was more than just the desire to find ramson
that drove her out of the safety of her burrow. She had
felt ill at ease for several days, unhappy, uncertain—as if
there was something that needed seeing to just around the
corner, but she didn't know what. She had kept looking
over her shoulder. It nagged at her and made her restless,
so the journey to find the ramson was a good way of giving way to her restlessness. There had been a shower
sometime in the night, and as the morning warmed, the
wood's floor grew steamy, while droplets of rain fell off
the bramble and ivy where Rebecca had to take to the
surface.

Quite what "white stars" referred to, she wasn't sure,
but the rest seemed to make sense. "You'll know the place
by the perfume, if you can call it that," she was told, and
she spent a happy morning sniffing her way along the
pasture edge, seeking out a "perfume" that wasn't quite a
perfume.

Lower and lower down the hill she went, among
the long summer grasses and bracken, and stopping with
delight by a stray wild honeysuckle that entwined itself
among a stand of brambles. Scent after scent came to her
—nettles, oak bark, ants, cow dung, the most delicate
aroma of fungi, but nothing that smelled like the way
ramson sounded.

Still, it was a nice day and that part of the wood felt
safe, provided you didn't stray too far beyond the cover
of the trees. By midmorning she was sleepy and dozed
off in a warm, dry old burrow she found.

She awoke in a delicious summertime reverie, when
each thought comes crystal clear but leisurely. She was
aware of birdsong around her and the gentle buzz of flies
and bees along the edge of the wood. The thought she
was thinking was how curious it is that some parts of the
wood seem safer than others, carrying in their every plant
and creature a greater sense of peace and calm. She had
mentioned this feeling to other moles before now, but they
looked puzzled and didn't seem to understand what she
was talking about.

Still, on a day like this, what did it matter what other

moles thought? Indeed, it didn't even matter much that she couldn't find the wild garlic, because there were plenty of other things to experience.

She listened to a blackbird hopping impatiently about the wood's floor, turning over this and that in search of grubs; she came upon a dusty little ants' nest and, as once before, tried licking up one or two. They tasted horrible and she spat them out again.

"Oh, well," she sighed happily, "if *everything* tasted nice, then *nothing* would taste nice, would it?" And with this thought she wandered straight into the range of a strong, clinging smell that was not horrible and yet not exactly nice . . . but definitely attractive, and began to make her way hopefully toward it.

She would have pressed straight on, but stopped when she heard the quiet singing of a mole ahead of her among the undergrowth. There wasn't any tune to the song, but it had a tune; there weren't any words, either, but it had words; you couldn't say the voice was much . . . but it was lovely to listen to.

In other places in the wood Rebecca would have backed carefully away, unwilling to risk attack, even if moles who sang songs were rarely aggressive. But here, in this part of the wood, on this particular August day, she had never felt safer. So she made a semiburrowing noise to announce politely that she was about and then went cheerfully forward through the undergrowth from beyond which the singing was coming.

There, right before her, was the singer—and the ramson. A female was crouched with head on one side among a clump of tall green plants with long, floppy, oval leaves that curled and fell back on themselves. She was quite old, by the look of her fur, and as happy as anymole Rebecca had ever seen. Between snatches of song, she was sniffing the plants up and down, almost as if caressing them.

The mole, who did not seem to notice Rebecca, was smallish, the tall plants all around her perhaps making her seem rather smaller than she was. But her shoulders were sturdy and there was a great solidity about her that reminded Rebecca of an oak root poking out of the ground to which there is a great deal more than the eye can see or the snout scent.

"Why, hello, dear," the mole said, without looking around, "I wondered how long it would be before you summoned up enough sense to come and introduce yourself."

Rebecca started forward but the old female raised a paw to signal that Rebecca should wait where she was while she finished whatever she was doing with the ramsons.

"It's best for you to wait there while I do this. I'm just getting these ramsons used to the idea that I'm going to pick one or two of them. It might slow things down if you came here among them."

She sang a little more, touched one or two of the stems, peered at them through wrinkled eyes, and finally said "There, now! That's all right! They're almost ready!"

Finally she turned to Rebecca, who saw what she had already sensed, that her face was one of the kindliest and most sympathetic she had ever looked upon.

"So they're ramsons, are they?" exclaimed Rebecca, finally unable to resist the temptation to run forward and sniff at the leaves and stem of the one nearest to her. The flowers, which were withered and nearly done, were too high for her to reach, though their scent was strong enough to smell without getting near. Even so, Rebecca noticed something curious. "It's strange," she said, "how they smell more at a distance than close to."

"It's not strange at all, as a matter of fact," said the other mole, coming over to where Rebecca was standing. "It's inevitable. If you can understand why and believe it, then you'll hold a secret in your heart for which many moles you meet will have cause to be grateful."

Before Rebecca could ask what this mystery meant, the mole asked, "What's your name, dear?"

"Rebecca. Mandrake's daughter."

"And Sarah's child, if I'm not mistaken. Well, child, my name's Rose."

"Oh, at last!" exclaimed Rebecca. "Rose the Healer! They said you'd know about ramsons and lots of things like that, and here you are to tell me!"

Rose laughed gaily and Rebecca began asking questions so infectiously that Rose quietly settled herself down in a spot warmed by the sun, for she knew she would be asked a lot more before this young thing had done with her.

But what Rebecca wanted to know about most of all was the little rhyme about ramsons she had heard. "I couldn't see what it could possibly mean," she said, "unless it was that you can only pick them at dawn when the stars have shone. But then . . . well . . . that would mean you could pick them at any season, and I'm sure *that* wouldn't be right."

"Why wouldn't it be right, my love?" Rose asked the question quite seriously, the cheerful content in her face subtly replaced by an excited curiosity about what Rebecca had said.

"Well, because there's only certain times you can pick plants and herbs like ramsons—I mean, times of seasons. Looking at growing things, I've often thought that they weren't exactly *ready* but I'm not sure ready for what."

"What mole told you there were only certain times?" asked Rose, now quite serious.

"Well, no mole exactly. My mother, Sarah, told me about some of the plants, and other, older moles told me names and rhymes and how you can use them for healing, but no mole said when to pick them. Well . . . the plants told me!"

Rebecca finally got this out with some difficulty; she had never thought about it before, though it had always seemed obvious enough to her. "Isn't it obvious?" she finally asked.

Rose looked at her for quite a long time, her head on one side. Then she said firmly, "It's not obvious at all; in fact . . ." But a blackbird hopped and scurried near her, seeming to break her line of thought. So Rebecca asked, "Well, what does that rhyme mean?"

Rose laughed. "It's the flowers, Rebecca; they're like lovely, white stars when they come out. Here, I'll show you . . ." And she led Rebecca through the clumps of ramson to a plant in a dark part of the wood over which an oak branch had fallen so that its growth had been stunted.

"Look!" said Rose, pointing to the moist shadows by the branch. There, among the small ramson leaves, Rebecca saw a stalk with a cluster of white flowers whose pointed petals were sharp and bright against the gentle, pale green of the long leaves. Several of the flowers were withered, but one or two were still fresh and their smell strong.

"You'll often find in a clump of plants that one or two flower very late, or their flowers stay longer after the others have developed toward seed. Perhaps the sun doesn't reach them, perhaps, as with this one, they are stunted by accident; or perhaps, like some moles, they just naturally take a long time to develop. Never ever pick those ones, my love, never ever. They're very special. Their spirit has a special beauty."

Again Rebecca wanted to ask why, but Rose turned away and went slowly back to where they had been sitting before, touching the stems of the bigger ramsons with her paws as she passed them. The subject seemed closed.

"Anyway, you can see now what the rhyme means, can't you?" said Rose.

"Yes," said Rebecca, but rather vaguely, because something had occurred to her. "Do stars look like that?" she asked Rose.

It was a good question. Everymole knows that stars shine some nights, usually when the moon is strong. But, of course, moles cannot see them. It had never occurred to Rebecca to wonder what mole it was that had been able to see stars so that other moles knew about them with such certainty that they never questioned their existence.

Rose thought about Rebecca's question for some time. Indeed, it prompted a whole series of thoughts in her mind far beyond the question itself. The fact was that, in a very short space of time, Rebecca had made a deep impression on Rose. She had liked her from the first moment she scented her hesitating beyond the undergrowth, uncertain whether to show herself or not. But liking is one thing, feeling awe is another. And that's what Rose felt.

Rose had been a healer in the pastures and Duncton Wood for many moleyears past and had felt many times the great wonder of the life about her which she was sometimes graced to have the special power to cherish and preserve. She was loving and modest in her service to other moles, going to them when they needed her and expecting nothing in return. Some, however, would bring to her useful herbs which grew near their tunnels, while others would tell her the stories and tales that had been told them by their parents, knowing they delighted her. She loved to tell stories herself, especially to the youngsters in spring (when she noticed with a smile that many adults would stop to listen as well). But she never spoke about one mole to another or of Duncton Wood in the pastures—or the pastures in Duncton Wood. Such knowledge was her own and she never passed on the secrets of the moles she helped and healed.

But a healer's life may sometimes be a lonely one, and in recent moleyears Rose, who had been getting older, had felt the weariness of forever being a prop to other moles and never being able to seek support for herself when she needed it. Naturally she scolded herself for such thoughts, or chewed some dried flowers of yellow meadowsweet which she gathered from where it grew down near the Marsh End and blossomed in summer. "Nothing like this to cheer up a mole," she would tell herself, but some melancholies will never quite leave, even from the heart of a healer.

On the dawn of this particular day, Rose had been drawn out of her burrow and over to Duncton Wood by an impulse compounded of unease and excitement. She never questioned such impulses—they had a will of their own, and a purpose, too, which it was beyond anymole to fathom. A mole resisted them at her, or his, peril. All she knew was that somewhere in the system there was a mole in deep trouble who in some way needed her help. Where the mole was, what the trouble was, or what mole it might be she had no idea. But the need to pick ramsons was part of the impulse and that in itself was unusual, since she had already gathered her stock of ramsons for drying in June, when they were flowering most widely. Still, with ramsons the fresh plant is always best, and if the impulse said "Go and pick some" Rose would do just that.

She had not been at all surprised when another mole joined her—though she had half expected whatever mole it was to be the one in need of help. That, however, did not seem to be the case.

To add to her puzzlement, and subsequently to create a sense of awe in her, Rebecca said several things that suggested she knew a great deal instinctively about plants and their powers, which she did not yet *know* she knew. Sensing this, Rose had deliberately not elaborated on several of the more important questions that Rebecca had raised almost unconsciously. The question of why the smell of wild garlic may seem stronger farther off than close by, for example, involved explanations of why it

is that the smaller the dose of a herb a healer gives, the
more potent may be the impact.

Rebecca's understanding of the fact that plants talked
to her was also difficult to explain to her without, in a
curious way, jeopardizing her ability to listen.

For knowledge, Rose had painfully discovered, was a
very different thing from wisdom and common sense and
may often come in the way of both. The sight of such
innocent wisdom as she saw in Sarah's and Mandrake's
child made Rose hesitate to try to explain these things.
Faced by it, she felt her own ignorance, not as a negative
thing but as a simple fact. And she saw again what her
weariness, age and occasional loneliness had made her
forget: that each mole is graced with different virtues,
just as each herb is. She sensed that Rebecca had many
graces and the awe she felt was of the power of the
Stone that had put them there.

These thoughts ran through Rose's mind while she considered Rebecca's question about the stars. She wished
she had more power with words to explain the answer,
though it was a wish that did her an injustice, since
Rose could often explain things that other moles, who
seemed more articulate, could somehow never grasp.

She sighed and wondered where to start. She looked
around her, at the ramsons, at the cluttered undergrowth
of thorns and dark leaves, and at the light sky above
and beyond.

It was the gentle sound of a warm breeze in the trees
that helped her. "Do you know what the top of a tree
looks like?" she asked Rebecca.

"Well, of course!" said Rebecca. "We've all been
shown fallen branches with leaves on—they look like
that."

"Can you remember the first time you saw one?" asked
Rose.

"Oh, yes, it was disappointing!" She paused, but Rose
stayed silent, so she continued. "Well, I mean . . . before
you see them, you imagine them, don't you? And the
roots of trees were so big, and the noise their tops made
in the wind so powerful, that I imagined that trees went
up and up forever into the sky, and their tops were each
as big as the whole of Duncton Wood put together. So
when someone said 'That's a top of a tree' I was disappointed!"

Rose laughed sympathetically—she had once felt just the same. "But really, my dear, treetops aren't just branches and leaves, are they? Did you *see* the noise of the wind, for example? I'm sure you didn't. Did you see all the branches together? Well, of course, you couldn't have. There are a lot of things, the most important things, which you can *never* see and can only learn about in your own way. Just as the treetop you saw couldn't tell you everything about treetops, so the starlike flowers of ramsons only hint at what stars are really like."

"But how does anymole know what they're like?" persisted Rebecca. "How can a mole be certain that they're *there?*"

A strange thing happened to Rebecca as she asked this question. As it hung in the air between them, she saw very clearly that it was a question impossible for Rose to answer. Perhaps it was because Rose was not trying to answer it that she saw this; perhaps it was also that she understood instinctively that Rose *knew* there were stars, even though she had never seen one. In that moment, Rebecca understood something quite different from what she had been asking about, that there are a lot of things moles can only come to know for themselves. Why, she had thought she knew all about treetops when she "saw" one, but, of course, she didn't! Why, they really are majestic and powerful just as I thought they were when I was a pup! she exclaimed to herself. It didn't matter what stars looked like—Rose knew they were there and perhaps one day she would really know it, too.

"Oh, I wish I could answer your question," exclaimed Rose, "but there are so many things that a mole can't explain. You see, if you tried to explain to most moles about plants talking to you, they . . ."

"I have, and they didn't," sighed Rebecca. "I've given up trying!"

"Well, it's like that with most important things. A mole will come to know things if he's going to, and no amount of talking about it will make him understand if he's not going to. And even if he or she is going to get to know something, it's no good trying to hurry the process up—it happens when it's meant to and there's nothing you or I can do about it. Well, perhaps we can encourage it sometimes."

Rebecca liked talking to Rose because she talked to

her as an equal. She made her feel that she wasn't just a youngster who hadn't mated yet. She made her feel that her paws were firmly on the ground.

"Now," said Rose firmly, "I really must finish these ramsons off. You sit there quietly and listen if you like. You'll want to ask questions, I wouldn't wonder, but you won't get any answers from me while I'm talking to the plants."

Rose's eyes twinkled with affection at both Rebecca and the ramsons and she re-entered the clump of wild garlic and began her strange enchanting song again. Her voice went gently up and down, in and out, as if weaving and winding among the stalks and leaves of the ramsons like thin wisps of mist among the trees on an early summer's morning.

Gradually Rebecca noticed that she seemed to be talking to two or three plants in particular and though Rebecca couldn't see that they looked different from the others, they definitely were, in some way. They seemed more . . . more . . . *there.*

Suddenly Rose's words became more distinct and Rebecca heard her singing

> *Wild flower, kind flower*
> *Petals for the sick;*
> *Wild plant, kind plant*
> *A healing for the ill.*
> *Leaves for the sorrowful*
> *And stem for the sad*
> *Bless them with your essence*
> *And their bodies will be glad.*

As Rose sang these words, she picked a stalk from each of the plants she had been concentrating on, touching the rest of each plant gently with a paw. Then she brought the stalks over to where Rebecca was and placed them on the ground by her.

"All over, all done," she said, yawning. "Oh, I am tired today!" Then she told Rebecca, "Now, don't you forget about picking plants at the right time, although you already seem to know something about that."

But before Rebecca could ask herself if she did know something about it, Rose continued: "And never pick too many, because you won't need them. The less you use, the further they go—that's why you can smell them better from farther off than near to."

"But I don't understand what you mean at all," said Rebecca, "or what you meant before when you said . . ."

Once more Rose didn't let her finish. Instead she laughed and said, "Now, Rebecca, my love, you take 'understand' right out of your vocabulary as quickly as you can and then you'll understand all the faster. I don't understand anything myself, my dear, not one single thing. Well, of course, I *do*, so that's silly. I understand that when you pick plants you must get on and use them, otherwise you'll lose so much."

"I don't understand again . . . ," sighed Rebecca. Rose didn't seem to answer any of her questions. "What do you *mean*, Rose?" she asked finally.

"That's better! What I mean is that generally when plants are ready to pick, they're ready to use, which is what I've got to do with these now. There's a mole that needs me in Duncton and I really only came here just to pick these and take them with me."

By now it was midafternoon and the wood had a warm, sleepy air about it. There was little birdsound, for with the passing of spring and early summer, their calls and songs had died away, leaving only the trills and whistles of yellowhammer and greenfinch along the woodland's edge. Sometimes, as now, the distant harsh call of a crow would come cawing through the wood high above their heads, making it seem vast and roomy in the summer stillness.

It was hard to think that anymole could be ill on such an afternoon, but as Rebecca automatically followed Rose as she made her way toward the wood's edge, she wondered again about the unease she had been feeling for so many days.

"Rose?"

"Mmm, my love, what is it?"

"Can I come with you?"

"No, my dear, not yet. I'll let you come one day when you're ready."

"Rose?"

"My love?"

"Which mole is it that's ill? There was real concern in her voice, for the unease she had felt seemed now to turn into a sense that a mole *was* ill and was calling her from somewhere in the wood, for she could feel the suffering almost as if it was her own. She looked about as if expecting to see some suffering mole right there before them both.

"I don't know," replied Rose quietly. "I often feel the call for help long before I know what it is, or which mole is calling."

By now Rebecca's afternoon content had been replaced by a restless unease as the strange feelings of distress she had felt, and which she had put aside, returned ten times more strongly. Oh, she could feel another mole's pain and it was drawing her somewhere . . . where? She looked again about the still wood where only ants stirred and bees and wasps hummed.

"Rose?" She spoke the name almost as a call for help. "When a mole is ill how can you feel it? Is it like . . . a . . . well, like a restless breeze that pulls you along, or a tunnel sucking you into its darkness, or a storm rising in the sky higher and higher until you feel you'll burst with it? Is it like that, Rose?"

As Rebecca spoke, Rose felt a great releasing flow through her body, as if she was returning to a welcoming burrow whose nest was warm and where she could lay her head and sleep at last. She had only ever once heard another mole describe the force of compassionate love that pulls a healer from her burrow, however weary she may be, so that she may find the strength to tend and cherish the distressed and sick. The last mole that spoke such words to her was the old female who had first taught her about healing. In all those long and often lonely mole-years since, she had forgotten how gentle was the sound of a healer's voice when it sounded in her own ears.

From the moment she had scented Rebecca coming with the wildflower smell of her kindness and youth, Rose had sensed, but not dared to believe, that another healer was near. Everything Rebecca had said to her had shown that her instinct was right, but again and again, as they had talked, Rose had not dared to accept the idea, for fear that it was her own hopes rather than the Stone's desire talking. But now, hearing Rebecca describe the restless impulse that leads a healer to the sick, she knew that her instinct about Rebecca had been right from the first.

"Yes," she said, "that's what it's like, Rebecca. That's what it will always be like."

If only she had the power to save this young creature from the pain and suffering the process of becoming a healer seemed so often to bring. But she had learned long ago that there were things no mole could change— a mole's freedom lay only in finding the courage to face with truth the darkness and light which the Stone would bring.

"Well, if it's like that," said Rebecca firmly, surprising herself with what she was saying so boldly, "then I think the mole you're going to is called Bracken. You'll find him somewhere up on the Ancient System. He was a friend of Hulver's when Hulver . . . before my . . . before Hulver . . . He told me to take care of Bracken but I didn't know what he meant, since I didn't even know him and have never met him."

Rebecca continued, less excitedly and more slowly as, with a brief glance to the south where the Ancient System lay, she turned to face her own part of the wood. "Hulver did say to take care of him but, well, perhaps he just meant for me to mention his name to you so you'd know. Mekkins told me he was dead, but I knew he wasn't. In fact, I thought he was all right at first, but now I think something's wrong—I've been feeling that restless feeling for days, but I didn't know what it was. It's what brought me over here today."

She finally stopped and Rose could feel how troubled she was. "I'll take care of him, my love, just as you would—try not to fret about him, for he will be safe."

"Who is he, Rose? Why is he special?"

Rose could only shake her head, for she did not know the answer. She only understood that Rebecca, too, was special, more special than anymole in Duncton could know, thought Rose, looking at her passionate innocence and watching her light-hearted ways.

"You leave your Bracken to me for the time being. I *will* take care of him, really I will." Rose moved gently over to Rebecca and nuzzled her in the soft part between shoulder and neck. "My dearest creature," she whispered. Then, taking up the ramson, she turned back toward the wood's edge so that she might take a route along it up to the Ancient System, and was gone.

❧ 10 ❧

THE Ancient System took in the injured Bracken as a mother tending a gravely hurt pup. It caressed him with its silence, soothed him with its darkness, and its labyrinths were to give him space in which to find himself again.

He was badly hurt. The wound where Mandrake's talons had torn into his left shoulder quickly turned septic so that even the strength that had allowed him to pull himself into the precipitous cliff face entrance ebbed away. He could do no more than crawl up and down the tunnel where he first arrived, taking whatever worms and beetles he found there.

For the first two or three days he looked forward to recovering and heading off into the tunnels beyond. The one he found himself in was big and well burrowed, its roof arching above his head and the pale chalk-dusted soil in which it was hewn catching the light that came in from the cliff opening.

But soon his interest in the Ancient System left him, as the poison in his wound seeped by degrees to the rest of his body and all he could do was to lie in the tunnel groaning and gasping with pain and distress.

The roots of his illness lay deeper than the wound itself. They went back to the trials and humiliations of his puphood, his uneasy passage into June, and the final shock of seeing the death, in the Stone clearing, of the one mole in whose presence he had begun to feel himself.

With the passage of each day, each one that succeeded it became longer and more painful. The agony of his shoulder spread to all parts of his body so that everything about him seemed to ache and throb. At the same time, the spirit that had started to grow in him in Hulver's presence began to wither as the hopes and interests in his mind became replaced by despair and weariness. As each passing day brought again the painful light from the tunnel end, it showed his fur to be more clogged and fading, while his snout and mouth were soon running with fever and disease.

His hunt for food became slower and more dragging,

while even the slowest of dank grubs seemed to find the power to escape his painful attempts to catch them. Once, a red cardinal beetle fell down on its back before his snout and gasping mouth. Nightmarelike, he watched it struggling to turn itself over and escape, while he, even more slowly, tried to bring his paw to bear on it. But his limb was like a root stuck in deep and paining ground, and by the time he finally dragged it to its target, the beetle had maneuvered itself upright, waved its antennae around to find an escape route, and was gone—its shiny redness lost in the swirling blackness of the tunnel beyond and Bracken's own tortured mind.

There were fresh roots enough, and the occasional live catch to keep him from dying quickly. His decline was gradual as, with too little food and moisture, the poison racked his body more and more and his sense of time, of place, of life itself, changed to a sense of eternal suffering. As week after week went by and summer took over the surface above, he slowly began to starve. Time lost its meaning.

Memories came back to him, clear and painful. Root, Wheatear, Burrhead. So much torment. A snatch of one of Aspen's stories and he would be crying in the vale of its words, the tears running furrows down his fur and hot and salty into his open mouth. Sometimes he seemed to hear rasping shouts directed at himself, or the thunderous sound of pursuit, but it was only the gasping of his own stricken voice and the shiver of his fevered paws on the tunnel floor.

Beyond the tunnel in which he lay so ill, the tunnels of the Ancient System turned this way and that, echoing the rhythms of emptiness that had occupied them for so many generations. From far off, though Bracken was too ill to hear it, there sometimes came the soft hiss of a minor roof-fall; or the plop and sliding back to safety of a worm; or the creaking, primal vibration of a tree root as it moved massively a fraction of a hairsbreadth in its growth among the tunnels.

Until the day came at the beginning of August, after weeks of illness, when he had no more strength even to eat the food that presented itself to him. A great lobworm that arced in and out of the tunnel wall seemed to sense that the mole who lay beneath him was not dangerous, and ran its pink, moist length over Bracken's

flanks, snaking in a curl of life along his back and fur.
A black, shining beetle, caught for a moment in the
light from the cliff end, stood poised before Bracken's
snout, its antennae questing and curious at the mole that
seemed dead and yet still made a faint noise of desperate
life. A flea hopped and bristled in the dust in which
Bracken lay, out of his fur and into it, and then out once
again.

Yet, in these hours of decline, he did not want to
die. Deep, deep within his heart the pup who had had
the strength to find his lonely way up out of the westside
and onto the slopes now stretched his soft paws out and
called for help. Beyond the seeping wound and fading
body, the spirit that moves a pup to bleat or a beaten
male to raise his talons one last time went out, insubstan-
tial as mist, vulnerable as an autumn leaf before an eastern wind. But who could hear?

What mole could know that on a warm August night,
when the rest of Duncton lay at peace, a precious mole
lay dying in the dark of a forgotten tunnel?

Only one, and she was at that moment by the Stone
and able to hear his unspoken cry. Rose had come the
long, weary way up the wood's edge and then cut into
the wood to the Stone, and now crouched praying that
it might lead her to the mole whose call both she and
Rebecca had heard. It was not that she doubted she
would find him—it did not occur to her that she would
not—but rather that she needed the Stone to lead her.
Now that she was on the Ancient System, she sensed
that her meeting with Rebecca and the desperate call
from Bracken were all part of a profound change that
was coming over the system, and perhaps all systems.

Rose could almost smell the forces for love and evil
that intertwined in the air about her and shuddered in
the tunnels below. She had never in her life entered the
tunnels around the Stone, though she had long ago known
that one day she might, when she had the strength.

Now she prayed for the Stone's help that she might
be able to aid whatever mole it was that was embroiled
in a battle with darkness and death and held so little
light in his talons to combat them with.

She left the clearing and took almost the same route
across the Ancient System as the one along which Bracken
had fled before Mandrake. She went slowly, too tired

to move fast, and snouted this way and that as she went —the drag of disease always strongest straight ahead. The summer day was long over, and high cloud hid whatever moon there might have been. The beech trees rustled cleanly above her, seeming to echo the dry rustle of the old leaves through which she made her way.

She could sense the deep past of the Ancient System all around her, rich with the love and suffering that are the residue of generation on generation of lives.

Still carrying the ramsons she had picked with Rebecca, Rose found her way to the part of the cliff over which Bracken had fallen, but was confused for a while by the lack of any obvious tunnel entrance. But finally her instinct told her where to dig and she burrowed down quickly, having carefully placed the ramsons clear of where the burrowed soil would fall, and after some tiring digging and a couple of rests, she broke into the tunnel between the cliff face and where Bracken lay. Long before she fully entered the tunnel, she knew that he was there. She could smell the heaviness of disease and hear the terrible rasping sound of the very ill.

"Oh my dearest," she whispered as she entered the tunnel and made her way along it to where she could see Bracken lying. He was huddled to one side of the tunnel, his back paws limp, and his snout and forepaws lost in the darkness ahead. His coat was grimy with dirt and round the terrible wound in his left shoulder were the congealings of blood and the spreading of poison. The tunnel floor about him was grimy with droppings and half-eaten food.

She touched him very, very gently on his good shoulder and whispered softly to him, but he did not respond at all, his breathing short and painful, his eyes closed, his snout bearing the pallor of near-death.

She could see how close to death he was, and how deeply he had suffered. Yet she was puzzled by the fact that the injury itself, though deep and unpleasant, was no worse than many she had seen and from which other moles, surely no fitter than Bracken had been, had recovered without any help at all. Such thoughts were natural to Rose, who treated anymole in trouble by trying to see what were the causes of his distress, knowing that more often than not they were different from what the victims themselves thought they were.

How often had a mole come to her with aches and pains in his shoulders which he had treated by massaging his haunches with comfrey; how often had she treated a loss of smell, the most terrible affliction for anymole, by buffeting the mole's back? Rose's treatments often seemed bizarre, but they worked.

She suspected that Bracken's illness lay not so much in the wound as in Bracken himself, and perhaps in the way the wound had been inflicted. Clearly, it had been done when he was in a state of distress and weakness . . . well, she couldn't very well ask him.

She began by gently caressing him and grooming his fur, so that slowly she could feel each part of his body relax under her paws and snout until his breathing grew a bit more peaceful and his paws a little less limp. This took her many hours, for he was so weak that she had to be very slow and gentle.

After this she cleaned the wound itself, using juice from the ramson, whose stinging smell also served to purify the air of the tunnel. He groaned a little when she did this, but not much, though he restlessly moved his head from one side to another in his unconsciousness.

She let him alone for a while so that she herself might sleep, and the day above had started again and the August sun was well into the beech trees, all yellow, gray and green, before she woke. She scurried up and down the tunnel, found a worm or two for herself and a couple of beetles, and even went to the cliff end of the tunnel whose precipitous drop made her gasp with awe as a morning breeze raced up from the cliff face below. Then, awake and recovered, she went back to Bracken.

He was alive and young, that was the best she could say. She sensed again the great struggle of darkness and light about him, as if all these conflicting forces were concentrated in his broken body which lay lost in this great place, teetering on the edge of a black void.

She placed one of her paws on each side of his face, closed her eyes, and began to pass into him her own healing love for life with a force and power she had never used before, or been able to use.

He was for her at once the frailest pup she had ever touched and all the hurt moles who had ever asked her for help. He was, too, all the many moles who had *never* asked her, not knowing they were troubled, to whom she had given her healing love.

There was no prayer in the meaning of the words she spoke, which were a running brook of love sounds and gentleness, of my love my dear my sweet thing, creature of love my laughter my whole-souled joy . . . the prayer lay in her whole being and it did not ask for help but praised the divine power that could still hold onto such life in so much suffering.

Her prayer, and the love of it, flowed through Bracken and beyond them both to the forgotten burrows and tunnels on whose edge he lay. Perhaps, too, it traveled out into the trees of the Ancient System, which now stood dappled in a morning sun, and it danced with the light and caressed the smooth gray branches of the beech trees and whispered amid the shining green of their leaves.

How long Rose gave herself to the healing of Bracken she never knew, for she was lost to the world as she did it. But long before she had finished, the sun on the surface declined toward the pastures and a wood pigeon had flapped and cooed in the evening light.

When, finally, she took her paws from Bracken's head, her aging fur was running with sweat and hung with exhaustion, and she looked as if she had been on a journey to the edge of life itself, and only just been able to return.

All her strength was gone. She was too tired even to find food and to wonder whether, after all, she had done enough. She simply lay down where she was, one of her paws touching his neck and her old body close to him— and fell asleep. She stirred sometimes when he stirred, and whispered gentleness into his ears and battling soul.

For three days, perhaps four, Rose stayed tending Bracken and cherishing the life in him back to hope and light. No mole can be certain of the time it took, and Boswell of Uffington, in the account he later scribed, says that there are events in moles' lives against which the measure of time becomes measureless, and "this one meeting between the loving Rose and Bracken of Duncton Wood was surely one of them."

However, the day came when Rose knew that Bracken, though not fully healed, was at least safe—as safe as a mole can ever be against the force of evil. His breathing became deeper and more rhythmic, his weak paws now moved restlessly with life, his groans no longer held the

agony she had first heard in them. He stirred at last into
consciousness and whispered words of Hulver and Rebecca the Healer . . . "Rebecca, Rebecca . . . ," though
he did not seem to know that Rose was there with him.

At last she left him, still only on the verge of conscious
health again, finding first for him in the tunnels some food
which she placed ready at his side. So many times she
had left moles like this, healed as best she knew how but
seeming so vulnerable before the rest of the journey into
health and wholeness which, finally, they must make for
themselves. Never had she been so reluctant to leave a
mole, and never had she said the ancient journey blessing
of Rebecca the Healer with such appeal to the forces of
light and love which abound in even the darkest places:

May the healing of Rebecca
Encompass your going and returning;
The peace of the White Moles be yours in the travel
And may you return home safeguarded.

And she might have said the blessing for herself as well,
for she had a long journey to her own burrow before her
and was very weary—more tired than she had ever been.

She left the tunnel by the way she had come, covered
over the entrance she had made with leaf litter and soil,
and tried to shake the fatigue from her old body. It was
dusk, a good time to travel at least, but it was an effort
even to put one paw in front of the other as she made for
the Stone—the first stage of her journey.

"I'm getting old," she said to herself, "and a little
weary. Why, my home burrow has never seemed quite
so far away as it does now." The atmosphere among the
great trees of the Ancient System was much calmer than
when she had arrived, and less confused.

When she reached the Stone clearing it was night, and
she paused there to rest and reflect, feeling the richness of
Duncton stretching beyond the slopes beneath her. Something very powerful was going on, bigger than the system
she loved, perhaps even more important than all the moles
who lived there or had made their lives there in the past,
and whom she had so long cared for and tended.

So much was changing. She had known of the change
even before Mandrake came—indeed, she saw that he
was a part of it and not a cause of it. Hulver and Bindle

were both gone, killed near this very spot, and other old moles she knew were all gone as well.

It occurred to her that she was one of the oldest moles in Duncton or on the pastures and she found herself thinking again "I *am* getting old!" She looked down at her paws and rubbed her snout and face against them, smiling gently at the silly thought. For above her, the tilted Stone rose in the night, the great tree roots black around its base, and she chided herself with the thought that no mole was ever old in the Stone. "Why, you mustn't make me say such foolish things!" she said to the Stone, in the chatty way she always spoke to it. "Or even let me think them."

With that she began to make her way slowly and carefully down the slopes by the edge of the wood, taking her thoughts and aging body to the warmth of her home burrow. And to sleep.

ROSE had chosen the moment of her departure wisely, for the following dawn Bracken finally awoke with a clear head but a terribly weakened body. He was aching and wretched, and a little ill-tempered, but at least he could see and hear the waking world around him. See, that is, the dawning light coming into the tunnel, and hear the morning breeze by the cliff and a chorus of wrens and greenfinch and the chaffer of a young jackdaw somewhere among the trees.

His shoulder still hurt terribly, but the pain was now confined to the wound itself and did not spread evilly through his body to his very eyes, and snout, and sensibility. He could control it.

He had the feeling that he was not alone, for the burrow smelled fresh and lived in. Curious! He dozed and awoke and dozed again, until he finally awoke hungry as a pup. And there was food ready for him. Strange. "I must have gotten it for myself," he thought, though he couldn't remember . . . anything.

Yes . . yes he could. Illness and dark and a great red cardinal beetle that was coming to him and struggling with him . . . and a worm and a black beetle much bigger than he that were trying to destroy him, take him away . . . Bracken shuddered and started to eat the food, asking no more questions of himself.

Though he was hungry, he managed less than half a worm. He was so unused to eating. But he managed to nibble at the stem of a . . . but he didn't know the plant's name. It tasted fresh and good. Strange again. He looked around the tunnel, half expecting to see a friendly mole, but there was none—just high, arching walls and a well-made floor that stretched into the darkness ahead.

For a moment he wanted to raise himself fully to his paws and start exploring the Ancient System which, he realized with a thrill, now lay ahead for him to explore whenever he wanted. But the moment he tried to move, he knew how weak he was and it was several days before he felt able to do more than struggle painfully up and down the tunnel he was already in, picking up what food he could find.

They were strange days of pain and content. His shoulder hurt whenever he moved and yet a restlessness to get started drove him on to use it more and more, despite the pain. In doing so, he learned that pain is a clumsy word, describing as one something that is a thousand feelings, not all of them unpleasant. The ache in his head, the searing pain if he worked his shoulder too much, the dull moaning of his stomach as it became used to food again—they were all different. He learned to welcome the step into pain that he had to take when he awoke and stretch his limbs and work his body back into himself.

Quite where the content of these days came from he did not know, but it was there alongside him as if a companionable mole were in the tunnel with him. He was restless, impatient, ill-tempered with his weakness, but beneath it all he felt a happy certainty that so much lay ahead for which he, himself, had found the strength. In his mole-months of illness, stretching from the last week of June to the start of August, he had matured a great deal. He could dimly remember, as a pleasant dream, the caresses and gentleness of a mole very close to him, but thought it must be some recreation of his own of the Rebecca of old times Hulver had talked about. He might indeed, had he been asked, have talked of Rebecca the legendary Healer as a real force in the system, so persistent was the idea that she had been there with him. But Rose? No, he never knew that she had been there.

Perhaps, deep down, he knew, but preferred to think that he gave himself the strength to survive, and so forgot. Certainly he forgot other important things as well. He forgot that he nearly died. He forgot the swirling forces of evil into whose darkness he had looked. He forgot the power of light by whose strength he had been kept back from the void. He forgot again the memories of puphood that early in his illness had flooded back. In forgetting all these things, he lost as well the lessons they might have taught him, or the releases their memory might have brought.

At the same time, he remembered things as they never were: he, and only he, had found the power to heal himself; that pain and suffering quickly pass; that Mandrake and Rune were, after all was said and done, just moles.

Just moles? No mole is just a mole. A mole may have to learn a lesson many times before he knows its truth, especially one like Bracken.

He finally woke up one dawn a few moledays into August, knowing that at last he had strength and desire enough to start exploring the Ancient System. Most of all he wanted to get his bearings, for few moles were quite so uncomfortable as Bracken, the greatest explorer of his generation, when they didn't know *exactly* where they were.

He ran first to the cliff end of the tunnel, to pay his respects to the spot where he had found a second life and to take one final look into the daylight before plunging back into the unknown tunnels and discoveries behind. Grass, cudweed and brambles hung waving across the tunnel from the surface above. He listened to the soft-loud-soft buzz of nectar-seeking flies and wasps taking advantage of the blue harebells and bright yellow furze that grew on this sunlit eastern part of the wood.

The smell of summer was warm and sweet and it was only then, taking it in, that he realized by its heavier dryness compared with June, how many molemonths had passed in nightmare illness. Well, now he was better, and the time had come, at last, to explore.

He turned around and started forward on a journey into tunnels and burrows, dangers and marvels, that no mole had ventured near for generations.

It was only when he was well past the farthest point he had reached previously in his search for food that Bracken noticed the deepening quality of sound in the tunnel he was traveling down. It crept forward toward him, at first no more precise than the backwash of a mixed wind on rough grass. But then, with each step he took, its quality became richer. The sound of sliding soil came whispering from the unknown labyrinths beyond; then the moan of wind at some twist or turn, gathered into the tunnel from some distant exposure; into these came the harsher, mysterious creaking of a subterranean tree root in stress—but whether from round the corner or many tunnels away, he could not tell; then the sudden scuttle of a beetle; and mixing with it all, the echo and re-echo of his own pawsteps running forward ahead of him and returning from some wall beyond in the dark.

The wall turned out to be the far side of a much bigger tunnel into which the one he had started from entered at right angles. As he stepped into it, the sounds he had heard redoubled in richness and complexity, and quite took his breath away. If there was any truth in the old mole saying "You can tell a mole by the sounds of his tunnels," then surely the moles who built this system were wise and cunning indeed.

For when a mole burrows a tunnel, he takes heed of the acoustics it creates—not for his entertainment, but so that he might gauge from the sounds it carries to him at any one point potential danger or possible food. A tunnel has to be good to carry the vibrations of a worm more than fifty moleyards: it has to be superbly designed to carry the slinking of a rival much more than one hundred moleyards. This being so, the air currents in a system are very important—for while earth vibrations may carry fifty moleyards and sound in a still system perhaps two hundred, air currents help carry sound a great deal farther, and scent as well. But air currents do not happen—they are designed, and it was this aspect of the tunnel into which he entered that impressed Bracken. For the air currents were subtle and complex, the moles achieving the difficult art (in many systems long forgotten) of creating tunnels in which air flows in different directions at different levels—as water may do in a river, or wind often does in a steep valley.

The advantage of such air currents to a mole who knows them is that they allow him to "read" his tunnels in two directions at once, and sometimes, if he is at an intersection or crosstunnel, even more.

At first Bracken could not easily interpret the sounds he heard or the scents either. That would take time. Though from the scents he could tell that there were no moles about, nor did he expect any. There were, however, other animal smells—voles, certainly, but they'll grab any temporary burrow they can get, and if that includes the entrance to a deserted mole tunnel, well and good; the more sinister, sharp smell of weasel came to him, too, though from a long, long way off; but nothing else that was specific, except for the clean, dry smell of fresh vegetation whose roots and scent he realized must enter the Ancient System in many places.

This play on his ears and snout was intoxicating

enough, but the impression of the great tunnel he was in was only completed by its awesome size and evident age. Its wall and roof towered above him, giving the immediate impression that it had been burrowed in some long-distant age, when giant moles roamed the earth. The walls were hard and a little chalky, the floors smooth and well packed, while the curves of its roof and corners, and where subsidiary tunnels joined it, were subtle and sinewy.

Set into the walls at irregular intervals were the gray-white roundels of enormous flints, plump with curves and hollows, which added not only to the curious flowing appearance of the tunnels but created a feeling of great antiquity as well.

It occurred to Bracken how extraordinary it was that moles had been able to move these great stones so that they might fit the tunnel—so deliberate did their setting seem—but then he saw that, by some miracle of orientation, the tunnel had been burrowed to fit the existing position of the stones. It was as if, in some way, the ancient moles had taken their cue not from any desire to impose a pattern on virgin soil but from the pattern set by whatever power it was that had first placed the stones. The feeling of age and venerability the tunnel gave him was such that he almost tiptoed along so he wouldn't disturb the ancient peace.

What he did disturb, however, was the deposit of fine white chalk dust that had settled through time on the floor and rougher parts of the walls. The first big drift he came to he mistook for a rise in the floor, and went unthinking into it so that particles rose about him in a great choking cloud of dust, and he backed away from it, sneezing and gasping, his fur all white.

After that, he watched carefully for the thicker drifts, after a while getting used to the fact that the chalk tended to be deposited on alternate sides of the great tunnel, creating a winding path of clearer floor down the center of the tunnel—which added to the impression the tunnel gave to a mole traveling down it of dancing or weaving along past the immovable stones of time.

Bracken did not enter any of the subsidiary tunnels that ran off this bigger tunnel on his first two days of exploration. He was too tired and too cautious. His explorations of the westside, Barrow Vale and the slopes in May and June had taught him that exploration is best done carefully until a mole has a grasp of the orientation of the tunnels accessible from it.

He quickly established that what he had come to regard as the peripheral communal tunnel of the Ancient System ran, at this point anyway, parallel with the cliff's edge and roughly one hundred moleyards in from it. It ran on up toward the top of the hill where he and Hulver had lain hidden before Midsummer Night, and back down toward the easternmost side of the slopes. There was only one other tunnel running back to the cliff's edge as did the first one he had found himself in—and this, too, fell sheer to the void below.

On the third day of his new exploration, Bracken traveled a little way down one of the tunnels that branched off toward the center of the Ancient System, which was the part he most wanted to reach. The tunnel was smaller than the communal one from which it led out, just as elegantly burrowed, and flints still lined its walls.

He was only a few moleyards into it before he saw ahead of him the well-rounded entrance into a burrow. He approached with heart beating rapidly and breath held, for in any system it is the burrows that bring home the fact that moles actually once lived and ate, slept and fought there. He entered it a little nervously, automatically sniffing at the entrance for the scent of life, though he knew that there could be none there. The burrow was bigger than those in the present system, and oval instead of round. Its soil was the same gray-white of the tunnels, the walls were smooth and held no flints, and on its floor lay the dusty fibers of some long-since-perished nesting material. The whole effect was sparse and cold, and try as he might, he could not *imagine* moles living there in some past time; he felt the age of the burrow, but no warm sense of its past life.

It was the same farther on—the same oval burrow, the same sparseness, the same disappointing inability to reach back to the moles who must once have lived there. Quite what Bracken expected he didn't know, but ever since he had first heard of the Ancient System the idea of its past life had excited his imagination. Now he was here—well, he wanted more than he could have.

He explored down all the subsidiary tunnels leading toward the center of the wood, which were in reach of

the base he had established for himself in his original
tunnel. He gradually got used to the rich sound and by
association and deduction was able to start to interpret it.
At the same time, and without knowing it, he built up his
strength again so that when he was ready for more am-
bitious exploration, he was fit enough for it as well.

It was the second week of August when he made the
decision to press forward to where he reckoned the center
of the system would be, and not try and return in one day
but to make do with whatever burrow he could find. By
now, the great communal tunnel that had so impressed
him at the start was familiar, its curves and twists still
mysterious and beautiful, but the initial awe he had felt
was replaced by a certain proprietorial confidence. He
felt there was nothing more it could tell him and that
having conquered it, so to speak, he might as well move
on to better things.

With this dangerously complacent attitude, Bracken
left what was in fact no more than the periphery of the
Ancient System and struck westward toward its very center. He took the biggest of the subsidiary tunnels and,
ignoring all side turns and burrow entrances, pressed on
down it, anxious to see if he could find something like a
center to the system.

Bracken's sense of direction was, as ever, very accurate, for the tunnel went directly west toward where he
was certain the Stone itself stood.

However, he was overoptimistic about the speed he
would make, for after two or three hundred moleyards,
the tunnel's condition deteriorated rapidly as it sloped upward nearer the surface and entered an area of softer,
blacker soil. There were frequent roof-falls to burrow
through; they had cascaded down in the long-distant past
and opened the way for superficial vegetation to send
down its roots, winding and confused among what had
once been a perfect tunnel. At the same time, the roots
of trees impinged on the tunnel, sometimes sending a root
shaft vertically through it, so that he had to squeeze his
way past, while more than once, an old root ran along
the tunnel itself, melding into the soil around it and losing
the tunnel in a debris of mold that he did not much like
burrowing through.

So his progress became slow, and his early hopes of a
quick passage to the marvels that he hoped lay ahead

were lost in the sweat and toil of pressing forward. The
tunnel was not so deep in the ground as the big communal one from which he had started, and had a more
temporary air about it and, somehow, somewhere, lost
the awesome sense of the past he had felt initially.

This feeling was accentuated by the fact that the mar-
velous richness of sound in the earlier tunnel was muffled
and lost in the confusion of roof-fall and roots he was
battling through. He began to feel isolated and cut off in
a way he had not felt before, and to have a sense that he
was lost forever in the ruins of a system that was now
empty of life and interest.

So strong did this feeling become that more than once
he was tempted to burrow up to the surface and press on
across it to a point where the Ancient System might have
more to offer. Only his desire truly to explore the Ancient
System, coupled with a real fear of the dangers from
predators on the open surface above him, kept him pressing on through the ruined tunnel. Until finally, and suddenly, he was tired. His left shoulder grew aching and
heavy, throbbing where the wound had been, while the
sounds in the tunnel seemed to fade and swell, whirling
in a dizzy way about him, so that he knew he must rest.

He chose one of the many subsidiary runs off the tunnel he had been going down and found a small burrow
a few moleyards into it. It was dusty and infiltrated from
above with the white fronds of roots, but at least it gave
him a floor on which to sleep and a secure roof over his
head. But he was too fatigued to fall into sleep immediately, dozing instead, while listening to the muffled sounds
about him.

If he fell asleep, he did not notice it, for he awoke
with a start and the crystal-clear conviction that the
sound about him was different from any sound he had
heard before in the Ancient System. It had a depth and
resonance that suggested . . . that said . . . he couldn't
say what. He could hear, but he could not put words to
it. But he was suddenly afraid in a way he had never
known before—a fear not of possible hurt to his body,
but of some wonder, some depth, that once felt or seen
would strip away something from him and leave a route-
way of vulnerability running to his very soul.

But just as a pup may often face some danger so enormous that he cannot even comprehend it and innocently

stand before it like an anemone in a gale, so Bracken
now only briefly acknowledged this fear. He shook himself awake, got up, and was off down the tunnel with
renewed excitement, convinced that the most grueling
part of the journey was over and that the deeper sound
ahead heralded a discovery that would take him at last
to the heart of the system.

He was right. The tunnel began to enter a harder chalk
subsoil and to drop down to still and ancient depths
where all windsound began to fade away, to be replaced
by frightening creakings and distant groanings.

The tunnel ran deeper and deeper and then leveled off,
the floor covered by dust and grime that had been disturbed by no creature for generations. The sound of his
pawsteps was muffled by dust, and when he scratched his
claws along the wall, the sound traveled ahead but did
not echo back, rather losing itself in some great void at
the end of the tunnel. He soon found out why. The tunnel
emerged into a chamber, the size of which took Bracken's
breath away. It was so big that had his paws not been
on solid ground, he might have thought he was floating
in space itself. The chamber was full of the mysterious
creakings and strainings he had heard before, coming
from its far side. The walls actually stretched ruggedly
to his right and left but appeared to stretch in a straight
line and not in the curve he was used to from other big
chambers he had been in. A curving wall, after all, sug-
gests that a place has confines. A straight wall in a
chamber hints at massive size.

Bracken crouched down in the protection of his little
tunnel entrance and began to feel his way mentally into
the place. Its roof soared so high above him that its
height seemed even farther off than its unknown, unseen
walls. He let out a brief call to test the echo, and it
traveled away from him, falling into silence until he had
almost given it up before far, far from the distance, the
echo returned, small and lorn. As he was thinking about
what this meant another echo came back from his call,
this time from somewhere high above him. Then finally
one more, from way off to the right.

He explored first to the right and then around the
perimeter to the left, stopping in each case only when
he reached either end of the massive wall that towered
darkly on the far side of the chamber.

The wall cast fear into him, for it was curiously carved, with great swirling crevices and jagged embossments that gave it an eerie power to distort and amplify any sound that came up against it. The sound of Bracken's pawfalls became the tramp tramp tramp of an army of great moles, causing him to peer furtively about him in the dark to see if these phantoms were really there. An intake of breath became a dark gasp of horror so convincing that it made him feel the fear it sounded like. As for a hum, which he tried, *that* turned into the deep chant of dark and malevolent moles.

Such was the power of these echoes or sounds that Bracken was at first reluctant to progress to its very center. But as it was from that murky and unseen depth that the creakings and stressings that vibrated about the chamber came, he knew that finally he would have to penetrate into it.

He thought about what he had found. Three tunnels on one side of the chamber, three on the other, all radiating to different parts of the system. Six in all, not counting the tiny tunnel that had led him here, and which he suspected had been burrowed in secret as a special way for some mole, or moles, in the past. Six tunnels. Was there, then, a seventh, leading through to the Stone clearing which must surely lie beyond this great embossed wall, and which must lie farther along it?

Slowly he set off, stepping out several moleyards from the wall so he could see ahead just a little better, and so his hums would not be quite so powerful.

The sounds, when he briefly created them by a tentative hum—he did not want to provoke the same reaction as before—now evoked a feeling of vulnerable good spirits in him, less jerky than before but quite without the smooth gentleness of the first set of sounds. He felt that at any moment they would take him plummeting down to misery again, and stopped humming, though it was difficult to stop the feeling continuing and changing as he went on. He looked at the wall, whose carvings were clear but getting more complex again, the lines spiraling and looping from ground to shoulder height and sometimes beyond.

He tried humming louder to see what would happen, and what happened was not pleasant. The sound had a dark quality to it. At first it was distant, coming from somewhere high up the wall some way beyond, hanging off the overhang and easily forgotten if he concentrated on the more pleasant sounds that came to him straight off the wall. But this became harder the farther he went, and, despite himself and his fear of being caught up again in dark sound, he continued to hum so that the darkness in the sound grew blacker and its lightness fled behind him to where the more melodious patterns and wall carvings were. This black sound began to overwhelm him and he began to push and stagger forward as if losing his sense of direction, trying to catch up with his breath and stop his own throat sending out these unnatural sounds that pulled him onward and on.

In front of him, a great jag of flint, black and shiny, rose up from the floor, set solid in the wall and tapering down into the floor. Its top was so sharp and fine that it was translucent, and a mole could have cut a single whisker with it. Bracken staggered around it to face another jag of flint, bigger than the first, that appeared to thrust toward him. He ran on, whimpering with fear. The sounds were dark, blacker and more and more owl-like, and he struggled desperately with himself to stop making them, his paw rattling its talons against his throat, scratching himself to stop the noise, conquer the terror. . . . Until there were no more flints and his breath came out shallower and he managed to twist his mouth to his paw and stop the sound, saliva running onto his talons with the effort. There was another set of the jagged chertlike rock beyond him, the same as the ones he had just passed by. They ran into the wall. His eyes followed their line upward to the great beak of shiny cold flint that curved up to two massive roundels of black-silver eyes, all of which seemed to form the massive face of an owl infinitely evil to look on. Its black, shiny flint seemed to give it a shimmering light.

The sound he had stopped making still echoed about the chamber, swirling blackly somewhere between him and the wall, caught between the flint talons that shot out on either side of him and seemed to draw him to the center of the wall. His eyes fell slowly and fearfully from those of the great owl to the wall beneath, the part that lay under the beak and between the great black talons. The part that lay straight ahead of him.

What he saw there made him gasp in horror. For there,

ahead of him, was the start of the last tunnel, the seventh, the one he had been seeking; and crouched at the entrance, its head resting between its paws, the round, black voids of its eye sockets looking straight at him, was the blanched skeleton of a massive mole.

Beyond it he caught the full blast of the straining, creaking sounds he had first heard when he entered the chamber. Sliding, rasping, slowly crushing and melding, the rasp of wood on living wood, a sound like old branches rubbing against each other on a wild night, only below ground.

Then he knew what it was he was hearing: the sound of the roots of the great beeches that surrounded the Stone clearing and into which he now knew with terror this seventh tunnel must lead. As he listened, the sounds seemed to come to him through the gaunt holes of the skull's eyes, or spat out at him from its vicious teeth, or sought to entangle him in its collapsed rib bones scattered on the ground behind the skull.

To reach the center of the system he would have to face the living roots he could hear but yet not see; and to reach them he would have to pass by this massive skeleton that seemed to carry the very essence of the root sounds themselves.

But not now, not at this moment. The fears he had so far controlled exploded inside him and turning, breath gasping, he started to run from the mole body in panic, heading across the great chamber and making instinctively for the tunnel to the northeast, which carried the scent of oaks and worms, and of a life that was now and that he needed.

AUGUST is an untidy month in Duncton Wood, when the leaves of the trees have lost both the virgin greenness in which they gloried up to June and their rich, rustling maturity, which was one of the pleasures of July. Now they are past their best. Here and there, passing August rain brings one or two leaves down, green but limp, onto the wood's brown floor to die among the great blowzy fern and insinuating ivy into which they have fallen.

Birdsong wanes down to the fidgeting of yellowhammer and greenfinch at the wood's edge and along some of its more open paths and vales, while in its heart only the call of rooks, with the flapping of their wings, makes a noise that carries. Still, on the occasional hot day, when the sun forms warm pools of yellow light among the rich green undergrowth, a stag beetle may suddenly rise and buzz through the air, or ants rustle, or gall wasps drone. And then a mole in Barrow Vale may yawn and stretch and another may affect to ask what the fuss is all about.

While a mole on the surface might think, as the vagrant sun catches the pink petals of bramble flower, that spring is suddenly back again and it is wild cherry blossom that is on show. But not for long. Let the high banking clouds smother the sun and the brambles look again like what they truly are, a tangled untidiness bearing wavering petals which never seem quite to know how to stay crisp and neat. Still, what's it matter? What mole cares? There must be something better to talk about. . . .

Chatter. Gossip. Rumor. The three consorts of August. One for the lazy, one for the idle, and the third for the bored.

For the older moles of Duncton, the ones who have seen at least one Longest Night through, the main source of chatter and gossip in August lies in the doings of the youngsters. They have by now left the home burrow far behind and, after a molemonth or two of scurrying about in shallow runs and burrows, are just beginning to establish themselves—the ones who have survived, that is. For many have been taken by owls or lost strength in territorial fights and, unable to find sufficient food, died a lingering death in hot July to be pecked at by crows or colonized by carrion flies and egg-laying beetles.

These struggles go on into the middle of August and many a Barrow Vale mole, complacent in the knowledge of having his or her own territory (though not *too* complacent because some of these westside youngsters are still very hungry indeed for territory), will pass the time of day with the kind of talk that begins "Have you heard what happened to . . . ?" or "One of them marshenders had the effrontery to. . . ." And so on, and so forth.

In an August when things are well settled by the third week and when there is enough food about and a mole gets bored, rumor may take over from gossip. Who can say where it comes from or why one story seems more fascinating than another? Some rumors fly on a breeze of hope to float about the burrows brightly and give pleasure to those who hear them, and those who pass them on. Others sneak in on the winds of discontent, shadows on whispered conversations whose dark pleasures lie in the fact that if what they say will happen really does, it will be somewhere else, to some other poor mole.

Occasionally, very rarely, a rumor may come which contains both the seeds of hope and the germs of discontent, and seems to herald change of a kind that will affect everymole, not just one.

Such a rumor arose that August in Duncton Wood, and unknowingly Bracken was the cause of it.

His panic flight from the Chamber of Dark Sound (as he now called it) took him toward the slopes, and the pleasant woodland scent of the tunnel lured him finally outside. But his surface senses had been dulled by the long time underground and by his illness, and without realizing what he had done, he went straight into the path of a westside youngster who was establishing his territory. Bracken looked so wild and desolate that the youngster (who was no older than Bracken himself) fled back to his home burrow with a garbled story of a wild monster mole he had seen coming from the Ancient System. The story soon got round the westside, and what good August story it was for moles to get their teeth into!

Then Bracken was spotted over on the eastside, and an exaggerated version got back to Barrow Vale—a wild mole seen on the Ancient System, massive and fearless, who would kill anymole that tried to get near him.

It was enough to get the rumor going even more strongly, and the eastsiders, a superstitious lot, resurrected an old legend that one day the Stone would send its own mole to bring havoc on the system as a punishment— though for what no mole was certain. And it was from this story that Bracken unwittingly gained himself an awesome name that became the subject of rumor, thrilling fears, and an exodus of youngsters who might otherwise have tried to make territory near the slopes: he became the Stone Mole.

"Aye, he's up there all right, you mark my words; and he'll be down this way, I shouldn't wonder," was how one Barrow Vale gossip put it, his words heavy with complacent warning. "Just been biding his time, he has, just waiting for the right moment, and now he's come. The eastsiders call him the Stone Mole, and that isn't such a bad name if you ask me . . ."

When Mandrake first heard the story, he thought it was amusing, and laughed. Probably some pasture mole gone astray, he thought. Well, he'd sort it all out when he felt like it. As for Rune, he latched onto anything that had possibilities for his own advancement, and there was a way the Stone Mole rumor could help him. His smile was smug with the potential of it all.

Had Bracken any inkling that such a rumor had gained ground, he would have been amazed. He regretted the contacts with moles he had so unsuccessfully made on two different occasions since he emerged out of the confines of the Ancient System, because he now reckoned that it was best, on the whole, to continue to lie low.

The first, with the mole on the west side of the slopes, was just an accident. Nothing he could do about that. The second was more regrettable, since it was born out of a desire in him to make contact with somemole somewhere after such a long isolation. The two old eastsiders looked friendly enough—and what a relief it had been to hear mole being talked. It was almost like listening to Hulver himself talking, so learned did they seem. And they used one or two words of the old language that Hulver had sometimes used. Spurred on by the promise of this and their seeming gentleness, he had come out into the open after listening to them for a while, and approached them.

When they challenged him with the traditional greeting, he tried to answer as best he could but, well, he wasn't sure quite where to say he had come from and, anyway, he was so unused to talking to another mole, let alone moles, that somehow he stumbled over his words. Then they looked frightened and ran away from him and he looked back behind him to see if there was some big mole or other creature that was threatening them, not realizing that it was he, himself, they were running from.

This incident saddened Bracken, for it made him feel isolated and lost and left him craving contact with another mole, anymole, even more. The idea that they were running from him dawned on him slowly as he scratched his side and felt his fur still hanging loose on his gaunt body, while he thought of the two older moles so plump and sleek who had fled from him.

"I must look a pretty sight," he whispered to himself, snouting first at his flanks, then at his scarred shoulder, and finally rubbing his paws down his thin face.

Bracken did not know it, but he looked a lot better than when he had first emerged from the Ancient System's tunnel and started to live in the warmer air and wormier soil of the slope surface. But while a mole will normally recover from injury or illness very fast, swinging back from near death to full health in a matter of moledays, one that has been as ill as Bracken had been, both physically and emotionally, may take moleweeks or even moleyears to recover fully. Just as such illness may be moleyears in the making, so the route back to health may be moleyears in the finding.

Still, physically at least, he was improving. In the days that followed the distressing incident near the eastside, he took it easy, eating as much as he could, sleeping a great deal and keeping well hidden. He still wanted to make contact with another mole, more and more so as he began to feel healthier, but he was regaining his normal caution and would try to be more careful next time.

It was perhaps three or four moledays into September before he returned to the Ancient System tunnels by the way he had come out. His intention was to explore the periphery of the tunnels on the slope side so that when, and if, he made contact with a mole again, he would have a good working knowledge of the system's main routes and be able to escape back into them if he needed to.

It was in this period that Bracken began to perfect his peculiar—some might say unique—talents for exploration and route-finding. He already had an instinctive grasp of the strategy that distinguishes an explorer (able rapidly to establish his sense of place in a widespread system) from an orienteer, able to grasp only the minutiae of tunnel directions in a smaller area. The key to this strategy lies in getting to know the outline of a system before exploring its detail—which was what he was now doing for the Ancient System.

Bracken now knew that there were two parts to the Ancient System—superficial summer tunnels which, on the edges, were bigger, forming an all-round peripheral system serving the central core; and a deeper, probably more ancient, set of tunnels, whose area was much more restricted and where food supply was likely to be a major problem except in the winter moleyears, when worms were driven deeper underground. He suspected that the big communal tunnel he had first entered from the cliffside formed a wide encirclement of the whole summer system, and this was soon confirmed by his following it from the slopes right round to the cliffside. It petered out, somewhat, farther on, where it turned northward on the west side and he did not bother to burrow his way through the many roof-falls in there. Instead, he pursued it back past the slopes and north of the Stone clearing where, again, it continued its circle round the whole system and faded again as it turned southward. From this great circling tunnel there were several routes radiating into the center.

First, he must find his courage and return to the deeper system where, though he dreaded doing it, he must make his way to the Chamber of Dark Sound and somehow past that long-dead mole.

But before doing that, Bracken decided—perhaps more as a way of delaying the day when he must go back to the deeper tunnels—to find out what tunnels lay between the summer communal route on the east side and the slopes beneath, to where, here and there, the present Duncton system reached. His objective, for he liked to have one, was to make his way to Hulver's tunnels, for he was convinced that the sealed-off tunnels he had seen in them, and puzzled over, must lead up into the Ancient System. It was there, where Hulver himself had lived and had tried so hard to maintain a living link between the old and the new, that the physical link must lie. Bracken wanted to establish the fact of it before doing anything else.

It was in this period of a moleweek or so that Bracken began to perfect another of his strong talents for exploration and route-finding. His accidental discovery that a mole may use sound to make carved walls "speak" had made him think about the possibility of using sound on ordinary walls in ordinary tunnels.

Of course, he already did this instinctively to some extent, using, for example, the echo-back of his pawsteps from a wall ahead to gauge how far he had to travel before reaching it. But until now Bracken had only done this in the tunnels he knew—and the soil in the Duncton system was too soft and absorbent ever to allow moles there to refine this technique very much. Up here, however, the soil was harder and much more responsive to sound and vibration, and now Bracken began to exploit the fact. He spent long periods trying different sounds on particular stretches of tunnels, learning to read the tunnel ahead from the sound it sent back. A straight tunnel running into a T-junction sent back a much clearer signal than a similar tunnel that had twists and turns; a tunnel with many burrows off it was more muted and richer-sounding than a similar tunnel with simple runs off it; softer soil—of which there were pockets on the Ancient System—was less responsive than harder soil and deeper sounds had to be used on it to get a maximum return of echo. Different sounds had to be used to maximize the information coming back from even clear-sounding tunnels—too sharp a sound, for example, in a responsive tunnel came back so fast and its echo repeated so often that it drowned itself in its own sound, and the information was lost.

So Bracken proceeded on his explorations, testing different sounds, trying out different thumps and scratches with his paws, and generally making enough noise to frighten a whole system of moles, let alone one, had they been there. But to Bracken it seemed that no mole would ever be there and, protected by his sense of isolation (though often regarding the fact of it as a curse), he went on in his humming, sounding, scratching, thumping way turning the art of exploration into a science.

It did not occur to him, as he made his rambling approach through the peripheral tunnels toward Hulver's old system, that another mole might have occupied them. But so it was. She was a female, and her name was Rue, and in her time she had littered well. Then, in the early summer, Mandrake himself had loomed, one terrible day, into her burrow and turned her out of the cosy tunnels beyond Barrow Vale, which she had occupied for mole-years, to make way for his darling daughter, Rebecca.

Rue didn't have a chance, and believed Mandrake's growling threat that if she so much as showed herself on Rebecca's territory or anywhere near Barrow Vale, he would maim or kill her.

She had already been distressed by her inability to litter that spring, though she had mated more than once. The sounds of other pup cries upset her and gradually she found she ate less and that her heart was not in keeping the burrows and tunnel tidy, though she was normally a very neat mole.

Already dispirited, she was easy prey to Mandrake's will and so became yet another victim of his unpredictable moods. Rue suddenly found herself competing with the new crop of youngsters for territory. She was a small mole and, coming as she did originally from the eastside, was not a great fighter. She certainly wasn't weak or even gentle, like some of the eastside moles, but she was no match for the bigger Duncton ones. The system she had won for herself, and that Rebecca had taken over, lay between two richer ones held by stronger moles and to some extent was neutral territory—perhaps that was why she had managed to hold on to it so long.

May, June and July were one long nightmare for Rue as she scratched about for a living wherever she could. Cut off by Mandrake's threat from her friends and the territory she knew, she became scraggy and disheveled, and her eyes began to wear the look of a female on the way to defeat—one who faces a mateless future and a territoryless death. She might have made for the Marsh End nearest where she was brought up, but that was moleyears and moleyears before, in times that she had long stopped thinking of, and in her present state it seemed a hazardous journey to make. And marshenders do not take kindly to strangers. Driven from one tunnel to the next, barely escaping with her life more than once, so real are the threats to an aging mole who falls from territory and grace, she slowly found herself in August making toward the one place where old moles may, before the shadow of age creeps right over them, find a temporary security and some vague hope—the slopes.

For younger moles the name is literally dreadful, for it puts into their minds the possibility that they, too, might one day wake up with aches in their backs and shoulders and find that they cannot move, or hear, so well as once they could. But Rue was nowhere near that stage, though to all outward appearances she might have seemed to be.

She grubbed about the quiet surface of the slopes, fearful of the owls said to haunt the heights above, running from temporary hide to temporary burrow, meeting aggression from one or two slopesiders whose tunnels she crossed until, one day, she came to a tunnel that smelled empty and deserted.

It was an outlier from Hulver's old system and had not been reoccupied by any other mole since he had gone forever from it in June.

She waited by it for three moledays, keeping her snout low and listening with care to see if there was mole somewhere about. Badgers she heard, from the humpy ground somewhere toward the eastside; crows she heard and saw; a fox prowled past quite close, but she smelled him long before he came and did not even bother to hide as youngsters often did before they learned better, because she knew that a fox will not touch a mole. "A fox may be a mole's best friend, when his path with ours doth wend" said the old eastside proverb she had learned when she was a pup. The fox sniffed about and tiptoed away.

Apart from that, nothing. So, after three moledays, Rue made her way timidly toward Hulver's old tunnels and could smell the emptiness all around. Oh! she sighed, though she hardly dared let the relief sound in her voice.

Suddenly bold, she darted this way and that in the tunnels, snouting out one tunnel after another, running from burrow to burrow. There was only a faint whiff of weasel at the end of one, but she sealed it off all the same.

She didn't yet dare to eat down there, so she found
some worms and took them out into a temporary burrow
on the surface nearby. Then she returned and completed
her exploration, eventually finding the central burrow,
the one where Bracken had crouched miserably after
Hulver's departure for the June elder meeting and which,
to her delight, was as deserted as everywhere else. In
fact, although the place needed a little dust cleared away
at one or two tunnel junctions and the nesting material
was old, the whole place seemed to her tired eyes as
bright as a primrose, and she sensed a peaceful air about
it, which she could not know was one of the legacies
left behind by old Hulver.

Rue was overjoyed. Her whole appearance changed
from the hunched-up, aged mole she was becoming to one
full of the joy of a place of her own and something to
care for. Indeed, she began to sing a song the like of which
these tunnels, and most others on the slopes, had not heard
in generations—the song a youngster mole traditionally
sings when, after the summer is over and the autumn is
setting in, she has found a place of her own and can relax into it for the winter:

> Rue's found a cleansome home,
> Rue's got a place.
> Let sun and moon and stars go roam,
> Rue's got a place.

Then, with her tail held higher than it had been for
molemonths, she busied herself with replacing the nesting
material, shoring up one or two entrances, and, most important of all, finding where the best spots for food were.

Three moleweeks later, when September was well
started and the leaves on the beech trees on the surface
were beginning to dry and mellow with the onset of autumn, Bracken solved the problem of which tunnel led
down to Hulver's system. He had had difficulties, because the tunnels seemed to have been made deliberately
complex here, but slowly, and by occasional recourse to
the surface, he made his way in the right direction until
the whole pattern fell into place and he found the tunnel
that led resolutely down the slopes to the point where

Hulver's system started—or stopped, depending on a mole's point of view.

He had now developed, almost to a science, his system of sound exploration to establish what lay ahead, and seeing that the tunnel was in softer soil more typical of the lower slopes, he called ahead with a deep roaring sound that traveled well and got a good response in this kind of soil.

The response it gave was the one he hoped for—a clean echo back, though far in the distance. It meant that the tunnel ran down to a dead end, the end being the seal he had seen from the other side in Hulver's tunnel. He ran on down, occasionally making an uncharacteristic whooping sound from the sheer pleasure of having finally found his way right round the Ancient System and established, he was almost certain, the site of its link with the present Duncton system. This was an important moment for Bracken, not so much because he wanted to go into the present system, but rather because it satisfied the desire he had had since puphood to get a grasp of how the Ancient System related geographically with everything else. "Where *is* the Ancient System— where does it start and where does it go?" he had once asked Burrhead. Now he would know.

He ran on down the tunnel almost as excited as when he had reached the Stone for the first time. Soon he heard the echo of his pawsteps coming back, *pitter pat pat patter, pitter pat pat patter,* drumming back to him in an escalating pattern of soft sound as the end of the tunnel got nearer and nearer and then finally came in sight straight ahead of him. As he reached it, he let out a shout of pleasure, for surely the tunnel was the right size, in the right direction . . . it was just a matter of finding a way through to the other side without leaving any clues for any Duncton mole who might, at some future time, come along.

The sound of his shout echoed back past him and on up the tunnel down which he had just run, where it was lost in the darkness of ever-shifting air currents. The tunnel here was dusty and he saw at once that the seal was as it had appeared on the other side—hard-packed soil. He was at the end! Again he let out a laugh or shout of pleasure, crouching down on the dusty floor of the tunnel with contented relief.

And Rue heard it. She *thought* she had heard sounds before, distant sounds like a mole running and shouting, sounds from *outside* her tunnels. She had run about seeking their source, determined to fight to the end for the tunnels she had found with such difficulty and which nothing would make her give up. Perhaps, three mole-weeks before, when she had first come here, she would not have been so determined. But now she was strong again and though the tunnels were not a patch on the system Mandrake had turned her out of—at least from a food point of view—they were hers. She had busied herself to make them comfortable for the approach of autumn and they smelled sweet from the nesting material she had brought in and rustled with the sound of beech leaves. Her cache of worms was well stocked and she had cleaned everywhere. It was hers, and nothing would force her out.

The sounds did not come from up on the surface into whose night air she snouted and listened fruitlessly. Down below again she listened and distinctly heard the sound of Bracken's approaching pawsteps, soft but persistent in her tunnels. She darted about, eliminating one tunnel after another as their source, until she took the old half-finished tunnel that lay past her burrow and led up toward the higher slopes, and the sound seemed to come from there. She went up it very, very hesitantly, because being dead-end, any creature there would have to fight, and a fight is best avoided if it can be.

The sound came stronger . . . *pitter pat pat patter pitter pat pat patter* . . . a running mole. *Surely* a running mole! Rue, trembling with apprehension, approached the tunnel end and looked up at the blank wall which, on this side, had been covered over with a thin layer of dried mud.

The sounds were coming from beyond her tunnels. Higher up the slope. From the direction of the Ancient System. Rue's eyes widened, and she waited, not knowing what to do or how to move. How can a mole fight an enemy who isn't there?

Beyond the wall she heard the pawsteps stop. She heard a triumphant shout or laugh—she couldn't tell which—and the settling of a body on the ground. She not only heard that, she felt its vibration as well. Her heart in her mouth, her mouth slightly open, she waited. Behind her her bright tunnels, her sweet place, seemed to darken and blur as she wondered if perhaps she should run after all.

Rue waited in the silence that now settled on the tunnels as, beyond the seal, Bracken got his breath back. She knew that the slightest clumsy movement on her part would send a vibration, and possibly even a sound, through to whatever creature it was beyond.

Bracken looked about him with pleasure, and then up at the blunt end to the tunnel formed by the seal. It looked like a mass of consolidated and close-packed soil and was not likely to give him much difficulty now that he had regained so much of his physical health and strength. He did not intend to break the seal right down, because he wanted no mole to know what lay on this side of it. But he wanted to make a hole big enough to peer through and establish without any doubt that this was the link. So he would make one, burrow his way up onto the surface, re-enter Hulver's tunnels and make his way up to the seal to confirm its position in the tunnels.

He got up, turned to the blank face of the seal, and in an exultant gesture, spread his talons wide, reached as high as he could, and brought them crashing down on the seal, ripping them vertically down its length. The noise that followed was indescribably terrible. For, unknown to Bracken, or to Rue who crouched so near on the other side, the seal was, in fact, massive flint covered over only thinly with soil and debris. Bracken's talons cut through the veneer of long-dried soil with ease, and scraped down the flint beneath with such a screeching scratch that the sound was like a million blackthorns flying in the air.

The soil fell away before him to reveal the great flint underneath and Bracken had to cover his ears with his paws to block out the terrible sound he had made.

While, on the other side, unknown to Bracken, Rue heard the terrible sound, and it was like an owl killing its prey. In that moment she forgot all her resolutions to stay and defend her territory. All she knew was that there was a mole beyond the Stone who could make owls appear and screech at their victims. She turned away in fear and ran away out of her new home, desperately making for the communal tunnel down to Barrow Vale, where, if she survived that far, she could tell her tale of a dreadful mole from the Ancient System and the owl that seemed to screech at his command.

She could not know what effect the sound of her fleeing would have on Bracken. His talons smarting from their confrontation with the impregnable flint, its sound dying away, he heard a mole beyond the stone fleeing away.

Nothing could have told him more clearly than this flint that it was here that the Ancient System ended, or started, depending on which side you came from. Nothing could have driven home to him more forcibly than the sound of yet another mole running from him, to whom he meant no harm, that he was forever dispossessed of the Duncton system in which he had grown up. It was no longer his system. He was not of it. He was of the Ancient System now, and alone in it. Its tunnels, its wormless depths, its mysterious secrets, its aching isolation and loneliness, were his, and his territory.

His mood changed from exultation to a grim despair.

He looked at the great flint and knew it would be useless to try to dig a way round it. Still, at least he could confirm that the seal was where he thought it was in Hulver's old tunnels, and perhaps stay in them for a few moledays, or until whatever mole it was that had run off came back. When he did, Bracken would retire gracefully. For the time being, however, he simply could not face going back to the confines of the Ancient System—which, though it was now his place, was too lonely for him to bear quite yet.

13

WITH Rue's sudden appearance in Barrow Vale one morning, frightened, disheveled and with a genuine tale of horror to tell, the rumor of a giant mole in the Ancient System turned into solid fact. She happened to arrive at a time when both Mandrake and Rune were away in the system, so that before news reached them, she had told her story to everymole who wanted to listen to it—which *was* every mole.

But the story did not only bring Mandrake and Rune hot-pawing it back to Barrow Vale; it also brought Rebecca, who, since her meeting with Rose, had grown much more independent. Perhaps having her own tunnels had something to do with it as well, for she seemed to throw off any sense of the constraints that Mandrake's bullying and rules of conduct had put on her and started living with a joy and spirit that Duncton females rarely showed. If there was laughter in the system, hers were the tunnels it seemed to come from; if there were tears, hers was the place where a mole might find comfort; if there were moles having a good feast, hers was the place where they had it.

In no sense was Rebecca willfully disobedient to Mandrake, about whom, and to the amazement of all moles who knew her, she never had a hard or harsh thing to say. "I love him," she would declare, as if such a love could forgive the many cruelties and unkindnesses all the system knew he had imposed on her. Which, indeed, it could. The fact was that Rebecca did not seem the least affected by Mandrake's attitude to her. But however great her love for him, her love for life and for living was greater. It was as if she was driven by a force for joy and love quite out of her control, and anymole who came into contact with her fell under its spell and got carried along by it. She seemed not only to affect other moles, but other creatures and plants as well, as other moles like Mekkins, who took to visiting her, soon noticed. The trees, the plants, the creatures of the wood—all seemed brighter and happier around Rebecca's burrows. Hers was the place where the nightingale sang; hers was the place where the sun seemed to shine; nowhere else did wood violets look quite so lovely in the sun.

And Rebecca herself was the picture of health and happiness. Her coat was full and glossy, catching even the most delicate of summer dawn lights in its sheen, and beautifully warm and dark when the sun shone full upon it. She had grown since the spring and was big for a female, equal in size to some of the smaller males, and though not so graceful as her mother, Sarah, she was a thousand times more feminine.

She would touch and rough-play, and cry "Look!," pointing to some rambling eglantine or scurrying beetle whose beauty and life caught her eye, which she always seemed to want to share with another mole. But for many, her enthusiasms were sometimes almost embarrassing in their exuberance, for it doesn't do for an adult to dance and play too much, does it?

So that sometimes, when Rebecca was quite alone and lying still in the evening or watching the light change in the early morning, there was a subtle sadness about her of which she herself was barely aware, and if she had been, she could not have known its cause. Sometimes in her dreams she wished that she might meet a mole who would play and dance with her and make her laugh and sing with the same abandon to life that she gave to others.

There were only two moles who understood this unseen sadness in her life. One was Sarah, who was now more a friend than a mother and who, though more sedate than Rebecca, would sometimes giggle like a pup and they would lose themselves in each other's fun. The other was Mekkins who, since that day in July when he had conceived such a powerful affection for her, had often stopped by near her burrow and spent some summer time there. Of all the males she knew, he was the one with the greatest force for life, the only one whose wit was sharp enough and whose humor was wide enough, and whose experience was sufficiently great, for Rebecca to feel in his presence an expansion of herself that she did not feel with the others. She loved his marshend language and irreverence.

Curiously, it was these two, who loved and cared for Rebecca most of all, who were the least concerned by the change that started to come over her in the end of August. She began to become restless and stayed for moledays down in her burrow, seeing no joy in the fading summer sun, no fun in the flocking of starlings and pigeons that were the early heralds of autumn. For the first time since she had left her home burrow she became angry with other moles, snarling at them if they came too near or presumed (as they had often done before) on her good humor and generosity. Sometimes, when she heard another mole coming, she would hide herself and not answer its calls.

But Sarah and Mekkins understood in their different ways. The fact was that Rebecca was beginning to need a mate. Or rather a mating and a litter, since Duncton moles rarely pair for more than a few moledays.

When Mandrake had forbidden her to go near a male in the spring, she had a craving for a mate and a need to celebrate the busy life she saw about her with the feel of a litter inside and the joy of pups in her tunnels. There had been times in early June when the sound of other females' growing pups had left her feeling bereft and lost. But these feelings had faded as the summer advanced until, at the start of September, this much stronger and more specific desire for a mate came to her.

Then sometimes she would remember, with a dark excitement, the time Rune had followed her down into the tunnels, chasing after her and she had been scared, knowing what he wanted. She hated him and yet (and this she could not understand) again and again the secret memory of the mating ritual he had started and Mandrake had stopped short, coupled with the dark, assured malevolence of Rune, came back to her.

It was Mekkins who, in the middle of September, brought her the sensational news that the Stone Mole, as the eastsiders had first called him, had been sighted by a female called Rue who, at this very moment, was telling everymole in Barrow about it.

"Course it's a load of rubbish. I mean, it's got to be, hasn't it? You've only got to look at this mole, and I've seen her, to see she's as nervous as a pup and would think a dormouse was a monster. They say that she's been through a hard time . . ." Mekkins knew perfectly well that it was Rue whom Mandrake had turned out of these very tunnels to make way for Rebecca, but knowing Rebecca as he did, he realized that if she knew, she would be the first to go impetuously rushing off to offer Rue back her tunnels. Rebecca would learn in time that there're some things a mole can't do much about.

Mekkins went on: "Anyway, it's had the inevitable effect of making the Stone Mole rumor the number-one talking point all over the bloody system." He laughed, and Rebecca shared his laugh.

Rebecca believed that the Stone Mole was Bracken, with a conviction born of the faith put into her by Hulver just before the June elder meeting; as for Mekkins, he almost believed it too, and the very least that Rebecca's certainty did for him was to remove him from taking part in the gossip about the Stone Mole and make him see most of it for the nonsense it truly was. This objectivity about something everymole else got worked up about was perhaps characteristic of Mekkins anyway, for he had maintained his unique position as a buffer between the marshenders and the main system only by the extreme independence of his spirit and actions. He was perhaps the only mole in the system uncorrupted by any fear of Mandrake.

It had been the eastsiders who had first labeled whatever it was up in the Ancient System the Stone Mole. Mekkins told Rebecca that story and thrilled to see the pleasure it gave her to have her belief that Bracken was still alive confirmed. He was puzzled that she should be so concerned about a mole she had never met, but with Rebecca, well, she was concerned about so many things so enthusiastically that one more shouldn't be a surprise. And she had explained the impact Hulver's conversation had had on her.

After that, he brought her the "news" of the Stone Mole as it came along, and there was plenty of it. Nothing highlighted the system's decline in morale under Mandrake's thrall so well as everymole's willingness to believe that anything out of the ordinary that happened in the system was the Stone Mole's doing. It was as if the whole system were looking for a savior, if only a fictional one, to rid them of Mandrake and his henchmoles. If a windbroken branch was found at the foot of a tree, it had been done by the Stone Mole; if a badger left his trail in moist soil down near the marsh, the Stone Mole had passed that way; if weasels had a fight and left a mess on the ground, why, of course, the Stone Mole did it!

Mekkins and Rebecca laughed together at these stories, for even Rebecca, eager as she was to have her hopes confirmed, could not believe them all when a mole as skeptical as Mekkins was her mentor.

But even Mekkins was surprised at something that happened just a few moledays before the arrival of Rue and provided almost the perfect preface of violence to it. One night, over on the westside adjacent to the pastures, there were screechings and unearthly growlings as two creatures locked together in combat late at night. The woodland silence was shattered by it, and many moles trembled to hear the fatal sounds carrying down into their burrows.

Everything finally fell silent as dawn broke, and some brave westsider, whose burrows lay nearby, crept out to find, hanging limp from the pasture fence in the cold, dull light of very early morning, a massive owl, savaged to death. One wing was entangled in the barbed wire of the fence, the body tilting from it down onto the ground, its talons hooked and dead. One eye was staring open, its yellow glare overtaken by a lifeless, opaque haze; the stomach and neck were bloody with gore, while the only movement was in the soft downy feathers of its inner legs when the morning breeze stirred them where they were not stiff with dried blood.

Burrhead was summoned, and he immediately sent henchmoles to get Mandrake and Rune, for a dead owl is a rare sight for a mole and something the elders should see. And the word quickly got about that the Stone Mole had killed an owl!

The only mole not visibly shaken by the sight was Mandrake himself—even Rune seemed put out by it, looking at the body sideways and unwilling to get too close to it. Mandrake doubted whether the owl had been killed by mole at all—the descriptions of the unearthly growling that had been heard, presumably sounds made by the mole's successful adversary, sounded very like a wild farm cat to him. But then, he thought, looking contemptuously around at the miserable Duncton moles gathered there, he was forgetting that this lot had never seen a farm, let alone a farm cat. They had never even been out of their own system.

But he didn't say anything—he had his own strategy for dealing with the Stone Mole rumor and it hinged on fostering the system's fear and awe of the Stone Mole until he felt the time was right to make an excursion to the Ancient System and kill it. Or rather, find some scapegoat mole and kill him in privacy in such a way as to impress on these miserable moles that only one mole was in charge in Duncton Wood and that was himself. Mandrake was beginning to get heartily sick of the Stone Mole rumor and was looking forward to putting into effect his simple plan to scotch it at one fell blow.

Meanwhile, his sense of bloody drama had not left him. As the rest of the moles hemmed and hawed at the sight of the owl, and Rune looked at it in his sneaking way, Mandrake went up to it and plunged his right paw, talons outstretched, into the owl's torn breast and smeared the blood over his face fur. Then, turning on the moles, he looked at each of them in turn and laughed. They looked shocked and frightened at his actions, as if believing that in some way he would now be able to inflict the owl curse on them. Then he licked his talons with relish and, with a mighty blow, knocked the owl's wing in such a way that the body fell onto the ground with a thump.

"Any mole here like a taste of owl as well?" he taunted them. "Good for the health, it is," he mocked.

The moles slunk away, excitement over, aware once again of Mandrake's brutish power. And even Rune, who had strategies within strategies of his own for dealing with the Stone Mole and Mandrake together, could not help wondering, as he looked at Mandrake exulting in the owl's gore, whether this bestial mole might not kill them all before he had a chance to take power for himself.

News of this incident was soon all over the system, and Mekkins regretted that he had not been near enough to witness it. So the Stone Mole was an owl-killer as well now! By the time he got near where the owl had died, it had long since been taken by some predator and only feathers and dried blood on the grass remained. The story impressed him, and it impressed Rebecca, too, elevating the already overimaginative idea of Bracken she had in her into almost heroic status.

Against this background, the sudden arrival of Rue on the scene caused a sensation, and when Mekkins told Rebecca of it, she determined to get to Barrow Vale before Mandrake and Rune did and talk for herself to the mole who claimed to have gotten to within a few molefeet of the Stone Mole. The idea of the journey appealed to her newfound restlessness for mating and gave her something concrete to do. She would be careful, she promised Mekkins, who was against her going, but she *would* go.

Rebecca reached Barrow Vale in safety, but she never got to Rue in time. For just as she entered among the wider Barrow Vale tunnels, a chilling voice called out to her from the shadows of a side tunnel. "Rebecca!" it said. "Now this is a surprise, it really is. You in Barrow Vale of all moles, come to gossip away with the best of them? Well, well."

Rune came out of the dark and stood boldly in front of her, moving slowly toward her as he spoke each word and forcing her back toward the side tunnel. Rune always seemed to be where he could inflict most evil, and he began to weave his black spell on Rebecca now. The moment he saw her so fortuitously he could scent she was ready for mating. Now, ever bold, ever opportunistic, he began resolutely to impose his sensual maleness on her. Rebecca hated him, but her body did not. She could have run, she could have raised her talons, she could have done a thousand things to get away. But instead, her snout fell low and her body tensed as her eyes were held by his bold gaze and she retreated before him.

"Well, now, it must be a long time since we met, yes . . . back in the spring, wasn't it, when you were hardly more than a pup . . . but one who's grown into an adult, a female, ripe with life, from what I've heard . . ."

She hated his words, she hated his stare that outstared hers, she hated the secret knowledge he seemed to have that he was going to take her then and there whatever she wanted, his slinky body bold and sure within hers, she hated him . . . and yet her breathing grew shallow with the excitement of it, and her eyes grew dim with the darkness of his bigger body coming closer and closer to her. Perhaps after all this was all mating was: just sensual darkness. She could wonder only vaguely where the light in the mating excitement was, where the joy she had sensed would be found.

Rune stopped talking and moved up to her, sniffing at her from snout to tail and then back to snout again. The sound of other moles in the main Barrow Vale tunnels nearby seemed to recede and grow distant, and though she wanted to move and run, her body also wanted to drown in his darkness as Rebecca relaxed before his power to do what no other moles she had met dared do, which was to master her. She did not want to feel the moment of his touch but craved his talons in her fur and shuddered and gasped when the first touch came, confident and assured, upon her. She stood tense and bound by instinctive desire, her haunches shivering very slightly and her mating scent growing moister and stronger as he circled about closer and closer with his sensual strength binding her.

She was ready for him, almost thrusting her haunches at him, and he could take her just when he wanted, just as he wanted . . .

"Rune! Rune, sir!" The henchmole's voice carried down the tunnel toward him and then the sound of the henchmole running down to them. "Rune, sir! Mandrake wants you."

The henchmole stopped some way from Rune before he could see what female he was with, for the salty, mating scent hung in the air and carried with it the threat that Rune might attack to kill for being disturbed. In the spring a mole was more careful, but September matings were a rarer thing. The henchmole backed slowly away, repeating "It's Mandrake, sir, he's got a mole he wants you to see and listen to. He's got Rue from the slopes."

Rune turned to look at him, the voice growing louder in his ears as he pulled himself back from the encirclement of Rebecca to the demands of Mandrake. He heard Rebecca's breathing change and saw her tense and move away very slightly, and he saw that his moment had gone, for the time being. I'll have you yet, he promised himself, looking at her beautiful coat and now only half-open haunches. I'll take you any way I want. With that, and without a word to her, he left, following the henchmole to go to Mandrake and this tiresome mole from the slopes.

For a long time after he had gone, Rebecca stayed where he had left her, feeling enshadowed and grimy. The talon touch that had excited her so much moments before now hung heavy on her. She could smell his scent in the air where he had left it, and it seemed dry and cold, making her shiver with disgust.

She had no more desire to stay in Barrow Vale, even though she had only just arrived. If Mandrake and Rune had got hold of Rue, she would have little chance of talking to her without Mandrake finding out she was there and causing trouble. And she was so tired of that from him. She wondered why something so simple as mating seemed to be so complicated.

Eventually, it was the possibility that Rune might come back and find her there, or that he would tell Mandrake that she was in Barrow Vale, that made Rebecca leave. But she had no desire to return to her tunnels. Instead, she circled her way through Barrow Vale in the direction opposite that in which Rune had gone with the henchmole, keeping to the shadows and avoiding conversation with other moles until she found herself leaving by an entrance that led toward the westside.

Well! She had heard so much about it and never dared to go there. Now was her chance! She stayed on the surface for only a short time, found what smelled like a communal tunnel, and shook the shadows of Rune and Barrow Vale from her fur as she headed off on the longest journey she had begun since going down to the Marsh End and meeting Rose the Healer.

If the thought had crossed Rue's mind, as she rushed in a panic down to Barrow Vale, that she would eventually be summoned into the elder burrow to tell her story to Mandrake, she might have thought twice about heading down there in the first place. She was terrified of him and had never forgotten his threat to kill her if she ever tried to return to her tunnels again.

But on her third day in Barrow Vale, a henchmole ambled up to her, pushed away the moles who were gathered around her, and said, "Yer ter jump to it and come wiv me dahn to the Elder Burrer: Mandrake wants to talk to yer." She stared at him in terror and could not move a muscle. "Come on then, look sharp. And for Stone's sake clean yerself up a bit, because although Mandrake won't notice, Rune's goin' to be there and 'e will."

The henchmole, a roly-poly bully of a southern westsider, almost had to drag her along to get her there, and when finally he shoved her into the presence of Mandrake and Rune, cuffing and cursing as he did, she felt certain she was going to be killed on the spot. Her paws trembled and she did not dare at first look up at the looming presence above her. When she finally did, it seemed that Mandrake's eyes were black holes deep in his face.

"So this is the female who claims to have heard mole noises coming from the Ancient System," said Rune to Mandrake in a voice so accusatory that it made it sound as if Rue had set out to tell lies and deliberately deceive Mandrake himself.

Mandrake looked full on her and she quailed before his gaze, everything suddenly cast for her into slow motion as he shifted his massive weight from one side to the other and scratched the side of his face with the biggest talon she had ever seen.

"Mmm . . .," he growled. "What's your name, girl?"

"R-Rue," she faltered.

"Rue." He said the name as if it were the name of a mole long lost in the pit of despair. "Rue. Mmm . . . you used to live over by . . ." He didn't finish the sentence, and to fill the gap she nodded her head eagerly, feeling an inclination to say anything to save herself from the death that she felt certain was about to come her way. Something like "It really doesn't matter that you forced me out of my tunnels, I don't mind, I'm only an insignificant little mole and you can do what you like to me only please don't . . ." As it was, she didn't need to say anything, since she looked as abject and pathetic as she felt.

"I have heard of your story and I'm not wasting time hearing it again here," said Mandrake. "You will take us to your tunnels and show us where you heard what you claim to have heard."

"Yes, sir," whispered Rue.

Rune suddenly poked his snout forward until it was only inches from hers, and she felt the power of his contempt on her.

"*Did* you hear noises, or did you make it up to draw attention to your miserable little self?" he asked.

Rue started to whimper at this. She was so frightened and cowered back, stuttering out that "n-n-no mole could tell a lie in the Elder Burrow." The thought had not occurred to Rune, who would tell a lie in front of the Stone itself if need be, but what did occur to them was that Rue was too grubby and unintelligent to make up such a bold lie.

So it was that Barrow Vale was treated to the rare sight of a quaking Rue leading the mighty Mandrake and Rune, along with the attendant henchmole, through their tunnels and on to the communal one leading toward the slopes.

Rue, however, was a poor leader. She felt nervous and sick at the strain of it all and at one point actually collapsed, unable to go on. "Get her food," snapped Rune impatiently to the henchmole, who did so with ill grace.

"Last bloody time I find worms for a female, I can tell you that," he muttered angrily as he hurled three worms down before her in the tunnel where she lay. Rune noted this remark down in his memory. He didn't trust moles who lost their tempers over something as trivial as that, or even lost their tempers at all.

"Well now, is her ladyship ready to move her ass forward then?" asked the henchmole sarcastically when she had eaten the food. She nodded and got up, feeling very shaky and nervous, for to add to her fear of Mandrake and Rune, there was her apprehension about what might be waiting for them in her tunnel.

Eventually she reached the end of the communal tunnel, led them out onto the surface, and from there pressed on the last few hundred moleyards to her tunnels.

"Well!" said Rune when they got there, with sarcasm lurking behind the good-humored tone in his voice. "This is where it all happened, is it?"

Rue nodded her head miserably. She felt she was going to be attacked at any moment by one of them, or perhaps all of them.

"Why didn't you say that this was Hulver's old system right from the start?" Rune spoke the words silkily, but to Rue they sounded as threatening as a thousand moles. And she didn't understand what he meant at all.

Her terror, her general miserableness, now gave way to tears and she gulped her next words out: "I don't know what you mean. I only did what you said. This is where I heard it and there is a mole up there on the higher slopes and I don't know if his name is Hulver or anything. I didn't even know moles lived in the Ancient System and I don't know what you want me to say or do."

"Be quiet!" Mandrake brought her flood of tearful words to a short, sharp stop as he raised his talons by a tunnel entrance and snouted inside. "There is a mole here, or has been recently," he said tersely. "You two wait here and let no mole out, no mole. I will see what

we may find, for there is a scent here like none I have
found before in the Ancient System—dry and dusty, old
in its impression but fresh in its strength." With that, Mandrake boldly went into the tunnels, while Rune covered
those entrances that lay nearby and the henchmole went
off to cover more.

Mandrake was right—Bracken had been in the tunnels, having gone there for comfort after Rue had fled
four moledays before. But he was getting wiser and, having worked out that if any mole returned it would almost
certainly do so from the direction of the communal tunnel, he had kept himself as far over the other side of the
tunnels as possible, with a line of retreat ready. On hearing the arrival of several moles, and in particular the
whimpering of a female, he quietly crept out of the tunnels by a little entrance higher up the slopes, which he
blocked behind him, and made his way down into the
tunnel on the far side of the stone seal. He was very cautious, indeed, and blocked up each tunnel as he went.

Mandrake explored the tunnels in a no-nonsense fash-
ion, quite ready to do battle with whatever creature he
might find there. The scent puzzled him, for it was
strange and strong, but he could not trace its source. He
called the others down, and Rue, still trembling, led them
past the main burrow up to the stone seal. She told them
what she had heard, pointing a talon at the blank wall of
the seal on the far side of which, unknown to any of
them, Bracken crouched listening.

Mandrake sent Rue and the henchmole back to her
burrow while he and Rune discussed the situation.

"Mmm . . . It's a seal, that's for sure," mumbled Mandrake, "which means there must be a tunnel beyond it."

"A tunnel leading into the Ancient System?" Rune
asked it as a question, for he liked Mandrake to feel he
had the initiative all the time, but it was more an obvious
statement of fact. Mandrake nodded.

"No wonder Hulver chose to live here, where he
could be so close to his beloved dead tunnels of the past,"
said Rune.

Mandrake looked up at the seal and finally decided
what he must do. A bold gesture was needed. He still
doubted very much that there was anymole in the Ancient
System—indeed, if there had been, whatever it was
would surely have destroyed the seal and entered these
tunnels. The fact that something had suggested to Mandrake that it was, as he always suspected, just an ordinary

mole—whom, when the time came, he would kill. If he
was in the forgotten tunnels beyond, then well and good,
let him know that Mandrake was here. He raised his
massive talons to the seal, not knowing that beneath its
cover of packed soil it was massive flint, and brought
them down upon it, just as Bracken had done.

But this time the result was startlingly different. Again
there was the terrifying screeching sound that Rue had
told them about, but from behind the mass of dust
and debris something far more frightening appeared. As
the covering peeled away under Mandrake's blow and
the dust settled, there, staring at them all, and bigger
even than Mandrake, was an image of an owl just like
the one Bracken had already found in the Chamber of
Dark Sound. Its eyes, its beak, its talons—each was
picked out through the calcite covering of the flint so
that they shone black with the hard, glossy shine of
the raw stone underneath, while the screech of talon on
flint sounded harshly about them, as it had sounded
about Rue before, seeming to come from the owl face
itself.

Their reactions to this sudden apparition were all different. Rue simply covered her ears with her paws,
looked at the image forming in front of her and fled to
her burrow. The henchmole staggered back from the
sound and sight, his mouth open, trying to say something in his fear and surprise, but failing.

At first sight of the owl face, Mandrake reared up
snarling before it, his talons poised on a level with the
owl's eyes, and his mouth open and ready for any kind
of fighting. He was feeling that at last, in this system to
which life had so miserably driven him, he had an adversary worth facing. And in that moment of poised action, he crossed over a boundary beyond which a mole
never again knows physical fear.

Crouched behind him, Rune's response was altogether
different. It was an inward reaction, for outwardly he
showed little or no response—a momentary look of surprise, an instinctive clawing of talons, but no more than
that. But as Rune looked into the sudden black eyes
of the owl face that materialized before him, he saw
the power for evil which he had pursued for so long.
His pulse quickened, he gazed with excited awe on the
owl face, and he shivered with a frisson of sensuality far
deeper, and for him far more exciting, than any he had

felt with Rebecca. With her he was in charge and playing a game; here, he was surrendering his will to what, for him, was the only reality of life, its dark and arcane side where a mole may learn to agonize the souls of others by wielding the same black power that seemed to lie behind the shining flint eyes of the owl.

For each mole these moments lasted a very long time; for all of them together they lasted for no longer than it takes to draw breath. Then Mandrake's paws dropped as he saw that the owl was no more than an image; the henchmole tried to recover his nonchalant stance, and Rune almost purred with pleasure at the sight before them. Rue's screams could be heard coming up the tunnel from her burrow.

"Shut her up," ordered Mandrake without taking his eyes off the image before him. The henchmole left the burrow.

"Well, well!" said Mandrake robustly. "So at long last the decaying Duncton system has actually sprung a surprise. You know what it is, don't you, Rune?"

"I have an idea," lied Rune. It was the pleasant face of power, as far as he was concerned.

"I have seen such images before," said Mandrake, "in burrows far from here. They were used by ancient moles to create fear in the minds of moles who might feel tempted to see what secrets lie in the tunnels beyond. Very effective on some moles, not much use on a mole like me. See, they don't really protect anything worth protecting. It's all nonsense, isn't it? Just a joke that ought to make a mole laugh."

Meanwhile, Bracken, who was listening to this from his vantage point beyond the flint but could not fully understand what was happening, had heard Mandrake's blow on the stone and seen its effect—for it was so powerful it sent some remnants of the soil cover on his side down onto the tunnel floor and onto his coat as well. He didn't dare shake it off for fear that he might be heard. Then a silence followed the terrible screech of talon on stone: he heard one of the moles scream and pawsteps fading away, he heard what sounded like Mandrake himself snarl with rage, but then nothing more for some moments. Until Mandrake's deep voice gave an inaudible command, and then a little muffled by the stone between, said "You know what this is, don't you, Rune?"

So Rune was there! But what was "this"? He listened on.

The conversation that followed was largely meaningless to Bracken until, at last, Mandrake said that he had seen "owl faces like this" in a system he had lived in for a short time "on my way from Siabod."

So there was an owl face on the far side of the stone! And it was a scaring-off device.

Beyond the stone, Mandrake and Rune finished their discussion. "So, for the time being, we'll leave it as it is," Mandrake was saying. "We will create the impression that we have faced great dangers—an idea which will no doubt be reinforced by that shambling henchmole, who seemed very frightened indeed."

Then he added: "I'm glad you weren't affected by it, Rune—I wouldn't want to think that you are afraid of things like this." He tapped the owl beak with his talons, the sound echoing into the ancient tunnels beyond, way past Bracken.

Rune smiled, pitying Mandrake for taking the owl so lightly. "We know better," he was effectively saying to himself, "we of the dark powers, we of the black beak and talon, we of the impenetrable eye."

Mandrake took his talons from the flint before him with an unaccustomed shiver. The stone was very cold and there was something in the way that Rune was looking at him which had the same blank quality of the owl's eyes. He didn't like Rune. You can't trust a mole like him. Mandrake turned his back on the owl and left down the tunnel toward Rue's burrow. His gait was suddenly heavy and ponderous and he felt tired. Tired and old. It was true that in his confrontation with the owl image he had, finally, lost all sense of physical fear, though Mandrake lived in too great a haze of anger and confusion to know the fact. But when a mole loses such fear, the freedom he finds may serve only to make him prey to the darker, more perilous fears that lurk beyond all moles' bodies and inhabit their minds.

Rune watched him go down the tunnel, perceiving the new fatigue in his movements as only a mole of his diabolic insight possibly could. Rune looked back to the black eyes of the owl, then forward again at Mandrake, and knew that the hour when he would take power in Duncton was getting nearer.

Lacking any instruction, Rue followed the three big moles up out of the tunnels and onto the surface, where she crouched, blinking in the light, wondering what was going to happen to her.

"Shall I have her killed?" asked Rune, looking at Mandrake and aware that the henchmole was itching to do it. Rue cowered pathetically back, staring at the big henchmole who she knew hated her. Too cowed even to raise her talons in self-defense. She knew she was going to die.

Mandrake looked round at her. It would be wrong, quite wrong to say that the light of pity shone in his heart. Pity was a word that Mandrake never knew. It was sheer tiredness with the effort of violence. Time was when he would have nodded his head, and Rune would have raised his talon as a signal, and the henchmole would have plunged his talons as a pleasant job. Not now.

"What's the point?" said Mandrake, looking blankly at Rue. Rune and the henchmole looked at Rue with complete contempt and then all three of them turned away from her as if she did not exist anymore. And the sense that she was so worthless that she wasn't worth killing was so great in Rue that she just crouched there stunned, unable even to relax in the knowledge that at last they had gone and she was safe. Then she started to cry, for she could not follow them back to Barrow Vale and she could not return into the tunnels that had started to be her home. She seemed to have nowhere to go. In her misery she wanted to do nothing but die, to forget the system into which she regretted ever having been born.

And there, a few molehours later, exposed in the open and vulnerable to owl attack, Bracken found her. He had heard her first, for after the moles had gone from the tunnels, he crept over there himself and, having established there was no mole there, went up onto the surface where he heard the shaky breathing and occasional sobs and he quietly went out to see who it might be.

He watched her for a long time, puzzled that she should stay crouched out in the open as dangerous dusk fell and trying to decide for one last time whether he should risk making contact with another mole.

Finally he came forward to her with enough noise for her to know that he was there. She looked at him but did not run away as he expected. Instead, her snout lowered in a gesture of total defeat and she asked him quietly, "Have you come to kill me?"

Such a thought was so far from his mind—indeed, it was so far from his experience—that it quite took his breath away. He saw that she was small and bedraggled and seemed very frightened, while he (and he looked at the now much glossier fur above his paws and felt the much more powerful muscles that had developed since he had started to regain his strength) was fit and well and must seem confident. Why, he was an adult, and a male, and strong!

Bracken laughed and said that the only killing he knew of was when moles tried to do it to him. She sniffled and wiped her face with her paw, comforted by his laugh but troubled by the curious wildness about his appearance and the strength that seemed to come from him, even though he wasn't as big as that Rune and the henchmole. As for that Mandrake, well . . . no mole was as big as him!

"What mole are you, and where are you from?" Bracken asked.

"My name is Rue from beyond Barrow Vale," she said, "but my tunnels were taken away by . . . they were taken from me. I lived here until the Stone Mole came. What mole are you?"

"Bracken, from the westside." The answer was, in his own mind at least, untrue, for he was really of the Ancient System now. But ever cautious, Bracken had worked out that if he should meet another mole, he would first find out where they were from and then say he was from anywhere else but the Ancient System.

"I knew Hulver," he added, by way of explaining why he was there. There was a pause while they considered what to say next. Then each asked a question simultaneously.

"Who's Hulver?" asked Rue. "Who's the Stone Mole?" wondered Bracken. They laughed, their mutual interruption breaking the awkwardness between them. They each sensed that the other meant no harm.

"It's a bit unsafe staying here," said Bracken. "It would be safer in the tunnel."

"Oh, I can't go in there," said Rue, horrified. "The owl's there."

"Yes, I know," said Bracken to her surprise. "That's what I want to see."

After a lot of persuasion, he managed to get Rue back into the safety of the tunnels, telling her that the owl would not attack her and, should Mandrake and Rune return, he knew a quick way out to safety. But it was more the simple fact that he so obviously intended not to harm her, and even seemed to have her safety at heart, that finally got her back to the burrow at the heart of Hulver's system. He even went so far as to get her some worms, and without any difficulty either, since he seemed to know the tunnels quite well. Once fed, they snuggled down on either side of the burrow, where they answered each other's questions about Hulver and the Stone Mole. Bracken told Rue all about Hulver and Rue explained what she knew, and had heard, about the Stone Mole. He realized long before she got to her own experience in these very same tunnels that he, himself, was the Stone Mole.

"Show me where it happened," he asked her.

"Oh, I couldn't," whispered Rue, who had worked herself up to a terror just telling the story.

"It won't hurt you," said Bracken. "It's only an image."

"How do you know?" asked Rue.

A mole like Rune would not have answered this question, for he would have known that a mole's power often lies in keeping others ignorant, and that it was in Bracken's interest that no mole knew who he truly was. But Bracken was not aware that he had an interest, being more concerned to reassure Rue, who was the first mole who had been friendly toward him since Hulver himself.

However, there is a difference between naïveté and ingenuousness, and Bracken's fault, if fault it was, was that he was naïve. He told her no more than that he had been into the tunnel behind the great flint and possibly what she had heard had been his noise and actions on the other side—as he had heard Mandrake's earlier that day. As for the sights he had seen in the Ancient System, and the sounds he had heard, there was something about them that warned him to keep them secret. Some things, especially when a mole does not understand them, are best honored by being kept secret in the heart rather than scattered to the winds as words.

Rue would only go so far as the last curve in the tunnel

leading to the great flint seal, peering on from there nervously as Bracken went on to the end, raising his voice over his shoulder to keep her reassured.

He told her "It is just an image, just a carving—something the ancient moles used to do to frighten other moles away." He raised his talons to the flint on a level with the curve of the beak and scratched it very slightly to show how the sound was made, and its screech whispered round the tunnel like a distant echo of the terrifying sounds he had heard before. She started to cover her ears again, and Bracken stopped. He looked at the owl face, surprised to find that it held no fear for him as the other one had. Looking at it, he felt a different mole from the one who had looked at the others, and he hoped that at last he had found the strength to delve back into the tunnels and make his way to the Chamber of Dark Sound, and beyond.

"Is there a giant mole in there?" asked Rue.

"There aren't any moles in there at all, not a single one."

"But the Stone Mole lives there!" Rumors die hard, even when the subject of them is there to put the record straight.

It was late and both of them needed sleep. Bracken thought it wiser to abandon the main burrow, since Mandrake and Rune might come back at any time, and so they occupied instead tunnels to the west of Hulver's system, where a few abandoned tunnels remained from some system of the past.

Even then, Rue might have been reluctant to stay there had not Bracken said that he would stay on a few moledays to help her seal up the connection between these tunnels and the others, so that Rue would have the makings of a system of her own. It was no hardship to him and, indeed, sometime before dawn, he awoke briefly to hear Rue's deep, peaceful breathing in a burrow nearby the tunnel where he slept, and was grateful to have company again, even if only temporarily.

Rue was a survivor, and recovered fast from her ordeal. With Bracken there to help her seal off her new system and to burrow out one or two new tunnels and entrances, it very soon took shape. Better than that, it gave Bracken an opportunity to put into practice one or two of the subtleties of shape and sound he had observed in the Ancient System as he created a couple of bigger-

than-normal tunnels which Rue looked at in surprise and
soon adopted with pleasure. Somehow they managed to
pick up the sound of the September rustles of beech
leaves from the surface, where hints of the autumn were
just beginning to show, and carry them on into the more
traditional tunnels that were the basis of her new system.

There was change in the air. The distant smell of autumn. And not so distant either when the wind blew,
carrying a few beech leaves down to the wood's floor or
scurrying the more crinkled leaves of the few oaks that
grew on the slopes along between the trees.

After three moledays, the tunnels began to look spick
and span and Rue said "Are these your tunnels?"

It was a strange question, for Bracken had never
thought for one moment that they were. His future lay
with the Ancient System and his time here was a welcome respite from pursuing his explorations of it to
the end. The question was Rue's way of asking him
when he was leaving. She was restless and increasingly
proprietorial about the place and wanted him gone. She
wanted to dwell in her own place, or so it seemed to
Bracken.

He looked wearily in the direction of the higher slopes
and knew that he must be off. He was beginning to like
Rue now that he had seen the nervousness fall off her
to be replaced by the good sense that was her nature.
She made a mole feel comfortable, even if not always
welcome. But that was the way with some females, Burrhead had once told him. Sometimes he was surprised to
find that he even felt aggressive, like an adult male, toward her.

"Are these your tunnels?" The question still waited
between them. Well, of course they weren't. He felt he
wanted to mock-fight with her and pretend they were
and to let their laughter fill the place with sound, as once
or twice his laughter had mingled with Wheatear's when
they were very young pups and when Root wasn't around
to break up their games.

"No, they're yours. You know that, Rue."

"Yes," she said. "Yes." And she got up, restless and
a little irritable and though he didn't want to go, he felt
he should.

Outside, above the biggest beech on the higher slopes,
the September sky was changing. Now blue and clear,
now white and cloudy, as the morning hesitated over

whether it was the remnant of a defeated summer or the vanguard of a new autumn.

"Well, I'll go, then," said Bracken, a little miserably, as he led the way to one of the entrances higher up the slopes. Rue stayed in the burrow as she watched his departure. She was glad to see him go, because there was an uneasy power about him like some of the youngsters she had had who had not yet learned their strength and are clumsy in their ignorance. Only this mole's strength wasn't physical but something else. He was such a strange mole to be with.

September. Such a funny month for a female who hasn't mated in the spring. September. And the morning in the sky above seemed to decide to be a part of autumn.

Somewhere near the entrance where Bracken paused, his sense of isolation very rapidly returning, a great plop of rain fell; and then another, almost into the entrance itself, spattering onto Bracken's face and hiding drops of silver in his fur. With a sigh he left the shelter of the tunnel.

The air Bracken stepped out into was getting heavier by the minute with the pressure of an impending storm, and the blue, clear patches in the sky, now pushed to the end of the wood, were disappearing fast, squeezed out by the heavy gray clouds that darkened the sky and told of the coming of the first autumn storm.

Several more drops of rain, and Bracken turned to look at Rue again, but he couldn't make her out any more in the shadows of the entrance, so he turned away and set off, swinging spontaneously to the southwest toward the Stone rather than toward the place where he could get back into the Ancient System.

"If the Stone calls you," Hulver had told him, "you go to it, because it knows best." In his misery and renewed loneliness, as he left Rue and her tunnels behind, the Stone was calling Bracken, and he obeyed its command.

Down among the shadows of her tunnel entrance, Rue watched him go, cursing herself as a fool for letting him go just yet, but remembering with a little giggle, which made her sound almost a youngster again, that males, even strange ones like Bracken, have a habit of coming back again when they are needed. Especially by females.

14

FROM the moment Rebecca left Barrow Vale for the westside, after Rune had been called away to hear Rue's story, she saw what she was doing as a journey of discovery. Perhaps she wanted to find the pastures and to test their scent; perhaps to press on up the legendary slopes to see the Stone; perhaps even to make contact with Bracken at last, though she was now a little nervous of doing so, because part of the price she had paid for holding on with such conviction to the idea that he was alive was that she believed him to be, at the very least, a mole almost as big and powerful as Mandrake himself.

But these were the vaguest of hopes, for Rebecca lived more in the delightful present than most moles, having little time for reveries concerning herself when there was so much to see, to do, and feel *now*. And as her journey coincided with the start of autumn in Duncton Wood, there was the excitement of the wood's sudden surrender to the season of change for her to enjoy.

On the second day, when far off to the east and up on the slopes Rune and Mandrake were leaving Hulver's burrows after investigating Rue's story, Rebecca awoke to a morning when the wood's floor was draped and decorated with a thousand dew-hung cobwebs. They ran in ladders and cascades of wet brightness up and down the untidy brambles, in and out of the ground ivy, over and around the dead twigs of fallen branches. About them the ground was moist and almost steamy, for it was still warm from the summer, and the sun that replaced the drizzle of the previous few days still had the strength to start drying the moistures onto which its light fell.

Sometimes, as Rebecca traveled on the surface, a spider would retreat into its silk-lined nest, its front legs poised tense against possible assault as she passed. Sometimes one of her front paws would catch a long anchor thread from a cobweb, which would stretch as she pulled past and then break, the web to which it was attached trembling as one of its supports was pulled away and the dew caught in its symmetry, suddenly dropping and falling to the bramble thorns or fallen leaves beneath, leaving the cobweb bereft of light.

Later the same morning, in a more open vale of the wood, she found herself face to face with the tiny red fruit of wild strawberries which brightened the shadows of their crumpled and serrated leaves and among which stood a few pink flowers of rosebay willowherb rose, tall as a small shrub and far beyond Rebecca's sight. But at least she could sniff at some of the blackberries, still hard and green, whose hairs tickled her snout and stopped her trying to nibble at them.

Rebecca at once grew happier and more restless with each passing sight, each exciting sound; the autumn made her want to run through the wood as fast as a fox, or be blown about it with the random abandon of the seeds of dandelion, which flurried and floated over the more open space.

As for the pastures, well! When she reached them, she found that they were fresher up here than she remembered from lower down by the Marsh End where she had said goodbye to Rose. She did not venture out of the long grass and rough hawthorn bushes that lay just inside under the barbed-wire fence that kept the cows out of the wood, because she was a little nervous of doing so—but the more she snouted out through the grass to the vast sky-strewn openness beyond, the more her excitement began to overcome her fear of the pastures or its moles.

On the third day Rebecca lost all track of time as the autumn continued its slow change about her and, as on different days in the spring and summer, she wandered from one delight to another. Squirrels nervously hopping between trees; starlings flocking and feeding in flurries of squealing sound; leaf-falls from a tall and gentle ash, whose leaves always fall earlier than other trees' in the wood. While there were some things she had at last gotten used to and found she could take pleasure in rather than run from—like the crashing about of an old hedgehog at dusk who grubbed about an area of leaf mold she had been interested in and which seemed to make so much noise that she wondered if he would scare away even the trees themselves.

With her fourth dawn away from Barrow Vale, the dew was thick on the pastures and Rebecca woke in the temporary burrow she had made near them, feeling at one with

the change that now moved so excitedly about her,
rather than just a delighted observer of it. From its first
moment, the day seemed to carry her along so that she
surrendered to its will and did whatever it seemed to
want. She was as hungry as ever on waking, but this put
no urgency at all into her stretching and grooming, which
became a timeless exercise in self-content. Time did not
matter. Eventually, her coat glossy and her eyes happy,
she burrowed about for food before taking to the surface
to see the day. And the day seemed so free with itself that
it almost asked that she should break free from the grass
of the wood's edge and go out onto the fresh pastures, the
cool dew catching her paws and belly.

Because this part of the wood faced the west, the sun
had not yet reached it, casting instead the shadow of the
trees way out across the pasture. Beyond, the sun hit the
grass and dried the dew, the area of tree shadow receding
as the sun rose higher in the sky and swung south.
The edge of the shadow and the area still bedewed shrank
steadily from west and south as the morning advanced,
and in it, near her burrow but now clear out on the pasture, Rebecca stayed, listening, watching and scenting
the day. Behind her, the barbed wire marked the edge of
the wood, and here and there along it, tufts of cow's hair
vibrated a little, the only evidence of a morning breeze.
Even if Mandrake himself had asked Rebecca to move
she might well not have done so, for she could smell a
scent of such excitement that she knew without thinking
about it that it was the one she had been seeking
for weeks past. For as the shadow of the trees shrank toward her, two big male pasture moles followed it up the
pastures, down among their tunnels, then up and rolling
across the surface, playing hide and seek and catch-as-
catch-can with each other. It was a morning in which a
mole should dance and smile and forget that summer was
yesterday and tomorrow may bring an autumn storm. A
morning to live in.

The two moles were slimmer and more lithe than Duncton moles, but just as powerful as the strongest westsider,
their coats just a shade lighter. They seemed to know
each other so well that they did not really talk as
they played, preferring to laugh and roll and touch and
mock-fight with each other as they made their way to-

ward the dark wall of the west side of the wood, its shadow receding before them.

The light morning breeze coming up the pastures carried their scent to where Rebecca crouched. The scent was male and new: strong and exciting. It was distant enough for her to want to run out toward it, to increase the chance that the males—though she did not know there were two of them—might scent her out. And run she did, or rather she danced across the dew-covered grass toward where the shadow stopped and the sun started, the male scent fresh like new-cropped grass, different from Duncton scents. As she danced, she did not even think of the risk she was taking, or how dangerous it would have seemed to most Duncton moles. She was Rebecca, there was the massive exhilaration of autumn soaring in the air around her, she wanted a mate, and a male was so near, somewhere near.

And one of them was. He had run on ahead, in and out of tunnels, toward where the pastures were still in shadow and where the dew had not yet dried out. On and on he ran, laughing and snouting back over his shoulder to see if the other was following near. On and on . . .

"Cairn! Cairn!" the one who was lagging behind called ahead, his voice deep and authoritative. "Don't go too near the wood without me, you never know if there are Duncton moles about near the edge. Cairn!" The name was called with love and good humor and without real fear that any harm was about. This was a morning in which to live to the full, rather than to sneak about.

Cairn ran on, laughing, snouting over his shoulder to see how far ahead he was and drawn on by such a sweet wildflower smell ahead. When, Oh! And a tumble. And a snarl. And Rebecca. Rebecca and Cairn. Tense and staring at each other, Rebecca's talons hard in the ground and Cairn looking to see and snouting to scent if there were other males about.

"Cairn . . . Cair . . . ," and the other arrived, and all three crouched suddenly tense in the still wet grass as the sun rose on into the sky and the shadow of the trees swept on toward the wood, passing over all three so that they were all in the sun, and Rebecca's coat was glossy with excitement and bedabbled with dew. And all their breaths were tense with excitement.

Rebecca moved first. She turned with what was meant

to be a mock-snarl, but came out more as a gay laugh
and started for the wood, but seeing the dewy shadows
there, twisted and turned in a circle back into the sun;
Cairn followed, with deep growls that delighted Rebecca
and finally made her turn to face him, talons out, watching him come toward her with exaggerated care, first one
paw, then another, snout quivering. He was magnificent:
each move he made had a muscular grace that made her
want to run forward and push and tumble him, to see
him spring up and mock-fight with her.

"My name's Cairn," he said, and snout to snout they
looked at each other, Rebecca's head very slightly to one
side, her back warmed by the morning sun and her talons
shiny with dew.

The other mole came toward her from her right and
looked at them both crouched opposite each other, and
then, settling down, said, "And I'm Stonecrop, just in case
you're interested."

Rebecca laughed, and sighed, and looked at him. He
was heavier than Cairn and if anything more powerful
and his coat was a little darker. Then she looked back at
Cairn.

"What mole are you, and where are you from?" Cairn
asked. It was the ritual question but one that Rebecca
had not been asked before, except in fun or mockery.

"I'm Rebecca, of Duncton Wood." As she said her
name it seemed that nothing had ever been so real to her
before and that, suddenly, she was out of the shadows in
which she had lived and fully herself, and playing in the
light without waiting for more questions she ran between
them and away, and she heard Cairn say "Rebecca!" and
heard him chase after her. Then Stonecrop laughed, deep
and strong as she liked to hear a male laugh, and suddenly they were all chasing and running and mock-
fighting in the sun, paw on face, face on flank, flank on
paw, paw entwined with paw again. And each of their
laughters seemed to go into and come out of each other's,
Rebecca's higher, female laughter mixing a gay silver
lightness into their deeper laughs and growls of content.

Until, when the morning was fat with the September
sun and the shadows of the trees by the wood had narrowed down to a sliver of dark, they were all still again,
crouching under the protection of some faded common
thistle, well out on the pastures and quite near one of the

entrances to a tunnel the two males had used on their way up toward the wood.

"So you're pasture moles! They said you were all vicious and dangerous!" exclaimed Rebecca, content and safe in their company.

"And they said you were all dark and broody and lived in shadows weaving spells," said Cairn.

Then they talked and asked so many questions of her that she couldn't find time to answer them all. They were fascinated by the fact that Duncton Wood had a central place for moles in Barrow Vale because, according to Stonecrop, "We don't have such a place at all, except where a couple of communal tunnels meet and you can have a chat down there, if you feel like it."

But they knew more about Duncton than she had expected, given there was so little contact between the two systems, and that she, herself, had learned nothing about the pastures. They knew of the Stone, "Though it's very dangerous and is protected by dangerous Duncton Wood spirit moles who could turn a pasture mole into the root of a tree by a glance and imprison him there forever until the tree dies and his spirit is released," explained Cairn.

"What happens then?" asked Rebecca, thinking that roots had never seemed sinister before to her but wondering if now she could ever look at one again without wondering if a mole was imprisoned inside.

"No mole is sure," continued Stonecrop. "And I personally don't believe it. Have you been to the Stone?" he asked Rebecca.

"No, it's a long way from where I live. I was going to it, well, sort of heading in that direction, when I stopped by the pastures. But it's not an evil place. Well, it can't be, because the Stone's there and the Stone protects us."

"Is it true you've got scribemoles living in Duncton Wood?" asked Cairn.

"Scribemoles?" Rebecca wasn't sure what he meant. She had heard of them in stories Sarah had told her, but they don't exist any more. "No, we haven't any of them. That was long ago and they only ever came here for a short time."

"What lies beyond the pastures?" asked Rebecca. Even asking the question made her nervous.

"Never been down there, have we, Stonecrop?"

"Nope. Too dangerous. But I've always said I would go—it's no good living in fear of things, is it?"

"Does Rose live in the pasture system?" asked Rebecca. "Rose the Healer?"

"Down near the marshes, isn't she, Cairn?"

"That's right," said Cairn, "though you never know where she's going to pop up next."

Rebecca laughed—at least there was one thing in common between the two systems.

Behind her, the wood murmured with birdsound. The morning was warm and they had talked enough. Two magpies played at the wood's edge, chucking to each other. One took off from the shadows into the sun out across the pastures below them, and then its mate followed their flight swift and direct, as if each second of life was precious and not one should be wasted.

With a laugh and a tumble, Stonecrop was suddenly gone, back to the tunnel, "Because it's time I found more to eat and you two found yourselves a burrow. I'll remember not to tell anymole, Cairn; you don't want gossip!"

Rebecca ran after him, rough-tumbling her farewell to him and feeling suddenly his solid strength. Cairn had a lightness of spirit and a grace that Stonecrop lacked, and yet she felt, as she pushed at Stonecrop and she seemed to make no impression on him, that there was only one other mole who had felt so solid and strong, and that was Mandrake, but his strength was corrupted while Stonecrop's was pure.

Stonecrop turned and looked down at her. His gaze was very direct. "Take care of him, Rebecca, because I love him," he said simply, his voice strong as roots.

Cairn watched them both, wanting and yet not wanting his brother to go. Rebecca turned back to him away from Stonecrop, whose sudden somber solidity had frightened her just a little, and made her want to run even more with the lightness of Cairn, which seemed to match the day so well.

They mock-fought and play-scratched their way to the wood, twisting and turning their snouts into each other, fur mingling with fur; now Rebecca leading, and now Cairn. She loved the way his shoulder bore down on hers because he was so powerful and big, and she loved the lightness of his spirit mingling with the powerful desire that lay behind the stronger and stronger way he touched her and pushed against her.

They ran from the warmth of the middle of the day to the warmth of her tunnel, down and then along into the buried darkness of its burrow.

He snouted her deliciously so that she sighed and gasped and cried out with pleasure, while his breathing became heavier and he moaned into her and his talons rough-scratched her back as she surrendered to his pulling of her this way and that and he gave himself to her rounder, deeper warmth and softer caresses.

Where she had been tensely expectant with Rune, she was gently relaxed with Cairn. First one flank was hard against hers, then another, then his paws and talons up her back and his belly sliding over her fur, higher and bigger and his scent all around her and his talons softly into her shoulders and neck and his snout down toward hers from above, but most of all his flanks behind, over and between; as his paws possessed her in front his flanks possessed her from behind, and they were both together, his talons her exquisite pain, his breathing her sighs, his fur her fur, her warmth his heat, her softness his joy, her depths his light, his power her power, and their power her light.

"Rebecca, Rebecca," whispered Cairn, her body as big and warm to him as a home burrow, his body as strong and safe to her as a whole system. Their words of love like no other words either had spoken before, each one a sigh of happiness. Two innocent moles in the darkness of a burrow, whose mating is the joy in the color of a wildflower, or the changing light of sun on dappled water.

"Rebecca, Rebecca," sighed Cairn.

"Cairn, oh, Cairn," she echoed in reply as they shifted caressingly into each other's paws and fur and their bodies were full of the content of satisfied surrender.

Evil. It snouts out good as a stinking hellebore finds out the sun in the very darkest part of the wood where it grows.

Evil. It hides in the shadows near which innocents play in the light, taking a thousand forms, some as hideous as disease and most as subtle as snakes.

Evil. No better name for Rune, who could sniff out the scent of goodness and convert it to the stench of corrupted innocence.

Rune. He snouted out with dark knowledge that somewhere, away in the westside, there was something pure
and good to get his bleak talons into, something to do
with Rebecca, who had left Barrow Vale before he came
back from Hulver's tunnels and who had not returned to
her own tunnels, according to the henchmole he had sent
there to see. So Rune set off for the westside.

How did he know? Who can say why shadows pass
their way? Except that a mole like Rune can always
stick out a talon and find trouble—for a mole like him *is*
trouble.

So secretly and shadowly Rune left Barrow Vale and
set off for the westside, snout poking into tunnel after
tunnel and burrow after burrow, not knowing exactly
what he sought but knowing he would find it.

And find them he did, scenting her deliciousness in the
shadows of the wood's edge and then cutting back and
forth along toward it like a fox quartering a wood. Until
he found what he was snouting for—the entrance to a
burrow from whose depths came the smell of Rebecca
and the smell of a male. Rune smiled, stretched his
talons, and started down boldly into the tunnel without
any other thought than the pleasure of killing. There was
only one mole in Duncton he was afraid of, and that was
Mandrake.

Rebecca tensed the moment she smelled his odor,
turning to face the burrow entrance, even before Cairn
knew there was trouble.

"Is it another male?" asked Cairn quietly and calmly,
coming to Rebecca's side and then easing himself ahead
of her nearer the entrance, where he could defend his
right.

"No, it's Rune. A Duncton elder. He's dangerous,
Cairn, and he'll fight to kill."

Cairn laughed out loud, just as Stonecrop, his brother,
had laughed the several lifetimes before when they had
all met out on the pastures. A deep laugh that mocked
the sly odor of Rune's coming.

Rune said nothing, but came to the burrow entrance
slowly, his eyes taking in the size of the tunnel, the possibilities of blocking and turning, and the size of the entrance where Rebecca and her consort lay hiding from
him. He liked a fight, especially one which he knew before he started that he was going to win.

It wasn't hard to win a fight when a male was trapped in a temporary burrow with no room to move and all he, Rune, had to do was to power-thrust his talons into the darkness and feel the soft fur, or even better, the vulnerable snout of his opponent yield before him.

Yet Cairn laughed. He had been in just this position so many times with Stonecrop, who was a master of fighting, that he knew exactly what to do about it. Instead of pushing forward boldly into his opponent's thrust as most males would have done, he fell back, pushing Rebecca behind him and keeping as far away from the entrance as possible. Rune's shadow fell across it and, as fast as it did so, Rune plunged forward and round into the entrance, his talons shooting forward to where Cairn was reared up ready and waiting. They brushed his fur but went no farther. There was a momentary pause as Rune puzzled over the contact he had failed to make, and taking the advantage of it Cairn lunged forward into the fleshy part of Rune's paw, a searing plunge of sharp talons that forced Rune to withdraw with a twist and a cry of pain.

As he did so, Cairn lunged forward, plunged out of the entrance with his left talon, straight into Rune's left shoulder and narrowly missing his snout. The whole thing was done with such speed that Cairn was back in the burrow and crouched still and waiting before Rebecca knew what had happened. They could hear the sharp, hurt breathing of Rune in the tunnel beyond, as he fell silent and thought what to do.

Then all was movement, as Rebecca heard a growling and a snarl, saw a rush forward by Cairn, heard a hissing from Rune and the two moles were attacking each other at the entrance, the dark body of Rune now in full sight, the lighter fur of Cairn contrasting with his blackness. For a moment both fell back; but then Cairn lunged forward again and was out into the tunnel driving Rune back down it toward the entrance. "Be careful, Cairn," called Rebecca desperately after him. "He's not just a mole, he's Rune. Be careful."

But Cairn was not a defensive fighter and Rune's retreat gave him the false impression that this was a fight to be easily won. When he heard Rebecca's voice, Cairn laughed and drove forcibly forward. But Rune, too, was strengthened by its sound.

Rune saw that the mole he was fighting was young but strong, and no fool, and that it would be cunning, not strength, that defeated him. And for Rune, what was worse and increased his hatred of this mole still more than the fact that he seemed to be Rebecca's mate was that he was a pasture mole. The fresh cropped-grass scent on Cairn sickened Rune, used as he was to the rotting of leaf mold in the shadow of the wood in which he habitually slunk.

So Rune backed slowly away, avoiding the worst of the blows that the young pasture mole powerfully directed at him, as he worked toward the maneuver that would allow him to inflict the fatal talon thrust that he had made his speciality.

Cairn pressed on, impressed by Rune's ability to avoid his fastest and most dangerous blows and to use the tunnel to prevent him from getting round and under him; warned, too, by the way Rune seemed to keep even his snarls under control.

For a moment, almost experimentally, Cairn relaxed in the face of his opponent's retreat and immediately, without a moment's hesitation and with no sign of the fear that a mole might mistakenly have thought would go with his retreat, Rune came in with a talon thrust which twisted and tore into Cairn's cheek, drawing blood onto his face fur, on which a thin trickle wound down to his snout.

The thrust brought a sudden stillness to both moles as each looked to find a move that would bring the opportunity for real damage to the other.

It was Rune who broke the deadlock. He suddenly turned and thrust back out of the tunnel to the surface, the start of the maneuver he had used many times before as a preface to defeating a mole who seemed stronger than he. With a snarling roar, Cairn lunged after his retreating form as Rebecca, who saw the back of him disappearing out to the surface, called urgently, "Be careful, he's *Rune*." She could have made no other word sound so black.

Her warning was right, for Rune knew that in the moment that a mole runs up toward the surface he instinctively hesitates to enter out onto it because he is about to lose the protection of the tunnel's darkness. In that moment of hesitation, another mole, one waiting as

Rune did now, with his talons poised for the kill by the entrance, can thrust back down into the tunnel on the mole who is coming out, and with luck administer a fatal snout-blow.

Rune's ploy might well have worked but for the chance that the mole he happened to be fighting had fought so many times with Stonecrop, whose prowess as a fighter was almost a legend in the pastures. The trick Rune was trying was an old one and Cairn's rapid pursuit, powered forward by his back paws so that his front paws could be protectively outstretched, was the answer Stonecrop had devised to it.

Neither mole won this round of fight. Cairn was caught by Rune's downward thrust as he came charging out, though only on the arm and shoulder, while Rune suffered a wound to his face. Then, on the surface, unrestricted by tunnel or burrow, the two moles rolled into thrusting clinch after cutting lunge, back paws scratching and kicking, front talons trying to plunge a fatal wound.

About them the sky became overshadowed by the threat of a storm, and instead of the light being bright it was, for a morning, almost gloomy dark. While far beyond the trees in whose stormy shade they now fought, the first great drops of rain of a storm started to fall, sporadic at first, but then growing more heavy and persistent.

It was the same rain into which, far off to the east on the slopes, Bracken was at that very moment setting off from Rue's new burrows for the Stone, which loomed, like the storm itself, over all the moles in Duncton Wood.

As the rain started to fall heavily on them both, Rune sensed that Cairn was the stronger and not much less the cunning, either. Rune might be lucky to find a fatal thrust. His speed might win the day. But he would have to be lucky, and the luck might not run his way, and anyway—why take a risk in killing a mole when there was a much surer way of doing it? There was another mole in Duncton much stronger than either of them who would relish the chance to kill Rebecca's mate—the more so if he came from the pastures.

So Rune's dark mind raced as he parried and thrust Cairn's blows, while the rain fell ever more thickly through the open trees of the wood's edge onto their fur,

mingling with their wounds and blood and obscuring their
sight and sense of each other.

Then Cairn charged on Rune once more, stronger and
more confident now that he was out in the open, and
caught him terribly on the haunch. In that moment, Rune
decided that, for the time being, he had had enough. He
would retreat into the wood, slowly enough to lure Cairn
on with him, and take him slowly and surely toward the
haunts of the westside where this pasture mole might be
killed; and if not there, then lure him even to Mandrake,
whose talons would take pleasure in doing the deed and
who would surely give Rune credit for bringing this mole
to him.

Rune ran back, turned and snarled, and ran back some
more into the wood, making Cairn follow as he pursued
the bloodlust that told him to kill this dark and vicious
Duncton mole, and made him forget Rebecca in the tunnel behind him.

As they retreated into the rain and dark of the wood,
she emerged from the tunnel entrance and listened to
their noise slowly die away. She wanted to chase after
them and join Cairn in his assault on Rune. But in a
mating fight, which surely this was, it wasn't for a female
to do more than wait. But everything in Rebecca told her
to chase after them, to help her Cairn; yet she stayed,
hesitating by the entrance in the rain, confused by the
sudden attack, hoping that at any moment Cairn would
come back with the blood of Rune on his talons.

But as the stormclouds burgeoned and grew heavier
over the pastures and wood, darkening everything with
its steady rain, Cairn followed the retreating Rune deeper
and deeper into the wood, leaving Rebecca crouched and
desolate and quite alone.

Each minute that passed left Rebecca more miserable
and lost. The sound of the rain seemed to confuse her
and drain her of strength, and she had no idea what had
happened, where her mate might be or whether or not
he might be injured. Once she advanced out into the rain,
toward the way they had gone, and called out "Cairn,
Cairn. . . ," but she could only hear rain and see wet
foliage and undergrowth. Then she crept back into the
burrow to wait some more.

At last she grew fearful for Cairn and this made her
fearful for herself. For if he had been defeated, then

Rune might come back and find her there. But surely her Cairn could not have been defeated? But perhaps he had been, and she should have tried . . .

So, for the first time in her life, questions and worries of life and death began to darken Rebecca's mind. The truth was that so much had happened to her so happily in the previous twenty-four molehours that the sudden appearance out of a dark sky of Rune had shocked her into being confused and upset. To have had taken from her so violently the very thing she had been seeking for so many molemonths left her frightened and insecure and doubting the very impulse for life and joy that had brought her so trustingly over to the pastures in the first place. Now the deafening rain seemed the mirror of her torrent of fears.

Until at last, panicked by the threat of Rune's possible return, she took to the surface again, though uncertain where to go. She turned at first toward the westside but stopped for fear that Rune, if he was coming back, would come that way. She hesitated before the pastures, for without Cairn and Stonecrop to accompany her there, they seemed dangerous; the more so because a great herd of cattle, which had silently drifted up the pastures through the day, now stood silent and massive beyond the fence, their hooves dirty from the mud that was forming there.

Miserably she turned yet again, this time toward the slopes to the south—but what could she find there but more desolation and emptiness? Everywhere seemed hopeless now that her mate was gone.

Such a time may come suddenly to anymole, in any place, at any time. When suddenly the sun's light is gone and all falls gloomy and dark and each drop of rain that thunders to the ground seems reminder that a mole is forever alone, seeming forever lost. But though the sun is gone, there is an unseen light that may seem far off and dim, and whose rays may touch the heart and not the mind. Yet such a light, vague and hard to make out though it is, may draw a mole forward far, far more powerfully than any sun.

And such a light drew her now, up along the wood's edge on the western side of the slopes, higher and higher up the hill, where the oaks thinned away to tall beeches, which even in the rain gave the wood a lighter, loftier look. Each massive beech she passed seemed to will her on as it stood, solid and powerful, the green lichen covering its base almost luminescent in the shady light of a darkening afternoon that had taken over from a gloomy morning. She hardly knew where she was going, or that she *was* going, and when she wandered in her desolation from the path that led her higher and higher, the massive trees seemed to sway her back toward the light that perhaps they could see far more clearly than she could that day. Higher and higher, until the wood's floor leveled off and she swung in from the pastures toward a great clearing that drummed with the sound of rain. At its center stood a Stone, enwrapped by the roots of a tree. The Stone itself. And on the west side of the clearing, crouched so still that he might almost have been a part of the wood, was a mole, shiny with rain, smaller than Cairn, who faced away from her as he looked out through the trees to the west.

Bracken had been there for several molehours, from the time the rain had begun to fall, thick and wet. His few days with Rue in Hulver's old tunnels, which might have left him feeling less lonely after his initial exploration of the Ancient System, had had the opposite effect. He had left her as the rain started, and trekked miserably up the hill toward the Stone, for no reason that he understood. Back to the Stone.

He had looked at it for a long time, feeling alternately resigned to its impassivity and angry with it just being there and "doing" nothing. Then he was angry with Hulver, who had said the Stone held everything, a promise which did not seem to be fulfilled now that Bracken was alone and desolate before it.

Finally Bracken had started to weep tears from a well of lonely desolation so deep that they shook his whole body in their sadness. Tears which mingled with the rain that tumbled on his face and fell with it to the ground which, slowly, took them in and carried his grief for its own. Then he had turned away from the Stone and went to crouch, still miserable, in the spot to the west side of the clearing which lay toward Uffington where the Holy Moles were said to be.

Some time later he started to speak to the Stone behind him and to Uffington far off before him, not knowing that what he was doing was praying. He asked for the Stone's help in his search for strength. He asked for the strength to continue his exploration of the Ancient System. He asked for help.

At first, the wind lashed the trees, which swayed and whipped each other in the wet, far above where Bracken crouched. But then the wind died and solid rain poured down, the same that seemed to deafen desolate Rebecca as she heard Cairn and Rune disappear deeper into the wood, and it ran in rivulets down the tree trunks round the Stone clearing, turning the leaf mold into a sodden carpet, cold and wet.

And the noise! The endless random drumming of the rain drowning every other sound—not a scurrying fox, or a scampering rabbit, or a scuffling mole could be heard above the noise. Until, when all creatures had found their burrows, except those like Bracken and Rebecca who had been caught out by trouble, the wood was as still in the rain as a lost and forgotten tunnel.

Then a peace crept slowly over Bracken. A peace that was mingled with the sighs of the understanding that came with the knowledge that he *was* alone and that moles like Mandrake and Rune, who could chase after a Stone Mole that did not exist, were surely no less alone than he. A peace that came with the certainty that it didn't matter where he lived, and if the Stone had brought him to the Ancient System, he might just as well explore it to the end.

So, as Rebecca began her own weary ascent of the hill in the rain, Bracken fell into the peace that follows the tears of a prayer spoken truly from the heart, surrounded by suffering and darkness. The words that Hulver had taught him now came back and each one seemed to carry a meaning for him now he had not seen when he first recited them:

> *The grace of form*
> *The grace of goodness*
> *The grace of suffering*
> *The grace of wisdom*
> *The grace of true words*
> *The grace of trust*
> *The grace of whole-souled loveliness.*

Then his mind fell silent for a time and he saw for a moment past the impenetrable, impassive face of the Stone into the world of trust and love beyond it.

Weary, her wet paws sore, her mind dazed and upset, Rebecca crouched down in the Stone clearing looking up at the Stone, unafraid of the strange mole who crouched off to her right in the pouring rain. She stared at the Stone for a long time, wondering at its size and majesty, losing herself in its strength.

Finally she grew cold and shivery, but found that her panic and confusion had gone, and she just wanted to get back to the tunnels of Duncton where she could shelter for a while and then try to find Cairn again.

She approached the mole on the edge of the clearing carefully, for fear of disturbing him, for he seemed not to have noticed her. There was a patch of sanicle into which she went and made her way round to him. At first she might almost have thought he was dead, so still did he crouch, looking away through the trees somewhere out to the west. But rain seems to sink into a dead creature, leaving no light, whereas with this mole there was about him the light of the few brighter parts of the sky which lay over to the west and were reflected in the sheen of his wet fur.

She watched him longer than she intended, for a great sense of peace seemed to come from him, even though he was small and hunched and seemed, in a way, almost afraid. She wondered for a moment who he might be and decided he must be one of the pasture moles. The thought that he might be Bracken never occurred to her, for her idea of Bracken was that he would be at least as big as Stonecrop or Mandrake, and quite unafraid. She wanted to get dry and warm again and back to the Duncton tunnels. But she needed help to get there, for the strength that had carried her up the hill had deserted her now, and she was weary.

Little by little the heavy rain began to fade and the drumming noise it had been making for so long became a patter again as individual droplets, falling through the trees that surrounded them, could be heard once more. Slowly the sky began to lighten from the west.

As this happened, the mole Rebecca was watching turned to face her, looking at her in an abstracted kind of way. Neither could have known how unutterably weary the other was. But just as Bracken sensed that the mole before him was anxious and lost, so Rebecca sensed that he, too, had been lost and lonely. It gave her the strength to speak to him, and in other circumstances would have been enough for Rebecca to run forward and make his eyes light up with her own vital joy, just as she had done sometimes with her brothers, and Mekkins, and Rose. And even, had she known it, with Mandrake.

But she was too tired to follow this impulse and instead came forward just a little and said "I'm lost. How do I get back into the system?"

The mention of the word *system* made Bracken look past her in its general direction down the slopes, as he remembered that it really was no longer his system. He was *not* of it. He had little desire or need to return to it, but then, what did it matter? And anyway, it was a pleasant feeling to have a mole ask him to do something to help. He looked at Rebecca and thought to himself that he wanted to help her because she . . . well, there was something warm about her that . . . but he didn't have words for it, or even clear thoughts.

"I'm a Duncton mole, you know," she added. He *knew* that—he could tell by her fresh wood scent that reminded him of the sunny surface of Barrow Vale when he had seen it at its best in early summer.

Bracken was especially pleased to be asked by a mole from the system to find a route. It was the first time (apart from the odd occasion with Root and Wheatear in their puphood) when somemole had asked him the way and there was almost nothing Bracken liked better than to exercise his unusual ability to navigate.

"Come on," he found himself saying happily. "I'll show you." And he was off past her, leading her down by a way he remembered to an entrance which must lie just beyond the slopes and from where she could find her own way on. He liked the feel of running down the slopes, this way and that, through the wet foliage, with another mole following, who depended on his skill. He enjoyed it so much that he was sorry when they got there and had to turn to her and say "There you are! I told you it was easy!"

He looked at her looking at him and wanted to stay and ask all sorts of things. But somehow the way she

was looking at him stopped him asking the questions he
was framing and left him mute, as she came forward
and touched him on his shoulder where the scar was fading under cover of new fur. She did it with such gentleness that the words he wanted to say were quite gone
and he felt suddenly achingly vulnerable as he let a
route into his heart open up that pride, or fear, or vanity,
would never again quite be able to close. He wanted to
go up close to her and touch her in his own turn, nuzzling his snout into the soft fur of her neck. The feeling
frightened him and he wanted to run away from it, and
from her, and the system.

"What's your name?" she asked gently.

"I'm Bracken," he blurted out. Then he did run, turning away from the entrance where they had been crouching and making for the slopes. As he ran, he felt a relief
that he was gone from her, but he could still feel the
touch of her caress on his shoulder where once his terrible wound had ached so much; and though he was
glad she was gone, he wished he had asked her name.

He did not hear her call out to him "My name is Rebecca," or see her run a little way toward the way he
had gone, nor did he see her stop and look up toward
the slopes to which he had returned before turning away
herself into the tunnels of the system.

II

REBECCA

15

THE silence of the Stone. A mole may listen for a lifetime and not hear it. Or it may touch him at birth and
seem to protect him with its power for the tasks that he
must face.

Such a mole was Boswell, scribemole of Uffington,
where the Holy Burrows lie, who is now known and beloved of all moles as Blessed Boswell.

Yet there was a time when his vow of obedience had
shaken his heart as day after day he prayed and medi-
tated in solitude by the Blowing Stone that lies at the foot
of Uffington Hill—a stone whose special power for truth
everymole knows. He was seeking the guidance he needed
before making his now-legendary decision to break his
vows and make the trek over chalk hills and clay vales,
across river and marsh, to the Ancient System of Duncton.

The time was September, the same in which Bracken
and Rebecca first met, and the weather was changeable.
A storm had come in from the east, the direction of Duncton Wood. It obscured the top of Uffington Hill in rain
and mist, leaving Boswell below it, isolated and alone
with the Blowing Stone, to make up his mind. At the
height of the storm, the wind was strong and it wound
and raced around the hollow convolutions of the Stone
until at last it sounded the deep vibrating note that cast
all doubts aside and filled his heart with the terrible
certainty that he must make the perilous journey.

He had already asked that he might do so, going with
his master, Skeat, to the Holy Mole himself and begging
to be allowed dispensation to risk the long trek to Duncton. But, though with kindness and compassion, he was
refused, just as Skeat had warned he would be.

"You're far too valuable here, Boswell, for no mole
knows the secrets of the libraries as well as you do, or
the old language, which even the scribes forget. And

anyway," and here Skeat looked sadly on Boswell, "you know you can never make such a journey and survive. Others might, perhaps, but not you, Boswell."

Boswell would not have stood a chance. He had been cursed at birth with a crippled paw, whose talons were weak and useless and with which he only barely had enough strength to limp about, always struggling to catch up with the other pups. It was perhaps a miracle that he survived long enough for Skeat to come across him—or perhaps a reflection of the fact that he had the intelligence to steer clear of trouble.

Skeat himself had first found Boswell in a system near Uffington and brought him for his own protection to the Holy Burrows. He said that he saw in his quickness and intelligence, and in his awe of the Stone, something that should not be lost when he grew too old to stay in his home burrow and was forced to fight for a place of his own.

He was put to work in the libraries at Uffington where, before he ever became a scribe, he learned to take care of the ancient books with a love and feeling that other scribes said was a joy to behold.

Some said he was natural-born to the libraries, where his fur, flecked with gray as it was, blended with the white of the chalk walls and made him seem, in some lights, as ancient as the books themselves. They soon grew fond of the sight of his frail form, struggling sometimes with the bigger books but refusing all help, and would smile to see him.

He became a scribe very young and quickly distinguished himself for his work on some of the most sacred texts of all. The Book of Earth, as it now exists in its edited form, is substantially Boswell's work; the Book of Light, so long an obscure text that few moles understood, was translated and explained by Boswell alone. And all this while he was still young and had seen through only one Longest Night.

But one spring, the same spring in which Bracken was born, Boswell seemed to change. Only Skeat, of all the masters, correctly linked the change with a text that Boswell one day found in the course of his delvings in the dark places of the libraries. It was a piece of bark manuscript and appeared to have been hidden deliberately. It

had upon it the most holy seal of all—the seal of white
birch bark: the seal of a White Mole.

He took this find to Skeat, his master, who took it to the
Holy Mole himself, who opened it in the presence only of
Skeat. It was written in the old language and began:
"Sevene Stillstoones, sevene Bookes makede, Alle but
oone been come to grounde . . . ," which in translation
reads

> *Seven stillstones, seven books made*
> *All, but one, have come to ground.*
> *First, the Stone of Earth for living*
> *Second, Stone for Suffering mole;*
> *Third of Fighting, born of bloodshed*
> > *Fourth of Darkness, born in death;*
> > *Fifth for Healing, born through touching.*
> > *Sixth of pure Light, born of love.*
> *Now we wait on*
> *For the last Stone*
> *Without which the circle gapes*
> *And the Seventh*
> *Lost and last book,*
> *By whose words we may be blessed.*
>
> *Find the lost Book, send the last Stone*
> *Bring them back to Uffington.*
> > *Send a mole in courage living*
> > *And a mole compassionate*
> > *With a third and last to bind them*
> > *By the warmest light of love.*
> *Song of silence*
> *Dance of mystery*
> *From their love one more will come . . .*
> *He the Stone holds*
> *He the Book brings*
> *His the Silence of the Stone.*

The enormous significance of this text was immediately
obvious to both the Holy Mole and to Skeat. For it confirmed a belief, held by generation on generation of
scribemoles, that there were, indeed, seven holy books and
not six—the number Uffington actually had. And if there

were seven books, there must be a seventh Stillstone, for
each of the six books in Uffington had its counterpart in a
Stillstone, as the special stones associated with the seven
books were known, whose location in the deepest parts of
Uffington was a secret known only to the Holy Mole and
the masters. What the two moles immediately debated
was whether this text answered the two great mysteries
about the lost book: where it was, and what was its subject. And also whether or not there was a seventh Stillstone. But, as scholars so often do, they failed to come to
any clear answer.

When the system heard that this text had been found
and what its contents were, there was an enormous excitement, for surely its discovery was some kind of sign.
Inevitably a great many scribes, particularly the younger,
more aggressive ones who liked a bit of action, asked to be
allowed to leave Uffington to search for the lost Stillstone
and the lost book.

But Boswell, who felt the same urge himself, was
excluded from this clamoring, for how could a defenseless mole such as he ever leave Uffington? He lost himself
in work in the libraries, pursuing the one course of search
for the seventh book open to him. He began a massive,
solitary search for other material in the library in the same
script as that of the manuscript he had found. He himself has recorded this search elsewhere, but what is
important here is that in the Midsummer after the spring
in which he made the initial discovery, he found a reference in an entry which *was* written in the same script, in
one of the Rolls of the Systems, the books that record the
findings of the wandering scribes, as they were then
known, about the systems they had visited. It referred to
"Duncton, a system separated from the world by the rivers that surround three sides of it, which has tunnels of
great subtlety and wisdom."

In itself this entry was not unusual. What was remarkable was the effect it had on him. It seemed to him as he
read it that he heard a calling to him from it, as if from
an old mole lost in a place from which he could not escape, asking him to come.

He himself doubted this voice, believing it to be but his
vanity and pride making an excuse for him to follow the
urgings he felt to leave the system. But, over the weeks
that followed, it persisted and eventually he too asked

permission of the Holy Mole to see if he could find the system, whose location was known, though no scribe had visited it—or at least returned from it—for many generations.

He asked three times, and each time his request was refused. So finally, that September, the same in which Bracken and Rebecca first met, he trekked down to the Blowing Stone and began his vigil for truth by it. And so it was there, in the light brought to him by storm and by the grace of the Stone, he made his decision, even though it meant breaking his vows. It is said that he begged the forgiveness of the Holy Mole himself and that it was given to him "for all the things you have done for Uffington and for all the things the Stone may allow you to do outside."

It is also said, though there is no record of this, that Skeat accompanied his protégé and friend to the end of the eastern part of Uffington Hill, where, sadly, he must have watched Boswell slowly make the start of his journey.

There, too, we must leave him to make his perilous journey alone. It will be a long time before we hear of him again, for Duncton was distant and those days were dark and dangerous.

Yet as he starts upon it, let us repeat, as Skeat did then, the ancient journey blessing, which is traditionally said as a plea to the Stone after a beloved one is going at last from our protection:

May the peace of your power
Encompass him, going and returning;
May the peace of the White Mole be his in the travel.
And may he return home safeguarded.

16

CAIRN'S vengeful chase after Rune eventually gave way
to common sense. The deeper he got into the wood the
more its great trees oppressed him, for he was only used to
open sky, fresh wind and tunnels that were sparse and
smelled dry.

But he was at first reluctant to turn back. For one thing,
his brother Stonecrop had told him once "Never leave a
fight half fought," which Cairn took to mean that an opponent was best killed rather than left free to sneak off
and remain a danger.

Also, Cairn sensed that Rune was not truly beaten anyway and probably had some trick prepared. And then
again, this Rune might bring other Duncton moles to attack him, and Cairn had no inflated sense of his own
prowess. He could have beaten Rune, he knew that, but
not two Runes, or three. So, finally, Cairn gave up the
chase and turned back to try to find his mate.

Out on the pastures this would have been easy for him,
but here in the wood with so many strange smells
and sounds, and with the heavy rain half-obscuring everything, Cairn found it impossible, and he was lost in the
wood for hours trying to find his way back to the
pastures. Eventually, when the rain lightened and a breeze
returned, fortunately from the west, he got a scent of the
pastures and was able to head directly for them and from
there to the temporary burrow where he had left Rebecca.

He called out her name as he went down, but he could
sense without waiting for the silence that greeted him that
she was gone. Probably to look for him.

But how wet and forlorn the place looked bereft of her.
How dank and desolate the wet wood about seemed, just
as it always had when he had come near it from the pastures. How cold their burrow was with only the fresh
wood scent of Rebecca there to give it a feeling of life
and love.

He waited in the burrow, tending the scratches and
wounds he had received in his fight with Rune and feeling
lost. He wanted to see her again, if only to confirm that
she had not been a dream—though, he thought ruefully,

his wounds from Rune were evidence enough that she was not.

Rebecca, too, was miserable throughout that same night, for though she was tired, she could not sleep with fretting for her Cairn. When dawn came, and it came very slowly, she made her way back to the surface near the pastures, where the air was cool and clear from yesterday's storm and sun was beginning to shine. The wood gave her the feeling that it had shaken off the trial of the storm and was there again for moles to enjoy, sliding into autumn it was true, but with enough green leaf about to catch the morning sun and make a mole feel that he, or she, was back in summer again.

As soon as Rebecca came to the little clearing where her temporary burrow was, she knew that he was there waiting for her. Oh, she could smell again the strong young scent of the open pastures, where the wind blew and shadows seemed few and far between. She sighed for happiness and crept as quietly as she could into the tunnel, hoping to surprise Cairn, but he was ready for her. She heard him stir and laugh as he delighted in her scent coming to him, and there he was, waiting in the burrow, her Cairn! Her love! His love, Rebecca!

How quiet they both were, and how content. She tended for a while to his scratches and wounds, especially the one he had received on his face as he had run out of the tunnel after Rune. What special attention she gave to that one! What sighings and caresses, what entwinings and delights, what peaceful rest and waking dreams! How close they were!

"Rebecca, Rebecca!"

"Cairn my love, my wildflower."

They smiled and laughed and giggled to be so near, fur once more mingling with fur, and haunch soft against haunch. For a while they even mock-fought, until Cairn's wound got scratched again and he surrendered in defeat to his Rebecca, and she licked and tended to him once more. Then they slept again, the sweet sleep of love satisfied.

"Been in a fight, have you Rune?" Mandrake asked the question with good humor, for after the confrontation with the owl face in Hulver's tunnels he had felt weary, and in no mood to deal with the sycophantic mumblings

of the henchmoles, so was glad to see Rune back again
from wherever he had been.

When he entered the elder burrow where Mandrake
was crouched, Rune had placed himself carefully out of
the shadows where his wounds and scratches might be
clearly seen. He had done so wearily and in seeming
pain, his snout low but making a consciously brave effort
to look cheerful.

"Not exactly a fight, Mandrake, but it is of no matter,
I hope."

"Mmm?" Mandrake's growl indicated that he wanted
to know more.

"It's nothing," said Rune. "At least, I hope it's nothing."

He paused to give time for the doubt to sink into Mandrake's mind and then said lightly, "Well! Everything's
quiet in Barrow Vale. That's something!"

"Where have you been, Rune?" asked Mandrake, his
curiosity now successfully aroused.

Rune sighed, licked his wounds, scratched, twisted and
turned, coughed, put a brave smile onto his shadowy
face, sighed again, and finally said: "Do you know where
Rebecca is at the moment?"

"No. Where?" asked Mandrake, puzzlement taking
over from curiosity.

"Ah! I thought . . . nothing. I must be wrong."

Mandrake got up and came closer to Rune. "What did
you think?" he asked more intensely.

Rune demurred. Then he said, "At any rate if there is
anywhere in the system where danger and treachery can
have least effect it is in the westside. Most of the henchmoles come from there. Very loyal to you and the
system."

"Danger? Treachery?" There was a hint of irritation in
Mandrake's voice, a touch of anger.

"We must always be prepared for them, you have
taught me that." Rune stopped again and Mandrake
waited for him to go on. Eventually he did, but deliberately onto another subject.

"Autumn is starting, Mandrake. A time of change. But
what a summer! You must have been proud of Rebecca,
then."

"Proud?"

"Such innocence, in the summer. Such warmth, when

the sun was shining. So beautiful, then. She's not here in Barrow Vale now?"

"Should she be?"

"She was. After she left her burrows a few days ago. But perhaps she's gone back there now, and I'm wrong."

"Wrong? What is that you're saying, Rune? Come on, out with it."

"Fears are not always founded in fact. They are best left unspoken until they are known to be true. And then a mole may root out danger and treachery."

"Treachery? Rebecca? What is that you mean?" Mandrake was becoming angry, though not exactly with Rune himself, since no mole had been more loyal to him.

"What mole did you fight?" persisted Mandrake.

"A mole I hope that Rebecca has not met," replied Rune, adding quickly "but we will soon know . . . if Rebecca is back in her tunnels, I mean. I did not want to worry you about fears which, though black as shadows, may yet be groundless. You have other things to worry about and I am ever concerned to keep such smaller worries from you." Rune scratched himself again and smiled weakly at Mandrake, grimacing as if in pain.

"What mole?" asked Mandrake.

"A pasture mole," said Rune.

"You killed him?" asked Mandrake.

"I wish I had. But there was more than one. Perhaps I killed one of them." He paused as if he were thinking and Mandrake waited impatiently for him to go on. Finally, he did.

"We must be more wary of the pasture moles, for they are getting subtler in their ways of attack, subtler than they once were. You know what I think, Mandrake?"

Involuntarily Mandrake came closer, thinking that at last Rune would say what was on his mind.

"I think that a pasture mole likes nothing more than to take a Duncton female, the younger and more innocent the better, and to have her for his own, hard haunch hard into soft young haunch. To take her in the safety of the wood's edge and to leave her to litter in shameful secrecy a brood of squawling pasture pups in the heart of Duncton Wood."

As this image hung between them, a henchmole poked his snout through the entrance into the elder burrow in which Mandrake and Rune were talking and, seeing that they were silent, whispered: "Rune, sir, Rune! She is not there!"

"Who is not where?" thundered Mandrake, putting the frustration he felt at Rune's careful vagueness onto the henchmole, who stumbled and stuttered and looked desperately at Rune for help.

Rune merely lowered his snout and shook his head sadly.

"Well?" demanded Mandrake of the henchmole.

"Er—well—it's Rebecca. She's not in her tunnels."

"Where is she, then?" roared Mandrake.

"I . . . we . . . don't know, Mandrake, sir," whispered the henchmole.

"Rune?" Mandrake turned aggressively back to Rune.

"This was what I feared. This was what I hoped could not be true. Ah, Rebecca!"

"Get out," shouted Mandrake at the henchmole. Then, turning to Rune, he said "You had better start at the beginning, Rune."

"There is not much more to say now, Mandrake. Only things to do. . . . But you know why Rebecca came to Barrow Vale?"

"Why?"

"September is a time of change. Leaves may be a delicate green in June, but by September they decay. Somemoles mate in September . . . somemoles like it, want it . . . then. Or *now,* I should say."

"Mating . . . Rebecca . . . now . . ." The elements were beginning to combine into swirling red and black poison in Mandrake's mind.

"On the wood's edge, near the pastures," went on Rune, adding hastily, but deliberately not hastily enough, an explanation of what he meant: "That's where I've been. Fighting pasture moles who had taken a Duncton female into their darkness and done to her what she allowed them to do. Treachery and danger."

"You mean Rebecca?" asked Mandrake, enraged but fascinated at the same time. With each word that Rune now spoke a picture of his Rebecca, his daughter Rebecca, his untouched child, hardened on the edge of his mind where no mole at first likes to look, but to which a jealous mole may easily be drawn. A picture of fur and darkness, of moving haunches and talon scratches on backs, of moist snouts long and pointing and open mouths, and white teeth and sensual smiles in the dark of a forbidden burrow. And his Rebecca among them. His daughter!

"Rebecca? With pasture moles? I hope not," said Rune. "I'm certain she couldn't," he added, but with too little conviction to satisfy Mandrake.

Rune's plans ran deep, deeper perhaps than even he realized. He recognized Mandrake's jealousy for Rebecca because he had felt something of it himself, though being cold and cerebral his was the jealousy of nonpossession rather than of blood right and lust, as Mandrake's was. He thought of Rebecca and Cairn, and his eyes had the black glitter of the owl face in Hulver's tunnels, for evil takes its greatest pleasure in tearing the innocence and happiness from the face of joy.

"Did you see her there?" demanded Mandrake, now shaking with anger and the need for action.

"I heard a female there, taking her pleasure with a mole or moles. A Duncton female from the scent. Thrusting her open haunches to a male, or males, from the pastures. She was there . . . but whether or not it was Rebecca I cannot be sure."

"Rebecca?"

"Perhaps it was another female, but I cannot be certain," said Rune.

His Rebecca. His child. Her haunches open to another male. . . . Mandrake shook with the thought of it until finally he shouted the words that Rune most wanted to hear. "Take me there and let me see!"

Yet even then Rune pretended to hesitate. "Perhaps it is but a mistake, a silliness on my part. It was raining, a heavy storm; the senses play tricks in such weather. I may be very wrong and no mole would wish harm on a mole such as Rebecca, sweet Rebecca, less than I."

"Take me there," ordered Mandrake with a terrible coldness in his voice that warmed Rune's heart.

Night-time, and Rebecca and her Cairn slept on. Night-time, and the urgent pounding of Mandrake's heavy pawsteps grew nearer and nearer to the wood's edge. Night-time, and up in the black and barkless wastes of a dead elm, the yellow eyes of an owl stared down and down at the wood floor beneath, talons itching round the branch they clasped as it waited for the sight and smell of prey.

Mandrake and Rune finally broke out onto the surface of the wood, near the pasture, just before dawn, when

the only sound is the distant squeal of a field mouse or
bank vole taken by a tawny owl. At such a moment only
troubles wake a mole and make him toss and turn in his
half-sleep; only a cold wind disturbs the wood floor and
makes a bramble thorn rasp against its own hard stem;
only a cold moon casts a light, though even that is fading
as the moon sinks down beyond the distant vales.

Cairn stirred. He knew that his time with Rebecca was
almost up. Rebecca moved even closer, even more content. She had mated and she would litter. She knew it
with sweet certainty. But she knew that Cairn, her love,
was restless and that dawn was coming. He wanted to
return now to his own system to find the tunnels he felt
safe in and talk again to his brother, Stonecrop.

Rebecca and he had come together in joy but both
wanted to part now, as mated moles eventually must.
Rebecca sighed, nuzzling him close and smiling, for she
was thinking of the pups he had given her, while Cairn
smiled to think of Rebecca with her pups, tumbling
and playing with them, suckling them to her body,
against whose soft warmth he now lay.

Close by, and getting closer, massive Mandrake and
Rune crept along the edge, Rune pretending to snout his
way there with difficulty, though knowing very well exactly where he was leading Mandrake.

"Here," hissed Rune.

"Where?" demanded Mandrake.

"There." Rune pointed, his talon indicating the entrance to Rebecca's temporary burrow, the disturbed
earth rough and shadowy around it in the dim, cold light.

Meanwhile, for Rebecca and Cairn the minutes that
had once seemed hours now turned to seconds as their
time together sped by. Soon it would be dawn and they
would part. They began to talk the sweet goodbyes of
lovers, but as they did so, there was a snarl and a roar
and it seemed as if the tunnel outside their burrow was
filled with the movement of a thousand predators. It was
Mandrake who, remembering what Rune had told him,
or seemed to have told him, had broken the sullen stillness of the last of the night and moved hugely into the
tunnel leading to the burrow with his talons ready to kill,
and kill powerfully, anymole, male or female, that showed
its snout.

Moments after this sudden disturbance, and as Cairn
instinctively turned with his talons to the burrow en-

trance, there came the scent that Rebecca knew too well
and which made her cry out in fear. The odor of Mandrake. It was strong and aggressive and angry, and it put
fear into the heart of even Cairn, who waited now a second time to defend his right to Rebecca. But this time he
did not laugh, and when Rebecca started to tell him who
it was, he pushed her back and away, for he knew he
would need all his concentration to survive this fight.

Somewhere farther down the tunnel there was movement and they heard the deep rasping voice of Mandrake
saying "Stay out on the surface, Rune, for this is my task.
I will kill them myself."

Rebecca wanted to run out past Cairn, to protect him
from the terror that was coming and that such a mole as
he could surely never imagine could exist. But if he could
not have imagined it before, he knew it now, for even
his bold young heart sickened at the smell of Mandrake's rage and quailed before the sight of Mandrake's
mighty talons lunging suddenly through the murk of the
tunnel and straight toward his snout. That would have
been as far as most moles ever got with Mandrake. But
not Cairn, for he was powerful and very quick and had
fought enough times on his own account to know how
to avoid the first lunges of a fight without becoming impaled upon the second.

Cairn did not even strike a blow before he retreated
into the burrow and crouched, appalled by the sight he
had seen approaching him as Mandrake's smoldering size
seemed to fill the tunnel before him.

Mandrake crouched for a moment in silence beyond
the entrance, looking at them both, surprised at Cairn's
size. But though Cairn was bigger even than Burrhead,
who was the biggest Duncton mole next to Mandrake,
he was not as big as Mandrake himself.

Cairn snarled, his great shoulders flexed and ready,
as Rebecca whispered urgently to him from the end of
the burrow where his movement had forced her: "Run
if you can, my love, for no mole has ever defeated him
and none ever will. Oh, run, my Cairn!"

If Cairn had not already mated with Rebecca he
would have fought to the death there and then, and died.
But he *had* mated and their time was over, and more
than anything else, more now even than Rebecca, he
wanted to be back in the fresh air of the pastures, where

he would not be surrounded by alien scents and evil moles.

"If I escape," he said to Rebecca without looking at her, for his every sense was concentrated on the burrow entrance through which Mandrake was wondering how to pass without exposing his snout too much, "I will return and we will mate again." He spoke the words quite clearly so that Mandrake would hear them, for he hoped they would enrage Mandrake enough for him to move carelessly and give him the chance he needed to give Mandrake a wounding thrust with his talons.

Mandrake reacted by rearing up and plunging his talons at Cairn once more; he, instead of retreating, came viciously forward with his own talons, the two becoming locked in a bloody struggle at the entrance to the burrow.

When one or other of the two great males hit the side of the entrance, the whole burrow shook and earth flew, as Rebecca watched them, at first helpless and confused. As she did so, a powerful and unwanted excitement ran through her, a forbidden and obscene excitement that she tried to blot from her mind: the excitement of seeing the two huge males, both of whom she loved, fighting for her.

There was a momentary lull in the fight as Mandrake stepped back in preparation for a complete push forward into the burrow, and in the lull she could hear her Cairn's desperate gasping of breath as his snout lowered from the enormous effort he had had to make to survive so far. It was this hopeless sound that made Rebecca act.

As Mandrake plunged forward into the burrow, she powered her way past Cairn, with her talons out for Mandrake and a cry of "Run, Cairn, run!" Mandrake moved to one side to avoid Rebecca, at the same time trying to land his talons on the suddenly rapidly moving Cairn, but he was too late, and Cairn was past him and out into the tunnel and running down toward the entrance to the surface.

Mandrake swung back through the entrance, knocking part of its lintel of solid earth flying, and managed to bring his talons with terrible force onto Cairn's fleeing back. Cairn grunted with terrible pain but pulled himself away, leaving Mandrake's talons hanging still for a moment in the middle of the tunnel, covered with his blood. Then he ran on, down the tunnel, the sound of Mandrake snarling and massive behind him. Then up desperately through the entrance, an instinctive memory of the trick Rune had tried to play before making him power his front paws ahead of him with talons splayed out, into the graying night.

But Rune was not to be caught a second time. He crouched to one side of the entrance and, as Cairn came out, plunged his talons with deadly accuracy toward the pasture mole's snout and face. One tore through the left side of the snout, another cut savagely into his left eye, in one terrible instant turning Cairn's face into an open wound that, after no more than a second, began to pour blood.

At the same time, behind him in the tunnel, Mandrake brought down his talons a second time on Cairn, this time tearing his haunches and hind quarters and only failing to stop the fleeing pasture mole dead in his tracks because Cairn's initial thrust out of the tunnel was so powerful.

Cairn staggered heavily forward, swinging instinctively round toward Rune, whom he could now only vaguely see through the haze of pain and blood round his face, catching him savagely in the breast with a cutting sweep of his talons that, had they been lunging instead of swinging, would certainly have killed Rune. As it was, the blow was sufficient to knock him backward past the entrance and to give Cairn time to turn to the fresh air and openness that he could sense off to his right. He began to run and stagger toward it with the desperation of a mole who has faced death, who may soon die, but who seeks one last chance to live.

He might still have been caught by Mandrake, had Mandrake wished it. But as the great mole squatted back ready to burst out of the entrance, he heard Rebecca whimpering and crying in the burrow where she had, for one brief second, blocked Mandrake's way and allowed Cairn to escape, and savagely, the blood of her mate on his talons and fur, he turned back toward the burrow.

As his shadow blackened the entrance to the burrow again and he entered it, Rebecca stopped sobbing and looked up at him. She saw again the great scars made by talons that ran and rumpled down his face, and the new talonscores that Cairn had made on his shoulders, which were bloody and red. She felt the power of his presence over her, and looked up at him as her mother, Sarah, must once have done; she looked into his angry eyes that saw so little and yet sought so much.

She thought he was going to kill her and expected the talons he had raised above his head to strike down upon her. They did come down, massively, not to kill her but to possess her as, without a word and with only the sound of anger in the burrow, he took her, he took her, he took her for his own, savaging his way into her as the burrow exploded about them both into a redness and black, and shafts of light and terrible pain. Rebecca! Rebecca!

She did not know if it was Mandrake who cried her name through the exquisite storm of agony in the burrow about her, and inside her, or a memory of her beloved Cairn saying it. Or whether it was another memory, of she herself calling it into the wet wood up through the slopes after Bracken had left her. My name is Rebecca! Or perhaps she was calling out her name to herself as she drowned in the flood of bloodlust that came over her.

Until, at last, she knew it *was* herself, and Mandrake, too. Rebecca! Rebecca! He spoke it deeply into her, his body in her and, for that brief moment, hers.

"Rebecca!" he repeated as he finally pulled away and back into the world of darkness in which he lived but from which, for a moment, he had escaped with her as he once had with Sarah.

"Rebecca," she said softly, crying and shuddering with pain and loss.

"Rebecca . . . ," whispered Cairn as he crawled up the hill along the wood's edge by the pasture with a throbbing of pain in his back and haunches and head that was almost too much to bear. "Rebecca," he whispered into the deaf grass that swayed toward him and struck his snout powerfully, "find my brother Stonecrop for me. Send him to help me."

But no answer and no Stonecrop came, and he stumbled desperately on, unwilling to stay still where he might be found, yet afraid to break cover onto the pasture from the longer grass by the wood's edge because he would be too slow to avoid any owl that saw him. On he struggled up the hill, not knowing that he was getting nearer and nearer to the Stone or that across its soaring face, now gray with dawn, the first dead beech leaves of autumn were beginning to fall.

17

IT was among a fresh-fallen scatter of beech leaves near the Stone that Bracken first saw him. He was trying to run, but in fact only just crawling, and Bracken had never seen a mole so terribly wounded yet still alive. His snout and cheek were crushed, his shoulders and flanks ragged red, his left eye torn and blinded, and his back legs seemed only good for dragging along, while his hind quarters had suffered deep wounds which seemed the result of several massive talon thrusts.

Bracken had never sensed such suffering in a mole, and perhaps he himself was only able to do so because of what he had suffered in the tunnel by the cliff before Rose the Healer came.

The injured mole advanced a little way toward the Stone, tried to snout up at it for a short while, but then staggered and slued round to one side. For a moment Bracken thought he was coming straight at him, where he crouched half visible on the other side of the Stone, and he grew frightened. It was as if death itself was approaching him. But the mole did not see Bracken and anyway swung round again, gasping and panting with pain and effort, as he dragged himself slowly across the clearing away from the Stone and toward the pastures.

As he disappeared into the undergrowth, Bracken felt the pain as if it were his own. There was a sense of loss and failure over the mole that made Bracken want to run after him and say "No. It's not like that, it's not." Though why he wanted to say such a thing, or about what, he did not know.

The mole's progress was not hard to follow, for he made a lot of noise and, despite his fear, Bracken followed him. He staggered this way and that, crashing painfully through some brambles and leaving a red-brown smear of blood on a young sapling he brushed against. The more Bracken watched him the less he was afraid and the more he wanted to help in some way. There *must* be something he could do. Fetch Rose? He would never know where to find her. Rue? Too far, and he doubted if she would want to leave her tunnels having only just refound them.

He remembered that once Hulver had told him that the juice of cammock was good for rubbing into wounds, but he didn't even know what it looked like, whether it was in season, or where to find it. And anyway, looking at this hurt creature, whose wounds looked all the worse for him being so big and once-powerful, Bracken thought that there was no herb that would help him now.

What would Hulver have done? He would have comforted the mole by talking gently to him. It was this conviction that made Bracken finally break cover, though he did it with some care—approaching the mole from his right side from where, given his wounds, he could more easily see and scent Bracken. He deliberately made a noise as he came near and the mole came to a clumsy halt.

"It's all right," said Bracken, "I will not harm you."

The mole turned his snout painfully toward Bracken and even tried to raise himself on his back paws for a few terrible seconds.

"It's all right," said Bracken again. "I may be able to help."

"Where are the pastures?" asked the mole. "Where are my tunnels?"

"The pastures are only fifty moleyards more," said Bracken. "Not far." Bracken turned toward them and led the way, slowing down when he sensed that even though he was going at a snail's pace, it was still too fast for the other mole. Finally they reached the wood's edge where the long grass grew on the wood side of the fence, stirred by the wind that always seemed to come off the pastures.

The mole slumped down, snout low, and Bracken asked "What's your name?"

"Cairn. From the pastures." For him to say that took a long time, for his voice came slowly and with pain.

"Did a Duncton mole do this," asked Bracken, "*because* you're from the pastures?"

"It was a mating fight. I took a woodmole for a mate. A mole called Rune found us. Do you know Rune?"

There was fear in Cairn's voice, for it occurred to him that Bracken might be one of Rune's friends. But then the thought weakened into hopelessness; if he was, so what? It didn't matter any more. He knew he was going to die.

"Rune!" exclaimed Bracken. "Yes. I know Rune. Everymole in Duncton does."

"He found us several days ago and I fought him and chased him away; I should have killed him. It was my first mating fight. He brought another mole and I could not fight him. Not to win. His name was Mandrake."

Bracken looked with renewed horror at Cairn. No living mole knew better than he what that meant. Surely there was something he could do.

Cairn seemed lost in a world of his own, for his head hung down onto the ground, tilted to one side so the wound did not touch the grass, and the only movement was his quick, shallow breathing that made one of his limp paws twist fractionally to the left and then back again with each in-and-out of his breath.

It occurred to Bracken finally that if only he could get Cairn to go a little way farther up the hill to where the Stone faced the west toward far-off Uffington, the line on which he himself had automatically crouched when he had first come to the Stone and on which Hulver had died, there might be some power for comfort there.

Somehow he coaxed Cairn along, though each step was painful, until at last Bracken could sense that they were in the right place. Cairn seemed to sense it, too, for he slumped down again with a sigh. His breathing grew easier and he was happy to be able to point his snout out over the pastures he loved. It was afternoon and the sky was light, with a few high clouds and some haze far off below them over the vales.

It was peaceful there and as Bracken faced in the direction of Uffington and felt its power coming to them, with the strength of the Stone from behind, a peace was beginning to fall on the broken and suffering Cairn.

"Tell me about the Stone," he whispered. "She talked about the Stone. She said, Rebecca told me, that she came up to the Stone after I left her to chase the Rune mole away. She talked a little about it."

"But no mole has been here," said Bracken, until he remembered that a mole had. A female. And he felt again her caress on his shoulder and knew that *she* had been Rebecca. If only he had stayed to ask her name. If only. For some reason this discovery made him feel at one with Cairn, and he began to understand something of the sense of loss he carried with him.

"Was your mate Mandrake's Rebecca?" asked Bracken needlessly.

Cairn nodded painfully.

Bracken moved closer to Cairn, flank against flank, trying to warm his body with his own as it grew colder and weaker.

"Talk to me, Bracken. Tell me about the Stone. Tell me about Rebecca."

What could Bracken say? He knew little about either, far too little when he thought about it. And what comfort can a mole give to one so injured?

"The Stone is the center of the Ancient System," he began, wondering how to go on. "And . . . and it's so big that a mole cannot see the top of it. It soars up like a tree without leaf or branch. But you must have seen it when I first saw you, for you were by it."

Cairn said nothing, so Bracken continued. "It's where the rituals are carried out, on Longest Night and Midsummer Night, and in the old days rituals now long forgotten were carried out there. They say it will always protect you, but—" But Bracken did not believe that. It had not protected him or Hulver from Mandrake. It had not miraculously healed Cairn when he came near the Stone.

Yet—yet the more Bracken saw of the Stone, and was near it, the more he felt its power and understood that it did hold an awesome mystery that a mole was unwise to turn his back on.

"Tell me about Rebecca," said Cairn quietly.

"Well, I don't know much about her, only what other moles have said. She's big for a female and lives down beyond Barrow Vale; somewhere near Mandrake, I was told once. I've heard them say she's beautiful."

He thought of the mole he had guided back to the system two days before and wondered if she *was* beautiful. It hadn't occurred to him.

"She was always getting into trouble when she was a youngster—you should have heard the stories they told about her in Barrow Vale! Eating worms she shouldn't, getting her brothers lost accidentally on purpose—that sort of thing. Hulver said something about her once (he was an old mole I knew once), he said that she was so full of life that it frightened other moles. But then, a lot of things he said didn't make much sense, though I think they meant something."

Bracken stopped for a moment, but from the way Cairn

moved and looked at him, he could tell he was enjoying him talking like this and so Bracken continued.

So he told him the full story about Rebecca stealing the worms from the elder burrows. As he told it, however, a sense of panic began to creep over him, for he sensed that Cairn was slipping away from him—or at least his body was. It was getting stiller and colder, and his breathing was becoming almost imperceptible.

When Bracken finally stopped talking and could think of nothing else to say, Cairn did not even try to look around at him, though his uninjured eye was half open and looking over the pastures. For a moment Bracken thought that he was . . . but then Cairn began to talk.

"She told me that story in our burrow when we mated, and how frightened she was when she was questioned by Mandrake about the worms. Having fought with him and lost, I know she was right to be frightened. There is no mole like Mandrake in the pasture system, and no mole like that Rune either." Each word was painful for him and occasionally he shifted his body heavily, as if in an effort to make it easier for him to speak, and Bracken saw that every word he spoke must have meant a great deal for him to have suffered the pain of getting it out.

Cairn went on. "She said she couldn't understand what all the fuss was about and didn't see why they didn't find more worms, which they must have done anyway."

Bracken nodded but said nothing, not wanting to interrupt Cairn's painful flow of words.

"Rebecca said she couldn't understand why behaving 'naturally,' as she put it, should be such a crime. What was worse for her was that Mandrake made her be polite with the other moles—which, as she didn't like some of them, was 'unnatural.' She was made to speak only when she was spoken to—which must have been hard for her." Cairn almost managed a little laugh and Bracken saw his face wrinkling a little, where it could, into lines of love and affection for his Rebecca.

"Why does all this have to happen?" asked Cairn, his words now so weak that Bracken could hardly hear them. "Why do moles sometimes get so angry that they kill each other? What was wrong with me and Rebecca being together? I was just going when they came. A few more minutes and I would have been gone. A few minutes and it would have been different. You ask your Stone why. I'd like to know what it answers."

Cairn turned with great difficulty to Bracken and the bewilderment in his voice was replaced by real pride as he said "She was my first mate." Bracken hardly dared draw breath for the frailty he now saw in the once-powerful mole beside him. "She was my only mate," he said softly.

"Then Mandrake came and just took it away. Him and that Rune mole. I could have killed him before." There was a long silence that Bracken did not try to break. Finally Cairn found the strength to go on: "He's killed me. If Stonecrop had been there we would have killed them both. He's my brother. He can fight like no other mole in the pastures. Why does a mole like Mandrake come? Why me?"

Why him, Bracken wondered. *Why* him? At that moment he could have wished almost any other mole to be suffering in Cairn's place, himself included. *Why* him?

"Why not me?" Bracken muttered to himself, not realizing that he too had suffered and might yet suffer much, much more.

"I don't know the answer to anything," said Bracken, "at least to anything like that."

Cairn suddenly began to tremble violently and when Bracken put a paw on his back to comfort and still him, he found the fur was wet with cold sweat. The blood of the wounds on his face and back had congealed, though a trickle of fresh blood still flowed down from the wounds at his back haunches; fresh blood from the wound on his back had trickled between the two moles and hardened their fur together.

The evening was near enough for the air to have started to cool, but far enough for the sky still to be light.

"Have you the strength to move?" Bracken asked. "I could help you across the pastures to one of your tunnels and perhaps somemole could try to find Rose the Healer." It was a brave suggestion, for if pasture moles had found Bracken with Cairn in this condition they would have killed him first and asked questions afterward.

But Cairn shook his head and settled even farther into the thick grass, leaning his weight even more against Bracken's body.

"It's a good spot, this," he whispered. "You chose well.

One half of me in the wood where I mated, the other half in the pastures where I lived."

There was a very long silence between them, then Cairn said: "There's so much, Bracken, so much more to it than I thought. Well, I didn't think before now. But you'll have time to find it."

Bracken heard the first stirrings of the evening wind in the beech trees above them. A few autumn leaves drifted leisurely down, bouncing somewhere above and behind them against the branches through which they fell. There was the sudden flap of a wood pigeon somewhere along the wood's edge below them. High above there was the soaring trilling of a skylark, sometimes strong, sometimes distant, dropping and rising against the wind in the sky. The sun, which had not really shone all afternoon, was dropping below the great mauve bank of cloud that had hidden it and was now pale and a little watery because far off, over where it hung in the sky, there had been rain. For a few minutes its rays below the cloud were light and golden, but as it sank further and further, they began to redden, and the bank of cloud it had left behind changed from mauve to a magnificent purple that faded into deep pink at the edges.

Find what? wondered Bracken. What was it Cairn had seen that had the power to put peace into his body, despite his wounds and agony? Bracken felt lonely suddenly, even though he had never ever been so close to anymole as he was now to Cairn, flank to flank, haunch to haunch.

He wanted to help Cairn so much, but did not know what more he could do, not knowing that he had already done far more than most moles ever could. Cairn trembled violently again, and Bracken put his paw softly on his great hurt back, holding him still and warming him as best he could with his own body.

"Tell me about Rebecca again," whispered Cairn, so softly that Bracken had to bend his head to hear, so that it almost touched Cairn's. "Tell me everything that you know about her."

Then, at last, Bracken sensed what he must say to Cairn. He must give to Cairn something that lay in his heart and spirit, rather than his mind. He must weave a tale of truth for Cairn about a mole he didn't know but whose spirit, for one brief caressing moment, had touched his own. He must honor that memory and through it bring

the peace and comfort that Cairn yearned for and which
he could until then only have got from Rebecca and
Stonecrop, two moles who loved him. At that fearful moment, Bracken must make the effort to love Cairn.

"Rebecca is a giving mole," he began, "a wonderful
mole—" and his pawhold on Cairn grew softer yet infinitely stronger as he began to weave a picture of Rebecca,
finding his words from the woods that surely she, too,
must love; from the wildflowers that she danced by and
whose scent she knew; weaving words from the breeze
that had so often rustled his fur, as it must have rustled
hers.

"Rebecca is the wildflower that grows in spring, whose
leaves are the freshest green; she is as strong and graceful
as the tallest grass that grows down by the Marsh End.
Rebecca's laughter and dance are like the sun dappling
the wood's floor when the trees sway lightly in the summer
wind. Hers is the love of life itself, and love with her is as
big and strong as a great oak tree, with a thousand
branches for its feelings and a million trembling leaves for
its caresses. And because your heart was open to hers,
the love you found was far, far greater than the love each
of you gave. If Rebecca were here now, she would take
away your agony and desolation because she would be all
you need, and all you are. As you are, and have been, for
her . . ."

Bracken spoke to Cairn with the same voice of power
that had come from him once in the Stone clearing, on
Midsummer Night; the voice of an adult who is blessed
for a moment to see far beyond himself. A voice that
spoke words that drew on his own heart's deepest yearn-
ings and gave the answers to his heart's own despairs.
Expressing to Cairn the love that lies waiting in everymole.

"But Rebecca *is* here, Cairn, for she has touched your
heart forever with her love. There is nothing you
can know or feel that she has not already given you and
with which you are not already touched. Hers is the love
in the very earth and burrows in which we live and sleep;
hers is the sun that warms us in the morning; hers is the
bliss of sleep that brings us peace and sees our troubles
through. She is there in the pastures where you and Stonecrop ran, as she has always been and always will be; she
is behind us in the wood among the trees and flowers; she

is the love in which you made your life. She is here, Cairn, she is here with you now."

But Cairn did not hear Bracken's final words, for in the peace that Bracken brought him, his agonies were gone and his injuries mattered no more.

He died with Bracken's paw on his back, holding him close, the fur of their flanks mingling as one.

"She is there in the pastures," Bracken had said, and Cairn had run there to join her, to dance with his Rebecca again across the dew-touched grass, their paws warmed at last in a rising sun. They had run and danced with Stonecrop in the warmth of the sun, which grew lighter and brighter about them until all was pure and white; and all that remained was the pattern of their dance on the pastures by Duncton Wood, where their paws and bodies had caught the morning dew.

The sun set slowly behind the distant hills, casting reds and pinks into the darkening sky above, while the vales beneath Duncton Hill grew misty blue before they fell into darkness. As the last light of the sun faded from the trees that rose behind Bracken, he finally took his paw from Cairn's back and moved away from his body.

He felt a terrible desolation. It was as if Cairn had gone to the world of the living, leaving him in a place of the dead.

He crept away from Cairn's cold body back into the wood and across to the Stone. For a time, as darkness fell, he stayed there, his tail moving restlessly this way and that as the only sign of how unsettled and without a place he felt.

He wanted another mole to talk to him, as he had talked to Cairn. He wanted to be touched by another mole. He wanted thereby to find that last portion of the courage he would need to return to the Ancient System, as he knew he very soon must.

But not yet—not now; not with the bleak reality of Cairn's death and the lost warmth of those words of love he himself had spoken and which hung over him like a shroud.

But there *was* a mole who knew who he was and might, for a short time, give him the reminder of life that he needed—Rue. When the thought came to him in the darkness, he did not hesitate over its possibility for one moment, but ran busily out of the Stone clearing and diagonally down across the slopes, wondering if she would be surprised to see him again so soon.

Up on the pastures, Stonecrop resolutely continued the search for his brother he had started in the afternoon, calling Cairn's name softly into the wood. Cairn had been gone too long and there was a smell of danger in the air that worried Stonecrop. He had delayed, not out of fear for Duncton Wood, for Stonecrop held little fear for anything, but out of affection and reverence for his brother's privacy.

But finally he had gone into the wood and found the temporary burrow where he could tell his brother had been, and where there were signs of fighting. There was fear and terror in the air of the burrow that put a dreadful urgency into Stonecrop's search.

Indeed, the stench of fear was so unpleasant in the abandoned burrow that he could not stay in it and ran out onto the surface. He moved carefully about the area of trampled vegetation around the tunnel entrance trying to work out what had happened. He had no fear at all of Duncton moles discovering him there, for he was powerful and strong, bigger and more solid than Cairn. So he searched the little clearing without fear, working out where Cairn had gone.

He must have been injured, or he would have returned to the pastures. He would not have gone deeper into the woods, for fear of other Duncton moles. Stonecrop searched the area between the tunnel entrance and wood's edge and finally found a clue of disturbed and bloodied vegetation that suggested that Cairn had been that way, keeping to the cover by the wood's edge and heading uphill.

Stonecrop's progress was slow, for he stopped every few yards calling and shouting about, knowing that his brother might be so injured that he was unable to respond to his call. So it was that the evening was late, the night had come and Bracken was long gone, before Stonecrop finally found Cairn's body.

Even in death he recognized his brother's beloved scent, the scent of openness and freedom and of running through sparse earth and fresh grass. He was shocked by how terribly injured Cairn had been and dazed by the fact that he would never play and mock-fight and laugh with Cairn again. He looked out at the dark pastures so overcome by a sense of unreality that he almost expected Cairn to come running over to him and say "It's all a joke. *That's* not me." But it was, and at last he sank down into a crouch, too full of grief to move, or think, or do anything.

Much later a chill breeze made him shiver and he got up stiffly. He snouted at the long grass and fence that formed an immediate backdrop to where his brother lay, and past into the rustlings and swayings of the great beech trees above, now lost in the darkness, and anger began to overtake him at last. He hated the dark wood where so much evil seemed to happen and he now hated everymole within it. Nothing, not even the beguiling Rebecca mole, was worth his brother's life. His breath came more quickly, he seemed to grow even bigger in his anger, and had anything moved before him at that moment, he would certainly have attacked it. But nothing moved and only his brother was there, still and cold. And not his brother any more.

"You should have called for me," he whispered. "I would have come. I would always have come." Then he did what seemed a strange thing—he took one of his brother's front paws in his mouth and dragged the body out onto the pastures. It was no longer stiff; that stage had passed, and its limbs and head flopped in the grass as he dragged it along, moving with some difficulty as he was going backward. At last he seemed satisfied with the distance he had gone and let the paw drop, looking up in the direction of the treetops he could not see. "Better to be owl fodder on the pastures he loved than prey to some skulking scavenger in the grass," he was thinking.

He looked again at the injuries and thought bitterly, "He must have been killed in a mating fight, but by two moles by the look of it. We don't fight like that on the pastures— we don't need to."

With that he turned back down the hill, keeping very close to the edge of the wood and moving as fast as he could. He had one last job to do before he returned to the pasture tunnels.

He made his way back to Rebecca's temporary burrow and went straight down it again and crouched there very still. He breathed in the sickening odor left there by

Cairn's attackers—it was so unpleasant that it made him
a little dizzy—until the fear it had initially put into even
him was replaced by the anger he had felt up on top of
the hill. He breathed it in so that he would never forget
it, for he knew it was the scent of the Duncton mole who
had killed his brother.

"I'll know you for a Duncton mole if ever I meet you,"
Stonecrop whispered menacingly into the tunnels, "and I
won't forget the smell of this wood either. I hope neither
was the last odor that my brother smelled but I won't
mind if they are mine, so long as my talons first reach
the mole whose stench this is."

When he was quite sure he would know the smell
again, and that it would cause him anger and not fear,
he ran as quickly as he could out of the tunnel, across to
the wood's edge, and out into the fresh air of the pastures.

Rue laughed a little laugh of pleasure when she realized it was Bracken from the Ancient System hesitating
about outside her tunnels. She recognized that he was not
dangerous from his noisiness and diffidence about entering her tunnels and the fact that he had approached from
the direction of the pastures suggested who it might be.
She went up to one of the entrances and the sight and
scent of him confirmed it. So she laughed, because she
was more than glad to see him. But she wouldn't make it
easy, oh no! Not she!

In the three days since he had left, she had been ever
so busy. Scurrying about cleaning the place of dust and
old vegetation, and finding the best place for worms—
just as she had in the adjacent Hulver's tunnels. She sang
songs to herself that she had not sung since puphood and
which she had forgotten that she knew. She shored up
one of two tunnels, sealed all the entrances that lay toward Hulver's tunnels and started to extend the system
on the other side. She made her burrow in the tunnel that
Bracken had burrowed for her because it had such a
lovely quality of sound to it—just as he had said it would
have—and then she slept in it long and peacefully, like a
log. When she awoke it was a lovely misty September
dawn and as she poked her snout out of one of the entrances and looked about, and then came back into her
tunnels again, she asked herself, "What's it all for? What
do *I* want such a well-burrowed system for?"

She answered herself as quickly as a September mist clears on a sunny morning: "For mating. That's what!" She fancied having an autumn litter. She fancied hearing pup cries up here on the slopes where those old stick-in-the-muds down in Barrow Vale said no mole ever had litters. Too ascetic and dangerous, they said.

So when she heard Bracken snouting about outside soon afterward, she could not help laughing for the pleasure of it and with delight that her life seemed to be taking a turn for the better at last. So she started the pretense that she didn't want to see him by running up to an entrance where he was wondering whether or not to enter and saying "It's *my* system now, Bracken, so even though you did stay here once, you can't any more." She even pretended to snarl a bit and scratched the wall with her talons.

Bracken crouched out on the surface listening to these goings on in some puzzlement. He could *hear* what she said but it didn't match up with the nice way she smelled. He had been near plenty of hostile systems in his time and none had ever smelled quite so welcoming as these tunnels of Rue's.

Bracken hesitated at the entrance, not quite sure of himself, but not so dim as to think that he could really be hurt by Rue. "Hullo!" he said, in as friendly and open a way as he could muster when Rue reappeared. "I was just passing!"

At this Rue laughed out loud, scratched the side of the tunnel a bit more, then backed a bit down the tunnel snarling and growling in a delightfully pathetic way that invited Bracken to follow her down the tunnel, which he did.

"Um," he began, "what a lot you've done here!" This turned her snarls into giggles and he laughed, too, and soon they were playing such a delicious game of scratching, snarling and talking nonsense that Bracken began to enjoy and relax into it. He wasn't quite sure of Rue—he thought correctly that this was her system now and that he must not take liberties with it—but he knew that for the time being at least she wanted him to be there.

Suddenly Rue ran off, and Bracken heard her crunching away at a worm. He stayed where he was and soon she came back, bringing one for him. They ate in silent intimacy. When they looked at each other again, she was

a bit meeker and her eyes were shiny and her mouth
open. She crouched still and he came up to her, snouting
around her, diffidently at first but then more boldly, more
deeply. He liked the delicious moistness of her, he liked
her snouting at him, under him, over his soft parts that
grew harder, he liked her smiles as if she knew a delightful secret that she wasn't going to tell him, but much,
much better, that she was going to show him. He
scratched her with his paw, nuzzled hard into her, pressed
himself closer and closer to her, as she twittered and
champed and swung her back round to him and then
back-quartered into him and he into her.

"He's like a pup," she thought delightedly, because she
had never mated before with a mole who was barely an
adult. But when he finally understood what it was about,
and was on her and taking her, she was surprised at his
strength and laughed with pleasure at his delight in her
and at the shuddering way he relaxed into her.

Afterward, he didn't want to leave her at all and they
went into the main burrow and snuggled into a dreamy
sleep with hardly a word spoken between them. Sometime, when evening had come, she awoke to find him
deliciously snouting at her again and pushing a little
clumsily at her so that, half asleep, she swung back into
him and he into her, and with his last shudder in her,
he was snuggling back to her and asleep again. Oh, he
was so simple and young!

Sometime later in the night he again woke up, this
time properly, and lay with her fur warm on his, giving
him the illusion that his whole body was cocooned into
her. He thought of the things that had happened in the
last two days and simply could not believe, in the total
comfort in which he now lay, that they *had* happened.

When they finally awoke, it was dawn again and the
magic and amusement of the mating with Rue was quite
finished. He sensed that she wanted him gone, so that her
tunnels were hers alone once more, and so was any litter
that she might have. But he didn't mind. The pattern of
the last few days had fallen into place and as he left her
burrow and headed off down the tunnel he himself had
burrowed, he found he was at last looking forward to
going back to the Ancient System where he would enter
the Chamber of Dark Sound again, and explore the seventh tunnel if he could and whatever secrets lay at its
end.

WITH Cairn's death, the shadows that had been looming so long over Duncton Wood began, one by one, to fall. Spirits crept lower, danger seemed to lurk in every shadow, the chatter in Barrow Vale fell muted, and even the weather deteriorated into a succession of cold mists and rain that robbed the autumn wood of its color and turned the falling leaves into a dank mess.

Few moles traveled, fewer smiled. It was as if the wood was waiting for the fulfillment of a curse. While even those visits which might normally have been a source for cheer turned out, for some moles at least, to be the harbingers of doom.

Just such a visit was made to Mekkins in the Marsh End in mid-October by Rose the Healer, whose normally cheerful face had not been seen in Duncton for several months. When Mekkins saw her, he guessed why. She looked as if she had been ill, for her face was drawn and her flanks thin and only her eyes, warm and gentle, though touched now, it seemed to Mekkins, with a hint of sadness, had anything of the old Rose in them.

" 'Ello, 'ello," Mekkins greeted her, hiding his alarm and sounding as cheerful as he could. "And 'ow 'ave you been keeping?"

"A little tired, my dear, I'm afraid," she said.

They talked a little about the Marsh End, and two or three moles that Rose liked to keep an eye on, and then Rose came straight to the point.

"It's you I've come to see, Mekkins," she began.

"Why? Nothing wrong with me, is there?" he laughed.

"No! No! Not that I can see. You only ever needed me when you were a pup, my love, and that was from sheer overindulgence in worms, as I remember!" She paused, looked at him with a great deal of affection, and then fell serious again.

"No, it's not that. Mekkins, I have come to warn you of a danger in which the system is going to need your help and all your skills. I have seen it coming for many years from before Mandrake came, from even before you were born. I experienced something of the power of the darkness to come in July, when I was summoned to help a certain mole up in the Ancient System . . ."

"Bracken?" asked Mekkins quietly. "*Is* he alive?"

"You know something of this, then?" asked Rose.

"Well, I know something's going on like, I mean you can feel it in the bloody trees, can't you?"

Rose smiled bleakly at this. She had hesitated about coming to talk to Mekkins, for no healer likes to talk of his or her own fears, or of other moles they have treated. But now she was glad she had, for however cunning he was in his handling of the Marsh End, and however much he had enjoyed the power of being an elder, she sensed that he could be trusted.

"Bracken carries a secret, but I doubt very much if he knows what it is. Perhaps he will never know and has no need to. Don't ask me what it is because I don't know myself. But whatever it is, he carries with it a burden the size and pain of which neither of us will ever comprehend. When I went to help him, I felt the force of its darkness sapping me of strength. I have been ill because of it and I doubt that I will ever recover the strength I once had. There is such fear about, Mekkins, of a kind you perhaps do not know. May the Stone help you never to know it."

Rose shifted wearily in the burrow where they crouched and then asked: "How well do you know Rebecca?"

Mekkins told her, describing how they had got to know each other in the summer and how fond of her he had become. Rose could hear from his voice, and see in his eyes, that his affection for Rebecca ran far deeper than fondness. She saw with relief that she had done the right thing to talk to him.

"Much is going to depend on these two moles, Bracken and Rebecca, and neither of them may ever know it. Somehow you will have to help watch over them until they are strong enough to stand alone, though what you must do I cannot say, but I suspect it will need great courage, which I know you have. But, most of all, you must trust them both, hard though it may sometimes be. In a pup trust is the most natural of emotions; in an adult it may often be the hardest. Without it nothing can be healed."

They talked on a little, but Rose had said the most

important things she wanted to say and she was tired, so Mekkins saw her back toward her tunnels, as far as the pastures. When she had gone, he wasn't sure if he knew exactly what it was she had said, but he understood enough to know that he must watch over Rebecca and, if the opportunity ever arose, over Bracken as well. He would go to Rebecca now.

But he was too late. Try as he did in the next few days, Mekkins could get no nearer to Rebecca's tunnels than the henchmoles who guarded each exit. The most he got from one of them was that Rebecca was being kept in her system by order of Mandrake until she littered.

"So, she is going to 'ave a litter, is she?" he said, surprised.

"Oh, yeh," said the other. "There's no doubt of that. She's already big with it. But it's more than my life's worth to let you near her. Well, you know how it is with Mandrake's orders . . ."

Mekkins did, but he didn't like it. There was trouble in the air, and forboding, and it seemed the worse for hanging about the tunnels which had been so full of life and joy in the summer.

"Fair enough, mate," said Mekkins. "But if you get to see her, you tell her there's Mekkins has been by and that 'e's always down the Marsh End if she needs 'im. Right?"

"If I can, I will. I don't like it any more than you do, chum. Now, you get goin', Mekkins, because our orders are to keep everymole away, even elders."

Rebecca lay on her side, trembling in her burrow. She could feel her young moving inside her and sometimes now even see their sudden movements as some tiny limb or embryonic head pushed against the tight soft fur below her belly.

"Oh, my loves," she whispered to them. "Oh, my darlings, my wildflowers, may I have the strength to protect you."

Two henchmoles crouched by the entrance to her burrow, silent, morose and pitiless. They had been specially picked for the task by Rune, acting on Mandrake's orders.

They had come unexpectedly several days before, just

when Rebecca was beginning to rejoice in her litter to come and make the delightful preparations of nesting a new burrow that she had so long looked forward to.

She had tried to fight with them, angry on behalf of herself and her young, but one of the henchmoles had cuffed her so hard across the snout that she fell back into her burrow almost unconscious. She had not been allowed out of the tunnel since, and food was brought to her. She was angry, she demanded to see Mandrake, or even Rune; she begged to be allowed to see Sarah. But it was useless and no mole came to see her. Faced by the henchmoles' silence and ignorance of her, she was overtaken by a creeping loneliness, and with it a terrible fear for her young.

The most they would let her do, and only because the unpleasantness was too much for them, was to allow her to switch to another burrow while hers was cleaned out and new nesting material put there. "And this is doing you a favor, lass," said one of them unpleasantly, "because Rune said to keep you where you were. But I'm buggered if I'm going to crouch in the way of your stink."

For Rebecca, who was the cleanest and brightest of moles, and whose burrows had always celebrated with their scents and cheer the best of the life in the wood, this was a terrible thing.

As her young grew inside her, she grew more fearful and her eyes, once so bright with joy, took on a sad and haunted look. She whispered for her mother, Sarah, begging her to hear her and come and help. And sometimes her mind wandered from its present pain to that day when she had danced with Stonecrop and Cairn on the pastures in the grass. Oh, Cairn, please help me, she entreated, fearing he would never come. Not knowing he was dead.

She tried to maintain her strength, knowing that it would be needed when the birth came, but fear and the desperate hopelessness over whatever it was that was coming began to take it from her. Until, at last, all she could do was to pray, beseeching the Stone to hear her and send its help. Prayers that were mingled with the tears and desperate love she felt for her growing young.

She lost track of time and her sense of things seemed to change. Soon, the only thing that mattered, the only hope she felt she had, was that Mandrake might come to see her. Then, surely, she could make him see!

One day she woke out of her nightmare drowsiness to the sound of whispers in the tunnel outside and the sight of two black eyes looking coldly at her from the entrance. It was Rune.

"I hoped she would have got rid of them by now," he was saying to one of the henchmoles. "A pity. Give her less food and hit her when you feel like it. She's bred with a pasture mole and ought to be killed. But Mandrake . . ." Rune shrugged and turned away.

Rebecca got up heavily and tried to call to him, moving as quickly as she could to the entrance, and begging him. But he was gone, and one of the henchmoles hit her and she fell down. And one of her young moved inside her as she lay there and she wept until fear overtook her and she lay trembling in the terrible silence.

She began to have fantasies and nightmares. In one of them her burrow was falling on her and she dug desperately at the wall trying to escape . . . to be waked by the angry shouts of the henchmoles and the discovery that in her sleep she had started to burrow at the walls. In another, she was lost in a storm on a hill and there was a mole there, crouching, who surely would give her help and show her the way, but when she asked him and he turned to face her, it was Rune. Rune, laughing at her!

Until suddenly, at last, her pups began to be born. "Oh!" she cried, "oh, no, my loves. Not yet! Not yet! Not here . . .," and her eyes searched the burrow fearfully and she saw, her nightmare realized, that watching her was the massive form of Mandrake, his eyes cold and full of hate. Just watching her, as the pains drove into her, and she begged for her young not to be born.

"She's giving birth to her pasture pups," she heard a voice hiss in the shadows next to Mandrake. "Which no mole here wants to see alive," said Rune.

"Oh, no," she gasped. "Not here, my flowers, not here. Oh, Cairn, my—" but they started to come, eyes blind, snouts pink, wet with blood and water, floppy as green wet leaves, tiny mouths mewing and seeking her teats. For a moment she saw them all. Four, or was it five altogether? Perfect and alive, their bleatings pure with life in her cursed burrow, their mewings drowned by a

voice that urgently hissed "They must be killed, Mandrake. They must go," and she tried to gather them to
her, to protect them in the crescent of her soft belly and
teats, to thrust away the cold, black talons that came
among them, stabbing and stealing them, hurting them
and making them bleat in their blindness. She tried to
raise herself through her nightmare weakness and strike
out into the darkness of bloody talons before her. She
tried so hard to protect them as their bleats weakened
or turned into pathetic last squeals and their mouths
tried to suckle her teats even as they died in the darkness that lay between her and Mandrake. And in that
moment, when he was murderous and full of hate before her, when he could not see, he could not see, it
was not her love for him that he destroyed but her trust
in life itself. And evil smiled to see its work well done.

Until there was nothing but death and darkness before her, for the sounds of her litter were gone, and only
her voice remained whispering endlessly into the silence:
"Forgive me. Forgive me. Forgive me . . ."

And all of them were gone. Mandrake, Rune, the
two henchmoles who had guarded the burrow and all
the henchmoles around her entrances, leaving Rebecca
alone in her burrow, and free now to go where she
pleased.

19

IF Bracken's adulthood may be said to have started with his almost casual mating with Rue, his long march into maturity started somewhere in the depths of the Ancient System to which he returned after leaving her. There he began the first exploration of its center since its desertion, isolation, and final forgetting so many generations before.

But if he hoped, as he approached the Chamber of Dark Sound once more, that this time he would be quite unafraid, his hopes were shattered into a thousand fears when he got there. He could not see the owl face from the east side to which he came, but the chamber echoed with its dark menace even before he got there. Summoning all his courage, he made his way straight across the floor of the chamber toward where the owl face towered, his snout trembling with apprehension and his fur sensitive to the slightest danger.

Finally he came near enough once more to see the dark glint of the flint parts of the face, and to look into the eye cavities of the mole skeleton that crouched at the entrance of the tunnel beneath.

And what relief! The skull and skeleton seemed suddenly no more than the white bones they were, and Bracken saw that they could do him no harm. He had lived into death with Cairn and now, looking at this long-dead creature, he could only feel sorrow for its passing and wonder what strange story lay behind its presence here. He was afraid, certainly, but no longer of a mere skeleton.

Shiny walls of flint rose on either side of it, gray flint rather than black, and stepping carefully past the skull, he passed through the entrance into the seventh tunnel.

It was simple and uncarved and not as big as other ancient tunnels, and it ran only a short way before it cut into a tunnel that curved away to the right and left.

He traveled carefully round this tunnel, which was roughly circular, as rapidly as he could, disturbing the chalk dust that had settled there through the ages and which flurried behind him in his haste. Its walls were of hard chalk subsoil, roughly burrowed, and it was clearly

231

no more than a passageway. It took a long time to do the
full circuit, but when he had, he had a very much clearer
idea of what he must do.

In addition to the entrance he had joined it by, the
circular tunnel had a total of eight different entrances
leading off it. Of these, seven were flint-lined and led on
toward the center of the circle. From each came a curious
murmuring, confusing rather than fearful, and not unlike
the distant chatter of male moles—sometimes one sound
rose a little above the rest, at others there was a momentary lull.

The eighth entrance was simply a tunnel leading away
from the circle on the far side where he had first entered.
Here and there on the outer edge of the circle there was a
root, half buried, sliding down the wall from above, which
suggested that his location was in that treeless circle that
surrounded the outer edge of the Stone clearing, adjacent
to the trees that formed it, which meant that he still had
the roots of the massive beeches that formed the clearing
itself to pass through.

It took him three hours or so to make the full circuit,
and since, at this depth, there was no food supply at all
and he was hungry and tired, he returned to the Chamber
of Dark Sound and cut across it to the eastern entrance,
along which he knew he would have no trouble finding
food.

He returned after a good sleep, carefully bringing with
him some worms, which he stored in a cache in the circular tunnel; and then he went into the nearest of the
flint-lined entrances toward the murmur of sound, anxious
to get on with what he hoped was the final exploration
into the heart of the Ancient System.

The tunnel was small and crudely burrowed into the
subsoil, with a packed floor, rough walls and a simple
rounding for the roof. After a short way, it split into two
and, taking the right-hand fork, Bracken found that it almost immediately split into two again. Worse, the tunnel began to curve confusingly and then cut across other
tunnels, and split yet more times. To add to this spatial
confusion, the deeper he got, the louder the stressed murmuring he had just heard so ominously in the Chamber
of Dark Sound became, while the echoes of his pawsteps
kept coming back to him, running in from all directions,
tripping over themselves in their eagerness to confuse

him, disappearing off behind him. Until he stopped, lost, and with no idea of whether he was going forward or backward, away from the center of the system or toward it.

It took him two long hours to find his way back again, and then only with the greatest skill and patience as he marked each turn and thought carefully back to the twists and turns he could remember.

It was while he was in the worrying process of doing this, crouching and thinking what to do next and making no noise himself, that he began to suspect what the vague murmurings he had first heard were, or seemed to be. They were muffled and soft, but there was enough edge and harshness to the louder of them for him to think that they must be the sound of the roots of the beech trees that protected the buried part of the Stone. He was getting closer.

When he finally got back to the safety of the circular tunnel and had eaten, he was sufficiently stirred by the realization of how near he was to want to go back quickly and try again.

What followed took him not minutes or hours but five days, and is now regarded as one of the greatest feats of tunnel analysis by any single mole. For the tunnel of echoes into which Bracken had entered, and in which he might easily have been lost and never heard of again, had been deliberately designed by the ancient moles to protect the Stone from just such interlopers as Bracken. Once, it had been protected by living moles as well, and he certainly would not have gotten as far as even the Chamber of Dark Sound. But the original designers of the system had foreseen that some catastrophe might one day overtake it, as it clearly had, and so had provided the Stone with the extra protection of the tunnels whose challenge Bracken now faced.

His approach was careful and methodical, and it took a very long time. He began by marking each split or subsidiary tunnel he came to in such a way that only one route that he took was the "main" one. When it circled back on itself or led to a dead end, he remarked it, thus trying one permutation after another. He progressed slowly at first, but then found that at some points in the tunnels the sound of the roots was louder, perhaps nearer, and he rerouted his chief route in the direction of the sound. Because of the subtlety of the echoes, this often led him round, back to a way he had come, or again to dead ends. But slowly the route he developed did seem to go deeper into the circle and the roots' sounds grew louder yet again, but just when it seemed to him that he was about to get there—wherever *there* was—they only led him nowhere.

But then he began to notice a new element in the tunnels that went with the sound—tunnel vibrations. As the sound began to define itself more clearly into stresses and creaks, long moans and pullings, so, too, matching vibrations came down the tunnel and he felt them with his paws: shakings, jolts and shudderings.

His excitement grew. As the sound got louder, the tunnel grew straighter until, pressing rapidly on and with no side turnings to worry about, he was suddenly out of it at last, and had successfully passed through the labyrinth of echoes into a place whose sights and shuddering sounds were of such enormity that he crouched there dumbfounded.

He was among the living roots of one of the gigantic beeches that protected the Stone, and they moved continually in response to the eternal swayings and stressings of the wind-touched tree whose trunk and branches they fed and supported. From a darkness high above him they plunged down through the soil, massive and vibrant, twisting down through the chalky floor on which he crouched. They stretched beyond him in a tangle of verticals and angles, some massive and thick, others fine and thin: some entwined about each other, some vibrating tautly. Each made some kind of noise, each noise was different. The whole made a sound that was distorted and tangled, like a thicket of dry brambles blown by the wind. There was no clear path ahead, for the roots snaked down this way and that, and their continuous movement gave him the impression that if there was a route, it was always changing.

To add to his confusion and sense of there being no direction ahead, there were no walls to the chamber into which he had entered. The roots not only stretched in a terrifying tangle into the distance ahead of him, but to either side as well.

He noticed that imprisoned among some of the tight vertical tangle of the roots were great lumps of hard soil or rock, which seemed either to have fallen from the ceiling or been lifted bodily from the floor, imprisoned in a cage of living, moving bars. Sometimes dust or small fragments fell from them as a result of the stress they were under. He saw plunging from ceiling to floor one root which seemed to pull upward periodically and then sink back. With each upward pull, a long boulder of chalk rose higher and higher from where the root left the ground until, before Bracken's startled eyes, the fragment, which was many times bigger than himself, pulled out of the ground and toppled with a crash of dust and fragments onto the floor of the chamber, breaking one of the thinner roots, which twanged loudly into the darkness above as it did so.

In some places the roots seemed to have forced themselves through the floor so powerfully that great fissures and crevices radiated dangerously from them, and when the roots moved dust and sound seemed to fly up from the jagged depths beneath.

Bracken looked on this terrifying scene for a very long time before turning his back on it and returning through the circuitous, echoing tunnels whose labyrinths absorbed the rootsound behind him, back to the outer circular tunnel. He was not yet ready to press on among the roots themselves.

It was at this point that Bracken showed again his special skill and foresight as an explorer. Some instinct, perhaps an awe of the venerable place he was in, told him that he must not leave the route he had found so clearly marked as it now was. And so, after more rest and food, he set himself to memorize it, slowly removing each marking the further his memory took him toward the roots.

Until at last he could run the whole route almost by instinct, navigating the labyrinths all the way to the Chamber of Roots without any need of markers. Only then was he even prepared to press on, but even then he did not do so. Instead, he began his exploration of another of the entrances, progressing up it the same way, though finding his task much easier now that he had done the same thing already.

In this way Bracken taught himself to find his way among three of the ways into the center and in doing so discovered, or rather deduced, that the labyrinth of echoes was interconnected right round the perimeter of the Stone, while the Chamber of Roots was really one big chamber, with no walls but those formed by roots. Though what lay beyond them he did not yet know and was a mystery he would need great courage and fortune to solve.

Yet, when the hour came to set off among the roots themselves, his attempt to pass through was a failure, and a curious one. It was not that he was afraid of the roots exactly, though their massive movement and confusing noise was enough to terrify anymole; nor was it that it would not have been possible to find his way into them in much the same way as he had through the labyrinth of echoes. It was subtler than that.

In his first attempt, for example, he got no farther than perhaps ten moleyards before his mind began to wander and he began to wonder *why* he was there and what the point was. He was out of the Chamber of Roots almost before he knew what he was doing, and only two or three hours later wondered why he had not gone on.

Another time he made a more determined effort and indeed got farther into a complex of roots from which he could no longer see the entrance to the chamber. But then the roots got denser and more sinewy, even the marks he made just behind him on the ground seemed to start disappearing, and he got the feeling that he was being watched from somewhere to his left. By mole? By beast? He felt panic coming over him and, try as he might to control it, he could not—though it cleared the moment he turned round and started back, stumbling quickly through the noise and heaving roots, afraid for a time that he would not find the way out again.

He tried once more, on a day that must have been calm on the surface, for the roots were whispering quietly, and he did quite well until he suddenly felt a pleasant tiredness coming over him and the roots ahead seemed to open out invitingly for him to lie down. . . . He had to shake himself to keep awake, only realizing when he did so that what lay ahead of him was a great crevice, wide and deep, and delving down to a rugged darkness from which slidings and hissings of thin roots seemed to come. Once more he turned back.

Each time he got back to the entrance of the chamber, however, these curious feelings immediately cleared and, looking back at the roots, they seemed their normal, massive, threatening selves, but no more than that.

Finally, he decided to take a break—perhaps, after all, the time had come to return to the surface, for he had been involved in this exploration for many days. He had lost his sense of timing, thinking that perhaps only fifteen or twenty days had passed since he had left Rue, yet when he finally reached the surface he was surprised to find it was chilly, even though it was afternoon. The wood was filled with the chill light of the end of October, when most of the leaves have gone and the wind stirs the remainder irritably.

Then he knew that he must have been gone for many moleweeks and wondered what it was about the Ancient System that made a mole seem to lose his sense of time.

Bracken shivered at the cold and felt in need of company. Well, he could visit Rue; she was always glad to see him—and always glad to see him go! He laughed a little as he bustled off down the slopes to see her, thinking that he was getting to know her ways, and how pleasant it was to feel the fresh air in his fur and smell the clear scents of the wood again.

He would laugh even more when he got there, and learn something about a kind of mole he had never had anything to do with—young pups. For Rue had littered just a few days before and, for the time being at least, would be delighted to see Bracken again, provided he didn't come into her birth-burrow uninvited. He could fetch a few worms now and again, and keep away intruders.

20

A cold wind blew on the wood's surface above Rebecca's burrows where the snout of a brave mole quivered in the shadow of a root. He was the henchmole who had finally refused to let Mekkins enter Rebecca's tunnels but who had promised to deliver his message and, shocked by what had happened though still fearful for his own safety, he had crept back in the depth of the night to see if there was anything he could to—ostensibly to help Rebecca but in truth to rid himself of the uneasiness he felt at being a party, however coerced, to what had happened.

He crept down the deserted tunnels to her burrow, ready to retreat at the slightest danger. He was a tough mole, a henchmole of experience, an aggressive westsider, but what he saw when he got there made him tremble with a fear greater than any he had ever felt before a fight, or after a close-won victory.

Rebecca lay still as death on the far side of the burrow. The bodies of her five young lay about the burrow, tangled up with nesting material, scattered like leaves. He picked his way with a beating heart among them and it was only when he was close up to her and he heard the soft moaning of her breathing, distant as a falling pulse, that he was sure that she was still alive.

What use his message now? For a moment he wanted none of it, telling himself "I don't know what the hell this has to do with me. Stone knows what I'm doing here—they'll kill me if they find out. What a bloody mess this is!"

Then he cuffed her lightly with his paw and said gruffly, "Here you—you wake up. Got to get you out of here quick. Wake up! Come on, lass . . ."

Rebecca stirred and was then awake instantly. She started to scream and he cuffed her again, none too softly.

"I'm not going to hurt you," he said, "but we'll both cop it if they find me here, so shut up!" She fell silent, looking at him fearfully.

"I know a mole who can help you," he said more

gently. "Name of Mekkins. He tried to see you before
. . . before this bloody thing happened."

Rebecca did not respond.

"Come on, love," he said suddenly, gruffly gentle, "you
can't stay here. Got to get you away . . ." He quickly
pulled her to her paws and, talking desperately fast so
that her attention would not wander to the dead litter
about her, he hurried her out of the burrow, down the
tunnel, and up to the entrance. But when she got into the
night air, she seemed to come round to understanding
where she was and what had happened. She started to
shiver violently and sob out words, so shaken by her distress that it was a long time before he could make out
what she wanted. "I c–c–can't leave them there," she
seemed to be saying. "I c–c–can't."

He was impatient with this, very conscious that the
noise she was making might easily attract the attention
of a mole like Rune, prone to skulk about at night, or
even an owl. But hard though he tried, she would not
leave. At last he said brutally, "Right! You're on your
own, then! I'm off . . ." and off he went.

But not far. His heart wouldn't let him. Instead, he
crouched in the protective shadow of the root he had
first hidden by and watched over her, thinking that she
would soon come to her senses. But what he then witnessed was the ancient and instinctive ritual of a bereft
mother.

She turned back down into the tunnel and after a long
wait, in which he almost decided to leave her to her fate,
she came back out into the night. She was carrying one of
her dead young by the scruff of the neck, just as a
mother carries a squalling pup. This one hung down limp
and dead, and she laid it on the surface by the tunnel
entrance. Then, one by one, she brought out the other
four and laid them where the wind might touch them and
the owls come and take them.

Then he watched as she crouched in the shadows by
them, whispering words of love and sorrow, chanting the
ancient songs of the bereft, whose words and sounds of
loss have no need of being set down or learned, for they
are written in the depths of every soul.

Then she crouched down with them to wait for the
owls to come. But *he* was not going to wait for that and
ran back over to her and said "Come on, Rebecca, come

on, love. There's nothing more you can do. There's nothing left to do."

He became angry again and said: "If you don't bloody well come now, then I really will push off. I'm only doing this for Mekkins. Come *on!*" And, more or less dragged along by him, she went with him, shaking and sobbing to leave all she had left of her litter behind in the night, tiny and pathetic on the cold surface of the wood.

No record has been kept of how this unnamed henchmole succeeded in leading Rebecca down to the Marsh End and how he protected her from the marshenders until Mekkins was found. But it is in such forgotten moles as he, as well as in those whose names are recorded in the books of Uffington, that the actions of truth and love fulfill themselves. So, nameless though he is, let him be remembered.

Mekkins took one look at Rebecca, out of whom all spirit of life had gone, and knew without being told what had happened, and what to do.

Half pushing, half carrying and constantly urging her, he took her toward the east side of the Marsh End, where the soil is dank and the vegetation heavy; a place in the wood where no mole goes and fallen wood rots unnoticed.

"Where are you taking me?" she whispered hopelessly, more than once.

"Somewhere Mandrake and Rune will never find you, and where you'll have time to find your strength again."

"I don't want to be alone," she sobbed, "not here in this terrible place."

"It's all right, Rebecca," he soothed her, "you won't be. There's a mole there will help you. She's known trouble herself and will know what to do."

But Rebecca became afraid again and refused for a while to go on.

"Look, my love," said Mekkins, desolate to see Rebecca so changed. "There's nowhere else I can take you. Mandrake and Rune will be after you—they'll want you killed. I *know* them. It's a miracle you're still alive as it is, though perhaps, at the time, that's something even Mandrake couldn't do. Not to you he couldn't."

At this second mention of his name Rebecca sobbed again and then fell into a torpor of desolation. But when Mekkins urged her on, she agreed, as if everything was hopeless and even resistance was futile. Mekkins saw then that she wanted to die.

They came at last to a far corner of the wood which edged the marsh and where the wind carried into the wood's depths the eerie call of marsh birds unknown to mole—snipe, curlew and clamorous red-shank—telling of the wet desolation all moles fear. It was a damp and dismal place where Mekkins finally stopped, by a dank and diseased-looking entrance, hung over with rotting wood. He peered into it and was about to call down, when an aged, frightened voice whispered out of its dead depths: "Disease! There is disease here! Disease and death!"

Rebecca shrank back, pleading with Mekkins to take her away, but he put a paw on hers and said, "Don't worry. It's not as bad as it sounds. She only says things like that to keep others away."

He turned back to the entrance. " 'Ere, Curlew! Don't be so daft! It's Mekkins. . . . I've got a friend with me for you to meet."

"I have no friends here," the voice said again, "only the darkness of disease, only the dankness of the earth."

Mekkins shrugged his shoulders and, with an encouraging pat on Rebecca's shoulder, pushed her down the burrow ahead of him.

The tunnel was both dank *and* dark and it was a long time before she could make out clearly the appearance of the old female who, muttering and cursing, retreated before them. "Trouble is," whispered Mekkins, "she lives alone so much that she takes a while to get used to strangers. And she likes to put on a bit of an act at first. But she's got a heart of gold and if she takes to you, she'll see you right as rain."

At last Rebecca could see her clearly and had she been anything less than near collapse, she might well have run away there and then.

Curlew was small and wasted, her whole body twisted subtly out of true by some past disease or abnormality; she had no fur on much of her face and what there was on her thin flanks was sparse and gray. Her front paws were almost translucent with weakness.

But her eyes! It was if they had, temporarily, taken refuge in the wrong body, for they were bright and warm with kindness and compassion, beautiful with life, and

Rebecca realized that the frightened voice that had come up to them really had been an act.

The moment Curlew saw Rebecca clearly, she came forward, though a little diffidently, and said "My dear!" in a voice of such compassion that Rebecca knew that she, too, had suffered in some terrible way and that she understood. Then Rebecca settled down, weary beyond words but feeling safer than she had for a very long time. She crouched down in the corner of Curlew's little burrow, with its wet walls and miserable air, settled her snout between her paws, and simply closed her eyes.

"This mole is Rebecca from Barrow Vale," said Mekkins. "And she needs help and protection. That's why I've brought her here, Curlew, 'cos I reckon you'll know how to get a bit of life back into her."

Rebecca felt a gentle paw caressing her face and heard a gentler voice saying, as if from a great distance, "It's all right, my dear, you're safe now, quite safe." And then she fell asleep.

When Mekkins told Curlew the story of what had happened, she sighed to hear it, speaking of "the wickedness of it" and the "dark shadows that curse Duncton," looking at the sleeping Rebecca, the tears in kind eyes running down her bald face.

She too had wanted a litter, but the disease that struck her down in her first summer so long before had forever deprived her of the chance. No male would take her and the story in the Marsh End for a long time was that she went simple as a result and was taken by an owl.

But this was not so—as Mekkins, in one of his explorations of the perimeter of the Marsh End when he was a youngster, found out. He came across her little system, burrowed in a ramshackle way in the soft wet soil, and for a long time got no response but "There's disease here" from her. Until, bit by bit, he cajoled his way into her tunnels and there found Curlew, who had had no contact with anymole for many years, preferring to hide her disfigurement in the isolated place she chose to live. Unlike other moles who had seen her in the past, he showed no fear of her and treated her as he would any other mole. Then, over the years, he had seen her change, losing some of her shyness and finding more and more peace in her life and teaching him that a mole may live alone for many years and learn a great deal of wisdom and find much love in the small things about its tunnels.

She refused to leave her tunnels because, as she explained, this was probably the only place in the system where her weak paws could manage to burrow and repair tunnels, and then only untidily. But yes, she had known sadness, and had always wanted young of her own, though now she knew she could never have them. It was knowing this that made Mekkins bring Rebecca here, for surely Curlew would take care of her as if she were a pup of her own.

But in the next few days, Rebecca's condition got steadily worse. She grew weaker and more and more unresponsive, hardly bothering to eat the food that Mekkins and Curlew brought her. The light had gone out of her eyes and the gloss from her fur, which now hung about her like dead ivy.

On the fourth night she was there, Curlew went to wake up Mekkins, prodding him urgently and asking him to come.

"She's dying, Mekkins, and there's not much anymole can do. Her teats are hard with unsuckled milk and they're swollen and are paining her in her troubled sleep. I think we may be too late to save her."

Mekkins looked at Rebecca, his snout low with grief and desolation, his eyes restless with the need to do something for her. "Rebecca," he whispered to her. "Rebecca. It's Mekkins! You're safe now. Listen, Rebecca!"

She stirred and turned a little to him, her forehead furrowed and her eyes hauntingly lost. "Listen to what?" she whispered. "They've all gone. I heard the last of their cries. He's taken them."

"But there's so much, Rebecca, so much. The flowers you love, the ones you showed me in the summer, they'll come again. And spring, that'll come, you'll see . . ." But Mekkins couldn't go on. He could find no words to say because he could not think of a reason why she should want to live. If only Rose were here, he thought, she'd know what to say.

Looking at her there, he felt himself almost absurdly strong and healthy, realizing what a gift it was, almost for the first time. But he would have given it all to see Rebecca look up at him with the laugh and dance in her eyes that he remembered and loved so well.

He left her and Curlew and went grimly up to the
tunnel entrance and stayed there looking into the night.
From somewhere off in the marshes came the haunting
single call of a solitary snipe. Otherwise the wood
seemed to be settling into the darkness of winter.

Yet, as he crouched there, upset and frustrated, from
the light-filled recesses of his soul, where the cherished
things of the heart lie still and waiting, there came a
memory of the Stone. Not as he had last seen it, with the
blood of Hulver and Bindle staining its shadow, but as he
had first seen it so long ago when he was little more than
a pup and had been led up Duncton Hill on the long
trek, when there was no shame in celebrating Midsummer.

It had stood massive, awe-inspiring and, somehow,
safe, and he had looked up at it, as the elders did their
chanting, and all had faded away from his mind but its
size and majesty, and his sense that he was part of it.
In the many moleyears since, he had only ever thought
of the Stone as a distant thing, for the sense of grace that
flowed into him then was overshadowed by the fighting
and living, and the mating, that was the reality of Duncton in his time.

But now the grace returned, distant and uncertain, but
there all the same. He turned back down into the tunnels
and went straight to Curlew.

"How long can she live?" he asked her.

"I don't know," she faltered. "There are herbs I know,
healing charms I heard my mother say. But she may cling
on for a few more days. . . ."

"She must," he said urgently, "she must. For a few days
you must make her. I have to go, but I will be back."

"Where to?" asked Curlew, suddenly afraid to be left
alone, with Rebecca now so certain to die.

"I'm going to the Stone, Curlew, to ask for its 'elp. I
don't know nothing about praying but I'm bloody well
going to try."

It took him a full night and day of travel to reach the
massive, silent Stone. Mekkins had never prayed in his
life before and so, lacking any preconceived idea of how
a mole should pray, he spoke to it as he would to anymole. "She's a good mole, better than anymole I know, so

why's she dying? What's the use in it? Look . . . I'll do anything I can do to 'elp her out . . ."

"Look 'ere," tried Mekkins again, his paws now touching the base of the Stone, "there can't be any sense in lettin' her die now, can there? I've seen her dance in the sun and say her rhymes and all sorts of things and you didn't make her learn to do those things so she should die like she is. You made her so that other moles could understand 'ow to live properly in this forsaken bloody system of ours."

But still the Stone stood silent, its cold height rising above and beyond Mekkins' vision to the nearly leafless branches of beech trees high above, which made an interlocking craze of silhouettes against the bleak white clouds of the October dusk.

He crouched by the Stone for a long time saying nothing. He had nothing to say. He looked around at the trees, then at his own strong paws, and then out across the lower wood in the direction of Marsh End. Then he got angry and started shouting at the Stone, almost attacking it in his anger: "What the 'ell are you anyway?" he shouted. "I come all the way 'ere to ask for your help and I ain't never asked for your 'elp before and all you do is nothing at all. Just stand there silent. Silent as the stone you are. You know what? You're nothing, that's what you are, nothing!"

Wild anger flowed through Mekkins, feelings of a power and rage he had never felt before. They were the more powerful for the sense he felt of the Stone's betrayal of the feeling of grace and hope that had inspired him to come so far in the first place. He turned away from the Stone and half hit, half collapsed on the ground, his movements as restless as the roots that ran this way and that around the Stone and formed the dark shadows at its base.

He half sobbed, half shouted in his rage until, slowly, the hatred for what was happening to Rebecca and his anger at the Stone began to fade into weariness and helplessness, so that even his strong shoulders and sturdy body could not stop wilting and sagging into a posture of defeat. He turned back to the Stone, his snout low and his anger quite gone.

" 'Elp her," he whispered finally to the Stone. " 'Elp her for my sake," he said simply.

Mekkins finally left the Stone as dawn was rising the next morning. His spirits were too low for him to want to face the chatter of westside or Barrow Vale, so he turned east, taking a route by the central slopes and contouring his way round, and slowly down toward tunnels that would eventually lead to the Marsh End.

His route took him by Hulver's old system and it was as he passed near it that he felt the faintest of vibrations and smelled the faintest of cheerful scents. He stopped and snouted about, glad to know there was life here again and then, finding an entrance, he went down into it, careful to make plenty of noise so as not to take anymole by surprise.

Anymole? Moles more like! The place was alive with the sound of pups, bleating and mewing and stirring, and the sound of a mother shushing them still.

Pups on the slopes! It was the first time he had ever heard of such a thing and if there was one thing in the world to raise his spirits a little at that moment, it was their sound.

There was a scurrying and muttering somewhere in the tunnels ahead where the litter was. Then a mole came running aggressively down the tunnel at him, stopping ready with her talons raised.

"It's all right," he said gently, "I'm not here for harm, just to pass the time of day like. I'm Mekkins the elder, from the Marsh End."

"What are you doing here?" asked Rue.

"I've been to the Stone."

"Oh!" She sounded surprised and came closer and snouted at him.

"Sounds like you got yourself a litter," said Mekkins cheerfully. "Can I look?"

She nodded. She knew of Mekkins. He was all right, played fair, they said.

"Got a worm or two to spare?" asked Mekkins, pressing his luck.

"You've got a nerve," said Rue. "But as it happens I have."

She turned round and ran on before him, back to her litter, and he followed very slowly, knowing how sensitive mothers can be.

Her burrow was a joy to look into. There she was, curled up with four pups suckling at her teats, bleating occasionally when they lost their grip, wrestling with each other for the best place, and milk spattering their pink snouts and pale young whiskers. Their eyes were blind and their paws as floppy as wet grass. Rue twittered and whiffled at them, guiding their mouths to her nipples and cooing love sounds at their feeble antics. One of the pups did a mewing cartwheel backward and Rue laughed fondly, saying "Come on, my sweet," pulling him back. It was only as she lifted him up to her nipples that Mekkins saw that there was a fifth pup there, smaller than the rest, lost among the melée of the paws and questing snouts. He was feeble and lacked the vigor of the others, seeming unable even to suck.

"The runt," said Rue matter-of-factly. "I've tried to make him feed but he only manages when the rest take a break and that isn't often. He's growing weaker by the hour. There's always a weak one in a litter of five. Of course, he's a male—they're always the ones."

But Mekkins wasn't listening. He was thinking, his mind was racing, and an idea was forming in his mind swifter than lightning. An idea so ridiculous that he might make it work.

He took a tentative step into the burrow, at which Rue immediately tensed. "There's a female I know," he said at last, "who lost her litter. She's ill from want of suck. That's why I went to the Stone—to ask it to help her." He looked meaningfully at the little feeble pup being climbed all over by the other four. Its mews were too weak for him to hear them above their noise, but he could see its mouth desperately forming the sounds.

Rue looked at him. "What you're saying is that he might survive with her, whereas he definitely won't with me. You may be right and you may be wrong." Slowly Rue relaxed.

She went back to tending the more vigorous four and somehow shifted a bit so the fifth fell away and got lost by itself in the nesting material between Rue and Mekkins. Slowly, with great care, he eased himself toward the little thing. Rue studiously ignored them both.

Then Mekkins gently bent down to the tiny pup, took it up in his mouth by the scruff of the neck, and lifted it off the ground. It swung loose from his mouth, eyes blind and paws waving weakly. Mekkins hesitated for only a moment before turning to the entrance and going back

into the tunnel and then, as fast as he could go, down to
its entrance. Rue did not even look up after he had gone.
"My sweet things," she whispered to the healthy four,
"my loves."

As Mekkins was about to exit on the surface, he heard
sounds behind him and thinking that Rue had, after all,
changed her mind, turned round to face her and found
himself looking into the face of a young adult male, with
gray fur and wary eyes. The pup hung in the air between
them.

"Take care of him," said the young male. His voice
was strong but strangely haunting, and it made Mekkins
stop quite still, for surely he had heard it before. Before
high summer he had heard it . . . coming out of the dark
on Midsummer Night, coming from the Stone clearing.
The voice of Bracken. Feeling suddenly that he and the
system were in the grip of forces whose power and destiny
were beyond imagining, the pup in his mouth stirred
feebly and Mekkins was gone, up into the light of early
morning, racing down the slopes, running with the little
pup swinging helplessly in front of him, as he ran desperately, without pause, to the distant isolated place where
Rebecca lay dying.

Never had the smell of decaying wood and rotting leaf
mold—the smell of the most forsaken part of Duncton
Wood—felt so good to Mekkins. It meant that he was
back.

Down then into Curlew's dark tunnels, along to her
burrow, desperate eyes at its entrance looking to see if
Rebecca . . . if Rebecca was . . . , and a gasp from
Curlew that had a thousand different feelings in it.

Mekkins placed the pup at Rebecca's belly, nudging
it to her hard and swollen nipples, pushing it forward
almost clumsily in his desperation to see it take suck.
And when it did not, whispering to Rebecca, whose eyes
were closed and whose breathing was shallow, "Rebecca!
Rebecca! I've brought you a pup!"

"They've all gone," she moaned in a dead voice. "All
gone."

"He's here. Look at him. *Look* at him," whispered
Mekkins gently, his eyes looking hopelessly to Curlew as
the pup, too feeble to suck on its own, fell back to the

shadows of her belly, its own tiny belly hurrying in and out, in and out, as if its life were being gasped away.

"Just look at him, my dear," said Curlew, her snout caressing Rebecca's face. "Just try."

But Rebecca was not even interested, and try as they did, the pup could not seem to suck at her nipples, though it mewed softly and its mouth opened to try.

"Rebecca," said Mekkins, again desperately, "please listen, my love. Try to help him. Try to give him your love. He needs you."

But still she only stirred slightly and though she looked round at the pup for a moment, seemed to have no interest.

Mekkins sought for something to say, just as he had searched for something to say at the Stone. His eyes were wild, his mind distraught, and he searched desperately about until, suddenly, the words of Bracken came to him again. "Take care of him," he had said and he saw an image of Bracken's face, looking at him so deeply.

Mekkins turned back to Rebecca once more, put his snout to her ear, and said urgently: "You must try. You must try. The pup is Bracken's young. He's *Bracken's* pup!"

What mole can say how soon a pup knows that its mother is gone? However it is, and will always be, the pup suddenly bleated out its sense of eternal loss. Not the quiet mewing that had been too soft to hear in Rue's burrow, nor the feeble bleats he had made while trying to reach Rebecca's teats. But the loud cry into the wilderness of loss, so that as Mekkins said "He's Bracken's pup" Rebecca seemed to hear the pup's cry as if it was her own.

Her snout slowly turned round and down to the bleating thing, ran gently over its body, sniffled at its tiny paws; her tongue ran softly over its dry snout and she curled the protection of her body around it and guided it to one of her teats. The pup fell away, but she tried again. And again. Beginning to whisper words of encouragement as soft as its gentle mews, nudging it to her, pushing her teat to its mouth, moistening her own teat with her tongue to help, giving it her love. Until at last, before the breathless gaze of Curlew and Mekkins, the pup at last began to suckle, the noise of it filling the

burrow like the sound of soft spring rain falling among
dry grass.

While behind them, unnoticed in the shadows of the
tunnel outside the burrow, Bracken crept silently away.
He had used all his skills to follow Mekkins' desperate
race to Curlew's burrow so that he might watch over
the safety of his son. Had danger loomed, had a badger
come by, had Mandrake himself come like a black cloud
out of the night, Bracken would surely have given fight,
so that his son, carried on by Mekkins, might be safe.

So, unnoticed, he had watched over the safety of his
son. He had crept into the tunnel after Mekkins and
watched unobserved, only realizing, because she was so
changed, that it was Rebecca who was lying there when
Mekkins said her name. He watched as the pup faltered
and weakened, willing him to try again. Until the pup
had bleated his heart out in one last cry and Rebecca
had at last turned her face gently to him and, unknowingly, taken his son for her own.

Only then did Bracken creep softly away. Out again
onto the surface of this dark and wet part of the wood,
back up south to the hill and toward the Ancient System, to which he seemed forever enchained.

21

THEY called the pup Comfrey, after the healing herb that grew by the wood's edge near Curlew's tunnels and which, she said, had kept Rebecca alive in the two days Mekkins was away at the Stone.

For many long days they worried over him, all three nurturing and cherishing life into him until he was able to suckle of his own accord, and his sounds were those of the eagerness of a growing mole rather than the desperation of a dying one.

But though Rebecca tended to him, whispering her love to him, it still seemed to Mekkins that some light in her had gone out and that there was a weariness with, or lack of belief in, the very life of which she had once been the greatest celebrant.

When November came, Mekkins could stay no longer and left to attend to Marsh End affairs and, though he did not say so, to see what he could find out about any search that might be being made for Rebecca.

"I'll take good care of her Mekkins, so don't you go fretting," said Curlew as he left. "Comfrey will be all right now, a little weak perhaps but even the slightest plants bear flowers. And as for Rebecca, she'll take time to recover, but recover she will, you'll see."

Mekkins was touched by the change that had come over Curlew herself since Rebecca, and then Comfrey, had come. They seemed to have put new life into her and the mole he remembered as being so frightened and withdrawn was now bustling with activity and full of purpose. Things certainly work out in a strange way, he thought to himself as he departed, and that was something to take comfort from.

When he got back to the Marsh End and heard what had been happening in the system, he realized how right Rose had been to warn that dark days were coming. They were already there. For fear and terror were taking Duncton over, as the henchmoles, mainly westsiders, were beginning to get so powerful that they were out of control.

There were random attacks on eastsiders and marshenders; there were takeovers of tunnels by henchmole gangs; there was even a killing in Barrow Vale itself, the one place in the system where a mole traditionally felt completely safe on neutral ground.

At the root of the problem was the change that had come over Mandrake which had started, the gossips were quick to point out, from the night he and Rune had killed Rebecca's young. In the early days of Mandrake's thrall, if there had been killing to be done it was done by Mandrake himself. He kept tight control of the henchmoles, whom he selected himself and who obeyed no mole but he. Slowly, subtly, darkly, Rune began to gain power. By acting as a buffer between the henchmoles on one hand and Mandrake on the other, he gained the confidence of both. A mole like Burrhead, who was the leading westside henchmole, preferred to work through Rune than directly with Mandrake, who was too unpredictable. He made a mole like Burrhead stumble over his words and feel stupid; Rune was so much more understanding. . . .

By the Midsummer after Bracken's birth, Rune had the direct loyalty of all the henchmoles, many of whom had gained their positions by his preferment, and one way or another (mainly by his guile) those henchmoles originally selected by Mandrake were frozen out. Rumors were set against them, for example, so that Mandrake no longer trusted them. At one elder burrow meeting, two of them, whose reputation with Mandrake had been poisoned by Rune's slanders, were killed by Mandrake himself in front of all. So savagely was it done that only Rune smiled; there was something sensual in death for him.

After the death of Hulver, or, more particularly, ever since Mandrake had been so shocked to hear those words of grace spoken by Bracken—the voice of the Stone, as it seemed to Mandrake—he had slowly lost interest in the power he had won for himself. No mole doubted he was in charge, not even Rune, but he preferred to let Rune exercise power for him, with occasional excursions into mindless brutality just to show who was in charge.

Most moles in Duncton, including Mandrake, assumed that Rebecca had been taken by an owl along with her litter after their killing. But seemingly worse, for Mandrake, was the fact that his mate, Sarah, who had opposed the killing of the litter from the start, had been taken by owl as well—at the same time as Rebecca. The sudden loss of his mate and daughter seemed to mark the start of Mandrake's decline into distracted brutality. He would suddenly appear in Barrow Vale and spend hours sitting brooding, while the moles there would quietly disappear. Sometimes he was heard to attack the walls of his tunnels in great lumbering crashes and to mutter to himself in the language of Siabod. Words that sounded like curses, and ravings no mole could understand.

He became obsessed, too, by the Stone Mole, a rumor that had never died out. Indeed, the incident with Rebecca got tangled up with the Stone Mole, who was said (and Mandrake appeared to believe it in some way) to have mated with Rebecca. Oh, yes! Haven't you heard? The pups Mandrake killed were the Stone Mole's pups!

No mole quite believed this, and yet it was a good story . . . so rumors feed on themselves.

As for the reports of her death, these were so confused that no mole could really tell what the truth was. Mandrake himself believed her dead but there were others, Rune among them, who were not so sure. Some even said—but this was the wild gossip of those who had exhausted the titillation in every other story—that she had escaped from the system with a single pup who had not died in the assault and was rearing him as a second Stone Mole to come and avenge his siblings' deaths. "Typical Rebecca!" some said, not knowing that the Rebecca they had known was no more, alive or dead.

Mekkins garnered all these stories in visits to Barrow Vale, for Marsh End was too cut off and unpopular to be a good source for gossip. He trusted the henchmole who had so bravely led Rebecca down to the Marsh End to keep quiet—it was in his interests to do so.

More serious was the possibility that the news of Rebecca's existence and whereabouts might leak from the Marsh End, where a few moles must have guessed at it. He began to think that if there was any way for Rebecca to leave the system he should find it. For surely if they ever did discover her, especially with Comfrey, then she *would* be killed. It was to discuss this that he himself decided to risk a journey to the pastures to see if he could locate Rose for her advice and help. He wanted, in any case, to bring her back to Curlew's burrow to take a look at Rebecca and see if she could inject into her a greater will to live again.

Meanwhile, the Stone Mole rumor was resurrected periodically by glimpses of Bracken, who now had such a command of the Ancient System—except for its most central part, whose exploration still defeated him—that he did not mind taking a few risks. In fact, for him it was quite fun. But he was seen only down on the slopes, for as the atmosphere of fear in the wood increased, no mole ventured too far from his burrow, and none up onto the hill itself.

Bracken's visits to the slopes were principally to see Rue and her thriving litter—Violet, Coltsfoot, Beech and Pipple.

Bracken had tried several more times to find his way through the Chamber of Roots but finally gave up when, one windy day when the roots were viciously active below ground, he got cut off by a deep and treacherous fissure that appeared in the floor and took a long and dangerous time to find another way out again, while the roots got noisier and noisier and seemed to want to entwine themselves about him and take him for their own. He was determined to return one day and find some way of completing the exploration, but meanwhile decided to create tunnels of his own.

He established his tunnels at the wood's edge beyond the Stone clearing, quite near the spot where Cairn had died. His choice was decided principally by the existence of the second tunnel leading out of (or into) the circular tunnel around the Chamber of Echoes. The tunnel was a slight affair, meandering here and there and eventually petering out to the west of the Stone. Bracken constructed a clever series of tunnels that connected up with it in a deliberately confusing and roundabout way, designed to put off any inquisitive mole who found his own tunnels. He liked the idea of having access to the Ancient System underground but saw danger in creating a direct route.

Meanwhile, Duncton Wood declined toward winter. The winds off the pastures grew grayer and colder, and the last of the leaves blew in desolate flurries off the trees, leaving just a few dead ones hanging on the beech and oak trees as a reminder of the summer now long gone. The only green that remained was the ivy that hung off some of the older trees, some mistletoe that had colonized the occasional oak on the lower westside, and near Barrow Vale a holly tree or two, whose shining, prickly leaves and clusters of red berries seemed the only splash of color in the whole wood.

Creature after creature disappeared from sight. Most of the birds had gone, while the gray squirrels, which had scampered their way over the trunks and branches of the oaks or across the wood floor between the beeches all spring and summer, began, one by one, to disappear into the nooks and holes in which they hibernated.

A colony of pipistrelle bats found out the hollow dead elm in the lower wood and, after wheeling and circling round it dusk after dusk, settled down to sleep the winter through in the safety of its dark inaccessibility. Insects like wasps and ladybirds crawled away under the looser patches of tree bark while hedgehogs, after growing slow and dozy, finally chose their spots for sleep as well, curling up under a cover of leaves and mold with only the very slightest trembling of their snouts to tell that they were still alive.

Then, as November gave way to December, the Duncton moles responded to winter by clearing out their deeper runs, shoring them up where necessary, blocking off colder entrances, and crouching still in the cold darkness of a system, and a season, bowed down by gloom. For hours a mole's only movement might be the shivering of flanks or a sullen search for food, while the only sounds carried in on the wet, cold wind were the periodic crackings and fallings of twigs and branches, or the flap of a magpie's wings whose black sheen reflected a gray sky.

Yet, however bowed down a system may be, nothing can quite destroy the spark of excitement that comes to everymole's breast with the start of the third week of December and the approach of Longest Night. For even in the darkest hour there is a distant star, a tiny light of hope whose glimmer, though far off, is enough to thrill the most despairing heart.

Longest Night! The time when youngsters grow silly with expectation and adults grow young with memory. The time when a mole may forget the icy months still to come in the knowledge that the imminent passage of Longest Night means that the days are beginning—however unlikely it seems—to shorten once more. Longest Night! The time when darkness and light hang in a balance and the mystery of life is remembered again.

Then are the old tales told and the ancient songs sung. Of the coming of Ballagan; of the finding of the first Stone, of its splitting into the seven hundred Stones; of Ballagan's mate, Vervain of the West Stone; of their struggle with darkness on the first Longest Night; of their sons and daughters and the founding of the first system; of Ballagan's discovery of the first Book, and Vervain's discovery of the second. But most beloved tale of all, and the one all moles like to hear again on Longest Night, of how Linden, last son of Ballagan and Vervain, made the trek with the books to Uffington and then learned to read them, and in the course of one Longest Night, became a White Mole, thereby allowing the Stone's healing power for love and silence to pass through him to all moles.

In honor of Linden at least somemoles in every system traditionally trek to the Stone (or whatever feature in their system represents it) on Longest Night. And what an exciting memory *that* is for those who take part, as jokes, smiles, giggles, whimsies, buffoonery, tomfoolery and games mix with prayers, silence and mystery in an evening of pilgrimage. Then back to the burrows for a feast and a chatter and a tale well told; and then sleep, if there's time, before waking at last in the knowledge that Longest Night has been survived and the long journey toward spring has begun.

As this particular Longest Night approached, many Duncton moles thought to themselves that one way or another they ought to make the trek to the Stone this time, having been deterred from doing so by Mandrake's outright threats on the previous Longest Night. This time their fear was greater and morale lower—yet it is just at such times that thoughts turn naturally to the Stone, and the need to ask for its help. So many moles secretly planned to make the trek, though few admitted they were making plans to do so. As December entered its third week, the system began to buzz with excitement and chatter as moles cleaned out their burrows and made their plans, and laughed with pleasure at the prospect of Longest Night.

But there are always moles—and always will be—who, through character or circumstances, decide they cannot join in the gregarious fun in the approach of Longest Night. Bracken was one of them. He could, it is true, have spent a little time with Rue, assuming she would have allowed it, but the spirit was not in him. At the very moment when most moles in the system were finding a little relief from the shadows of winter in the celebration to come, he found himself falling into an uneasy sadness.

Some days he would go to the edge of the wood and look across the pastures and wonder if, after all, his first impulse on coming to the Stone might have been the best —to leave the system altogether and make his way to whatever lay beyond it in the direction of Uffington. Other days he found himself crouched in anguished silence in its shadows, wondering whether, after all, its power was imaginary—demanding then to see the power, to feel it. Or again, he would think about the Chamber of Roots and wonder why he could not cross it—and then ask himself how he could consider leaving the system if he had failed even to explore the system's most secret part. "What will I find out there," he would whisper to himself as he looked across the pastures, "if I can't even follow my snout in *here?*"

He was lonely. He wanted to talk to a mole again as he had talked so long before to Hulver; he wanted to learn something from a mole who could tell him what to learn. He wanted knowledge, but did not know where to find it. And Longest Night, which he knew was near, and when all moles shared a joy together, simply underlined the fact of his isolation from the Stone, from the heart of the Ancient System, and from all other moles.

"Rebecca! 'Ere, Rebecca! I've got a surprise for you, my girl!" It was Mekkins, full of joy of the season and suddenly back in Curlew's burrow with many a whisper and a laugh on the way down the tunnel to it. He had brought Rose.

She took one look at Rebecca and said, "My love, how frail and thin you have become. This certainly will *not* do." She said it kindly but firmly, crouching down snout to snout with Rebecca and examining her with motherly care.

"I'm sorry, Rose," said Rebecca. "I'm sorry," she whispered. "I'm sorry." And faced by Rose's love, she started to cry as she had never cried, ever before. She tried for a moment to stop, for little Comfrey, who was snuggled up against her, started up frightened, but Curlew took

him to her and played a game with him, which had him
and Mekkins running out into the tunnel, leaving Rose
and Rebecca alone together. So that Rebecca could cry.

Rose was too wise to think that jollying Rebecca along
to get her out of her depression would be useful. She
saw that much of Rebecca's spirit had been killed and
its rebirth was not something a healer could do quickly
by herself. As she talked to Rebecca and heard the indifference to life in her voice, Rose saw that the best
she could do was to push her in the right direction and
trust to the Stone that she would finally be able to find
the right way for herself.

When Rose watched Rebecca play with Comfrey, she
was pleased to see that there, at least, was something she
wanted to do, though she saw that even Rebecca's interest in Comfrey was sometimes little more than dutiful.
The sounds of love were there, for sure, but spontaneous
love, or trust, or faith, or hope, or life? These were the
drives that Rebecca had had so much of before, but
which somehow she seemed not to be able to pass on to
Comfrey, for they were no longer in her.

The pup was growing well, Rose observed, but he
would need to be given much more than food and grooming if he was to reflect in his life some of the quality that
Rebecca had once had in hers, and surely still could have.

"But how?" asked Mekkins, who understood well what
was wrong with Rebecca. "What can we do to make her
see that, terrible though the death of her litter has been,
life, for her, has barely begun?"

"Mekkins, my dear, you have a good heart, I sometimes think better than anymole I know! But Rebecca's
problem lies deeper than in simply having things to live
for. You see, my love, she has experienced evil—she
has seen it with her eyes, smelled it with her snout, and
felt its dark talons tearing inside her body. It tears at
her still. She has felt enough of its power to destroy an
ordinary mole but, as the coming of Comfrey shows, she
is in some ways graced and surely a special mole. The
only power that can heal her lies in the Stone—though
you must understand she may never be the same kind
of mole that you once knew. If a mole feels evil as she
has done, only the light in the Stone can erase its shadow.
Then may she continue to grow again."

"But how can she be made to see it?" asked Mekkins.

"There is no way a mole such as I, or you, can predict how the power of the Stone will be felt, or when. Often we may not even know if it *has* been. But Longest Night is coming and I think Rebecca should make the trek to the Stone. Perhaps, if she goes near it, something of her spirit will be reborn . . ."

"But what about Comfrey, and how will she get there?"

"You will guide her there, Mekkins, and Curlew will take care of Comfrey—something I suspect she has prayed she might be able to do—by herself for a while. He is no longer suckling and she can look after him very well by herself."

But what seemed a good idea to Rose, and eventually to Mekkins, did not appeal to Rebecca. She simply was not interested. She shook her head. She said she would not leave Comfrey. She said it was too far and Mekkins had done too much. She said there was no point. She grew angry with them all and attacked the idea that the Stone was anything more than mystic nonsense beloved of silly old moles. She had a temper tantrum.

Until, the problem still unresolved, Rose herself had to leave to get back to the pastures in time for Longest Night. Mekkins accompanied her, for she was now growing old and frail. Her last words to him when they came to the woody edge on the west side of Marsh End were "You must try once more to get her to go, Mekkins. The fact that she is so opposed to going convinces me that she should go—even if you have to drag her there!" They both laughed a little at the idea, but their laughter was sad.

"I'll do the best I can," said Mekkins.

"I know you will, my love," said Rose. "I always knew you would. The day will come when all moles will remember you and will take heart from the story of your loyalty and of what you did for Rebecca."

"Me, Rose? Don't be silly!" said Mekkins. Adding "Now you take care of yourself on those pastures, and have a good Longest Night."

"And you," said Rose, running back and nuzzling him. "And you, too, my love." Then with a smile of affection they parted. And hour by hour Longest Night crept nearer.

BRACKEN knew when the trek to the Stone on Longest
Night had begun by the sound of chitter and chatter
and laughter coming from the clearing—he could even
hear it in his deepest burrow, to which he moved in a
sullen irritation. Somemoles, who evidently did not know
the best way to the Stone, wandered over the surface
above his tunnels telling their stories, singing ridiculous
songs, racing and dancing about, and generally annoying
him. He wanted none of it.

But as the evening drew on, the sounds changed from
revelry to reverence—for the first moles there were always the ones who came simply for the fun of the trip
and wanted to get it over as quickly as possible so that
they could get back to their burrows for the real festivi-
ties.

Only later did those who were moved by the mystery
of Longest Night and remembered Linden, the first White
Mole, with real thanksgiving in their hearts, come in
ones and twos and crouch in reverence by the Stone.

By this time Bracken was too restless with annoyance
at the disturbance of his peace—or what he considered
his peace—to be able to stay still, and so crept as near
as he could to the Stone to watch the proceedings. He
felt alienated from each mole there, and from the Stone
itself, and watched it all almost as if he was not breathing the same air or sharing the same cold frosty December night as anymole else. There was moon low to the
east which, since the night was clear, cast its light into
the Stone clearing, the Stone a black silhouette in the
center, the moles forming gently moving shadows around
it. The shadow of the Stone ran directly toward Bracken
when he arrived, shortening and swinging to the south
as the evening passed on when the moon rose and swung
to the north in the sky.

Moles continually came and went from the clearing,
with a little banter and gentle laughter on the edge, but
none at the center itself.

Bracken heard snatches of their conversation: "You
here as well this time?" "Why, bless me, I ain't seen you

since July, and what a good time *that* was . . ." "Bit bloody parky up here, isn't it?" "Goin' to be a cold winter if you ask me . . ." Each phrase that came to him reminded him of how alone he was and without a friend. He thought again of visiting Rue, but somehow she wasn't what he wanted on Longest Night, though what that was he didn't know. He scratched himself miserably, looked balefully at the moon through the trees and turned his attention to the moles in the center of the clearing near the Stone. There was silence and a great sense of awe in their communal presence. Some crouched peacefully, occasionally raising their snouts slowly to look up at the Stone, almost as if they thought that something so awesome might suddenly go away. Others intoned prayers to themselves which Bracken could not hear, while some, mainly eastsiders he guessed (for theirs were the traditions nearest to the ancient ones) half sang, half intoned their prayers in a dialect Bracken could not understand.

Others spoke prayers of unaffected simplicity loud enough for him to hear. "Thank you, Stone, for the joys you have given and for the strength I have been blessed with. . . . Take care of Duncton and let it see your light. . . . My heart is in thy silence, Stone, only let me hear it. . . ." Again and again he heard moles, both males and females, whispering the same final little prayer, "Only take us to the silence"—words he had heard Hulver himself say from time to time.

Occasionally several of the moles there would appear to start saying the same prayer simultaneously; their voices would join in unison, creating a kind of spoken song of great power which would, for a moment, take Bracken's heart out of himself and transport it into something of the mystery of Longest Night.

As the night wore on and grew colder, the moon rising and the Stone's shadow turning toward the lower part of the wood while growing smaller at the same time, Bracken was touched by something of these moles' faith, and the Stone began to seem less distant from him than he had thought. He wanted to run out into the center and ask one of the older ones to explain about the Stone to him; he thirsted for knowledge of it. But he did not have the courage. Sometimes he wanted to join in their prayers, but he did not know the words.

Slowly, the numbers in the clearing declined until he began to have to search its shadows to locate the few moles left, mainly the very old ones, and he realized that the Stone trek was almost over. From down on the slopes even the sound of the songs and revels of departing moles faded, until as one by one all the moles in the clearing left and Bracken was left quite alone.

A bleak despair began to creep over him, for he felt he had seen a glimpse of some sweet mystery into whose light he wanted to go, but for which he needed a mole to guide him. He had never missed old Hulver so much as at that moment; surely, thought Bracken through tears that stopped him even seeing the Stone, he would have shared his Longest Night with me. Self-pity mixed with a real sense of loss as he crouched in the shadows beyond the clearing, and he sighed for the burden he felt himself to be carrying, and the night deepened into a still, cold silence all about him.

The moonlight was now strong enough to catch the condensation of his outward breaths into the cold air and the wood fell very still. The dead brown beech leaves on the floor of the Stone clearing looked pale white, and the surrounding vegetation was black around them.

On impulse, Bracken advanced toward the Stone, out of the undergrowth in which he had been hiding, not sure what he was doing but very conscious of himself alone in the wood. He wanted to say something to the Stone, not a prayer so much as an affirmation that he was there before it, waiting for something to happen. He felt he had been waiting a long time. He also felt unsettled and angry and very conscious of his own lonely existence.

For lack of anything better to do, he went up to the Stone and touched it with his paws to see if, after all, there was more to it than there seemed to be. But there was nothing but its unyielding rough surface, nothing at all.

He waited like this a long time until, somewhere in the darkness beyond, not far off in the shadows by the clearing's edge, past the great tree whose roots encircled the Stone, he heard a scurry and a slide.

A whispered "Ssh!" came out of the darkness into the moonlight where he lay. He turned his snout toward it aggressively, wondering what it was. Then he sensed mole.

A deep silence fell as Bracken waited, every sense stretched, his snout poised still as stone and his face whiskers stiff as pine needles.

But not for long. For very soon the anger that had been building up all night replaced the defensive care with which he had first responded to the noise.

"What mole is there, and why?" he demanded, getting up from where he was and approaching through the moonlight toward the impenetrable shadows around and beyond the tree roots.

A rustle. The sneak of a talon. A whisper again.

"I said what mole is there!" Bracken said again, his talons tensing and his body angry beyond his mind.

A movement, a scurry, an intake of breath and as a snout pushed out from the blackness half into the shadow, a voice accompanied it saying " 'Ello, Bracken. It's me, Mekkins. You know! We met . . ."

"What do you want?" demanded Bracken, tensing even more. Mekkins' friendliness upset him more than if he had been hostile. He wanted no part in friendliness.

"I'm Mekkins. I met you in Rue's burrows . . ."

Bracken was getting more angry by the second, an irrational anger born out of despair. At that moment he would probably have been angry at anything that moved. Bracken could feel anger overtaking him and was almost enjoying the feeling, even though the anger was absolutely real.

"Look, Bracken," said Mekkins, advancing toward him in a conciliatory way, "it's Longest Night and a time for celebration, not . . ."

"I don't care if it's Longest *Minute,*" shouted Bracken. "I don't want you here. There's been enough moles up here disturbing me . . ." He was shaking with anger and began the ritual advance on Mekkins that prefaced a fight —paws stiff, tail high, snout pointed stiffly forward.

At this, Mekkins, no slouch when it came to combat, narrowed his eyes and protracted his talons—he might have been asked to watch over Bracken, but there was absolutely no way he was going to allow himself to be assaulted just like that.

Then, a voice came hesitantly out of the shadows. "Bracken?"—and there stood Rebecca in the moonlight.

She immediately moved in front of Mekkins toward him.

"Bracken?" she said again, touching him with her paw as she had once touched him before. Only this time it was as if she did not believe that he could be Bracken. She spoke as if she was in a terrible nightmare; the frailty and fear in her voice seemed to hang over them all.

He turned his eyes away from Mekkins to Rebecca and looked at her. He was shaking with anger and tension but it slowly died away as he seemed to wake from some nightmare of his own and saw before him a mole so hurt in spirit that his anger and pain was nothing. He thought slowly, Is *this* Rebecca?

He was appalled by how thin she was, how stooped. Was this Cairn's Rebecca? The same he had met here by the Stone? There was puzzled entreaty in her eyes and he saw with utter clarity that she had been so hurt in some way that she could not stand his anger with Mekkins, or the threat in his voice. Words formed very slowly in his mind and when they were ready he said them.

"It's all right." Then, more softly, "It's all right." He paused and then said, as if he were calling out from some depth in which he was trapped: "Rebecca?" He advanced forward just a fraction and reached out a paw toward her. "Rebecca?"

Mekkins crouched quite still. It seemed to him that he could hear two moles calling out to each other from some lost place of their own and, more important, they seemed to hear each other. The Stone rose high above them all, most of it black with shadow, but with a thin line of moonlight delineating one plunging edge of it. When he looked again at Bracken and Rebecca, they were even closer together, Rebecca speaking to him as if he were Comfrey, which in a way he was; while he spoke to her with a gentleness Mekkins had never heard an adult male speak with before, except to a pup, a tiny lost daughter perhaps. Rebecca seemed to be crying, or sobbing, or was she laughing? She was doing something, at least. Then they were nuzzling each other, snouting softly at each other and whether the sounds they made were of tears or joy, sobs or laughter Mekkins could not tell. They were the sounds of discovered love.

It's Longest Night! thought Mekkins to himself, filled

suddenly with a sense of its joyous mystery and witnessing for himself the power of the Stone to make moles see each other. It's Longest Night! Involuntarily he began to sing a little song to himself and wander around the clearing to get a view of the Stone on the side that was lit by the moon.

Beneath it, Rebecca and Bracken seemed almost still, for Rebecca's nuzzlings were of the gentlest, quietest sort, while Bracken's paw caresses were of the softest and most tender.

"It's Longest Night!" said Bracken to her. "Do you realize?"

"Yes!" she said. "Yes, I do! Mekkins!" she called across the clearing. "Do you know what tonight is?"

He answered with a Marsh End ditty, and Rebecca started to laugh with a hint of the old freedom Mekkins had thought he would never hear again, the laughter that put hope into a mole's heart. But it was deeper and quieter than it had once been. She stopped suddenly and turned again to Bracken and just looked at him. And he looked at her. Why, she understands, he was thinking. He knows! she said to herself.

"Where are the worms then?" said Mekkins. "Where's the feast? I don't know about you, Rebecca, but I ain't come all the way up 'ere just to sing a song and get no food. Where is it, then?"

Bracken almost fell over himself thinking how he could get the best worms and other things together in the shortest possible time, while at the same time thinking that his burrow wasn't big enough for all of them—or was it? —and what was the best way to take them, and try to sing a song as well; while Rebecca kept laughing and looking serious and then a little sad, and then dancing a bit and Mekkins thinking there had never been such a good spot or such nice moles as this spot and these moles, at that particular moment. . . . Oh! surely there weren't three more excited or happy moles in the whole of Duncton Wood, and any one of them would have been hard put to it to explain quite why! Except . . . well . . . it's Longest Night, of course! When a mole realizes there are other things, bigger things, than even the biggest fears and most terrible worries. That's the magic of it, that's its mystery. And so, with a song and a dance in his steps,

Bracken led them out of the Stone clearing and down the tunnels to his biggest burrow.

"Well, that was some feast, that was!" declared Mekkins sometime deep in the night, paws on his stomach and full contentment on his face. And with that, his eyes closed, his head began to nod and his mouth fell gently open as he gave himself up to a deep and delicious sleep.

He might equally have said "That was some occasion, that was!" for surely the Ancient System had not been within sound of such tale-telling, singing, joking, guzzling, speechifying (mainly by Mekkins) and laughing, smiling, grinning (mainly by Bracken) and rhyming, molelore, and enchantment (Rebecca's) in generations. What excitement for Mekkins and Rebecca to enter tunnels burrowed into the chalk soil, with its gray-white shadows, which made a mole feel close to the past and the Stone; what a joy for Bracken to hear the sound of friendly moles in his tunnels, which he had burrowed in isolation and shared only with his own silence until now.

They all asked each other dozens of questions and listened spellbound to each other's tales. Rebecca hardly dared to breathe when Bracken described to her his first entry into the Chamber of Dark Sound, while Bracken laughed to hear how the story of the Stone Mole had grown to such proportions all over the system. As for Mekkins, his real joy was to see something of the old Rebecca return, though it was a richer, less impetuous sense of life that she now had. And to see that there was something between these two young moles that gave joy in an older mole like him to see, and which anymole with half a heart would want to cherish and protect. But he wondered if it was just something that had happened on Longest Night and which, in the morning, might not seem quite so powerful as it did now. Still, a mole mustn't go spoiling the present by fearing the future, he thought to himself, and so, more than content with the joy of the night, he finally fell asleep.

Bracken, on one side of the main burrow, and Rebecca on the other, both with their snouts between their paws, fell into thinking the warm, random thoughts of the contented tired. Mekkins' laughing, spring, dangers past, Rose, Rune, Rue, echoing tunnels, Curlew's eyes, Comfrey, Cairn, Cairn, oh Cairn, the Stone, what a time it's been and how much has happened . . .

"Bracken?"

"Mmm?" Her voice sounded so good in his burrow. He wanted her to repeat his name again.

"Bracken? Do you believe in the Stone?"

He did not think about the answer but rather wallowed with it in an image of the Stone, wondering what the question meant. He could say he didn't know, and that was true; but it wasn't really because he knew there was something there. Why, there was so much he hadn't told them. He had got as far as the circular tunnel with the seven entrances into the central part, but after that he had felt it unwise to go on and had steered the conversation away.

"I don't know," he said finally, "do you?"

She wanted to say "No," to shout "No!" because she didn't, she couldn't, it had let her litter die, it let those talons come down, there was no Stone, there was nothing, nothing; except that an image of Comfrey came to her suddenly and she saw that there *was* something. There was so much they hadn't talked about, she and Bracken, she thought to herself.

She raised her head off her paws and looked at him, and found that he was looking at her so deeply that her body seemed to fall away and only her heart or her soul was there; while it seemed to Bracken, when she raised her head to look at him, that there was nothing he could not tell her if she wanted to know, and that most of all, he would like to tell her about the Stone, for that was finally where everything, for good or ill, seemed to be.

He started to say her name again and to move a little toward her, but then he looked beyond her to the entrance to the burrow and thought beyond that to the tunnels he had created, and beyond them to the secret way he had made to the circular tunnel, and on beyond, racing along left and right, into the labyrinths with echoes all around and his skin and fur, his whole body, calling to the Stone, and great shadows of roots, great falls and rises of roots, silent and completely motionless, while beyond them, calling him, beyond them . . .

Bracken got up and, without looking back to Rebecca, went to the entrance, snouting down it toward where the

secret tunnels lay. Rebecca followed him silently as if
they were one mole, not two, both moving together down
the tunnels toward something that pulled them from the
direction of the Stone. They moved quite fast but completely without effort and there was no fear at all, just a
certainty that somewhere ahead the Stone was expecting
them.

As they ran into the ins and outs of Bracken's confusing tunnels to the center, they could both feel the Ancient
System alive before them, stretching far beyond in tunnel
after tunnel, alive with the warm spirit of Longest Night.
There was no fear at all.

Bracken led on into the circular tunnel and turned right
through one of the flint entrances and into the labyrinth
of echoes, pausing for a moment for Rebecca to catch up.
The pattering of her paws echoed on into the darkness
ahead of them and she whispered: "Listen. Listen! Oh,
it's so beautiful. Listen!"

Bracken ran now into the sound of the echoes, twisting
and turning each way and every way toward the roots,
not even checking the way he went with his memory, for
he no longer needed to, he could hear the way ahead, he
knew the way, he knew the way. His Rebecca was close
with him, her paws pattering with his, her warmth behind
him, they were twisting and turning, weaving and wend-
ing their way together, as one mole, running as one, no
effort, their bodies in unison.

"Oh, listen!" he could hear her whispering, or hear the
echoes of her whisper, whispering, "Listen, listen, my
love, my love . . ." deeper and deeper into the labyrinths
until the confusion of whispering echoes was all about
them but they were one mole together, so beautiful, so
beautifully echoing around them until at last they were
there by the roots, shadows and falls of rising roots as
silent and utterly motionless as the trees on the surface
in the still night to which they belonged.

"Listen, my love, listen!" whispered Rebecca, running
ahead of him without pause and entering first among the
great roots which rose massive above her and he following
her paws, following her warmth, following his Rebecca,
my love my love, the echoes following them both from
the labyrinths behind them, fading away behind as they
entered deeper and deeper among the roots, one mole
running, moving as one, each mole knowing the route as

one. The roots grew bigger and thicker, twining about this way and that, seeming to open before them, the sound of their silence all about them, the sound of silence running ahead of them, Rebecca running on without fear and Bracken behind and fissures in front and over them, over them, on and round, and through and under and over and beyond and on past the roots for shadow after shadow each twist falling straight, each turn not a turn, the route so easy, so easy for them both together.

Then, as suddenly as they had entered the Chamber of Roots, they reached its end, which was a massive impregnable wall rising up into darkness and made of hard chalk subsoil with great nodules of flint poking out of it like the snouts of huge moles. Their eyes traveled from one brooding shape to another, and then behind them, back to the mass of roots that now seemed quite impassable but through which, somehow, they had come. It was a fearsome sight but neither Bracken nor Rebecca felt fear, for they now looked at the ancient world about them as if they were pups in a world in which harm did not exist.

Bracken now took the lead, turning left along the wall and following its rough and ancient surface round, and round, until they came, as he knew they would without knowing, to an entrance to a tunnel. It was small, crudely burrowed by some mole for whom shape and form no longer mattered. Its floor sloped roughly downward, twisting among the flints that were held in the chalk and determined the detail, though not the general direction, of the tunnel.

From beyond it an ancient sound came, the sound that had been heard for whole ages and eras before even moles roamed the earth; the sound that accompanies the rise and fall, and rise again, of trees and woods and whole forests of trees. The sound of an ancient tree whose huge trunk carries the vibrations of both life and death. The sound of a tree whose roots are alive on the outside and carry life up into the new wood and branches but whose central core is now dry and sacrificed and whose hollow secret darkness stretching high out above the surface may be the home of bats or insects, butterflies or birds, but which below ground, where Bracken and Rebecca were, only carries the sound of a sleeping life that waits to be reborn in the wood's decay.

They had arrived at the roots of the tree that encircled the Stone in the center of the clearing. The tunnel now was burrowed out between living and dead roots—these dead roots' stillness being the peace against which the life of the living roots was set. The roots plunged down into the ancient tunnel, forcing them to squeeze round or between them on and on, now, more slowly and with a deepening sense of being at one with each other and the system that radiated all about them.

The farther they advanced along the tunnel, the more its walls seemed to be made up of roots as well as chalk, so that they had the feeling that the tree was all around them, the final guardian of the Stone.

The tunnel grew smaller about them, the dryness of its walls now catching their fur as they advanced and its sound deepened and hollowed ahead of them so that Bracken slowed still more, recognizing from its pattern that ahead of them lay a chamber greater than any he had discovered in the Ancient System so far.

There was a mass of debris and dust ahead that blocked the lower half of the tunnel and over whose top Bracken could not see. Cautiously he pushed it forward with his right paw, trying to flatten it down a bit, but it just fell forward and away, the debris sliding away from him in an avalanche, dust rising, and then a long, long silence before, far below them, it cascaded and echoed down onto some unknown, unvisited floor. As the dust cleared, they saw ahead of them the vast round of the old tree's central hollow, which rose above them to unknown heights of ancient wood, and below to where the debris had fallen. The tunnel gave way to a precipitous path torn out of the side of the hollow and round which they started now to go, the wall of soft wood on their right flank, a void of darkness on their left. It spiraled round and down, and they followed it slowly, feeling as if they were traveling into a past that held in its waiting silence the future as well.

Then Bracken stopped and, half turning back to Rebecca—the narrow path would allow him no more movement than that—he pointed a talon at a sight ahead of them that made her gasp with wonder.

It was a massive jutting, jagged corner of stone, *the* Stone, around which the tree had girt itself and whose roots had pushed and pulled at it so that in their embrace the great Stone had tilted up and forward toward the west, toward Uffington until here, deep below ground, the corner of the base on which it had originally stood had risen off the ground and ridden into the hollow depth of the tree itself.

The path traversed right down to the Stone, and then under it, leaving the wall of the hollow as it followed the massive, and now dead, root that had first, as a tendril thinner than a single hair of fur, crept under the Stone so long ago.

Into this holy secret place Bracken and Rebecca now moved, the base of the Stone now actually above them and plunging down ahead of them to the very center of the Stone and the Ancient System itself.

Then the path widened onto a floor, if floor it was that was half chalk, half soil, half debris, all crossed and intertwined with the arms and bent haunches of long-dead roots. The Stone base was above them still, but as they advanced still farther, clambering over the ancient obstructions in their way, they saw that it plunged suddenly down some distance ahead to form a kind of hollow or cave beyond which, no doubt, the farthest part of the Stone had buried itself finally into the chalk, mirroring in its depth the heights of the other part of the base which tilted above them.

They could only see the top half of this hollow because the roots were bigger than they were and they had to climb over each one. The nearer they got, the more they could see that one last great root had grown across most of the hollow, sealing it off at the bottom and leaving only a thin gap at the top. As they got near they both stopped at once.

"Listen!" whispered Bracken.

"Look!" whispered Rebecca.

As they crouched there, they heard from behind them the soft sound of the ancient tree, stirring and stressing in slow, long sounds, sounds more beautiful than either of them had ever heard, for in its movement it carried both the sound and the silence of life itself: the sound of old winds, the sounds of new life, the sound of moisture, the sound of warm wood, of cold wind, of the sun.

While they could see above them, on the roof of the hollow cave blocked by the root, a glimmering light like the shimmering sun from a moving stream up onto the gnarled bark of a willow that stretches out over it.

Bracken moved forward and began to burrow under the root—which was easy, because the ground was loose and dry while the root itself was soft with age. Rebecca joined him, burrowing silently by his side, each pushing out the soil and debris behind them, advancing toward the sealed cave of the Stone. It was easy, so easy. Until at last one of Bracken's burrowing thrusts pushed forward into nothing and he stopped and held his paw there and turned to Rebecca, who stretched her own paw forward and through, and together they pulled the last of the soil and root seal down.

As they did so their fur, their outstretched talons, their eyes, the tunnel about them . . . all was covered in a glimmering white light, whose source lay on the floor of the hollow cave into which they had found a way.

It was stone, no bigger than a mole's paw, oval, smooth and translucent, and from its center came a light that was not bright like the sun, nor cold like the moon, nor fierce like an owl's eye. Rather, it was a light like that which fills a raindrop caught by a soft, warm morning sun. As they advanced toward it, it seemed to change a thousand times each second, as the quality of light on a spring day changes with each station of the sun and shift in humidity in the air. Its glimmering had the endless fascination of the shifting windsound in an ash tree, whose leaves seem to dissect the wind into a thousand different whispers.

Its rays shone and shot about the burrow in which it lay, lighting up first this side and then that, casting shadow here and chasing shadow there, always changing, never ending.

Bracken slowly, fearfully, stretched out a talon to touch it, but Rebecca ran to him and pulled him back, whispering "Don't. There's no need to touch it."

But Bracken only smiled, for never in his life had he seen or dreamed of anything so beautiful or felt at such peace, and he reached out again. Rebecca's paw rested on his shoulder, her breath held still, for she, too, wanted to touch the stone. Then, as his paw touched it, its light was suddenly gone, and the burrow was plunged into a darkness so thick that a mole could not breathe.

Rebecca gasped, Bracken pulled back, and as his paw

left the smooth stone, the feel of it like the softest moss on his skin, the light in the center of the stone glimmered dimly again and then, like some creature that has curled up in defense and uncurls when the danger is gone, it slowly came to life and light once more, the light advancing about them like a new dawn.

They looked at each other in wonder, and then round at the burrow, noticing for the first time that its floor was strewn with vegetation and material so dry it fell to dust almost as they moved. Yet from it came the subtlest and the sweetest fragrances that either had ever smelled.

Verbena, feverfew, woodruff and thyme, camomile and bergamot, germander, mint, and rose . . . blending into the fragrance of a warm spring and a celebration of summer, with a hint of the fruits of autumn and a touch of winter snow. It was so subtle, yet so essential to the burrow, that Rebecca stretched out her paws as if to touch it, and failing, turned back to Bracken and touched him.

She caressed him with a wonder that made her gasp and sigh, for by the glimmering light of the stone he seemed more beautiful than any mole she had ever seen. His fur gray and his eyes soft. Bracken turned to her and touched the soft fur of her face, his eyes alight with a sense of the life that he saw within her which was of a force and power he had never before felt within himself. They moved closer to each other, the stone to their side and the wonder of the world within each other's gaze.

Then they crouched nuzzling each other and sighing, saying words of trust and love, joy and intent, the jumbled words of love whose nonsense makes a greater sense than any reasoned sentence ever can.

They drifted in and out of their newfound world, talking and laughing softly together, Bracken sometimes raising himself and looking down at Rebecca, running his talons through her fur, almost shoving and pushing at her as if he disbelieved that anything so beautiful could be at once outside his body and within his heart. They were pup and mother to each other, father and mate, friend and lover all at once, coming closer and closer to each other in their discovery of trust and love.

And then, surrounded by the silence of the stone, they began to talk the things that had been in their hearts so heavily for so long and healing each other of their memory. Rebecca's lost litter, Bracken's isolation in the Ancient System, Comfrey, their son by circumstance, and Cairn, oh Cairn. Sometimes they wept, sometimes their tears were dried by their laughter, sometimes they reached out to be touched, sometimes they lay still, but always the light of stone glimmered and shone in the burrow about them.

Bracken told her about the death of Cairn, repeating the words he had said to him about Rebecca at the end: "She is the wildflower that grows in spring, she is as graceful as the swaying branches of the ash, as light as pussy willow caught by sun, she is . . ." and as he talked, using words he half remembered, he began to say them to her direct, his body against hers, her paws on his face, his snout to her neck fur, her body caressingly warm against him. "Yours is the love of life itself, yours is the life that flows from wood to pasture, from hill to vale; yours is the love in the tunnels of Uffington; yours is the love in the hearts of the White Moles.

"That's what I told him, Rebecca, that's what I said," whispered Bracken to her. "I could feel his pain, the terrible pain they made him feel; and I could feel his love for you, I could feel it . . ."

"I know," she replied. "I know, my own wildflower, my sweet love, I know . . . I love you, I love you," she said, and he said, endlessly, over and over again.

At their side the light from the center of the stone flared and flickered all around, and cast their shadows out onto the roots and walls of the chamber beyond the burrow where they crouched, where they mingled into one shadow, one shape, which shimmered and moved with the light. How many minutes or hours they stayed together in this state of loving grace no mole can say, or cares to try. But there came a time when, just as they had moved with one accord on their journey there, so they simultaneously began to be restless and to lose their sense of being at one with each other and the stone, in whose depth they had found such peace. Perhaps it was their imagination, but the stone in the burrow seemed to flicker and glimmer more intermittently.

Bracken suddenly found he was hungry, Rebecca that she wanted to get back to Comfrey. They began to feel the love they had touched slipping away. Both of them tried to reach out for it with new endearments of love and passion, deeper sighs and heavier caresses, for it was too sweet to lose. But it seemed to them to be fleeing away to some world they could not reach, whereas, in truth, it was they who were fleeing away from it as they returned to the world of time and worry, fears and fretting heaviness.

Bracken turned to look at the stone again, for he knew he must soon leave and he wanted to remember it. After all, this was the heart of the system he had sought so long to explore. He looked at it now (as it seemed to him) more objectively, from the illusory world of time he and Rebecca were so reluctantly reinhabiting, and it no longer seemed quite so smooth or quite so oval as it had before. There was a delicate whorl of interlocking shadows on it . . . not shadows, but carvings, or rather embossments, like those he had seen before on a cruder and grander scale on the wall of the Chamber of Dark Sound.

"I know those patterns," he said, half to himself. "I know their power. If you hum, they will make a music back to you." He half reached out toward the stone, as if warming his paws at its light, and began to hum. The burrow was soon filled with sounds in return, some far lighter and more beautiful then the most wonderful he had heard from the wall, others far darker and more unbearable.

Rebecca began to writhe and gasp as the beginnings of a scream formed inside her, while Bracken felt fear and panic overtaking him. He stopped humming and reached out involuntarily to the stone, as if trying to stop the sound coming from it, and as he touched it, the light plunged out once more, casting them not only into darkness but into a depth of despair—a sense of loss—that brought horror to them and made them both gasp for each other instinctively.

As Bracken's paw left to touch Rebecca, the light slowly returned again and their sense of loss began to fade. This time Bracken could feel the impression of the stone on his paw, not smooth like moss, but more like an embossed abrasion, like a pain that had a shape to it. Yet when he looked, there was nothing there.

"Come on, Rebecca, we must go," he said, and without looking back he turned out of the burrow, down the big tunnel they had dug, and away under the rising ceiling of the stone. Rebecca followed, more distressed than he and kept close behind, fearful that he would go too fast. But this feeling lasted only for a short time and when they had climbed the root path back to the hollow of the tree and the stone was behind them, they stopped and looked around, wondering again at the size of the stone, beginning to wonder what it was they had seen, and felt.

"Will we ever come here again?" asked Rebecca.

Bracken whispered that he didn't know, that he didn't understand quite where they had been, and started again on the trek up the path. The sound in the tree hollow was now more stressed and great shatterings of straining noise cascaded about them, like the sound of lightning they could not see, great rumblings of a power so great that they felt they were nothing in the middle of a storm. There was windnoise, too, and the path ahead of them seemed to tremble or sway, not much but enough to suggest that out on the surface a morning wind was already awakening and stirring the tree that guarded the great Stone in the clearing.

As they reached the entrance to the hollow, they heard even more fearful sounds coming from the tunnel beyond, and as they ran down it, faster and faster, they saw that the roots of the tree were beginning to stress and strain. They ran and pushed, and Bracken herded Rebecca through the roots threatening to crush them, on and on now, anxious to get out. They felt they had stolen the sight of something sacred and the noise was pursuing them to take it back.

When they got past the outer roots of the great tree, they made their way down the rough tunnel back to the roots, but it was like running from the talons of an owl into the fatal rushing of a flood. For the Chamber of Roots was now filled with sinister sliding and pullings, terrible rackings and stretchings, crushings and stranglings, as the mass of roots, which had been so still when they first passed through them, started to respond to the wind on the surface.

Bracken looked up to the roof of the chamber, wondering if they could escape that way, by burrowing up somehow onto the surface—but it was too high, and the jags of thrusting flint too difficult to negotiate.

Rebecca ran forward to the heaving roots and Bracken followed to stop her. "It's impossible!" he shouted over the noise. "We'll be lost forever in there."

But Rebecca twisted away from his grasp and ran between the first roots, shouting back to him, "Think of the stone we saw, think of its protection . . . ," and she was gone among them.

He stretched a paw after her, hesitating for a moment, but then, feeling again the strange itching impression of the stone on his paw, he remembered the light of the stone and ran after her. They twisted their way among the treacherous roots—each movement forward just in time to escape the crushing behind them of roots between which they had passed, a path opening up before them as roots parted just in time for them to escape the opening of fissures in the ground or the crashing down of debris from above. On and on they went, Bracken following his Rebecca, Rebecca feeling that Bracken was pressing her on from behind, two moles as one, one mole escaping the roots. Always thinking of, and clutching onto, the memory of the stone and its glimmering light, always trying to hold that in their hearts to keep at bay the horror around them. Each moment held a terrible death for them, each moment was a miraculous escape, until their breathing came gasping and desperate and they felt they could not run on through the racking darkness of the roots. On and on until they were led forward by instinct and trust as a blind pup might find its mother's teats.

Then they were clear, back to the entrance into the labyrinth of echoes, the roots reaching out at them from behind, trying to pull them back as Bracken led them out through the labyrinths into the sudden, unbelievable silence of the circular tunnel.

Without a word to each other they wended their way back to Bracken's burrow, where they found Mekkins still asleep, paws curled to his belly and a contented purr coming from his mouth. They looked at each other in deep silence, there being no words to express the joy and then the dark they had experienced together.

In the peace and homely comfort of his own burrow, Bracken could barely believe that he had seen what he had, and the memory, both good and bad, seemed already to be slipping away. To remember it was too much for him to want to face.

For Rebecca, however, the memory was clear and she guessed that they had seen something more wonderful than some moles ever dream of. She touched Bracken with her paw to tell him that it was real and that he must not let it slip away, but he only looked at her in a kind of dawning fear, compounded partly of a sense of loss of what he could not quite remember, partly from having faced for a moment a truth he could face no longer.

Then they slept the fitful sleep of the deeply tired, waking only to the sound of Mekkins' singing as he groomed and stretched himself in preparation for leaving with Rebecca.

They said few words—indeed, Mekkins said most of the farewells. But they touched again and Bracken knew that Rebecca and he had, for a time at least, been at one with one another and that a part of himself was forever in her heart, as part of her would always be in his.

He saw them as far as the Stone clearing where, for a brief moment, they looked up at the great Stone, leaning into the morning wind, the beech branches waving against a cold white sky above it.

When they were gone, he turned back to his tunnel and down to his burrow where he crouched in silence, a sense of wonder and disbelief mixing with a terrible feeling of loss. His left paw vaguely itched or burned, but when he looked at it, there was nothing there. But the irritation stayed with him and eventually, with his right paw, he tried to scratch the pattern that he had felt on the stone onto the burrow floor, an interlacing of lines and circles. Again and again he traced in the dust, scratching it out with his paw until slowly it seemed to come right. Again and again, until, like the tunnels in the Chamber of Echoes, he knew it by heart. The itch began to fade and as it did so, he began to sink into a deep sleep, his right paw still extended where it was tracing the pattern of the burrow stone yet again, before he finally slept.

23

WITH the passing of Longest Night, which he spent completely alone, Mandrake sank finally into obsessive madness. He ranged about his tunnels, or Barrow Vale, muttering and cursing violently, often in the rough hard tongue of Siabod, the language of his fathers. Occasionally he caught some unfortunate mole unawares and —whether young or old, male or female—would attack it savagely for some imagined wrong it had done, leaving it wounded or, more than once, dead.

Trembling moles would hide in tunnels and burrows as he passed heavily by, wondering at his continual calling out for Sarah and Rebecca, whom he no longer seemed to think were dead but gone to the Stone Mole in the Ancient System, leaving him alone and forsaken. As the days slipped by into cold January, he could be heard sounding curses in his own language: "Arthur, helgi Siabod, a'm dial am eu colled trwy ddodi ei felltith ar Faenwadd Duncton"—"May Arthur, hound of Siabod, avenge for me their loss by bringing his curse on the Stone Mole of Duncton." Arthur was the legendary hound of Siabod who was believed to protect its holy stones, though none in Duncton knew of his name then.

Any lesser mole than Mandrake would have been killed by other moles, or driven out of the system, but there was none in Duncton prepared to start a fight with him. And only one—Rune—with the courage even to talk to him.

Rune listened with almost a purr of pleasure to his ravings about the Stone Mole and his threats to summon the mythical Arthur. He knew that with each day that passed, the system was slipping out of Mandrake's talons and into his own. It was just a matter of time and opportunity.

Inevitably, plots were made against Mandrake, especially since the murder of Rebecca's litter, which had appalled so many moles, as Rune had hoped it would. Rune positively licked his lips with pleasure when dithering henchmole after henchmole came to him with some feeble plot or other. "A group of us feel, and it's only a feeling, and we wouldn't do anything without your ap-

proval and support, Rune, sir, that the system is overdue
for a change . . ."

"Well, I'm sure that as long as Mandrake is here
in good health and in charge we none of us need
worry . . . ," Rune would reply hypocritically to would-
be revolutionaries in his maddeningly measured and reasonable way. And they would retreat, murmuring to each
other "Rune's too loyal for his own good!" or "Far too
modest, that Rune—doesn't realize his own worth."

But if there was going to be a revolution (and that was
precisely what Rune intended there should be), it would
be done in his own way and in his own time. And as
Mandrake's ravings about the Stone Mole got worse, he
began to see that there *was* a way, and its path lay toward the Ancient System.

So the shadows on the system continued to fall, and
with them the bitterest weather of winter came. The first
snow fell after two cold days in the second week of January and though it did not stick, the skies remained gray
and cold, and the wood silent but for the wind. Then, in
the third week of January, it turned even more bitter and
thick snow finally came, the silent brightness it brought to
the wood almost a relief after the previous gloom.

The winds drove the snow into the tree trunks so that
on some of them, especially the rougher-barked oak, the
snow formed a vertical line on the windward side, making
the trees seem even higher and more ethereal than they
normally did in snow. The brambles, which retained their
leaves through much of the winter, were bowed down
with white, while the orange stalks of the dead bracken,
lost until now against the leaf-fall of autumn, stood out
brightly against the snow. While, but for the occasional
dropping of dead twigs and the odd branch under the
weight of snow, the wood fell into a cold, white silence.

The shadows cast by Mandrake's rule did not fall on
all burrows equally. Some, like the tunnels of Rue and of
Curlew, were brighter for the presence of growing pups.
Rue's four were lively and, by the third week of January, beginning to have minds of their own, chattering
and squabbling among themselves so much that Rue was
glad that they were able to look after themselves so much
more, only clustering around her and half-heartedly suckling when they had had enough of each other's company
and fancied a snuggle.

Curlew's burrow was quieter, not only because there was just a single pup there, but because he was far less advanced than Rue's other four.

Comfrey was thin and nervous, sticking close to Rebecca or Curlew, or both if he could, and by the time the snow came had not learned to talk with any fluency. He would try as best he could, but the words came out stutteringly and he often broke off in midsentence as if he had lost interest in what he was trying to say.

"R–R–Rebecca? I want the . . . ," and he would trail off, looking somewhere else, as Rebecca looked up inquiringly and asked him what it was he wanted. Often he seemed to have forgotten.

Mekkins stayed on for only two days after he had delivered Rebecca back safely—just time enough to confirm that the change for the better that he saw coming over her on Longest Night, whose causes he did not fully understand, was lasting. Then he left them to it—partly because no male likes to be away from his own burrow too long in January, when the females are just beginning to get restless for the mating season and the males are beginning to extend their territory.

So, when the deep snow came, it was just Rebecca, Curlew and a fascinated Comfrey there.

"Where has the g–g–ground gone?" asked Comfrey when he first saw the snow. Then "Where did it come from? What is it? H–How long has it come for?"

His slowness of speech did not stop him asking a dozen questions, many of which neither Rebecca nor Curlew could answer. But Rebecca did her best—for she remembered her own insatiable curiosity as a pup about the wood—and to Curlew's delight the two would sit and talk away, the burrow filled with Rebecca's laughter and Comfrey's hesitating, serious voice. He never laughed and rarely smiled, yet managed to convey a sense of excitement and fascination with the world about him. But he hated Rebecca to leave the burrow for too long and would stand by the burrow entrance, looking miserably up the tunnel, and nothing Curlew could say would take the worried furrows from the thin fur on his forehead.

When the snows came and the males in the system began to be more aggressive, Rune knew that he must soon take a chance on his own revolution. The time was

right, for there was nothing like a bit of premating aggression to put the henchmoles into the right frame of
mind to follow his lead and oust Mandrake. But it had
to be done subtly.

His opportunity came during a conversation with Mandrake—monologue is a better word—which convinced
Rune that the system's long-standing leader was, indeed,
demented.

"Have you seen the Stone Mole, Rune?" asked Mandrake, having summoned him into his tunnels with a
roaring shout around Barrow Vale. "Well?"

"I? No . . . I have not," said Rune carefully.

Mandrake smiled a terrible smile of triumph.

"Ah! But I have, you see. I know!"

Rune was a study in unctuous silence.

"I have spoken to the Stone Mole," added Mandrake
softly. "I know he means harm to the system and I have
told him I will kill him." Mandrake's black eyes widened
horribly and he nodded his head. "I will. Yes I will. I'll
kill him."

There was a long silence.

"Only you could do such a thing," began Rune sooth-
ingly, wondering if his opportunity to get Mandrake up
to the Ancient System and isolate him there, which was
his intention, was now coming.

Mandrake grew irrationally angry at this: he did not
need Rune to tell him what he could do or could not do.
Whatmole was Rune to say such a thing? Always poking
his snout into things. Perhaps he was the one who told
the Stone Mole to take Sarah away, and Rebecca?
Wouldn't put it past him. Slimy little bastard is Rune.
Interfering little hypocrite. Mandrake turned to Rune to
strike him with his talons so that he would learn what not
to say . . . But Rune was gone. Rune was not crouching
where he had been. There, there were only black shadows
where Rune had been, shades of darkness where Rune-
mole Rune had gone. And there *would* be, for Mandrake
was not even facing where Rune had been and still
was; Mandrake did not want to put his talons into anymole again; Mandrake was mumbling into a dark corner
of his own imagining, mumbling to himself in his loneliness.

He knew the Stone Mole was waiting for him and he
was afraid, and he had never felt fear, no not that, not

fear. He didn't like fear, so he would go to that ancient place where the voice in the Midsummer Night was and where the old mole died never even struggling, no fear in *his* eyes. Old whatwashisname? Before Sarah, before Rebecca, remember? He had been a pup but he couldn't remember or could he remember, remember his talons soft like Rebecca's had been when she was born he remembered that, no blizzard though. But snow, now. They don't know the cold. Only Siabod moles know cold. Take them up Cwmoer and the whole bloody lot would freeze. Arthur would have a feast, see? What did Y Wrach used to say? Crai by mryd rhag lledfryd heno. Melancholy as hell she was, the old bitch. Call this Duncton snow cold? They should try the ice on Castell y Gwynt.

Mandrake's massive body moved uncomfortably in the dark, his own dark, aching with the lifelong effort of seeing beyond the whirling blizzard in his mind and failing, always not quite seeing, but remembering that he might have, with Sarah, who surely could hear him calling when he took her and he tried to say something but his body and the darkness wouldn't let him. Yes, she heard him calling out of the blizzard oh Sarah, she heard him out of the Siabod ice. He remembered that. Or was it Rebecca? With Rebecca. On and in Rebecca when she heard him . . . yes she did! She *heard* him. Where is she now? Where is she?

Rune watched the slow tears on Mandrake's face pitilessly and called them madness. He had raised his talons to strike the wall and then muttered, and now turned mumbling and with tears wetting his rough old face fur. He's past it, gloated Rune.

"You must go to the Ancient System and find the Stone Mole," said Rune finally and bravely, "and you must kill him for us."

Mandrake looked at his talons, twisted with fighting and killing, and his snout lowered. He was thinking of when they were in Rebecca's fur, his Rebecca.

"Yes," he said wearily. "Will you come with me, Rune?"

"Yes," said Rune, thinking that a lot of henchmoles would not be far behind either.

"Yes, you come along, Rune, you might help me find Sarah." He wasn't going to mention Rebecca because he didn't want Rune helping him to find her. No.

How was Rue to know that her youngsters had mischievously burrowed a way into Hulver's old tunnels?
What wisdom could ever have told her that Mandrake
and Rune would happen that way? When trouble comes
calling a mole had better not waste time asking such questions else the impossibility of answering them and so
finding some *reason* for tragedy will drive him, or her,
mad.

But one day, when the world was quiet because the
snow was thick and all the pups had gone off somewhere,
Rue was suddenly alert with a mother's foreknowledge
that something is dreadfully wrong. It was Violet who
came running, frightened as a pup should never be frightened.

"What's happened?" Rue asked urgently.

"There's two big moles and they've got Beech and
they're *hitting* him." Rue started to run the way Violet
had come, calling out *"Show* me."

What Violet had reported was not strictly true. Mandrake and Rune had entered Hulver's burrows and gone
straight to the sealed tunnel that led into the Ancient System. They had not even considered that the tunnels would
be occupied, and the lack of sound and smell seemed to
prove them right.

Mandrake started without ado to burrow around the
flint seal and, quite quickly, made sufficient of a passage
to get through to the other side if he wanted. He
had sniffed the cold air of the Ancient System, looked into
its depths and was working himself up into a rage prepar-
atory to setting off by himself into its silent depths, to root
out and kill the Stone Mole.

Then Rune heard a rustle behind them and caught
sight of the youngsters, watching. Mandrake, unpredict-
ably, laughed. Rune, predictably, saw as quick as a talon
thrust that there might be some use for these youngsters.
They were all of them about to run off, but there was
such ice in Rune's gaze that they froze trembling to the
wall—all except Violet, who was behind and slipped back
into the shadows.

Mandrake came out of the tunnel he had made, peered
heavily at them, shook his head, and was gone into the
blackness of the Ancient System with a chuckle and a
roar, leaving Rune with the youngsters.

Beech was nearest, so Rune picked on him. "Well,

well," he said sneeringly at him, "and who are we, then?"

"Beech, sir," whispered Beech. Rune stretched out a talon and cuffed him hard enough to hurt.

"Really?" smiled Rune, hitting him again. The other youngsters' eyes widened in fear and they started to tremble.

"Who's your mother then, Beech, sir?" said Rune, approaching near him so that Beech felt he was being engulfed by darkness. Beech couldn't take his eyes off Rune's; Coltsfoot and Pipple simply stared at him in horror as if they were transfixed by a talon to the tunnel wall.

"She's Rue, sir," said Beech. He looked round at his brothers and sisters for help, his mouth trembling in his struggle not to cry, for he thought that if he did, he might be punished still more. It was at this point that Violet slipped away to run and find Rue.

Until Rue's name was mentioned, Rune was merely enjoying himself putting terror into the hearts of these youngsters; once it came out, his mind began to race with possibilities. The opportunity he was seeking, and which he knew would come eventually if he was patient enough, had arrived.

Rue was the mole who had first reported hearing the Stone Mole in the Ancient System—a report that in Rune's view was hysterical and unfounded. But that was no matter—her name was remembered sympathetically in Barrow Vale. What a terrible thing it would be—would it not?—if Mandrake was proved to have killed some of Rue's litter—a litter she had bravely reared up on the slopes all by herself, et cetera and so forth. And after he had done away with Rebecca's brood! Rune looked down at the pathetic Beech, thinking that there's nothing like fear to confuse a mind.

Then he heard a calling and a running, the cry of a mother to her litter, and a look of hope came into the stricken eyes of little Beech. So Rue was coming, was she? Perfect timing!

With a talon thrust quicker than a pup can bleat, Rune killed Beech, his body and a few drops of blood falling in a slump against the tunnel wall.

He watched coldly when Rue arrived and a look of horror came over her face and a choking to her throat as she looked disbelievingly at Beech and then up at Rune.

"Very sad," said Rune. "Very unpleasant. The work of

Mandrake, I'm afraid, wasn't it?" He looked menacingly at
Coltsfoot and Pipple; he could not see Violet, who
was some way behind Rue and sensibly staying there. The
two youngsters nodded silently. Rue could see they were
terrified, too afraid even to run to her. She went to them.

Rune looked at her and said, "You will go to Barrow
Vale and report that Mandrake has tried to kill your litter
and that Rune has managed to save all but one of them.
Tell them that Rune wants the henchmoles to muster. Tell
them that Rune is coming."

Rue started to back away, eyes wide, protectively pulling two youngsters with her.

Rune loomed toward her. "That won't be necessary,"
he smiled. "They'll slow your progress, and anyway, I will
protect them from Mandrake should he return." He
reached out his paws for them, talons loose, and she
looked into his evil eyes, every instinct telling her to push
them behind her and fight . . . and yet if she did, they
would surely die, whereas this way, Rune's way, there
could be a chance.

"Will they be all right?"

"Of course," nodded Rune, "they'll be safer here than
tagging along with you. I will block up the entrance into
the Ancient System, making it more difficult for Mandrake to return and then hide elsewhere in these tunnels.
If Mandrake returns, which he may very soon do, I will
fight him for you, for I hate him as you do, as we all do.
Now the time has come to resist him, so run to Barrow
Vale now, not only for your system's sake but for your
litter's, too."

Rue's grasp of Coltsfoot and Pipple loosened. Perhaps
he was telling the truth. She looked round for Violet, and
not seeing her decided not to mention her.

"Take care of them," she whispered desperately, then
she turned and ran for their lives toward Barrow Vale.

The two youngsters looked up at Rune, feeling utterly
betrayed and now quite terrified. Rune looked down at
them and as his smile faded, he pulled back his paw swiftly
and with a lunge powerful enough to make him grunt a
little with its effort, he stabbed Coltsfoot to death.

Pipple simply turned and ran, his tiny paws desperately
trying to carry him away from Rune, who watched him go
and then nonchalantly trotted after him, letting him run
for a twist and turn or two of the tunnel. Unwittingly, Pip-

ple ran straight into the place where Violet was hiding and the two simply crouched transfixed as Rune came upon them in a side tunnel.

"Well!" said Rune, "how many more of you are there?"

"There's four of us altogether," said Violet.

Just two left, then, said Rune to himself. He decided to leave one alive just so it could tell the story to the henchmoles. Whichever one it was would be too confused to know the truth, and too terrified to tell it if he did. He wondered coldly which one to kill.

"What are your names?" asked Rune.

"I'm Violet," said Violet, "and he's Pipple." Pipple looked up at Rune and put his paw for safety on his sister's flank.

"Pipple?" ruminated Rune. He didn't like the name. So he killed Pipple.

"My name's Mandrake," lied Rune to Violet, just to confuse the youngster further. And with that he went back to the main tunnel and headed off for Barrow Vale, slowly enough to let Rue get there ahead of him and create some panic before he arrived.

Violet crouched in the tunnel looking at the crumpled Pipple. His eyes were closed and his mouth hung open. "Pipple?" she faltered. "Pipple?" She touched him, but he didn't move.

She ran down the tunnel, back to where they had been, and found Coltsfoot. "Coltsfoot?" she said, her voice faltering in fear about the tunnel. But she didn't move either.

Then on toward where Beech had been . . . surely he would be there. Yes, he was, but there was blood on him. He wasn't like Beech any more.

Violet looked in panic around the tunnel, not even seeing the owl face that glowered down at her from the flint seal. All she knew was that she could not return down the tunnel where that big mole who had hurt Beech, Pipple and Coltsfoot had gone. She was too afraid to do that.

So she turned instead to the tunnel by the side of the flint that went into the hill where that other big mole had gone, the one who had laughed. Perhaps he would help them. He would know what to do to help Beech and Pipple and Coltsfoot. So, panicked and half-sobbing, Violet clambered over the fresh earth burrowed out by Man-

drake and went into the echoing depths of the Ancient
System, fear behind her and Mandrake somewhere in the
darkness ahead.

Rune's plan worked. It could hardly do otherwise. Rue
had given such a garbled version of what had happened,
and was in such a state of shock, that everymole became
convinced that it was Mandrake who had killed one of
her young, and Mandrake who was now lurking in the
Ancient System, possibly with the Stone Mole himself,
ready to wreak vengeance on Duncton.

Moles gathered in panic in Barrow Vale, and when
Rune arrived he was greeted like the savior he wanted to
appear to be. The time, he told them, had come for the
system to act. The Stone had sent Mandrake to test the
system's courage and strength and it must now act by
killing him and prove to the Stone that they would not
accept such an evil leader.

In the next few hours, henchmoles flocked into Barrow
Vale, and even some eastsiders, hearing the news, came
and offered their help.

Rune fueled their anger by cynically sending Rue back
to her tunnels—with a henchmole to "watch over her"—to
collect her young, who he said he had had to leave there
so that he could get himself to Barrow Vale quickly. The
terrible story she brought back, that her young were dead
or gone, which the henchmole confirmed, gave Rune the
final impetus he needed to create a sense of communal
outrage with Mandrake and set the moles gathered in
Barrow Vale on the path to destroy Mandrake and "anymole still in his thrall."

Rune made various speeches, the most predictable of
which ended with the words "These are troubled times
and at a time when we lack a leader we must stand firm
together . . ."

At the words *lack a leader* there were cries of dissent
and dismay from the attendant henchmoles, who clam-
ored to let him know that he was far too modest, he was
their leader, *would* he lead them? It was finally Burrhead
himself who proposed it, a suggestion Rune accepted "reluctantly" and "for the time being" and with the thought
to himself that life can sometimes be very simple.

It was now only a matter of time before Rune led the
henchmoles back up to the tunnel into the Ancient Sys-

tem and then marched through their aged depths to find
and kill Mandrake.

There was only one small cloud on Rune's horizon,
and that was the uncooperative attitude of the Marsh
End to his new rule.

"I see no marshenders lending their support here in
Barrow Vale," he said smoothly to Mekkins, who had
put in an appearance to see what was going on.

"Disease," lied Mekkins, taking a tip from Curlew's
methods of isolating herself. "Been dropping like flies in
the Marsh End, they have. Often do this time of year,
just before the mating season is about to start. There's
not a mole down there doesn't want to give his support,
Rune—in fact, I had to physically restrain a whole pack
of them from coming up here. There's no love lost for
Mandrake down our way, you know. But I felt it was too
big a risk, mate, too much trouble."

Rune didn't like Mekkins—far too disrespectful. Nor
did he entirely believe his story. But there were other
things to think about and the marshenders' failure to help
oust Mandrake would be just the excuse he was going to
need when it came to doing what he had long wanted to
do—wipe out the marshenders, Mekkins included.

As for Mekkins, he slipped quietly back to the Marsh
End, where he had plans of his own to see to. He was
well aware of the threat to it and had worked various
ideas out, which he now intended to put into practice. At
the same time, he had to think how he was going to protect Rebecca and Comfrey now that they could expect
trouble down that way, and the first thing he was going to
do was to work out where to move them to, for surely
where they were was now too isolated and exposed
should Rune and the henchmoles choose to take over the
system from Mandrake.

It took two days for Mandrake to make his way to the
Chamber of Dark Sound, where he stood in the center
and roared out his challenge to the Stone Mole. His noise
came back in echoes from the carved wall with the flint
owl face at its center a hundredfold, but had no effect on
him. His obsessions seemed to have given him a sublime
courage, or ignorance, of where he was and what he was
doing. He believed the Stone Mole was there and so he
called out to him. He was afraid, but not of a sound that

had no effect on him, and the feeling of fear was so alien
to him, being Mandrake, that he could only turn and face
it with his talons—a courage that few moles would have
easily understood.

Violet, wandering disconsolately among the tunnels,
heard the roaring and *was* afraid, but not thinking it
came from "the big mole," redoubled her efforts to find
him, thinking he would protect her from everything, and
perhaps still help her siblings. She did not really understand that they were dead.

She found him eventually sleeping in one of the entrances to the great chamber and without ado, woke him
up. Her presence confused him. She wasn't the Stone
Mole. She wasn't Sarah. She wasn't Rebecca. He had
been a youngster himself. Yes.

She prattled on about Coltsfoot and Pipple and Beech
and a big mole. She obviously knew where the Stone
Mole was. Perhaps she was a spy. Cunning. But not as
cunning as he. He would keep an eye on her, keep her
within a talon's reach. Yes, he would! Better still, he'd get
her to show him where the Stone Mole was. Yes. Cunning
and clever.

Violet could not understand him. He was alternately
kind and angry. He wanted her to lead him somewhere
after a *stonemole,* and she didn't know what that was. So
to avoid him getting angry she led him here and there
among the tunnels, her tiny form ahead of his brooding
mass as he muttered "Cunning," and "You're a clever
one, but not as clever as Mandrake," and told her stories
about a mole he knew called Rebecca, his Rebecca, who
did disobedient things and was with the stonemole, whatever it was.

But they were not alone in the tunnels, for another
mole, who knew the ins and outs of the system better
than anymole ever had, flitted from shadow to shadow,
ahead and behind, looking after them round corners,
watching in agonies as Mandrake threatened Violet,
watching with relief when he talked more softly to her,
and wondering, wondering, how to get her away from
Mandrake's talons.

It was Bracken, who had heard the roarings and had
come to investigate. He had recognized Violet as his and
Rue's daughter, and was able, in horror, to piece together
something of what had happened from Violet's pathetic

conversation with the demented Mandrake. And he knew that he must act very soon if she, too, was not to be killed.

Outside, the weather was as troubled and changeable as the life of the moles underground. After two days of still coldness the snow had begun to melt, falling with phuts and plops and dollops from the trees, spraying down through the branches, and pitting the snow on the floor of the wood into thousands of minicraters. Here and there a fox's tracks wove among the trees, and where the badgers lived down on the eastside, the snow was roughed and dirtied by soil and debris from their sets.

Then a moist, wet wind came, and the snow began to thaw slowly, making the ground sodden and slushy and the pastures a mixture of green and yellow grass and remnant snow in the hollows where the wind had gathered it. While out on the marshes beyond Marsh End, the snow melted into the water and mud, and at night froze and was deadly still. Then wind again, and change. Uncomfortable weather that did not know which way it was going to go.

24

As far as he could, Bracken always kept himself between Mandrake and the Chamber of Dark Sound, because then, if he was spotted, he could retreat to the relative safety of the central tunnels beyond the chamber in which, should he be chased there, Mandrake would certainly lose himself.

The precaution was wise, for the moment inevitably came when Mandrake sensed his presence.

"Shush, girl," he said to Violet. "I think I hear the Stone Mole ahead."

Bracken froze and tried to steal away, but Mandrake had heard and was after him, all his old savage speed still there.

Bracken raced ahead, his knowledge of the tunnels making up for Mandrake's extraordinary speed. He reached the Chamber of Dark Sound, raced across it to the seventh entrance, where the mole skeleton still lay undisturbed, but instead of running on he halted between the two great flintstones that stood either side of it and turned to face the chamber. He waited until Mandrake was about to enter and then began to hum softly up into the convolutions of the terrible owl face above. The effect was extraordinary. The noises that had so terrified him when he was in front of it now sounded out beyond him and gave the impression of having great strength and power. His very talons and shoulders seemed bigger, his sight more deadly clear. He seemed to be able to see across the chamber, which normally was not quite possible, and there to catch sight of Mandrake, halted and baffled, moving as if in slow motion, struggling forward into a sound that clearly caused him great fear and distress. Bracken watched him almost dispassionately, seeing his massive size, each limb seeming as big as a mole, the eyes red with aggression, but fearing none of it. He knew with certainty that so long as he sounded the noise, Mandrake would never be able to reach him.

But the effect of the sound was soon subtler and more evil than that. It began to make Bracken want to torment Mandrake, to hurt him, it made him feel that he really was as powerful as the owl looked; it made him want to kill Mandrake. Worse, it made him start to forget that his real aim was to get Violet away from Mandrake and the Ancient System. For his now dispassionate gaze fell not only on Mandrake but also on Violet, who had followed into the chamber after him and now stood, apparently unaffected by the sound, in its center.

Bracken's talons protracted forward, his back reared up and his snout arched cruelly down, his mouth and teeth setting into a rigor of humming as he felt himself losing control of his body and the hum began to take him over, its evil sound beginning to creep into his spirit.

It was Violet who stopped him. She watched puzzled as Mandrake writhed and thrashed about at the noise, which was only a nasty noise as far as she was concerned, and then she wandered over toward its source. She saw a white skeleton, but that didn't worry her because she had no idea what it was, and anyway, what crouched by it was far more interesting. It was a mole that stood like stone, its eyes wide and its teeth clenched. It had terribly big talons, all stretched out. It was humming. It was the stonemole! The thing Mandrake was looking for! She ran forward to it and touched it and oh . . . it was *real,* it had fur just like her . . .

The touch of her paw broke the spell of the hum and slowly he relaxed, and then fell silent, the sound fading out in the chamber as both he and Mandrake seemed to come out of a nightmare.

Poor Violet, upset by shock after shock, started to cry; Mandrake, hearing her, started running toward them both. Bracken stepped forward, put a paw round her shoulders, and pulled her back through the flint entrance.

"Violet," he said urgently. "Listen! Run down this tunnel and go into the first entrance you see in the tunnel it comes into. Hide in the shadows there. I'll come. Run!"

She only half recognized him, but she knew his voice, he was a mole who knew Rue. Oh, that was a relief! And she was running, she was running, and perhaps he'd help. "Run!" he shouted after her, "run!"

It was as Bracken turned back into the chamber to face Mandrake, who was now halfway across it, and coming inexorably toward him, that the whole chamber was filled with another sound, one that took them both totally by surprise—the pattering of a hundred running paws, and of grim mutterings of moles, angry and full of blood-lust.

Mandrake stopped and turned round, his back to

Bracken, and both saw first one mole, then two, then five more pouring through the eastern tunnel entrance that marked the tunnel running up from the slopes. It was Rune and the henchmoles and more beside, and they were chanting "Kill him, kill him!" and massing ready to charge Mandrake down.

"There he is!" cried Rune, pointing a taloned paw at Mandrake.

Mandrake looked at them uncomprehendingly. He wasn't interested in them. He had the Stone Mole almost at the end of his talons and he wasn't going to waste time on Rune and a bunch of henchmoles. Were they threatening *him?* He laughed, shook his head, turned his back contemptuously on them and started forward again to pursue Bracken.

"He's running!" cried Rune triumphantly, and that was enough to give the moles the courage they needed to begin their assault on Mandrake. Several of them reached him before he reached the flint entrance and thrust their claws at him with screams and shouts. One got in the way of his back paws and made him half trip, forcing him to stop. He turned to face them again, and as he did so Bracken, unseen by anymole, took the opportunity of running off down the tunnel to find Violet and slip away. The Duncton system was clearly going mad.

In amid the moles, Mandrake rose up magnificently, and with a mighty sweep of his right taloned paw, killed three moles with one terrible blow. He had not forgotten how to fight. He stepped back, throwing, as he did so, another two off his huge back. His left paw thrust viciously forward and two moles crumpled up screaming below his snout. His movements were not hasty or rapid, but had the leisurely grace of a confident fighter who had never in his life been beaten. With dead or dying moles around him, he stepped back once more, swinging his right paw back so that two more moles went flying forward into the mass who had been clamoring to get at him. He laughed and then roared, and the moles hesitated, the ones in front no longer willing to go forward to what seemed a certain, and cruel, death. Only Rune was still there and shouted out again for moles to kill. Mandrake might, indeed, have killed Rune there and then, but he remembered that his main purpose was to kill the Stone Mole, not this sniveling rabble or Rune.

He backed into the flint entrance, watching as the

moles still came slowly forward on him. He saw the great
flints on either side of the entrance, raised a paw to each
of them, dug his talons deeply into the soil behind them,
and with one massive roaring and grunting effort, pulled
down the two flints in a mass of dust and debris before
them all, blocking the entrance completely and leaving
himself free to pursue the Stone Mole.

As he ran off, the remaining flint capstone over the
entrance broke free from the soil above it and crashed
onto the flints below, and from out of their dust and
debris, all that Rune and the other moles could now see
were the gaunt, hollow eyes of the skull of a long-dead
mole, the rest of its skeleton lost under a mass of impassable debris.

Bracken almost carried Violet round the circular tunnel and out into his own burrows, he was so anxious to
get her out of the Ancient System and away from Mandrake. And himself, too, for that matter.

He went as fast as he could straight up the entrance
nearest the pastures and then out onto the surface, where
a gray morning was well advanced and the ground was
wet from the thaw of snow. And there they were almost
immediately seen by a henchmole—one of the many
Rune had prudently posted all around the surface of the
Ancient System for just such a possibility as this. Only it
was Mandrake Rune had expected to try to escape, not
some other mole. Bracken dived back down into his tunnels, pushing Violet roughly ahead of him and, knowing
that the henchmole would delay some while before he
risked chasing down after him, made for a different exit.

The fact that they were so nearly caught was a blessing
in disguise, for it warned Bracken of the dangers they
now faced. It seemed to him that the only possibility open
to him was to get as far away from the top of the hill
as possible, to somewhere where they could find friends.
And that meant Rebecca's hideaway down in the eastern
Marsh End.

Of their trek down there, which took almost three days,
almost every terrifying detail is known, for it was a memory that Violet was to carry with her for the rest of her
life and accounts of which now lie recorded in the Rolls
of the Systems in the libraries of Uffington.

What Violet never said, however, was that the real
reason for their delay was her incredible slowness and

her inability to understand the danger they were in. At moments when they were close to being sighted by pursuing henchmoles, or when Bracken was despairing of ever keeping her alive, or when the cold of January seemed certain to freeze them both to death, she would ask some irrelevant question like "Who *is* that stonemole, then?" or "Do you really know where we're going because I'm getting bored?" or "If *he* was Mandrake, who was that big mole?" Or she would declare in a loud voice that would shatter the silence they were trying to sneak through "I'm hungry!"

But while she may have driven Bracken mad, perhaps her continual puppish ebullience kept his spirits up as well.

They were under pressure from henchmoles from the moment they started down the slopes toward the eastside. On their flanks, behind, sometimes in front, henchmoles chased them, cutting back and forth in numbers across the wood's floor to find their scent and track them down. Bracken avoided them, partly by sticking to the surface the whole time—except for once, when he had to use a tunnel to escape several henchmoles coming for them from different directions—but mainly by his extraordinary ability, developed in his long period of solo exploration in the Ancient System, to foresee route alternatives and take the one that would confound his enemies. He himself later pinned his success on the fact that thawing snow created temporary rivulets, particularly just below the slopes, which masked their scent tracks.

However, they avoided rather than lost their pursuers and by the third day, when they were nearing Curlew's burrows, they were being very hard-pressed. The more so because, unknown to Bracken, the pressure to find them had been increased by Rune's decision to join the search and abandon Mandrake to the central part of the Ancient System, where he seemed content to stay. Henchmoles only remained up there to monitor his movements while Rune rapidly went down the slopes to find out who these two moles were who had escaped so mysteriously from the Ancient System.

By the time Bracken realized in horror that his own arrival might lead to the discovery of Rebecca and Comfrey and Curlew by leading the henchmoles to their tunnels, it was too late—henchmoles seemed to have cut off any other route. All he could do was to make a final dash ahead and hope he would be in time to warn Rebecca.

On the afternoon of the third day, when the weather was turning bitterly cold again and the light in the wood was gloomy and dark, Bracken finally reached the entrance to Curlew's tunnel. Henchmoles were not far behind and so he pushed Violet down it with an instruction (which he had scant hope would be carried out) for her to warn them that he was there, and turned round to ward off any henchmole who might come and surprise them.

Violet tottered complainingly down into the tunnels, saying she was hungry and she hoped there was some *nice* mole around who would do the proper thing and produce a worm or two, or three, and that Bracken never answered any of her questions, and aren't there any moles here *at all?* She found herself face to face with Mekkins, who had advanced warily up the tunnel to see what the fuss was about.

"Hullo," said Mekkins, "and who are you, then?"

"Violet, I'm hungry."

"Yes, so I heard. I expect Rebecca'll find you something."

"He's up there," said Violet, looking back up the tunnel, "he said to warn you."

When Mekkins saw Bracken, he was relieved to see him safe but shocked at how terribly weary he was. But a moment's account of what had happened soon explained why.

"I've come 'ere myself to take them away," said Mekkins, "'cos I could see the way things are goin'. There's only one place where they'll be safe, and that's out of the system."

"But where?" asked Bracken.

"With Rose, on the pastures. It'll be risky getting them there and might even be risky once they're there, because Rose's protection may not be enough. But anywhere else . . . Well . . ."

Bracken was almost falling off his paws with tiredness. But still he snouted into the gloom for signs of henchmoles.

"They'll not come this far yet, surely?" said Mekkins.

"Yes they will," sighed Bracken. "There seems to be so many of them and they're so determined to find us that they keep on and on. They nearly caught us several times. You've got to get out of here, Mekkins. I'm sorry . . ."

"Listen, chum. You've worked a bloody marvel. The

more I know about you and Rebecca, the less I understand. But don't *you* say you're *sorry*. Now look, there's no sign of them at the moment, and it would take them a while to find these tunnels anyway, so you go down and rest for a bit and I'll keep a watch out and come down later to work out what to do. You send Curlew up as well, 'cos there's something she can do . . ."

Mekkins had nothing for Curlew to do at all, but he knew that Rebecca had been worried about Bracken. Let 'em have a few minutes together for Stone's sake, he said to himself. Don't ask me what it's about, he added, shaking his head and turning his attention to the gathering dark.

But Mekkins' sentimentality was misplaced. Bracken was too tired, Rebecca already too aware of the dangers in the system, and Comfrey too afraid of Bracken's size and different smell for there to be much between any of them. Only Violet seemed unaffected by it all. Bracken laid his head on his paws and looked curiously at the thin and nervous Comfrey. Why, he liked Violet better! As for Rebecca and him, neither could believe that they had really made a journey to the center of the system together. Surely that was two different moles? The burrow was small and cramped, the atmosphere fearful, and everything in flux. There was the feeling that nothing could be permanent and that the system of Mandrake was giving way to something worse. As for Bracken, he was beginning to feel tired of running, always running, and half felt inclined to go out onto the surface and do some final battle with the henchmoles. But then he fell asleep.

Rebecca watched over him, wondering as she looked, almost for the first time, at a mole she hardly knew, and who seemed a stranger, why she was so moved by every start and turn in his fitful and uneasy sleep. Who is he? she wondered. She wanted to draw Comfrey to her and say to him "Look, that's your father, his name's Bracken, he's a brave mole." But wisely she let him be.

Comfrey was having problems of his own, anyway, with Violet—who might just as well have woken from a long refreshing sleep for all the sign she showed of tiredness from a three-day escape from Rune's henchmoles.

"What's your name?" she asked him.

"C–C–Comfrey," he finally got out.

"Why can't you speak properly?"

Silence.

"Well, at least you could ask *my* name, which is Violet."

"Where do you come from?" tried Comfrey.

"Rue's tunnels, near where the Stone Mole lives."

"Who's the St—Stone Mole?"

"He is, silly," said Violet, pointing at the sleeping Bracken. Violet turned away, looking a little miserable. Now that Bracken was asleep, she felt alone. He was all she had.

Rebecca stretched a motherly paw to her and pulled her to her flank. "Why don't you tell me what happened, my love," said Rebecca, and bit by bit Violet did, her little defenses dropping as she relaxed at last into a mole who seemed almost as cuddly as Rue. "What's going to happen?" Violet asked much later. Rebecca could see how alone she was, and how near to tears. Bracken's daughter, Bracken's son. He couldn't have done more for them. Now perhaps she could care for them while they grew up.

"Rebecca! Bracken!" It was Curlew, running back into the burrow. "Wake up, Bracken! The henchmoles are coming!" How Curlew had changed since Rebecca had first come! True, her fur was still rough and patchy—but her spirits were so full and high, and her body straighter and prouder than it had been. "You've got to leave, Rebecca, almost immediately," she said.

Mekkins came running down. "They're almost here," he said, "and they'll find these tunnels very soon. There's an exit nearer the marshes and I'll take you all out by that."

Bracken did not move. He did not even get up. He was tired of running. "You go, I'll stay. I can hold them back for a while."

As Mekkins and Rebecca started to argue, Bracken got up and slowly faced them. His gaze was clear and there was an enormous authority about what he said that left no mole there in any doubt that he would do what he intended.

"I led them here and I'll lead them away again, in a different direction to where you're going. Don't worry, Mekkins, I won't try to fight them all by myself. But with luck I can lead them off your scent, and you, Rebecca and these two," he pointed to Comfrey and Violet, "can get away to Rose the Healer."

Violet started to protest, but Bracken gazed at her with

such strength and love that she simply retreated back to
Rebecca's flank and waited for once for the adults to
do whatever they had to do. "Rebecca will take care of
you and I'll be back," Bracken said gently to her. "And
don't you chatter so much this time!"

For a moment Rebecca and Bracken stared across the
burrow at each other and the light that seemed to have
gone from them shone again, and time was not important. Why, it's there and always will be, thought Rebecca,
knowing it was true.

"I'm not going either," said Curlew suddenly. "These
are my tunnels and they've served me well, and I'll defend
them. I couldn't live anywhere else, anyway." Her mind
was quite made up so that, with a shake of his head in
puzzlement, Mekkins led Rebecca and the youngsters
away, and the burrow was suddenly silent of them.

"There's a tunnel I'll show you, off to the east," said
Curlew. "It goes for quite a way. If they come, I've
got a way of holding them up for a bit so you go down
there and lead them off away from the west, where Mekkins will be. Every little bit gives them time."

With a thumping overhead and shouts, the henchmoles
did come, not long after, and Curlew tried her old trick
on them. "There's disease here, contagious disease," she
hissed up the tunnel at them.

It worked for a while until a cold authoritative voice
came out of the bitter night to the henchmole who was
hesitating.

"Get down there now or I'll kill you with my own talons," it said. Down in the central burrow, Bracken recognized with a shudder the voice of Rune. So he was here!
And then there was a thump and a gasp, and old Curlew
was outnumbered and outfought as the henchmoles rushed
past her and down to where Bracken crouched.

He raced away down the tunnel she had shown him
and out into the night, and chased desperately this way
and that across the frozen ground, making as much noise
as possible and heading for the north and east toward
the marsh. Henchmoles were thick on the ground, and
more than once he came face to face with one before
twisting away into the dark, saved only by their own
confusion at each other's noise. Sometimes he hid in
silence and let them chase around him; then, when they
seemed to be drifting back to the west, toward where
Rebecca, Violet and Comfrey might be with Mekkins, he

would make a noise again and they would swing back toward him.

If the night was cold, the dawn was colder. It rose bleakly on a wood full of hate and fear. There was a hoarfrost on the trees and ground which gave the wood a deceptive white calm but meant that the slightest movement brought a crackling of frozen leaves and vegetation.

Bracken was now very tired and responded with a start of alarm at every movement around him. He wanted to run back, or forward, or wherever they were and say "Here I am. Here! It's over. You've got what you want!"

Then a henchmole moved somewhere and he was off again, paw in front of paw, twisting and turning and trying to think ahead of himself, trying not to drown in his own breathlessness and succumb at last to the tiredness he felt. Noises all around, and white-coated twigs and leaves that would have seemed delicate and beautiful had a mole had time to look.

On through the lightening mauve of dawn, nearer and nearer to the wood's edge, nearer and nearer now to the marsh. He could sense the dreadful space stretching out somewhere beyond the trees and tried to cut away from it back into the bigger trees. But henchmoles were there, more of them running, distant shouts, nearby sneakings of talons on the frosty ground. He was forced nearer and nearer to the marsh.

Sounds to the right and left, the fearful light and space ahead, no other way to go for a desperate mole, paw after paw unsteadily in front of each other, shoulders aching with effort.

Then he was out of the wood and tumbling down a short bank under an old wire fence to a wall of alien marsh grass and the smell of the unknown. Off to the right two henchmoles came out of the wood as well, down the bank, looked right and then left and saw him; and they were coming, coming, their paws and talons pounding, bigger and nearer with each moment. He looked back along the marsh grass to his left toward the west and there were other henchmoles, several, sneaking steadily along toward him. Desperate, he turned around to look back up the bank he had fallen down, so steep, so tired, each gasp a pain for life. Perhaps he could make it back into the wood, perhaps his near-dead, aching legs would take him back. Perhaps.

Then Rune was there. Rune out on the bank looking down at him. A nightmare come true. Rune triumphant. Rune about to say something. Rune's mouth open and his talons ready, as left and right the henchmoles came.

Bracken turned away from them all and faced the still, frosted wall of tall, haggard grass, diving into it and through, a final chase to his own destruction. Through the grass, leaving the shouts, into an alien world where the birds have eerie calls and slow flapping wings and long, sharp beaks big enough to kill a mole. Running once more, but with the voices fading at last behind him.

"He's gone into the marsh, the silly bugger!"

"Who was 'e then? Never seen him before."

"E'll be drownded or eaten 'fore the hour's done."

"Who was he, Rune?"

"Somemole we'll wait for, that's who. So patrol this edge until I'm satisfied he's gone for good," said Rune.

Silence came and the wood was gone forever behind Bracken as he wearily wended his way over the tussocks and ice of the frozen marsh. No food, no shelter, little hope. Lost in a frozen waste. No good going back.

On he went into a fearful day, with whispers of wind in the reeds above his head, the frozen debris of an alien world at his paws. And hunger bearing him down. A long day of fear, a night of rustling ahead. Another dawn came, a day of gnawing at dry grass stems and snouting out the dangers that seemed to wait at every turn. Another afternoon. A sudden spell of bright, cold sun that made him feel as vulnerable as a flea on an open paw. Night and cold. Day and fear. A starting up of blustering winds as hunger weakened him step by step. The carcass of a dead and frozen bird, torn by other scavengers more used to the marsh than he. A tearing of teeth at it, something to eat, a frozen survival, and then black crows wheeling from the sky and down at him, and he was off again, shaken by the cawings and wheelings of blacksheen wings.

Then the worst horror, the ultimate fear of every mole in nightmare straits: oozing mud. The wind brought a thaw and that brought a softening to the grasses, and a heaving to the ground. Where it had been solid to his tired paws, it now squelched wet. Where it had supported his weight, it now let him sink. His belly was covered in the slime of mud as finally, and desperately, he dragged himself on. Everything gone, why cling to life? But what makes a mole fight death? What force drags one tired paw before the other?

His progress—where, he wondered?—grew slower. If he stopped, he sank, if he went on, he grew more and more in need of sleep. A great crow dived from the white sky again, wheeling and calling about him. On and on, with talons ready, Bracken tried his best.

His best was just good enough, for as the marsh thawed out behind him, the frost quite gone, and pockets of water appeared again where ice had been, Bracken neared a wall that skirted its northern edge. The grass adjacent to it was a little drier and he was on it, and up to the wall, and suddenly alive for a moment more as the crows wheeled about and he looked for cover. The smell of a hole, damp and cool, and he was chasing to it . . . along the wall to a great round drainage pipe set into it, and into its dank shelter. Behind, against the white sky, there was the flutter of a black wing, the hang of a dark gray claw, the tap of a death beak. He turned away in fear into the strange round tunnel and started down it, only trying to stop himself when it was too late. For it sloped down steeply, its bottom was slimy with mud and as the sides were too wide for him to reach to grip, he could not stop himself sliding faster and faster down it, a tired anger mounting in him to be falling to his death like this.

Then, slipping helplessly toward a bright light, where the tunnel ended in a void, he fell tumbling in a shower of mud and water into a concrete drainageway, beyond the marsh and wall.

He opened his eyes into a waking nightmare. For fighting and clawing at each other in the mud and slime that had fallen with him onto the hard ground of the drainage channel were two moles, both intent, it seemed, on finding any worms or other food that had come from the pipe in his fall. There was something wild and desperate about each of them—their fur was unkempt and their flanks thin from starvation, and one of them was rapidly losing the fight. Indeed, so unequal was the struggle that the smaller of the two was simply retreating from the other when Bracken first fully realized what was happening.

With one final clout, the bigger one turned back to where Bracken lay, to search for food in peace, the other

watching from a distance, hoping, perhaps, to pick up
a scrap or two.

All this Bracken took in very quickly, and as he did
so he felt himself suddenly lifted onto his paws by a
sense of anger and outrage. Had he run and run and run
from fighting in Duncton only to find himself landing
straight into more fighting even in this evil-smelling
place?

It was as if his frustration with Rune and Mandrake,
at Cairn's death and the henchmoles, even back to Root
and Wheatear—all moles who had faced him in one way
or another with fighting from which he had run—had finally boiled over into rage. He snarled, his talons extended, and without any more ado he attacked the bigger
mole viciously. There was no fear in what he was doing,
and little thought. He simply crashed down his paws and
talons, grunting and snarling with each lunge, encouraged
to even greater violence by each successful contact with
his surprised and then frightened adversary. For a moment, the mole fought back, but then, lowering his snout
in a gesture of defeat, he turned tail and ran off down
the channel, out of the range of Bracken's sight.

Bracken watched him go, shaking with anger, and
then turned to the smaller mole who crouched quite still
looking at him. Quite what Bracken expected he did not
know—but certainly not the response he got. For, instead of showing any thanks for his deliverance from
the bigger mole or any acquiescence to Bracken's superiority, or even any fear, he had the nerve to ask "Whatmole are you, and where are you from?"—the traditional
greetings of the superior mole to the inferior.

Bracken was so taken back by this insolence that he
very nearly started laying into this mole as well, but
then the sight of one so weak and pathetic-looking being
so bold struck him as frankly comic.

"You've got a nerve," he said. "My name's Bracken,
from Duncton Wood."

This appeared to have as startling an effect on the
small mole as his own question had had on Bracken.

He darted forward, limping in a curious way as if he
was injured, and exclaimed, "You mean the Duncton
system?" Bracken began to nod and then said: "And
whatmole are you, for Stone's sake?"

"Boswell of Uffington," the mole replied.

III

BRACKEN

UFFINGTON! No single word could have heartened Bracken more at that moment. A mole from Uffington! It had always been Hulver's greatest wish that he should live to see such a thing and now, here in this strange place, Bracken had been led to just such a mole by the Stone's grace.

His excitement was, however, tinged by a sense of disappointment, for this Boswell did not in any way look as Bracken had imagined one of the legendary moles from Uffington would look. He was small and crippled, his weak paw making him walk in a darting, hobbling way that had his head swinging to the left—the side of his weak paw—then up away from the ground on his right and then down again. His coat was a very dark gray flecked with white and he looked half-starved.

He spoke in a quick staccato way as if he could not get his thoughts out fast enough to keep up with his words, and he had a habit of interrupting Bracken when he spoke with a "Yes, yes," as if he knew what he was going to say before he said it. Which, often, he did.

Despite his overt weakness he seemed quite unafraid, although a semblance of fear—very like that he had shown before the other mole—would sometimes cross his face. Bracken soon realized that this was a guise, a kind of mask he wore to appear so pathetic that no mole would wish to persist in attacking. Perhaps that's why he's managed to survive, thought Bracken, whose only knowledge of crippled moles was that they never survived their first summer because they could not get territory of their own.

Perhaps the most disconcerting quality he had lay in the way his eyes, small and bright as a bark beetle's wing, fixed Bracken with a gaze so direct and penetrating that at first Bracken felt positively shifty looking at him.

"So you're from Duncton, are you?" said Boswell, before Bracken could get a word in. "Just the mole I've been looking for."

"Well, it would be nice to know a bit more . . ."

"Yes, yes," interrupted Boswell, "all in good time. Right now there's *no* time. If you want to rest you had better forget it. We've got to get out of here as fast as we can."

"*We've* got to—" started Bracken, who had no intention of allying himself to anymole just like that, whether he came from Uffington or not.

"That's right. *We*. You can try it on your own but you won't succeed."

It did not take Boswell very long to persuade Bracken that they—and his *they* included the other mole, who now lurked near them looking both angry and fearful at the same time—were in a desperate situation.

The place into which Bracken had fallen was a long, narrow drainage channel made of a smooth unnatural stone, which smelled wrong and had high impassable walls. On one side was the marsh, on the other side an embankment that rose massively upward and sloped away out of sight. But though Bracken could not see its end, he could smell and hear what was there—creatures whose noise was loud and rumbling, so great, indeed, that the very ground shook with their passing and whose smell was so sick with death that it made a mole's snout go numb.

"Roaring owls," said Boswell obscurely.

"Owls?"

"Seen them myself. I came here *down* that embankment two nights ago. There's a flat path at the top, wide as a mole's system, and the roaring owls fly along just above it. You wait till night comes and you'll see what I mean."

By this time the third mole, whom Bracken had driven away, slunk back within earshot. He seemed to want to join in the discussion and nodded his head when Boswell was describing the owls.

"Their gaze is so fierce that you can see it at night even down here. It's like fire," he said, creeping over to them.

"Fire?" queried Bracken, who had never heard the word.

"Like hot sun," said the other, "only it kills everything it touches."

As if this weren't enough, they went on to explain that the channel they were in was plagued by carrion crows and the occasional kestrel, which dived and pecked at any creature alive or dead caught in it. They had taken a mole only hours before Bracken's arrival, and constantly squabbled and pecked over a dead hare that lay away farther down the channel.

"There's no cover here. You can't burrow. And the stench of the roaring owls is enough to kill a mole," exclaimed Boswell.

"And there's no food—that's why . . . ," the other mole didn't finish; he didn't want to remind Bracken of the circumstances of their first meeting.

"What's your name?" asked Bracken, taking the initiative for the first time.

"Mullion, from the pasture system. It's near Duncton Hill."

"I *have* heard of it," said Bracken irritably.

"He hadn't," said Mullion, pointing at Boswell.

They talked for a while—Bracken was too tired to do much else—and kept well in to the side of the channel, using some plant debris as cover. It seemed that Mullion had come over the marshes a week before, when it was frozen, in search of a mole who had left the pastures. A friend of his, he said. As for Boswell, he had made his way along the path used by the roaring owls, nearly been hypnotized by them, and then slipped and tumbled headlong down the embankment, trying to escape crows one night. Bracken wanted to know much more about him and where he had come and why, but this was not the moment. The lack of food showed on them both, and the fact that Mullion had survived a full week said much for his basic strength.

Bracken was aware that he had brought them both some kind of hope, though why he could not imagine.

"We've both tried everything," said Boswell.

"Why did you say a mole couldn't do it by himself but might together with others?" Bracken asked him.

"No reason, just instinct. A mole like me only survives with others, you see." He looked at his crippled paw and shrugged. "Moles don't often realize that two's better than one."

"Or three's better than two," said Mullion.

"Quite," said Boswell.

They looked at Bracken, waiting for him to speak, and for the first time in his life Bracken understood that he had to lead other moles. They were right; there was no time. With each passing hour he would grow weaker, as Mullion had done. Better get on with it.

At that moment, as a reminder of the dangers they faced, the cawing above them of a crow, which hung as a shadow in the sky, shattered through the constant rumbling noise of the roaring owls as it lunged down toward where they crouched, its eyes peering down into the channel. Its claws hung loose, relaxed and deadly under its body as its harsh caw shot about them. Then it wheeled away again.

"Right," said Bracken, "we're getting out of here. There must be a way. I'm going to have a look around for myself. Don't move—and don't fight. I'll be back and we'll work out something."

They watched him creep off along the bottom of the wall, a look of hope in Mullion's eyes and a look of confidence in Boswell's.

The channel, which was about two hundred moleyards long, had few features. Its walls were smooth and impossible to climb; its floor was wet with drifts of sand where water had flooded in the past. At either end the channel was cut off abruptly by a deeper channel that appeared to flow from the marsh and on through the embankment by huge tunnels visible to Bracken but inaccessible because the water flow was too fast and furious, and now very nearly on a level with the channel he was in. Five pipes, like the one he had tumbled down, drained into it from the marsh, ten or twelve molefeet above the bottom of the channel, which sloped gently down from a central point either way to the bigger, lateral drainageways at the bottom. Water drained steadily down from the five pipes.

On the embankment side there were a couple of evil-smelling pipes set into the wall and sloping up into the darkness of the embankment itself, their outlets low enough for Bracken to be able to snout out the fumes and stench that came from them. From the black stains running from them down the wall he guessed that they were unpleasant inside.

The sense of exposure was quite frightening—no mole likes to be on unburrowable ground. As Bracken was thinking about what to do, he heard a shout behind him, and Mullion came running.

"The water's rising," he said. "It's creeping up toward where we were from the other channel."

He was right. The thaw of the snow and ice on the marsh must have brought a rush of water into the bigger channels and now it was creeping quite steadily up toward them from either end of the channel.

"Well, we can't fly," said Bracken sardonically, "so we had better do something."

A check down the other end, where Bracken had been, confirmed that the level had risen even since he had last been there. The dead hare, which lay grotesquely huddled against the channel wall and smelled of death, began to flop and float about in the rising waters, while their channel began to grow wet and treacherous from the increasing outflow from the marsh-drainage pipes leading into it.

"What about those tunnels up into the embankment?" he said finally to them both.

"It's what I said," said Boswell, "but Mullion says it's not possible."

"Too steep and slippery, quite apart from the poisonous smell. You can't even get started," said Mullion.

The water crept nearer and they all moved up toward the center of the channel. The walls seemed higher and more impassable with each second, almost leaning over and crushing down upon them.

"What about swimming out?" said Mullion.

"Never swum in my life," said Bracken.

"You'd learn quick enough," said Boswell. "Even I can do it. But the water in those channels is too fierce."

At the far end of the channel a massive white-and-gray gull dived squawking on the hare, which was now half submerged in water. There was a plash and splash as the gull's claws swept the water, trying vainly to lift the hare out, and then it was up and away into the dull sky. A black beetle suddenly came crawling by along the sand, heading up the center of the channel, as if it knew that the water was rising. Mullion took it for his own and crunched it nervously as they all thought what to do.

Bracken went and took another look up into the round tunnel pipes into the embankment and then impatiently scrambled up into one of them. His back paws had almost disappeared before he came sliding out again and fell into a roll on the channel floor.

"See what I mean?" said Mullion. He was beginning to sound desperate.

"No, I don't," said Bracken. "You can get a grip if you stretch far enough ahead because I could feel that the tunnel has an edge across it—it's not all smooth like the marsh one I came down." He climbed up again, Mullion nudging him up a little from behind and this time his whole body disappeared and he was gone.

"What's he doing?" asked Mullion, increasingly worried by the water at his paws.

"Finding a way out, I expect," said Boswell calmly. Then he added for Mullion's benefit, "It's not as bad as it seems, you know. We can all swim if necessary—though our chances would be low. But we're not going to drown in the next five minutes."

There were shouts from the pipe and Bracken came slithering down backward out of it, covered in mud. He hung for a moment from its edge, his back paws scrabbling for a hold on the smooth wall, and then fell the short distance to the channel floor.

"Well, it's possible, I suppose," he said breathlessly. "It doesn't go anywhere much because there's no wind current and I can sense that it doesn't. But at the very least we might—if we're careful and if you do exactly what I say—avoid the water when it rises. There might even be some food up there—though how it would survive in that roaring-owl stench I don't know."

The water began to rise toward their bellies and was now threatening to sweep them off their feet as Bracken quickly outlined his plan. The pipe was in sections, each unfortunately longer than the length of a mole. But where they joined there was a gap in the pipe large enough to sneak a talon or two in and hold a mole secure.

"The trouble is," said Bracken, "negotiating your way up to the next hold—that's how I slipped the first time."

"Are we taking *him?*" asked Mullion suddenly, looking at Boswell.

"Yes," said Bracken coldly, in a voice that allowed no argument. His plan was that Mullion should go first, being biggest, and stretch forward to the hold Bracken had managed to reach. Then Boswell should follow, clambering up over Mullion to get a grip—a thought that seemed to annoy Mullion and amuse Boswell, who was the only one among them apparently quite unaffected by the position they faced. Then Mullion was to go to the next hold as Bracken joined Boswell, who then went on up to Mullion again.

"That's the theory. Now let's get on with it," said Bracken urgently, the water now almost lifting Boswell off his feet. "And remember you two—one slip and we'll probably all go sliding down into this lot."

The pipe was far more slippery with mud and slime than Mullion expected and it took him several attempts even to get up into it, and then only with Bracken pushing, while Boswell in turn hung onto Bracken as the water steadily rose about them.

"Come on!" urged Bracken, giving Mullion a final heave from behind to help him stretch blindly into the darkness and fight his way up to the first hold. He got to it just as his back paws began to slide away from under him and hung there gasping for a few moments before bringing his other paw forward and getting a secure grip. The gap between the two sections of pipe was quite wide and the hold was good enough to let him rest for a little as his back paws found a better grip and he distributed his weight securely. There was a thin trickle of muddy water running down the bottom of the pipe, getting into his snout and fur. The smell in the pipe went to his snout so powerfully that it disoriented him and made him feel nauseous. But he hung on—he wasn't going to let a Duncton mole think pasture moles were always quite so nervous as he had been before. Behind him he felt Boswell pulling tentatively at his back paw and then somehow levering himself along him with gasps and pants.

"Just in time," said Boswell, joining him at the first hold. "The water was getting so dangerous that Bracken virtually threw me up."

Behind them they heard Bracken working his way up and then call out: "On you go, Mullion, so I can come on up."

And on Mullion went, inch by slippery inch, paws constantly seeming about to slip out of control. Then up struggled Boswell again, even finding time to comment:

"Not a nice place to live, this!" The round tunnel was cold, wet and dark about them. Behind them they could hear Bracken talking himself on: "Now, if I put this one there, and this one here, then I'll get a better grip and . . . ," a habit he had acquired from so many months alone in the Ancient System and one that, in moments of crisis, he was never to lose.

The higher they went the steeper the pipe seemed to get and the more nervous each became as the consequences of a slip became increasingly serious. A mole slipping from this height would probably be so stunned in the fall that he would drown in the swirling water at the foot of the pipe.

Here and there the gap between the pipes was quite wide and gave them points at which they could rest—for lying outstretched in the steep tunnel, hanging on only by talons, was very tiring.

It was when they reached about the fifteenth stretch of pipe that Mullion suddenly, and without warning, slipped. He fell back onto Boswell without even a chance to cry out, and Boswell slipped back onto Bracken under his weight. For a moment Bracken felt his own grip going, the slimy, odorous tunnel suddenly witness to a desperate struggle to maintain a hold on life—but above him, Mullion managed to get a grip again and Boswell, his back paws bouncing all over Bracken's snout, recovered himself as well.

"Thank you," said Bracken acidly.

"Sorry," shouted Mullion down the pipe. He was feeling very weak, but really his performance so far was extraordinary for a mole who had been so weakened by starvation.

A short while later, the pipe leveled off to a less steep slope and they were all able to have a rest. The water flow down it, however, was cold and dank and Boswell was beginning to shiver.

"Well! Well!" said Bracken, trying to keep up morale. "I wonder where we go from here!" From the darkness far below them they could hear a splashing and rushing of water as if the channel where they had been was now as flooded as the ones at its ends had been. It sounded a long way away, and nearer at hand they could hear the occasional drip of water, hollow and ringing through the pipe.

"I don't think this tunnel goes anywhere, but we can

try," said Bracken. The next few sections were easy, though Bracken stayed carefully behind, watching over their progress—he knew how weak they both were. But then there was a hopeless shout from Mullion: "I can't go on—it's almost vertical now." And it was. The pipes twisted upward and offered no further holds.

"We'll just have to burrow out from here, then," said Boswell, picking with his good paw at the earth and grit that lay between two sections of the pipe near which they were crouched. But it was Bracken who had to do it and it proved a long, slow job, partly because the embankment was made of hard-packed soil with all sorts of obstacles like pieces of square rock he had to burrow round, but also because he was so very tired. He seemed barely to have stopped moving since his escape from the Ancient System back in Duncton four days before. But he tried to put that out of his mind, for he knew his chances of ever returning to Duncton were now slim, even supposing he wanted to.

It took him over two hours before a pawthrust broke through the surface of the embankment. He emerged tentatively; Boswell had warned him of the steepness of the slope, and there were the roaring owls to beware of.

Night had fallen and the first thing he saw—and it made him retreat into the tunnel—was the glare of a roaring owl's eyes racing toward him out of darkness, and the growing crescendo of its rumbling flight. The noise was so loud that it stunned him and the stench was many times more nauseating than that in the tunnel. It made his eyes water and his snout ache. And below there was the roar of running water.

He retreated down into the tunnel.

"Well, we can get out, but it's so dangerous there that we had better work out what to do," he said.

"There is little you can do except move as fast as possible," said Boswell. "From what I've seen, we'll have to cross the owl paths and head off along their edge to the west. We'll be very exposed—not only to the roaring owls but to crows and other predators that may be about."

"At night, up here?" queried Mullion.

"Death hangs in the air at any time," said Boswell. "With luck we'll be able to get off the path by the way I originally came and there'll be food to find when we get there. But whatever you do, do not look directly

into the eyes of a roaring owl, as it will instantly hypno-
tize you."

The climb up the burrowed tunnel was no problem,
since it was small enough for them to flex their limbs
against the sides, but once out onto the wet slope they
were in continual danger. The passing owls were snout-
shatteringly loud, and each one left its wave of noisome
smells which so disorientated them that they nearly lost
their grips more than once. Indeed, Bracken, used as he
was to the clear air of Duncton Hill, started to faint
and had not Boswell, at risk to himself, put his paw hard
against Bracken's back, he might easily have slipped back
down into the wet running darkness from which they
were trying to escape.

Thus, slowly and dangerously, they climbed a mountain whose top they were afraid of reaching. When they
got there it was far worse than either Bracken or Mullion
could ever have imagined. The noise, the stench, the
flashing owl gazes! They all kept their snouts down and
their eyes averted for fear of being transfixed by the owls'
gaze—but even so, they could see the light of the owl eyes
flashing and shooting on the grubby wet grass that grew
on top of the embankment, and the ground continually
trembled with their passing.

"Whatever you do, and whatever happens, do not look
round at the roaring owls," repeated Boswell. "Once they
have transfixed you with their gaze, they will crush you
with their talons."

The owls passed intermittently from both directions—
the ones on the nearer path going one way and on the
farther path the other. The three moles waited for a lull
before looking up and across—but it was too murky to see
much and their snouts were so upset by the fumes and
vibrations that they could not snout out much either.
Bracken felt a lassitude growing over him. His will to
move was fading. He wanted to crouch down and sleep.
He wanted . . . , until Boswell nudged him. "Come *on*,
we must move. They are so powerful they can confuse you and put you to sleep without even touching you.
Come on!"

It was suddenly Boswell who was leading them, for he
seemed to have the power to fight the weakness this terrible place put into a mole.

"Listen!" he said urgently. "We will run across to the area between the two paths . . ."

"But if they see us," faltered Mullion, looking up just a little at the owl gazes about them.

"They mustn't, and you mustn't let them. Wait until I start and then follow, and do not look toward them, however near they may seem."

Boswell waited for another lull and then was suddenly off through the grass and onto a hard, wide path that smelled of death. In the distance an owl's gaze shone up into the sky, round across the marshes behind them and then along the path toward them, casting their three shadows before it. "Run!" gasped Boswell, hobbling across the road as fast as he could, the road so wide, the danger getting so near. "Run!" The path stretched hard and black ahead of them as the roaring owl grew nearer, its noise shaking the air about them and its gaze bright and moving on their fur.

Fast as they ran, the roaring owl seemed to fly faster toward them, getting bigger as the edge of the path they could now just see ahead of them seemed to retreat. Each pawstep forward seemed to take a lifetime, each second brought the owl bigger and nearer, its eyes brighter as they tried to reach the center, as Boswell trailed behind the other two.

"Run!" It was Bracken's voice shouting out over the owl noise, urging Boswell on to the safety of the central edge. And he was almost there, his paws almost among the sparse vegetation that scraped a living there, when the roaring owl loomed mightily above him and roared past, the wind from its wings so powerful that he was bowled several moleyards along the road.

In the silence that followed, Bracken and Mullion watching in dread, Boswell turned back on his paws, shook himself, and ran at last to join them. "Running's not my strong point," he said, and Bracken shook his head in disbelief that a mole should make a joke of nearly dying. There was more to Boswell than met the eye.

The central strip between the paths offered them some cover, though the creatures still flew close by in each direction and every time they did so, the world seemed to be replaced for a few moments by hell itself.

It was Boswell, once again, who urged them on, running out into the darkness of a lull once more, the others following.

None of them knew quite what happened next. However it was, Mullion forgot himself when he was halfway across and looked up at another approaching owl, its eyes catching his into a transfixation of horror. He stopped and turned toward it and it was only when the other two were across and looked back that they realized what had happened. There Mullion crouched, snout toward the approaching owl, quite still and waiting for death. It was Bracken who gasped, but Boswell who acted. He darted out into the path again, hobbled over to Mullion as fast as he could and went between him and the roaring owl. Bracken could not hear what he said but he saw him shouting, saw him cuff Mullion and saw Mullion shake himself as if awaking and then Mullion turned and ran toward him to safety.

But then something worse followed, the sight of which Bracken would never forget. As Boswell stood poised to follow Mullion, lit up by the owl's gaze, there was the sudden ghostly shadow of a ragged translucent white in the sky as from it there dropped, at terrible speed, a tawny owl, its feathers caught in the glare and its talons heading straight for Boswell. The roaring owl noise got louder and louder, the tawny owl fluttered for a moment above Boswell, its wings shining and shadowy with light, and then down the last few moleyards onto Boswell. There was a squeal, a fluttering of wings as the owl started to rise again, with Boswell as its limp prey. But beyond it, on the far path, a roaring owl passed by and the wind from its wings seemed to beat the tawny owl back down toward the ground, straight into the murderous path of the one that had caught Mullion in its gaze. There was a rush and a thump, a squeal, and a flying of feathers and the roaring owl passed by, taking with it the tawny owl and Boswell. Silence. Nothing. Bracken stared at the path in disbelief. He looked at Mullion, who looked despairingly at him and then into the path again.

"It even eats its own kind," whispered Mullion.

"But . . . ," began Bracken, utterly shocked by what had happened. Another roaring owl passed. Silence again. Boswell had gone.

They retreated into the cover of the grass on this side of the path.

"We had better get out of here," said Mullion matter-of-factly. "Which way did he want us to go?"

"To the west," said a voice from the darkness behind them. It was Boswell! He was covered with blood. "Not going without me, are you?"

Bracken ran back to him, reaching forward before Boswell collapsed from his injuries.

"It's owl's blood, not mine," said Boswell. "He got killed when the roaring owl went over him, but I didn't. It went over me, too, but by the Stone's grace his talons missed me. Now. Shall we get going? Again." Even his normal calm sounded just a little shaky.

They followed him down the path under cover of the grass that grew there, so shocked by what had nearly happened that the proximity of other roaring owls going by no longer disturbed them. They hid each time a yellow gaze lit up the path and grass near them, then went on again, until the night grew deep and the roaring owls came less often.

Until at last they came to a part where the path gave way to gravel and then a wall, creeping along its edge, round its far corner, and then blissfully away from the path and down an embankment again, this one drier and less steep. As they went down, they moved into a beautiful darkness, the sounds and gazes of the owls now high above them, and never had Bracken appreciated more the moving stillness of his own world.

Boswell insisted on leading them on along the edge of a field—to get them away from the owl paths as quickly as possible—until there was no more than a distant occasional roar, and they were back in the elements of earth and silence and rustling that they knew. A quick, tired digging of temporary burrows, a snouting out of a couple of worms each, and then tumbling head over heels and falling down a dreamland embankment of moss and soft grass into the sleep of the tired and safe.

⤜ৡ 26 ৡ⤛

THEY stayed for several weeks near the field to which
Boswell had led them. Not only were they all tired and
in need of rest and food to regain their strength, but
February was just starting and with it the worst of the
winter. The thaw was soon followed by more snow, which
gave way to freezing rain that finally slunk into miserable
cold days when the nights dragged on and on and the
days were so gloomy they barely got started before they
were finished.

Mullion, being a pasture mole and used to open
ground, stayed out in the field, quickly taking the opportunity of the thaw to create a simple but extensive system deep enough underground to avoid the frost, which
when it came again, drove worms and grubs down into
his tunnels. His lines of freshly dug molehills began to
poke out of the snow for a wide area over the field.

Bracken hunted around along the edge of the field until he found a small copse just beyond the fence farthest
from where they first came, where he created a more
complex Duncton Wood-style of system, with subtly con-
necting tunnels and secret entrances concealed by long
grass or leaf mold.

As for Boswell, he refused Bracken's offer to help to
build tunnels and worked slowly on his own to create his
own system—starting it from inside an abandoned rabbit
tunnel. Bracken was surprised at how big Boswell insisted
on burrowing his tunnels and it took him several days
before he realized that the feeling of familiarity they gave
him, as if he had been there before, came from the fact
that they were not unlike some of the tunnels in the
Ancient System.

But it did not need this to prompt him to satisfy his
curiosity about Uffington. Indeed, he could hardly wait
for Boswell to recover from their ordeal before asking
him a dozen questions. His curiosity was matched by Boswell's about Duncton. But asking questions is one thing,
giving answers quite another. The fact was that Bracken
was not very eager to talk about it in detail. So he merely
outlined the system's geography, described its personality,

explained where he had come from, but affected vagueness about the Ancient System and never even mentioned Rebecca.

These glimpses scarcely satisfied Boswell, whose eagerness after so many moleyears to talk to the one mole he had met who knew anything about Duncton was only tempered by Bracken's almost painful inability to talk in detail about it. He guessed its causes and, with a compassion and wisdom that Bracken did not realize, eventually stopped seeking the information he felt he needed to pursue his quest to Duncton.

In fact, his self-denial in not pressing Bracken surprised him, for if there was one vice of which he was aware in himself it was impatience. Again and again he had caused annoyance and trouble with other moles he had met since leaving Uffington with his habit of saying too directly what he thought, and his habit of jumping five paces ahead of anymole talking to him.

His fault lay in his own quick intelligence, which made it almost painful for him to have to sit and listen to somemole prattling on toward a point that was perfectly obvious the moment he opened his mouth.

With Bracken he found he did not feel this frustration —not that Bracken's thinking was so swift and clear that he never wandered in talk; he did, but there was a quality in Bracken that roused in Boswell feelings he had not known before and swamped any impatience he might have felt. It was as if Bracken had unknowingly opened a tunnel for Boswell into a world of suffering and joy he had never entered before.

The books he had read, the writing he had learned to scribe and interpret, the two works he himself had worked on all seemed quite irrelevant beside the unfamiliar breathless feeling of being on a brink of something when talking with Bracken.

He saw, too, that Bracken himself was not aware that he had this effect—perhaps not even aware of the sufferings and joys whose power was revealed so well in the way he sometimes talked and by the way his eyes would seem to seek out, even in the burrow where they crouched, the moles he mentioned or the places he described so reluctantly, all of which he had so recently left behind.

He mentioned a mole called Hulver, for example, with

a tremble in his voice, as if he had not got used to the
fact that Hulver had died long before, violently it seemed.
Yet when Boswell asked a little more about him, Bracken
avoided the subject, saying, "He was only an old mole I
knew who talked too much!" But the look in his eyes
betrayed how much more Hulver meant to him than that.

Then there was a mole called Rebecca, of whom, when
he finally mentioned her, Bracken said, "She was a mole
I met in a rainstorm by the Stone on top of the hill. She
was as lost up there as I was, in a different way, and she
touched me." Bracken's voice had lowered when he said
this, as his snout had, and for a moment Boswell felt as
if he was walking with Bracken through the silence of a
forgotten wood that even a single breath would blow
away. Which, indeed, it did. For Bracken changed when
pressed about Rebecca and laughed about her, pretending
she was just "one of the Duncton females, and a very
pretty one, too."

It was the same with the Ancient System, which was
what Boswell wanted most to know about. Bracken said
hardly anything about it, but when it did get mentioned,
his whole body seemed to alternate between fear and
peace and Boswell felt he was watching a changeable
spring day pass by.

It was seeing these things in Bracken that made Boswell, who was so quick with words and so used to the
learned cut and thrust of Uffington, understand that
the message in something a mole says may lie not in the
words spoken, or the sense imparted, but in the impulse
of feeling behind them which they themselves may
change or distort. The more he spoke with Bracken, the
more he had the feeling that the Stone itself had brought
them together and that this strange mole was one he
would follow wherever he went. It seemed to Boswell
that Bracken held in his heart a secret of which he was
not aware but whose revelation was a joy and pain to
which, in some way, both of them must surrender themselves.

So it was that Boswell's initial impatience with
Bracken's unwillingness to talk about Duncton in detail
gave way to an affectionate silence from whose simplicity
Boswell really began to hear the words the other spoke
and, through him, the words all moles speak.

There was another way in which his dialogue with

Bracken was a new experience for him as well: the fact
that since the preceding September, when he had left
Uffington to come to Duncton, a period of several moleyears, he had become increasingly unwilling to talk about
the sacred Holy Burrows to anymole. Yet when Bracken
started asking him questions so enthusiastically, he found
only pleasure in giving him the answers. His reluctance
simply vanished.

"What are they *like?*" asked Bracken. "And do scribemoles still live there?"

"They are on top of a chalk plateau many thousands
of molefeet high, which is steep to its north side and
gentle to the south. The tunnels are very big and spacious,
unlike any tunnels I have seen since elsewhere. It is the
most peaceful place I know."

"But what are the Holy Burrows?"

"A group of burrows in the center of the Uffington
system where only moles who have taken certain vows
of obedience may live. Fighting is not allowed. Many of
the moles there decide to stop talking and live in a silence
of contemplation. Those that talk try only to say those
things that are essential and truthful."

"Are they all White Moles?" asked Bracken, fascinated
by everything Boswell was saying.

"No, none of them is. There are no White Moles—
well, there were once, starting with the first of them all,
Linden, the last son of Ballagan and Vervain . . ."

"Yes. They tell that story in our system, though I've
only heard it vaguely because it's one normally only for
Longest Night and I was . . . well . . . nowhere where
stories like that were told on Longest Night."

So, piece by piece, Boswell told Bracken about Uffington and its lore, learning something about it himself too
as he talked, for he had never really thought about it
objectively before. He realized that he missed the Holy
Burrows, the libraries and some of the moles there, like
Skeat, whom he had grown up to know so well; yet he
saw, too, how ignorant he had been of the world outside
and how many of the scribemoles he had known, for all
their learning and wit, worshiped the Stone through ignorance rather than wisdom. Perhaps Uffington was as
much in decline as so many of the systems he had passed
through seemed to be.

"Why did you leave?" Bracken had asked. And Bos-

well had told him, describing as best he could the urge
he had felt to leave, though not mentioning that it was
to Duncton that he had felt directed to come.

He even recited the text he had found hidden in the
depths of the libraries, the indirect cause of his breaking
his vows and departing for Duncton.

> Seven stillstones, seven Books made,
> All but one have come to ground.
> > First, the Stone of Earth for Living
> > Second, Stone for Suffering mole;
> > Third of Fighting, born of bloodshed
> > Fourth of Darkness, born in death;
> > Fifth for Healing, born through touching
> > Sixth of pure Light, born of love.
>
> Now we wait on
> For the last Stone
> Without which the circle gapes
> And the Seventh
> Lost and last book,
> By whose words we may be blessed.

As Boswell was about to recite the second stanza, Bracken
interrupted.

"What's all that mean?" he asked.

"Well, it's obvious, it's saying that—"

"No. I mean, what's a Stillstone?"

It had not occurred to Boswell that he didn't know such
a simple thing.

"There are six of them—well, seven, according to this
text—but the ones that are known are somewhere in the
Holy Burrows where only the Holy Mole and the masters
have seen them. They are Stones that legend says contain
the essence of the seven Holy Books, one Stone for each
book. I've never seen them myself, of course, but they say
in Uffington that each one contains a kind of light, like the
sun or moon only colored, one for each book. They—"

"How big are they?" interrupted Bracken. He almost
whispered it, an extraordinary sense of being carried along
on a great wind or flood overtaking him and stilling him
to the ground.

"Well, I've no idea, since the masters never spoke of
them; indeed, it is forbidden to speak to the masters about

them. But—well—scribemoles like a chat like anyone else."

"What are they for, exactly?"

"It's a good question, and one every newcomer to Uffington asks. The best answer is in the Book of Light, though I can't remember it well enough to quote exactly. But it explains that each book has a Stone so that by looking at it a reader of the book may be reminded that truth lies not in scribed words but only in the heart that scribed them and the heart that reads them, just as the light lies inside the Stone and not outside it."

Bracken fell silent. He was thinking of the stone he and Rebecca had found in the Ancient System. He felt at once full of wonder and very frightened. Had it been a Stillstone? *Was* it the Seventh Stillstone? He wished he could reach out and touch Rebecca now, just as he had then. He wished her paws were round him. He silently begged the Stone to keep her safe, and his paw, the one that had touched the stone in the Ancient System, began to burn and ache. He looked at it, but there was nothing there.

"Probably doesn't make much sense," said Boswell, thinking his silence meant incomprehension.

"No," said Bracken. "I was just thinking . . . I was wondering. . . . Well, what the Seventh Stone is, the last one, the one in that verse?"

"The Seventh Stone is a Stillstone; it doesn't have a name. But the last book, the Seventh Book—ah! Well! That's the question every scribemole in Uffington wants an answer to. No mole knows—it is not written anywhere."

Boswell fell silent, thinking. Then he said, "Of course, everymole has made guesses—the most popular being that it's the Book of Love, but I don't think that's likely. For one thing, anymole who's read the Book of Light knows that that's the one about love, really, which the sacred text confirms; and anyway, love isn't exactly an easy word to define, is it? It's not absolute, like fighting or earth, if you see what I mean. No. It's not love. The other idea in Uffington about the Seventh Stone is that it is simply the Book of the Stone. Makes sense in lots of ways."

Bracken rubbed his paw, which was still itching. He had the impulse to scratch out the pattern from the stone in the Ancient System on the burrow floor, but some deep instinct told him that much though he wanted to, he must give no mole any clue of what he and Rebecca had seen. It was something they had shared, for some reason he didn't know, but it would be wrong to the Stone itself to talk about it.

He looked at Boswell and, just as Boswell had felt that his destiny was in some way tied to Bracken, so now in his own turn Bracken sensed that this strange Boswell, so full of information and knowledge, was a precious mole, a mole to protect; and he understood why the Stone had protected him from the certain death that surely went with his being crippled, and as he did so he saw, or felt he saw, that in some way the burden of protecting Boswell had somehow passed to him.

As February passed into March and the heavy, bitter gloom of the past long weeks gave way to changeable cold winds and rain, with an odd hour or two of watery sun, Mullion grew increasingly restless.

He had kept very much to himself since they had arrived in the field, not out of any hostility but because the winter months are a time when pasture moles lie still, not having the protection of a wood or its undergrowth overhead. But then, as the weather began to improve, he started burrowing at a shallower level, throwing up a new set of molehills in place of the ones he had created when they first came, and which had now been beaten down into muddy remnants of themselves by the weather.

Occasionally he came over for a chat—principally to try to satisfy his curiosity about Duncton Wood, in whose shadow he had lived through two Longest Nights. Bracken's monosyllabic answers about it confirmed his belief that the Duncton moles were a silent, secretive lot, prone to keeping things to themselves—a theory he expounded to Boswell one day.

"No doubt about it, Boswell. Those Duncton moles are shifty and dangerous, like what we've always been told by our elders. They do strange rituals in that wood of theirs, and weave evil spells. They'd turn a mole into a root as soon as look at him. You wouldn't get me within a long tunnel's length of that place."

Suddenly afraid that Boswell might pass all this on to Bracken who, though younger, had beaten him in a fight, he added: "Mind you, I've got nothing against *Bracken*—look at the way he got us out of that channel! I admire a mole with what my father used to call re-sources. Know what I mean?"

Boswell did and smiled. Mullion yawned and stretched himself.

"We've got to have a talk about where we're going. Can't stay here much longer, that's obvious. I mean, there's nothing here, is there? Maybe a few moles about somewhere, but I haven't seen signs of any yet. And any-way, there's somewhere I want to go to. . . ."

Boswell listened, as talking with Bracken had taught him to. Now that Mullion had fattened up, he had lost some of the aggression he had shown when they had first found themselves imprisoned together in the channel and Boswell got on well with him. He was a big mole, as pasture moles generally were, but a little clumsy. Inclined to bump into entrances when he entered burrows and throw out molehill soil a bit too enthusiastically so that it fell in a mess. But he was good-natured with it—which made the objective he had in mind when he had first left the pastures slightly comic.

It seemed there was a story current in the pastures that there was a mole come from the north who now lived in the nearby system of Nuneham, a fighter who taught other moles to fight. No mole knew his name, but the story was that he was not staying in the Nuneham system for long. Several pasture moles had left to join him to see what they could learn, and Mullion, who had been undecided about whether to join them, had changed his mind and set off later on his own.

"Then I came a cropper in the channel and thought that was it. But now, what with spring coming along soon and this being only a temporary place for the winter, I reckon it would be good to see if we could get to the Nuneham system."

"What you mean is that you want us to go with you because three is safer than one," said Boswell.

"That's about it," Mullion agreed. "Unless you've got a better suggestion."

Boswell knew what he, personally, wanted to do, what he *must* do, but he also realized that Bracken was not yet ready even to think about returning to Duncton. At the same time, Mullion's story interested him, for (as he explained to Bracken after Mullion had put his plan to him himself) there were many accounts of such wandering fighters in the records of Uffington. Indeed, the Book of Fighting had been written by one of them after he had taken his vows, among them the vow not to fight again.

"Seems a funny thing to do then—write a book about it!" declared Bracken.

"The book is not about fighting but about how not to have the need to fight," said Boswell mysteriously.

"Where is this place, Mullion?"

Mullion hesitated, then admitted he wasn't sure. One of the elders in the system had told him to "keep his snout to the Stone" but he was not sure what that meant and the explanation was not very clear.

"Is there a Stone at the system of Nuneham, then?" asked Bracken. Mullion did not know.

The Stone, always the Stone. Bracken remembered the pull of the Stone, the power on its line between Duncton and Uffington. He knew what the elder meant.

"Do you know what direction it's in?" persisted Bracken.

"The story was, and it came from the mole who came to the pastures and had been to this Nuneham place, that it was toward the north."

"If there is a Stone there, I may be able to snout it out," said Bracken, surprised at his own audacity. He left them in the burrow and went up onto the surface and out into the field, where he crouched in some grass by a stand of last summer's thistles, wondering quite what he was doing. It was midmorning and cold but the grass in the field, unlike the thistles, was just beginning to have a bit of life in it again, while from up in one of the bushes among the trees where his tunnels were, the shrill song of a blackbird, powerful and urgent, came across the field.

Bracken thought of the Stone, the Duncton Stone, and looked automatically toward where he knew, without knowing, it must be. Its pull had been there all the time, only he had not bothered to think of it before. But he did not face it directly—it made him feel too desolate and lost to do that.

He turned his back to it and snouted out again, seeing if he could feel any other pulls. Well, of course, there was Uffington; he could feel that. Deep and distant but always strong. He crouched silent and still, letting his mind wander out of his body and around the horizon in the circle. It was hard not to be continually pulled by Duncton and Uffington, the two Stone pulls with which he was familiar, but slowly he forgot them, putting them in the background of his body and mind and seeing what else he could feel.

Nuneham. He tried to reach out to it somehow. If it had a Stone, then surely he would feel it as well! But he suddenly grew tired and ran back for cover again.

For several days Bracken was irritable and wandered about on the surface alone, confirming once more Mullion's prejudices about Duncton moles generally.

But Boswell understood well what he was trying to do, and realized that few moles had the ability to follow the Stones, and that it was sometimes hard for them. He had already seen how, if they talked about Uffington, Bracken unconsciously aligned himself to its direction and when they referred to Duncton, he would look over his shoulder in what Boswell imagined to be its direction, though Bracken never aligned himself directly to it.

"Leave him alone to his own thoughts for a few days, Mullion," advised Boswell, knowing how impatient and restless the pasture mole was becoming. "He got us out of the channel—he may be able to find the way to Nuneham."

"He's so secretive he won't even say if he's willing," complained Mullion, "and I want to get going."

Four or five nights later, Boswell was waked by Bracken well past midnight. "Here. Wake up and come outside!" said Bracken urgently.

Boswell followed him onto the surface.

"I think Nuneham's over there," said Bracken, pointing a talon to the northwest and aligning his body as well. "I woke up a short time ago and could feel it in my body. I know it's there. There's a Stone there, though it's not nearly as strong as Duncton's. I can *feel* it." He sounded happier than he had for days and Boswell could sense and share his excitement with him.

"We'll go there," said Bracken. "I'll lead you there."

He looked out into the night and then swung back toward Uffington. "I've always felt the pull of Uffington from the moment I first went to the Stone," he said. He glanced briefly over his shoulder to the east where Duncton lay, and then back, with relief, to where he said

Nuneham was. Boswell could almost feel the pulls of the Stones that Bracken felt. Involuntarily he ran forward and touched Bracken's shoulder with his good paw.

"We'll all go there, together," said Boswell.

"I wouldn't leave you here," said Bracken seriously, misunderstanding him, adding lightly to hide the way he felt: "Anyway, you haven't told me all you know about Uffington yet!"

Boswell understood what Bracken meant and felt suddenly warmed by the power of his protection. It had been a long, cold journey from Uffington but now, watching Bracken returning to his burrow through the night ahead of him, Boswell felt that at last he had arrived.

REBECCA'S escape with Comfrey and Violet from Duncton was made possible only by Mekkins' intricate knowledge of the Marsh End, which allowed them to elude the henchmoles who sighted them almost immediately after Bracken's departure into the marsh.

Even then they were not safe, for they were found trying to make their way to Rose's tunnels by a group of pasture moles who very nearly killed them. The only thing that saved them was Rebecca's pleas that they at least be allowed to see Rose—whose name the pasture moles seemed to respect—and also by the audacity of Mekkins' defense of the three of them.

"You bloody well take your paws off of me, and let us talk to Rose the Healer! And don't give me any of your lip, chum, because otherwise I'll get *really* narked."

The pasture moles did not understand all the words, but they could make sense of the sentiment—and even the biggest of them quailed slightly at the sight of Mekkins in a rage. Duncton moles had a reputation for being brave and cunning fighters.

When Rose finally came, brought by an uneasy pasture mole, the first thing that Mekkins said was " 'Ere, Rose, tell this bleeding lot of pasture moles that we've not come 'ere to take over the pasture system all by ourselves. We're not bloody stupid. And anyway," he added, looking contemptuously around, "and begging your pardon, but this ain't exactly the place I'd choose to settle down!"

Rose smiled at them all, though she knew that this was an escape and not a visit. She had long suspected that this might happen.

"It's all right," she said. "This is Mekkins of the Duncton system and other moles I know. He is an elder and an honorable mole, even if he does seem a little rude at times."

"Yes—well—sorry," muttered Mekkins, shaking his shoulders and looking chastened. "But they needn't have been so rough with Rebecca and the youngsters. This is

Rose, you two," he added, turning to Comfrey and Violet, "so you say hello."

"Hello!" said Violet, running up to Rose immediately.

Comfrey just looked at her, moving to hide behind Rebecca.

"Hello, my dears," said Rose. "Now Mekkins had better tell me what has happened."

Rose quickly insisted on installing Rebecca and the youngsters in a burrow near her own, though the pasture moles muttered that it wasn't right, and they'd better not get up to any of their Duncton Wood hanky-panky *here*. And to make sure they didn't, they said they would post some guards by the burrow to make sure, while they went and conferred with one of their elders.

Mekkins found this hard to take, especially as he was now very anxious to get back to the Marsh End, but did not want to risk leaving Rebecca here until he was sure it was safe for her. He suggested that he go with the pasture moles to see their elders for himself.

"No way, mate," said the toughest of the pasture moles. "No way. We're not having you spying on us, casting those spells and rituals you get up to in Duncton Wood. No! You stay right here and just shut up until we decide what to do. And think yourself lucky that Rose knows you, otherwise . . ." He stabbed a talon into the air to indicate what would otherwise happen.

However, after two days of complaints and anger, Mekkins was finally summoned to meet a pasture elder somewhere deep in the pasture system. By then Rose had made it quite clear that she felt that Rebecca must stay with her and Comfrey and Violet, too, until they were more independent. "Which won't be all that long, my love, by the way they're already settling down," she said. And it was true, for Violet was beginning to get on with even the pasture moles and Comfrey finding new questions to ask Rose every hour, now that he had gotten used to her.

The place that Mekkins was taken to by four of the toughest moles he had ever seen outside the westside of Duncton (guardmoles, they called themselves) was way down in the pastures through a series of long, sparse tunnels with far fewer burrows off them than he was used

to. The pasture moles seemed thinner on the ground—
but then he could see that worms were not so plentiful
out here either.

Finally they reached a structure that Mekkins had
heard of but never seen—a fortress, a massive molehill
with burrows on several levels both above and below
ground connected by linked tunnels. There was a big,
round central burrow that was wider but not so high as
the elder burrow in Barrow Vale. Its walls were dry and
well burrowed, and its floor covered in comfortable nesting material, mainly dry thistles and grass. He was ush-
ered none too gently into the burrow where, at one end,
a big, dark-gray mole crouched, his talons splayed
loosely before him and his snout sleepily lowered over
them. His eyes were half closed, but his voice, when he
finally used it after a long silence, was wide awake.

"Name?"

"My name's Mekkins, and I . . ."

"System?"

"Don't be so daft!" said Mekkins, more than irritated.
"I'm from Duncton, aren't I?"

The guardmoles moved heavily forward at this rude-
ness, but the big mole raised one paw to stop them.

"Just answer my questions," he said. "Purpose?"

"What do you mean, 'purpose'?" said Mekkins.

"What are you doing here?"

"The moles I brought—that's Rebecca and her two
youngsters—had a spot of bother. They were being attacked. I knew Rose would help them so I brought them."

"Why should we let them stay here?"

Mekkins opened his mouth to answer, but couldn't
think of anything to say that would make any sense to a
mole that didn't know Rebecca.

"Well?"

"Because Rose trusts her; that's the best reason I can
give," said Mekkins.

Suddenly and unexpectedly the mole smiled. It was a
slow, warm smile which took the aggression right out of
Mekkins.

"A very good reason, if I may say so, a very good
reason. Very good." The mole got up and came over to
where Mekkins was crouched between the guardmoles.
With a pleasant nod he dismissed them, leaving him alone
with Mekkins.

"My name's Brome," he said, "and despite appearances I'm glad to see you. Rose warned me that there was trouble coming and she even mentioned your name as a mole to trust. I did not think we would meet so soon. Sorry about my guardmoles, but you can't change generations of hostility overnight and there's no reason why we should. Except that if you believe Rose, which I do, the time is coming when hostility isn't going to matter much one way or another. Now, since you are on pasture territory, I think it is reasonable that you tell me about your system first. All these warnings by Rose are fair enough, but I have to run a system and I can't do it on vague guesses and surmises. So what's happening?"

He spoke pleasantly but with great authority, treating Mekkins as an equal and instilling in him a sense of trust that Mekkins, well used to judging moles quickly, was prepared to believe. These were funny times and the more friends a mole had the better, as far as he was concerned. So he told Brome exactly what the problem was and how the system had changed and been corrupted under Mandrake—a mole, it turned out, who had done a great deal of damage in the pastures en route to Duncton. Mekkins described how Rune was in the process of taking over Duncton and what the implications were for his own Marsh End.

Mekkins told him something too about Rebecca, saying there was no reason the pastures should suddenly take her into their system except that he, Mekkins, believed she held some kind of destiny in herself for more than just a couple of youngsters. And so did Rose.

Brome listened to this with great interest, for it seemed to him to have a lot to do with what he wanted to say to this first senior mole of Duncton he had met. But first he had to decide if he could trust Mekkins.

"Tell me, Mekkins," he said quietly, "what do you know of the Stone?"

Brome noticed that Mekkins' manner changed. It became more personal, less weighted by the many considerations a leader has, even if only of part of a system like Marsh End.

"Do you mean the Stone generally?" asked Mekkins, looking around in a quiet way. "Or the Duncton Stone in particular?"

"Is there a difference?" asked Brome.

Mekkins hesitated. He had never talked about the Stone to another mole in his life, not even since he had gone to it for Rebecca's sake and it had answered his prayers. Since then he had been in deep awe of it and hesitated now to talk to another mole who might not understand his words. Finally he said: "The Duncton Stone has great power and may still be the true heart of our system, as it once was the heart in reality—when moles lived only on top of the hill. We've been cut off from it, though, by the likes of Mandrake and Rune, who I've told you about." Then he added in a rush: "If you want to know what I think, the Stone is the most important thing Duncton's got."

Brome nodded. He looked pleased by this reply but said nothing. For a moment it was his turn to hesitate, but then he settled down farther onto his paws with the air of a mole who, after a very long time keeping something to himself, has decided that the moment has come to tell it all. He trusted Mekkins.

"You've got to understand that in my system we are brought up to believe that Duncton moles are spell-weavers and evil, that the wood is dangerous to go near and that the Stone on top of the hill—which we have all heard about—is an evil Stone."

Mekkins looked visibly surprised at this.

"Well, that's how it is. Now, plenty of moles here believe in the Stone as an idea—something to worship, if you like. And we've got our rituals, like any other system. But we're a big, diverse system and in recent years have been plagued by fighting and factions, just as other systems such as your own have. When at about the time I took control here, I got talking to Rose about this and that, and she told me, to my surprise, that she had been to your Stone several times. 'It's about as evil as a buttercup,' she said. Well, one night I decided to go and see for myself—a bit risky, but something drove me to it."

"Yeh! The Stone's like that," murmured Mekkins.

"Well, of course it wasn't evil, it was inspiring. I couldn't even describe the effect it had."

"Don't worry," said Mekkins with a conspiratorial grin. "I think I know."

"I might have left it at that but for something that happened last September. One of our moles, Cairn, got killed in your system. A mating fight. His brother is . . . I

should say *was* because he has left our system now . . .
a mole called Stonecrop, who was the most important
fighter this system has ever seen. He wanted to lead a
group of moles over to Duncton and avenge Cairn's death.
One way or another I persuaded them out of it—frankly,
I was worried about the consequences. But somehow it
made me think about whether it *would* be worth invading
Duncton."

Mekkins began to look worried, but Brome laughed.
"Don't worry. Hear me out. What I concluded was that if
there was anything at all in Duncton Wood we wanted
it was the Stone. Or rather, access to the Stone. It would
give our moles the kind of focusing point that might stop
the pointless feuds that keep developing here. And anyway, half of Duncton Hill is made up of the pastures,
isn't it? And taken together—the two systems, that is—
the Stone is a natural center."

Mekkins looked decidedly worried. The implications of
what Brome was saying were very obvious to him.

Brome continued. "Now, the reason I mention all this
to you is principally because if you want my help down
in the Marsh End against your Rune, which I think you
may, then I'm going to want yours, up on top of the hill.
I don't want territory. I want access."

"The thin end of the root," said Mekkins cynically.

"Maybe. Maybe not," said Brome. "But it might just
stop the killing and feuding that goes on between the systems, and within my own."

"What's this to do with me?" asked Mekkins.

"I don't know—yet," said Brome. "But I've got a feeling that when Rose told me that you were a mole to be
trusted, she meant you might have a bigger part to play
than perhaps you expect in the changes she is talking
about."

Mekkins and Brome looked at each other as two
equals, poised before great events are about to take place
which would affect and change everything they knew.
Mekkins smiled at last.

"You're quite a mole, you are, Brome. We could do
with a mole like you in Duncton."

Brome laughed and cuffed him lightly on the shoulder,
as if to seal a trust between them.

"By the way," he said, "if that Rebecca of yours is the
one who mated with Cairn, which I noticed you avoided

even hinting at, you had better warn her not to mention it. There's pasture moles who wouldn't like to know she's in the system. You see, Cairn's brother Stonecrop was a very special mole and he's missed. If they thought a mole who, even indirectly, caused his departure from the system was here, they might not like it."

Mekkins smiled noncommittally. He turned to go.

"*Is* she that mole?" asked Brome.

"Yes," said Mekkins. He didn't like lies.

"She must be quite somemole," said Brome.

"She is," said Mekkins. With that their discussion was over, and after a short visit back to Rose's burrow, in which he passed on Brome's advice to Rebecca, Mekkins went hurriedly back to see what was happening in Duncton Wood.

Rose's burrow was one of the untidiest, and loveliest, Rebecca had ever seen. It was the kind in which youngsters could wander delightedly from object to object and lose themselves in reveries of wonder and play. Its walls had been burrowed in a rough and homely way, with an occasional roundel of stone left protruding, because Rose liked it that way, which cast friendly shadows and pillows of shade.

Just inside the entrance, and half blocking it, was a pile of dried leaves and flowers of woodruff, whose hay-like scent, said Rose, was the quickest way of reminding a returning mole that sanity lies inside her burrow more often than outside it. Next to this was a scatter of beech-nut husks and near them, the two mingling together at the edges, a collection of black elderberries, dried and grizzled into hardness.

There were several flints around the floor of the burrow, one of them flat-topped and obviously used by Rose as a surface on which to crush herbs, for it was covered by the crushed and shredded foliage of white horehound, whose thyme-scent made that corner of the burrow like an open field of its own to moles who closed their eyes and let the scent take them over.

"Yes, my love, that's why I never quite finish crushing them all, because, you see, every time I try, the delicious scent quite takes me over!" said Rose, explaining the clutter of horehound stems and leaving them exactly where they were.

On the far wall opposite the entrance Rose had made her own special nest, a soft pile of blue-runner leaves intermingled with the dried petals of eglantine and wild lavender. Rose had let Violet sleep there one day, though inevitably she complained that it was "uncomfortable and bumpy," which indeed it was, since some of the rose hips which Rose had gathered and heaped nearby had "inexplicably" rolled into her nest and she had never noticed them.

There was a dusty, dried-out red cardinal beetle shell by one wall, which Rose had never bothered to move since "it crawled down here one summer's day and peacefully spent the evening watching me do something or other—I can't quite remember what—and then died!" Violet didn't like it much, but Comfrey found its color —a deep red ochre—beautiful, and he liked the obscure shine of its dead wings.

In the center of the burrow and draped with other herbs and stems, all dusty, dry and green with age, was a long, gnarled flint of pinks and blues whose shape seemed to change with the hour of the day and the angle at which a mole chose to look at it. "Oh, no. *It* doesn't change," explained Rose to Rebecca when they were talking one day, "*you* do."

From this fragrant burrow Rose had made her life's work of healing Duncton and pasture moles alike. By the time Rebecca came so desperately to her in the last week of that cold January, Rose was reaching the end of her long life. Even in the time since just before Longest Night, when Rebecca had last seen her, Rose had slowed and aged. She suffered pains now in her shoulders and back paws, which made movement difficult so that she tended to prefer to settle into one position at a time, moving only her head to keep track of Rebecca and the youngsters when they were in her burrow. She liked to see a mole's eyes when she spoke to him, or her, and despite her pain, her own eyes were as still and warm as ever.

At the same time she slept more, sometimes drifting in and out of sleeping and waking as a scatter of dandelion silk rises and falls on a warm evening wind in September. As the days went by, she seemed to say less and less and to smile more, and round her came a peace that descended even on Violet, whose normal ebullience grew quieter and gentler when she was near Rose.

Comfrey had quickly overcome his initial wariness of Rose and, together with Violet, he would spend long hours with her as she told them tales and legends of the system. Violet liked the dramatic ones, with heroes and villains dashing about from tunnel to tunnel while Comfrey preferred to hear Rose tell stories of the flowers and trees, whose lore and mysteries held him spellbound.

Rose began each of her tales the same way—"From my heart to your heart I tell this tale that its blessing may touch you as it has touched me"—and Comfrey would snuggle down, while Violet looked all expectant as the magic of the story wove them into its fabric.

Although Rebecca was not aware of it, it was almost unknown for a mole to enter Rose's burrow, and word quickly got about among the pasture moles that "that Rebecca from Duncton must be very special, because Rose the Healer lets her *inside* her burrow. *Inside!*"

They were right to remark on it, for to Rose, Rebecca *was* very special. She had seen the power for life in Rebecca from the first, and valuing it as she did, understood better than anymole, better even than Mekkins, how near to a death of spirit the murder of her litter by Mandrake had brought her.

Even in Rebecca's care of Comfrey, which could hardly have been more tender and loving—and now, in her acceptance of Violet—even now Rose could see that Rebecca had lost much trust in life. Sometimes there was a far-off sadness in the way Rebecca caressed Comfrey, or a sudden frailty in the laughter that had once always been so full and free.

So Rose opened her burrow to Rebecca and the youngsters, knowing that with the Stone's grace, Rebecca might find again some of the life she had lost touch with. Rose did not waste time or breath on regretting what had happened. She had known since their first meeting that Rebecca would be a healer, and she knew that healing can only come from a heart that has seen the dark as well as the light. She feared that for Rebecca there was more to come, far more than she herself had ever known and she silently prayed that the Stone would help her give to Rebecca the strength and trust to find her way alone when she, Rose, was gone.

It was for this reason that Rose was insistent that the youngsters should, for a period every day, leave her together alone with Rebecca—indeed, she made sure that the more friendly of the pasture guardmoles, who still hung about, took Violet and Comfrey under their care and kept them occupied.

These were times of talk and silence, times in which Rose imparted to Rebecca her knowledge of herbs and healing lore and a trust in the Stone—a time in which there continued inside Rebecca the healing that had started with her communion with Bracken on Longest Night, in the silence of the Stone.

She taught Rebecca by instinct rather than design, for her mind was as delightfully illogical as her burrow. Rhymes and sayings, thoughts and words, ideas and laughter all came to their own pace and in their own way, and Rebecca was barely conscious that she was learning anything. Like the old flower-rhyme that Rose taught her one day to illustrate the herbs that give a burrow a nice, long-lasting scent, and which Rebecca only discovered she remembered many moleyears later.

> *Germander and marjoram*
> *Basil, meadowsweet,*
> *Daisy-tops and tansies*
> *Fennel with burnet;*
> *Roses in August*
> *Lavender in June*
> *Maudlin and red mint—*
> *None will go too soon.*

They talked about a thousand things, but what Rose most put into Rebecca's mind were seeds of thought to grow, rather than finished plants to fade. And she waited for Rebecca to ask the questions.

"Rose?"

"Mmm, my love?"

"How do you know how to help a mole when you think he needs help?"

"You don't know, my dear. You never know. You may have an idea but you don't *know*. No . . . you see, they *tell* you. What you have to learn is to understand what they are trying to say, because if there's one thing certain, they won't know themselves! In fact, Rebecca, one of the burdens healers have to bear is most moles' inability to say what it is that's wrong with them. Mind you, if they knew—*really* knew—then there probably wouldn't be anything wrong." Rose crouched in silence, Rebecca letting the words sink in. Then Rose added "The best way to start is to touch them gently with your paw just as you touch Comfrey when he needs comforting. Touching tells you far more than words ever can."

Another time, Rose suddenly broke a long silence in which she had seemed to be sleeping and said "You can tell what's wrong with a mole by the way they stand. Illness and disease, even that which starts in the mind, always shows in the body. The easiest things to heal are injuries after a mating fight—give them a push here, a shove there, and a word of encouragement all over and they're soon as right as rain. How I used to love to get my paws on those rough, westside males!" They both laughed at the thought, and Rose explained: "You see, they use their bodies for fighting so much that they can feel what's wrong better than most moles, and they soon go back into place. As a matter of fact, fighting isn't as bad as some moles make out. It teaches a mole to appreciate what he's got. Too much fear and too little action spoils a body. That's what was wrong with that Bracken of yours!"

As the weeks passed and February reached its chilly end, Rose began to encourage Rebecca to make sure each day to find time to crouch by herself and "not think" for a while.

"What do you mean, Rose?"

"You just do it, my love, and don't think about it. You'll find that every burrow has its best spot for crouching and doing nothing and in my burrow it's over by that plant where the horehound scent's so pleasant. You can start right now. You just go over there and close your eyes and don't think, while I do my best to tidy up a bit. But don't mind me."

As Rose slowly moved about, Rebecca tried, but after a few minutes her voice came to Rose across the burrow. "It's impossible not to think! Thoughts keep coming to replace the ones I've just got rid of!"

"Yes, I know," said Rose unsympathetically, "it *is* trying. But you won't find it helps to talk."

That first time Rebecca managed it for only ten minutes before she gave up in exasperation, claiming that she had better go and see what the youngsters were up to. But Rose kept her at it and gradually, as March progressed, Rebecca found she was positively looking forward to her time of not thinking every day.

When this happened, Rose, who was only repeating what her own teacher had taught her so many years before, started to suggest that instead of thinking of nothing, she try thinking about *one* thing each time. It was the spear thistle that grew on the pasture above Rose's tunnel and would soon be showing life again that she had to think about first time. Then, variously, such things and ideas as oak trees, owls, stones, the Stone, darkness, talons and warmth.

One day Rebecca started to weep when she was doing this, and Rose let her, glad to see that at last some of her grief was leaving her. Later, Rebecca spoke about it, saying, "I remembered running up the hill one day, after Cairn had left to fight Rune—I told you—and it was raining and I was running. I was so confused, running this way and that until somehow I found I was up at the Stone . . ."

"Somehow?"

When Rose interjected like this, Rebecca knew it was important to find an answer. How *had* she found her way up the hill? She thought back, and she was among those great gray beech trees again, with the rain falling between them and she was turning, running . . . why, it was the beech trees swaying with her, urging her this way and that, swaying her back to the light at the top of the hill where the Stone was, as if *they* knew where she should go and were telling her . . .

"Was *that* it, then?" she asked herself and Rose.

"Only you can really tell, my dear. But I know that the trees and plants tell me many things I wouldn't otherwise know. Sometimes I think they help to guide me to a mole who needs help—otherwise I can't think how I've so often found my way so quickly to a mole. If you doubt me, go on to the surface in Duncton Wood after a really bad storm, when the trees have been whipped and shattered by the wind, and branches have fallen: you can feel that the trees are shaken and desolate by what has happened, for their feeling is in the very air, mixed with relief as well."

So, bit by bit, Rose passed over some of the heritage of her wisdom to Rebecca, who one day, she knew, would take over her task of healing.

By mid-March, the two youngsters, particularly Violet, were growing increasingly independent. Violet was already growing fast and had managed to make friends with some pasture youngsters from an autumn litter, so they saw less and less of her, though she came back to sleep in Rebecca's burrow most days.

Comfrey still liked to stay near Rebecca, though lately he had taken to sleeping in a burrow of his own making. Inspired by Rose, he had grown increasingly interested in herbs and flowers, and was forever asking when he would be able to go out on the surface and see more for himself.

"You'll have to wait a week or two more yet before the first ones start coming, my sweet thing," said Rose, "though I expect you'd find a few snowdrops here and there now. And winter aconite. But soon there'll be celandine and bluebells and after that, in April, there's ground ivy, bugle, all sorts of ferns starting up and oh! you're so lucky!" Rose suddenly looked sad and nostalgic, as if she knew that she'd never see such delights again.

"Of course you will, Rose," said Rebecca. "The warm weather's nearly here now. Why, there'll be the sound of pup cries in Duncton soon, and probably in the pastures as well . . ." But Rebecca couldn't go on. Rose was looking at her with eyes that said she knew how old she was and how near the end. And Rebecca could never say anything but the truth to Rose.

Now, subtly, their relationship deepened and changed. It was as if Rose felt there was no more she could tell Rebecca—her beloved Rebecca—and now she must trust to the Stone that Rebecca could find her own way. There were long hours of silence between them; times when the best words were silent. A time when Rose showed Rebecca that she trusted her and in doing so helped Rebecca learn to trust in life again. A time when Rebecca began to see, and fear, that she might soon have to take over Rose's task of healing. Oh! She knew so little! A time when Rose's sleep grew longer and more troubled with pain, and her talk began to wander and her sense of peace to deepen, so that the very burrow seemed to hush and grow more still: its shadows darkening, its aromas and scents more delicate and distant, and Rebecca now rarely leaving Rose alone as she slept in her nest.

The pasture moles seemed to sense that Rose's work was nearly done, for they shushed the youngsters in the tunnels outside and the pasture moles spoke in low voices, and brought food to save Rebecca from having to get it.

Some of what Rose whispered to herself aloud in those last days Rebecca understood; other parts she remembered, and somehow made sense of in later years when she had greater wisdom; and some made no sense at all.

She was old Rose now, her breathing shorter and shallower, her snout hardly moving, the bliss of having Rebecca near her in the dark, moving gently in her burrow soothing her pains, laughing still with that Violet, naughty minx, and Cairn of Bracken of the Ancient System my love my sweet thing she said to him do you remember? Bracken up in the dark tunnel where I lost so much strength giving it to Bracken so he could learn to love so many moles had come her way one by one so much fear so much unnecessary things. Rebecca knew everything already poor child she didn't know no good telling her sweet child her Bracken she would love.

"Rebecca! Rebecca!" she whispered in the burrow where the scent was sweet.

"Yes, my love," said Rebecca. Her fur on mine, nuzzling me my love my words her love in me Rebecca Rebecca shivering a shiver where's your Bracken who I saw, where . . .

"What is it, Rose?"

"Where's Bracken do you know where . . . Bracken?"

"I told you, Rose, he's gone, he's gone, but I know he's safe I can feel it like the beech trees, like I knew before when . . ."

"I went to him" On the hill and you helped me you did . . .

"Yes, Rose, sleep, Rose, sleep my dearest Rose."

I stayed by the Stone afterward looking darkness in the night great trees beech trees sway and roots and I knew it was you and Bracken around us you and Bracken Rebecca you and Bracken would be around us all . .

"Yes, Rose."

You wept at last and I knew it would come like you

did to the hill your wet tears had to come on your face on my fur at last. Now. No need my dear no need.

And her old voice died away, leaving only the sound of Rebecca's tears, muffled by sweet Rose's fur.

"Where's Rose gone?" Violet asked the guardmole, who hesitated because he didn't know.

"She's gone to the St–Stone," said Comfrey, angry with himself for always stuttering on the word that mattered most.

"How do you know?" asked Violet.

"I just d–do," said Comfrey, who *did* know, because Rose told him once that all the plants come from the Stone and plants were no different from moles and he said where do they go when they wither and die in the winter and she said they go to the Stone, which is everywhere, so they must do, and that's where Rose has gone. But it's no good telling Violet that, because the words wouldn't come out right.

But he could tell Rebecca, because she knew and he could find her up by the entrance on the surface in the sun where she went afterward and was now. He would run, he *was* running, running into tears, and he couldn't help it. Oh, where was Rose, he sobbed.

Rebecca would know.

IT took Bracken, Boswell and Mullion until the middle of April to make their way to the Nuneham system—a time in which Mullion frequently threatened to leave them because "Bracken obviously does not know the way and all this Stone stuff is a load of nonsense," as he put it.

Bracken himself did not say much. He could feel the Stone's pull but was not confident enough about it to be willing to argue with Mullion, if he did not want to follow him. Boswell had more faith than either of them, and it was his moderation, and occasional calling of Mullion's bluff—for the pasture mole really did not want to go it alone—that kept them together.

They faced many difficulties and dangers: the country they had to cross was mainly wet and low-lying and often slow to cross, while since it was the mating season they had to avoid penetrating too deeply into any of the systems they came near. But gradually Bracken found that the pull of the Stone got stronger and stronger until there came a day when they asked a mole they met if he knew where Nuneham was and he answered, with a look that showed he thought they were stupid, "Aye, this is it. It was Nuneham you said, warn't it?"

Bracken immediately asked where the Stone was and how hostile Nuneham moles were likely to be.

"Oh, well, I wouldn't worry about that too much. Nuneham ain't what it was, you know. The river's moved in the last few generations and flooded the place out so much that there isn't a system worth speaking of any more. Just a few old-timers like me who keep their snouts out of trouble. . . . You'll find the Stone yonder." He waved a talon westward down the tunnel where they had met and scurried off in the opposite direction.

"Here!" shouted Mullion after him. "Wait a minute!" He ran off after the mole and Bracken and Boswell heard him ask "You got any idea if there's a mole here who's a fighter, come from the north?"

"You're not the first as has asked that, I can tell you! Well, there is and there isn't. I never met en myself. Plenty comes to find en and most go away disappointed,

Some claim they found en, but won't never say where or when."

"Where do you think we could find him?" asked Mullion.

"Beyond the Stone, that's where most things be," said the mole. "There was several moles like you come on through here not so long back, couple of weeks it war. Big like you they was. They found en and they didn't."

"What do you mean?" asked Mullion.

"Well, now, there was four of en and I met three of en after, up by Stone as it happens, and they said they looked about and they reckoned en didn't exist. But one of en oo warn't with them anymore, he was waiting a bit longer to see and not going back with the others."

"Where to?" asked Mullion excitedly.

"Ask the worms, don't ask me. I don't go gallivantin' about the countryside like you youngsters do." With that he really did leave, and Mullion came back to the others.

"Hear that? Sounds like the four pasture moles I mentioned have been here before us. I wonder who stayed behind?"

They found the Nuneham Stone with no difficulty—all the tunnels seemed to lead to it. It was wide and bulbous in shape, much less tall than the Duncton Stone, and stood on a bluff of deep green pasture grass overlooking a slow and meandering river that lay below, beyond several fields of lush green pasture. Patches of blue creeping speedwell, a few early dandelions and the darker leaves of young bugle shoots grew among the grass by the Stone, whose general appearance disappointed Bracken. He had expected something much more impressive.

"Each Stone is different," explained Boswell, "and they can all teach you something. Try to spend some time in silence by any Stone you come to before examining it too closely—that way you may get to know it faster."

Bracken complied—he trusted Boswell's advice on anything to do with the Stone—and since it was late afternoon, and the surface felt safe, he was willing to crouch for a while in the open. From beyond the Stone he could hear the sound of chaffinch, yellowhammer and blackbirds busy in some hedge he could not see, and to the mixed sound of their warbles, notes and songs, he let himself listen to the Nuneham Stone. It seemed a friendly, peaceful place.

Mullion, however, could not crouch still and had no desire to. He wanted to go searching for the fighting mole, and also to see if he was right and that the pasture moles had indeed been there.

It was only when evening started drawing in, bringing with it the risk of predators, that Bracken and Boswell returned to the tunnels and pressed on beyond the Stone, calling out for Mullion, who had disappeared.

The tunnels were like those in the pastures by Duncton Wood, sparse, long and straight, with relatively few burrows or side runs, but the impression they gave was very different. For one thing, the soil was richer and darker, and having an element of sand or gravel in it from some distant past when the river had deposited its alluvium this high up the valley side, it tended to soften and slide in places, giving the tunnels a discarded air. There was an untidy litter on some of the tunnel floors while what burrow entrances there were were untidy and unkempt.

Once or twice they heard and saw moles nearby, but there was no feeling of hostility or even curiosity about them, and they, too, seemed to be coming and going rather than stopping still.

"There aren't even any pup cries up here," observed Bracken to Boswell. "In fact, I haven't seen or smelled a female yet."

Boswell was content to follow Bracken, whose instincts in route-finding he trusted absolutely, and so they wandered from tunnel to tunnel, generally slightly uphill, occasionally calling out for Mullion, though they knew that they could always meet him back at the Stone again.

Being April, the nights were still cold and as nightfall began outside, a chill settled down into the tunnel. They had some food and then decided to press on uphill to any outer limit the tunnels might have, and there to sleep.

But then, as they advanced, Bracken began to grow restless, feeling that he was going somewhere definite, though where, he had no idea. He scurried on forward, only occasionally stopping to look around and check that Boswell was behind him and to let him catch up.

"Have you noticed that the tunnel is suddenly getting tidier and neater?" asked Boswell, limping forward to where Bracken was waiting for him on one of these slopes. "Somemole's cleared the litter and shored up some of these crumbling walls," he added.

And as he spoke, there was a heavy tread in the tunnel ahead of them which stopped someway beyond in the darkness.

"Whatmole is there?" asked a strong, deep voice from the depths behind. It was neither friendly nor hostile.

They pressed forward until they came to a big central chamber in which several routes met, on the far side of which crouched a very powerful-looking mole. He was slim compared with a Duncton mole and his fur was light. He was enormously muscular and strong—the kind of mole whose size only tells when a normal mole goes near him, and whichever way he stands he seems to feel dwarfed.

His face fur was thick and dark-silvery, his eyes full of self-confidence. Bracken noticed that his back paws were unusually large and that he crouched full square on the ground, giving the impression that he was ready to spring into action at any moment.

"Whatmoles are you?" he repeated.

But before Bracken could reply, his manner, until now quite neutral, suddenly changed. His big snout came forward toward Bracken and sniffed at him, his front paws pushed powerfully into the chamber floor as his eyes narrowed and his tail started to twitch angrily. There was a deep growling from his throat as, very slowly, he drew himself up to his full height.

Bracken stopped quite still, his mind racing after reasons for this sudden hostility. Not finding any but being unwilling to argue, he backed away toward the entrance through which they had come, pushing Boswell protectively behind him. Better to have it out verbally from a position in which it was possible to retreat.

"I said whatmoles are you and where are you from?" repeated the mole, more angry by the second.

"I am Bracken of . . ."

"Duncton Wood?" roared the mole inquisitorially. "From Duncton Wood are you?"

He came powerfully toward Bracken, his size seeming to double with each forward step he took. And before Bracken could even say a word or raise his talons to defend himself, the mole was on to him and had thrust a paw just behind his shoulder and with one massive heave pulled him round into the center of the chamber. For a moment the mole looked back at Boswell, snouted at him and then turned away dismissively, back to Bracken again.

"I would know your smell anywhere," he thundered, bringing down a massive talon blow in such a way that it did not seriously injure Bracken but cut across his shoulder and hurled him backward several steps. His power and speed were extraordinary and Bracken was still desperately trying to think what was happening before the mole brought his left paw swinging round and tore a talon's cut along his flank. As Bracken staggered back gasping and frightened, a line of blood appearing on his fur, he watched as behind the great mole Boswell hobbled forward bravely to strike uselessly at the mole with one paw. With a terrible backward kick he sent his back paw shattering into Boswell's face and he fell back against the wall behind and slumped across the entrance they had come in by.

Despite his shock and cuts, this sight of Boswell, who he knew had never harmed anymole in his life, being knocked unconscious, brought to Bracken the kind of rage he had felt overtake him when he had first confronted Mullion in the channel beyond the marsh.

He raised his talons, stepped back to give himself more room, and then lunged forward toward the mole's eyes and snout with all his power. He missed wildly, however. When he got there, the great mole moved easily out of his path, leaving his talons stabbing at the air, while the mole laughed cruelly at him. And then grew serious.

"What's it feel like, Duncton mole? What's it feel like?" he roared.

Bracken charged again, but this time the great mole simply leaned up and backward and Bracken could not even reach his face with his talons. He tried bringing them down on the mole's shoulders but he simply stepped sideways, letting Bracken fall vulnerably forward, carried by the force of his own futile blow.

By now Bracken was gasping for breath, and frightened, as he looked desperately around the burrow for his adversary. The mole was now behind him, talons loose and relaxed, mocking him in his inability even to hit him.

Then he said "Is this what you're trying to do?" and lunged a blow forward that caught Bracken powerfully below his shoulder and made him sound a deep grunt of pain, the sound of a mole who knows that a few more such blows will mean death.

"Or this?" said the mole, suddenly swinging round and kicking him so hard that for a moment it seemed that the chamber was collapsing about him as he fell back against the wall where Boswell still lay, now groaning and beginning to stir.

Bracken tried to move but couldn't. A thousand painful weights seemed to be dragging each limb down. The great mole started toward him, talons out, and a look in his eyes such as Bracken had only once seen in anymole's, and that was Mandrake's as he came toward him in the Chamber of Dark Sound.

He tried to pull himself up, but even his head would not move as he wanted it to, seeming to slur to one side with a mouth that hung open and gasping with pain. The mole came nearer, the talons of one paw rising. He was saying something but there was such pain in Bracken's head that he could not hear—only see the mouthings of accusation, and recognize the word "Duncton Duncton," and then, as talons rose over him, he knew with terrible certainty that he and Boswell were going to die. His head turned uselessly to look at Boswell, by the entrance, still lying where he had been thrown by the mole's kick. Bracken tried to speak, tried to say "Why?"—tried to push his body back into the wall, through the wall, out of the chamber to escape the talons, the fear like a root round his throat.

But then the talons stopped, the mole's head turned away to look at the entrance near where Boswell lay and then at something beyond it. The mole's motion slowed to stillness and a look of surprise came on his face and his body started to turn aggressively toward the entrance when, through it, there came a snout, then a face, and then the front half of a mole; an old mole, a frail mole, a mole whose coat was wrinkled with age and whose movement were hardly movement at all.

Sound returned to Bracken's ears.

"So there's another one of you!" roared the big mole.

The old mole half smiled; he turned toward where Bracken and Boswell lay and was suddenly there between them and the big mole, crouching down and facing him.

"Then three of you can die," shouted the big mole,

moving suddenly forward again. How does a mole re-member something impossible but which he has seen happen? He remembers it as a dream.

So it was a dream to Bracken as the great mole lunged toward them and the wrinkled old mole moved forward and away, perhaps lunging gently with one paw and the great mole was suddenly falling backward, wheeling round and back against the far wall of the chamber. Then the old mole was in the middle of the chamber, crouched quiet again and the attacker coming forward with a mas-sive lunge of both paws.

In Bracken's dream the old mole stepped, or rather seemed to float, to one side and with the softest of flicks of one of his back paws sent the great mole shuddering into the side wall of the chamber. A dream, but a dream with sounds. For Bracken could hear the pained gasping of the great mole and the scrabbling of its paws as it tried to right itself and staggered round for a third attempt. But even as it drew itself ready, the old mole, whose smile never seemed to leave his face and whose eyes stayed clear and calm, stepped forward slowly as if time had stood still especially for him, and gave the big mole the gentlest of blows with his left paw, which made him fall back into unconsciousness, as if he had been struck by some massive storm-torn oak branch.

The dream seemed to continue. As Bracken watched, still half conscious, he heard a fifth mole slowly enter the chamber on his left. He turned his throbbing head to-ward it and there he saw Mullion standing open-mouthed, taking in the scene before him. Bracken could almost hear Mullion's thoughts think themselves.

Three moles lying around the chamber walls as if swept aside by a raging storm and in the center an old mole crouched still and peaceful, aged paws stretched harm-lessly before him, snout settling down comfortably onto them. Impossible! Mullion was thinking.

Oh no, it's not, thought Bracken. And then, Oh no, you don't as Mullion started angrily toward the old mole. But he got up, turned his snout to Mullion, seemed suddenly more powerful than anything Bracken had ever seen in his life, and without so much as a flexing talon, brought Mullion to a respectful halt.

The dream ended. To his right Bracken saw the big mole stirring and heard him groan and gasp. To his left he felt Boswell's paw, against which he had fallen, moving as the mole from Uffington slowly came to. He felt himself stretching aching and pained as he righted himself back to his paws, and turned to look at the old mole again.

"It would be a courtesy if you told me your names," said the old mole in a kindly, wise voice.

"Mullion, of the pasture system," said Mullion, awed and respectful.

"Bracken of Duncton," said Bracken. The old mole turned to look at him, nodded gently and said nothing. He turned to the big mole at the side of the chamber, who raised his snout, shook it, and said "My name is Stonecrop, also of the pasture system."

At this, both Bracken and Mullion started with surprise. Stonecrop! thought Bracken. Stonecrop. Brother of Cairn. Known to Rebecca. So *that* was why . . .

"Stonecrop!" said Mullion delightedly, but with the old mole so much in command he did not dare move.

The old mole smiled and turned to Boswell who, instead of saying his name, got up slowly and moved out into the chamber before him.

"My name is Boswell of Uffington," he said, lowering his snout respectfully to the old mole.

"May the blessings of the Stone be with you, as they must have been to have brought you safely so far from the Holy Burrows," the old mole said to him. "And may they be with the rest of you. My name is Medlar of the North and it would be better if there were no fighting in these tunnels—not at any rate by moles such as yourselves who are prey to ignorance and fear." He said this severely, as a father might to a recalcitrant youngster.

Then he turned to Mullion and said gently, "I think you have come to learn how to fight, but I tell you, your nature is not that of a fighter but a friend. Anymole that counts you as a friend will be stronger by far than if he stood alone."

Medlar turned to the other three and looked at each of them in turn and then said: "I do not know what forces have brought you here, or indeed have led me here myself. But in all my long life I have never met three moles who have more to learn about the way of fighting, or have given me the sense that they will learn as much. I hesitate to speak of this and after it will say little more on the sub-

ject. Each of us has a task and with the Stone's grace only
may he fulfill it. All moles may choose to be a fighter if
they wish, though many do so who are not fitted for that
way. All moles perhaps may be warriors, too, though few,
too few, can find the way to it. My task is to try to show
you the difference between a fighter and a warrior and it
may not be what you expect.

"Each of you stands now in a tunnel, the start of which
is far behind you, the end of which is far ahead. I am but
a mole who meets you on the way. Others ahead of me
will talk to you as well, and many try to take you down
false paths with them. These are your real opponents. Do
not give in. Some will invent ways of distracting you.
Learn to recognize them. Only the spirit in your heart
will keep you going. Hear it. Follow it. Let courage and
patience enter your talons and love of your opponents
enter your heart."

Medlar looked round at each of them in turn again. As
he looked at Bracken, his old eyes kind and wrinkled
with age, Bracken felt as if his soul was stripped bare and
this strange mole knew everything there was to know
about him. Bracken felt at once frightened and exultant.

"Now," said Medlar, "leave me here and go and sleep,
for each of you has made a long journey to get here—and
each must soon make a long journey again. So our time is
short. Eat and sleep and tomorrow I will begin to show
you what you need to do."

TOMORROW came, and with it the start of what, for Bracken, was to be the first long period of settled peace in his life. For the days and nights passed slowly, sliding through the mole-months as April gave way to May, and May grew warm with sunshine and birdsong, until a full moleyear had gone by.

It was a time in which Bracken learned to stop worrying about physical danger as he and the other moles concentrated on the guidance that Medlar gave them. Like Hulver, Medlar gave a mole the feeling that when he crouched in a burrow, time chose to crouch still with him, and from this stillness some of Medlar's wisdom went out to all of them.

Each took something different from him, though it was to be a very long time before any of them understood what he was teaching them. For as well as the curious exercises he made them do—Boswell, for instance, had to attack a wall "in slow motion" for many days in succession, while Bracken had to crouch opposite Mullion and guess "what he was thinking and whether he likes you or not"—he instructed them in the art of sitting still and doing nothing, "which is where you will meet your first, and perhaps your only real opponent—yourselves."

But for his extraordinary display of fighting skill against Stonecrop, and the sense of truth he seemed to carry in everything he did, all three of them, at one time or another, might well have given up what seemed a fruitless effort.

As Stonecrop—who soon learned to respect Bracken—was to say one night, "I've come here to learn how to fight, not to sit on my belly all day trying to think about nothing." Yet there was never a time when all three wanted to leave all at once and, indeed, at any one time there was always at least one of them who positively felt he was learning something, though none of them was ever quite sure what.

The fact was that Medlar had seen from the first that the three moles who appeared in the chamber so unexpectedly each had unusual abilities in some directions and were underdeveloped in others. Stonecrop, for example, was one of the most physically harmonious moles he had ever met but for the key fact that his mind was unpeaceful and often confused and full of anger about his brother's death, so that he could never be a really good fighter because he was not at one with himself. So Medlar made him sit still and give time for the anger to evaporate.

Boswell, on the other paw, was one of the most spiritually developed moles Medlar had come across—indeed, Boswell was to teach Medlar a great deal about the philosophy of the Stone in talks they had to which Bracken listened, though Stonecrop and Mullion found them boring.

But Medlar understood clearly Boswell's difficulty in believing that he could extend the use of his body into something as straightforwardly physical as fighting—a natural doubt, given his deformity. But if there was one thing Medlar had learned in his years of showing others how to fight, it was that most moles underestimated what they were capable of doing, killing off their own instincts with the false opinions others held of them.

As for Bracken, Medlar found him the most interesting of the three. It was obvious to Medlar from the moment he first saw him that he was a mole of enormous physical and mental stamina. But it was only slowly that Medlar understood that the fugitive life he had lived, alone with himself and with real danger, had given him no way of valuing the strengths he truly had. He was like a hungry mole who is too insensitive to see that food lies all around him. Medlar's task was to make him see the qualities he had developed inside himself without knowing it—an ability to act independently and alone for long periods, and very real physical power.

Medlar's skill lay in making each of the three moles not only see these different qualities in themselves but actually to experience them, the only way to pursue truth that he knew. "You may tell a mole ten times he is strong and he may believe you, but he will still remain weak; only let him experience his own strength once, and he will always be strong," he was fond of saying. So he made Stonecrop experience stillness, Boswell experience gracefulness and Bracken experience his own independence and staying power.

Bracken's view of Medlar—and indeed of Boswell,

Mullion and Stonecrop—changed several times as the molemonths went by. His early awe gave way to exasperation at having to do such pointless-seeming things, and then blind trust took over when he found he could do things that were difficult; then a kind of cocksure disrespect when he thought it was all very easy; and then when molemonths had passed, he discovered a new awe bordering on love when he understood that Medlar was teaching him things, without him knowing it, whose very conception he could not even have had at first. Like the question that Medlar had first raised with them about how a great fighter loves his opponent.

His insight of the truth of this came one day when he was engaged in a mock fight with Stonecrop. By now the two moles had an affectionate relationship and were certainly close enough not to wish to harm each other. Bracken was no longer afraid of Stonecrop because he had discovered that though smaller, he was able to move faster and could turn Stonecrop's size and power back against himself by, for example, using it to add power to his own talon thrusts. As they were engaged in sparring in this way, Medlar suddenly called out: "Right! Now make the fight real. Try to kill each other."

So great was their trust in Medlar that their hesitation was only temporary as each saw the other's stance change into a real threat. The fight grew slower and more intense and Bracken found to his surprise that he seemed to be not so much fighting against Stonecrop as engaged in a ritual dance *with* him—a feeling that soon gave way to the sense that, for the moment at least, he *was* Stonecrop and that when Stonecrop lunged toward him, he was able to counteract the move instinctively because he was making Stonecrop's lunge himself. "Stop!" called Medlar, and the two, who had both experienced this sense of oneness in the fight, or "love," as Medlar called it, found their bodies now experienced a curious sense of loss as the fight ended. Neither was in the slighest bit hurt.

Experience like this also taught Bracken to appreciate that a fight between moles is not, at root, a physical thing at all, but a spiritual confrontation. The very idea of spirit was a new one to him and he only learned of it in himself by being made to observe it in other moles. Mullion, for example, had a friendly, weak spirit with no "hardness" or "force" to it and it was only when Bracken himself sensed this that he understood Medlar's immediate rejection of Mullion as a fighter.

"But it is his real spirit," said Medlar, "and it is therefore a powerful one, but it is not the spirit of a fighter. Win the loyalty of his spirit, however, and you are strong indeed."

Bracken found that Stonecrop, on the other hand, had a very hard and powerful spirit, though one that was inflexible and therefore, in Medlar's terms, fairly easy to get round. In his own mind, Bracken came to understand this by thinking of Stonecrop as a series of burrows and tunnels, not unlike the Barrow Vale, where, if a mole kept his head and spirit firm, he would eventually find a way through. It was understanding this that cleared Bracken of his fear of Stonecrop—and simultaneously made Stonecrop more respectful of Bracken.

As these insights about fighting came to Bracken, he began to understand other things that Medlar had taught. One of them was the idea that there is no such thing as a talon lunge *by itself:* a proper fighter lunges with his whole body, which for Medlar meant with his whole spirit.

"If you understand this, Bracken, you have the way into your true strength. So many moles think that they will succeed by making their lunges more and more powerful—but a gentle touch from the paw of an old mole like me is a thousand times more powerful because I make it with my whole spirit, whereas they use only their muscles." And, as if to prove the point, Medlar seemed to do no more than touch Bracken on his shoulder and he found himself tumbling back across the chamber.

Sometimes Bracken saw things suddenly as if a rush of sunlight had all at once filled a gap between trees—and this often happened when he was watching Medlar instruct one of the others. One day, when Boswell was the willing victim, Medlar suddenly yawned and crouched down. Involuntarily Boswell followed suit, thinking that Medlar was taking a rest. Or *was* it just that? As Boswell relaxed, Medlar attacked him viciously and, taken by surprise, Boswell almost crumpled up before them.

"A weak spirit will follow a strong spirit and copy what it does," said Medlar. "You tense up, he will tense up; but you relax and he will relax, as Boswell just did. In a fight, if you gain dominance of spirit and *then* relax, your opponent will do the same and in that moment you can kill him, as I could have killed Boswell. Learn to read your opponent's spirit.

"It will help you do this if you make him strike at you first with his talons. Indeed, among great fighters the one who strikes first will always lose the fight. Striking betrays weakness of spirit."

"Well, that would mean that really great fighters never need to strike a blow," said Bracken dubiously.

"Exactly," said Medlar.

One day, Medlar invited Stonecrop to kill him. Stonecrop thought it was a joke, or some kind of trap—which, in a sense, it was, though not quite as Stonecrop imagined. Medlar became angry with his hesitation (or seemed to be, none of them was ever sure with Medlar) and he started viciously attacking Stonecrop, who became angry in his turn. In the midst of the fight, Medlar dropped his guard and repeated "Kill me, Stonecrop," and crouched quite still, waiting. There was a hush lasting a long time as Stonecrop's talons hung poised above Medlar's upturned snout. Suddenly he dropped his talons and relaxed, saying "You want to die!"

Medlar laughed and said "Perhaps I do, but do not turn your back on what you have learned. You see, I am no longer afraid of death and for another mole to meet that attitude is a very fearful thing. A mole who no longer fears death is very powerful because his opponents are then faced by nothing but their own fears. This is very hard to understand, very hard to feel. When you can see that there is no difference between life and death and that you are already dead, then not only will you be more alive than you have ever been but it may be that at last you can accept the task that the Stone has got for you. When that happens you will be a warrior."

Bracken found it hard to understand these ideas but the exercises Medlar made him do made him *feel* the truth of them and so come to know them from within rather than from without. Discussing them with Boswell, he discovered that while Boswell often understood them better, he found it harder to feel them—neither was sure which was best, or worst.

So the molemonths passed, and the meadow grass on the surface of the Nuneham system began to grow green and lush with the coming of June. More and more grasses

and flowers appeared, as the early spring plants gave
way to red and white clover, the waving pink flowers of
ragged robin, while white clusters of sneezewort and pink
cuckoo flowers grew down nearer the river where, in moments of relaxation, the moles occasionally explored.
While the river itself flowed more languidly, tiny whirl-
pools of water catching and circling into nothing at its
edge, where the shadows of tall reed, reedmace and fluttering yellow flag fell; and the occasional chub or roach
took food on the surface, the roundling circlets of their
rise traveling and fading slowly with the flow.

Then, quite suddenly, Bracken began to miss Duncton
Wood. He missed the high cover of green leaves, always
rustling above, and the different sounds of birds—blackbird and thrush, treecreeper and chaffinch—scurrying and
hopping, some on the surface, others on the branches,
their massed song at daybreak sharper and much clearer
than the more diffused song out here of a system in the
open. He missed the beech trees he had grown to love.
He missed the darker rich smell of the tunnels, where
the worms moved easily, and the surface litter, so much
richer in grubs and insects than green grass.

He missed the sound of a Duncton voice. He missed
Rue. But most of all, and most mysteriously to him, he
missed Rebecca. The more he sat and didn't think, as
Medlar insisted that he should, the more he learned to
feel the spirit of Stonecrop or Boswell, and of himself;
the more he turned to face the world about him through
learning how to fight . . . the more he missed Rebecca.

There were days when her memory would nag at him,
and he would look about him as if the world was incom-
plete, and there was something just outside his reach
which needed to be put in place for it all to be right
again. He remembered running through the chamber of
roots beneath the Stone, when she was ahead of him. He
could feel her touch on his shoulder and her voice, gentler and yet fuller than any birdsong he had ever heard,
as it spoke again to him. My love. My sweet love. She
had said those words to him, she had, she did, my love,
my Rebecca. And the stone beneath the Stone, the stone
that had glimmered and played its light around them!
The Stillstone! He had touched it; he could still feel its
pattern on his paw, and could scratch it on the ground
and wonder at it, thinking of her. She had touched his

fur, and he remembered touching hers, he did, he had, his love Rebecca.

Talking about her did not help, or any other of his Duncton memories. One day he suddenly took it into his head to tell Stonecrop about Cairn. He told him just as it was, the terrible love and ache of it all, his spirit turning weak from the telling. He said again what he had said then about Rebecca, and Stonecrop nodded because he remembered her. Stonecrop didn't say much but just heaved his body sadly, the look in his eyes a mixture of loss and anger, and disgust at the memory of Mandrake's odor in a temporary burrow by a wood's edge, a smell he had not forgotten.

No, talking was no use. Bracken tried to tell Boswell about the stone in the heart of the Ancient System but the words died in his mouth and he could not take Boswell past the Chamber of Echoes in his account, lying— "No, no. I couldn't get through, it's impossible"—and the lie was better than betraying the memory of the glimmering stone where he and Rebecca were . . . what? Where we *were* was the best way he could tell it to himself. Bracken wanted to leave Nuneham.

So did Stonecrop, and Mullion as well; while Boswell left those things to Bracken, whose words were sometimes jumbled and confused but whose instincts he trusted and would always follow, as the Stone itself seemed to have insructed him to do. Medlar agreed. He had known before any of them that there was no more he could do—a mole must learn the rest himself. And anyway, he had more to learn himself, and a place he must go to.

"You will find there is much more to learn," Medlar said finally at the end of the first week of June, "and that none of it is very far from your heart. Indeed, I will let you into a secret!" Medlar said this jovially, for he was relieved that his task was done. June was a time to travel, and he wanted to leave Nuneham himself and head for Uffington, to where, he knew now, he had always been going.

"You do not have to *learn* anything. You know it all already. Each one of you. It's all here!" And he thumped his old chest cheerfully, laughing gaily as if everything was really so simple that it was absurd worrying about it, which it was.

"As for fighting, when you no longer need to fight at

all, you will know when you have learned enough. This is
not a mystery but a simple fact. A real fighter does not
need to raise one single talon to quell an opponent—unless it be to teach him a lesson of the crudest sort!" Medlar looked at Stonecrop when he said this, remembering
their first meeting, and then laughed again.

"We are living in a strange time, which is why I am
going to Uffington. By the Stone's grace I will get there.
As for you, each of you has the strength to be a warrior,
as we all have."

They said their farewells at night by the Nuneham
Stone. Medlar spoke to each of them in turn—including
Mullion, of whom he had grown especially fond—and
then said a prayer to the Stone itself. Boswell said a
prayer as well and then uttered the journey blessing on
Medlar. And when Medlar had gone, he said it again, so
that its protection would go with old Medlar, who had
awakened so much in all their hearts.

The June moon was waxing and strong. "We'll travel
all together," said Bracken with a strong spirit which they
all respected, even Stonecrop. "We'll head straight for the
Duncton Stone. Just look at the moon! You know what it
means for a Duncton mole? Midsummer's coming! And
there's words I've promised to say by the Stone on Midsummer Night."

"We'll have to push it to get there that quick," said
Stonecrop.

"We will!" said Bracken. He stayed on alone by the
Nuneham Stone for a moment after the others had set
off, his snout pointing toward Duncton, whose pull he
could feel and which would get stronger as the moon got
fuller and the days advanced toward Midsummer. And
looking at it, and then in the direction of Duncton Wood,
he remembered another light, white, glimmering, and
whispered "Rebecca, Rebecca," and laughed aloud into
the night.

FEW springs had ever been as miserable in spirit as that in which Rune consolidated his power in Duncton Wood. Under his black thrall the system became in fact what the pasture moles had always feared it was—a place where evil spells are woven by minds that lurk in darkness and by moles whose smiles are as warm as the welcome an owl gives to its prey.

Rune's power came initially from the vicious loyalty of the henchmoles whose favor he had fostered so successfully under Mandrake, and who now did his bidding whenever it came, and for whatever purpose.

He was well aware that since the henchmoles had given him power, they could, in theory at least, take it away again. For this reason, once he was installed as leader of the Duncton system, he began a policy of winning their gratitude by granting them favors of territory and matings and securing their fear by imposing particularly cruel and rough punishment on those henchmoles who transgressed his deliberately arbitrary rules. He had noticed how Mandrake had made everymole fear him by occasionally picking on one at random and killing or maiming him for all to see.

Rune's method was more subtle and perhaps even more effective. He would arbitrarily select a henchmole and accuse him of a crime that had not been a crime the day before, and was not one again in the days that followed. Perhaps a henchmole had killed another one unnecessarily in a mating fight—nothing normally wrong with that at all in Rune's system: the more killing the better! But suddenly, out of the blue, that mole would be accused of harming Duncton by attacking a colleague and a friend, and Rune would throw his fate open to the whim of the groups of trusty henchmoles who always stayed close by him, currying his favor. Great was their joy not to be the victim; pleasantly were their sadistic imaginations stretched to think of a way of punishing him. Injure him and leave him for the owls to take alive? Crush his snout and let him die slowly in full view of Barrow Vale? Whatever was decided Rune liked to watch, and he rarely left a scene of punishment without his own talons being covered in blood and his unpleasant laughter carrying above that of the rest.

At the same time, he encouraged henchmoles to spy on each other and on other moles, and to tell him what they had found out. His punishments for moles successfully accused were always grim and form one of the cruelest, and saddest, periods in the history of Duncton. Maimings, blindings, snout-crushings and enforced cannibalism—the list is as long, as dark and as bloody as each individual death the henchmoles devised.

By the beginning of March, Rune had the henchmoles completely under his control, and with them all the system but the Marsh End. That he preferred to leave alone for a while longer, for fear that the disease that had broken out there—a rumor successfully propagated by Mekkins, who intended to resist Rune in every way he could—would spread into the main system. But if a henchmole could get hold of a wandering marshender, that was fine, and what cruel pleasure was had by all before the poor creature died!

As March had begun and the mating season got under way, there was a certain decrease of the violence, for it had served its purpose and the henchmoles deserved to take their pleasures in mating and fighting among themselves and others. The sight of the big and bullying westsiders, from whose ranks most of the henchmoles came, as they roamed about seeking mates became familiar in all the system, where females waited in abject fear, and males from such areas as the eastside and around Barrow Vale preferred to scurry away and hide, lest they be lured into a mating fight they could not win.

The henchmoles did not, however, always have things their own way. One female called Oxlip, who lived near the Marsh End, objected to the invasion of her tunnels by a henchmole and, with a combination of cunning and sheer anger, succeeded not only in killing him but also injured another henchmole who was lurking nearby.

Rune's reaction was to kill the injured one who reported the incident "for bringing shame to the henchmoles" and then to send others to find the female. They failed, for Oxlip turned north to the Marsh End, where Mekkins accepted her as a marshender, glad to have anymole brave enough to fight and flee from the henchmoles.

But just as spiders suddenly appear from nowhere in

damp September, so does evil manifest itself when a mole like Rune takes power. Strange, dark creatures of moles, diseased in mind, distorted in body, began to appear from the darkness in which they had so long lurked and gather in the shadows that surrounded Rune. An old female from the eastside, for example, appeared one day in Barrow Vale—her thin and haggard appearance and the cast of danger in her body all so threatening that the henchmole who found her and dared not touch her took her to Rune.

Although her origin was vaguely known—she said herself that she came from beyond the eastside—no mole knew her name. The henchmole called her Nightshade and Rune very quickly seemed to take to her, liking to have her misshapen form lurking in the tunnels and burrows from which he ruled Duncton. He saw the silly, superstitious fear she caused others and so exploited it. It was said that she knew dark and secret rituals banished from Duncton by the moles of the Ancient System and handed down in some outback of the eastside by generation after generation of moles waiting for just such a moment as this. However it was, no henchmole dared to risk angering her or getting in her way before dawn, when she liked to squirm about the surface muttering and cursing to herself and casting spells that left an odor in the air.

Evil showed itself in other ways, too. Duncton's normally bright and cheerful spring wildflowers seemed to grow prematurely withered out of the ground—wood anemones drooping, the white petals mottled and limp, while even the normally ebullient dog's mercury grew rank and fetid where its spiky leaves pierced last year's dead undergrowth. The sun, normally bright and warm for at least a few days at the end of March, stayed distant and watery, and even when its rays broke through the cloud they were chilly, and the light they cast was cold.

The trees were slow to take leaf, and by mid-April only the hawthorn and occasional horse chestnut was beginning to show green in its buds, miserable against the black trunks and leafless trees that gave the wood a wintry air.

Ordinary moles in the system did their best to keep their snouts out of trouble, staying as quietly as they could in their own tunnels or giving them up without a struggle if some bully of a henchmole fancied taking them. Some sought to find favor and settled old territorial scores by reporting their harmless neighbors to the henchmoles. Others crouched and shivered in their burrows, stirring only to find food, their spirits lowering as the weeks went by.

The fear and stress found their evil way into the very life of the system itself, for far fewer females became pregnant, and of those that did, far more than usual aborted their litter and went pupless into April. Such females were vulnerable to attack, for they were already weak, and Rune made his displeasure with them known. Those who littered were, however, favored—not because of the joy their pups might bring but because their young might make henchmoles in the future, and it was to the future that Rune's black mind was looking.

As April advanced, Rune, the only mole in Duncton Wood who seemed positively glowing with health, began to relax about the possible return of Mandrake, which he had seen initially as a serious threat. Mandrake had last been seen bringing down the great flints in the Chamber of Dark Sound to halt the henchmoles' assault upon him, and since then, nothing had been heard. Rune had left several henchmoles at key points around the Ancient System—at Hulver's old tunnels, by Bracken's tunnels in the area between the Stone clearing and the pastures, and a few other points where tunnels started. But Mandrake was never seen or heard, and Rune began to suspect that the inevitable had happened and that Mandrake had died in lonely madness somewhere in the forgotten tunnels, or perhaps had left the system altogether to seek out some other place as he had once sought out Duncton. But wherever he was, the henchmoles would never allow him back now.

In any case, as the warmer weather finally and reluctantly began to arrive in the second week of May, Rune became preoccupied with an idea that had been growing in his mind for many moleyears. He wanted to attack the pasture system.

He had suspected for a long time that the pasture moles were not as strong as the Duncton moles feared they were. The number of incidents between the two systems had declined steadily over the moleyears, and it was significant to him that there was no reaction from the pastures after the attack on Cairn. Rune wrongly assumed that the injured Cairn had made his way back to the pastures and from this believed that had the pasture moles been really powerful, they would have attacked Duncton, or at least sought reprisals. But even in the mating season, when there were usually a few incursions, nothing happened.

Rune decided that the time had come to launch a limited assault on the pastures. It was with this objective in mind that he started to gather his henchmoles on the westside at the end of May.

The death of Rose was a deep loss to the pasture system, where she was much loved, and in particular to Brome, who had always revered the trust and advice she had given and that had helped him to take control of the pastures peacefully and with justice.

When her death was reported to him, he had set off at once for Rose's burrows, for it is the tradition in the pastures that the burrows of a healer are sealed by a mole or moles to whom they have been close. When he got there, he found the tunnels and burrows deserted except for the body of Rose, and a guardmole led him to her main tunnel's exit on the surface where Rebecca was crouched, snout pointing across the open grass to the darkness of the wood she loved. She had a youngster at her side.

Because he was uncertain how to address a mole who had, by all accounts, lived closer than any other ever had to Rose, if only for the last few molemonths, he said rather formally "It is the custom to seal the burrow."

Rebecca turned and looked at him, tiredness and loss in her eyes, but a sense of peace as well. Used as Brome was to deference from other moles, he was surprised but relieved to sense none at all in this Rebecca, only a sorrow for the passing of a mole she had obviously loved as well.

"In our system, it is the custom to let the owls have their way," she said, quietly smiling to him as a token of her sense of his loss.

A little discomfited by the directness of her gaze, Brome asked "What's *his* name?" looking at Comfrey. Rebecca said nothing, making it clear that Comfrey was old enough to reply for himself.

"My name's C—C—Comfrey," he said, looking at Brome with his curious mixture of timidity and interest, "and I'm from D—D—Duncton Wood." Brome nodded and smiled, but Comfrey went on. "My father was Bracken who went into the marshes. H–He's coming back."

Brome had heard about the sad story of Bracken from Mekkins, so he smiled again and nodded his head vaguely, thinking that this was some kind story Rebecca had reassured the youngster with, for no mole returns from the marshes. To his astonishment he saw a look on Rebecca's face that seemed almost angry with him, as if she suspected this thought and wished to underline that what she had told Comfrey was indeed true.

This mute exchange surprised Brome and he looked at Rebecca more closely, his curiosity sliding very quickly into a kind of uneasy awe. Never before had he been in the presence of a mole who gave him the impression that she knew exactly what he was feeling. He saw as well that she was very beautiful, with a coat of dark, silvery gray, whose sheen held the light of a clear sky after rain.

He had a dozen things in his mind to say, but they all fell away before her still gaze and he said what was in his heart: "What are we going to do, Rebecca?" She came forward and touched him for a second, a touch that reassured him, and then she led the way back to Rose's tunnels where, without another word, they sealed the tunnels together, soil falling on their fur as with burrowing sweeps of their paws they retreated before it. It was the pasture way of doing things.

"Will you stay here?" he asked. It was really a plea, for such a mole could bring nothing but good to the system and the pastures had lost much in the passing of Rose.

She nodded, suddenly weary, for she knew that Rose had left her the task of filling her place as healer, a prospect that seemed unreal and impossible to achieve. There was so much she didn't know and so many things she wished she had asked. So she would be a healer and for the time being she would stay here, for there was nowhere else she could go—certainly not to Duncton, not yet. It was Brome's turn to sense what was in her mind, for he came nearer her and crouched quietly, his big limbs stretched comfortably by the untidy seal of soil they had just made as he said: "It will be all right here, you know. There are many moles that will need you."

For a while he hesitated to say more, but finally said "There may be problems if they know that you and Cairn . . ."

Rebecca looked sharply at him and his words froze in his mouth. Rebecca had a power in her he had never seen before in anymole. "The only way possible for a healer is to live in the truth," she said. "Cairn and I mated, and he was killed by Mandrake and Rune, two Duncton moles."

"Well," said Brome, "I will see that all moles know who you are and why you are here. Only *you* can allay any doubts or fears or hostility they may have."

"If Stonecrop were here and I could talk to him, he would understand," she said.

Brome shook his head sadly. "Stonecrop left the system —he wanted to avenge Cairn's death—but I persuaded him that it would not be right, or safe." Rebecca smiled, for that was just what Stonecrop would have wanted to do.

"He heard that a great fighter had come to a system said to be quite near here, beyond the pastures, and in company with other moles he went off to find him. The others have come back, but Stonecrop was not with them."

Rebecca lowered her head. Stonecrop dead, or lost? Another mole gone? Cairn, Bracken, Hulver, Stonecrop, Mandrake. Why so many? She felt as if they were all leaving her, and immediately felt that the thought was wrong. I'm so self-centered! she scolded herself. Then she said: "Bracken was with Cairn when he died," as if to reassure Brome about Cairn's death, and through him other pasture moles.

"Who is this Bracken? Everymole I meet from Duncton seems to mention him—you, Mekkins, even Comfrey. Was he one of your mates?" She shook her head. "He was a mole who lived in the Ancient System by the Stone —he knew the tunnels there better than anymole ever has. He is a very special mole."

"But he's lost if he's gone out onto the marsh—no mole ever comes back from there," said Brome.

"*He* will," said Rebecca, closing the subject.

Rebecca made her own tunnels quite near where Rose's had been—but how bare her burrow seemed compared with the cluttered, untidy place that Rose's was! How she missed the scents and smells of a thousand different herbs!

She saw little of Violet, who had a sort of a burrow of her own nearby but was rarely seen near it for she was quickly getting absorbed into the pasture system and even beginning to speak in the quicker, higher intonation of the pasture moles. Comfrey stayed near—big enough now to make his own burrow, digging it into a long and winding shape, quite unlike any burrow Rebecca had ever seen before. He preferred her not to enter it, and, like Rose, seemed inherently untidy, though always clean.

The fascination with herbs that Rose had inspired in him persisted, and his first long expedition away from Rebecca and the burrows arose out of it. He heard her say one day that she missed the smells of herbs and looked forward to the day when she could go back to Duncton and get some. The following day he disappeared. He returned two days later with a lot of noise and deposited outside her burrow a pile of fresh light-green leaves.

"It's ch—chamomile," he said matter-of-factly. "Just the leaves. The flowers aren't out yet, b—but when they are I'll get you some. The leaves smell fresh."

Something else happened that same day that made her feel that at last the clouds that had been above her so long were beginning to lift. There was a timid scratching near her burrow, and when she looked outside, a young and nervous-looking female was standing there in a worried sort of way. She started back when Rebecca appeared and seemed to find difficulty saying anything. She looked very miserable.

"What is it, my love?" asked Rebecca gently. The female stayed where she was, dug her talons nervously in and out of the soil of the tunnel floor, and eventually managed to say "Violet said you would help."

Rebecca went forward to her until they were almost touching and asked "Are you a friend of Violet's?" The female nodded, but said nothing. "What's worrying you?" asked Rebecca gently.

For a moment the female swayed back and forth, her eyes fixed in a mute appeal on Rebecca, and then burst out "I don't know!" in a voice of despair and started to cry. Rebecca touched her with her paw, felt that her fur was clammy and cold and her head too hot, and somehow she caressed her, held her, touched her, and the female slowly calmed and settled down. Rebecca found herself muttering healing words softly to her, nothing talk, talk about the herbs she wished she had, talk from one heart to another whose individual words are of no account. Until eventually the female got up, eyes bright, and with barely a word went off down the tunnel, leaving Rebecca quite exhausted.

A few days later a male came, saying, "You helped a friend of mine and I don't think there's anything wrong with me, and I don't know why I'm here, in fact, I think I'll go away again, it hurts here, well not there *exactly*, I don't know why I didn't see to it before, for years actually . . ." And so, by word of mouth, Rebecca's work as a healer gently began.

Rune finally launched his attack on the pasture system in mid-June in a spirit of cold curiosity. Like every other aggressive mole in Duncton, he was interested to find out what the pastures, and the moles who lived in them, were like. This factor, coupled with a few well-chosen words to his henchmoles about how "pasture moles periodically murder our females and youngsters" and how "the pride of Duncton Wood is threatened by these cowardly moles" and so on and so forth, was sufficient to give the henchmoles the motive they needed to pass over the wood's edge and onto the pastures, and from there to make the trek to find tunnels down which they could mount their attack.

But Rune was no fool and he was well aware of the dangers inherent in leading a body of moles who had no experience at all in warfare. So he was also curious to see how the henchmoles would perform as an attacking group and to find out what lessons he might learn for future, more serious affrays.

His caution was wise. The assault on the pastures might well have been a complete disaster had not the pasture moles been as ill-prepared for a sudden night attack as he was in making it, and had he not had a superiority of numbers. His objective was to locate and kill a few pasture moles and this was only achieved by the henchmoles with a great deal of rushing about, shouting, bumping into each other, wounding one another by mistake, and generally inefficient turmoil. They killed four moles, wounded seven and frightened a dozen more.

However, they were also very nearly cut off from the wood by a rapid and efficient counterattack led by Brome, and they retreated, as they had arrived, in disarray. Near-disasters are, however, usually labeled complete victories by cunning leaders and this one was no exception. It was true that the henchmoles lost three of their number, but once back in the westside with no sign of pursuit by the pasture moles, they celebrated the "victory" as if they had conquered the whole of the pasture system in two hours' work, recalling the deeds of their lost colleagues with relish.

Rune learned many things from this attack, the most immediately applicable being his need to appoint a tough deputy he could trust to keep the henchmoles in control when he was not around. He gave the task to the trusty westsider Burrhead, knowing that his loyalty was sound and that he did not have sufficient wit to attempt to lead a coup on Rune's position.

He also decided he must quickly and ruthlessly inculcate group efficiency into the henchmoles—which he set about doing immediately, knowing there would be little time to lose before he heard from the pasture moles.

The repercussions of this attack in the pastures, in the Marsh End and, finally, in Duncton Wood itself, were many and complex. Perhaps the most significant was Brome's decision to take reprisals against Duncton—a move more or less forced upon him by the anger of the pasture moles at the savagery of Rune's attack. Brome was, in fact, reluctant to counterattack, since what little he had seen of the stocky Duncton moles suggested that they were individually far more powerful as fighters than pasture moles, even though they were not always as big. There was an evil viciousness about the moles of Duncton, whose fur was generally so dark and whose bodies smelled of the dank wood. And who fought with cold ruthlessness.

For this reason, rather than enter into Duncton Wood his method was to lure them onto the pastures one evening with a deliberately weak attack and spurious retreat by the wood's edge, where he felt he could outmaneuver them. But he was wrong.

Rune had ruthlessly and efficiently disciplined his henchmoles, and they followed the fleeing pasture moles so fast that they had killed most of them before they had advanced sufficiently to fall into the trap Brome had prepared. Suspecting it, Rune cunningly stopped his forces from advancing directly, circling instead through the unknown pasture tunnels in the belief that they might outflank the pasture moles in their own system. At the same time, Rune left sufficient henchmoles to guard the wood's edge, with various small but very fast runners to keep the two groups in touch with each other.

Rune finally led his henchmoles into a vicious and bloody attack on Brome's moles, coming at speed from an unexpected direction and moving forward with a solid resolution that took the pasture moles by surprise.

Brome's reaction was wise, unimpressive, but saved the day. He retreated on all sides, using his popularity with the pasture moles to persuade them to follow his advice and retreat quickly so that the Duncton moles would have no mole to fight. The move was so effective that the impetus of the Duncton henchmoles was lost as they found burrow after burrow empty, and tunnel after tunnel echoing only with the sound of their own slowing paws and the groans of badly injured pasture moles left behind in the flight.

At the same time, Brome sent two of his most trusted moles northeast toward the distant Marsh End to take Rebecca with them, and with her help to try to win the support of Mekkins. It was a long shot, but Brome saw clearly that a temporary retreat might indirectly win victory while a permanent retreat meant defeat. He would soon have to attack again, and the more friends he had, the better.

Rune's cunning as leader improved every moment, and with his now-customary speed of action he withdrew all the henchmoles back to the westside, much against their wishes.

"Have I not led you to victory so far?" he asked the doubters coldly. "Trust me to do so now. This trick will bring the pasture moles back."

For two days there was an uneasy silence as the normally clear, sparse tunnels of the pastures, now deserted, began to reek of the stench of the dead, whose decay was hastened by the onset of summery June weather. During the day, birdsong filled the wood, skylarks hung on the air above the high pastures, and the fresh green of the leaves of Duncton Wood glistened and danced with sunshine before the warm June breeze.

But underground, moles on both sides were tense and anxious as each waited for the other to make a move.

Brome advanced his moles back to their original positions, at first puzzled by the Duncton moles' disappearance, then seeing its logic. Rune must have guessed that after successfully killing so many pasture moles, their remaining forces would not want actually to enter the wood itself.

In the course of this advance, Brome was unexpectedly visited by Rebecca. She had refused to accompany his moles to the Marsh End, or even to show them the way, without first understanding what was going on. She did not like mass fighting and wanted no part in causing it. And anyway, she felt she should be where she could help. She shivered at the smell of carnage in the tunnels and her first words to Brome were the simple advice that he had best arrange for the dead to be dragged to the surface for the owls "or there won't be a system worth living in anyway."

This simple advice was to be the cause of one of the many remarkable myths that grew up around Rebecca. For soon after it was done, the surface above the pasture was covered not by a plague of owls but by a mass of bristling, cawing, fighting crows, pecking at the dead moles and putting fear into the advance guards of the Duncton moles, watching out for signs of pasture movement.

The idea that the pasture moles "had the crows on their side," as one of the scouts put it, was fearful indeed. While among the pasture moles the arrival of the crows, simultaneous as it was with the coming of the mysterious, though increasingly popular Duncton healer, created the idea that Rebecca had the power to summon crows!

"If Mekkins were to support us from the north," explained Brome, "then it would probably be worth our while standing our ground. We cannot retreat again, but I do not think we have the skill or strength to resist these Duncton moles by ourselves."

Rebecca was doubtful. Fighting was not something she liked, although she conceded it was sometimes necessary.

"Whatmole is leading the moles from Duncton?" she asked curiously.

Brome shrugged. "He's a good fighter, that's for sure. Several of our moles report seeing a cunning-looking mole apparently in charge, quite big, very dark and with as evil a glitter about him as you would find in any nightmare."

"Rune!" whispered Rebecca. Yes, in that case she

would do what Brome wanted and try to summon Mekkins' help.

"It's all right," she said. "I will go to the Marsh End
—let's hope Mekkins is still secure. I want to go. Things
are happening down there, I think. Here too. It's all
changing, Brome, and whatever you try to do, there's
nothing you can do—but you *must* try." She laughed at
his bewilderment at her words and added: "I only half
understand what I'm saying myself. It's all right!"

As Brome watched her leave, he thought to himself that
there were times when she spoke with the same mysterious certainty Rose sometimes had. As if she saw a world
he could not see and there were no words to describe the
realities within it. Yet as she left alone, how vulnerable
she seemed, and for the first time he saw very clearly how
much in need of protection she really was.

Two days later, as night fell, the battle started up again,
first as a skirmish up near the wood's edge where some
pasture moles went scouting about, and then a full-scale
battle in the pasture tunnels themselves.

It was bloody and confused as under Brome's quiet
leadership every pasture mole stood his ground against
the brutal assault of the Duncton henchmoles. Brome
had sensibly blocked several side tunnels, making it difficult for the henchmoles to advance in mass, and that
much easier for them to be picked off one by one. But
soon the henchmoles did manage their circling tactics
again and the battle raged back and forth from tunnel to
tunnel with little pattern except that slowly the pasture
moles began to retreat, moving back steadily toward bigger tunnels where, once the henchmoles were established,
they would have room to maneuver and crush the pasture
moles with their greater ruthlessness and nerve. It was not
that the pasture moles lacked courage—just the opposite
—but somehow they did not have the will to win that
Rune inspired in his own moles.

The fighting eventually began to concentrate in a central chamber formed by the crossing of two communal
tunnels. The pasture moles occupied the part that led directly away from the direction of the wood and toward
the center of their own system. Rune's henchmoles occupied the wood side of the chamber and the side tunnels that radiated north and south from it. Powerful talon

thrusts and lunges jabbed out from the dark, moving mass
of the henchmoles toward the group of pasture moles
whose light coats showed up the blood from their cuts and
wounds more easily. Brome now stood resolutely at their
head.

There was a continuous angry growl to the air as the
moles fought back and forth, panting and grunting with
the effort of staying alive. Gradually, subtly, as pasture
mole after mole fell and the henchmoles advanced across
the chamber, there came the feeling among all of them
that a critical point in the struggle had been reached.
Brome moved right to the front of his moles, fighting
strongly and encouraging them to stand firm. While behind the mass of henchmoles, wounded but not seriously,
Rune slid back and forth, encouraging a mole here, warning one there, shouting out orders to them all.

"Kill their leader . . . go for their leader," he shouted,
gesticulating through the fighting talons and noise toward
Brome.

Brome stood solid, now surrounded by his most loyal
fighters, eyes narrowed with concentration and aggression, his great, strong body and calm stance the central
part of the pasture defense. He had tried pushing forward but the henchmoles were too strong and stolid in
their positions, and inch by inch he was retreating. To
his left a pasture mole had rolled over onto his side,
blood running from his mouth, and a henchmole was on
top of him pushing forward in his determination to reach
Brome. To Brome's right, the henchmoles pulled back and
forth, trying to get round one of their own number who
had fallen bloodily from an accurate blow to his snout.
The talons cut and thrust so fast that had the sturdiest
thistle clump suddenly sprouted up between the two
camps, it would have been torn to shreds in seconds.

"Stand firm!" roared Brome to his forces, but he feared
in his heart that the cry was vain. "Hold fast!" he shouted,
pressing suddenly forward in an effort to show his moles
that they could make headway if only they would try. . . .

As he did so, the henchmoles wavered very slightly, so
subtly that only Brome himself noticed it—but it was
enough for him to shout and lunge forward again, the
pasture moles encouraged by his bravery.

And then the henchmoles *were* wavering and looking
uncertainly behind themselves as there came confusion

in the tunnel from the north. Screams and shouts, different noises, the roar of new moles arriving and a wavering, even by Rune, who turned to see what the commotion was and then found himself pressed back by a retreat of his own forces from the chamber as, with roars and shouts, a gang of marshenders burst into the chamber.

At their head was Mekkins, swearing and cursing at his own forces, and everymole else's, flailing his talons before him like the whipping branches of a blackthorn in a thunderstorm.

"Kill the buggers," he was shouting. "Give 'em every bloody thing they've asked for!" He lunged forward and Brome, hardly daring to believe his eyes, saw that among the forces behind Mekkins—as motley and vicious a band of moles as he'd ever seen—were males and females, big and small, all wiry and quick and fighting in a raggle-taggle way but with resolution that made the rest of them look half asleep.

Then, as suddenly as they had arrived, the henchmoles were in retreat as the harsh cold voice of Rune rose above their heads and he shouted "Fall back in order!" and "Take it slowly!" until, fighting every inch of the way, back the henchmoles went to run back toward the direction of the wood, leaving several of their dead and wounded blocking the tunnel up which they ran.

For a moment there was silence in the chamber as the remaining pasture moles and marshenders looked at each other in disbelief. Then the noise of relief and cheers as Brome and Mekkins were congratulating each other and there was excited chattering and laughter, drowning the groans of the dying; and the sight of very tired moles, who had stared at death, falling into a fatigue deeper than many of them had ever known as they realized that it was over.

But was it? After the victory cheers had died down and the wounded had been cared for and most moles fell asleep, Mekkins remained uneasy, as he had been from the moment Rune had suddenly withdrawn his forces from the chamber. You never could trust that Rune. Nothing he ever did was as simple as it seemed. But in the first flush of victory such doubts were submerged, and only hours later did the doubts come back. He *was* uneasy. Something was wrong. He didn't know what.

"Are you thinking they'll come back here?" asked

Brome, who had carefully placed some guardmoles higher
up the tunnels toward the wood to watch for just such a
possibility.

"I don't know," said Mekkins, thinking and thinking.
Unless . . . unless! A shiver of horror ran through him.
He looked quickly around to see which of his moles were
about and then he was urgently gathering them together,
his seriousness putting a pall on the cheer in the tunnels.

It was obvious. You should *never* take Rune at face
value. Mekkins was right—never trust Rune. He had not
retreated to defeat, but cleverly seized the opportunity
presented to him by the appearance of so many marshenders on the pastures to redeploy his forces, tired though
they were, out of the pastures and down to the now defenseless Marsh End. For there, as he must have guessed,
only the spring youngsters remained with a few of the
older females—offering him the perfect opportunity to
wipe out the next generation of marshenders, and make
their annihilation from the system so much easier. . . . As
for disease, well! they wouldn't all be here if that story
was true. Never trust that Mekkins!

Then Mekkins was running, with three of his strongest
moles at his side, up on the surface and ignoring the owls
. . . running across the pastures, down the slopes toward
the Marsh End, with the other moles following behind.
Running through the night with a terrible fear at his paws
to spur him on, an icy coldness in his heart to keep him
company. It was so obvious!

Down, down through the night, the warm air no comfort to their fur, down toward the Marsh End that lay
below them still and strangely silent. Running on and
down to the edge of the wood itself, and there stopping
and listening for sounds, hoping that somewhere they
would see a youngster who should be aburrow, a female
who couldn't sleep, some kind of Marsh End life. But
there was nothing.

Then, creeping skillfully by secret Marsh End routes
toward the tunnels themselves, and his terrible fear confirmed—for the sound of the deep bully voices of henchmoles could be heard in the tunnels where Marsh End
youngsters had so recently run and played and females
gossiped.

No good four of them attacking—best find out the
worst. Creeping again by secret ways, looking for what
they feared to find—the massacre of their youngsters.

Henchmoles here and there but no bodies yet . . . and then to the central place, in and out of the shadows, fugitives in their own tunnels, seeking the sight that would make them fugitives for life. Were they all dead, all killed?

It was only after peering down into many tunnels that Mekkins and his three friends began to realize that there were *no* Marsh End youngsters or females here at all, dead or alive. Not a single one.

"They've all gone!" said Mekkins. "They've gone!" And it was confirmed by a conversation they overheard between two henchmoles: "Bloody waste of time, this jaunt were. That Mekkins must have taken the whole pack of them onto the pastures, youngsters and all! Cunning little bugger, isn't he?"

But "that" Mekkins had done nothing of the kind. Mekkins crouched in the shadows as a sense of wonder and disbelief settled over him. They could not *all* have gone!

"But they have!" said one of the three with him. They checked again on the surface, down to the marsh edge, creeping silently along for fear of disturbing the henchmoles, peering into tunnel after tunnel and burrows when they could. But not a sign of life could they find. Just a few grumbling henchmoles in deserted tunnels of Marsh End.

They stopped still again up on the surface, which was bright with the cold light of a nearly full moon. Out from the marshes came the call of curlew and snipe, calls which every one of the four had heard a thousand times and which they barely noticed. Leaves of oak and ash rustled gently above them, catching the moonshine. Mekkins looked about him in wonder and then, very slowly, his face and snout rose to point up toward the moon.

"It's nearly full strength," he murmured to himself. "Nearly full. You know what tomorrow will be?" There was silence, so he answered his own question: "It'll be Midsummer Night, that's what day it is." He turned away from the marsh to face southward, up toward the distant hill now sunk in wooded darkness, where the Stone stood waiting.

"You know where youngsters go for Midsummer Night, don't you? I think I know where ours have gone. They've not gone, they've bloody well escaped!" Then he laughed gently with wonder and relief and added "And I've got a damn good idea who's leading 'em there!"

REBECCA had sensed something wrong in Duncton Wood
two hours after Mekkins had left in the early evening with
a band of Marsh End males and the stronger females to
enter the pastures to try to help Brome. They had gone off
amid excited chatter and cheering, eager to be a party to
a possible defeat of Rune.

But Rebecca had stayed behind and only later did she
begin to know why. Something *was* wrong. She had the
same impending fear she had felt on that night when
Rune and Mandrake had come and killed her litter. She
went up onto the surface, where the light of the rising
moon against a still sky was just beginning to filter among
the trees and fall weakly on the wood's floor, and snouted
up in the direction of Barrow Vale. Dark shadows, talons,
the shifting unease of danger was what she sensed. She
went down into the tunnels where burrow after burrow
was filled with the gentle sound of youngsters, some still
suckling, others rolling and fighting each other with the
strength and independence they had found by the third
week of June.

Mothers relaxed with their young, a few older, litterless females gossiped among themselves, chattering about
the excitement of seeing Mekkins off "to give that Rune a
taste of his own violence."

It was quiet and peaceful with just a hint of laughter
in the air. Rebecca paced about uneasily, the few marshenders who met her smiling, for they knew from Mekkins
who she was and that she was a healer like Rose had
been.

"Tell us a story, Rebecca!" a giggling youngster asked
her, pushed forward by his less bold siblings. She touched
him, shook her head and passed on, her tail twitching
with tension. Something was wrong. Then up onto the surface again and the growing feeling that there was a terrible danger coming through the night, down here where
only youngsters played and females were unprotected.

Birdcalls drifted in from the marshes, as they had on
the night Bracken had gone; a tree occasionally stirred
and whispered in a breeze that ran above the wood but
not on its still floor.

Fear began to come into her, her eyes widened in the night, her snout pointed and pointed to the dark toward Barrow Vale. She felt that she was the only thing protecting the Marsh End . . . from what? The moon rose slowly, stronger, full, the sky finally turning black, and somewhere a small branch fell rolling through the fresh-leaved branches of a tree, tumbling round and down leisurely until it hit the wood floor and all was silent again.

There was danger, and it was coming. And she knew suddenly, and with a ruthless certainty, that she must take them away to somewhere safe where no hurt could befall them. These youngsters were in her protection, just as once her own litter had been. *This* time there would be no mistakes.

So powerful was her sense of danger and so determined her resolution, there was no argument. The females with litters heard her in silence, her instinct for protection of the young soon becoming theirs.

Urgent whispers, silent runnings through tunnels, low voices, scurrying, sleepy youngsters suddenly awake and standing still waiting for instructions, last-minute checkings of more distant tunnels and then off together through the tunnels to the east, where no mole likes to go. Where that Curlew had lived. Youngsters running and scrabbling to keep up, calm fear of mothers knowing they must not panic, away and away through the night tunnels, to where the soil is damper and the smell is strange.

Rebecca leading them, away from a danger she had not yet seen but which *was* coming, toward a place to rest on the east side of the Marsh End and then on, the massed sound of escaping paws pattering in the silent night.

On and on she led them, letting none lag behind, the youngsters holding back their tears and tiredness before the urgent seriousness of adult moles.

Even at Curlew's place there was no safety in the air. The wood was too still in the light of a nearly full moon. Where to take them? Where to lead? Again and again her snout led her round and up toward the distant slopes where once, on Longest Night, she had gone with Mekkins. Beyond, the Stone waited. It always waited. A full moon, and nearly Midsummer, when the Stone blessed the young. One day to get there, sneaking through the wood. She could try along the east side, up on the surface, pray to the Stone and take them there. The Stone would protect them on Midsummer Night. On to the Stone.

Mekkins and the moles who had followed him finally got back to Brome in the pasture system at dawn, fatigued beyond sleep.

"They've gone," Mekkins said blankly to Brome. "Rebecca must have taken the Marsh End youngsters over to the east side so that Rune and the henchmoles couldn't get them. She'll probably try to reach the Stone. We'll have to help . . ." But his body could hardly hold itself straight he was so tired, and his eyes could not focus.

"Try to sleep," urged Brome, "and when we have all rested we will work out what to do. We will help you as you helped us. If need be our moles will die for your youngsters."

Mekkins awoke restless and worried. It was late morning and the tunnels of the pastures were light with warm air and the soft smell of summer wafting down from the surface. Then a curious, distant rumbling slowly filled the tunnels as he woke up, quite unlike any sound he had ever heard, and it brought him wide awake and out into the communal before he could blink twice more. A passing pasture mole must have seen his concern, for he said the single word *cows* as he went by. The rumbling stopped and started, passing overhead like a summer day's cloud that hides the sun for a while in its passing. "Cows!" muttered Mekkins in a grumbling voice, finding a tunnel to the surface, and going to see them close to. He smelled them before he got there, heavy and sweet, and then watched their black and white flanks swaying and stalling above his gaze against a blue sky, the tearing sound of the grass they grazed filling the tunnels and mixing with the slow sound of their chewing and breathing and chomping and thumping of their hooves. All harmless and sad. Bloody cows!

The wood was too distant for Mekkins to see, but the sun was high enough to have caught its western edge billowing green above the pasture, dark at its base where the trunks and shadows were and then bright-lit greens of great branches of leaves, thousands on millions; and a shimmer of the lightest blue haze covering them all as soft flaps and sounds of lazing birds, mainly wood pigeon and magpie, broke out through the haze and drifted over the pasture toward him. A couple of young thistle plants, spikes still soft with youth, cast a shadow on the entrance where he crouched.

He would lead them to the Stone, for it was Midsummer, and tonight, surely, that was where they should be. They would wait for the safety of dusk and then start the trek toward the high wood, into the rustling shade of the beeches as the day drew in, and then over to the Stone. He was restless and worried, but never had he had so much faith in the Stone.

Brome joined him, snouted out into the air, and said "It's the kind of day pasture moles love, when the young can play and us adults can find a bit of food early and then laze around doing nothing!"

"We ain't no different," said Mekkins. "Pasture, wood . . . moles don't change. Not really." He told Brome his plan and Brome nodded: he knew it would be hard to persuade his own forces to follow Mekkins so soon into Duncton Wood, but if he had to kick them all the way there he would see they went. And anyway, wasn't this what they needed—access to the Stone? They would see when they got there, just as he had. There was nothing worthwhile in the world that a mole didn't have to fight for.

As the warm day slid imperceptibly into the evening of Midsummer Night, Rebecca moved silently among the sleeping mothers and youngsters where they lay hiding and resting in an old tunnel she had found for them.

The mothers dozed rather than slept, looking anxiously over the young who snuggled against them to see that they were safe. Some of the youngsters lay separately, paws out and snouts stretched, like the young adults they almost were. As Rebecca passed them by, she was aware that they looked at her with mute concern, just to see if she was really confident that where she was leading them was all right and that she knew they would be safe. She could sense that panic was not far below their seeming calm, and knew that if it broke out they would all be lost. So she went by calmly, deliberately slowly, saying a word here, pushing a youngster out of the main tunnel there, every second seeming an hour to her.

She was almost reluctant to leave, for once they got to

the Stone, what then? It was like leading them to the edge of a void with the enemy behind and wondering how, exactly, they were going to fly to safety when they got there. She had no wings for them.

Henchmoles *were* about. Earlier she had met one, scurrying busily down toward Barrow Vale, and with the rest of them freezing into the wood's floor, he had questioned her briefly and she lied that she was from the eastside. "Well, get on back there now, you know the rules. If I weren't in a hurry you'd feel the strength of my paw!" Big and mindless his voice was, and the youngsters from the Marsh End shivered when they heard it, their mothers' eyes silent on them, imploring them to keep quite still.

As dusk began to fall, Rebecca led them off on the trek again, cutting straight up the slopes to the Ancient System. There, the massive gray trunks of the beech trees soared above as the last light of the sun died in the highest leaves against the sky, turning in seconds from pinks and greens to the rustling warm gray that would soon be a thousand tiny black silhouettes. Nearer the wood's floor great beech branches looped down from the main trunks and hung still and low, the leaves getting lighter green as darkness fell, for they were set against darkening shadows rather than a lighter evening sky as the leaves high above were.

Occasionally a youngster would stop, from tiredness or plain awe, and look up and around into the massed depths of the trees, like nothing ever seen in the danker closed-in Marsh End. The bleak hooting of a tawny owl cut suddenly through the night from somewhere on the slopes below them, and as they froze to a halt, a distant echoing answer came back from somewhere higher up the hill toward the Stone.

"Ssh!" hushed Rebecca softly; "hussh," for she was used to the sound and in a way it gave her confidence. It was the sound of her wood and it was a long time since she had heard it. "They're no more dangerous to us here than those eerie birdcalls *you* get from off the marshes," she said reassuringly, though it wasn't quite true. But if an owl came, well, that was that! But she could feel the Stone get nearer and trusted in its protection.

She ran ahead in the dark, having made them spread out among the roots of two adjacent beech trees, so that she could see if the Stone was clear of mole. When she got there, the light was just as it had been the night before, with a moon beginning to show and cast a thin, milky glare in the Stone clearing. At first she could not see the Stone, but then it was there, stretched up into the dark of the sky, the leaves of the beech tree that stood so near it rustling in the night above. It was the start of Midsummer Night, and the full cycle of seasons had run since the last Midsummer, when Hulver had died. Mandrake. Rune. Bracken. Curlew. The image of them rushed and mixed in her mind—so many moleyears had passed! Why, she was an adult; many of the mothers with young whom she had led up here were younger than she was.

There was an air of expectation in the clearing before her. It seemed to wait as she remembered Barrow Vale had sometimes waited for some old storyteller to set the place alive with the action of a tale of old.

She ran back and brought the marshenders forward to the edge of the clearing, hiding them in the shadows by its edge on the safer side, away from the slopes. They were glad to rest but hungry, and Rebecca let them go into the darkness to seek some food, litter by litter, telling them to be quiet and quick about it. In such a place, and with so much heavy expectation in the air, they did not need much telling. Most of them just stared from the shadows across the clearing at the Stone, and waited.

The night air cooled slowly as the full moon rose behind the trees, its light filtering down into the clearing and making it seem almost bright against the shadows of the wood around, which grew blacker and more impenetrable. None of them knew what they were waiting for and all Rebecca could do was to look up at the Stone in the center of the clearing, now rugged and gray in the moonlight, and pray that in its depths it would find protection for these young. She felt that it was their life that was in her charge, rather than their personalities, and, indeed, she was indifferent to them individually. She comforted them, or touched them, if need be, but it was their force for life that she cherished.

To their left, through the wood and by the pastures at the wood's edge, the wind stirred high in the branches, running lightly through the trees toward them. Then again, stronger. Then stillness. Then wind rippled away over the slopes, disappeared into the night across the wood to the vales and silent places of the eastside. A youngster rustled and was hushed. Another snuggled closer to its mother, half its face lost in her fur, eyes opening and closing toward sleep.

It was Midsummer Night, and bit by bit the wood was beginning to be alive with the rustles of movement. Wind? Moles? Predators? It was the night the Stone gave its traditional blessing to the young.

If there was one mole who knew what Midsummer meant better than any other, it was Bracken, who had been the fearful witness to the terrible death of Hulver in this very spot twelve moleyears before on the last Midsummer Night. Then he had spoken the words of the Midsummer blessing, moving himself toward adulthood as he said them. Now, Bracken was nearly back, rustling into the long grass and old year's leaves at the wood's edge as he re-entered his Duncton Wood.

"We'll soon be there, Boswell," he whispered, "and you'll see the Stone at last." Behind them Mullion and Stonecrop crept, wishing they could go straight down to their own tunnels on the pastures but agreeable to sticking with Bracken right to the very foot of the Stone. And anyway, they wanted to see it.

"We'll approach slowly and silently, because I don't know who may be up here tonight. If Mandrake has gone and Rune has taken charge, then he may be here. Rune doesn't like the Stone, especially at this time of old rituals. He'll want to see that no ritual is said."

They crept forward so silently that the first Rebecca knew of them was when she saw the shadow of a mole sliding out of the darkness on the far side of the clearing to stand, in bold silhouette, looking at the Stone. Then another mole, smaller, came out, and even in the moonlight Rebecca could tell that he was limping as his snout moved forward and up with each sequence of steps. Then two more moles, one very large, who looked around the clearing a little uneasily before stopping and settling his gaze as well on the Stone.

"Well, I've got to say it! You've got us here, Bracken!" said the big mole.

The world seemed suddenly an unreal place to Rebecca as the name Bracken came across the clearing to her. She looked in wonder at the four moles, trying to make out from the confusion of their silhouettes whether one of them was indeed her Bracken.

Then the small mole spoke, his calm, clear voice full of awe and reverence as he broke away from the other four and went right up to the Stone. "So I have finally reached the Duncton system," he said. "So many moleyears in the travel and all of them survived only by the Stone's grace."

Rebecca watched him fascinated, while her heart raced for Bracken, if Bracken it was. The small mole put a paw to the Stone, touched it, and then turned and faced the other three and said quietly "You know there is nothing else but the Stone. Finally, there is nothing else."

His head turned a little toward Rebecca, where she crouched in the shadow of the wood, and for the first time she saw his face. His fur was gray in the moonlight; seeing him for the first time, his eyes clear and soft, his face filled with the peace of the Stone, Rebecca felt she had never before seen anymole who made her sense the wonder of the Stone so much. The three in the clearing seemed to sense it too, for they all stayed quite still, though she could not tell if they were looking at the small mole or at the Stone that soared so high above him.

"Am I glad to be back!" said one of them, moving out clearly into the light. "I never would have known how much!" And Rebecca saw that it *was* Bracken, it was *her* Bracken, safe and well, and back in the wood they both loved. She had come unknowing to the Stone and he had come as well as, if she had thought about it, she should have known he would on Midsummer Night.

In the shadows, the youngsters' eyes peered at her, trying to see what she wanted to do, wondering if these moles were enemies from whom they should run. She turned to them and smiled, touching the one nearest her, and as they relaxed in her confidence, she turned back to the clearing and started out into the moonlight toward Bracken, her shadow running before her.

It seemed to Bracken, and to the others as well, that Rebecca appeared out of the night and before the Stone as if she was part of a mystery in which all things—the moonlight, the trees in silhouette against it, the wood, the Stone, her presence and the darkness behind her—were at one with each other. It was as if, for a moment, he was able to see beyond Rebecca to the powers of life, and death, that had brought her there at that moment and from which she was not separate but a part.

"Rebecca," he said, for there was no other word.

"My love," she said, saying what he felt.

"Rebecca?" he said again, advancing toward her, all sounds and sights of the night but her quite gone from him.

"Yes," she said softly. Then they nuzzled each other as soft as the softest fur, because he almost thought she was a dream and she knew he was her love, and their touching again was as precious as life. They nuzzled each other's neck and face, she smiling and he serious, she purring and he growling, his body strong and big to her at last, no more the fugitive mole she once had seen. My love, they said together, where have you been? Where have you been?

Their greeting took no longer than it takes to see the beauty in the moonlit Stone; then she was laughing in the night and saying "Boswell? From Uffington? From Uffington!" and "Stonecrop, dearest creature," and then to Mullion, shy before her, whom she cuffed gently because there was no need to be shy. And back to Bracken, who was looking at the Stone, touching the Stone as Boswell had done and understanding that there is no love but in the Stone. And thinking that there was nothing that could disturb a love strong and clear as theirs. Nothing!

Nothing? There was a crashing through the wood from the pasture's edge, a running and drumming of mole paws, and each one of them was suddenly tense and separate, turning to face the noise, with great Stonecrop moving to their front. Moles were coming, but the nearer they got to the clearing, the more Stonecrop relaxed, as Medlar had made him understand he must. Boswell was the same, his eyes clear into the darkness of the rustling sound, while Bracken sighed and stepped forward to be beside Stonecrop. The three had learned their lessons well. Behind them Mullion stood more tensely, uncertain what to do, while Rebecca silently crossed the clearing to where the youngsters lay, staying in the light and unable to see them, but signaling with a smile for them to stay still and feel safe.

The advancing moles came quickly and, without even a pause, broke cover from the wood into the clearing, only then stopping to look at where Bracken and the others stood ranked by the Stone. There was silence on both sides as each took a moment to recognize each other.

It was Brome and Mekkins, come from the pastures with pasture and Marsh End moles, but it was one of the Marsh End females in the shadows behind Rebecca who broke the silence.

"And where the 'ell have you been, Mekkins my lad!" she said ironically, breaking cover herself.

Mekkins smiled but ignored her, turning instead to Brome and saying "There you are, Brome, me old mate. I said they'd be here, and they are. And where's Rebecca? Come on, she's not normally bashful!" Rebecca moved forward and laughed and everymole relaxed. And then Mekkins was surprise itself when he saw Bracken, and Brome was lost in delight when there were Stonecrop and Mullion before him.

There was relief and reunion, levity and laughter, but not for long. It was Mekkins, speaking in a whisper to Bracken, Stonecrop, Brome and Rebecca, who gave them the warning that, in his heart, Bracken had feared.

"There's a bloody army of henchmoles coming up here with you know which mole leading them. Brome put a couple of his moles over by the wood's edge at dusk, just to see if they could learn anything and they did. Them henchmoles are the worst blabbermouths you could wish to meet and they found out that, sure enough, Rune is planning to bring the whole lot of 'em up 'ere to see that there's no way anymole can celebrate Midsummer Night."

Mekkins looked round at them all and grinned. "Well, of course there ain't no way I'm going to leave 'ere and since by some miracle of the Stone's magic we seem to 'ave none other than Bracken 'imself come along 'specially for the occasion, the only mole in Duncton who knows the blessing, I suggest we sit tight, get rid of Rune when 'e comes, get on wiv the ritual blessing and show these Marsh End youngsters what tonight's all about."

They all turned to Bracken who, not for the first time, was surprised to find that they were looking to him for some kind of lead. It was as if, by virtue of his having lived near the Ancient System for so long, they regarded him as in some way the guardian of the Stone and all its secrets. It was a role he felt inadequate to play, since he did not think he knew enough about the Stone, and was very conscious that what little he did know came from

Hulver, who had known so much more. Boswell sensed his doubt, and to encourage him said "What do you think we should do, Bracken?"

Bracken looked up at the Stone for a moment and then said simply "We must say the blessing. Hulver said it twelve moleyears ago, with only Bindle to help him and myself—though I was too young to protect him, just as these youngsters are too young to protect us, though one day theirs will be the strength to decide and to do what must be done. May the Stone give them its help as it has helped each one of us."

He looked slowly at them all in turn, his eyes falling finally on Rebecca's and staying there longest. As he spoke, his voice had gradually grown more powerful and now, as he continued, its strength and force brought all the moles gathering around him in silence.

"In another hour or so, when the moon is at its peak, it will be the moment to say the blessing before our great Stone. Its power travels to all the other stones set up in the chosen systems by Ballagan, the first Holy Mole. This is not a night for fighting, but for peace and blessing. But the time in which we live is strange and troubled." He turned and pointed up at the Stone, whose crevices and facets seemed infinitely complex in the moonlight. "Look at our Great Stone," he said, feeling as he did so its power flowing into him, and his ideas, his very voice, taken over by it as they had been once before when he had spoken to Cairn about Rebecca, and found his words flowing from a source beyond himself.

"Look at the Duncton Stone! It should stand straight and tall like the trees around it. But see how it tilts over toward the west, where Uffington lies! The system of which it is so much a part is decayed, and it tilts for weakness at the knowledge, seeking the help of Uffington. I tell you all that the day will come when by our strength this Stone will stand aright again, proud of the system from whose strength it will soar to the sky and whose power we will not question or, like Rune, try to corrupt. It will stand as straight as the mighty Ballagan set it and when it does all moles shall know that our system has been healed.

"This is not a night for fighting and Midsummer is not the time for blood. But I tell you that until the time comes when the Stone is the true center of our system once more, then those who know that there is nothing without the Stone must fight for their belief. I, who have run so often in fear from the talons of death, will run no more, but stand and face what comes with talons of my own. Their strength comes from the power and the silence that lies within the Stone and which each of us may hear and feel.

"It is no sin to run, and if any want to go, then let them go in peace. But the hour has finally come when everymole, whether from Duncton Wood or the pastures, or Uffington itself, must stand and fight if their belief is in the Stone. Let each one of you look at it now and decide." Bracken pointed again at the Stone and everymole there, including the youngsters, looked at the Stone in the light of his words. Not a single mole moved until, one by one, they turned back to look again at Bracken. The night was stirring now with wind and around them in the wood were heavy movements in the undergrowth first on one side and then on another. The sound of henchmoles closing in. It was too late for anymole there to escape.

"Let the youngsters gather round the flanks of the Stone, which will protect them, and let the rest range themselves closely about the clearing, for soon Rune will be here. Let pasture mole mingle with Duncton mole and let us all fight as one."

Then around them, in the darkness beyond the clearing, there were creepings and peerings, whisperings and plottings, slinkings and dark talons massing for attack. Somewhere in the darkness Rune crouched, listening to the sounds about him, waiting for his forces to mass themselves completely around the Stone clearing. He was smiling. There *had* been a moment when they should have attacked him—when he was coming up the slopes and feared an ambush—but now the advantage was his. Why, the fools were gathered in the moonlight by the Stone where they could be seen clearly and smelled. The sniveling little Marsh End youngsters were gathered round the Stone with them, waiting to be comfortably killed by his henchmoles, who would take pleasure in catching up with moles who had escaped them down at the Marsh End. Henchmoles do not like being made to feel foolish.

Near Rune, Nightshade slipped her body among the contorted and twisted shadows of the smaller roots of a beech tree—shapes it fitted perfectly. Her talons wound

and wove with continuous movement as if she were caressing the night air into dangerous shapes as she snouted
out the Stone beyond the darkness. She was casting spells
for victory.

"When the moon is at its peak, Rune, I want to be free
with the Stone, yes . . . mm . . . to wipe the blood of
the young into its holes and crevices and make a curse on
all the marshenders unfortunate enough to survive. What
a pity if they all died. Yes . . . mm . . ."

Her voice was slimy, like a dying worm, but it clung to
the mind of any who heard it, suffocating any thought of
love or light or color that might already be there and
aborting any about to be born. Rune, however, wallowed
in its sound. Nightshade had waited a long time for this
night, as had the dark and treacherous generations whose
dark endeavors had produced her, and other moles like
her who had lived on the edge of the system until the
darkness of Rune sucked them inside it and to the very
heart of Barrow Vale. Yes . . . mm . . .

The first attack was swift, sudden and very deadly. Five
henchmoles broke cover into the clearing, ran straight
across to where a group of marshender males stood ready,
and with swift and fatal lunges killed four moles where
they crouched. Just like that. The blood had barely
started to flow before they were gone again, and as the
natural movement of the defenders of the Stone swayed
toward the shadows into which they had disappeared, another attack was launched from a different direction, this
time to where Stonecrop and Bracken stood, side by side.
Perhaps sensing how dangerous these two were, the
attackers sidestepped them and two more moles went
down before Bracken, with a relaxed lunge, felled one
where it stood and so injured another that it took only a
quick kick from Stonecrop to finish him off.

Rebecca stood to one side of them, facing the darkness,
while around the base of the Stone, among the beech
roots gathered there, the youngsters huddled, their mothers forming a final protective rank around them.

The battle was sporadic at first as one quick thrust of
attack followed another—a technique already rehearsed
by Rune. But it was effective, for the moles of the Stone
lost more with each attack than they were able to kill
and, the light of the full moon being on them and the at-

tackers coming out of darkness, the advantage was with Rune.

It was to Rune's credit as a leader that this series of attacks lasted as long as it did before finally breaking down into a concerted onslaught onto the besieged moles of the Stone at two different points. On one side, Stonecrop and Bracken, Rebecca and Brome headed the defense; on the other Mekkins and Mullion stood the main ground. All fought differently—Stonecrop with a massive slow soberness that was utterly ruthless—taking blows that would be fatal to other moles as if they were nothing and then launching his own devastating lunges; Bracken was quicker and more subtle, parrying here, cutting there, and killing whenever he could; Mekkins, as usual, swore aloud with every blow, roaring "Take that, you bastard" and "Oh, no you don't, brother" with every lunge, and "Sod it" when he missed. Brome fought more like Stonecrop but a little less effectively, for he lacked the total concentration Stonecrop had learned; Rebecca was fast, vicious and magnificent, shouting and screaming with anger, snarling at the biggest moles, cutting and thrusting where she could, fearing none. While somewhere just behind Brome and Bracken, Boswell stood firm as well, striking when he could but most useful for the cries of warning he calmly gave to each of the stronger fighters in front of him who were so preoccupied with their individual struggles that they often did not see a threat from another angle.

But one by one they suffered cuts and injuries that slowed them, as around them their colleagues began to fall. Some dead, some too injured to fight, a few too tired to raise their paws and defend themselves. Oxlip, the female who had escaped to the Marsh End, fell and died by Mekkins' side. Mullion, too, was grimly wounded and fell back behind his own lines, life leaving him.

The moon shone on, its light cold on the terrible scene of carnage it lit so clearly. It reached a peak and then began its waning descent, and still the battle went on with no word of Midsummer blessing said.

The moles around the Stone began to retreat back toward it, leaving their dead and wounded before them as the henchmoles, black and tough as ever, climbed over the stricken bodies and pressed forward.

Then Rune appeared out of the night, the twisted

shape of Nightshade at his side waiting by the clearing
edge with glee in her eyes, while he pressed forward suddenly into the bloodiest of the melée, leading his henchmoles on for the last part of the fight. There always
seemed to be more henchmoles coming, and more, and
always fewer and fewer moles able to stand and face
their onslaught. They slowly retreated, back toward the
Stone, and as the retreat set in, Rebecca instinctively went
behind the front line to rally the mothers of the youngsters behind her so that, if necessary, they could put up
a last defense.

The youngsters, seeing now the great floodtide of
henchmoles bearing down on them, stopped only by
Bracken, Stonecrop, Brome, Mekkins and a few others
who stood their ground, began to whimper, their sound
a pathetic addition to the screams of triumph and death
that rose and fell in the clearing.

Then Brome staggered and fell, lost under a torrent
of terrible lunges, and with his death the resolution of the
other pasture moles began to weaken and they all retreated even farther back. Seeing his advantage, Rune
pressed even harder on them, his black talons cutting and
stabbing before him, shiny with blood in the moonlight.
Behind him, beyond the mass of murderous henchmoles
that backed him up, Bracken could see for a moment the
sinister shape of Nightshade, whom he did not recognize,
slinking gleefully about the clearing's edge as if waiting to
take her pickings of the dead.

Rebecca rose up magnificently behind him, eyes flashing with anger and determination, the youngsters huddled
behind her, the Stone soaring up above them, almost
hanging over them all as it tilted over toward the west.

"Trust in the Stone!" she shouted, her voice carrying to
them all. "Trust in Bracken and the Stone!" Her words
carried even to Rune, who until then had not seen her
clearly, and he faltered, as if uncertain whether she was
really living or come back from the dead. Then he heard
that it *was* her and she was shouting the name of Bracken.
His eyes narrowed, he wondered whether he was fighting
an army of ghost moles, for he remembered Bracken now;
then, as ever, coolness returned and he fought on even
more strongly, eager to get to the mole who must be
Bracken—the tough one who stood fighting between the

great mole from the pastures and Mekkins. That was him. He was the one to kill, before the massacre.

His talons razed through the face fur of Bracken, and other henchmoles, sensing his intent, pressed toward Bracken as well, each trying to get their talons in his fur or snout.

The noise was terrible. Screams. Roaring. But then another roaring. The sound came through like sudden winds in trees, a roaring louder than any they had yet heard. A monstrous roaring, accompanied by blunderings and crashings in the wood beyond the clearing, a sound made by no henchmole that had ever lived.

Rune and his moles ignored it, fighting on to kill Bracken and the others. But facing the darkness of the wood as they were, Bracken and Stonecrop and Mekkins, blood flowing freely from their tired limbs, could not but see the sudden huge shadow that appeared at the wood's edge, ten times bigger it seemed than the slinking form of Nightshade over which it loomed.

It surged forward, caught the moonlight and became clear, a sight more fearful than a thousand henchmoles poised to kill.

It was Mandrake—and he had not looked more terrifying since that spring day, so many moleyears before, when he had appeared at the wood's edge and slaughtered his way into Duncton.

"It's Mandrake!" cried Bracken, his voice suddenly clear and strong in the night.

Rune and his moles stepped back for a moment, turning back to see what it was. Mandrake stood facing them all, his eyes black and impenetrable as the most savage night, fur hanging in great folds about his massive body, his snout as ever like a talon before him.

Nightshade turned round to look as well, but with one single blow of his right paw he swept her bloodily away, her body lifeless before it touched the ground. Mandrake was back.

If days of destiny lead to a final hour and that hour reaches a last minute in whose seconds decisions that form life are made, this was it. Rune tried to grab it.

"Here is the Stone Mole," he shouted, pointing his talons at Bracken. "He is the Stone Mole. Help us kill him, Mandrake." He turned back to complete the onslaught on Bracken, a cunning and brave maneuver by Rune.

Mandrake said no word and only a vibrating growl came from him as he looked at them all. His gaze settled not on Bracken but on Rebecca behind him, and behind her to the youngsters gathered, terrified, around her.

"Rebecca!" he roared suddenly, moving forward like a black storm cloud across a windy, moonlit sky. "Rebecca!" And his huge paws began to flay right and left, taking with each blow one or two or three henchmoles out of his path. Rune's forces fell around him at Mandrake's advance, and at last Rune himself, seeing his support going and his ploy failing, slunk to one side as Mandrake continued his advance, not on Bracken, not on Mekkins, not on Stonecrop, but toward Rebecca beyond them. "Rebecca!" he cried. "Rebecca!"

There came from him a smell so rank, so disgusting in its anger and wretched rage, that Mekkins and Bracken fell back before it, closing in front of Rebecca and raising their talons to protect her. But its effect on Stonecrop was just the opposite. He had smelled that odor before—in a temporary burrow where Rebecca and his brother, Cairn, had mated. *This* was the odor on which he had sworn to take revenge. He moved his own great body forward, his fur lighter and his muscles tauter than Mandrake's, and with one massive lunge stopped Mandrake in his tracks.

It was the first time since Mandrake had left the frozen slopes of Siabod so many long and cruel moleyears before that anymole had stood so solid in his path. He reared up, looking at Stonecrop as if he was in some way surprised to see him, as if he expected no mole at all to be there. As if the very nature of the world itself had suddenly changed.

Every lesson Stonecrop had learned from Medlar now came into play. Sensing Mandrake's surprise, Stonecrop acted immediately, lunging forward with a talon cut that scored another wound on Mandrake's lined and pitted face.

Then Mandrake did a strange thing. Instead of immediately counterattacking, he seemed to try to peer round Stonecrop as if baffled by an obstruction on a path that had once been clear; trying to get a better look at Rebecca and calling, crying "Rebecca! Rebecca!" And still he did not try to strike Stonecrop back.

Behind Stonecrop, Bracken turned to Rebecca, who was trying to come forward toward Mandrake as she herself called out from some terrible distance "Oh Mandrake, Mandrake!"

Stonecrop hesitated, not knowing whether to yield to his desire to try and kill Cairn's murderer or to listen to some half-heard instinct that told him . . . told him something he could not quite catch . . . something desolate in Rebecca's voice.

There was movement behind him as Bracken and Mekkins forcibly stopped Rebecca running forward and Bracken shouted grimly "Kill him, Stonecrop. Kill him!" Then, as Rebecca let forth a terrible cry of "No . . . no . . ." that seemed to fill the clearing, and beyond it the beech trees and beyond them the whole of Duncton Wood with despair, Stonecrop lunged forward against Mandrake again.

"He will kill *you*," shouted Bracken, as Rebecca's talons tore at him and Mekkins in her desperation to go to her father. "He wants to save me," she cried, as once more Mandrake roared out "Rebecca, I'm here, Rebecca," and she heard him cry, his voice calling from out of a blizzard of icy winds and sleet that ravaged the high slopes of Siabod, where once, so long ago and so terribly, he had been born. She heard his cries of "Rebecca, Rebecca" as the cries of a pup which feels itself lost forever in a storm, she heard them as the mewings and bleatings of a litter she could not save. Her talons tore uselessly, desperately, into the face and fur and flanks of Bracken as beyond him she saw Stonecrop bear down at last on Mandrake, beginning, lunge by terrible lunge, to kill him. There were growlings and roars, there was blood on angry talons, but most of all, and worst, there was the huge impersonal back of Stonecrop, his massive shoulders working methodically forward as lunge after cut after talon thrust he destroyed Mandrake before her eyes. Mandrake's cries of "Rebecca!" continued between grunts of horrid pain and the last tired lunges of a fighter who has no more will to fight; the last calls of pup in a blizzard whose cold has taken him for its own. And then they grew weaker, despairing, and finally fell silent until, at last, Stonecrop seemed to be hitting not straight ahead of

him but down, near the ground, where Mandrake had
fallen into his own blood, his paws feeble and his breath
weakening, his eyes closing, and finally, his life force
gone. Then Stonecrop was over him, shoulders weak from
the kill, Mandrake's blood on his paws and fur, the living
looking at the dead.

He turned back toward the Stone where Rebecca now
crouched, Mekkins and Bracken still holding her, and
each of them saw that his face was contorted by a horror
of something his eyes had seen and his talons felt. Then
he said, almost by way of explanation and with unnatural calm: "He killed Cairn. He killed your litter. He . . ."

"He loved me," shouted Rebecca. "He was calling for
me. And I couldn't . . . You wouldn't . . . let me . . ."
Then her sobs were wild and desperate, a weeping for
something that can never be brought back, while to
Bracken it seemed that they were not just for Mandrake,
but for all the moles who lay dead and dying about the
Stone clearing—Brome, Mullion, Oxlip, Burrhead, his
own father now dead before him, pasture moles, Duncton
moles, males and females, and Rebecca's tears seemed
for them all. Worst of all, they were for him as well.

He tried to comfort her but she pulled away, looking
at him from a cold and far-off place he knew he could
never reach. His hold on her fell limp and she crossed
over to where Mandrake lay, paused for a moment as
she touched his head gently, looked back at Bracken and
Stonecrop with a fierce and cold pity, and then went out
of the clearing and into the dark.

No stabbing talon could ever have thrust itself with
such pain into Bracken's heart as that terrible look from
Rebecca before she turned her back on him and was gone.
He felt himself cut off from life itself. He ran from the
Stone toward the clearing edge calling "Rebecca, Rebecca," but the name did not seem to carry, and even
the light in the clearing grew weaker as the moon began
its fall behind the trees.

Then Boswell's voice came to him gently from the
Stone. "Say the blessing, Bracken, say the Midsummer
blessing for the young."

Bracken turned to look back at the Stone, which stood
darker now, the bodies of the dead moles about it no
more than rounded shadows in the weakening light. He
could see the snouts of the youngsters they had saved

moving and bobbing by the Stone, with the bigger forms of their mothers about them. A stronger shaft of light seemed to fall on Boswell, who stood to one side of the Stone, his eyes compassionately on Bracken, to whom it seemed that Boswell was part of the Stone, a living part.

He was weak and utterly desolate and his breathing came quicker and more shallow as if he was going to weep. He had lost his Rebecca. He knew it as certainly as he knew it was night.

"Say the blessing, Bracken," whispered Boswell—or did he shout it?—"Rune has gone, the Stone has given its protection."

The Stone has given its protection to everymole but me, Bracken thought bitterly. And Rebecca.

He came forward, moving slightly to the right to stand to the west of the Stone, in the direction in which it tilted. He looked up at its highest point, the only part that still caught the moonlight clearly, and began to speak words he had learned so reluctantly, so long ago. First the prefatory chants that he did not even know he knew, and then finally, the last words of the blessing:

> *We bathe their paws in showers of dew*
> *We free their fur with wind from the West*
> *We bring them . . . choice . . . soil*
> *Sunlight in . . . life . . .*

As his voice faltered and caught sobbing in his throat, Boswell's voice joined him, its strength giving him strength and its faith giving him a kind of desolate hope. The voice of Boswell spoke from some ancient past that stretched back to a time before even the tunnels around them were made, and which went forward to a future that trembled now in his heart:

> *We ask they be blessed*
> *With a sevenfold blessing . . .*
> > *The grace of form*
> > *The grace of goodness*
> > *The grace of suffering*
> > *The grace of wisdom*
> > *The grace of true words*
> > *The grace of trust*
> > *The grace of whole-souled loveliness.*

If Bracken's voice faltered as he spoke the words none there noticed it, for Boswell's voice mingled powerfully with it as, without knowing what he was doing, Bracken moved among the youngsters, touching them as his Rebecca might have done.

> *We bathe their paws in showers of light*
> *We free their souls with talons of love*
> *We ask that they hear the silent Stone.*

So Boswell knows the words as well, thought Bracken, vaguely. Then who is Boswell? he asked himself.

"The wood is safe," Bracken found himself saying to the Marsh End mothers, "so take your youngsters back to the Marsh End." Then, one by one, the moles left the Stone—the pasture moles cutting off westward through the wood, Stonecrop leaving with them, as the marshenders began their long trek home. There were henchmoles there, but Bracken saw they were no longer threatening, just ordinary moles who had lost their way. They began to cluster silently around Bracken, Mekkins and Boswell, looking to them for guidance, and Bracken noticed that beyond them other Duncton moles came from out of the shadows—eastsiders, females from the westside, moles from the slopes all scraggy with age. Even some of the marshenders stayed behind with Bracken. Then they began to whisper in a curious, almost primitive, chanting way, "Barrow Vale, Barrow Vale, Barrow Vale . . ." and Bracken knew he must lead them there. He turned his back on the Stone to take up the power Mandrake had held, and then Rune, and that had destroyed both of them.

Among the moles who followed Bracken down, gleefully chanting "Barrow Vale" and then "Bracken, Bracken," there was only one who stayed silent and yet who truly loved him. And that was Boswell, who followed limping behind, trying to keep up with them so that he could always keep Bracken in his sight.

DUNCTON Wood quickly settled down to summer and
Bracken's rule. There was some preliminary skirmishing
with the remnants of the henchmoles, some of whom
claimed that since Rune had not been killed and was
nowhere to be found, there was no reason to think that
he wasn't coming back. But Bracken quickly put a stop to
this with a couple of swift and deadly fights against the
toughest of the remaining henchmoles, which killed one
and injured the other.

By the first week of July all was quiet and Bracken
was in total command and the henchmoles were but a
memory fading into the shadows from whence they had
come, as Bracken's days became taken up with the settle-
ment of the usual disputes and wrangles that beset any
system in the idle months of summer, when the only real
interest lies in what territory the youngsters are winning
for themselves.

The summer grew increasingly hot. Not the occasional
heat of a couple of days that gives way rapidly to great
lumbering cumulus clouds that sail across the face of the
sun and remind moles to enjoy the sun while they may
but the heat that starts slowly and then simply stays,
beating down day after day and making green leaves begin to look wan and desperate in its hazy stillness. The
kind of heat that produces an endless palling stillness
through which the sun seems almost to filter itself of good
cheer, becoming instead faceless and impersonal. Rain,
when it fell, was almost dry before it hit the ground, and
by the third week of July it seemed to have been all used
up.

Against this background, Bracken's rule settled into rou-
tine. He gave advice and help when it was sought and
visited the pastures, where Stonecrop had assumed control, agreeing that the Stone should be made accessible to
any pasture mole who wanted to visit it. Soon there was a
feeling of lightness and relief in both systems and Bracken
began to feel, with some justice, that in most respects
Duncton Wood was a better place than it had been for
many many moleyears.

Yet all was *not* well. As the molemonths passed into August, he began to change in ways that were imperceptible to himself. For one thing, it proved impossible to remain as accessible and friendly as he had initially been to everymole who came to see him.

Most moles seemed to want to set him apart, eager to respect him, and to listen with irritating seriousness to what he said. Others, even the biggest westsiders, seemed afraid of him and his initial attempts to put them at their ease gave way eventually to an unconscious contempt for them and a subtly growing idea that, yes, indeed, he must be a special mole and perhaps everything he said *was* interesting.

When he wanted things done, he began to find it easier to be tough and terse in issuing instructions than careful and polite. It was much less fuss, and anyway, as he grumbled to Boswell in an irritated rationalization of his growing autocracy, the moles of Duncton liked to be led and have their minds made up for them.

It was easier, too, to have other moles do certain things for him—to listen to complaints, to advise on which issue Bracken would, or would not, prefer to make his own judgment about personally—and so a corpus of moles, many of them from Barrow Vale and a few from the eastside, began to grow up who acted as a buffer between Bracken and everymole else.

There was nothing unusual or sinister about such a development—most systems have something like it at one time or another—but in Bracken it combined, unfortunately, with his own growing unspoken restlessness, whose causes he did not seek to know, since he was not even aware of the changes overtaking him.

He became irritable and sharp; some of his judgments were hasty and ill-advised. He stepped in on one territorial dispute, for example, up near the slopes between youngsters who should have been left to settle it themselves, and so caused resentment all round. Whole days would pass when he refused to talk to anymole, preferring to stay in his tunnels near Barrow Vale or wander over to the more deserted areas of the slopes.

The only mole who retained constant contact with him was Boswell, though even to Boswell Bracken was increasingly offhand and indifferent.

In Barrow Vale they began to call Bracken standoffish

and superior, though his achievements in getting rid of
Rune, in being the one to order the killing of Mandrake,
and his now-legendary crossing of the marsh were sufficient for no mole to doubt that he was their leader.

But soon there were other things to gossip about, like
the continuing hot weather which, it was said (though no
mole was sure by whom), was beginning to affect the
worm supply on the pastures and some of the marshenders were saying that the marshes were smelling terrible and hadn't been so bad in living memory, while
everymole agreed that the heat and dryness was enough
to make a mole thoroughly irritable, not to say fed up,
wasn't it?

But while other moles thought of other things, Boswell
concerned himself about what lay at the root of the
change in Bracken. He had been bleak witness to the
terrible shock that crossed Bracken's face when Rebecca
left them in the clearing on Midsummer Night, since
when, so far as he knew, the two had not met again.
Now he could not help but notice that whereas Bracken
had once talked often of Rebecca, especially on their
journey from Nuneham, he never mentioned her name
now, although sometimes, in the presence of one of the
brighter younger females or up on the surface when a
wind ran among the trees, he would see Bracken look
about him sadly, his normal mask of cool command dropping for a while, as if there were something nearby he
thought he had lost.

Boswell was too wise to raise this with Bracken directly,
but if, as it sometimes did, the subject of healing came
up or some particular work Rebecca had been doing
somewhere in the pastures or Duncton was mentioned,
he would try to draw Bracken onto the subject, believing
that talking might help. But it didn't. Bracken did not
seem to mind mention of her name, but he did not react
to it except to utter some general comment like "The
system is lucky to have a mole like Rebecca for its healer
—in fact, it's a miracle we've got a mole so good in
succession to Rose," but there was something too studiously careful about these comments to convince or satisfy
Boswell.

At the same time, Rebecca was rarely seen anywhere
near Barrow Vale, a fact made far more of by Boswell
and Mekkins, who discussed it together, than it was

worth, since in her own time Rose had rarely bothered
with Barrow Vale. When moles need healing the best
place to do it, she used to say, is in the privacy of their
burrows, not on public view in Barrow Vale.

Rebecca had stayed on the pastures in the tunnels she
created for herself after Rose's death, and little had
changed; Comfrey still lived nearby, still strange and
nervous, with a great love of herbs and plants and unwilling to let Rebecca go too far from him for too long:
partly, perhaps, from his own insecurity but also, though
Boswell was never to guess it, because in his own way
he protected Rebecca from despair. Sometimes he would
travel off in search of new herbs, but he had a knack of
making his path cross near where Rebecca was—and
seemed, too, to sense what herbs she needed, for often he
would appear suddenly in some remote corner of one of
the systems with the very herb she needed for some healing process. There was a great trust and peace between
the two, and by virtue of his attachment to her Comfrey
went unmolested wherever he wished in the systems,
which allowed him to develop in time as wide a knowledge of where the medicinal plants of the two systems
were as any mole had ever had.

Violet had now been completely absorbed into the
pasture system and lost all contact with Rebecca and, of
course, Bracken.

But as for Rebecca coming to see Bracken, it just
never happened, and it wasn't the kind of thing a mole
would want to raise with Rebecca. A healer does not
have problems as far as anymole else is concerned. And
even if she had, Rebecca gave no sign of it at all except
to Comfrey, who saw far more than even she ever suspected.

What was worse for Boswell was that he saw clearly
how Bracken's coldness about Rebecca affected the way
he thought about the Stone. Bracken no longer revered
the Stone but became inclined to make ironic or cynical
remarks about it—"It's all an illusion, which may please
some moles, but they'll soon grow out of it" or, on an
occasion when Boswell dared to suggest that it would be
a good idea to go to the Stone to pray for rain, Bracken
said, "If it sends rain, Boswell, it'll send a flood; that's
the way your Stone amuses itself when it answers
prayers."

As for visiting the Stone, or the Ancient System, which Boswell still desperately wanted to do in Bracken's company, there was no quicker way to make Bracken coldly angry than to suggest it. There was only one absolute rule with Bracken, and that was that no mole was to visit the tunnels of the Ancient System, in any circumstances. They could go to the Stone if they wanted, though it was probably a waste of their time.

Boswell was at first very frustrated by all this, not only because he loved Bracken as he had loved no mole, but also because he wanted to pursue the quest he had come to Duncton Wood to fulfill—to find the Seventh Stillstone and the Seventh Book, which he was convinced were there. He would talk to other moles he met about the system, seeking out the oldest ones with longest memories, trying to find clues in the stories they told that might guide him forward. He would even tell them about Uffington if they asked or he thought it might encourage them to revive memories of their own system. He might have been tempted to visit there himself but for the sense he had that it was Bracken, and Bracken alone, who would guide him there.

But as time went by a curious thing happened: Boswell began to lose the urgent desire he had first felt to find the Seventh Book. He began to sense that there are some things, great things, which a mole should not reach out his talons for. He must learn to sit still and trust that they will come to him. This discovery served only to increase his awe for Bracken—for was it not Bracken's very recalcitrance that made him see it? He began to wonder whether, in some strange way, the Stone was working through Bracken far more powerfully than anymole could ever have dreamed of, which made him seek ways of quietly making life as caring and loving for Bracken as he could. Nothing gave him more pleasure than the fact that, despite Bracken's ill temper and contradictions, he never once told Boswell to leave him, but always seemed pleased in his awkward way for him to be there.

So it was quite without seeking it that Boswell discovered his first dramatic clue to the existence of the Seventh Book. It arose when he decided for himself to go to Rebecca in the pastures and see if he could not work some kind of reconciliation between her and

Bracken. An idea which, had he known Rebecca better, he would never have been innocent enough to try.

He made his way into the pastures with Mekkins' help, the marshender leaving him safely at the entrance to Rebecca's tunnels. Mekkins was no fool and could guess why Boswell had come and though, being more worldly wise, he feared the attempt would fail, he felt it best to stay clear of the whole thing and let the strange scribemole try.

He himself loved Rebecca too much to want her to stay so far apart from Bracken, and anyway, he had grown to respect Boswell, who seemed to know a lot of things, even if he was a bit daft when it came to understanding females, especially ones like Rebecca.

Rebecca greeted Boswell with real warmth. They had not met since Midsummer Night, but her travels about the systems had brought her into contact with many moles who were wide-eyed with fascination about the strange mole from Uffington "who do ask the queerest questions that ever I have heard, and do tell the strangest quaintest tales if 'e's a mind to it."

Boswell's response to Rebecca was not at all what he had expected it would be. He had come full of good intent, calmly and gently to talk to her about Bracken. But the moment he saw her again and found himself in the clear warmth of her smile, any words that he had rehearsed quite left him. He gazed on her with genuine delight, his bright intelligent eyes traveling quickly around her burrow, now nearly as full of herbs and flowers as Rose's had once been. He sensed the great reverence she felt in the life which she had pledged herself to help, and he saw far more about her than Mekkins could ever have given him credit for: he saw a brave mole whose warmth and love were real, but whose spirit bore the marks of loss as Bracken's did, but who did not pretend to herself it was not so.

He saw immediately how vulnerable she was. But what he did not see, and perhaps would never understand, was how, in his company, her spirit was able to begin to soar again into a freedom it had once taken for granted. Indeed, the feeling of lightheartedness that arose in her as soon as he crouched down, looked about him curiously and then fixed his gaze directly on her, took her by surprise. She wanted to laugh for the pleasure of it. More than that, she wanted to dance! She wanted to sing and play. What she did do was to smile and feel more delightfully foolish than she had for many a long molemonth.

"Why have you come to Duncton Wood?" she asked eagerly, quite unaware that she was the first mole to ask him this simple question or that it raised a subject that made his mission of reconciliation suddenly irrelevant.

"Well," he began, not sure where to begin.

"You must have come here for some reason, Boswell! It's a long way to come just to say Hello! and go away again."

"I think the Stone called me here, or told me to come," he said simply. He knew instinctively that she would understand what he meant by this, and he was right, for Rebecca nodded and said: "Yes, of course. But why?"

"It has to do with what the scribemoles of Uffington call the Seventh Book. You see, Rebecca, there are seven holy books and . . ." and he began to tell her, reciting the mysterious text he had found describing the other six books, and explaining at some length why it was so important that the Seventh Book was found.

"The Book will be found when it needs to be found, I expect—and anyway, perhaps what will happen is that the Book will find you." He knew what she meant, and of course she was right. Hadn't he told himself that no mole can try to reach out for such a thing?

As Boswell talked, Rebecca had grown happier and happier, for she saw clearly what it was about Boswell that made her feel so free. Every other mole she saw sought her help one way or another, whereas Boswell, despite appearances, did not need any healing that she could give. She was free with him because he did not need her. He asked nothing of her and because of it was strong enough to face the full spirit of her love for life, as if it were no more unusual than a tree or sunshine. She sighed to herself in bliss to feel it and closed her eyes with a smile as he talked.

It was only when he began to tell her of the Seven Stillstones that went with the books, and she realized that they were not huge stones like the one on top of Duncton Hill but smaller, that her sense of bliss was transmuted into the shiveringly awesome feeling that she and Boswell were touching something that made time and circumstances fall away into a different place.

Boswell sensed this feeling in her, for he stopped talking at once and asked: "Can you tell me something about any of this?" For the first time since he had come to Duncton he felt that the Stone was casting its light his way.

Then, very simply, Rebecca told him about what she and Bracken had seen and felt on Longest Night. She described it matter-of-factly and quite without mystery, though the fears, doubts and joys that had been a part of that night were a part of her description.

He listened to her, trembling with the same sense of awe that she had felt, and when she finished, his first comment was "So he *touched* the stone and its light faded? He touched it!"

"Does it matter?" she asked a little nervously, because he sounded shocked.

"I don't know, Rebecca. Perhaps not. I don't know."

"Hasn't Bracken told you anything about this at all?" she asked.

Boswell shook his head. "Nothing. In fact, he doesn't even like to talk about it. I've asked him to take me up to the Ancient System but he has ordered that no mole goes there. I think . . ." But he stopped, because what he thought was something that Rebecca perhaps ought not to hear.

"Yes?" said Rebecca who, as a healer, was more used than anymole in the two systems to moles who were reluctant to finish sentences. Usually the unspoken part of the sentence was what they had come to talk to her about. She didn't think this of Boswell, but habits die hard.

"I was going to say that I think his apparent dislike of the Ancient System, which extends to the Stone, as well you know, has a lot to do with you and him . . . well . . . not . . . ," said Boswell, searching vainly for the right words.

"Not being in touch?" said Rebecca.

"Exactly," smiled Boswell. "Yes, that's it!" He wanted to laugh, but Rebecca was not smiling. She was serious, and for the first time since he had been in her burrow her face expressed the sense of loss that he had sensed in her spirit when he first came.

Once more he saw how vulnerable she was. There were times when he felt acutely his own lack of wisdom and wished he knew how to comfort a mole. He was full to bursting with the desire to say something to Rebecca, but did not know the words. But he found himself saying "He loves you." Perhaps it was all he had come to say to Rebecca anyway.

"Does he know it?" asked Rebecca.

Boswell shook his head: he didn't know. He could not help wondering whether or not Rebecca knew that she loved Bracken. But then, what did those words mean unless they were expressed through the Stone, which, in the first place, they had been?

"When I think of him or hear his name, I think of Mandrake," said Rebecca quietly. "I think of him trying to reach out to me by the Stone and Bracken stopping me, stopping me."

"But it was Stonecrop who killed him," said Boswell.

"It wasn't that," whispered Rebecca, remembering. "Perhaps a fight is better than an owl, or disease, especially for Mandrake. Perhaps that was best. No, you see, Bracken *heard* Mandrake. He heard him calling me and because he was afraid he stopped me going, and Mandrake was left in that . . . place—" Rebecca could not go on. She cried freely, freer than she would have been before any other mole but Boswell. Boswell wished he had had the wisdom to understand.

But Bracken and Rebecca did meet, an accidental crossing of paths in the Marsh End where he and Boswell had been talking to Mekkins one day about what everymole now recognized was a drought, and getting more serious every day.

Bracken and Boswell were going down a tunnel. There was laughter ahead, a couple of females chatting, and then there was Rebecca, large as life. Bracken tensed and looked surly, even angry. Rebecca smiled, a shade too calmly Boswell thought, as he backed away to leave the two together.

"Rebecca!" exclaimed Bracken with false cheer, having recovered himself. "I hear good reports of your work —not only in Duncton but on the pasture as well."

"Hello, Bracken," said Rebecca quietly.

"Yes, again and again I come across moles who . . . ,"

and within Boswell's hearing Bracken launched into a shower of talk about everything but what was in his heart —his joy and confusion at seeing Rebecca again.

She said hardly a word during this prattle, except "yes" and "mmm" and "really?" but each word she spoke seemed slower and sadder than the last. But there was a point in their painful conversation when, for a brief moment, the light shone again. Bracken had gotten onto the subject of the drought and Rebecca suddenly said, ironically, "You should put a stop to it, Bracken. You're the leader of Duncton."

Bracken laughed a little too loudly and then said, "I'm not the Stone, Rebecca," and Boswell heard her soft reply: "No, my dear, you're not."

Bracken was silent, for he heard the love behind her reproof just as much as Boswell did, and he could not hide the sadness in his own eyes. For a moment he relaxed and looked directly into Rebecca's eyes—and she into his. And there was stillness between them again. Rebecca had seen that look before, one September in the fading of a rainstorm when Bracken had first told her his name. He had run off then, and he did it again now, barely saying goodbye before he was gone. And Rebecca was left with only a look of understanding from Boswell to weigh against the loss she felt, the frustration at Bracken's fear, and the feeling that in some way, surely, it was her fault. She could have done more: the same feeling she had so often and so sadly faced with Mandrake. And then she thought of Mandrake, whom she had loved so deeply, and wondered why Bracken had not heard his cries.

IN the third week of August, Stonecrop came over from
the pastures to see Bracken. They talked in the elder burrow with Boswell and a couple of other Duncton moles
present.

"The drought on the pastures is now getting very serious,
Bracken," started Stonecrop. "Perhaps you in the wood
are more protected than we are, and so do not realize
how critical it is becoming. The grass is turning yellow
with dryness; the soil is cracking and so hard for lack of
rain that our youngsters who have left their home burrows
cannot burrow tunnels and are being forced to live on the
surface in the few areas of longer grass that exist. Many
have been taken by owl and kestrel. The stronger ones
are fighting for older moles' territory and there is death
and violence in the system. Food is scarce and moles that
find a source of worms are keeping it secret, or killing
other moles who find out their secret, and there is a growing sense of distrust and treachery throughout the system."

"What can we do about it?" asked Bracken coldly. "Our
own food supply is poor and, I am told, getting worse."
He looked round at the others for confirmation. They
nodded, and Boswell thought to himself that there is nothing like a shortage of food to turn a system violently
against others and itself. He had heard of it, but never
seen it at first paw.

Bracken looked at Stonecrop unsympathetically. His job
now was to protect his system and if Stonecrop was going
to suggest, which it seemed likely that he was, that the
pasture moles should move in on Duncton where the food
supply was better, he would have to resist it. With force,
if necessary.

"My predecessor, Brome, who helped you save your
system and get rid of Rune—not to mention Mandrake—
believed that the Stone should be accessible to the pasture
moles," said Stonecrop.

"Well, isn't it?" asked Bracken irritably. He didn't like
being reminded about Brome and Rune and Mandrake,

not by Stonecrop of all moles. All that, and a lot more,
was over. It was gone.

"Does anymole *live* in the Ancient System now?" asked
Stonecrop unexpectedly.

The question brought an icy calm into Bracken's mind
as, keeping his face quite impassive, he worked out what
his response to the implication behind this question should
be. He wanted no pasture mole living in the Ancient System. There was something almost blasphemous about the
idea. *Blasphemous?* Bracken thought to himself that that
was a strange word for him to use. Why, for Stone's sake,
he didn't want *anymole* living in the Ancient System.

"If you are going to suggest that because no mole from
Duncton now lives in the Ancient System that pasture
moles might now live there, then . . ." he was about to
say, and thought better of it, that if that was what Stonecrop meant he had better forget about it. Right now.

However, if his time as leader of Duncton had taught
him anything, it was that blunt statements of intent were
sometimes less effective as a way of getting things done
than ambiguity. So he finished the sentence clumsily and
only half-convincingly: "then . . . this is something we
will naturally need to talk about carefully among ourselves. Trust me, Stonecrop, to see that we do our best."
But Stonecrop didn't like the indirect mole Bracken was
becoming and certainly didn't trust him much at all. Why,
it used to be so easy to talk to Bracken, didn't it? But he
hadn't smiled once. Where was his spirit gone?

After a few minutes of half-hearted talk, Stonecrop left
with only the promise that Bracken would let him have
an answer in the next few days. Well, a week at most.
But Stonecrop let it be known that he wasn't sure that he
would be able to hold his moles in control that long unless something changed very dramatically. If it didn't, and
Bracken remained uncooperative, then he would have to
consider whether the help his moles had given Bracken
did not give them the right to take the Ancient System
by force. . . .

The effect of Stonecrop's visit on Bracken was immediate. As soon as he had gone, he ordered the other Duncton moles out of the elder burrow and turned to Boswell.
"Right. We're going to the Ancient System to see what the
food situation is there. It was never up to much when I
lived there, but you never know, it might have changed.

But first we're going to find out what the position is in Duncton. I've been thinking this drought would soon go away, but we'd better face the fact that it might stay for many weeks yet, perhaps even months. We owe something to the pasture system. We had better make some plans, but you can't do that without facts.''

Boswell could hardly believe his ears. For the first time since Bracken had taken over the system he seemed to have real fire in his spirit. His eyes were brighter, there was a combativeness in the way he spoke. More than that, Stonecrop's suggestion seemed to have opened the way to Boswell finally getting to see the Ancient System with Bracken.

They went first to the westside, then down to see Mekkins in the Marsh End. They talked to mole after mole, getting a detailed picture of what effect the drought was having on the system. Then back to the tunnels of Barrow Vale, where the moles were at first surprised to see Bracken so personally interested in what they had to say, then falling over themselves to tell him their woes. Finally they went to the eastside before starting on the trek up the slopes toward the Ancient System.

By then the picture they had formed—not only from what they had been told but also from what they had seen —was a grim one. The system was on the verge of disarray and fights over food were already becoming more frequent.

Along the wood's edge, the normally green grass and burgeoning brambles had turned yellow in the dryness. Everything creaked and crackled for want of moisture. The very air itself seemed to be made of oppressive dust, the light was harsh and bare—though because of the pall of white haze that seemed to have fallen on the earth, the sun rarely shone directly. On some of the more exposed trees, particularly on their south-facing side, the leaves had dried and crinkled and turned prematurely autumnal. The moisture that normally stayed throughout the summer just beneath the first layer of leaf litter seemed all to have gone, and what grubs there were had buried themselves deeper than usual, along with all the worms, making the normal summer surface runs useless for getting food. The worms also seemed to have bred much less prolifically, so that there was a general shortage. It was not acute, but to survive a mole had to spend much longer each day, and range much farther, to find enough food. As a result there were more fights, for territory was more valuable, and anyway, any shortage of food makes moles aggressive and irritable. At the same time, the number of owls in the wood seemed to have increased—summer was always a bad time as the tawny owls' own young were learning to fly and feed, and took any young moles in the wood or on the pastures they laid their yellow eyes upon. By the end of August, however, this bloody threat was normally over, for the youngsters that were going to be taken had gone, and most moles were sensibly underground. This time, however, the weather seemed to have prolonged the owl threat, whose hanging presence added to the grim atmosphere in the wood.

Mole after mole complained to Boswell and Bracken that something was wrong, very wrong, and they were afraid, very afraid. The Stone was angry and something was going to happen to them. And everymole they met complained of something they themselves had noticed in Barrow Vale: there was an unpleasant infestation of fleas in the tunnels all over the system.

So it was in a mood of foreboding that Bracken and Boswell turned at last up to the slopes and toward the Ancient System. The slopes were more populated with youngsters than Bracken could ever remember having heard of. Unable to find territory in the main system because its residents were keeping a larger portion of it for themselves, many youngsters had come to the traditionally impoverished slopes and established a meager existence for themselves in the dilapidated tunnels that were distant remnants of the original migration from the Ancient System. They were a skinny, frightened, sorry lot, somehow symptomatic of the arid days through which the system was going. Most ran away and hid when Bracken and Boswell approached.

"The whole system's falling apart," growled Bracken once when this happened, unaware that just as once he had been afraid of fully mature adult males, so these timid youngsters were afraid of him. Had Boswell been by himself, the story might have been different, for Boswell was the most approachable of moles.

Hulver's old tunnels were unoccupied and they entered the ancient tunnels by the route carved out by the side of the owl face by Mandrake. As they did so, Boswell felt obliged to reveal to Bracken what Rebecca had told him about their experience together in the central part of the system and what they had found together under the Stone. But whereas before Stonecrop's visit Bracken would surely have been angry, now he seemed, if anything, relieved.

"Did she tell you all that? Well, it's true enough, though it seems so removed from *me* now that I sometimes think all that happened to two other moles. You can't go backward, Boswell."

Ostensibly they went to find out what the food supply would be like in the ancient tunnels, but having quickly established that it was no better there than anywhere else, the journey became a tour of the system conducted by Bracken for Boswell's benefit.

They stayed there for three days, and in that time Boswell learned more about Bracken than he had ever known before. They went over to the cliff edge where Bracken had first entered the system; they traveled down the communal tunnel toward the center of the system; and they entered tunnel after tunnel and poked their snouts into many burrows even Bracken had not seen before.

Bracken spoke simply about the past, speaking almost as if it were a different mole he was talking about, but describing all the fears and excitements of the original exploration.

"Really, when it comes down to it, there isn't much to see. It's a deserted system, that's all, with just the central part having any great interest . . . perhaps I'll show it to you before we go back to the main system," Bracken said mischievously, for he could see Boswell's excitement at everything they saw—and, indeed, it rubbed off onto him.

So, when they finally reached the Chamber of Dark Sound, they were both equally excited, and ran down the final length of tunnel toward the echoes like a couple of youngsters. Boswell noticed that Bracken's old good humor had come back—away from the main system he seemed more relaxed. Perhaps at heart he was a solitary mole, perhaps that was what was wrong—he could never be solitary in Barrow Vale.

The chamber was the same, except that the entrance to the tunnel to the most central part of the system had fallen in where Mandrake had destroyed it, and the half-buried bones of the henchmoles killed in the fall remained among the soil and rubbish. There was a way through, however, dug out no doubt by Mandrake in the time he lived in the tunnels alone.

The atmosphere, which had been dark and dangerous when Bracken first came there, was somehow lighter and more neutral. Bracken did not feel nervous about it, and dispassionately showed Boswell the embossed walls, whose patterns still gyrated and wound across its surface, changing into heavier, deeper patterns nearer and nearer the center where the owl face, still threatening, hung. How had he ever been afraid of it all!

"You know what I found out?" said Bracken, finding it strange to talk normally in this once-terrifying place. "If you hum in a certain way, you get sounds back." He was about to show how when Boswell suddenly looked warningly at him, raised a paw and said quietly: "Be careful, Bracken. You don't know what you're doing."

Bracken began to protest but, as sometimes happened, there was a quality of fierceness to Boswell's expression that made him hold back his words. His mouth opened and then shut, and it was Boswell who spoke.

"This wall is the work of long generations of graced moles. It is a wall of hope and warning and it is true that by humming in a certain way, something you have stumbled upon, you may get some of the power from its ancient script. There is a wall like this in Uffington, as there is one in each of the seven chosen systems. They are not to be played with and are traditionally guarded by a mole not only great in body, but wise in spirit as well. It was said that such a guard never left his place, which is at the center of the wall, whatever calamity befell."

Bracken remembered then the mole skeleton that had so frightened him in the entrance in the center of the wall, the seventh entrance. So that had been the guard, and some calamity had befallen the ancient system. Yet he had stayed. Something of the awe that Bracken had once felt was returning in the face of Boswell's transformation beneath the wall from follower to aide to teacher.

"What is the wall for, then?" asked Bracken rather humbly.

"It protects the most holy part of the system, the system beyond that entrance. Its shapes carry the voices of the moles of the past and the proper way to approach it is with a chant in the old language, which all scribemoles should know, though these days, alas, many do not know it well enough. If I were still a scribemole and bound by my vows, I would not be able to tell of this, or let you hear the language. But now, Bracken, I am beginning to see that the Stone works its wisdom in ways we cannot understand, and I think it has made me free so that you, who carry so much . . . may hear the proper sound of the wall."

"What do you mean 'carry so much'?" asked Bracken.

Boswell was getting sterner and stranger by the second, and Bracken felt almost intimidated. "We didn't meet by accident, Bracken—surely you know that. You have a destiny I do not understand. But I know it is so. And the Stone had blessed me to help you fulfill it. Rebecca . . . the Seventh Stillstone which . . . you were so unwilling to talk about . . . the shadows that have fallen and continue to fall on the Duncton system . . . they are all a part of it. Every system seems to be in disarray—Nuneham, the pastures, Duncton, and many that I passed through when I came here. No mole trusts the Stone; no mole trusts himself. Fear is written on every face." It was written on Bracken's as he listened to Boswell. Who was he? What did the Stone want of him?

Bracken began to shake with fear, for as Boswell spoke, his voice seemed to grow louder and more sonorous and his very language changed as word by word it slid into the old language, which Bracken could not understand. Sounds hard; sounds mellifluous; sounds mysterious. Yet he did understand that there was worse than warning in Boswell's words and that Boswell was more than mole . . . Boswell turned to the wall and his voice became a chant, in the language of the old moles, and it began to echo and reverberate a thousand times more powerfully than when Bracken had first discovered the effect a hum could have.

> *The stait of mole dois change and vary*
> *Now sound, now seik, now blith, now sary*
> *Now dansand mery, now like to dee*
> *Our plesance heir is all vaneglory;*
> *This fals warld is bot transitory*
> *The flesh is brukle the dark is sle*
> *We that in heill wes, and gladnes*
> *Are trublit now with gret seiknes*
> *And feblit with infermite . . .*

As he chanted these ancient words, few of which Bracken could understand, it was as if the wall echoed back the actual chant of ancient moles, powerful moles, and dark sound began to come at Bracken, louder and louder, so that he wanted to run from it. But whichever way he turned, however he tried to escape, it came louder at him, surrounding him in its catastrophe, running at him from every tunnel in the Ancient System, a storm of sound.

As he began to cry out for the terror of it, he thought only of himself and could not know that its echoes and reverberations traveled far beyond the chamber they were in, down the tunnels, booming and vibrating up to the surface, encircling and then issuing from the Stone itself, and then out over the slopes, down toward Barrow Vale, a sound of disaster.

Mekkins heard it, stopping in midsentence down in the Marsh End, shaking his head in puzzlement, then running to the surface and snouting up toward the distant Stone from where the deep chant of ancient moles seemed to be coming.

Comfrey heard it, in the shade of the wood's edge where he vainly sought herbs long since killed by the drought, and he turned toward the hill, the name Rebecca forming helplessly in his mouth as fear filled him and he sought the comfort her name always gave him.

Rebecca heard it, down in her burrows, and she knew that what it was they had been waiting· for for so long, for generations, perhaps before any of them had been born, had come.

Stonecrop heard it and mole after mole, like him, stopped what they were doing and paused fearfully, as the sound from the Stone came down to them like thunder through the trees.

"Stop!" cried Bracken to Boswell. "Stop the sound!" he shouted, turning this way and that in his desperation. And Boswell's voice began to soften and change back, his words still thundering but no longer echoing with dark sound, as Bracken heard him say "You argue with Stonecrop, you argue with Rebecca, you argue with yourself. All of you argue, but now the time is coming when you must listen to the Stone. Now the last shadow is falling."

Bracken stared at Boswell and saw that he too was shaking, sweating and afraid himself. He seemed possessed by some power that only reluctantly let him go and Bracken called again to him, no longer in fear, but in pity and compassion for them all.

The last shadow had fallen. The last shadow? It was with this mysterious knowledge hanging over them, and not knowing what it meant, that Bracken finally led Boswell—both of them very subdued—through the seventh entrance and on to the central core.

In this moment of long-awaited arrival at the heart of Duncton Boswell said nothing, for he felt the dread of a threat outside the ancient tunnels far more than the promise and excitement of finding the Seventh Book, or clues to it, within them. But they pressed on, Bracken leading them quickly to one of the entrances into the Chamber of Echoes, and from there, without faltering once, through the complex labyrinths where the echoes played among the chalky walls and on to the edge of the Chamber of Roots.

There they stopped and looked at the sinews and shadows of the roots massing before them, seeming utterly still for once, but even then sounding the whine and shrill of the subtlest of shiftings from some deep crevice or high cleft as the roots responded to the stresses of the trees. The drought extended even down there, for the air was dry and the root sounds were tauter and higher-pitched.

"The buried part of the Stone is beyond the roots," said Bracken, pointing half-heartedly at them, "and since we're here, we might as well try to get through. But . . . well, you'll see."

Bracken led slowly off among the roots, taking care to mark the ground from the beginning so that they could find their way out. But, as he expected, they did not get more than a few moleyards beyond the first of the roots before the lethargy and loss of purpose that had affected him before struck them both. A voice kept saying to each of them "What's the point?" and "You know you can't get through, it's too far" until they seemed to veer off the course Bracken was trying to lead them on, round and round, and out again, back to the edge.

"You see what I mean?" said Bracken. "I was only able to get through there with Rebecca. We just went straight through without any confusion at all. But if you want to get to the Stillstone, that's where you'll have to find a way through, Boswell."

Boswell was not really listening. He was uncomfortable and restless, feeling that something was nagging at him from behind, a looming shadow he could not quite make out.

Bracken said, "Come on, I'll get you out. Another time . . . I'll bring you here again. Anyway, there are things to do. I'll tell Stonecrop he can bring what moles he likes into the ancient tunnels. I'll go and see Rebecca. It will be all right, Boswell."

He saw that the things he must do were really quite simple, and as he did so, felt relieved and clear-headed. He might even have felt light-hearted but for the oppression of the drought and the feeling that Boswell, who was now so silent, was full of fear or dread.

He took them out by his own series of tunnels that led over toward the wood's edge, describing to Boswell how he had escaped through them with Violet. They found a little food there, but ate it quickly because they wanted to get back onto the surface and down the slopes to the main system. When they did, they found the air was still as dry as bone.

"It's just the same as it was!" said Bracken with relief, as if he had expected the whole wood to have disappeared. "That place can leave a mole full of fears! Nice to be out again!" He tried to be as positive and as cheerful as possible, but Boswell did not react.

"I can't see what you're so miserable about," said Bracken, exasperated. "There's nothing wrong—except the heat."

BUT the system was not quite the same. While they had been in the ancient tunnels, the sky had taken on an eerie, threatening color, as if a thunderstorm of heat was about to break but could never quite manage it. At the same time, the flea infestation, which Bracken and Boswell had noticed on their tour of the system, got suddenly worse. A mole could not enter the tunnels and burrows to the south of Barrow Vale without brown-orange fleas hopping on and off his face and paws, bristling among his fur and itching and biting. They seemed attracted to the fine layer of dust and grit that had formed on the floors of the tunnel with the drought, and although not at first easily seen, the floor was sometimes literally alive with them.

It was so bad in some places that moles began to avoid certain of the communal tunnels and even to abandon affected sections of their own tunnels. Many of the marshenders took the more drastic but effective step of gathering leaves and the yellow flowerheads of the fleabane that grew down near the marshes to spread about their tunnels, which had the unfortunate effect on the system of forcing the infestations farther toward the center, where the fleabane did not grow.

Such infestations had happened in summer before, though never so badly, but even this was regarded by the gossips of Barrow Vale as just another annoyance of an aggravating season. Certainly it was not of enough significance to stop Bracken deciding that, once he had had a rest from his tour of the tunnels, he would set off for the pastures to tell Stonecrop and the pasture moles that they could occupy the ancient tunnels if they really wanted to. Then he would go and see Rebecca, hoping that she would come close to him again.

But he was never to make either journey. As he was about to leave, Mekkins arrived from the Marsh End with some news so strange that he immediately accompanied him back, though taking a roundabout route to avoid the fleas.

It seemed that the day before, three moles had been

gathering fleabane by the marsh's edge, when from out among its dry rustling grasses two strange moles appeared. Never in living memory or legend had anymole ever come from across the marshes. The marshenders were hostile—two standing their ground very firmly while the other got reinforcements and sent to Mekkins. Mekkins came quickly and interrogated them. The two strangers were friendly to the point of abjection. They had come a long way, they said; the marsh was caked over with dryness and there was no problem with crossing it. No, they had not crossed over by any route which the roaring owls took—a suggestion Mekkins made to them on the basis of what Boswell had told him about what lay behind the marshes. No, they had come by some other way, though they seemed confused, or deliberately vague, about where. They kept asking questions themselves—what system was this, they wanted to know, and was everything all right.

Mekkins answered no questions, but let them come into one of the burrows nearest the marsh where there he put some guards on them while he went to get Bracken. His instinct was to kill them there and then, but he felt that their visit was so unusual, and times were so strange, that it was a good idea to give Bracken and Boswell the chance to talk to them.

So all three of them went back quickly to the Marsh End without pause, going right through toward the marsh itself. But before they got to the burrow where the strangers were being kept, they met the three Marsh End moles who had been guarding them coming toward them.

"Why the 'ell aren't you doin' what you should be?" demanded Mekkins. "Don't you tell me that them two buggers have scarpered." He looked very threatening.

One of the three spoke up: "It ain't that they've scarpered, Mekkins. Worse than that. They're dead!"

"Yes, suddenly took ill last night with Stone knows what, and as soon as you know it, they were gone," said another.

"*Both* of them?" asked Mekkins.

"Horrible it was," said the third. "In agony they were."

"Horrible it *is*," said the first mole. "Never smelled anything like it. You go an' see for yerself, Mekkins."

The two dead moles presented a pathetic sight. One

was still crouched upright on his paws, all hunched up with his snout tight between his legs, as if he had been trying to protect himself from a headlong wind. His eyes were terribly swollen, while his snout, what they could see of it, was red and sore, and his fur mottled and caked with sweat. The other was on his side, paws out stiff, his mouth agape. His soft, pale belly fur was lank and diseased-looking, and in the soft part where one of the back paws joined his body there was a gaping sore, yellow with pus. It was from this that a terrible stench of death that filled the burrow seemed to emanate. There was one other thing. The floor of the burrow was bristling with fleas whose one objective seemed the same: to get to the open sores on the mole's body. Some fleas were already there, sucking at the red-and-yellow patch. Others, satiated, occasionally lost their grip and fell off, their place taken immediately by new ones.

"But they looked all right when I left 'em to go and get Bracken," said Mekkins to one of the guardmoles.

"Well, we watched over them from the moment you went. Even offered 'em a worm or two, which is saying something these days, but they weren't interested. Said they weren't hungry. One of 'em got restless first and started sweating, a smelly kind of sweat. Then the other got all hot and bothered and says something like 'We're cursed, it will kill everymole.' So I asked him what he was on about and he said 'You'll soon find out' and started groaning and cursing while the other one—he's the one who's still on his paws—just sort of curled up and then shivered and started scratching his snout as if there was something on it, which there wasn't. Then they got steadily worse and worse and I sent somemole over to the pastures to get Rebecca because I thought she would help out, but that was early this morning and you've got here first. Then the one that was groaning stopped groaning and sort of his breath came faster'n faster and *he* shivered. Then before we knew where we were they were both dead, one just where he was and the other keeling over and ending up where 'e is now, on 'is side. Well, then we noticed the smell getting bad, and then the fleas seemed to get worse, though Stone knows where they come from because this burrow was pretty clear of 'em."

"What did they mean?" Bracken pondered aloud to

himself. " 'It will kill everymole' . . . What do you make
of it, Boswell?"

They turned to Boswell, who was looking closely at
the dead moles. If ever a mole looked as if he knew
more than he was saying, it was Boswell at that moment.
"The best thing you can do for the time being is to seal
that burrow," he said, not answering Bracken's question.

"This ain't the pasture system, me old mate," said
Mekkins. "They may do that there, but they ain't taken
over Duncton yet. I don't want a couple of diseased
strangers rotting in my tunnels, thank you very much."

Just as Bracken was about to step in and settle the
argument there was a commotion at the other end of
the tunnel and the mole who had been sent to get Rebecca appeared.

"She ain't there," he said. "Gone to deal with something or other over in the far pastures she has, so some
burk of a pasture mole told me. They're thick as lob-
worms, them lot. I left a message. Let's hope he's not too
thick to pass it on."

"Right. We'll wait till Rebecca gets back before deciding what to do with these two," said Bracken firmly.
"Now, can we go somewhere more pleasant, Mekkins?"

Two hours later one of the moles who had been guarding the two strangers began to sweat. Six hours later he
was dead. That same evening a mole came to tell Mekkins that two more who lived near the burrow where the
two strangers had died had been taken ill—sweating, irritable, very thirsty and weakening by the hour.

Bracken, now increasingly worried and restless for
something to do before Rebecca arrived, went to look at
them. Rebecca came straight from the pastures on re-
ceiving the message and it was here that she found
him. He was looking at their suffering and feeling the
agony of helplessness that the healthy feel before extreme
illness in another. If they heard him in the tunnel where
they were crouched motionless, they did not show it, and
they could not have seen or scented him, for the skin
around their eyes was painfully swollen and their snouts
were running with a foul-smelling mucus.

"Bracken?" It was Rebecca's voice, and then her touch.
"Bracken?"

He turned to her, his suffering for them so much a part of him that his gaze on her was direct and open. The last thing he was thinking about was Rebecca's attitude to him. "Can you help them?" he asked, but before the question was fully out he could see her answer. She looked tired and stricken.

"There are many moles like this on the pastures over on the far side," she said. "Somemoles came in from another system and must have brought the disease with them. One of them has been lucky and is not ill, but he says that most of the moles in his system died from the disease."

"The *whole* system?" whispered Bracken.

Rebecca nodded. "Bracken, there was nothing I could do for them. The ones who died didn't respond to anything I gave them. The one who lived—or has so far—didn't survive because of anything I did."

Mekkins suddenly joined them. "A couple of moles have come over from the eastside and there's death there now." He shrugged hopelessly. "You know what it is, don't you? It's the plague, and there's not a blind thing anymole can do about it—not even you, Rebecca."

"But Rose might—" she began. "She couldn't," said Mekkins firmly, "so put that idea out of your head."

Boswell joined them quietly as well, and all four looked at each other in a dawning horror. Each one had heard stories of the plague, though none knew the history of its terror more than Boswell, who had read some of the Rolls of the Systems, whose records had been mysteriously interrupted two or three times in molehistory when most of the chroniclers themselves had suddenly died or disappeared in a waste of history that reflected plague and only a single account had remained to tell the story.

"The shadow has fallen" was the phrase with which one of the most famous Rolls of the Systems ended, written as it had been by the last survivor, a scribemole, in a system to the west, whose account was left unfinished before he himself had died. It was the same phrase that Boswell, or the moles that possessed him, had used by the wall in the Chamber of Dark Sound.

But Boswell, who knew so much, had nothing to say.

Crouched together in the tunnel, the four began to feel the full weight of the waves of death that were roll-

ing toward them, a flood far more powerful than the one
Bracken and Boswell had faced in the drainage channel.
Then, hour by hour, the reports began to stream in.

"Five moles in the eastside . . ."

"A female in Barrow Vale itself . . ."

"Three westsiders, two males and a female . . ."

Panic and fear began to take over the system as each
began to fear for his or her life. Everymole sought some
remedy or escape and when moles found that Rebecca
was among them, with Mekkins, they besieged and be-
seeched her for help—for a charm, for a prayer, for a
herb that would save them. But the more they asked, the
more impotent Rebecca felt, for there was nothing her
normally healing words seemed able to do, and no herb
that she knew seemed to help.

By the third day, when Bracken and Boswell had
moved back to Barrow Vale to see if they could at least
control the panic, leaving Mekkins and Rebecca in the
Marsh End—the one because he wanted to be in his
own tunnels, the other because she felt instinctively that
that was where she could give most comfort—there were
so many dead in the system that the living could no longer
move them from where they had died. Dead, odorous
moles lay in tunnels, in burrows, halfway out of entrances, some even lay in the very place they had been
burrowing for worms before the plague crept up on them
and took them away.

Each corpse was flea-covered, each carried the stench
that the first two had had, and each showed the same
grim progress of symptoms. And the stifling heat that
continued seemed only to speed up the process of decay
and spread the smell of death.

By the third day there was not a mole in the system
who did not have a friend or close relative who had died.
Some had lost each one of their siblings; some had lost
each of their neighbors; many marveled to find themselves alive. In one or two places—on the slopes and in
parts of the westside—hardly a single mole died and the
moles marveled at their fortune, seeking vainly for an
explanation of it.

Then there was a lull for two days which brought sudden false hope, and the gossips in Barrow Vale, who
chattered now more wildly and more desperately, started
to say that the plague was over and Stone knows why

they had been spared but . . . but on the next day the plague returned, in a new form. It was as if, unable to kill all the moles quickly, it had adopted a new guise to take them in a different way, one that was slower.

Moles broke out in sores under their bellies and on their flanks, painless but odorous sores, which came with the sweating. Then swellings and nodules of hardness under the skin appeared on their faces and snouts, blocking them and making their breathing labored and terrible to hear. At the same time, the disease seemed to go to the lungs of the moles, causing them to cough and retch. And a mole that began to cough blood was a mole soon dead.

The system began to be filled with a strange moaning sound, the cries of moles in distress to whom there was none to minister, few to give comfort. Those that survived, untouched by the plague, seemed to wander about in a daze, unable to stay still in the face of such total tragedy but unable to help those suffering around them.

The system soon started to collapse around Bracken. Many of the moles who had been his executives and aides simply disappeared; others joined in the incessant talk that now took over the panic-stricken Barrow Vale, where moles seemed to find refuge in congregating together and discussing the latest plague news and noting with alarm and self-satisfaction which moles from among their number had gone. They noted that more moles seemed to die in the early morning before sunrise than at any other time, while more moles seemed to develop swellings around the belly and groin which developed into sores after two or three days. Death from the new form of plague took up to four days and the only one consolation that the moles could find was that not all the sufferers seemed to die, though most still did.

Not every mole panicked. At least one, Comfrey, stayed calm and left the pasture, crossed through the wood and began searching for something that a long time before he remembered Rose talking about. "If only I c–c–could remember *properly*," he scolded himself.

The talk in Barrow Vale soon concentrated on the idea that the plague came from the Stone and was its judgment on them, a punishment for a system that had let the old ways slip under the rule of Mandrake and Rune.

From this idea came the belief that the only way of combating the plague was to visit the Stone and touch it

—eagerly accepted confirmation of which was that one of the moles who had recovered from the plague had previously been up to the Stone and touched it, living proof that the Stone worked.

"Is it true, Boswell, or is it just another superstition?" asked Bracken, making it more a statement than a question. He had noticed that several moles who had been to the Stone had subsequently died and was cynical about the "explanations" offered by the Stone's proponents that these moles had transgressed in other ways and so the Stone did not favor them.

"In the sense you mean it is untrue," said Boswell, breaking the silence in which he had been lost for most of the time since the plague came upon them. "These moles do not understand that the Stone is not a power by itself. Its power is invested in each one of us, whether it is a power for good or for evil. If you touch the Stone with faith, perhaps that does release a power, but only one that exists already inside you. For all your cynicism, Bracken, you have that power as well."

"Can I stop myself getting the plague?" asked Bracken bitterly, thinking of the many who had died. "Could *they* have?"

Boswell was silent, which turned Bracken's bitterness into anger. He felt, as so many other moles did themselves, that the plague was in some way a judgment on him. But his feeling was the stronger for his being leader of the Duncton system and, though no other mole said it, he felt responsible for what was happening. Like Rebecca, he felt the terrible frustration of not being able to relieve the suffering, almost as if it was a guilt. He turned these feelings back on Boswell, and through him onto the Stone.

Boswell was silent.

"Where is this power of the Stone when it is most needed?" demanded Bracken angrily. "You're clever at making the Stone seem important, but when it's needed, really needed, what good is it? Why does it let this happen?" Bracken waved his paws around the tunnels of Barrow Vale, now full of frightened survivors of the plague, in a way that took in their fears and took in as well the dead, the stench of the dead and the distant moans of the dying.

"Well, Boswell?"

But Boswell was silent. He knew the Stone was inside Bracken and one day he would know it. The plague was no more a judgment on the system or the moles in it than the idea that the sun was a bonus for living a good life was true. The plague was a part of life, as death was, but Boswell did not know what words could express such thoughts in such a place as this.

"I will go to the Stone myself," he said finally.

"To pray?" mocked Bracken. "Or to touch the Stone so you don't get it . . ." His voice trailed off as he heard his own tired bitterness. He was so weary, and suddenly afraid now that Boswell was going to leave. Impulsively he went up to Boswell and stopped him leaving.

"What will happen to us all, to the system?" Boswell looked at him with those bright dark eyes that held such understanding and warmth to anymole willing to raise his own eyes and look into them. He understood Bracken's anger and torment, for he loved him with a love that grew stronger and fiercer in him day by day. He knew that a mole like Bracken might be angry with the Stone as well as in love with it. Indifference was the greatest threat.

"I will pray for you, Bracken, for Rebecca and for all moles . . ." but Bracken turned away again, thinking that prayers would be of no help to the moles in his system who had died already and to whom he had been unable to offer any protection. Yet his heart sank to see Boswell go. He wondered if he would ever see him again.

Four days and many more plague deaths later, Bracken had a visit in Barrow Vale from a marshender. His message was stark and simple: Mekkins was dead. Just like that. Mekkins was gone.

"Rebecca was with him but she couldn't do nothing," said the marshender, who had seen so much death that even Mekkins' death did not affect him. "Whatmole can? It's the Stone's curse, and we're powerless against it." Mekkins!

There was no need to be told how, or when, or where. The fact of it was enough to take the last strength from his body and for despair to take him over. It was as if some thief had sneaked into his burrow in the night and taken something from him without him seeing it and which he could never recover. Nothing could have under-

lined the tragedy that had overtaken the system more
than this. Mekkins! Who had talked to him only days
before, who was always aggressive and full of life; who
had done so much for him and Rebecca and so many
other moles.

He rose up from where he was crouched and began to
roar in his shock and rage, raising his living talons and
bringing them down on the walls of the elder burrow,
gasping out in his anger, grunting in his effort to attack
and attack the earth around him, spittle forming on his
mouth fur. He wanted to do something, anything, but there
was nothing. He wanted to run roaring through the tunnels to the Marsh End, but what was the point?

The marshender watched him. He had seen it all before. Anger, rage, prayers, the whole bleedin' lot. A bit
of roaring and raving wasn't goin' to do no good. Still,
didn't hurt, either. Better tell him the rest.

"Rebecca's got it as well. She's got the plague," said
the marshender.

Horror and fear rushed over Bracken's fur, then icy
calm. "Where is she?" he asked urgently.

"Stone knows," said the marshender. "She was only
just took with it when I left—sweatin' she was just like
the others. I reckoned it was the plague. I scarpered. I
mean, if the healer gets it, then Stone help us all."

Bracken was gone before he could say more, running
down through the system toward Mekkins' tunnels, for
that was where she would be. Running and running as if
death were chasing at his paws. Running and running
through the flea-ridden, death-smelling, stifling tunnels
with sweat in his fur and terrible visions of a dying Rebecca mixing with pictures of a dead Mekkins in his
mind, and prayers, more wild and desperate than any
he had ever felt tempted to utter running through his
head. "Keep her alive," he begged as he ran, "keep her
alive. Spare Rebecca . . . take me. Take me" as he ran
and ran.

She was not in Mekkins' burrow, where only Mekkins'
body lay, hunched and sore-ridden like the rest. Oh,
Mekkins! Mekkins!

Rebecca! He looked around wildly, not knowing where
to go, trying to think, trying to recover enough to think.
Rebecca! He ran from tunnel to tunnel, seeking a mole
to guide him to where she might be, meeting mole after

mole who looked at him stupidly when he asked "Where's Rebecca?" for they had problems of their own and how would they know where she was?

Why hadn't she come to him? Where would she have gone?

He began to run toward the pastures, thinking that she must have returned to her burrow, but only when he was nearly to the wood's edge did he remember that he didn't know exactly where she lived there—up near the higher pastures? Down where Rose once lived? And anyway . . . he paused in his running, sweat now shining in his fur and his breathing desperate with effort . . . it didn't feel right. He felt as if he was running away from her. He turned south, toward the Stone on top of the hill, the evening air in the tunnels around him heavy with dry heat and asked aloud "Where are you?" He wanted to call for her and hear her answer. He wanted Rebecca.

Where would she have gone? He crouched down and closed his eyes, thinking himself into her mind as best he could and wondering where she might have gone. The Stone? Barrow Vale? Where else was there?

Only one place, and it came to him quietly as he himself had once gone there. Curlew's burrow. The place she had gone when she had been so ill before and where, by the grace of the Stone, she had survived to take care of Comfrey. She must have gone there. He was so certain of it that a peace came to him as he got up and set off eastward across the Marsh End to the most forsaken part of the system. By the grace of the Stone . . . he prayed to it, subconsciously feeling guilty at asking it to keep her alive when he had doubted it so much. "If you keep her alive," he bargained, "I'll go to Uffington to give thanks. I'll do anything . . . only keep her alive."

It was a journey through death, for the marshenders seemed even more stricken than the moles around Barrow Vale and he came across body after body, or poor creatures dragging themselves along in their final hours. Or others, who seemed to have gone insane, whispering in a kind of daze "We have been saved from the plague, we had it we had it, and we have been saved. Praise the Stone for saving us. Praise the Stone . . ." And they reached out to touch Bracken as he passed them by, their faces and bodies still bearing the plague sores to show that it had, indeed, been their way, their eyes crazed by their deliverance.

Until at last he was into the eastern part of the Marsh End, whose surface was now hard and friable but still had something of the dank shadowiness that it had always held. He had not been here since he had been chased from it by Rune so long before when . . . he almost said to himself "when the world was right."

On and on he went, his heart quickening as he reached the end of the journey for what he might find when he got there.

It was night and he had been journeying one way or another since the early evening. "Only let her be alive," he whispered again as he reached the last few yards, "and nothing else will matter. I will go to Uffington and give thanks whatever the cost."

He found Curlew's old tunnels with little difficulty, but stopped short outside the entrance because something lay there he had not seen for a long time—a fresh flowerhead. Its petals were like a crocus, and a delicate mauve, its stalk white and vulnerable. Lying as it was among the aridness of drought-dusty, faded ivy that covered the tree trunk by the entrance and on top of rustling dry leaf mold, it presented a strange sight. He had never seen such a flower before and it made him pause and wonder at it before entering the tunnel carefully, snouting out ahead of him to see if life were there.

There was life all right, and plague. He could smell the terrible plague odor and hear movement of some kind. At least she was still alive. He approached noisily and called out ahead of himself "Rebecca! Rebecca! It's Bracken!" and ran on down.

He was met at the entrance to Curlew's old burrow not by Rebecca but by the stutter and stumble of Comfrey, whose thin snout peered out at him as he approached. "Hello, Br–Br–Bracken," he said.

Before Bracken even wondered what Comfrey was doing there he asked: "Is she *here?* Is she all right?"

"She's g–g–got the plague," stuttered Comfrey. "She's n–n–not very well."

Rebecca was crouched in the same corner she had occupied when she had been so ill before. Her eyes were swollen but not yet closed, while her mouth hung loose to ease her breathing. Already the swellings were starting on her face and snout. By her head on the floor lay the white shiny bulb part of a plant, the flower of which Bracken had seen on the surface.

Comfrey stepped forward to Rebecca. "You've got to eat it, R–Rebecca," he said to her softly, touching her face to draw her attention. "You've g–got to *try*."

"Rebecca," whispered Bracken. "It's me, Bracken."

She sighed and he saw that her eyes were running, though whether with tears or illness it was hard to say.

"Thank you," she whispered almost inaudibly.

"M–make her eat it," said Comfrey desperately to Bracken. "It will help her. I kn–kn–know it will."

"What is it?" asked Bracken.

"I got it from beyond the eastside where there's pasture near the marsh. It's called meadow saffron by the east-siders, though it's so rare that few of them have ever seen it. But I found it, and when I did I kn–kn–knew it was for R–Rebecca. I *knew* it. I always kn–know when she n–needs help. It's a special healing plant . . . I've often f–found plants when she needed them. But it's always been for a m–mole she's helping. I didn't know it was for her." He sounded desperate and kept pushing the white flesh of the bulb at Rebecca's mouth for her to take.

"You mustn't try to die," he said simply, almost scolding her. "It'll take you longer to get better if you d–d–don't eat it." Then he looked straight at Bracken as if reading his thoughts and said: "You don't have to worry about her dying. She won't." There was total faith in Comfrey's words.

If Bracken had not been in such a place at such a time he would have sworn that he saw a glimmer of the starting of a smile on Rebecca's plague-ridden face, or per-haps even a laugh.

"Rebecca," he said urgently. "Rebecca . . ." His voice changed almost to a command and he said, "You're bloody going to eat this thing Comfrey's got for you!" With that he took the bulb himself, bit off a piece, chewed it lightly into a mush, and putting it on his paw, started feeding it to Rebecca. She couldn't chew but she was able to take it piece by slow piece and swallow it, like a pup taking its first solid food.

As she did so, he too knew with absolute certainty that she was not going to die—or rather that Comfrey, for all

his hesitation, had spoken with such total faith in a voice
that Rebecca had heard, that she *could* not die.

"Most of them die because they don't eat anything and
b—because they can't breathe properly," said Comfrey
matter-of-factly, now content to watch over Rebecca and
Bracken as if they were one mole—and one who had given
him a rather unnecessary scare. "Rose told me about
meadow saffron in a rhyme she said once, b—b—but I
didn't know that 'pestilence' meant plague. Then an east-
sider told me, so I know."

Bracken did not take much of this in, though much
later Rebecca was to remember every word. The horror
of the plague for a mole was that the mind stayed quite
clear while the body would no longer obey it.

Perhaps Bracken sensed this, for he talked to her as if
she could hear him, treating her as if she were the most
precious thing in the world, as, indeed, she was. The ugliness as the plague swellings grew worse, the stench of
the sores when they came, the abjection of the affliction
. . . neither he nor Comfrey noticed or afterward remembered. It was Rebecca they loved, and she was not
a swelling or a sore but a mole who had tended so many
and suffered so much, and who, in their turn and in their
different ways, now tended her, both giving her something
different from their own spirits. Comfrey's certain knowledge that she would live was one strength: Bracken's
force of love was another.

Present with them in Curlew's burrows was a third
strength—the power of the prayers that Boswell spoke up
at the Stone, so far away, thinking of them both, and of
all the other moles of Duncton and the pastures which his
great love encompassed through the Stone.

Crouched up in the darkness of that long night, when
Rebecca lay so ill, perhaps sensing that she was, he whispered the prayers he had learned as a scribemole but
never thought he would himself have the power to say.
Though now, as he said them, they came as naturally as
breathing, each one calling out through him the blessing
of the silence of the Stone:

> *Power of the Stone come into thee*
> *All of thee in quiet*
> *Power of the sun come into thee*
> *A part of thee in warmth*

Power of the moon come into thee
A part of thee feel cool
Power of the rain come into thee
A part of thee refreshed
Power of death depart from thee
Taken by the Stone
Power of life return to thee
Borrowed from the Stone
Power of the Stone is with thee
For you are the Stone,
All of you the Stone.

He said it for the system's sake, he said it for the pastures, he said it for the moles he had seen suffer and the moles who would never know the Stone; he said it for Bracken, and he whispered it for Rebecca. And if its effect was to bring quiet and silence, this was the third strength that came into Curlew's burrows and accompanied Bracken and Comfrey and Rebecca on her journey through the plague.

And though its talons may have cast her down they took with them, when they finally left her three days later, the power that Mandrake's dreadful death had held over her. After two long days and nights she began to breathe easily, and on the fourth, she smiled again at last, and all of them could smile. And she had the strength to tell them both that they were her loves, as they had always been, father and son.

35

On the fifth day in Curlew's burrows, when Rebecca had almost recovered, a mist unlike any mist Bracken had ever seen came over the surface from the marsh. It was thin and swirling at first, noticeable more for its smell than its sight. It was dry and woody and smelled like some musky flower. Sometimes it was stronger, sometimes weaker and sometimes minute black dusty particles, light as the seedsails of rosebay willowherb, floated down in it.

Bracken did not know it, but it was the smoke of a fire that was spreading slowly across the dried-up marsh, crackling inexorably among the husky tall grass and reeds, curling and licking its way from reed stem to stem, its flaming reds and oranges paled by the sunlight. Here and there, where the reeds were thicker and the fire caught hold better, the smoke curled in thick waves of choking blue-gray, then rose and swirled away, revealing the brighter red of flames as they turned the yellow dry vegetation black and traveled on, leaving smoldering charred remnants behind.

Creatures ran in panic and confusion before it, many waiting as long as they could, for they had never seen a fire, then running before its heat and in the waves of panic of other creatures about it; fieldmice, a couple of voles, a hare that had strayed onto the dry marsh in search of food, and hundreds more.

A long olive grass snake delayed too long and its back-and-forth snaking became quicker and more rushed as it tried to escape, until smoke came into its throat and its shaking became a thrashing as the fire ran over and under it and its body curled and blackened into an agonized death, the skin cracking as the life in the flesh hissed out. The fire passed on, leaving the snake's burnt corpse behind with the other distortions of life among the ashes.

As the afternoon progressed, the mist by Curlew's burrows grew thicker and more difficult to breathe in, and the sounds in the wood no longer seemed right. The mist was beginning to smell in the burrow and though it smelled cleaner than the plague, a mole would be insane to stay there too long.

Rebecca was strong enough to move—indeed, for a full day she had begged Bracken to let her go out, but he had resisted the idea: best to take it easy. And anyway, where could they go that wasn't plague-ridden? Best to stay still. But now things were different and he was going to lead them up through the wood, away from the marsh, which he had never liked and from where this mist was drifting in.

"We're going," said Bracken. "Now."

The smoke on the surface was getting steadily thicker, but the evening sun could still penetrate into it, giving the wood a luminescent blue appearance, with the trees looming out of it palely. Black sooty specks of burnt grass drifted along with the smoke toward the interior of the wood, and Bracken led Rebecca and Comfrey along with them, instinctively following a route away from the advancing fire—which had now reached to within a few moleyards of the wood and whose urgently sharp crackling could be heard.

"What is it?" asked Comfrey, curious rather than afraid.

"I don't know," said Bracken, "but it's dangerous. Now come on."

But though Rebecca could move, she could not move fast, and with Comfrey unable to keep in a straight line for continually snouting after things and trying to satisfy his curiosity about them, their progress was slow.

Behind them the fire had reached the reed wall at the marsh edge and burst through it with low rustlings and crackles as orange flame licked at the dry grass of the bank that led up to the shrubs and smaller bushes that grew at the wood's edge. At one point it took hold and crossed to the bank, encouraged by the lightest of breezes that came off the marsh. Then, at another point. Then a third. Until the whole bank had taken, and the fire was sweeping up it through the shrubs to the first trees of the wood. As it reached them and started at the heavy dry leaf litter, the quality of the fire and smoke changed. It grew thicker and heavier as curls of gray-yellow smoke came from the leaf litter and the breeze carried it through the wood, where it overtook the lighter blue smoke with its white-yellow, and this drifted on more urgently into the wood, obscuring the sun, enshrouding the trees and soon catching up with the fleeing moles.

Bracken was more worried about Rebecca than Comfrey, for her strength was not as great as either of them had thought. He had taken a place behind them both and urged them on, especially Rebecca. "My love, you've got to keep going. It's getting thicker and the noises are louder. It is coming nearer." Behind them the crackle of the fire increased, changing here and there into a roar as it passed over what had been Curlew's burrows and trees and branches fell under its heat and destroyed her tunnels forever.

Sometimes, the breeze of smoke through the wood, which was getting stronger, carried a roaring of fire sound rather than just a crackle.

They ran on, smoke at their throats and eyes, now frightened by the thing that sounded so massive and threatening behind them, their own rustles and scamperings drowned by the fallings, crashings and roarings from the fire.

Once clear of the isolated area of woodland in which Curlew's tunnels were they came across entrances to tunnels into the system, and to get them away from the smoke Bracken led them down. The air was blissfully easier to breathe, but once down they noticed immediately the nauseating odor of plague and ahead of them saw the rotting body of a mole.

"Come," said Bracken wearily, "we had best stick to the surface."

Even in the short time they had been underground, the fire had advanced so much that they could feel that the temperature of the air had gone up and waves of heat were blowing up from behind them, with smoke and black soot. At one point Comfrey went off too far to the left and they lost him and had to stop and call until, scared and apologetic, he came spluttering back. "It's even worse over there," he said.

Bracken had memories of being chased through this same part of the wood by henchmoles, in the opposite direction, and remembered how they had advanced to his right and his left until they seemed to be all around him. He felt that the "thing" behind them was doing the same—and although he sensed it was impersonal, like rain, it was still frightening. Gradually the fire overtook them on the left and they veered away from it to the right, only to find its sound and roaring even louder there.

"Faster! Faster!" he urged them. "It mustn't catch us!" And they ran on.

The fire had taken hold of the whole of the Marsh End, surging through the dried bracken and leaf litter and crackling at the base of trees before turning their bark black, while higher tongues of flame leaped up from dry fern and bracken and caught at the leaves of the lower branches which took the flames, curling them into death as they raced over the tree's surface and then started at the twigs and branches as it took hold. Smoke billowed up from the wood, heavy with the feathery remnants of burning leaves and black ash, twisting and swirling into a great pall of smoke that drifted ahead of the fire through the drought-dry branches of the trees and undergrowth, toward the slopes.

Sometimes, among the soaring fragments of ash, a delicate white admiral butterfly or garish purple emperor tried to fly clear of the heat and smoke, beating frail wings unnaturally high into the air against the sucking and hurling currents, fluttering the last of its life away before smoke choked it and heat turned the beautiful wings into crumpled ash, and it fell back into the flames unrecognizable and lost.

Death licked and darted its flaming way among the heavy tree trunks and branches, where, beneath the once-protective bark, the larvae of stag beetles and longhorns or scuttling weevils found themselves trapped in the steam of boiling sap, their scrabbling bodies falling still as the fire burned away the life of tree after tree. While on the leaves, and especially the beloved oaks of Duncton Wood, the nobbles and carbuncles of the gall wasps and midges, where tiny young maggots lived in a cocoon of life, were suddenly gone, caught by a devastation more terrible than the plague that had swept the moles before and one from which none escaped.

Along the wood's edge, in advance of the flames, the grass was alive with fleeing creatures: dormice, unused to the light of day; squirrels, tails dancing in tune with their run and then stopping, still on two legs, to see if they could tell where the danger lay before running on again; stoats and bank voles, and, of course, those few moles who had survived the plague and been driven from their tunnels by the smell of danger. Creatures that were

normally foes now lost their internecine fears and ran, or
hopped, or hesitated, or fled as their nature and instincts
told them. Few dared to venture out of cover onto the
pastures, most preferring to run on through grass or undergrowth in advance of the fire, and hope that they
might escape it.

On the hilltop by the Stone, among the great beeches,
Boswell could sense the terrible devastation that was
spreading through the wood below. He could smell the
smoke, though the terrible pall that now covered the wood
as far as the slopes was behind his range of vision. And
he could not know that below him the ancient and noble
oaks of Barrow Vale were being taken forever by the
fire. He had heard the urgent wings of carrion crow high
in the branches, flapping blackly up through the smoke-
filled beech branches and out of the wood. Then the sudden flight of a spotted woodpecker, flying straight out of
its territory and ignoring any danger but the fire behind.
And an urgent scurrying of such normally unseen birds
as nuthatches and tree-creepers driven out of their cover
by panic.

There were other moles with Boswell, huddling by the
Stone, most of whom had come to touch the Stone to
avoid the plague and stayed there to avoid the danger in
the system below. One or two had come up from the
slopes, worried by the smoke and unnatural sounds.

Their only comfort was Boswell's calm and peaceful
presence, and to him they looked again and again for reassurance, shivering with fear despite the heat of the day
and the smoke, unwilling to flee beyond the Stone. Occasionally creatures ran across the clearing—a squirrel, a
stoat from somewhere down on the slopes—but the paw-
ful of moles stayed fast, waiting and waiting in the smell
of the fire and the sound of Boswell's prayers.

The fire finally caught up with Bracken, Rebecca and
Comfrey when they were halfway to the slopes. The
flames crackled and roared to their left and right, burning
branches fell crashing into the flames of the undergrowth,
the smoke began to choke them with its heat and they began to turn this way and that in an attempt to progress
further. Until at last there was nowhere to go, and the fire

was approaching from all around them, Bracken's fur singed by its sparks and flames.

It was then that they were forced underground again, into the plague-smelling, smoke-filled tunnels. Bracken led them down, past the dead and gaping bodies of moles, seeking out a tunnel or burrow that was smoke-free. To the left, to the right, through narrow tunnels they went, until they found a subsidiary tunnel that was clear—obviously because it led nowhere. Bracken saw Rebecca and Comfrey safely into it before following them and then sealing it up, so that no smoke could enter, and running on down it and making a second seal. The tunnel ran among the roots of an oak tree, thick and gnarled, and there they stopped, hoping that the danger would pass. They could hear the sound of the crashing fire above them, and worse, far worse, they could hear in the desperate sounds of the roots the useless fight of the tree against the fire that now overwhelmed it. Hissings and sobbings, groanings and cryings as the tree died above them, the roots sweating with its death. Branches crashing and cracking all about. Time stretched from desperate minutes into aching hours, and then on into an unseen dawn and another day.

Occasionally they heard thumps and crashings above them, or the tunnels vibrate from some far-off branchfall. But gradually thick silence fell, the only sense of the fire left to them being its smell, which filtered even into their sealed tunnels. The air in the tunnels grew heavy and warm with their confined presence, and fetid, too, though they could not tell it. They sweated and sighed, crouching in silence together, Bracken's flank to Rebecca's, and Rebecca's paw just touching Comfrey.

But at least they found a little food—some worms and grubs that had made their way to the tree's roots. At last the air became so unpleasant that they all wanted to move, and they were encouraged by the arrival of silence.

"Right," said Bracken, breaking the silence, "we're going to try to get out."

They broke through one seal and then, very slowly, poked a way through the other. The air beyond smelled of smoke but it was clear, and they passed without hesitation into it to find their way back to the surface.

"Rebecca!" said Comfrey as they ran down the tunnel.

"What is it, my sweet?" said Rebecca, her voice warm and healthy again.

"There's no smell of plague in the tunnel!" And it was true—the dead moles were still there but somehow they were dry and did not seem ever to have been moles.

"There's no fleas, either," said Bracken in wonder.

It was true—the smoke and heat from the fire had cleared the tunnels of plague.

The entrance they had come in by had gone beyond recognition, for a great branch had shattered through the dry soil and the tunnel was open to the air, its roof torn and black, warm ash and occasional swirlings of smoke playing where the roof had been.

Then they were out, onto what had once been the surface, but now laid black and waste, with not a hint of green in sight; just blackened roots of trees that had become no more than huge black thorns pointing ruggedly to the bare sky.

The surface felt exposed, as it did over on the pastures, and its air was heavy with the passage of the fire. They passed over the ashes of their wood, their black coats making them seem no more than shadows against its dark gray wastes. Where fire still smoldered at a root or branch, the smoke was swirled this way and that by a wind that seemed unable to make up its mind which way to blow. And the air hung heavier and heavier while the sky grew darker and more overcast. Ahead of them there was still an occasional crackle of fire, but it was sporadic and non-threatening and anyway, they could go no way other than up the slopes, for behind them their devastated wood stretched black and defeated, dead of all life.

The fire had stopped by the top of the slopes, turned back by the wider spacing of the trees and the lack of undergrowth. It had smoldered its way up among the first one or two of the beeches but could not get hold of the carpet of beech leaves or make headway against the massive bare trunks of the beech. One or two were charred, a few more blackened by soot, but none took the fire and it had stopped. It guttered and crackled still, but they were able to pick a way through it without trouble.

Rebecca let out a cry of sheer delight when they were able to get their paws on unburned leaf litter once more, and Bracken's pace quickened. His mind was a whirl of thoughts and feelings as tiredness mixed with relief, sadness with delight, excitement with apprehension. They headed straight for the Stone, the air about them faintly hazy from the smoke that drifted up from the wood.

Then they were there, the clearing ahead, the Stone looming up into the haze and then the Stone clear before them—and at its foot in a motley cluster of moles of all shapes and sizes, the moles who had survived the fire and, before it, the plague.

And Boswell was there. Their Boswell, greeting them with a touch and smile as a gasp of wonder greeted their arrival and they were surrounded by the moles, some of whom knew Rebecca, while others recognized Bracken and welcomed their leader back.

What mole can remember the laughter and blessings that were spoken then among the moles who had survived so much? What mole ever remembers such moments, when the past and the future are gone in the delight of life rediscovered and reclaimed? Each had a story to tell, each had struggled through surroundings of death. Not one mole there but Boswell failed to tell a story of how he or she had nearly died a dozen times. Only Boswell stayed silent, for he had come to the Stone before the fire even started, and prayed in its shadow asking that the plague might go and knowing that however his prayer was answered, it would not be in a way he could predict or understand. Fire was not part of his prayer, but a prayer answered is a grace, for it takes a mole beyond himself and his present life and starts him on his way again.

Boswell's prayer had been answered for good or bad— and who was he to question the Stone? The results now clustered about him. And he was their silent center. As he watched them, he began to understand better than any scribemole before him what the Seventh Book must be about, and why the color of its light was no color at all, but white. The color of silence. In the exultant activity of survival around the Stone, Boswell understood at last the name of the book he had sought so long. It was the Book of Silence, but where he would find it he could not guess.

Bracken, Rebecca and Comfrey were not the last moles to arrive. Some fifteen more came finally from off the pastures where they had crept as high as they could to escape the plague and then waited while the smoke and fire came up through Duncton Wood.

Their own system had been decimated by plague, and they brought the news that Stonecrop had died of it, and all the pasture elders. And somemole said that little Violet had died of it as well. So many gone! They were all gone but these few. Leaderless and lost.

As evening fell, the moles about the Stone began to fall silent and restless as one by one they whispered among themselves "What shall we do now? Where can we go?"

Bracken heard them, and though he was still their leader, he asked himself what good he had done any of them.

"What shall we do?" they began to ask it of him directly, waiting for him to tell them, to show them a way of living beyond the devastation that had overtaken them all. He heard them, but had no wish to lead anymole anywhere ever again. A mole had best lead himself. He turned to Rebecca and called her name.

She came to him silently, as if she knew what he was thinking, and together they moved away from the other moles to the west side of the clearing. Above them the trees stirred softly with a cool breeze and the air felt fresher than it had for months. The skies were still dark and the fraught color in it had gone, so that it looked gray with moisture.

"This is where you were crouching when I first met you, here," she said softly to him. "So long ago now."

He stared again out through the wood toward the west, as he had then. He could feel Uffington's pull as he always had and he turned to her and said "That's where Uffington lies. Rebecca . . . ," but he couldn't finish his sentence or even whatever thought lay behind it, for as he looked at her, and she at him, they knew that they were at one again and that she was part of him and now always would be. But . . . but . . . , and he stared out through the trees toward Uffington, through trees that shimmered and shook in his tears. He had fought through so much, as she had, but whenever they reached a point together again there was always something pulling. Uffington! Still looking out toward it, he reached out a paw and found hers, not daring to say what he would have liked to say. And anyway, there was no need, for she knew—she could tell.

"Rebecca?"

He had promised the Stone that he would go to Uffington if she survived, and she had. He had made a bargain with himself. They were at one with each other and yet a promise to the Stone that had brought them together now stood between them. He wished he understood better, and it wasn't so confused and that he could be at peace with the Stone. Perhaps the answer lay in Uffington, but he wished he could be certain.

"Rebecca," he said quietly. "I'm going to Uffington."

"I know, my dear," she whispered, her eyes fixed on the west whose sky was lighter for the dark angry clouds that now loomed around and above it.

He turned abruptly toward the Stone, and Boswell came toward him. "They want you to tell them what to do," he said.

"That's something no mole can do," he said softly, "and certainly not me. And anyway, I must leave Duncton."

"Where will you go?" asked Boswell, though he knew the answer and was smiling before Bracken gave it.

"Uffington," said Bracken. "And you're coming, Boswell."

"Yes," said Boswell. "Yes, that's right."

Bracken went to the moles by the Stone and looked gently at them. "There is only one place for you to go now that the wood is destroyed, and the pastures are plague-ridden." He waved his paw toward the beech trees behind the Stone. "A long time ago, for reasons we can never know, the moles who lived in the Ancient System left it. Many must have gone down the slopes and created a new system there, whose tunnels have been the inheritance of many of you. Some, perhaps only a few, must have left altogether, perhaps traveling on the long journey to Uffington, to give thanks for deliverance and to pay homage to the Stone. But they left an inheritance, and it is one that each of you may now accept if you wish it; the ancient tunnels which they left behind. They are yours to make of what you can. They lack only life, and the laughter and dance and cries of the young. I will show you them and leave you there, for I must go to distant Uffington." There was a groan among the moles, and a shaking of heads.

"I will give thanks that each of us has lived. But I will leave behind much of my spirit, which has dwelt already in the ancient tunnels where you will make a place of love; and I will leave behind Rebecca, who was

taught by Rose the Healer. Guard her well, for she is
your healer. Cherish her, as she will cherish you. And
trust the Stone as, slowly, I have come to do."

When Bracken had shown the moles the way into the
Ancient System and left them to discover the tunnels for
themselves and create a system born of the union of
Duncton and pasture moles, he returned with Boswell
and Rebecca to the Stone clearing.

Night was coming on fast, and the air was pleasantly
cool. Approaching them from the west was a front of
rain—rain that would end the drought, the first rain of
September.

It was a good time to go and they said very little.
What need three moles who love each other say when
they part?

"Take care, my love," whispered Rebecca. "Come
back to me." They touched and caressed and nuzzled,
and Boswell, too, felt the warmth of Rebecca's great love.

"I'll look after him," Boswell whispered to her, limping slowly out of the clearing after Bracken as they started
on their journey.

"I know you will," said Rebecca, thinking that she
could wish for no other mole than Boswell, however
great or strong, to protect her Bracken from the dangers
and trials that faced him.

Then they were gone into the night, toward Uffington,
their paws scuffling through dry leaves, leaving Rebecca
to crouch by the Stone as the first drops of rain began to
fall through the swaying beech leaves above and down
into the dry and blackened soil of the system below the
slopes, which had once been theirs. And then September
rain at last fell whose sound drowned out the final rustles
of Bracken and Boswell as they left Duncton Wood for
the dangerous world beyond.

IV

SIABOD

❧ 36 ❧

THE following March Bracken and Boswell finally came within a day's journey of the Blowing Stone, which stood at the foot of Uffington Hill, and more than six long moleyears had passed. They had faced every kind of physical danger moles can face—river, ice, owls and weasels, and marsh—and worse, had seen that system after system had been devastated by the plague. In many only a few solitary moles survived, turned half mad by the mystery of why they had not died or showing such a fear of strangers that Bracken and Boswell might have been the plague incarnate.

More than once their path crossed that of other wanderers, some looking for moles whom they could not believe were dead, while others were thin and unkempt and ate little, telling of the curse that had fallen on the world and the punishment that still waited each one of them.

These encounters, and the strain of the journey itself, had changed Bracken. His face fur was now lined and he had matured; at the same time he had filled out and become more powerful-looking so that he had something of the solid strength of his father Burrhead, though none of the heaviness. He was not aware of it himself (though Boswell was) but he was now a formidable mole to face, for his four paws were firmly on the ground and his gaze was often clear and direct, as from a settled heart. But recently there had come a weariness of spirit over him especially with the beginning of spring, which only Rebecca would have lifted from him. Days went by when he would talk little, and Boswell understood from the way he looked around and ahead at each turn in their journey that he was searching for the love they had made together.

Boswell had changed, too, though not physically. He was still thin and jerky in movement, his eyes darting this way and that with the great curiosity about life that

449

he had; his coat, shot through with gray as it was, was now fuller and more glossy than when Bracken had first met him in the drainage channel.

But the biggest change was in his spirit, which became ever more simple and laughing, so that a mole who didn't know him might almost have taken him for a fool. He saw laughter in the simplest things, and often when they were in difficulties it was his good humor that took the frown from Bracken's face. And often, too, Bracken's own laughter would never have started had not Boswell been there to show that a heart may be light even when circumstances are grim.

At last, on a gray March morning after days in which the pull of Uffington had become stronger and stronger, they came within sight of the Blowing Stone. Or rather within sound, for the day was windy and the first signal they had that they had reached Uffington were the low moans of the wind in the crevices and holes of the Stone, all of which carried in vibrating waves down into the vale up which they were traveling.

"Listen! *That's* the Blowing Stone," said Boswell.

"So we're almost there!" said Bracken, unable to believe that their long journey was nearly over.

Their pace quickened and soon the wind carried to them a scent Bracken had almost forgotten—beech trees. They were nearly on chalk again. Soon they came to a clump of beech and as they passed among it, the familiar roots, firm and powerful in the ground, the dry smell of chalk and beech leaf litter brought back to Bracken a memory of Duncton Hill, of the Ancient System and, most of all, of Rebecca. She was suddenly full in his heart again as, passing beyond the last of the beech trees, they came to the great Blowing Stone itself and crouched down thankfully in its presence.

It stood at the edge of a field, overshadowing a hedge that grew near it and had been weathered by wind and rain and sometimes ice into a thousand scoops and hollows, with holes in its upper parts which the moles could not see but which were the source of its moaning and hooting in the wind. It was split vertically along its natural cleavage as well, so that from some points it looked more like three stones than one.

Looming over it was the steep escarpment of Uffington Hill itself, which rose in sheer shadows of nearly vertical, tussocky grass, many hundreds of molefeet high. A mole's gaze had to tilt higher and higher, and still higher, before he saw the shadows end at the distant top of the hill and the white-gray March sky beyond.

"Over to the west, beyond the top of the hillface, that's where the Holy Burrows lie," said Boswell. "It takes half a day for most moles to climb it—a bit longer for me."

The day was drawing in, gray and cold, and they decided to stay where they were until full light before climbing the hill, eager though both of them were to get to the top. But they were tired and thankful for food and a temporary burrow near the Blowing Stone, falling asleep to the soft vibrations and moans of the Stone.

Because the escarpment faced north, dawn was a long time coming, and even when it came it seemed gloomy and wan. The wind had died and the March grass through which they started their climb was lank and dreary. But it soon became shorter and more wiry and their hearts began to fill with excitement as, step by step, they climbed up toward the goal they had aimed at for so long. At first, Bracken took the lead, but in his eagerness to get to the top, he so outpaced the limping Boswell that finally he stopped and let Boswell set the pace, and it seemed right that Boswell should take the lead.

The hillface grew steeper and steeper and their pace slower, and Bracken began to have the feeling that behind him there was nothing but clear air and a tumbling fall to somewhere far below. At the same time they felt the wind behind them, a wind that blew on even the calmest of days up the scarp face, flattening the grass upward and on toward the top.

Higher and higher they climbed until each step was accompanied by a pant and they could think of nothing but finding a talonhold in the next patch of rough grass ahead and summoning the strength to push themselves and pull themselves yet higher. The grass was tough, more like a set of long pine needles than the soft pasture and meadow grass of the valleys they had grown used to, and was a buff-yellow or brown rather than green, scorched in summer by sun and in winter by wind.

They stopped several times for a rest before Boswell said—or rather breathed: "Halfway. A good way to go yet."

Bracken looked above him and the scarp face still looked as massive as when they had first started. They

felt exposed, for the grass was now quite short and the
sky loomed hugely all around them, while the soil, which
showed through the grass in places, was dry and stony
with flakes of chalk and flint—not easy to burrow into
quickly if a kestrel happened along.

They pressed on, the wind coming stronger and colder
behind them all the time, blowing across their fur and
driving it forward like the grass beneath them. On they
went, the wind so battering them from behind that in the
final stretch it almost blew them up the hill and they
had to lean back a little into it to keep their balance.

Then the grass changed to a short, green pasture grass,
and the slope suddenly slackened to a final rolling stretch.
Fifteen moleyards, ten, five, and then, as simple as you
please, they were there together, on top of Uffington Hill,
at the end of their journey.

Bracken turned round, snouted into the shrill wind,
and looked out onto a sea of sky, massive above and
ahead of him and below, the hazy distance of fields and
grasslands, meadows and valley, trees, rivers and farm-
land. The wind was so strong that it took Bracken's
breath away and made his eyes water, and so noisy that
talking was impossible so that Boswell had to cuff him
lightly to draw his attention as he indicated that they
should retreat a little from the crest of the slope. They
did so, and within a matter of ten moleyards the wind
dropped to almost nothing and they could see and hear
and think again. Boswell turned away from the slope and
waved a paw to the west. "Uffington!" he said, excitement and apprehension in his voice. "By the Stone's
grace, and with its strength, I am back. May the stone
have preserved the moles I left behind."

Beyond him the clear grass swept into a tussocky distance. In the foreground it seemed as flat as the slope
had been steep, though over a distance it undulated
gently, soft, delicate curves that changed subtly whichever way a mole turned and never seemed to stay the
same.

"Well, come on then," said Boswell, winding his way
among old molehills flattened by wind and rain in which
flakes and chips of flint were mixed with the light soil,
until he came to a hill of fresh earth. Burrowing into it,
he led Bracken into the Holy Burrows at last.

The tunnels leading to the Holy Burrows were worn
smooth with age and venerable use. Generations on gen-

erations of scribemoles had trodden their way through the tunnels so that some of the protruding flints were rounded and shiny from the rubbing of flank fur, while the chalky floor was packed hard and shiny in places as well, so that near some of the entrances, the light coming in made the tunnel floor look like dimly lit ice.

"We're nearly there now," said Boswell, "though there aren't many moles about."

"I haven't seen *any*. Not a single one. But I can scent them all right. Uffington must have been affected by the plague like every other system," said Bracken brutally. "Better face the fact, Boswell."

"Well, well," said Boswell, "we'll soon know."

Boswell led them on down a tunnel whose size was equal to the biggest in the Ancient System but whose sculpting was more aged—very like the simple rounds and squares of the tunnel beyond the Chamber of Roots which led to the buried part of the Stone. It sloped steadily downhill for a while before leveling off, and Bracken sensed that they had entered a deeper and somehow more sacred part of the system. It was a place to move slowly in, and with grace, and one where, if a mole spoke at all, he did so in a low voice that did not disturb the peace.

"We are very near the libraries," said Boswell softly. "This is a holy place, Bracken, and it is best that you do not say anything to anymole we may meet. I do not think a mole who is not a scribemole has ever been here before, but nor do I remember anything in the writings or rules that is against it. But stay silent, move gently, and let me talk."

The tunnel entered a round chamber that was the confluence of three other major tunnels as well as two much smaller ones.

"That one leads to the Holy Burrows themselves," said Boswell, pointing to one that Bracken estimated ran westward, "while this one leads to the libraries." He led the way down it slowly. As Bracken followed him out of the chamber and into the tunnel, he could have sworn he saw a mole watching them from where, seconds before, there had been no mole, in the entrance to the tunnel to the Holy Burrows. He thought he saw him clearly, an old mole with a long-lean face and thin fur, but when he really looked, he wasn't there! Strange! Bracken looked around him, feeling that in this place time did not mean quite what it meant in other systems. But he had seen a mole! He hastened after Boswell, anxious to keep him in sight.

The tunnel steepened suddenly, going down deeper and deeper, until it was cast into semisolid chalk in which fissures and stratum lines were visible. The air was heavy with the slow echoes of their movement but there was no windsound now at all. The tunnel leveled off again, ran to an entrance, and then they were through it and into an enormous chamber whose end was too far off to see. It was too complex and confusing a place to take in all at once, and it was some moments before Bracken could even make out its main features.

It was not a simple oval or square but rather appeared to be a series of interconnected chambers with entrances between them big enough to allow a mole to see into the next chamber. There were arches and corners in the chamber, parts darker than others, and set into each of the many walls were surfaces on which were stacked what looked like pieces of bark and sometimes flakes of hard chalk. Above these surfaces were embossments like those in the Chamber of Dark Sound. There were stacks of bark on the floor as well, or piled against walls and, as far as Bracken was able to see into the linked chambers, there were more pieces of bark piled untidily there.

"Books," whispered Boswell. "This is the main library."

He was about to say more, and might have taken one of them down to show Bracken, when he was stopped short by a stirring at the far end of the chamber and a movement as what seemed a shadow changed into what looked like an ancient and gray-furred mole who was in the middle of a long yawn.

"Well! I don't know, I'm sure," the ancient mole muttered to himself, oblivious of their presence at the other end of the chamber. "I don't know. If I didn't put it where I should have, which is more than likely, then surely I would have put it here, which it seems I didn't. How they expect me to do all this by myself I really don't know. Come on, my beauty, where are you?" he said, snouting back and forth among some of the books and evidently hoping that one of them, which he had obviously lost, would pop out of its own accord and announce its hiding place.

Boswell signaled to Bracken to move back into the shadows and not say anything as he advanced slowly on the ancient mole. He got nearer and nearer, but the mole did not seem to notice, muttering to himself and peering impatiently here and there among the books, turning over one or two half-heartedly and leaving them where they fell. Eventually Boswell made a discreet scratching noise to announce himself.

"Yes, yes," said the old mole, "I'm coming. Can't do everything, you know. Anyway, is it *that* important?"

He darted forward to an enormous book and started to pull it down, but its weight was too much for him to take it bodily off the surface. But it slid off onto him all the same and his tottering old paws struggled to keep it under control. Boswell stepped forward and relieved him of the book.

"There we are!" said Boswell. The old mole looked at him at last, peering at him with a frown. "I know you," he said.

"Boswell," said Boswell.

"Mmm, something like that," said the old mole.

Boswell stepped back a little and hesitated for a moment before saying "Is it Quire? Are you Quire?"

"Yes, yes," said Quire. "Now what's *this?*" he muttered, peering at the book and then running his paw across its surface. He growled and grunted to himself and then stepped back, saying "Here, you tell me. I'm losing my feel. Can't even read any more. There was a time when I knew every book in the place by position alone, but since they changed it all round and then the plague came, it's all gone to wrack and ruin. I can't keep it up all by myself."

Bracken watched as Boswell examined the book. First he snouted rapidly over its surface. Then, for the first time ever in Bracken's presence, he used his withered left paw positively. He swung it onto the book and, with a gentle caressing motion beautiful to see, ran the paw across the embossments on the book's surface.

"It's the Avebury Hymnal, with an appendix of carols and lays," said Boswell.

"No, that's not the one. What I want is the Book of the Chosen Moles. You know . . ."

"Linden?"

"Do you know where it is?" asked the old mole eagerly.

"I know what it feels like," said Boswell, "at least I

think I can remember." He snouted rapidly along the
rows of books, muttering and twittering to himself, touching one book after another, half pulling out one or two,
shaking his head, umming and ahhing and, it seemed to
Bracken who had listened to their conversation without
understanding a word of it, having the time of his life.

"Got it," he announced finally, pulling another enormous book off the shelves. He ran his paw over it. "Linden's Book of Chosen Moles, with additions by sundry
paws," he read out.

"Not before time," said Quire ungratefully.

"Sorry," said Boswell.

"You youngsters are all the same. Think you know it
all. You wait till you're as old as me and you'll find you
know nothing at all." He peered at Boswell again. "Where
was it?" he asked.

"Where it always used to be."

"Damnation!" said Quire, almost lifting himself off
his paws with the violence of the word. "I can't get used
to the new system—always put books back in the wrong
place now. I know *you*, don't I? How did *you* survive the
plague?"

"I wasn't here," said Boswell. "I've been away."

"Oh, yes!" said Quire, seeming to remember but making
it obvious that he didn't. "Mmm. Which system?"

"Duncton."

"One of the Seven! Did you get there?"

"Yes," said Boswell, "I did."

"Good. Glad to have you back, especially since most of
the scribemoles here went away during the plague or suc-
cumbed to it, and there's hardly any left who know enough
about the library to be much use to me. I remember you.
Boswell, isn't it? Should have told me before. Crippled
but useful, as I remember. Where have you been?"

"Duncton," repeated Boswell patiently.

"Good. Glad to have you back," repeated Quire.
"They're in a bit of a flummox at the moment because
there's hardly enough moles to sing the song and even
though I offered my services to Skeat, he told me I was
not chosen. So anyway, you can help me here . . ."

He seemed about to dragoon Boswell into work when
three moles entered the chamber from one of the side
chambers.

They snouted about, saw Boswell, and there was a moment of absolute stillness as everymole looked at each other. It was Boswell who broke the silence.

"May the grace of the Stone be with you," he said. They relaxed a little.

"And with thee," said one of the three.

They continued to look at each other.

"I do not know you," said Boswell quietly, his voice echoing among the books, "but my name is Boswell. I have returned from a journey to Duncton Wood."

One of the moles darted forward and snouted at him, turned round, signaled to one of the others, who ran out of the entrance near where Bracken was crouched in the shadows. Soon several more moles joined them, none seeming to notice Bracken, who kept quite still as Boswell had told him.

As Boswell crouched there, the moles about him began a curious chanting, nearer speech than song, which was deep and rhythmic and to which Boswell occasionally responded. Bracken could not catch most of the words, which were in a language strange to him, but Boswell's response seemed to be "And with thee, and with thee . . . ," the same as one of the moles had spoken to him. He only recognized the word *thee* because he had heard Boswell speak it occasionally to very old moles they had met.

The moles were all shapes and sizes, and Bracken was disappointed to see that not one of them was white. Many were gray, and some just common or garden black, like him. But he had to admit that they did have an air of authority—a strange, quiet way of carrying themselves— that fitted well with the reverential air in the place and made him reluctant even to think of speaking or making a noise. He felt as if just being there was distrubing something precious and holy.

It was strange and exciting for him to see Boswell in this setting, for he saw how well he fitted here and, as it seemed to him, what enormous peace and authority emanated from Boswell. Bracken might not be able to tell what was being said, but he could sense that no mole there was going to attack Boswell and that was all he was really worried about. When the others had first come, he had been ready to leap forward and defend Boswell to the death.

Without warning, the chanting suddenly stopped and all the moles seemed to relax. Especially Quire, who had been fretting about behind Boswell and now said to one of the moles, "I've got it, here it is, the book *he* wants."

But before there was time to reply, there was a stir and a sound from one of the side chambers. Two older-looking moles came forward, both with calm, severe expressions on their faces, and their look about the library brought an immediate hush to all the moles there. They stepped to either side of the chamber entrance and a mole came forward in whose presence Bracken felt an immediate awe. He wanted to lower his snout in a gesture of submission and, indeed, he did so, but he could not help keeping his eyes open at the extraordinary scene before him.

The mole was old and thin, with a frail, silver-gray coat of fur that was patchy in places and the most kindly eyes that Bracken had ever seen. Bracken had seen him before, or thought he had: he was the mole who had seemed to be at the entrance to the Holy Burrows watching them as they entered the libraries. As he entered the chamber, the other moles cleared a path between him and Boswell, and Boswell, snout low, stepped forward a few paces toward him. And then they had a chanting exchange in the language Bracken could not understand.

"Steyn rix in thine herte," said Boswell.

"Staye thee hol and soint," said the Holy Mole.

"Me desire wot I none," replied Boswell.

"Blessed be thou and ful of blisse," finished the Holy Mole. A blessing, thought Bracken. That's what it was!

Then the Holy Mole smiled and Boswell stepped forward, and for a moment they nuzzled each other.

"Well, Boswell, so you have returned. By the Stone's grace you have come back!"

Boswell seemed unable to say anything, but looked at the Holy Mole almost with disbelief in his eyes.

"Yes," said the Holy Mole, "it really is Skeat, your old master. Look what they've done to me!" He laughed, a delightful laugh, very like the one that Boswell, in his moments of puppish delight in something, sometimes let forth.

"Well, well . . . I said the journey blessing when you left and here you are, so many moleyears later, to prove that a mole may trust its power. Have you nothing to say to your Skeat? Those few of us left who remember you are going to want to hear your story very much; and those others here, whom you will not know, will surely profit by it."

"Skeat, I . . ." As he said this, there was a slight gasp among the other moles and Skeat raised his paw, smiling.

"You're meant to call me Holiness, but . . . these are strange times and anyway, if I'm not mistaken, you were relieved of your vows." Then Skeat spoke to all of them rather than to Boswell, and said "Remember he has not been here for many moleyears—perhaps more than twenty, and has forgotten our ways. But then it is not our ways or rituals that express the truth in the Stone but what is in our hearts. The Stone has sent Boswell back to us, for what purpose none can tell, though I have my own ideas. But the Stone will not mind if he calls me Skeat, or any other name for that matter."

Turning to Boswell he said, "However, bringing a mole who is not a scribe into the Holy Burrows is just a trifle daring, even for you, Boswell. Who is he?" With that, Skeat turned slowly to where Bracken crouched in the shadows, thinking no mole knew he was there.

If a yawning crevice could have opened up and swallowed him there and then, or if the rows of books could have all collapsed on him, hiding him from view, Bracken would not have minded in the least. Fifty marauding moles, twenty weasels, ten owls . . . anything but the sudden exposure to the gaze of all those scribemoles.

He stepped forward reluctantly, out of the darkness by the tunnel entrance, hardly daring to breathe and, not knowing what else to do, he kept his snout low and waited.

"His name is Bracken," said Boswell, "and without his help I would not be here now and nor would there be anything to report of my quest for the Seventh Book." At this there was a sudden excited buzz of whispers among the moles. The Seventh Book! So Boswell was one of those who had gone in search for it so long ago, thought the new scribemoles who were wondering what this was all about. They gazed on Bracken with awe.

"He has also come to give thanks to the Stone for a mole who survived the plague. I have reason to give thanks to her myself, as many moles have."

Skeat stepped forward toward Bracken, going up to him and touching him gently on his right shoulder, just where another mole had touched him once, long, long

before, after they had met by the Stone. The feeling he
had then was the same as he had now, and he looked up
into Skeat's eyes as if no other mole existed. He was
close to tears.

"What is the mole's name?" asked Skeat gently, so
quietly that it was almost like a private conversation.

"Rebecca," whispered Bracken.

"May the Stone protect her and bless her with strength.
May you both have strength for the trials to come."

No other mole heard him say this blessing, not even
Boswell, and Skeat himself was surprised to find himself
saying it. But there was something about this mole Boswell had brought to Uffington that made him see again
something that he had often thought, though most
scribemoles and even masters forgot it: the Stone very
often works through moles who are far from Uffington's
peace and prayer, who may themselves never understand
the Stone or, indeed, may not even trust it. Such moles
may show a courage far greater than many a scribemole
shows in their pursuit of truth and their fulfillment of
the task the Stone has set. Their pain and suffering may
be as deeply felt and as spiritual as a scribemole's, or
one who worshipped the Stone. Skeat sensed that Bracken
was just such a mole.

Skeat turned back to Boswell and said "And what of
your quest for the Seventh Book? Did you succeed . . .?"
His question tailed off into nothing and an excited hush
fell over the scribemoles who were listening.

"I have not found the Seventh Book," said Boswell, a
ripple of disappointment running round the moles in the
library, "but Bracken of Duncton"—they all looked at
Bracken—"has, I believe, seen the Seventh Stillstone.
He knows where it is and has shown me."

There was absolute silence in the library.

"It is in a sacred place, a protected place, and one into
which no mole may simply go. Only a mole or moles
graced by the Stone, as Bracken was graced, may go there
and perhaps no mole in our lifetime will ever be able to
enter there again."

"A strange beginning, Boswell, and a story which,
when you both have rested and eaten, you had better
tell me of in full. There is much, too, for you to hear,
and if you are as you once were, you will ask me a dozen

questions for every one I answer! But not until you have eaten and rested."

With that Skeat raised one paw briefly to them all and said "In worde, werke, will and thought, make us meke and lowe in hert. And us to love as we shulde do."

As Skeat left, Bracken noticed that one of the two moles who had come in with him took the book Quire had been searching for and carried it off after the Holy Mole.

Then, thinking that if he wasn't "low in heart" he was certainly low in strength, Bracken willingly followed one of the scribemoles as he led them away to two simple burrows in the chalk soil where they found food was provided, and they were left to eat and sleep. Bracken found it hard to fall asleep for thinking about the strangeness of the Holy Burrows, and finally got up to go and have a chat with Boswell. But he found him fast asleep, head and snout curled onto his crippled paw as they always did when he was sleeping peacefully. Bracken did not disturb him but returned to his own burrow. It was only the memory of the private blessing Skeat had given to Rebecca and himself, and the consecration he felt that it imposed upon their love, that finally brought him the peace he needed before he, too, fell into a deep sleep.

In the course of their subsequent conversations with Skeat, which were held over a period of many weeks in a simple chamber along the tunnel that led to the Holy Burrows, with just one other mole in attendance, Bracken and Boswell were to learn much more about how the plague had ravaged the systems in general.

It had started in the north and traveled steadily southward, killing about nine out of ten moles who came into contact with it. It was regarded by the scribemoles as a judgment on moles by the Stone and, to their credit, a judgment on themselves as well when it struck Uffington, killing as many there as elsewhere.

Skeat had been the only master to survive and had accordingly, by the tradition of precedence, been elected Holy Mole—a task he had desired or expected and one he accepted with reluctance. One reason for this was that he sensed, as others in many different systems had, that the time in which they lived was one of great change and destiny. They needed a Holy Mole of greater wis-

dom and experience than he, and one who had seen into
the silence of the Stone far more deeply than he felt he
had.

But with such thoughts, genuinely modest as they were,
he did himself an injustice: Uffington, and through its
example all systems, needed in that troubled time a
leader who was strong enough to impose the unity and
trust the conditions of devastation demanded, while wise
enough to dispense with the rigid and sometimes inflexible rituals of the past.

It seemed that many of the plague survivors had felt,
as Bracken had, that they should visit Uffington to express their thanks to the Stone. Most had been unable or
unwilling to do this in person, preferring to visit the
nearest Stone, from where their prayers of thanksgiving
came to Uffington. That many such visits had been made
was known, because some scribemoles had, like Boswell,
survived and made their way back to Uffington, while a
very few nonscribes had come as well. Bracken was one,
but there had been others.

"We have had a visit from a mole who knows you
both and has spoken well of you: Medlar, from the
north."

So he had got here, after all! The news excited Bracken,
who was now a little less awed than he had been at first
in Skeat's presence and who, since Boswell wasn't going to
ask, boldly asked the question himself.

"Where is he?"

"It will not be possible to see him," said Skeat with a
certain finality to his voice. "May the Steyn rix in hys
herte," he added, words that seemed to have a special
significance for Boswell, who started a little at it and muttered a blessing under his breath. It was this that warned
Bracken from asking outright where Medlar was, and
this too that gave him the uncomfortable feeling that
there was a lot about the Holy Burrows that he did not
understand, and never would.

"With your visit we have now heard from all six of
the seven major systems—Duncton, Avebury, Uffington,
of course; Stonehenge, Castlerigg and Rollright," said
Skeat.

"What's the last one which you haven't heard from?"
asked Bracken.

"It's the great system of Siabod in North Wales. No

mole has come to Uffington who knows what has happened to it in the plague. Perhaps no mole survived, but I think that is unlikely . . . the Siabod moles are famous, or notorious, for their toughness. Of all the seven systems theirs is the least accessible and the most difficult to live in."

Bracken listened fascinated, for Siabod was Mandrake's old system, the one where they spoke a different language, even today.

"Is there a Stone there?" he asked, hoping to find out something more.

"Now *that* is something we would very much like to know! The records have no account of a Stone on the Siabod system itself, but there is a constant reference to a Stone or stones at a place nearby mysteriously called Castell y Gwynt, and there is a single reference in the records of Linden, referring to the travels of Ballagan to the 'Stones of Tryfan' which we think is a group of the Stones in this other place. Perhaps bigger than the rest."

"Why's it so important?" asked Bracken, his mind racing with these mysteries and strange names.

"Because while other systems come and go, the seven great systems have always been occupied and lived in. Some, like Duncton, have been cut off for long periods, but moles there have always finally come forward who have maintained the traditions laid down by Ballagan himself, as you yourselves have now. We do not know— we have never really known—if the moles of Siabod worship at whatever Stone it is that stands at Castell y Gwynt. Their language is different and no scribemole that I know has ever bothered to learn it."

"Does it matter?" asked Bracken, rather regretting the question when he saw the look of patient tolerance that flickered over Skeat's face for a moment.

"I think so, Bracken. We live in a time of trial and trouble. Worship of the Stone is really at the center of all moles' lives, although it has been forgotten by so many. But we in Uffington are to blame for that. There was a time when scribemoles visited each of the systems at least once in a generation and the seven main systems more regularly than that. And from those seven the strength would go out to the others. It is now no longer possible to visit Siabod. We have too few scribemoles even to service Uffington itself, but if we knew that the

Stone was at least honored in all of the seven systems,
that would be a start. And we do—for six of them. For
these have been visited and by the Stone's grace even
Duncton, so long cut off, has made itself felt again. But
Siabod . . . we know nothing of it. Siabod has always been
an exception. It requires a mole of exceptional fortitude
of spirit and body to reach it, let alone return from it."

Skeat was silent for a while before starting to talk
quietly again, almost as if thinking aloud. "The systems,
the worship of the Stone . . . it has all slipped into disarray. Now the plague. We have a chance to start again
—perhaps we already have, for your visit, like Medlar's
before you, fills me with hope. But what strength it
would give us in Uffington to know that all seven of the
major systems were centered on the Stone . . . to know
that Siabod, too, worships the Stone! You must both forgive an old mole his dreams. Perhaps this office makes a
mole overreach himself. Well, now, to other things."

He asked them a great many questions about Duncton,
a subject Bracken had not particularly enjoyed listening to
Boswell talk about in the library. There was something
special about his experience by the buried part of
the Stone with Rebecca that made him recoil instinctively
from having it talked about in public. However, Skeat
seemed to sense this and his manner was so gentle and
understanding that soon Bracken was describing what had
happened on two Longest Nights previously in a detail, and
with a passion that even Boswell had not heard.

Skeat wanted to know a great deal about the location
of the Stillstone after this—how accessible it was, what
the Chamber of Roots consisted of, whether any other
moles knew of it, and many things more—and his interest
and concern extended to the story of Bracken himself, and
Rebecca, Mandrake, Rune, Mekkins . . . they all played a
part in the story Bracken was induced to tell. And Skeat
was especially interested that Mandrake was said to be
from Siabod, and fell silent for a long time thinking about
it.

Then suddenly, it was over. Skeat had finished with his
questions and there seemed nothing more to say.

"Leave us now, Bracken, for I have to talk to Boswell
alone for a while . . ." and Bracken found himself
excluded, cut off from the mole with whom he had shared

everything for moleyears on end, and at a loose end in a system where the moles were strange and there were long silences, and great spaces, in which a mole like Bracken felt restless and uneasy. He was taken back to his burrow by a silent mole, who responded to all questions with a bland smile and a maddening shake of the head which might have been "yes" and might have been "no" but seemed most likely to be "perhaps." Yet when they arrived and the mole seemed about to leave, he hesitated and asked suddenly. "Did you really see the Seventh Stillstone?" And then, before Bracken could even begin to think what to say the mole added, "I'm sorry. I should not have asked such a thing."

But Bracken, a little fed up with all the secrecy, said boldly "Yes. I did!" and added with what he thought was obvious irony, "It was ten times as big as a mole and made a noise like a bumblebee." Bracken regretted this expression of irritability the moment he said it, for the mole scurried away as if he had been stung by a bee and no amount of calling after him would bring him back. With a sigh, Bracken returned to the burrow, laid himself down, and in no time at all was asleep. He had done more talking than he realized, and there is something about memories recalled in detail that makes a mole tired.

He was waked by Boswell saying "Bracken! Bracken! I'm sorry about all that. But it's not important . . ."

"What did he want to say to you?" asked Bracken, but immediately his voice died miserably in his mouth because he could see Boswell uncharacteristically stiffen and lower his snout, indicating that he didn't want to talk about it.

"I *can't* say, Bracken. You must try to understand that there are things here which are impossible to explain . . ."

"All I understand is that they've no use for what they call nonscribes around here," said Bracken angrily. "All this bloody way and there's secrets all around. What's this with Medlar, for example? Why can't he be seen?"

Boswell lowered his gaze to the floor, his normally peaceful face troubled with Bracken's feeling of being excluded, which, of course, he was being. Perhaps, though, what had happened to Medlar was something he could explain. Surely it would do no harm.

"Medlar has gone to a place which is to the west of Uffington Hill where the silent burrows are. It is not

far, perhaps two molemiles at most and it is connected to
Uffington by a tunnel."

"What happens there?" asked Bracken.

"Well, that's hard to explain. Nothing really. Nothing at
all. There are special burrows there in which certain moles,
only a very few, choose to live in and rarely leave. In fact,
the entrances are sealed up and they stay there in silence."

"What for?" asked Bracken, incredulous.

"Because they have reached a point where the only way
forward is sitting still. Do you remember what Medlar
used to say about the importance of doing that?"

"Is that what *he's* doing now, up there?"

Boswell nodded.

"But how does he stay alive?"

"Other moles bring him food. It is an honor to serve a
silent mole. At some time all novices take their turn in
serving them."

"What about fouling the burrow?" asked Bracken.

"They use two burrows. One of them is cleaned out by
the other moles. But, in fact, it is not a problem. After a
while, a silent mole eats less and less and the process
seems to purify him in a strange way."

"When do they come out?" Bracken wanted to know
next—he had never heard anything so extraordinary in
his life.

"No mole can say. Some can only bear it for a few
days, though that is very rare, for the preparation is careful. Medlar, for example, has been preparing for this for
many moleyears, probably without realizing it, although
his case is unusual since he comes from outside and is not
a scribemole in the normal way. Others, in fact most, stay
in the silent burrow for at least two moleyears, often very
much longer. Some choose never to emerge again and one
day, when no movement has been heard for a full moleyear, and when no food has been taken, the Holy Mole
orders that their burrow should be honorably sealed."

"But what do they *do?*"

"Pray. Meditate. Forget themselves. Learn something
of the glory of the Stone."

"What about the ones who come out?"

"What about them?"

"Well, what happens to them?"

"They continue to live ordinary lives. You have already
met one: Quire was in the silent burrow for ten mole-

years. But do not think his forgetfulness is as a result of that—he is very old now and, for all his bad temper, much honored."

"Do all scribemoles go there?"

Boswell laughed. He had never heard Bracken ask so many questions all at once.

"No, very few. It requires great strength and simplicity. Medlar is probably the only one there now, and I think it is significant that he is not a scribemole. As Skeat has said, we live in a strange time when traditions are changing. I do not know if a nonscribemole has ever been in the silent burrows before, but I do not see why they shouldn't. Getting close to the Stone is not a prerogative of the scribemoles only, as my journey to Duncton has shown me." He was referring to moles like Mekkins, Rebecca and Bracken himself who, in his opinion, had much to teach scribemoles. Hadn't he learned much himself from them, and had he not still so much to learn?

Boswell yawned, scratched himself, snouted this way and that and finally wandered off to his burrow to sleep. Bracken scouted around for some food and then returned to his own burrow to sleep, his mind full of images of moles in silent burrows. Uffington was a strange place, and he was not sure he liked it much. Well, he had done his bit and come here and thanked the Stone. The Holy—Skeat had blessed him, and Rebecca as well. His half-sleeping mind transmuted the image of silent burrows into one of the burrows he and Rebecca had found under the buried part of the Duncton Stone and he remembered them lying there together, touching and caressing, the light of the Stillstone all over the place, and he smiled, for nothing seemed more pleasant or comfortable. But then, as half-dreams often will, the image slid into something more fearful as he saw Rebecca in a silent burrow alone, waiting through the long moleyears, waiting and waiting, and he wanted to go to her *now* and take her protectively to him; as he wanted her now, in this strange place, where he was alone with Boswell. Tears wet his face fur, but the sudden pain of their separation was so strong in his mind that he did not notice them.

"Protect her," he whispered. "Protect her until I can return and protect her myself." And with this prayer to the Stone in his heart he fell asleep.

No mole is so strong or unfeeling that it does not suffer a time during a prolonged period of endurance when courage begins to fail and spirits sag.

Such a time came to Rebecca in March at about the time that, unknown to her, Bracken and Boswell arrived in Uffington. From the moment of Bracken's and Boswell's departure for Uffington, she had inspired the other dispirited Duncton and pasture moles into occupying the Ancient System with enthusiasm and determination. It was she who suggested that they should occupy the eastern half near the cliff, where the soil was a little more worm-full and the tunnels less immediately forbidding; it was she who stopped the pasture moles from occupying one section and the Duncton moles another, persuading them instead to mix and form a united group; it was Rebecca to whom the others came with their fears and doubts, hopes and ideas, and she who nudged one mole, twisted the paw of another, spent time with a third to ensure they lived in health and harmony.

For the other moles Rebecca was always available, always cheerful, always the one they could rely on, the one who made them see sense. And it was a task she took on willingly, for had not Rose taught her that a healer works in many different ways and will not even think about the fact that she puts herself last?

But in March, after the long moleyears of winter, her spirits were low and it became a terrible effort for her to appear, as she successfully did, ever cheerful and happy to deal with the other moles' problems. She had occupied the tunnels created by Bracken on the far side of the Stone near the pastures.

"A healer shouldn't live under the paws of other moles," Rose had once told her, "because she needs a space in which to find herself and the strength she needs to serve others." Rebecca not only followed this advice in choosing the location of her home burrow, but decided in March, when she felt so low, that it also meant she should spend rather more time alone occasionally. For a short period, at least.

This was, however, easier said than done, since as soon as moles suspect that a healer is no longer so available as she once was, they have the habit of finding a thousand excuses to go especially to see her. And how could Rebecca turn away a female who is worried that she won't litter or an older mole whose aches about the shoulders get unbearable when it tries to burrow? Or a mole who has damaged his paw right at the start of the mating season? So, day after day, always for one good reason or another, Rebecca found herself preoccupied with other moles when she should have been sitting quietly doing nothing. And she began to get more tired and more irritable; and as she did so, she felt more and more guilty about it—for wasn't she a healer and therefore must always be cheerful and good-natured?

But there were times when even with the best of wills she lapsed into distant and seeming coolness, and the mole who bore the brunt of this was Comfrey.

Comfrey had chosen to live away from the others down on the slopes, choosing a place on the very edge of where the fire had reached. His reason, he told Rebecca, was because there weren't enough herbs and flowers up among the "boring" beeches and he wanted to be near what remained of the wood to see if any of the plants had survived the fire.

He ranged far and wide in his pursuit of plants and almost every time he visited Rebecca, which he did when he returned from one of his trips, he would bring her something or other for her burrow. Even through the winter months he managed to find things: the red berries of cuckoo pint; gentle-scented fungi; and bright, shiny leaves of holly plants.

"Where do you find them?" she would ask.

He would shrug his shoulders and say he had been over beyond the eastside where the wood hadn't been touched by the fire. He often appeared when she was visiting in the Ancient System, with parts of plants he thought she might need and became regarded by many of the moles there with the same affectionate awe they held for Rebecca. Like Rebecca, he never seemed to expect thanks for what he did, regarding it more as something that just happened, like the weather.

Rebecca's occasional coldness to him in March upset him dreadfully. It happened in various ways, and always unexpectedly, as she slid away into a world of her own, no longer willing to make the effort to open herself to his stuttering and stumbling conversation.

"Hello, R—Rebecca!" he would say, putting a plant, or part of one, by her burrow entrance.

"That's nice," she would smile, her eyes drifting away from him and with none of the usual questions and laughter that he loved so much. Then silence, which would make him uneasy and he would stumble over himself trying to fill it. His thin face would crease with the effort of trying to find something to say which would lift the impersonal smile from her face, which he felt to be in some way his own fault.

"I've b—b—been a long way in the last few d—d—days," he might say.

"Have you?" Rebecca would respond dispassionately.

"Y—Yes, all the way d—down to the m—marsh."

Smiles. No questions. No encouragement.

"It was in—in—interesting," he might add weakly.

He would try for a bit longer, but was no good at it and when Rebecca was like that, his whole world seemed to grow dark and he wanted to escape.

Sometimes Rebecca would say she was sorry and it wasn't his fault. Other times she would let him go without saying a word, feeling a numbness within herself and unable to do anything but, eventually, weep. Or she would do busy things around her burrow, losing herself in rearranging it or cleaning out already-clean tunnels.

Sometimes he would stay quietly with her when she wept and hear the things she said, and could have said in the hearing of no other mole in Duncton, about how she had no strength to serve them all and how they came all the time and they needed her help and how she ought to have the strength to give it if she was to honor Rose's memory. She would weep and even scream sometimes. "Oh! Oh! Oh!" And he would listen to her, too slow in his speech to say anything, light only dawning in him very slowly that sometimes she needed a mole to run to, as he ran to her and the others did. It was then, too, that he wished there was a mole like Mekkins had been, whom she would rely on and lean against sometimes. He wished he was like that and not, as it seemed to him, so weak. Still, he could go to the Stone, which he did, and pray that perhaps the Stone would let Bracken come back so he could help Rebecca.

It was after one of these dispiriting times in March that Comfrey went to the Stone and crouched there, racking his brains about the way he could help. Several days later, Rebecca noticed that not a single mole had visited her, which was odd. She had never been left so blissfully and peacefully alone before. She began to worry about them and after fretting for a whole day, went down to see what was apaw.

The first mole she met, a female, looked surprised, even alarmed, saying "Oh! Rebecca!" and scampering away.

The second, a male well known for his habit of finding things wrong with himself when everything was all right really, because he needed Rebecca to tend to him once in a while, said a strange thing when he saw her. "Hullo, Rebecca! I'm just fine. Nothing troubling me at all . . . no, not a single thing!" he added with a merry, unnatural laugh.

She finally got the truth out of an old female who was genuinely unwell and whose distress she could sense before she even entered her burrow. It seemed that Comfrey had gone around the tunnels virtually ordering all moles to stay away from Rebecca "b–b–because she needs a rest." If any moles needed her desperately they must go to him on the slopes and he would do what he could for them without disturbing Rebecca. Which was an odd thing, because if there was one thing Comfrey didn't like, it was being disturbed in his own herb-laden burrow.

She went down to the slopes herself to see him and scolded him for what he had done—but very halfheartedly because, in truth, she could hardly remember anymole doing anything so kindly for her benefit and she loved him for the care he had taken and the love he had shown.

But her low spirits persisted as March progressed, increased rather than lifted by the exciting arrival of the first few litters in the ancient tunnels for many generations. Most of the females had mated and the first litters, although a little late, began to arrive toward the end of the month.

The excitement! The rushing! The chatter in the great old tunnels! The hurried, whispered thanks to the Stone! But at the end of the day, Rebecca, the loveliest mole in the system, the most beautiful, the one who so desired to cherish and nurture a litter of her own, remained mateless and litterless. The truth was that she might well have accepted one of the males in the system had they not all been so afraid of her, and in awe of her

healing power. But none dared step forward and she
thought wistfully of Cairn, of moles like Bracken and
Mekkins, and, yes, even of Mandrake. She wished that
the shadow of a male such as they had been would cross
the entrance to her tunnels. But then she told herself
that perhaps it wasn't just a mate she wanted, and she
dared to think it was Bracken alone she needed, whom
she loved and who she feared might never return. She let
herself weep for him, her face fur contorted with her
sense of loss and despair and with the weakness, as she
thought of it, of feeling such things. She looked out toward the west and trembled to think that he would never
come back.

Comfrey saw this side of her as well and wished there
was some comfort he could bring her, however slight.

It was in the second week of April, with the weather
still changeable and cold, that he tried once more to help.

He arrived at her tunnels and said "Let's go for a
w–w–walk."

He ignored her reluctance, her distance, her coldness
and her wish to be alone, and almost literally dragged her
out.

"Come on, Rebecca! You used to love going and
l–l–looking at things. Well, let's g–g–go and see if we can
find spring."

The weather could hardly have been less springlike,
being cold and damp, with the great leafless beech
branches swishing around irritably in a fretful wind. Rebecca was even more reluctant to go when Comfrey began
heading off down the slopes toward what the moles in the
Ancient System now called, ironically enough, the Old
Wood. She had not been back since the fire and found
she had a real fear of going there. It was all right for Comfrey; he was hardly old enough to remember it as it had
once been—the westside, the Marsh End, Barrow Vale
—and could not feel the loss now that it was all gone.

But he went off so quickly that she had to follow him
if only to stop him, and then she found she was twisting
and turning down the slopes behind him, her eyes softening as she settled happily into being led, and she remembered how Bracken had led her once down the slopes,
almost on this self-same route. Why! How big Comfrey
was now compared with the weakling he had once been!
He was thin and nervous, but he moved with a certain
assurance through the wood. It was good being led by

him. At the same time, there was an unusual air of secrecy, or suppressed excitement, about him that intrigued
her. Comfrey was a strange mole!

The slopes were covered in sludgy leaf litter—mostly
beech but with a few rotted oak leaves from the previous
moleyear and fresher ones that had blown up here from
the few oaks still standing after the fire—all in the narrow
zone at the bottom of the slope where both sets of trees
grew uncomfortably together.

Rebecca knew when they were approaching the fire-
devastated wood by the fact that the trees ahead suddenly lightened out, where once it had grown darker and
more dense as they had gone under the thicker mixture
of oak and ash branches and holly and hazel shrubs. The
wind was freer than before as well, and there was a silence
from the place ahead where once there might, even in
this weather, have been the startings of a spring bird
chorus.

Then they were there, among the stark, burnt stumps
that stood stiff and unnatural above the ashy wood floor.

"Comfrey! Comfrey!" called Rebecca, wanting to stop
him from going any farther into this desolate place, but
he ran on, pretending not to hear, which wasn't like him
either. Oh, Comfrey, she sighed, following on.

They skirted round blackened tree roots, over tangles
of ashy bramble skeletons, round jumbles of shattered,
burned branches, black and wet and lifeless. She looked
in vain for something she recognized, some scent, some
tunnel entrance, some shape to the roots that might tell
her where she was. But the air was dead of scent and
nothing was familiar, and anyway, Comfrey was running
on so fast that there was no time to stop and pause.

Here and there the wood floor was thick with a white,
sodden ash where the fire had been so hot that it had
reduced wood to bleached-out embers. In other places
the heavy rains of winter, unimpeded in their drainage by
undergrowth and living plant roots, had eroded out little
gulleys that zigzagged downward for a short way, with a
few flints and stones left clear of ash and soil in their cen-
ters, like miniature dry river beds.

Then she saw something among the ashes that brought
her to a startled halt. Fresh spring green it was, peeping
from among gray ash.

"Comfrey! Look! Stop, Comfrey, and look!" It was the
first pushings of a fern shoot, curled up tight and hairy,

parts of it green, fresh green, among the dead ashes. Then she saw another, which had forced aside two or three lumps of gray-black wood ash to get at the light and air for its growth.

"Comfrey! Stop!" Oh, she was so excited! There was life still in the soil of the burnt-down wood and it would come up in the next few weeks and cover the dead, white, gray, black ashes of the fire with a carpet of green.

But Comfrey didn't stop. He went on, darting this way and that, looking over his shoulder sometimes to see that she was following and then pressing on again. And he was smiling to himself, excited and pleased to see her excitement.

"Where are we going, Comfrey?" she called.

"Just to see if there are any plants growing here," he called back, not stopping.

"But there are, there *are*," she said, "didn't you see them?"

He rushed on, deeper and deeper into the Old Wood, over the charred surface, ignoring the great hulks of dead trees that stuck up into the gray, billowing sky, snout ever onward. She had never seen him move in such a straight line for so long. Not Comfrey, who tended to snout at everything he saw and ended up going opposite the direction from that in which he had set out and finding a different plant than the one he had been looking for.

But finally he stopped, breathless and trying to act natural. "Well, just a few ferns, and some thistles. Not much, I'm afraid. I thought we might see more . . . Still, we m—might as well press on a bit further."

"Where are we?" asked Rebecca, who was quite lost.

"I'm not sure," said Comfrey unconvincingly. "You take the lead, Rebecca, and I'll follow for a change." She turned one way, but he said "N–n–no. Go *that* way."

She did. The ground rose very slightly. She pressed on and then she ran straight into them. Not one, not two, not ten, but dozens of wood anemones, their green leaves perfect, their white and purple flowers half open and bespattered with shining raindroplets.

"Oh, Comfrey!" she said. "They're growing just as they always did. Anemones! Did I ever tell you . . . ?"

He nodded. Yes, she had. In Curlew's burrow she had told him. And her love for these flowers had inspired him with a love for all flowers and herbs. Yes, he knew she loved them, and how much.

"You knew they were here, didn't you, Comfrey?" she said, smiling gently at him.

"No, I d–d–didn't," he said, turning away because he hated to tell lies, even white ones. Then he added: "But I thought they'd come back. You know, after the f–fire."

Rebecca looked at them, wandering among them and letting their intricate pointed leaves brush against her, springing back on their long delicate stalks as she went by. The flowers were still young, their heads hanging down with the weakness of youth and many with their petals still to open. They had come back!

"Where is this place?" she asked, looking around at the wide circle of anemones with the stretching of burnt tree trunks and shrubs at its edge.

"It's Barrow Vale," said Comfrey.

"Oh!" she said.

"Rebecca?" whispered Comfrey, looking at the anemones with her, "you know that B–Bracken will come back, don't you. He *will*, you know."

Rebecca closed her eyes as a great wave of feeling, powerful and tearful, took her over. She felt weak and almost swayed and fell, and she started to weep, her tears as soft on her fur as the raindroplets on the green leaves of the wood anemones about her.

"Oh, Comfrey," she said, "Comfrey!" He had bullied and fooled her into coming, to show her these flowers to remind her that just as they had survived the fire, so, somehow, Bracken would survive and come back. But what made her weep was that Comfrey had thought to do it, loving her enough to think of a way to make her see again something of the joy in Duncton Wood that once, so long ago, she had so often celebrated and that she would not always have to stand alone. But what made her weep even more was the thought that if Bracken did return, then surely he, too, would love her enough to sit down sometimes, as Comfrey must have done, to think of ways to cherish her. "Oh, Comfrey!" she said again, going to him and nuzzling him close.

As she did so, a wonderful look of strength came into Comfrey's normally nervous face, for he had never, ever in his whole life, felt quite so proud.

"Rebecca, you're the best mole there is," he said without the trace of a stutter.

38

BRACKEN woke late one morning, long after dawn, with a head as heavy as a clod of wet clay. He lay drowsily uncomfortable for a long time, waiting for the aches behind his eyes and snout to clear away and the real world of the chalky burrow to take over from the troubled place of half-remembered dreams into which he thought he had awoken.

So it was some time, and gradually, before the awareness that something was wrong in Uffington fully came to him. The silence in Boswell's burrow was the first clue, a general feeling of abandonment the second.

He was up and into Boswell's burrow in a second, but he knew in his heart before he got there that his friend had gone. He hurried into the communal tunnels outside, thinking that there might be a scribemole about, but it was empty of life or even a hint of it. At first Bracken was curious rather than alarmed, but his curiosity soon gave way to something more urgent as he went down the first tunnel to the bigger one it joined, where there had, until now, always been some sound of scribemole about. Not a thing stirred. Only the far-off wind that whistled and moaned in the higher-level tunnels of Uffington and which could sometimes be heard down in the Holy Burrows.

Bracken headed for the chamber that Boswell had originally taken him to, and from which tunnels led to the libraries (into which he had been) and the Holy Burrows (into which he had not). As he passed through the chalky tunnel, he had the absurd feeling that he would never again see another mole alive and all he could have for companionship was the echoing sound of his own pawsteps.

This illusion was quickly shattered, though not in a way that gave him much cheer. Ahead he heard a sound. He stopped, snouted about, ran forward and two scribemoles, thin and bent, crossed the tunnel ahead of him, emerging from a small tunnel on one side and disappearing into one on the other, no more than a few molefeet from where he watched. They ignored him utterly, going past with snouts bowed and in a hushed and reverential way as if they had an appointment with Skeat himself.

He called after them—"Have you seen Boswell?"—but his voice sounded loud and almost blasphemous with the disturbance it made, and although one mole paused and looked back at him, neither said anything and both went on.

He wondered whether to follow them but decided to go on to the chamber where, surely, he would find some-mole.

When he got there, he found that a scribemole had been posted, rather like a henchmole, between the two major tunnels—the one leading to the libraries and the other to the Holy Burrows.

"Ah, hello!" said Bracken. "It's Boswell I'm looking for. Have you seen him?"

The scribemole appeared to be half asleep, his snout low as the others' had been and his eyes closed. Once again Bracken's words hung embarrassingly loud in the air until, when they died away, Bracken noticed that the scribemole was muttering or chanting to himself. Slowly he came out of what seemed a trance and looked with some surprise at Bracken.

"Are you Bracken of Duncton?" he asked, adding, before Bracken had a chance to reply, "Why are you here?"

"Why shouldn't I be?"

"Has no mole told you to go out onto the surface or to stay in the guest burrow?"

"No mole has told me anything," said Bracken a little ill-temperedly.

"It is best that you do one or the other. Just for today and tonight. Just until tomorrow. You'll find plenty of food in the high tunnels since all scribemoles must fast today. Though you know it would be appropriate if you did the same."

Bracken was annoyed by the mole's offhand manner and air of slight condescension and might well have been tempted to push past him to the libraries, or explore into the Holy Burrows, had not the possibility that he might embarrass Boswell in some way occurred to him.

"Look, mate," he said, adopting the tough familiarity of a marshender, "stop burrowing about the bush and tell me where Boswell is."

The mole shook his head and said "That is not pos-sible. If the Holy Mole has not told you what today is, then I certainly may not do so. Trust in the Stone and go back to your burrow and meditate in peace."

Stuff this, thought Bracken to himself, now thoroughly
annoyed and resisting the impulse to attack the scribemole. He turned back the way he had come, nodding his
head as if in agreement with the scribemole and thinking
that rather than have a confrontation he would simply
find some other way past the chamber. The thought
turned into action as soon as he got back to the tunnel
down which the two scribemoles, who had ignored him,
had gone. He paused there, crouched down, and for the
first time since he had come to Uffington felt his way into
the tunnels about him. It was exciting, like being back in
the ancient tunnels of Duncton, where everything was
unknown and all lay before him for him alone to find out.
Bracken liked nothing more than a challenge in which he
had to use his wits and talent for exploration.

As far as he could tell, everything happened to the
west of the chamber where he had been stopped. There
lay the libraries and the burrows, and beyond, according
to what Boswell had told him, lay the tunnel leading to
those mysterious silent burrows. He hesitated for only a
moment before heading off into the side tunnel, the way
the other two moles had gone, believing that if he could
find out their destination, he could solve the mystery of
where Boswell was, and what was so special about the
day.

For the next two hours Bracken enjoyed the thrill of
exploration and orientation once again, creeping along
the ancient, dusty tunnels that seemed much less used
than the others he had been in in Uffington and coming to
an exaggerated stop, sharp stop, at the slightest real or
imagined noise. He heard moles several times, and chanting more than once, but he avoided direct contact and
the one or two moles who went by near him never saw
him, for he hid in the many corners and shadows created
by the old flints that protruded from the walls or the complex intersections of tunnels' crossing points. Soon the
original object of his search—to find Boswell—was lost in
the sheer enjoyment of outwitting the scribemoles about
him.

But his game and his anonymity were brought to a
sudden halt when, turning a corner, he found, as he suspected that he eventually would, that he had by this
roundabout route made his way into the main library.
Quire was there, ferreting around among the books as
usual, and on seeing him Bracken was suddenly weary

of his game and the isolation it caused him. He greeted
Quire with a reverence he genuinely felt and explained
that he was in search of Boswell.

"Why should I know where he is, might I ask?" said
Quire, peering at Bracken. "Wait a minute—I know you.
You're the Duncton mole, aren't you? The one who's seen
the Seventh Stillstone. Where *is* Boswell?"

Patiently, Bracken explained what had happened and
how puzzled he was by the secrecy among the moles in
the tunnels that day.

Quire smiled and shrugged. "Yes, they do make rather
a meal of it. There's no mystery. Today is the day when
the secret song is sung. You know, Merton's task and all
that. Now *that* may be a mystery, but the fact of its being
sung is known to all moles. That's what all the fuss about
chosen moles was about, you see. They like to enter their
names in the book before the song is sung, all twenty-four
of them. You'll probably find, Bracken of Duncton, that
Boswell has been chosen. Hence the secret. We'll soon
know, since the Holy Mole will return the book tomorrow
with the new names neatly scribed. Of course, you're not
meant to read them but, well, the book's kept on
the shelves and it's an open secret. As a matter of fact,
there is an exceptional number of new chosen moles this
time because so many of the last lot died of the plague.
That's why you'll find there's not that many about. After
the devastation of the plague it's a miracle that there's
enough moles to sing the song."

"Where do they sing the song?" asked Bracken.

"Never been there myself, of course, not being chosen,
but it's somewhere up near the silent burrows. In a special chamber. Said to be the oldest in Uffington, though,
strictly speaking, it's not in Uffington but up where the
silent burrows are. About two molemiles yonder . . ." He
waved a paw toward the west.

"Could I get there?" asked Bracken.

"Whatever for?" asked Quire. "I never can understand
why you youngsters are always rushing off to see and
hear things somewhere else when there's plenty to see
and hear where you happen to be crouching at the moment. You'll be asking me next what I thought about all
those moleyears I was in the silent burrows. You wouldn't
be the first."

Bracken couldn't help laughing. It was true. Quire
wasn't as daft as he seemed. Then Quire laughed, too,

though his laughter rapidly degenerated into a wheezing and coughing through which he finally said "I thought about nothing, don't you see? Mind you, that's easier said than done for most."

There were times when Bracken thought himself completely stupid, when his brain seemed to register things so slowly that he found it embarrassing to contemplate the process as it happened. It happened now, as everything about him, all the secrecy and rushings about, fell into place. They were going to sing the same secret song that Hulver had once told him about when he told the story of Merton, and Merton's task. Linden had been the scribe who wrote about Merton, the selfsame scribe, presumably, who made the first entries into the Book of Chosen Moles. Why didn't somemole *say*, and then he wouldn't have got worried about Boswell. In fact, come to think of it, he felt proud of Boswell. Him, a chosen mole! A feeling of awe came over him . . . there was something special about a day when they sang a song that had been passed on in secret through generations and which was sung once in twelve moleyears, and which would only be sung to all moles and then by them when the Blowing Stone sounded seven times.

"Quire, have you ever heard the Blowing Stone sound?"

"Many times, many times. A mole may often hear it in a storm sounding the odd note. As a matter of fact, I once heard it sound three times in succession and it was that which made me decide to go to the silent burrows. It seemed significant at the time. I never regretted it."

"What did it sound like?"

"Oh dear! More questions? You can ask things until your snout turns blue, but you'll only ever really find the answers yourself. Now, why don't you stop asking questions and go up onto the surface and get some fresh air? Make your way up to the surface near the silent burrows and crouch among the grass and trees up there. It's a good place to be."

"How will I find it?"

"*More* questions? Go and try. And if you see Boswell anywhere tomorrow when it's over, tell him he hasn't finished here yet. I thought he said he was going to do some filing for me," and Quire turned away from Bracken and started poking about among the books. As Bracken set off out of the library to find a way to the surface, his spirit was very calm and peaceful. He might not be able to sing a song or take part in the special rituals the scribe-moles seemed involved in, but in his own Duncton way he could perhaps go and crouch on the surface and offer some invocation to the Stone on this special day, and think of Boswell, who perhaps needed a little extra strength in the next few hours.

Up through the tunnels he went, back the way he had first come with Boswell with a smile of affection for Quire on his face and moving with an air of reverence and peace which, though he did not know it, was exactly the same as that in which the two scribemoles had originally passed him by in the tunnel. The spirit of Uffington, ancient and reverent, had finally caught up with Bracken.

The weather was cold, wet, and messy, as gray sweeps of rain came across the vales below Uffington and swirled up the hill into the long, coarse grass into which Bracken emerged from the tunnels below. Not normally conditions in which a mole much likes to wander about, but Bracken did not mind, for there was a certain wild freshness about the air that suited his mood.

He headed westward, as Quire had suggested, and with his usual talent for finding the right route, soon came upon a run of long grass that gave him good protection and headed the right way. He did not know what he was looking for but, as often in the past, he knew he would find it when he got there. It was hard to say at what time of day he set off, because the sky was so overcast that the sun might as well not have existed.

But there was the feeling of late afternoon to the air when he finally began to think he ought to arrive somewhere, and the sky was beginning to gloom over even more. To the right of the line of grass in which he made his way was a plowed field of thin soil, more gray than brown and with many flakes of mottled blue flint and hard off-white chalk, and not a single sign of plant growth yet. To the left was a rutted, grassy track, potholed and puddly, where the soil and chalk had formed a light-gray clay. If Bracken had been able to fly up into the air, he would have seen what he knew by instinct, that the chalk downlands stretched far away all around him, except to the right, beyond the plowed field, where the chalk escarpment fell many hundreds of molefeet downward.

Then he heard a familiar and welcoming sound, the

rushing of wind through bare beech-tree branches and
twigs somewhere ahead. Its sound was subtle and variable,
so that at first he had to pause in his passage through the
long, whipping grass to catch it. But it soon got stronger
and more persistent and he had the illusion for a moment
that he was moving up the slopes of Duncton Hill toward
the beeches that surrounded the Stone.

The air was clearing of rain as the wind increased and
he found that he was, indeed, moving uphill and that
ahead the light was darker and more confused as the
great, tall shapes of the beech trees he had heard came
into view. They were thinner than the Duncton trees,
giving the illusion that they were taller, and stood in such
a neat, tight group that from the distance their branches
seemed to form one great crown, as if there were only
one tree there.

They were to the right of his path, fenced off all by
themselves in the middle of the plowed field he had
been skirting, so that he had to pick his way across the
wet earth, flints and chalk fragments to reach them. The
trees whipped and whistled high above him, and as he
entered among them he saw that they formed a single
oval stretching away from him, and there was such a
pool of quietness in the center where the wind was still
that it was like entering into a peaceful burrow.

Inside the oval, nearest to where he had entered it,
stood a sight more magnificent than any he had ever
seen on the surface before. Four great sarsen stones stood
in a gnarled, dark line with a gap in the middle between
them beyond which there were more stones sunk into
the ground. Among them were deep shadows and a wet,
dark stillness and they formed an entrance to a great
mound or barrow that stretched to the far edge of the
oval of beeches. There was an air of great solidity and
silence about the whole place, as if the very weather itself stopped and knocked before it entered. The sky
above formed a great oval of light, though for the time
being it was gloomy and lowering gray.

The grass in the oval was short and soft, and it covered the barrow behind the stones, although here and
there a smaller sarsen stone poked its gray, wet snout
out of it on the edge of the barrow and formed a pattern
that delineated its long shape.

Sensing that he was in a very holy place, Bracken

skirted around the edge of the stones and barrow at first, traveling its full length and then back the other side. Only when he had made a full circuit did he plunge into the gap between the stones, sniffing among them for mole-scent. There was nothing much, certainly nothing fresh, until he went right into a cell formed by the stones from beyond which, through gaps between them, he sensed the presence of recent mole activity. The scent was dry and a little mysterious, like sun-bleached wood or the husks of beech nuts. He fancied he sensed movement, secretive and silent, ritualistic and arcane—or was it vibrations from the great, shadowy stones about him, before which many a mole ritual must have been enacted, that he heard? He moved carefully and silently, as if the slightest movement would disturb the peace about him.

He was tempted to go beyond the stones into the cave through the gap between them, but one thing he had learned in exploration of a new place was that it was best to approach by the least obvious way. It was not that he was afraid for himself here so much as that he felt himself on the edge of some religious rite for the Stone and preferred to be as unobserved as possible. For this reason he retreated out of the stone caves and climbed up on top of the long barrow where, rather to his surprise, he found evidence of molehills, though they were old and half washed away by weather.

It was now growing dark and the wind had died a little so that the trees swayed only very slightly, whispering occasionally around the barrow and giving the impression of a growing calm. He snouted from one molehill to the next until he found one where the scent had completely gone and what remained of it was just wet and muddy. Experience now told him that such an entry was likely to be unobserved and forgotten, and he was right. The entrance was virtually blocked up with age and he had to burrow some way down, taking care to let no soil fall downward, before he found the tunnel he was looking for.

The soil was darker than the chalky soil he had gotten used to in Uffington, and the tunnel itself was smaller. It led along a short way and then down almost vertically, and then on again and down once more, as if he was dropping into a deeper and deeper silence. There was molescent about, but it was distant and still. It was as if he had descended vertically into a sleeping burrow, except that there was no burrow as such and, as far as he could see, there were no moles near.

The tunnel came to a sudden end, sealed irrecoverably by a massive sarsen stone. He put a paw to it and then his snout, sensing that beyond it lay something which would be very worthwhile seeing. Bracken very much wanted to get beyond it and was tempted to burrow round it until, feeling the hard, caked soil in which it was embedded, he realized that the attempt would make far too much noise. Yet, at the same time, he felt a sense of urgency to press on, a confusing mixture of awe and disregard for the place coming over him, with the same feeling of certainty that he would get through he had had in the Chamber of Roots with Rebecca when they had passed on to the buried Stone itself. He retreated, looking for the slightest burrowable chink in the wall.

Soon he found one, at the bottom corner of another sarsen stone that lined the wall and in which the soil was not packed so tight. Careful not to scratch the stone with his talons and so make a noise, he rapidly burrowed the chink bigger so that his snout was into the hole behind his paws, and then his shoulders, and he was pushing the dry soil behind him in great scoops, until the earth ahead collapsed forward and he was in a burrow or small chamber. There was an entrance on its far side and through it he could hear, from somewhere far off, even farther off than the scent, the faintest vibrations of voices, as if many moles were gathered together and whispering in a chamber that echoed their sound. He went through this chamber into a tunnel off which there were many turns to left and right. The walls were partly composed of dark earth and partly of dark-olive sarsen stones, which gave any sound in the tunnel a heavy thunking echo in which even the lightest cough might sound serious.

Bracken headed downward as fast as he could without making a noise, the mutterings and coughing sounds seeming to come from several directions at once and giving him the feeling that he was on the edge of something important which he could not quite reach. He sneaked his way along, keeping to the inside edge of the wall where it curved, just in case there were moles ahead. The sound of voices grew louder and richer and he very nearly stopped, convinced that at the next corner he would come to a great mass of moles. But each turn in the tunnel brought nothing but a louder and louder sound of the mole voices echoing around and past him.

Ahead, the air gained a spacious quality that warned him long before he reached it that he was about to approach a gap in the tunnel or a precipitous void, and he snouted ahead very carefully until, quite suddenly, the floor ahead disappeared and he found himself crouching at the end of a huge drop into the biggest, deepest chamber he had ever seen. It was not so wide as the Chamber of Dark Sound, but it was certainly deeper, and it was some moments before he could make out anything in it, though the echoing and coughing and throat-clearing that came up from below made it obvious that the moles he had heard were gathered somewhere in the gloom below.

The chamber was round and for the most part seemed to have been made of the sarsen stones, piled one on top of the other, to form a well-like wall that dropped way down below him and rose far above him into dark and echoing heights he could not even see.

This vertical drop had the effect of making the moles gathered far below him seem tiny, like ants, except that they crouched still and in order, a crescent of moles gathered about what, from above, looked like a jagged shadow but which, after a while, he made out to be a single stone on the floor of the chamber.

To one side of them was an entrance; leaning against the wall of the chamber, ready to seal it, was a great, round flint, shiny and blue and contrasting with the dull, rough texture of the sarsen.

A hush fell. There was a muttering among several of the moles, and two of them went over to the flint and started rocking it back and forth, for it was too heavy for them to heave in one go. Then Bracken saw that they were going to seal the entrance, and the only way that the flint was to be stopped from rolling past it was that there was a jag of flint set out from the wall, against which it would rest; and Bracken noticed another for the return journey when whatever they were going to do was finished, and they intended to unseal the entrance. For-ward, back-ward, forward, back . . . the rocking of the stone was taken up as a chant among the other moles as the great crunch, kerunch of the stone's movement began to vibrate about the chamber, spiraling rhythmically up the walls around toward where Bracken crouched, with his snout peeping over the edge from the squat, arched entrance from which he watched, and then booming its way upward into the echoing darkness above. The chant became slower, not faster, as the flint rocked farther back and farther forward, almost tipping over at last onto the flint set out of the wall, teetering, then back until, with one mighty effort and with a loud push from the moles, the flint rolled right forward and struck hard against the flint stop in the wall.

It was a moment which all those moles watching, especially ones who had never seen it before, like Bracken, would never forget. For as the flint struck the stop, a spark of stunning light leapt from between the two stones and filled the whole chamber with a light so bright that it seemed everything in the chamber was turned into iridescent white, except the shadows, which turned pitch-black. The outline of each mole on the chamber floor was delineated in frozen clarity, the edges of the sarsen stones and the flints themselves seemed as hard as ice, the arched entrance in which Bracken hid became an arched, black hole against the white surrounding wall, the very heights of the massive chamber itself might have been seen, had a mole been looking at them. But none was.

As the flints struck together and the light lit up the chamber for an eternal second, several of the moles, all older ones who had sung the song before, broke into a deep-voiced, rhythmic song that seemed cast as far back in time as the very stones of which the chamber was built. It was a song such as Bracken had never heard before, which took a mole's heart into itself and carried it, and his spirit, and his whole being in powerful steps toward the heart of the Stone itself. Bracken gasped and moved forward, unafraid of being observed so high, as from its very first notes the song took his spirit into its ancient being.

But as the last of the light from the clashing flints died away and he watched the singing moles below, he did not see one other sight that the spark had lit up and frozen even higher up in the chamber than he was, on the opposite side and crouched in a similar tunnel end. It was the face of Skeat, the Holy Mole, crouched in an entrance high above the chamber where, by long tradition, the Holy Moles who had sung the song themselves listened in silence to its subsequent singing.

But what Skeat saw, no other Holy Mole had ever suffered seeing, and it brought to his peaceful face a look of unutterable alarm. He had seen Bracken and realized in

that instant of white light that the song that had been secret for so many centuries was now being heard by a non-
scribe. It was for him a moment of terrible blasphemy. It
was as if the sacred song itself was being reviled and
sworn on; it was a kind of spiritual death. Shaking with
horror, Skeat turned away from the chamber and began
to make his way down the tunnel levels to where Bracken
was crouched.

Unaware that he had been observed, utterly conquered
by the first few notes of the song, Bracken rose into its
glory as, line by rhythmic line, its first verse was sung by
the older moles. He could not understand its words, which
were in the old language, but as it progressed he began to
understand its meaning with his deepest being. There was
a short pause, a voice of instruction, and then the second
verse started with more moles joining it, doubly as powerful in sound and richness as the first verse. With each line,
each word, each syllable, it seemed that the song gained
strength, as the moles that sang it gave their whole souls
into it, and it marched forward with them as an expression
of the power that impels all scribemoles forward, indeed,
all moles, toward the Stone from which they come and to
which they return.

As the third verse started, and even more of the
twenty-four moles joined in, Bracken began to weep in
his heart for the joy that the song surged into him.
With each glorious word its deep melody seemed to untie
the tangles in his heart about the Stone and the things he
had done, and the moles he had known, and forge them
into a powerful simplicity. He saw that everything he was
was of the Stone—everything he had done, and would do,
was of the Stone; Mandrake was of the Stone, Rune . . .
Mekkins . . . Hulver . . . Duncton . . . Boswell, beloved
Boswell was of the Stone . . . Rebecca was of the Stone
. . . and their love! Their love only had meaning in the
Stone, and he seemed almost to fly with the power of the
song for the glory that it brought to his spirit. And then, as
the fourth and strongest verse started and all the moles
were singing, and his own voice seemed to join them and
he was singing it, too, and it carried him even further as
its sound echoed and re-echoed around the chamber about
him and took him finally for a moment into the very silence of the Stone, where a mole is no mole but a part of
the glimmers and rays of the silence itself, unseen. As he
went there, he understood at last where he had been with

Rebecca and why he would always search until he found it with her once more.

Then the song was over as abruptly as it had begun. But for Bracken, as for the scribemoles who had sung it in the chamber below him, its sound continued on as its echoes died away only slowly in the chamber around them, and even more slowly in the higher peaks of the mountains of their spirits. The flint sealstone was rocked back and forth once more, until it rolled back into its resting place and opened up the chamber again, and one by one the chosen moles began to come out of the world into which the song had led them, through, but back into which there would now always be an entrance in their souls, which was the purpose of the singing of the song.

While high above them, crouched on the edge of the chamber wall, Bracken began to feel the enormous strength of peace and love and purpose which the song had put into him. But as the chamber focused before him once more and the slow sounds of the scribemoles below drifted up, he became aware of a commotion behind him, of a running and angry panting and, turning round, he saw Skeat, the Holy Mole, whose eyes were not filled with love and peace but with horror at the presence of Bracken.

From the place the song had taken him to and from which he was only slowly returning, Bracken seemed to see Skeat as if he was shouting against the force of a wind, so that the sound of his voice was lost and mute and his wild gestures bore no meaning.

Then the sound did come through, and the chamber behind him was filled with a terrible sound which caused the scribemoles below to stop and peer up into the dark, from where they heard a voice of terrible power cry:

"Bracken of Duncton, you are cursed by the Stone, you are cursed of the Stone, you are lost from its wonder, you are cut off from its love, you . . ." and they heard the sounds of scuffles and sobbings and terror above.

As Skeat had begun to curse Bracken, he stepped forward, toward him, and Bracken automatically stepped back to the very edge of the massive drop into the chamber, for what mole dares raise a paw to such a holy mole as Skeat? Everything was confused in Bracken's mind, for he could not even understand Skeat's words, or from where this terror had come to disturb the world of peace to which the song had carried him. He felt like a pup suddenly and violently cuffed by a mother or sibling who, until that moment, had only ever loved him. So he began to sob in unbelieving fear, weak with confusion, and retreating before a nightmare force. For his part, Skeat was quite as confused, for a Holy Mole is, as he himself had always said, only another mole at heart. What Bracken had done, or seemed to have done, had appalled him as nothing had ever in his life appalled him. He had run through the tunnels, round to this second viewing point, the sound of the song echoing in his ears and the picture of the intruding Bracken in his mind, but with what intent he had no idea.

When he saw Bracken, the curse came from him as if he had no control over it, and his confusion increased, growing even worse as Bracken retreated toward the void of the chamber behind, looking not like a guilty mole or one who thinks he has done something wrong, but like a pup who has lost his mother and needs help.

But Bracken was not a pup, but an adult who had survived to reach Uffington, and as he felt the danger of the precipice behind him, anger replaced confusion, aggression replaced love, and he instinctively lunged back toward old Skeat with his talons. But instead of retreating, Skeat came forward, for perhaps he saw, as a mole as wise as he must have seen, that Bracken's blasphemy was unconscious, while the power of the Stone's love in him was very strong. Perhaps Skeat wanted to take away the curse while its very sound still echoed about them; perhaps he wanted to touch Bracken to bring him back to peace. However it was, and no chronicler is certain on the point, not even Boswell himself who was there . . . however it was, Bracken mistook Skeat's advance for attack, swung round and into him again as Medlar had taught him to do so well, and with a gasp and a cry Skeat was plunging over the void of the chamber down, terribly, toward its depth, down to where the chosen moles were encircled, looking up in horror at the sounds above them, until he fell to his death among them, his frail old body still and bloody at their paws.

Far above them, Bracken crouched frozen in horror looking down, Skeat's blood on his talons and a black and terrible fear in his heart. And then, as gasps and shouts came up from below, he turned and ran, his paws pulling him desperately forward and up back through the tunnels he had come down, to get away from the crime he had committed and which lay dead on the floor of the chamber in whose echoing depth he had heard the silence of the Stone. But as he flew from the evil that he seemed to have done, he left behind as well hope and light of the Stone, a mole fleeing from light into darkness. Until, gasping and panting with effort, weeping and sobbing with fear, he emerged onto the surface again and ran without pause from the calm inside the oval of beeches around the long barrow, onto the rough and difficult plowed field now dark with night and gusty with wind, across which he began to escape toward the escarpment on the northern edge of Uffington Hill.

It was Boswell who found him, three days later, desolate and lost in the drizzle that enveloped the Blowing Stone. Boswell had left the prayers and chanting lamentations that followed Skeat's death in Uffington and had gone out onto the surface, turning by instinct down to the Stone toward which, in a time of his own despair, he had gone.

There Bracken crouched, muttering and half mad with grief and shame, with no direction in which to turn that did not seem blacker than the last. Had Boswell believed that his friend had deliberately killed Skeat, once his own beloved master, he might not have been there. But he could not and did not believe it, and the fact seemed confirmed by the presence of Bracken by the Stone before which he shivered and asked for help and guidance.

Boswell's gentle touch calmed him, and though Bracken could not bring himself to look straight at his friend, he asked the endless question that all moles faced by seeming evil ask: "Why?"

There was no answer, and never can be, and the two moles crouched together in a tragic silence, the wet drizzle of the last days of March heavy and thick on their fur.

Then, with a sigh, Bracken got to his paws and did something more brave than anything Boswell had ever known: he started the long weary climb back up Uffington Hill again to face the scribemoles into whose system he had brought such shame.

"Let them decide what is to become of me" were the only words he spoke to Boswell on the long, weary climb back.

It was the chosen moles who sat in judgment on Bracken, Boswell present but not among them, and they did it in the chamber where the song had been sung and Skeat had died, believing that his spirit would guide them in their decision.

After Bracken had told them what had happened, as far as he could remember it, and one or two points of detail were cleared up, there seemed nothing more to say at all, and they crouched in a deep silence which Bracken, in his guilt and before their calm, found almost unbearable. He would rather have faced the talons of Mandrake himself and accepted death there and then, than to face the silent and tragic meditation of the scribe-moles around him earnestly searching for a decision about his future.

Eventually, he, too, fell into a kind of trance and began to think of Skeat, of what little Boswell had told him and what little he had seen of him when they had talked. It was as he did so that an idea came to him, a suggestion, a possibility, that grew in his mind only slowly as light grows at dawn on a winter's morning. He broke the silence around him with it, speaking it out almost before the thought was clearly into his mind:

"There is one thing I could do, or try to do if the Stone would give me strength," he began, speaking in such a weak and broken voice that it was hard to hear him. There was a murmur among the chosen moles, and they looked up from their prayers at him.

"Skeat said that Uffington has heard from all the seven major systems but one. He said what strength it would give all moles if here, in Uffington, you know that the Stone was honored in the last system—the system of Siabod, of which little is now known. Let me go there and seek to fulfill the dream that Skeat had. If I never come back, then at least I will have tried; and if I return with information, or can myself honor the Stone there, then give me no thanks . . ." He bowed his snout and waited while his words sank in.

There was a chatter among the moles, and a voice said "A fine idea, except that this mole, should he ever reach Siabod, and even more unlikely reach the Stones of Tryfan which are believed to stand by the legendary Castell y Gwynt, would bring no honor to the Stone. What he has done means that he can pray for no mole but himself."

At this there was a murmur of agreement, and the light that had dawned in Bracken's heart began to flicker and die away into despair again. Until, very softly, a voice broke through the murmurings, the voice of Boswell, and the others fell silent.

"Then let me go with him," he said, "and if we reach this place called Siabod, *I* will speak the prayers of healing and forgiveness that Skeat, my former master, would have spoken, and I will call out the invocations of love through the Stone so that all will know that the Stone is honored in every system, even after the plague has cursed all moles."

As Boswell spoke, Bracken dared to look fully on him again at last, and felt the great power of his love, whose light and strength seemed capable of healing so much.

"Let me go with him," repeated Boswell, "and surely the Stone's will may be done."

There was a silence as the chosen moles considered Boswell's proposal and then the oldest one among them finally said:

"Steyn rix in thine herte."

"Staye thee hol and soint," chanted all the moles.

"Me desire wot we none," said Boswell, stepping forward to join Bracken and to face the rest of the scribemoles.

"Blessed be thou and ful of blisse," said the oldest mole, raising a paw to bless them and to give them the strength and forgiveness of the Stone. At which Boswell led Bracken out of the chamber and up through the tunnels to the main system of Uffington, and from there out onto the surface. Both knew the sacrifice they had made. For Boswell it was surely the end of his quest for the Seventh Book and the Stillstone; for Bracken, the fear now grew into certainty that he would never see his Rebecca again, and the promise he had made in his heart so many times to return and protect her could never be fulfilled. They found a temporary burrow away from the main system and food, and when they had slept and were refreshed, they set off together northward down the escarpment, veering off toward the dark northwest beyond whose dangerous distances the feared and unknown system of Siabod lay. Each leaving behind him the places and hopes they had cherished for so long.

39

By the time that Midsummer came round once more to
Duncton's Ancient System, the moles who had survived
in it to burrow and mate and litter through the spring
had formed a healthy and harmonious system. The tunnels they had recolonized smelled once more of the freshness of youth and echoed to the sound of growing litters and a laughter that would have brought a smile even
to the faces of the sternest moles who lived there originally.

Although the system had no leader, it was Rebecca
to whom all moles turned for help and guidance and
whose love for them all was the wellspring of so much
happiness. And by June, with the coming of summer, Rebecca had regained—or seemed to—much of her normal
joy in living.

So it was she who reminded them that Midsummer
Night was a time to gather quietly at the Stone and to
give thanks for the young; and who can say, as the warm
Midsummer evening drew in, that she did not hope that
her beloved Bracken might come again from off the
pastures, with Boswell at his side, and speak the special
blessing only he knew, which he had not had time to
teach another mole before he left.

Perhaps Comfrey suspected, or guessed, that Rebecca
had such dreams; perhaps he prayed to the Stone for
such a miracle to happen while making sure that he
stayed lovingly close to Rebecca all Midsummer Night
in case it did not.

All moles gathered by the Stone, the youngsters younger
than normal because of a lateness of littering, many of
them playing and gamboling among the roots and leaves,
hushed by the peace of their parents and Rebecca, who
moved among them whispering words of blessing that she
drew from memory and love and which surely spoke the
spirit, if not the words, the Stone intended on that special
night.

But no Bracken came, no Boswell hobbled into view:
though there was a time, later in the evening, when the
youngsters had been taken back to their home burrows

and only a few adults remained in silence by the Stone, the warm night air soft in their fur, when Rebecca knew in her heart that somewhere, far, far away, her Bracken was saying the blessing for them all and sending her his love as the same moon that shone down into the Stone clearing shone on his own dark fur. She hoped that just as Comfrey was by her, and had stayed with her all evening, so Boswell was near him. Dearest Boswell, she thought, my own sweet Bracken she smiled, hoping that the Stone would let him know how much she loved him.

Well, perhaps it could, perhaps it would, and *perhaps* became a word Rebecca grew tired of using. A mole must live where a Stone has put her, or him, and with those moles who happen by circumstances or fate to be living in the same system. And no mole was more aware than Rebecca, healer now to the system of Duncton, that hopes and memories are like winter aconite, a source of health and joy if used one way, a debilitating poison if used another. So, as the summer advanced, she put her Bracken from her mind and concentrated all her energies on helping the moles about her.

Their numbers grew rapidly. Under her care, most of the late spring litters survived and there was so much spare territory available in the Ancient System that there was little conflict, or death, when it came to the dispersal of the young in July and August. At the same time, the Stone, and perhaps the reputation of Rebecca, brought a steady flow of moles into Duncton, some from the outlying parts of the pasture system, others from far to the east, the old eastside, which had not been much affected by the fire. There was a good mixture of males and younger females in this influx and the system began to have a fuller, united feel about it—the main social center of the system being over to its east side where Bracken had first started his exploration.

There was a natural reluctance among the moles to go west into the Chamber of Dark Sound or beyond it toward where the Chamber of Echoes lay, and most moles lived on the east side of the ancient tunnels. Only Comfrey lived on the slopes, which gave him a reputation as an amiable eccentric, but he was respected for his enormous knowledge of the lore of plants and the role he was thought to have as adviser and protector of Rebecca. The mystery around him was enhanced by the fact that it was known that he traveled widely in his search for herbs, venturing right across the pastures, so it was said, and even down across the stricken Old Wood to the marshes.

Although the summer was generally sunless and chilly, in contrast with the preceding one, it was still a time for idleness: the rain had brought plenty of worms and grubs to the beech woods and the litters were quickly off parents' paws. So, once more, the Duncton moles slipped into their old habits of gossip and chatter and the telling of tales; and, memories being short and imaginations strong, many stories were told (and more created) of the deeds and adventures of Bracken, the mole who had rid the system of Mandrake and Rune and who had gone to Uffington with that Boswell, the mole from Uffington, to give thanks for deliverance from the plague.

Many a youngster heard the tale, and asked to be told again, of how Bracken crossed the marshes to "rescue Boswell," of how Bracken "ordered" Stonecrop to kill Mandrake before the Stone, of the plague and of Bracken's subsequent departure for the Holy Burrows.

"Will he come back one day?" was the question always asked, and most often greeted with a shrug and shake of the head and a statement like "These things happened many moleyears ago now, before last Longest Night, and what happened to Bracken and Boswell lies with the Stone."

Many stories linked Rebecca's name to Bracken and some even said that stuttering Comfrey was the result of their great love and supposed mating and was the cause of Mandrake's anger with Rebecca. As the mole-months of summer passed by into moleyears, the name of Mandrake became darker and blacker than it had ever been during his lifetime, and many moles refused even to talk of him. As for Rune, whose evil ran deeper than Mandrake's ever did, the moles were strangely silent about him, as if disease attached itself to anymole who even mentioned his name. When it was spoken (and what mole doesn't like from time to time to flirt with evil?), it was in hushes and in secret, and told in garbled form by siblings to each other who thought themselves daring and who gasped at the wickedness of it all. Rune and his henchmoles were routed by Bracken and Stonecrop, and Rune was forced to flee far away, where he died of the plague. Rune, it was said, did "things" to other moles, and made other moles do them as well, though what "things" were was never specified.

Rebecca heard these stories but never involved herself with them, refusing to be drawn on to the subject of Bracken or Mandrake or any other mole, except that sometimes she would tell tales of Rose the Healer, whom some still remembered, and would often make youngsters and adults alike laugh with her fond memories of Mekkins, the marshender who had more courage than anymole she knew.

The Old Wood was never visited now by the Duncton moles; its tunnels were believed to be dangerous because of the many moles who had died there of the plague and whose bodies were incarcerated there forever in the debris of the fire. But in fact, as Comfrey alone knew well, the wood was not as devastated as it had first seemed to be. True, all the shrubs had been killed by the fire, and many of the smaller trees like holly and hazel as well, while some of the oaks, particularly in the center of the wood where the fire was the strongest, had suffered total destruction of their crown canopies and so would die slowly for want of the means to take life from the sun and air.

But by the end of June, some tree life had returned to the stricken wood as well as a great deal of plant life. Some of the smaller trees had sent up suckers from their roots, like the aspen and, curiously, a couple of old and previously near-dead elm trees, while many of the oaks that had looked dead from ground level because their roots and lower trunk and branches had seemed so charred, had withstood the fire well, and their higher branches were putting on leaf and beginning to cast a little shade when the sun showed up over the derelict wood floor.

At the same time plant life, which Duncton had never seen before in such profusion because the wood was normally too dark to sustain it by Midsummer, began to blossom and grow among the ashes of the fire. Even in some of the most fire-wasted areas, creeping thistles, their tubers untouched by the fire, sent prickly green shoots up through the black, dead litter; in many areas, great banks of rosebay willowherb shoots were forming, their pink flowers not yet out but their thick stems and long, narrow leaves already giving a magnificent swaying life to the very areas where the fire had been thickest.

Other plants began to rejoice in the new freedom for growth they found, like the evergreen alkanet, whose luminescent tight blue flowers nestled among thick, hairy leaves that towered above a mole like Comfrey, casting shade for the occasional rabbit that came in off the pastures. Down by the marshes there were unaccustomed paths of swaying green watercress, and in the stretches of the wood where the spring rains had turned the wood ash into mud, yellow and pink comfrey had taken root, bigger than that which grew on drier, higher ground and a place for bees to buzz and saunter. Birdsong returned to the wood, though mainly from nesting birds in the less-burnt eastside, though the beating of wood-pigeon wings and the scurry of magpies was heard more clearly among the sparser trees.

The greens in the wood were lusher, too, because of persistent rains; so rich, indeed, that they seemed almost to bleed out into the sky, shining with life among the occasional horse chestnuts and furtive hawthorn on the wood's edge.

The "old" wood was a now-lost strange place, a secret place, where a mole like Comfrey could almost lose himself in wonder at the power of life over fire and nature's burgeoning disregard of death. It was a world Rebecca also ventured into more and more as the summer advanced from July into August, and the magnificent waving pinkreds of the rosebay willowherb came out at last like sunrise against a morning sky. She called them fireflowers, though whenever she did Comfrey corrected her, because he liked to get the names precisely right.

Both of them left the old tunnels alone, occasionally burrowing new tunnels for food and shelter but steering well clear of the old ones. In any case, as the summer advanced, bracken and bramble began to grow once more, thick grass grew here and there, and ground ivy filled the spaces between, so that there was plenty of safe ground cover for a mole. On a hot day, when the sun shone bright and strong and a convectional breeze caught the few remaining full trees, a mole might almost

think that he or she was back in the Duncton Wood of
old, before the troubles.

August passed and September came, with warm, settled
weather for its first two weeks, and not a mole in the
Ancient System seemed to need Rebecca's help. She spent
long days alone, basking in the vegetation-covered warmth
of the wood floor, listening to the last of the buzzing insects, watching the first of the dews and spiders come,
relaxing from a summer of work and rebuilding.

At the same time, the system settled at last into its own
patterns and rhythms as the excitement of the plague and
the fire finally gave way to a new generation who knew
them only as memories, and who grew tired of hearing
those old tales told. The young who had been pups in
spring now became adults, settling into their own territory
in the wide and expansive Ancient System and putting
their life into finding today's food rather than talking
about yesterday's battles.

Bracken, too, became a memory, an especially romantic and dramatic one it is true, but a memory all the
same. In the minds of the young, his leadership against
Rune and Mandrake was more legend than contemporary
history and though many a youngster crouched by the
Stone and gazed toward the west just as Bracken was
said to have done, few could really believe he still existed, or could now come back.

Then the first rains of September came and only Rebecca remembered Bracken as he had been and believed
he was still alive. Time after time she remembered Boswell's final reassurance to her—"I'll look after him"—
and she went to the Stone to pray that he might be given
the strength to do so. So many long moleyears gone and
she could barely remember what Bracken looked like . . .
only his touch and caress and the protection of his words
down beneath the Stone where the Stillstone had shone
upon them.

Sometimes she fancied she sensed that he was out there
far, far to the west where Uffington lay, until in the last
wet week of September she lost that sense and found
herself drawn uneasily toward the north, toward . . . oh,
where was it? Then she found herself aching to understand what it was calling her, sensing some terrible need
far greater than the demands made on her by the Duncton moles and drawing her to a place she felt she knew

and had once been shown, but which she could not remember. Oh, give me the strength, she prayed, give me the courage.

Some say now that it was a sudden vicious autumn hailstorm that reminded her of the blizzard that Mandrake had once dragged her into on the pastures, when she was a pup. Others, that it was simply that special sense she had always had of where her healing was needed. Whatever it was, she knew that one day soon she must leave Duncton and seek out Siabod, where her father had come from. Oh she remembered the blizzard now, and understood again the terrible cry from Mandrake she had heard, and which all her life with him she had never learned how to answer so that he could trust her love.

But the very absurdity of making such a journey, the inevitability of her dying on the way, was so great that for days she dared not even admit the possibility of doing it to herself.

"W–w–what's wrong, Rebecca?" asked Comfrey one evening by the Stone. "W–What is it?"

His voice trembled with loss and fear for he knew, or could sense, that Rebecca was preparing to go away from Duncton Wood, just as Bracken and Boswell had done.

Slowly she told of the calling from Siabod she had had, and as she did so she felt again the grip of Mandrake's talons on her back as he had turned her to face the blizzard.

"How will you f–f–find it?" trembled Comfrey, muttering miserably to himself.

"The Stones of Siabod will guide and protect me, just as they gave protection to Mandrake for so long. I'll follow the line between the Duncton Stone and where they stand, just as Bracken once found his way to the Nuneham Stone and back, and must have since found his way to Uffington. And beyond."

She tried to sound bold about it, to convince herself, but she didn't fool Comfrey. Yet he said something then that in a strange way gave her the strength she needed to finally leave Duncton:

"What will we do w–w–while you're gone?"

Oh, she smiled; oh she loved Comfrey! While she was gone! *While!* No mole, not even Mekkins, had ever had such faith in her as Comfrey. To tell Comfrey you would do something was as good as making a promise to the Stone, and so as a final affirmation of her faith in the decision to leave she said "While I'm gone"—and how she relished the phrase!—"*while* I'm away, you will be healer in the system for me."

Comfrey's eyes opened wide in astonishment and he looked in puzzlement at his gentle, hesitant paws.

"You know more about the healing herbs of the wood and how to use them than anymole Duncton has ever known," she said firmly, "and you knew Rose as I did, even though you were only a pup then. More important than this is that you have a faith in the Stone that runs very deep, and its power will always be with you, as it is already."

"Oh!" said Comfrey, for if Rebecca said it then it must be true.

Rebecca would have liked to leave there and then but she rightly sensed that she was such an integral part of the system's life that to leave without saying goodbye and trying to make others understand would be a betrayal of those who had given her love. So she said goodbye to each of them, saying again and again that she had faith in the Stone that she would be back, as they shook their heads and scuffed the ground with their paws.

Some were angry and bold enough to say "But what about Bracken and that Boswell? They never came back, did they? Got taken by owls if you ask me. Just as . . ." but not many dared finish the thought to her face.

"And who'll take your place?" asked others tearfully.

"Comfrey," she smiled.

"*Comfrey?* She must be bloody daft," they swore among themselves when she had gone to talk with other moles.

Yet when, finally, she left, taking a route down near the marsh by way of the pastures, it was to Comfrey that they turned and asked "Will she come back? *Will* she?"

"Yes she will," said Comfrey firmly, "because she's R–R–Rebecca and she will."

"And what about Bracken and Boswell?" reminded the doubters, the angry ones who felt most betrayed. "*They* never came back."

"I d–d–don't know about them. But she will."

But when they had all gone back to their burrows and

Comfrey was sure there wasn't a single mole to see, he felt all the loss and loneliness he had been trying to control begin to overwhelm him and he ran back and forth in the Stone clearing, peering first at the Stone and then out from the edge of the clearing toward where she had gone. All he could do was say Rebecca Rebecca to stop himself crying, until he couldn't even think her name without crying and wishing she was there for him to run to.

The Stone watched over him, its power in him and its silence finally there as well. Until when his grief had played itself out, and he had slept, and he was ready to face the system as its healer, he found that he had the strength never to doubt, not for one single solitary lonely moment throughout the long moleyears that followed, that Rebecca would come back. He was just looking after things while she was gone.

40

NOTHING more is known of Bracken's and Boswell's long journey between Uffington and Capel Garmon, which lies on the very threshold of the Siabod system itself, than has been recorded by Boswell himself. His account has left much technical information about the postplague state of the many systems the two moles passed through, but of the many long moleyears' travel, and what happened during it, he scribed little and said less.

It is known that the two moles spent Longest Night at Caer Caradoc, a system near the Welsh Marches, after which, says Boswell's account, "We were soon able to gain access to Offa's Dyke by which route Bracken of Duncton was able to find a rapid and safe approach for us to the forsaken system of Capel Garmon."

This brief sentence, which covers a period of many moleyears, gives no hint of the hard winter conditions through which they had to travel, or of the intriguing question of why they made for Capel Garmon. Certainly Boswell regarded Capel Garmon, a miserable and insignificant place now but for its association with these two courageous moles, as a turning point on their journey. Perhaps the stones that now squat lifeless and gray in that dank place still retained some of the power they have now entirely lost.

But the true answer can only be found by a mole who has crouched among the squalid, bare moorlands of Capel Garmon and turned his snout to the west and contemplated the fact that his long journey northward from the warmer south is over and he must now turn irrevocably west to the heights of worm-poor soils that are the grim prelude to the mass of Siabod itself.

But let the name of Capel Garmon send a shiver down the spine of *anymole* who knows what it feels like to crouch on the edge of a dark country into which he must, for whatever reason, reluctantly travel and from which death is a more certain gift than a safe return.

The two moles paused there for only two or three days before the hour came when Bracken crouched on the surface, his snout due west, and said: "We are near to Siabod now, Boswell; I can feel it and we must go while we still have strength." He was shivering and his voice

was strained because he was afraid of the power of Siabod. "We must go *now*."

Boswell smiled and nodded, for he had often heard
Bracken say the same thing when they faced a danger
ahead and he wanted to face it and get it over. Bracken
always found it hard to wait. But even Boswell felt a
sense of dread, for there was something worse than forsaken about a place where a system had once thrived
(according to the record of the Rolls of the Systems) but
of which there was now barely a sign. The soil was soggy
with rain and thawed snow, and there had already been
long stretches, many molemiles wide, in which they had
had to scratch around for hours to find a decent worm.
Now there was just the sodden rustling of last year's
bracken and heather and the plaintive bleating of grubby,
dung-caked sheep among the scattered bleakness of rocks
whose color was so dead that when light from the sky
touched them they seemed to turn it into shadow. Yet,
with the prospect of Siabod before them, even Capel
Garmon seemed a haven. But finally, wet, cold and hungry, the two moles made the turn west for the last part of
their journey. Yet, even at the grimmest moments, a
mole may see some reminder of hope, and Bracken saw
it. Among the lifeless stones through which they passed
he came upon a wet and stunted bush of gorse on which,
joyous in the April murk, was a cluster of orange-yellow
flowers, fresh as a happy spring. "They grow like that,
only bigger, up on the chalk downland above Duncton
Wood," he told Boswell, "and one day, if we ever get
out of this alive, I'll show you. I'd give anything to be
able to be there now!"

Although in the final stages of their journey to Capel
Garmon they had managed to avoid all contact with
roaring owls, the route on which Bracken now led them
took them steeply down into a river valley in which, as
they knew from experience, they would sooner or later
have to cross a roaring-owl route. In fact, it came sooner,
right at the bottom of a steep valley side. They were glad
to reach the bottom, for the valley side was wooded with
coniferous trees, never a good place to find food. They
pressed on over the roaring-owl way without difficulty,
using the technique they had developed over the moleyears—a long touch of the snout on the hard, unnatural
ground they found in such places and then, when both
agreed that there was no vibration, a fast dash across.

Once on the other side they found that the air was heavy with the scent of a deep, cold river and though tempted to press on and find it, for rivers were a good place for food, Bracken insisted that they stay higher up the valley by the roaring-owl way and follow along by the side of it. It was a wise decision, for this route took them to a bridge over the river from whose height they could hear that it would have been too fast and wide for them to have swum across safely. They waited until dusk before risking the bridge, but once across dropped right to the river's edge, where they found food on the thin strip of rough pasture fields that ran by its side.

On the side of the river from which they had come the ground rose steeply with massive coniferous trees covering it in darkness and stiff silence, while higher up on their own side a smattering of deciduous trees, mainly oaks and ash, gave way to rougher, starker ground that grew thicker with coniferous forest the higher it went. They pressed on downstream until, after only four or five molemiles, a tributary flowed down into the main river, a tumbling, rocky stream too rough for a mole ever to cross.

"But then, we don't need to," said Bracken. "That's where Siabod lies, off up this valley somewhere." He pointed his snout upstream and they both headed westward again, wondering what lay up the valley above them.

Their progress was mainly slow, for the valley was steep and rocky, but here and there it flattened out into sheep-pasture fields where the food was good and the going easy. But however flat the ground immediately ahead of them sometimes was, they were aware, constantly and claustrophobically, of the steep valley sides rising to their left and beyond the river to their right, and of the dark green forest that clothed it, out of which ugly snouts and flanks of gray-black rock protruded more and more frequently. Bracken felt he was taking them straight into a rocky trap from which, should they run into trouble, there would be no easy escape. The river raced and roared down past them and occasionally its sound was joined by the rumble and rattle of a roaring owl as it went by on the way that ran a little higher up the valley side.

Because the valley was so closed in they could get no sense of what lay beyond it, either to the side or straight ahead, while from down the valley and into their faces ran a continual run of bad weather, rain and wind, sometimes hail, and air that got colder and colder. It gave them the feeling that their situation was only going to get worse.

It was on the fourth day after crossing the bridge that they ran into their first snow—not falling from the sky, but lying in wet, streaky patches in hollows in the ground and several days old, judging from the way it had been trodden over and messed on by the sheep. It was grubby, half-thawed snow and it matched the place they were in. High above them, where bare rock was exposed, an occasional patch glared against the dark rise of trees, though these had now shed whatever snow had settled on them from their steep branches. As night fell, the temperature dropped and the snow patches began to freeze and crackle at a talon touch, their icy surfaces catching the last purple glimmer of daylight in the chill sky above.

It was on the following day, the fifth in their journey up the valley, that they met their first Siabod mole. It happened suddenly among some tussocky brown grass near the river's edge where they had gone to take a drink in a tiny backpool made accessible by treading sheep.

They heard his voice from the tussocks above before they saw him: "Beth yw eich enwau, a'ch cyfundrefn?" They did not understand the language at all, though from its tone and his stance it was obvious what it meant.

"We've come from Capel Garmon," said Bracken, to make things simple.

"In peace," added Boswell.

"Dieithriaid i Siabod, paham yr ydych yma?" His words were a question, but that was all they could tell. They waited in silence. If he was a Siabod mole, he was not what either of them had expected, which was a mole as big as Mandrake, and as fierce.

He was thin and wiry and had a wizened, suspicious expression on his face that spelled distrust. His snout was mean and pinched, and his fur looked more like a bedraggled teasel than anything else. His small black eyes traveled rapidly over them, taking in their strength, their relative size, Boswell's crippled paw, their positions (which was lower than his down by the water) and generally giving them the feeling that they were being picked over by the snoutiest little mole they had ever come across.

Then Boswell spoke again. "Siabod?" he asked.

The mole stared at them, his eyes flicking from one to the other, the faintest wrinkles of contempt forming in minute folds down the furless part of his snout.

"Southerners, are you?" he asked, speaking in ordinary mole so they could understand, but in such a way that the question was also accusation and with a harsh, mocking accent to the words.

But before they had time to reply, he darted back into the grass from which he had emerged and by the time Bracken had climbed up to it, was gone. Bracken called after him, shouted out that they intended no harm, asked him to come back, but the only reply lay in whatever words a mole cared to divine in the rushing and rippling of the cold, indifferent river.

"He's gone," said Bracken.

"Let's press on," said Boswell, "as you have said more than once. He'll be back."

"Yes, and with other moles. He was Siabod, all right. He spoke with the same accent Mandrake had," said Bracken.

"Well, I can't see where else he can be from up here," said Boswell, running along a little behind, "and that must have been Siabod he was speaking and—"

"He was so pathetic," said Bracken contemptuously. "He reminded me of nothing more than a wireworm in a tunnel when you expected to see a lobworm. Nasty little character he was. I mean, he might have helped us . . ." The anger in Bracken's words reflected his apprehension of what they might soon face.

They pressed on, a new life flowing through them now that they had made contact, if contact it was, with somemole, however contemptible he seemed to Bracken.

Indeed, they were so full of the encounter and the discussion of the possibilities of the first mole bringing others, and their decision just to push forward and see what happened, that they hardly noticed that the wood on their side of the river suddenly gave way to clear, rough pasture, while the valley widened out to their left into a gentler slope. As they moved forward, their snouts to the ground ahead and not looking up at the prospect that very slowly began to loom before them, they did not notice that beyond the now gentler valley side, off to their left, what looked like a mist was beginning to swirl in, swath after swath, among the upper branches of the highest trees. Not mist but low cloud, whose lower edge smoked like moist grass caught by fire, while beyond the gaps in these low clouds there was not more sky but a grim, great blackness, spattered here and there with specks of pure white that rose soaring like a wall high and massive above the valley: a mountain.

Because the mist was so pervasive and changeable, it would have been impossible, even had Bracken and Boswell been aware of the scene looming so high beyond them, to make out the complete shape of the gloomy heights above the valley side.

But no sooner were they conscious that the valley had widened and that the quality of windsound had grown deeper and heavier than the mist began to fall in waves toward them into the valley. At first it was only a thin veil that softened and deadened the russet and gray slopes behind it, but as it crept, swirled and surged lower, its higher parts grew thicker and the valley sides above them were lost in an impenetrable murk like the opaque off-white that slinks across the eyes of the creature going blind with age.

Then, faster than a forest fire, more silent than snow in the night, more unexpected than an owl's attack, the mist was down across the ground where they crouched, racing and running between them in cold and clammy fronds, robbing everything of color before masking everything in gray.

It was like no mist either of them had ever seen on the chalk downland they knew, where a mist generally came with cold, still air and a mole waited patiently for it to go. This one was moving and racing and challenging, a living mist that disoriented a mole by putting its chill around his snout and forming mysterious shapes in its layered depths that seemed to move around him, or make him feel *he* was moving when he was, in fact, crouching still.

"Boswell?" called Bracken to his friend who, though only a few moleyards away, was becoming obscured by the thickening white between them that not only cut off sight and smell but muffled and distorted sound as well.

"Boswell, stay close to me or we'll get separated."

When the two moles came together, each noticed that the other's fur was coated with the finest of condensation and that their talons were shiny wet with it.

With no reference points of sight or smell around them but the now-muffled river, they instinctively tried burrowing, but the ground was so wet and full of flat, granular stones that jarred the shallowest talon thrust that they gave it up.

"I don't like this one bit," said Bracken, looking around at the mist in which the light intensity continually changed as the layers between them and the sky thickened or thinned with the run of the breeze. "I've never felt so exposed in my life. Let's make for the river and we can find a temporary burrow in its bank."

Bracken started off one way, then paused and, shaking his head, went another before stopping and moving in yet a third.

"I think the river's *that* way," said Boswell, pointing in a fourth direction.

"No, I can distinctly hear it *that* way," said Bracken, pointing somewhere else and resolutely leading them toward where the sound of the river seemed, possibly, to come from. The mist moved about them, drifting one way, racing another, fading before them so that they caught a glimpse of a scatter of gray rock for a moment before it disappeared again, or a stand of grass appeared to their left or right.

Then they heard voices, harsh and quick, somewhere ahead; or was it behind? Siabod voices.

They stopped, snouting about themselves in confusion and for the first time in their long journeys together found they were totally lost. They could hear the river but not find it, and the only reference point they really had was each other.

"Best thing to do," said Bracken in a voice that made quite clear that it was what *he* was going to do whatever else happened, "is to crouch still and wait until it clears. And if those were moles we heard, I hope they find us, because they can lead us to somewhere safe."

He looked in the direction of the sky above them, seeking out a lighter part of the mist and hoping it might clear. Then the voices came back, from somewhere else, and there was a sudden rush and squeal of a massive herring gull in and out of the mist above them.

Time was as obscured as place, and neither mole could have said whether it was ten minutes or two hours before the mist began to clear as suddenly as it had begun. First they were able to see a greater distance along the ground as one patch moved off and was not so quickly replaced by another. Then the swirls above them parted for a moment to reveal, quite unexpectedly, the hint of a blue sky. The light brightened around them, and soon they were able to make out the direction of the sun itself, though it was too diffused to show its shape. The mist suddenly cleared to their right, bringing the sound of the river clearly to them once more, and there it lay, quite a way below them; without realizing they had moved across the valley and a little way up its side in their wandering. They were about to start off toward it when a voice sang out of the light mist that still lay ahead of them: "It's lost you are, is it?"

Bracken tensed and stepped a pace or two in front of Boswell, squinting to see if he could make out from the dark rocky shapes and shadows ahead where the mole was hidden. He felt angry and frustrated enough for a fight.

The mist rolled away and there were four moles ranged on the slope a little above them, the one they had seen and three others, all equally stunted and mean-looking.

"Siabod moles," murmured Boswell.

"Yes, we *are* lost, as a matter of fact," said Bracken boldly, "and we'd be obliged if you'd tell us where Siabod is."

There was a rapid crossfire of talk among the four moles which they could not understand before the smaller one, who had met them already, approached and said "And what would you be wanting with Siabod? It's not a place you just go to, you know."

"If you hadn't scarpered when you saw us before, we wouldn't have been mucking about in that bloody mess," said Bracken, waving a paw at the retreating mist and deciding that a bit of aggression wouldn't go amiss.

It went very amiss indeed. One of the other moles stepped forward and said in a high, angry voice, "Now don't you go talking to Bran like that, or you'll have something else to talk about, see?"

Bran smirked and stepped cockily forward in a way he had not dared to do when he was alone.

"Well?" he asked.

Bracken did not reply because he was engaged in a snout confrontation with the other mole, who did not impress him one bit. He had learned a great deal about aggression over the moleyears and could tell a phony when he saw one. Also, he was hungry and he was itching for a fight.

Boswell tried to defuse the situation by crouching down and beginning to explain why they were there by saying "We've come from Capel Garmon and are seeking to find Siabod and . . ." But it was no use. Bran foolishly darted forward, outraged at Bracken's apparent ignoring of him, and dared to cuff Bracken lightly on the snout.

Bracken did not hesitate. With a backsweep of his right paw he knocked Bran off his paws, while with a forward thrust with his left he lunged his talons into the other mole's shoulder and then swept him to the left with a powerful smack of his right paw. Then, facing the two big moles and rearing up before them, he said between angry gulps of breath: "Don't any of you try *anything* like that again. Now, where's Siabod?"

As he spoke, the answer soared high above him, behind the silent Siabod moles. Beyond the rim of the valley side the mist slowly cleared and rolled back out of the valley, revealing in the distance the cruel mass of a mountain whose shape was streaked with more and more snow the higher the eye traveled, between which rose steep masses of bare, black rock whose details were obscured by distance. Its size and impregnability seemed absolute. Angry gray clouds kissed at its highest peak, a sharp point that made a mole feel very small and distant.

"That's Siabod," spat Bran in a high, shaken voice.

"Good," said Boswell quietly, "and now that we've found it and got to know each other's strength, why don't we find a nice safe burrow somewhere and we'll try and explain why we're here."

"What's your names, then?" asked one of the bigger moles.

"Bracken of Duncton," said Bracken.

"Boswell of Uffington," said Boswell, a little wearily because the mention of Uffington rarely failed to have an effect on other moles. It was one of the few systems everymole seemed to have heard of. This time there was no exception.

"Why didn't you say so before, mole?" said one of them after a long, respectful pause.

"Now *there's* a fine thing!" said Bran, his crafty face cracking suddenly into what was for him a smile. "A mole from Uffington! An honor. A great honor."

And the four of them clustered around Boswell and led him up the valley side, leaving Bracken to trail along behind, feeling quite forgotten and a little foolish for having been so aggressive.

41

"YOU'RE never going to try to get to Castell y Gwynt!" exclaimed Bran after he and several other Siabod moles they met had heard their tale. There was a great shaking of heads and mutterings in Siabod, whose meaning was plain enough to Bracken: "insane," "mad," "crazy," "foolish," "idiots." But behind it all there was awe as well.

"You'll never do it, mole, you never will."

"Have none of you ever tried?" asked Bracken.

Bran repeated the question in Siabod, because they found that most moles there spoke no mole at all. There was another shaking of heads and a sullen silence.

"One mole tried a long time ago, but he never came back," said Bran. "You can't, see? There is evil up there, there is dangers like no danger anymole has ever faced and lived through. There's no food, for they say no worms live that high and there is Arthur the Hound of Siabod." Arthur! Was that what Mandrake had muttered to himself and shouted in his threats at Bracken in the Ancient System? wondered Bracken.

Neither Bracken nor Boswell mentioned Mandrake in their account, principally because they feared that if they told the full story, it might invoke hostility on them. Bracken had, after all, been responsible for his death. But now. . . .

"Do you know a Siabod mole called Mandrake?" asked Bracken slowly.

Bran looked startled, his mouth fell open, he looked nervously at the other moles, and one of them asked him to translate. When he did so there was rapid talk and looks of surprise.

"Well?" said Bracken.

"That's a strange question, isn't it?" said Bran carefully. "What makes you ask a question like that?"

Briefly Bracken told him. As he spoke Bran translated, but the moles never took their eyes off Bracken. The only bit that Bracken glossed over was how Mandrake had died.

"Tell them the truth," urged Boswell.

But Bracken shook his head. "Too risky," he said. "Later, perhaps."

"Well, do you know him?" asked Bracken again. But before Bran could answer, or would, one of the older moles there came forward with such authority that they realized that while Bran was their spokesman, this mole was their leader. He had seen perhaps four Longest Nights and he was a little on the tubby side, though his face was lined and scraggy as the others' were. He had intelligent eyes and a firm way with him that brought respect. He spoke rapidly to Bran in Siabod, while gesticulating at them both. Bran nodded rapidly and turned to them. "You're to go with Celyn, see? There's a mole he says you must meet."

With Bran taking the rear, they were led from the surface tunnels in which they had been talking higher and higher up the valley and out onto the surface. They did not resist this move because they had so often had the experience of being met by guardmoles or scouts at the periphery of a system and then being interrogated before being led into its heart and they had taken it for granted that this was what was happening to them when they were initially led into the tunnels lower down the valley. They rarely found out much about whatever moles they had met during such preliminary talks, and no longer expected to. The excitement started once they were led, as they were being led now, into the real heart of the system.

But this time the journey was unusually long and little was said. The system's peripheral tunnels were very variable, ranging from the crudest surface runs through an unpleasant, wormless peat soil that smelled of marsh to deep tunnels in a soft and sticky dark soil filled with gray, flat flakes of rusty-looking slate. The system seemed to have no clear pattern to it, and frequently they broke out onto the surface into nearly open tunnels through rough grass or among heather.

It was in one of these surface runs that they saw, off to their left, their first full view of Siabod, or Moel Siabod as Bran called it, speaking the words with a shiver in his voice that made him seem almost likable.

Now that they could make out its mass unobstructed by the valley side, they saw that it was even more imposing than they had at first thought, with great falls of black rock, misty with distance, rising in ugly snow-covered steps to the summit itself.

Once above the valley and past the gnarled oaks they found unexpectedly at its top beyond a stand of coniferous trees, the ground leveled out into an area of flat sheep pasture, green and relatively dry in some places, boggy and soppy with wet peat in others, all interspersed with rocky outcrops. They crossed this on the surface, keeping to a ground cover of heather and young bilberry which the surface runs had been cleverly designed to exploit to the full until at last they plunged underground once more into tunnels that gave them their first sense of being in a real, complete system.

In all their explorations and journeys, they had never seen tunnels quite so bare and bleak as these were. The soil was good, considering the miserable, wet peats they had crossed over and the bleached-out, ash-colored soils that had been encountered nearer the valley, for it was dark and well-structured and had the smell of food about it.

What was unusual was the way the tunnels exploited the great masses of smooth and jagged slate that thrust through it from below, its strata all at a steep angle to the level of the surface itself. Clearly, generations of moles had turned these rocks into natural routeways, burrowing tunnels which used the tilted slate as one massive wall on one side, with bare soil on the other. The effect was grim but powerful, for the tunnel's roofs—though most were more pointed or lanceolate than flat—were unusually high, and this no doubt created the moist, dour echo that was deeper and more primitive than the echoes drier chalk created.

Celyn, the older mole who had been leading them, stopped suddenly and crouched down, saying nothing.

"After we've eaten, we'll rest here and sleep in burrows nearby," said Bran. "There's still some way to go."

Food was brought to them by yet another scraggy, thin-faced mole like Bran who appeared with a bundle of worms that were mean and grubby little specimens by any normal standards.

Boswell ate them slowly, one by one, but Bracken, who was hungry, wolfed several down very fast before becoming aware that the chumping and crunching of his eating was the only sound in the tunnels about them apart from the distant drip, drip, drip of water off the slate. He slowed down and made a few overly appreciative remarks about them to cover the slight sense of embarrassment he felt. Food up here, he was beginning to realize, was a lot harder to come by than in the lowlands. It was not to be eaten too fast.

Only after they had eaten did they feel free to ask some questions about the Siabod system and where they were being taken. Most of the talking was done in Siabod by the bigger, older mole, and then translated by Bran.

What they heard about Siabod was familiar enough. The system had been decimated by the plague, which came to it later than to other systems but took a massive toll. The few moles left tended to live now on a narrow belt between where they had been interrogated and where they were now, where there was reasonably worm-full soil if a mole knew where to look.

There was no leader in the system because Siabod moles tended to follow the lead of a group of elders like Celyn. But he was at pains to explain that the system had been kept together during and since the plague by a mole he called Y Wrach—a guttural-sounding name that made the mole, whoever he was, sound like a curse.

"Oh, it's not a male, it's a female. Her name is Gwynbach, but most of the moles here have a nickname and hers has always been Y Wrach."

"And what does *that* mean in mole?" asked Bracken.

"Depends how you pronounce it, see? One way it means healer or spell-weaver, another way it means witch. You'll see why when you meet her."

"So we're going to meet her, are we?" said Bracken.

"You'll have to, now. Wouldn't be right not to, you know. Not after what you said about Mandrake. You see, she's the one who saved him . . ." And it was then that Bran began to tell them the tale that, long afterward, Boswell was to scribe so carefully in the Rolls of the Systems and which begins with the now-famous words "Mandrake was born and survived in conditions beyond even the nightmare of the toughest Siabod moles . . ."

When he got to the end of the chilling story, which carried into the heart of Bracken as he remembered Mandrake's despairing cry to Rebecca before he was killed by Stonecrop, Bran explained, "You see, Y Wrach was the female who found him. She liked wild places, she still does, and she heard him bleating up on the slopes where he had been born and carried him down by the scruff of his neck. They say there were those who wanted to kill him, being the last of a cursed litter, but she protected him and fought them off, dragging him about with her until he grew strong and then, when he did, teaching him to trust no mole, to despise all moles and to fight like no Siabod mole has ever fought. And he grew to be enormous and powerful, like no mole the system's ever seen before or since. You know what they called them then, being such a funny-looking pair? The fach and the fawr—which means the little and the big."

"But how can she still be alive?" asked Boswell. "She must be very old."

"She's seen six Longest Nights through at least," said Bran, "and though her senses are failing now, her mind's as sharp as a talon. Now the moles here bring her food, robbing themselves of it when it's scarce, just as she did for that Mandrake."

"But what happened to him? How did he come to leave the system?"

"He defied her. He was always like that, from the moment she found him, it's said. No mole ever understood why she looked after him, for there was never a word of love spoken by Y Wrach. Not to him or anymole. Nor between them. They fought from the start and it's said that the scars on her snout came from him, made when he finally left her."

"What did he do?" asked Bracken.

Bran turned to Celyn and consulted with him. The two talked rapidly in Siabod for a while until finally Bran came closer to Bracken and Boswell, speaking in a low voice as if he was going to be overheard by the passionless slate walls of the tunnel or the empty depths about them.

"He set off for Castell y Gwynt." Bran paused to let the words sink in before adding slowly, "That's what he did, see. That's what he did."

"But why?" asked Bracken. "Why?"

Bran ignored his question, his gaze fixed on some image in his imagination as he continued. "He must have gone up through Cwmoer because that's the only route

to the upper slopes, up into the desolate place where
Arthur the Hound lives. It was thought, until you told
your story, that he must have been torn to death. But he
must somehow have got through and then gone on up to
the wormless heights of Siabod and on to the holy Stones
of Castell y Gwynt." Bran paused and there was silence
among them.

"But why?" persisted Bracken.

"Why? What mole can say the true reason why a mole
risks death where every other mole fears to go? The reason he gave, as it is said, was that the Stone does not
exist. There is no Stone. Therefore the Stones themselves
mean nothing. He wanted to show that the Stone all moles
worship and Siabod moles have always revered is nothing. He wanted at once to show how he despised our
fears and mocked our belief. Remember, in those days
before the plague, all moles were made to worship the
Stone, but Y Wrach taught him not to, at least she told
him to take no part in our rituals. But then Mandrake
said, "What Stone can exist when such suffering as was
wrought by his own birth can exist? And after the plague
came a lot of us came to see he was right, see?"

The thought hung about them, each considering it in a
different way. For Boswell the answer was as simple and
as peaceful as sitting still; for Bracken, who had seen
plenty of suffering in his own time, it was a question he
had never been able to answer. For Bran, it was not much
worth thinking about. They could not tell what Celyn
thought at all.

"And she's still alive, after so long?" asked Boswell.
"What is it that she's waiting for?" He asked it with compassion, looking not at Bran but at Celyn. Bran repeated
the question in Siabod and Celyn answered it very softly.

"Well?" asked Bracken.

Bran laughed and shrugged. "He says that she thinks
that Mandrake will come back," he said.

Bracken had never actually said that Mandrake was
dead and now was even less sure what he should say.
But Boswell got him out of the difficulty.

"Take us to her," he said gently.

"But we need to rest, to sleep . . . ," complained Bran.

"Take us," Boswell repeated, saying the words to
Celyn, who seemed to understand and got up to lead the
way forward again.

The second journey consumed several molehours more and took them into tunnels whose size and appearance was more fearful than anything a Duncton mole could even have imagined. The slate walls began to tower higher and higher above them, the floor to widen so broadly that it was sometimes hard to make out the far side. To keep a straight track they had to stay close to one wall, though that was difficult sometimes because the continual running of water down the walls had created great pools on the floor, which was made of slate flakes rather than soil. In several places great tunnels entered the one they were traveling down and there was the continual sound of the running of underground streams and even in one place of some subterranean waterfall. The quality of the echo became deep and sonorous so that even the smallest paw sound seemed made by a giant mole.

"What moles burrowed these?" asked Bracken in awe at one point, his voice echoing harshly into the distance.

"Not moles," said Bran. "This is not the work of moles."

In some places there were great chambers of slate, higher than a hill, taller than the biggest beech tree, and littered about the flat, lifeless floors were twisted, jagged shapes of rusting metal such as they had seen sometimes near where roaring owls ran. The air was chill with a death that had been dead many generations before.

"She lives *here?*" asked Bracken.

"No, this is just a quick way to reach her when there's too much wet on the surface above. But we're nearly there, see," said Bran.

Celyn led them round another great chamber that echoed to the clatter of their paws on the slaty floor, then through a blissful mole-sized crack in the rock that sloped steeply upward but down which fresh cold air streamed. They scrambled up through the muck of slate fragments and muddy, fallen vegetation, scrabbling through sodden peat particles and back to near the surface into a proper tunnel, obviously mole-burrowed. Then out onto the surface where the evening was beginning to form in the angry gray sky. They could see Siabod more clearly now, nearer and more massive; more jagged, too, with black buttresses of rock jutting out and disrupting the smoother profile they had first seen and obscuring all but the highest part of the summit itself, over which gray mist lingered.

Then down into another tunnel, along for a quarter of a molemile, and into the tunnels of a damp and dismal little system that reminded Bracken of Curlew's burrows in what had once been the Marsh End.

"It's Celyn and Bran, Gwynbach," called Bran. "And some friends for you to meet."

They rounded a corner, went to a burrow entrance, and Celyn, signaling them to stop, entered. They heard him talking in Siabod and the murmur of a reply from a cracked and aged voice through which ran an edge as sharp as the thinnest of slate flakes. Celyn came out and beckoned Boswell and Bracken inside the burrow.

Y Wrach was crouched in a nest of dried mat grass and heather, and what pale fur she still had on her ancient body was gray and worn with age. Her face was contorted into a thousand wrinkles and her talons were short and worn—one had gone altogether—and their color was translucent gray rather than black. Her eyes were closed, blind and running, and Bracken noticed that her back paws were swollen out of shape by some disease or complaint that came with age. But her head movements were quick and acute, and she beckoned first Boswell and then Bracken over to her, seeming to know exactly where they crouched. She snouted at each one of them, running a paw over Boswell, lingering for a moment at his crippled paw and then pushing him away, turning to Bracken, whom she examined in the same way. He shuddered at her touch, which was like the caress of disease, but he noticed that Boswell was looking intently at her, compassion and warmth in his eyes—and more than that, respect.

"Pa waddod ydych, sy'n ddieithriaid yma? Dywedwch yn eich geiriau eich hunain a siaredwch o'r galon."

"She wants to know who you are and for you to tell her yourselves," said Bran.

"Well, I'm not sure that we ought to tell her everything . . ." As Bracken hesitated and stumbled over his words, Boswell quietly interrupted him, speaking to Celyn and ignoring Bran.

"Where shall we begin?" he asked.

Celyn hesitated and then, to Bracken's surprise, broke

into mole, which he spoke very well though with a harsher accent than Bran.

"Tell her what's in your heart. She will know it, anyway. I will translate."

There was something almost ritualistic about the way Boswell set about telling their story—quite unlike the matter-of-fact approach Bracken used. First he settled himself down comfortably, close to Y Wrach, closing his eyes for a short while almost as if he were praying or invoking some power he felt the occasion warranted. To his surprise, Bracken saw that the ancient mole started to do the same, the two of them engaged in a kind of crouching mutual trance.

Finally Boswell said, softly, "What I shall say is from my heart to your heart, told with the truth the Stone itself put there, and which I shall try to honor." He paused briefly, and Y Wrach nodded slightly, her snout bowed and her head a little on one side.

"My name is Boswell, scribemole of Uffington who has journeyed here for many long moleyears, through winter and snow, with news you have waited for for far longer than that. May the Stone give you strength to receive it."

He paused between each sentence so Celyn could translate, and imperceptibly Bran and Bracken retreated into the farther shadows of the burrow as Boswell and Y Wrach began their talk, almost as if it were private. Even Celyn soon seemed to fade away, his voice speaking their words to one another as if he himself was not there, so that soon it was just Boswell and the old female talking alone together.

"The mole I have come with, who brought me safely here, is Bracken from Duncton which, like Siabod, is one of the Great Systems. No mole may be trusted more." Y Wrach nodded gently, snouting over toward the shadows where Bracken crouched in silence.

"I will tell you of Mandrake, the mole of Siabod; I will tell you of changes that no mole may judge. I will ask you a favor of the great Stones of Siabod . . ." So Boswell began to tell their story, speaking in the traditional rhythmic way of scribemoles for whom truth is more important than time or effect, and who speak as moles can only ever truly speak, from one heart to another.

When Celyn reached the name of Mandrake in his translation, Y Wrach sighed very slightly and seemed to mutter to herself, peering blindly at Boswell and then round at the rest of them in the burrow, seeming suddenly to find more strength in her body and to hold herself more and more erect. Her face bore the pride of a difficult promise fulfilled. She spoke a few words in Siabod which Celyn translated simultaneously as she spoke them.

"Alas, Boswell, that you are not a female, for then, perhaps, there would be less need of words. Tell me of Mandrake whom I saved on the mountain, tell me it all and I will tell you its truth."

So Boswell began the tale, telling of Duncton and of all Mandrake did there. Telling of Rebecca and speaking of Rune, sometimes softly referring to Bracken for details that he did not know or could not remember having been told. Until at last, in a voice as hushed as nighttime snow, he told of the fight by the Stone and of the death of Mandrake.

There was a sigh from Y Wrach as he told of this and a shaking of her old lined head. Then Boswell continued, telling of the Seventh Stillstone, of the death of Skeat, of the plague, and of all things that had happened to bring them to Siabod. As he spoke, Bracken saw for the first time that, looked at in the way Boswell had told them, all these things were linked to Mandrake. But then he thought that in another way they were linked to Rebecca, or to Boswell, or to Uffington. And the Stone. Their story was all one.

There was a long silence before Y Wrach began in her own turn to speak. As she did so, she seemed to rear up and grow in size, the great slab of slate that formed one side of the burrow seeming to shrink behind her, a black backdrop to her gray and wrinkled form. She spoke in a singsong voice, different from the one she had first spoken in, and the words seemed to come not from her but through her, from a different generation of moles and from a mole who was young and speaking reluctantly through a body that had nearly done with life:

> Hen wyf i, ni'th oddiweddaf . . .
> Crai fy myrd rhag gofid haint . . .
> Gorddyar adar; gwlyb naint.
> Llewychyd lloer; oer dewaint.

> Ancient am I and do not comprehend you . . .
> I am wasted from painful disease . . .

> *Loud are birds; streams wet*
> *The moon shines; midnight is cold.*

The Siabod she spoke was more rhythmic and musical
than that Bracken had first heard from Bran and the other
moles down in the valley. And as Celyn's translation began, her own words seemed to form a wonderful, melodic
accompaniment to his own rendering of it, so that the
sense came from him, but the power and poetry of sound
came from her.

At first Bracken found it hard to follow what she
meant, until he realized that he was not listening to a
series of logical ideas or explanations of anything so much
as the outpouring of images and memories from the heart
of a mole who had struggled with age for many long
moleyears and whose life is better explained by the running of a stream than the exposition of a scribemole. At
the heart of all she said was her faith in Mandrake, or in
the life force within him, whose power she believed would
not have withered in the dull safety of burrows and tunnels, having survived the blizzard from which she saved
him.

> *Mandrake, I knew your nature*
> *Like the rush of an eagle in estuaries were you,*
> *Had I been fortunate you could have escaped*
> *But my misfortune was your life.*
> *My heart was withered from longing*
> *The buzzard has plunged on the heath*
> *Your black fur lost in the slate*
> *Of Siabod, or the hound's howls,*
> *Of Arthur, black as Llyn dur Arddu.*
> *I am wasted, disease has seized me.*
> *Mandrake, what part of you hears me?*
> *For you are coming again*
> *From the slate where you went*
> *Black among shadows. I hear you.*
> *Wind tosses starry flowers*
> *Snow drips among green fern*
> *No more will the buzzard see me*
> *But I will come in a circle*
> *A gyre of triumph; bare like the hill*
> *No fur, no grass; weak talons, soft rock*
>
> *This leaf, the wind whips it away*

Alas for its fate,
Old, born this year.
Young, reborn next.
So will you come back
So will I come back
So will you know me
So will I laugh at the black slate of Siabod
Though my heart withered from longing
In this life that you left me
And wind swept the last trees from the mountain.
So did I laugh in the blizzard that found you.
Lakes cold, their looks want warmth
Raven scutters in Castell y Gwynt
Beak on the ice where your talon went
Where the Stone's silence warned you
And Tryfan stands still.
I am wasted with melancholy tonight
That I was not there with you
Nor can ever be. Another will go
And you will come back.
Let the Stone see another
In Castell y Gwynt
Where the winds howl through stones
But Tryfan stands still.

As the chanting music of her voice fell away, Celyn spoke the final words and then there was a long silence in the burrow, Bracken never taking his eyes from her as the images she had invoked of age, and of quest, and of Mandrake to whom she spoke as if he was still alive melded in his mind and soared to the Stones of Siabod where he knew he must go.

But most of all he felt her love for Mandrake and her sense that in some way she, who had saved him, had yet failed him. And in hearing her speak, and understanding this truth behind her words, he understood at last Rebecca's love for Mandrake, which was the same. He remembered again, as he had so many times, that terrible cry by Mandrake when he was by the Stone, a cry he had heard but not known how to listen to. How can a mole answer such anguish? Where does he find the strength? So he looked on Y Wrach anew and wondered if there was anything that he might say to her, anything, that would bring her some comfort.

"Tell her about Rebecca," he said suddenly, his voice breaking the silence. And then, turning to Celyn, he said "Did you tell her?"

"She knows," said Boswell softly, and Celyn nodded.

"No," said Bracken, "I mean you must tell her I love her," for he knew it was the only way of letting this mole, who had waited so long, know that there was something of Mandrake that another mole loved.

"Tell her," said Bracken to Celyn.

Celyn spoke softly to Y Wrach, who put out to him an aged paw which he held in his own before she turned and faced Bracken directly. Then she came over to him slowly, her back paws moving with difficulty, and touched his paw with her own.

"Dywedwch wrthyf sut un ydi Rebecca!" she said softly.

Bracken looked over to Celyn for a translation.

"She says 'Tell me what Rebecca is like,' " he said.

Bracken looked at Y Wrach and wondered what he should say, what he could say. She was like . . . she was like . . .

"She is full of love and her fur is thick and glossy gray. She is big for a female but graceful as a rush in the wind. Her laughter is like sunshine. Life flows through her and she is powerful with it, and moles are afraid of the life she has but they come to her because they need it . . ." He trailed off into silence and Celyn's soft translation came to an end soon after and there was silence among them.

Bracken wondered at what he had said, because he had never thought those thoughts before about Rebecca. Was he afraid of her himself? Was it simply the life she had that he wanted?

He wanted to carry on speaking to Y Wrach but felt embarrassed with Celyn and Bran and Boswell there, and uncertain of his feelings. He tried to think himself back to the Stillstone with Rebecca, but it seemed too far away, so long ago, that it had happened to another mole. He wanted to cry. He wanted to sigh. He wanted Y Wrach to hold him. He wanted Rebecca.

"I love her," he mumbled, and Celyn repeated the words in Siabod. Y Wrach smiled and then looked a little fierce and then said something to him.

"She says she knows you love Mandrake's child Rebecca," said Celyn, "and that one day you may know it too."

Then Y Wrach began speaking again, though not in the chant she had used before.

"I did not want him to go, and warned him against it," repeated Celyn, once more translating her words, "but you who never saw him then, or ever watched him grow, can perhaps not understand the power that he had. The sky and the wind was in his fur, and though black clouds raced there, the sun lit its way as well. He had a power of life before which I saw that sad and empty Siabod, the system that you call one of the seven great systems, was but the carcass of a crow dashed against slate cliffs by a cold wind.

"They grew angry that I would not let them see the Stone crushed between the dead talons of their rituals or join their hopeless song. I told him that the Stone soars on Castell y Gwynt, not in these slated, wormless tunnels now fittingly punished by plague.

"But he grew to hate me as he hated them, and sought to mock us all by going there. Yet I knew that even Arthur, Hound of Siabod, could not rob him of his life, none could or ever will."

"But he's dead now," said Boswell softly, Celyn saying the words back to her.

She shook her head and laughed, her first laugh among them, a laugh as stunted but strong as hillside gorse.

"You have things to learn, Boswell. And you," she turned unerringly toward Bracken and raised an ancient paw at him. "You have things to learn, and things you must do, you who say you love Mandrake's child." She came forward slowly to Bracken and touched him, and this time her touch was like a warm, rippling breeze on his fur and he knew that she knew all that was inside him.

"You may have to lose her, Bracken of Duncton, before you find her. Just like I lost my Mandrake. And found him."

With this final mystery, which threw only fear into Bracken's heart, she fell silent and Celyn signaled that they should leave her.

They saw her only once more, two days later, when she led them to the end of her tunnels to the edge of a massive drop down into the quarried cliffs that, in the distance, edged the precipitous slopes up toward Siabod.

She snouted blindly over this precipice for some time before saying "The way onto Moel Siabod lies through there by the cliffs of Cwmoer. Beyond it, though no mole now knows them, stand the Stones you seek, and Tryfan, which you will never reach." She waved a paw over the precipice to her right. "Over there, as I remember too well, is a way back from these depths, but no mole may climb it—only tumble down."

The ground she pointed over was rough rock, with a few fragments of starved vegetation—frail parsley fern and battered bilberry—that rose steeply along the edge of the quarry and in the distance met its far heights.

"Up there, in a blizzard, was Mandrake born and there did I find him: a place for herring gull or crow or the dance of a fritillary in summer, but not for mole."

She turned back to the grim depths of slate below them which rose far into the distance in a jumble of massed rock fragments and forgotten ruins.

"That is where Arthur lives and where your path lies." She turned away, muttering finally to herself the words she had said before: "Hen wyf i, ni'th oddiweddaf."

"Ancient am I and do not comprehend."

Bracken looked up at Siabod and then back down into the place he would soon have to go to reach it, feeling that if she did not understand, what hope had he?

42

BRACKEN and Boswell crouched on the threshold of Cwmoer with the warnings of the Siabod moles in their ears and shadows in their hearts. A sleety snow had fallen in the night, layering the fragmented black rocks that lined its gaping valley walls with a thin wet whiteness that only added to the bleakness of the place.

Only Celyn had come with them, for though Bran had guided them back down the valley, he had refused to come anywhere near Cwmoer, hurrying away from them long before they reached it with barely a word of farewell, as if staying too long would bring upon him the same doom that would surely soon fall upon them.

But Celyn took them on along a route he had traveled for a dare as a pup, though he did not know its final stages, for the wind from the cwm had been so chillingly vicious then that he did not get that far. Now, however, he took them on as far as the rocky turning that revealed the start of Cwmoer.

There he stopped, and before leaving them wished them well and gave them one last piece of advice, born of his own long experience on the gentler slopes of Siabod on its eastern side.

"You will probably find this place even more wormscarce than those parts of Moel Siabod you have already seen. Many a mole has starved to death out on the soggy peat seeking food—or has been caught out in the open by buzzards or ravens, kestrel or merlin. Up here the streams often shelter food, so follow them if you're in doubt, however unpromising they may seem. There's plants, too, that like the soil that worms go for, but you'll not know most of them. Do you get orchids on the soil you come from—on what you call chalk?"

Boswell nodded, the memory of the delicate, curling orchids of the chalk seeming a distant, unattainable dream up here.

"Then watch out for one that's purple and in flower now. And starry saxifrage which Y Wrach mentioned, and which you saw coming here—you'll find that near worms and grubs. And sorrel, do you know that?"

This time it was Bracken who nodded, for they had fed near sorrel many, many times in the last few moleyears. Always a few worms near sorrel!

"There's one that grows up here in the worm-full soils, only a bit different from the one you see in the valley—it's got heart-shaped leaves, but its scent is much the same. It won't be blooming yet, but watch out for its leaves; they'll guide you to food."

He left them with a blessing in Siabod, disappearing back down the rough grass over which they had finally had to come, for the tunnels petered out some way before Cwmoer. They did not move for a while, preferring to stay in the safety of the clump of matgrass in which they were crouching while they worked out what to do.

To their left they could hear and smell the fush of a mountain stream whose noise and heavy splashing suggested that it was the one that took in all the many streamlets that raced and wound their secret ways down the sides of the cwm valley, even fuller now from the fall of snow overnight. A little way up the slope above them, to their right, the grass came to an abrupt stop where the final spewing of a steep and massive slate tip covered it. Not a plant grew on its uninviting face, which rose starkly toward the sky, hiding the base of the great buttress of rock that rose behind and far above it.

Of what lay straight ahead higher up the valley they could not sense, though its total distance, judging from the quality of wind-sound, and occasional bird cry in it, and what they had seen already from Y Wrach's tunnels, was perhaps six or seven molemiles—a five-hour trek.

"Let's press on as fast as we can to the head of the valley so that when we get there we'll have enough time and strength left to find a place for rest and food," said Bracken. "If this famous hound of theirs is here, so be it! There's nothing we can do about that. At least there's plenty of slate to hide away under out of reach of his legendary paws!" Bracken's lightheartedness was a poor cover for the unease he felt at the start of this grim journey.

They set off quickly, finding their way to a wide, slaty track that had the smell of roaring owls about it, with the stream on one side and the slate tip on the other. There were patches of sheep's fescue and matgrass here and there, a welcome break from the snow and slate, but otherwise their way was bleak and steep. The higher they got, the more oppressive they found the towering tip on their right—the more so because flurries of snow occasionally slid off the great flakes of gray and rusty-brown slate of

which it was formed, while in several places along the
track there had been rock slips from the tip and great
pieces of slate, many twice as thick as a mole and many
times longer, had spilled across the track, giving the whole
area an atmosphere of oppressive instability.

After an hour's steady climb in which they used out-
growths of grass for cover as much as possible, the slope
leveled off and the track slued round to the left onto a
bridge over the stream and round the left side of a long
lake that filled the valley floor ahead of them. Although
its water was clear, it appeared cold and black, because
of the reflection in it of the towering slate cliffs that rose
on its far edge. Black and impatient, little wavelets lapped
at the edge of the lake near the track on which they traveled: the whole effect was black and chill.

Here and there on the lake, though a mole could not
see it, there were runs of icy white, where the reflections
of the precipitous backdrop took in a steep side of snow-
covered grass between the cliffs.

To their left the peat gave way to shallow, rocky slopes
covered in drier grass and studded here and there by the
only cheerful color in the whole miserable scene, the
bright yellow petals of squat tormentil. But behind this
grass, too, the slope gradually steepened, rising eventually
to more overhangs of rock, or sheer black-gray faces where
only an occasional raven or crow moved, visible only when
they rose high enough to break out across the dull white
sky.

Bracken and Boswell now moved faster, for the track
was exposed ground, only pausing to rest at a spot where
a rivulet ran under the track in the peat to join the lake.
They expected to find food there but were wrong, and all
they could do was to rest and snout out at the sky for
predators.

Then on they went, right along the edge of the lake,
until that too lay behind them and they were rising again,
back among great steep jumbles of snow-covered slate
tips that edged the now increasingly rough and rocky
track.

They might by now have been lulled by the sheer un-
eventfulness of the journey into thinking that its dangers
had been exaggerated had they not quite suddenly moved
into a bank of the heavy odor of some creature they had
never faced before, whose path must have crossed the
slaty track a short time previously. Its scent had some-

thing of the wild deadness of the thick brown peat and something more of the savagery of a carnivore; worse, it held the vaguest hint of that stupefying smell that goes with roaring owl and which, if a mole is not careful, will dull his snout into senselessness.

They retreated off the track for a while, taking refuge by some loose slates among which matgrass was growing, and snouted out for a stronger indication of the scent, listening for movement or vibration.

"What creature was it?" asked Bracken.

Boswell shrugged and shook his head. He was frankly frightened. But as he watched Bracken stir and eventually snout out of the protection of the grass, he admired again, as he had admired so many times before, his friend's obstinate courage. So often it had been the only thing that had led him, Boswell of Uffington, a scribemole who was meant to know so much, forward into new awareness and wisdom.

There was a kind of courage Boswell had seen in moles many times that was born of ignorance and stupidity. Give such a mole a task, tell him to get on with it, and off he goes. But Bracken? He was not stupid, he had so many things he understood and sought to live for, and yet on he went in the wake of this fearful odor.

Truly the Stone was wise to have bound me to Bracken, thought Boswell, following with something near a rueful grin.

They very soon found they had good cause to fear, for as the path took them nearer to the stark rock face at the end of Cwmoer, leaving the lake now some way behind and below them, they moved straight into the terrible smell again, this time finding as well the awesome tracks of the creature that had made it. Each impression was at least half the size of a mole and comprised the five pad-marks like a dog, which at their forward edge had an additional deep gashline in the snow where a claw had left its mark. The space between each print was three or four times wider than they had seen in any creature's tracks and bigger by far than the tracks of even the biggest fox or badger, while the weight of the creature was such that, whereas their own tracks in the snow just broke the surface, these pressed right through to the black slate beneath. They looked like dog, but a monstrous dog, and one whose size would block out the very sky.

They now took a path that prudently meandered from

side to side of the track to seek out a route ahead that
went as near as possible to growths of matgrass or slate
crevices in case quick refuge was needed.

The pawmarks they had seen crossed their track and
rose impossibly in great, leaping bounds up the steep side
of the slate tip and over its distant top. Here and there,
though the two moles could not quite see it, the heaviness
of the creature had been too much for the sometimes
delicately balanced slates, and the tracks were marked by
slidings of snow and slate that had avalanched down the
face of the tip with its passing.

A hovering kestrel might have seen, in the wastes of
Cwmoer below, how the tracks dropped down on the far
side of the tip, bounded up another, wandered here and
there after the smell of sheep, and then dropped back
lower down the valley, padding across the snow-layered
grass and rocks until they cut back onto the very same
track up which Bracken and Boswell had labored an
hour or so before.

A kestrel might have left it at that, but a carrion crow,
who knows how to seek out death and feed off it, might
have seen that the tracks then ran clumsily back and forth
across the fresh moletracks, the snow by them stirred and
messed by the sniffing and slobbering of some great maw
until finally and inexorably they began to follow back
up the track after the scent the moles had left behind.

Meanwhile, Bracken and Boswell were beginning to
get tired. They seemed to have climbed and climbed all
day, with never a sniff of food before them. The walls
of the valley had closed in and now forced the track, and
them, round to the left, past a bluff that cut off any view
of the lake below and then up a much steeper incline on
the right-hand side of the now narrowing valley. Below
them the head stream of the cwm rushed icily down in
the direction they had come. They began to regret not
following it up because, as Celyn had suggested, they
might have found food somewhere along it. Now it was
too late, for the route down the valley side to it would be
too steep and slippery and so they pushed on up the track,
hoping that finally it would reach the head of the valley
and rejoin the river again.

As they went on, the sound of the river below became
slowly muffled by the infilling of yet another ugly tip of
slate, far bigger than any they had passed so far, that
looked as if the very head of the valley itself had slumped

forward in one massive, loose mound that rose higher and higher up the valley side, the river issuing forth at its foot, until the tip was level with the track on their left and soon rising above it. With this on their left and the final stages of the valley wall proper on their right, they were hemmed in on both sides so that if danger should come, they had little hope of moving to right or left unless to hide among the looser slates at the side of the tip.

But for the half-hearted snow about them, all was black and oppressive, and even the afternoon sky seemed to have turned the color of slate. There was no color left in the world at all, and the only sound was that of the stream, rushing below them somewhere through the depths of the tip, and other streamlets coursing their eternal way down the steep, echoing walls of the cwm that now, finally, had the two moles in the depths of its savage grip.

They grew fearful, with danger all around them—from shifting slate, from diving predator, from polecat and from monstrous hound—and never in all their travels had they felt a greater sense of foreboding.

The track rose sharply over a thin line of harder rock protruding from the valley side on their right and then suddenly before them into a tip-surrounded hollow, its far side towering above them, to the far right of which, over a rocky ledge, the stream that had been on their left tumbled in a waterfall through ruined slate and then under the track of loose slate before them. They looked back at the last of the cwm, and forward into a hollow that looked like a dark well, for barely any light seemed to reflect out of it. It was a moment at which Bracken would have given his very soul to catch one glimpse of sunshine on a bare face of white chalk, and to hear the run of a summer Duncton breeze through dry grasses, and orchids and blue harebells that lift the heart of the saddest mole. But beyond it surely there would be safety and food!

So down into the hollow they went, slipping here and there on snowy slates, lifeless wetness all around them and the rush of the waterfall growing louder all the time. There was not the scent of a single living plant to cheer them, and they knew without searching that they would have to climb back up out of this hollow even higher before having any hope of finding food.

It was only when they reached the bottom, with difficult steepness all about them and the feeling that the

slates might suddenly slide inward and bury them in their
jagged darkness forever, that they caught smell of the
creature again. The same savage smell they had had before, only fiercer and nearer.

As the stream rushed and bubbled and raced, they
heard over its noise what sounded like the rumble of
slate on slate but was, in fact, the first grim growlings of a
massive hound whose great paws and claws now covered
the tracks Bracken and Boswell had left minutes before
at the top of the hollow.

As Bracken stopped, turned and looked back the way
they had come, the scent and the sound melded into the
terrifying knowledge that a hound was on them. Arthur
of Siabod was at them and it seemed that the sky itself
had a snarling muzzle of teeth, that it had fiery yellow
eyes, that the slate tips were great living paws. Then the
sky, the tips around them and the very ground on which
they stood so defenselessly seemed to emit a scent of
death. His fur was yellow flecked with white, thick as
wire grass, his paws heavy, and his great head massive
as a bulwark of rock.

Arthur the Hound of Siabod tore down toward them
mockingly, his snarls the sound of pleasure as he raced
upon them, his great maw of flapping, loose flesh hanging
momentarily over them to take in their scent before racing away up the other side of the hollow where he turned
on loose slates, which flew away beneath his weight, and
began the pleasurable descent upon them once more.

Moles! It was usually better fun to dig them out from
where they shivered in fear among the slates to which he
had tracked them; even better to dig them out of the
valley meadows below Cwmoer, where they left a trail
any hound could follow. Only once before that he could
remember had mole come to Cwmoer itself, and that was
many killings ago. But if he could not sniff them out of
the slates or dig them out of the ground, he could play
with their fear of him right here, before shattering their
silky bodies against the slate and seeing their bloodstains
in the snow.

So, enjoying himself, Arthur tore down upon them
again, adding growls to his snarls, just for fun, because
living meat was so much more exciting than dead.

It was as the hound passed by a third time without
touching them that Bracken realized that they were being
played with and might yet have time to escape into the

many hollows off the track under the slates at the foot of the tip. He grabbed at Boswell and pushed him toward them, automatically shielding him as the hound began its fourth run upon them down the steep track.

Seeing them move, Arthur's great muscles rippled and flexed in his shoulders. He shifted his weight with the subtlety of a bird in flight, his back legs following his body in a swerve to the left as, to his delight, the moles pathetically scrabbled for shelter. With the slightest halts in motion and speed he effortlessly brought his great front paws hard on the ground just in front of their snouts, making them stop in panic and giving him the pleasurable whiff of their scent of fear.

They turned away, as he knew they would, and he swung his great rough-furred head to look at them, enjoying the flow of his great body as it turned sharply back on itself and he went in for a proper snout at them.

Bracken had stopped still when the hound came at them again, but as he went past, he pushed Boswell ahead again, turning back toward the hound. There are some threats so vast to a mole, so utterly beyond his sight, that resistance seems as absurd as a six-day mole pup fighting with its mother. And yet a pup does fight.

So, as Boswell ran on, Bracken turned back toward the great shining muzzle of Arthur and with all his body and spirit thrust out his talons at it as Medlar had so long before taught him. His talons were sharp, the lunge very powerful and it caught the hound with such surprise and sudden pain that he pulled massively back and growled for the first time with genuine anger.

With one great sweep of his paw he sought to catch both moles at once, the one who had struck out at him and the other who was fleeing. As Boswell dived beneath the massive slate toward which Bracken had pushed him, Arthur's claws, or one of them, ran searingly down Boswell's back, bringing an immediate rush of blood to it. This was sufficient to halt the swing of Arthur's paw enough for Bracken instinctively to sidestep its nearly fatal sweep, to snarl in his turn and to run under Arthur's gaping jaws after Boswell into the safety of the slate. A smaller adversary has some advantages. There was a great growling and snarling from above them as Arthur, angry but delightfully excited now, smelled the blood on his paw and hungrily thrust it under the slate, the claws scratching noisily at its edge. Getting a purchase on it, he strained to pull it aside but though it rocked and Bracken felt its weight lift and slide above him, it did not shift sufficiently to give Arthur access to the moles.

The slate was piled against another even bigger one, and it was to the shelter of this that Bracken now crawled, pulling the half-conscious Boswell with him. The hound lunged and thrust and barked about them, growling at his quarry, smelling the blood from Boswell's wound, hungry for the living flesh.

Then, as suddenly as his attack had begun, he fell silent, crouching down by the pile of slates where the moles were hiding, head on one side, paws stretched forward as he tried his next and often successful move—to wait for them to make a dash for it.

As the silence started, Bracken dared to breathe and turned to Boswell, whose wound he saw was deep and serious.

"Boswell! Can you hear me? Boswell! How much does it hurt?" Boswell only moaned, his eyes closed, and a curtain of blood from the long wound running down his left flank and turning his fur into a shiny, congealing bog.

The hound above them, whose odor was now all about their retreat, next tried scrabbling at the ground by the slates, great claws pumping up and down as he tried to dig them out. But the ground was hard with sharp fragments of slate and they gave as good as they got from Arthur's paws.

He sat down on his haunches once more and waited, pale eyes never leaving the slates, only a sullen twitch of his tail betraying the excited impatience he felt. He had sat like this before, for rabbit and weasel, vole and even for shrew. He had the patience to wait for mole.

The afternoon wore down into sullen gloomy skies as the same drift of weather that had brought wet snow the night before now carried thunderous rain toward the hills and mountain of Siabod. It came from the west in a great swath of lightning and noise, with a rolling of thunder and yellow, sudden light, into the darkest cwms of deeps of the dark mountains west of Siabod. Until, at last, it reached Siabod itself and as rain fell upon its peaks, lightning picked out its jagged summit against the dark evening clouds. Then, with a crack and a roar and flickering flashes of light, the storm began to roar around the great deep of Cwmoer, flattening the wavelets on the lake with pelting rain, breaking up the snow on the sullen slates, turning the streams all around them into torrents.

Like the rocky bluffs that stuck out of the valley's sides, Arthur's head stayed motionless in the rain, water running through his rough, tawny fur and dropping off the blue-black skin that hung from his lower jaw. His eyes stayed fixed on the two slates where the moles were still hiding as a thin run of surface water began to slide under them.

Its cold wet at first seeped under the slate, wetting Bracken's belly as he tried unsuccessfully to move himself and the now-unconscious Boswell out of its way. But soon water dripped and poured all around him, running through the cracks between the slates and along the impervious ground under them until everything was wet and cold.

But Bracken barely noticed it. Nor did he think very much now of the hound whose paws lay on the wet ground within sight from under the slate, waiting for their move. Bracken was thinking of Boswell. He had seen another mole die of an evening, up on Duncton Hill, and that one had not deserved such an end, either. He loved Boswell. The Stone knew how much. Now his friend would need food and shelter, warmth and love if he were to survive, but here they lay trapped, denied everything. Bracken had crouched in another storm, too, when he had started out across the vales that lay beneath Duncton Wood, wondering if one day he might go out among them as the moles of the Ancient System once had done. Now here he was.

As the storm crashed about him and the lightning shone on the wet ground around the slate, casting the shadow of Arthur into their retreat, such memories as these began to replace the fear Bracken had felt. He remembered being in the Chamber of Dark Sound with Mandrake coming toward him and starting the hum that created the sound that seemed to confuse Mandrake and cause him to stumble and hesitate in the center of the great chamber. He remembered, too, that great power that had come to him then, making his limbs feel bigger and his talons more and more powerful. And how Mandrake had stared over at him, afraid. Then the power had nearly overwhelmed him, for he was too young to know how to use it. Now he was older, stronger, and had learned something of the spirit of the warrior from Medlar.

Now something of the power Bracken had felt in different ways so many times before began to consolidate in him, tough as the slate that gave them protection. While Arthur, crouching in the storm, the rain pouring off him, let his tail fall still and shifted uncomfortably. Some deep instinct made him switch his gaze for a moment from the slates on the ground to the rain-swirled heights above him, searching for something he could not see.

There *had* been another mole here, the only other mole that had dared venture in his lifetime into Cwmoer. No good pretending he had forgotten, though many killings had assuaged the memory. A bigger, darker mole than either of these two, with talons as strong as a badger's.

That mole had faced him as well and not run away. Its odor was the fiercest of any creature he had ever faced. Faced! Does a hound talk of facing a mole? In his nightmare *he* did, when he remembered the power in the mole who had faced him contemptuously somewhere among these slate tips. He knew where. Slowly he admitted the memory to his mind and saw again the great mole who had snarled back at him near this very spot, talons as ready to kill as his own, and had finally passed him dismissively by, finally turning its back contemptuously on him and ignoring his howls.

Arthur's baleful eyes searched the great cliffs about him, feeling that something was there and was staring at him, wishing him ill and robbing him of his pleasure and will. He began to howl, while beneath the slate, Bracken began to move, stirring himself into the action which he knew he must take and which now no longer cast a single shadow of fear into his heart.

High up on the edge of the cwm, her blind eyes the color of the rain-filled mist that swirled and raced there, Y Wrach crouched at the end of the tunnels with her snout to the depths below. She had been waiting, a lifetime of waiting, waiting for the sound that now came up to her from the black depths beneath: the lost and bewildered howling of Arthur the Hound of Siabod, carried up on the storming winds and which signaled in some way she did not yet comprehend the return to her of Mandrake.

> *Gwyw calon rhag hiraeth*
> *Crai by myrd rhag lledfryd heno* . . .

she chanted.

> *My heart is withered from longing*
> *I am wasted from melancholy tonight*
> *But give me strength through this storm* . . .
> *Come Mandrake, hear his howling*
> *Give of your spirit, hard as the slate,*
> *Arc out your talons where buzzard floats*
> *The rocks are bare above* . . .

Her voice was harsh, spittle ran from her cracked mouth, and now the sound of the Siabod she spoke was not musical but fierce, invoking onto the mole who struggled in the cwm below the power he needed but which she could only partially give.

She felt the weight and waste of age upon her, but fought it off to pass down to Bracken what power she had, and more than that, to celebrate the trust she had that Mandrake was not dead and would come back.

She did not need eyes to see the struggle. She crouched, withered, fierce as hail, proud as the eye of an eagle. Rebecca, was that the name? It does not matter; it does not matter that he's dead, he's coming back.

She cried it out in Siabod, old Siabod, whose sounds are harsh and pity not the hound his cries. She shivered like a young female, she felt a tremble of life where any other mole would only sense a withered womb and see the obscene-seeming twistings of an ancient female whose cries no longer even sound the words of the old ancestral tongues but slide, or rather scream, into the eternal sound of a frightened female giving birth again. A second chance and bastard Mandrake you will come again and see the Stones whose light you saw before and never could forget, whatever darkness shadowed out its grace. You, come!

She cried out the words into the wind, spitting them down toward Arthur, drowning his howls as they sought a way out of Cwmoer, past whatever it was there, staring down at him, wishing him ill and sending him weakness and Bracken strength.

The rain lightened but the storm grew wilder as Bracken slowly and heavily backed his way out from under the great slate into the evening light under Arthur's great stare. The hound watched helpless, his flanks trembling from cold, though not a cold that any other creature felt, as the mole came out, rump first, dragging the other mole with him.

It was contemptuous, just like the other one whose presence now seemed to swirl about again, around this mole. It turned and faced him. Faced him! From its mouth, caught by the loose skin of its neck, heavy in the wind, hung the other mole.

Bracken stood solid in the storm, his Boswell hanging from him like a pup, and gazed in pity and anger on great Arthur, such a power in him now that it needed no raised talons to tell out its force.

He had picked up Boswell because he loved him and was going to see him live just as he had wanted Cairn to live. Ten hounds of Siabod would not stop him seeing Boswell live. So he picked him up with gentle love, dragged him from the retreat where he was dying from cold and wet and lack of food and boldly placed him down between the massive paws of Arthur.

Then he began to speak out the words that came to him from the silent Stone and made him, Bracken, seem ever greater and more powerful to Arthur, bigger and bigger, as behind him another mole seemed to rear, its great head scarred with fights; and Arthur's eyes widened in fear and he started to howl because his limbs refused to take him away from the horror as the mole began to speak words whose meaning he could not understand and yet were clear as claws.

"Arthur, Hound of Siabod, see the blood of Boswell you have spilled and freeze in fear before its flow. This is a holy mole and you are cursed for what you dared to do. You will help him live . . ."

It was the Stone that gave the words to Bracken, the Stone that made Arthur see the one thing that puts a fear into all spirits, however mighty the body that shields them—a mole that no longer fears death—and made him understand the intent of the words whose language he could not understand.

The mole needed help. Arthur turned suddenly and in three or four great bounds was up on the far edge of the hollow they were in and looking back down on Bracken, whining slightly to make him understand, as his mouth hung open and his breaths came out in miserable bursts as he waited for Bracken to follow.

Bracken looked up at him, then down at Boswell, then back up the steep slope to where Arthur stood. Wearily he bent down again and took up Boswell by the neck to carry him to wherever it was that the hound seemed to want to lead them.

Up toward Arthur he struggled, step by slow step, the roar of the stream to his right and the gray winds battering the rock faces behind and above him. Up and up he struggled, as once he had climbed the chalk escarpment of Uffington, each painful breath rasping out of his mouth between the folds of Boswell's neck skin which his teeth hung on to. Sometimes Boswell's crippled paw rocked limply against his struggling ones and sometimes, where Boswell's back dragged on the slates, it left behind a smear of blood, red on the dead gray slates.

Then he was up to where Arthur stood towering above him, the hound's great flanks breathing in and out as his head and face pointed this way and that across the flatter moor that ran beyond the quarry of Cwmoer. Until his gaze settled on a point where the stream flowed more gently, and he led Bracken across to it with infinite and troubled patience.

Bracken found himself at last by a gentler curve of the stream where saxifrage and heart-leaved sorrel grew, and he knew that they would find food and shelter there. He lay Boswell gently down and crouched, faltering now, by him, while the hound, his yellow eyes gazing down on them, wondered what they would want of him.

"Rebecca." Boswell whispered the name so softly that Bracken had to lean close to him and hear it again. Then Bracken said to himself wearily, "Oh yes, Rebecca. She would help if she were here. She would know how to save Boswell."

"Tell him," whispered Boswell, gulping with the strain of speaking, "tell him to find her. Tell him to seek her out."

Oh Boswell, said Bracken to himself, desolation coming over him. He got up from the hollow by the stream and stepped out into the wind. He ignored Arthur, who crouched waiting. He snouted into the wind and then southeastward toward where Duncton Wood lay so many hundreds of molemiles away. The words formed long be-

fore the idea did, for the idea was absurd and words are
easy: "Boswell needs you, Boswell needs you. Can you
hear him calling, give me the strength to heal him," and
as he spoke the words to himself the spirit of them became stronger in him and he began to feel again the
power of the Stone, and then the more specific force of
the Duncton Stone, and then a wild Siabod calling off
along the top of Cwmoer, wild and harsh in the wind, a
call of triumph, and he knew that the impossible was
possible. So he turned to great Arthur once more and
said "Go and find our healer, go and get Rebecca, go
away from Cwmoer and lead our healer here."

Arthur reared and shook in fear, his yellow eyes casting
about the moor and sky, his flanks trembling at whatever
it was this mole, this monster mole, wanted him to do. Go
and get Rebecca . . . the idea stormed about them. Perhaps
Bracken did not even speak its words. Perhaps their power
simply showed itself.

Arthur's paws scratched at the ground, his great head
swayed back and forth as Bracken began to think again
of Rebecca and the Stone and some deep sense of calling
came to Arthur. He bent his head down to the mole he
feared, and sniffed and snouted at him, taking in his
scent, and then raised his head and looked across the
moor away from Siabod and down into the valleys from
where the pulling was coming, aching to find the thing
they wanted.

"Bring Rebecca here. Bring our healer here."

And Arthur turned at last away from the hold of
Cwmoer, down through its falls and rocks by the way these
moles had come, away from their cries whose power in
breaking him had brought him such strange distress. He
bounded down the hills away from them until he found
the scent again, and it showed him whatever it was they
wanted him to bring back for them.

The Siabod moles heard him before they saw him, a
great hound in maddened distress: running over the surface, howling and scratching here and there with his great
paws. He surprised some on the surface and they thought
themselves dead when his great snout and maw came
down on them, sniffing at them. But then he dismissed
them, for they were not the scent he was looking for.

The Siabod moles tell of it still, of how Arthur followed

the scent of Bracken and Boswell down into the valley the way they had come, and of how they heard his howlings from near the river and then suddenly a thunderous barking, like a hound that has found its prey.

While Celyn himself, who heard the hound and later saw him clear as slate in the sun, made a song of it which told how Arthur came back from the valley carrying a mole that none of them had ever seen or scented before.

Rebecca never spoke of how Arthur found her, or much of her journey to Siabod, though she would have known that in a way Celyn's song was true. For though Arthur never carried her he did lead her up the valley and round to Cwmoer, watching over every inch of what to him must have seemed slow progress.

Massive and dangerous though he was, she knew he would never harm her for she was not afraid of him, as Mandrake was not afraid. How can a mole be afraid of a hound who carries such loss and craving as he did? And perhaps he sensed that she was *of* Mandrake, the monster mole, and that all of them were monsters who had a power that made him tremble. So he watched over her, running forward impatiently, and back to where she was struggling forward, then on again and urging her to come to where those other moles were waiting.

But if she was slow how could he know that she was with litter? No mole now knows or will ever know which mole was her mate. Though why she took him is obvious enough because it was spring and mating time, and had not Rebecca suffered enough litterless days on her own? Perhaps she feared she would never see another mating time. Perhaps she found a male somewhere below Siabod who sensed her desire and had none of the fears the Duncton males had in the presence of their healer.

Her pregnancy was nearing its term when Arthur found her and perhaps she would have let him carry her, as the ballads would have us believe, if she had not been thinking of her young. There are some things about which the histories of Uffington are silent.

Did she sense that it was to Bracken and Boswell that Arthur was leading her? Did she hear Bracken's call? Or did her instinct go even deeper and make her sense, as she passed up the shadowy paths of Cwmoer, that above the rock faces an ancient female was watching blindly, sensing that she was there, and then singing a cracked song into the wind in old Siabod, whose words spoke of Mandrake's return and wove tears into triumph?

Death and life, suffering and triumph are all one, they are all one, and disease or health, they matter not. They are all one was the theme of despair behind the jumble of suffering thoughts that overtook Boswell in the dreadful days following Arthur's departure.

While Bracken, between searching for food and forcing Boswell to eat what he could, tried to say no no no no in so many different ways and so to halt the slide into despair and death toward which Boswell's thoughts seemed to be leading him.

There is an intimacy between moles in a death burrow when one mole lies dying and another uselessly watches every shiver of pain, every weak smile of bravery, every shaking of fear, every sliding into puppish cries and sees the blood and the vomit and the messing that accompanies the stiflement of life. An intimacy and secretiveness which afterward make the healthy one forget what he saw and heard and smelled. Just as a mother forgets the messing her pup once caused, so does a mole who watched a loved one near death not feel disgust at the ugliness that goes with a body's decline.

So Boswell, so Bracken. But a decline from wounds is a different thing than from disease or age; its danger, and what may weigh the balance down, lies in the loss of spirit that dies with wounds—for without the will that made the first pup cry, no mole would ever have raised its head and laughed at the world about it.

So Boswell now. The days dragged by and Bracken barely slept. He talked to his beloved Boswell in images of warmth, answering each of Boswell's weakening despairs with whispered memories of life that he had seen or they had seen together.

Boswell's wound coursed deeply down his back, and though it did not fester or poison it seemed to have ripped out his will to live. He lay belly down, for any other position caused him worse pain, with his snout on one side to ease his breathing. His paws became as floppy as a pup's and of the food, mushed up, that Bracken tried to feed him, only a small part went down—the rest dribbling back out of his weak mouth.

But at least Boswell sometimes asked if Rebecca was

coming, and that, surely, said that he was still looking to a life beyond his pain.

Bracken dug out a temporary burrow for them both, but it was so shallow and the tunnel so short that light of day came in. And the cold of night as well. Days ran into nights which lost themselves in days, but there were so many times when Boswell seemed so weak that it was minutes that Bracken prayed for, not whole days.

"Let him hold on for one more hour . . . let him live until the rain has stopped . . . let him stay until the first light of dawn . . ." So Bracken pleaded with the Stone, begging that his friend might hold on to life until Rebecca came.

Until, at last, after eight days of waiting, Arthur returned. His paws were cut and bloody, his coat was covered in mud and grit and there were great cuts and gashes across his face where he had plunged through blackthorn and brambles, and a terrible cut under his left flank where, in leaping over some obstruction, the cut of steel had caught him.

But he had led Rebecca in safety over the molemiles, a journey that moles still celebrate with gratitude and pride, and he took her to the ground by the temporary burrow as gently as he had led her. Who she was, or what she was for, he did not know; but his journey was done and the cliffs of Cwmoer no longer seemed to want to press down upon him; and the great moles that had threatened him from the shadows were gone. He scratched at the ground, waited until Bracken came, and then turned wearily back down the track, his tail low and his body dragging with fatigue to hide in his own lair where he could forget these moles, or try to, and dream of summer days when no trouble like they brought bothered him.

The first thing Bracken noticed about Rebecca was that she was with litter, and not his litter. The second was that she was not the mole, the fictitious female, he had created in his imagination in the long moleyears of their separation. This was not the mole he had prayed for, whose memory had comforted him, whose caress had become in his mind like the music of water or wind. She was tired, she was older, she was worried.

"Rebecca!" he said, a little hostile.

"Bracken!" She smiled, seeing at once his confusion and disappointment. And seeing, too, how much thinner he had become—just as he had been when they met for the very first time. Did he know how wild his fur looked, or how lost his eyes? Did he know how nervous and ill at ease he was?

"It's Boswell, isn't it?" she asked. He nodded and took her down into the burrow where he crouched uneasily as she examined Boswell's wound. She asked Bracken questions about it, but less for the information they gave her (she got that from touching poor Boswell) than in the hope that they might put Bracken at his ease. But it was no good, and the hostility she sensed to her touching "his" Boswell finally made her ask him gently to leave her alone with Boswell "so that I can talk to him as a healer must and for no other reason than that."

Oh, she sighed as Bracken left, miserably; oh, my love! She was so tired and there was nothing, nothing in the world, that she desired more at that moment than Bracken's trusting touch and caress in her fur so that she could know that he was there with her, in love and silence. As she turned to Boswell she scolded herself for thinking, as Rose had done before her so many times, that she wished there were a mole who would one day reach out and touch her and let her rest.

Later, moleyears later, Boswell would say that his days of illness on Siabod were the days when he learned most about physical suffering. For a mole born with such a disadvantage as a withered paw, it was a remarkable thing that by the Stone's grace he so rarely suffered assault or direct physical hardship.

He knew, as Bracken did not, how important his contact with Rebecca was in those long days and nights. She stayed by him constantly (as close to him as Rose had once been to Bracken in the Ancient System), whispering her healing words and letting him find again, in the security of her warmth, the spirit and strength he had lost when Arthur wounded him so deeply.

Yet Boswell was a healer, too, and as he gained in strength, his own acceptance of her great love of life, which most moles found so hard to face, helped her through her final days before her litter came. Not many males, certainly very, very few scribemoles, have ever been so close to a female with litter as Boswell was in those strange healing days.

For Rebecca herself, the only hardship was Bracken's uneasy companionship to them both: he made another burrow for himself nearby and unstintingly found them food and whatever herbs he could that might be of help. When the weather grew colder, as it did two days after her arrival, he reburrowed the tunnels to insulate Boswell's burrow better.

But there was an air of distrust about Bracken's contact with Rebecca which put an impassable barrier between them so that, although both ached for an expression of love, neither knew how it could be done. The fact that she was with litter made him angry and turned and twisted in his mind and put a barrier of suspicion and jealousy before his eyes.

The time came when Rebecca made a burrow of her own and began gathering what nesting material she could from the sparse vegetation that grew by the stream where they lived. She did not want to litter there, for there was something grim and desolate about Siabod, but she did not trust herself to move back down through the Cwmoer, even with Bracken's help, and anyway, Boswell was still weak.

The weather turned colder and a bitter wind blew and began to put a layer of verglas on the rocks near their tunnels so that they became slippery and unsafe for even the steadiest talon. The matgrass snapped and crackled in the cold, darkness fell swiftly, the sun seemed lost forever, and the snow that had fallen the night before they had first come up Cwmoer, having half melted with the rain, had now permanently frozen on the rocks where it had stayed or lay dry and shiny among the tussocks of grass. Late spring in Siabod seemed to bring harsher weather than the cruelest winter in Duncton.

Now that Rebecca was living and spending more time in her own burrow, Bracken talked to Boswell more and found he was beginning to recover fast. As ever, Boswell was aware of, and upset by, his friend's distrust of Rebecca. Could they never see that the love they had was as strong as the sunshine? Why was Bracken such a fool, and Rebecca, who knew so much, unable to make Bracken see their love?

"Look after her, Bracken, because she needs your help, you know. I sometimes think you don't know how much she loves you . . ."

Bracken shrugged. "She's more concerned with that litter of hers than anything else," he said, betraying his real feelings. "But, of course, I'll do what I can. But a nesting female doesn't want males hanging about, every-mole knows that. They like to get on with it themselves."

It was night, and the wind stirred, fretting at the tunnel entrances, seeming to find a way into even the warmest spots. Outside the stream rushed and dashed against the rocks, grass chattered against the entrances, a night when only the most peaceful moles can fall easily to sleep.

Boswell was worried and concerned, but he didn't know what about. Bracken crouched talking to him in stops and starts, eyes flicking about the burrow, sentences cut off by the howl of the wind outside.

Rebecca, separated from them by two tunnels and the short surface run between, stirred restlessly. Her tail switched back and forth, she couldn't get her body comfortable now that it was so full and her litter was nosing and muzzling and turning inside her, limbs pushing under her smooth belly fur. She didn't like this Siabod. She didn't want her young born here among dark, peaty soil and slate fragments that cut a careless mole. She shuddered to think now of the dark falls of rock in Cwmoer beneath them and the Siabod heights some-where over the moor beyond from where the peat-colored river rushed down.

She wanted Bracken there, nearer than he was. She wanted to hear him stir outside, and not the wind. She wanted to call his name and know that he was there to say the silly things that mean so much; the silly things no male but Cairn had ever said to her when she was very young.

"Bracken, Bracken, Bracken," she whispered, looking at her swollen sides and trying to invoke not a mole so much as a peace and silence she had known when they had touched together by the glimmering Stillstone. She started to cry and then stopped, and then started again. She wanted him to come to her without being called. She wanted her litter to come in the warmth of his trust. She was so restless, so confused, and the burrow wasn't right any more, not here with those black slates outside in whose shadow Mandrake had been born.

She stirred yet again, rising clumsily to her paws and going first to the tunnel and then to the entrance and then snouting outside against the bitter wind that came down the moor. She looked over through the darkness toward where the entrances to Bracken's and Boswell's burrows lay and wished that Bracken was there on the surface to greet her.

She wished he would come over to her and whisper to her and hustle her back into the warmth of her burrow and say it was all right, it didn't matter where her litter was born. But she was restless and turned away upslope from the stream, thinking that perhaps there might be a better place for her litter nearby where the soil was less cold and a burrow could be free of these slates. She moved restlessly along, almost talking aloud to herself, telling her young that it wouldn't be long now and she loved them and they shouldn't be afraid; though she was —yes, she was—so afraid.

Bracken follow me follow me, she thought as she moved higher and higher in the darkness up the slopes to find somewhere better. The wind grew steadily colder, but Rebecca didn't notice; indeed, she was almost hot with sudden energy as she moved on steadily away from the safety of her burrow out onto the moor that rose round and above the quarried cliffs of Cwmoer.

Then, unnoticed, the first whipping sleets of snow came rushing with the wind. She laughed into the wind. She felt hot and alive in it and as the sleety snow whipped along more strongly through the darkness, she did not care.

I'll find a place for them soon, she said to herself, the grass changing to grassy rock, the flat turning to a slope that grew steeper and steeper as she contoured it, the cwm off to her right. There is a better place . . . but I haven't quite found it, she kept telling herself. The stream suddenly stopped her forward movement and she climbed up along it until the ground grew flatter where it had fanned out into braids of streamlets running among soft, boggy grass and moss, and she crossed it.

So Rebecca wandered, higher and higher up the slopes of Siabod to where the soils were thin as old fur and the return down the rocks that she was able to climb so easily became more and more difficult.

Perhaps she rested. Perhaps she drank at the chill water of the innumerable streamlets that coursed down the slopes and which she crossed without difficulty; always she must have been looking for soil and a place for a burrow that reminded her more of the peace and warmth of Duncton Wood. Until sometime in the night, as dawn approached, the energy that preceded the start of the birth of her litter must have begun to fail and Rebecca must have started to feel tired and desperate.

Sometime in the night, not too long before dawn, the real blizzard came. Sudden, cold and harsh—a driving and swirling of biting snow that stung a mole's snout and roared so loud that thinking became hard. The snow barely settled, preferred to race like moving ice across the surface; but then it began to form eddies and drifts to the lee side of the bigger rocks and to spread out from these in scatters of white. Nowhere safe for Rebecca to stop, so on she went, still certain that she could find a place where she could burrow down into stillness for the sake of herself and her litter.

Did she stop now and try to turn back and discover that it was impossible to go back without sliding and falling? Did she think to find a drift of snow and stop for safety there? Did she wander here and there, confused, and know that she was lost? The blizzard grew worse, creating a nightmare dawn in which the only sound is the rushing snow and the wind seems to tear at fur and eyes and talons and tail, flattening a mole that tries to move against it, toppling one over that tries to run with it.

It was sometime then that Bracken awoke and heard the blizzard's roar. He went immediately to Rebecca's tunnel, finding even the short run between the two a struggle to cross. But she was not there. He rushed back to Boswell's burrow, and the two called uselessly, Boswell coming to the entrance and peering out into the racing snow that fell in flurries of cold into his tunnel.

"Rebecca! Rebecca!" they called, but the blizzard was so loud that they could not even hear each other's call.

Bracken stepped full out into the blizzard and cried "Rebecca!" for he loved her, she was his love, and as panic and anger came over him at the thought of her loss, he pressed forward up the slope in the direction in which his instinct told him she had gone without even looking back to say a word to Boswell.

"Bracken! Bracken!" cried Boswell as the racing blizzard blotted out Bracken's retreating back and Boswell too tried to go after him, but was too weak and found it hard even to regain access to his tunnels.

While up through the blizzard Bracken went, trusting to his instinct to find Rebecca, who must have gone seeking a birth burrow as females in litter sometimes will. Oh, Rebecca! he cried out in despair as the icy, racing snow tore at him, Rebecca!

She wandered on through the blizzard, no longer in any set direction but disorientated and growing progressively weaker as the effort to find a place, any place she could litter, came over her. But not here, not here where the snow is thin as ice on the bare rock ground and shadows of half-seen boulders and shapes in the racing snow seem to loom; and where a litter would be lost. Not here!

Somewhere, sometime, Rebecca came across the fresh tracks of another mole in the thin snow. She looked at them disbelievingly until she thought, and then she knew, that it was Bracken, her Bracken, come for her, and she turned to follow them, for they were fresh and the racing snow hadn't even started to obscure them. "Bracken!" she must have called, trying to follow and catch up with him, "Bracken!"

Ahead of her, not knowing she was so close by, he pressed on even faster and called her name despairingly into the wind, Rebecca, Rebecca, Rebecca.

But try as she might, she was too tired and too heavy to move fast enough, and the tracks raced on ahead of her, beginning to fill with snow, growing fainter before her as her Bracken, trying to find her, moved farther and farther away from her. Then, finally, she lost the tracks and despair began to creep over her as she turned to the right, high above Cwmoer, to go with the wind, which was easier for her. And she knew that soon, in this waste, with the blizzard raging around, she would have to litter as Mandrake's mother had done. Oh my loves, she must have whispered, forgive me, forgive me, as she hopelessly sought a place where she might burrow on the black slate plateaus of Siabod.

Off to her left, far off now and growing farther, Bracken pressed on, fearing more and more that he had lost his Rebecca forever in the snow.

He stopped and snouted about into the blizzard all around trying to make contact with his love. Great falls of black rock now rose above him, covered in ice and with the thin half-snow of the blizzard swirling like white

mist aross their sheer faces. He did feel a pull from far,
far off to the northwest, a pull that he wrongly thought
might be his Rebecca calling. So he turned toward it and
away from his Rebecca, not knowing that up there,
through the wastes, far off, stood the great Stones of Castell y Gwynt, which had waited for mole for so long. He
thought he could feel his Rebecca there, and so he stumbled forward across the rocks and moors where the wind
was so strong that only the thinnest layer of snow settled.
He prayed to the Stones for his Rebecca as he began the
terrible trek that, unbeknown to him, would grant the last
wishes of Skeat that the Stone should be honored even in
these wastes; and to fulfill his promise to the scribemoles
of Uffington and Boswell as well. But he only thought of
Rebecca and of how somehow, somewhere, he had lost
her.

While Rebecca, lost now above Cwmoer in the white-
out of the blizzard, finally gave up her futile search for
safety and settled into the thin snow, her back curled
against the bitter wind, as one by one her litter began to
be born and from their very first moment she battled to
protect their lives just as Mandrake's mother had once
battled so bravely to protect his.

It was three full days before Boswell was able and
strong enough to move from his burrow out into the blizzard. He had thought a thousand times of what he should
do, knowing that he did not have the strength to go upslope into the storm, and only one possibility seemed to
slip and slide his way back down through Cwmoer and try
to find Arthur of Siabod and perhaps he would know what
to do. But he never could find him, wandering lower and
lower down Cwmoer in his weakness from the wound until
the time came that he had to find food and so give up the
search. Soon afterward he knew he would never find the
strength to go back up into the blizzard wastes above
Cwmoer. He had lost Bracken, lost Rebecca. The Seventh
Stillstone, the Seventh Book . . . they were not after all
his to find. He found that he could not even return to
Siabod, for the way by which he had come so recently
with Celyn and Bracken was blocked by snow and ice. So
he turned his back on Siabod and pointed his snout back
to the south, toward Uffington. Asking himself as he left
those futile questions to the Stone that anymole asks in the
face of pointless tragedy, all of which begin with *Why?*

❧ 43 ❧

THAT same day, Bracken, nearing starvation, found to his surprise that he was dropping rapidly into a valley where the snow was thicker, and he was able to burrow into its silence out of the blizzard. If the soil beneath had been anything else but wormless peat, he might have stayed still and waited for the blizzard to pass. But it was peat, and so on he had to go—sometimes through the snow itself, sometimes out on the surface where its depth was shallow. Until, at last, he was in a river valley where the soil was rich with food under the layer of snow.

For a whole day he was too tired and shocked to do more than rest and eat and regain his strength. But when he had, the pull from the northwest continued. What called him on? He knew it was no longer the hope of finding Rebecca, for Siabod was now far behind him. He crouched clear of the snow's edge by the river and looked across it through the continuing wind, sensing more great heights beyond him. His snout traveled the length of the great ridge on the far side of the valley and he began to know that there, where such power seemed to come from, must stand the Stones he had been sent to reach. Castell y Gwynt . . . Tryfan . . . Rebecca. He whispered the names into the wind, careless of his own life now that Rebecca was gone, and knowing that this was his final trek.

Even so, he shivered as he looked about the worm-full tunnels he had made by the river, and then up to the wastes from which he had no expectation of ever returning. He remembered something Celyn had said about the final climb having to be done fast to the Stones because the ground was wormless and then, impulsively, he was off—up the river to a bridge, across a way which even the roaring owls seemed to have abandoned to the snow, and then climbing once again with growing despair in his heart. So far to go, so little time.

Strange thoughts flew at him out of the wind and snow, most of them of Mandrake. It was as if he knew with certainty that this was the way Mandrake had come—up Cwmoer, over Siabod, and then up here. He remembered Mandrake again, his power and despair, but most of all he remembered Mandrake's last sad cries to Rebecca by the Duncton Stone, which he had not known how to listen to. Now, as he climbed onward and upward into the cold and rocks on the far side of the valley from Siabod, he spurred himself forward by telling himself that he was at last answering Mandrake's call. Cruel Mandrake, mad Mandrake, but a mole that Rebecca had loved. And if, as he climbed, he fancied he saw in the flurries of snow and the changing shadows of the contorted rocks the shape of a great and lumbering mole, what then? It no longer mattered. Y Wrach had said that Mandrake would come back. So let him come back, here now, to guide me with his knowledge and power to the great Stones, and to the Tryfan Stones themselves.

Celyn had been right; these heights *were* wormless. What worms ever live among acid peats or a surface where only rocks seem in place?

Steep, steeper, steeply dangerous drops fell beneath his slipping talons, which could hardly hold onto the icy rocks. Falls into black rocks far below, wind racing up sheer faces along whose very edge he had to climb. No place for moles.

Steeper and steeper, into the sky itself. Then suddenly, quite suddenly, the terrain was rounded and flat and on top of the world. Between blasts of wind he could make out square and random shapes of rocks stretching eerily away on flat ground, and piled like jumbled slates one on top of another, or toppled over on their sides, or rising in a fan like the spines of a dead hedgehog. Blacks and whites, snow and ice, eerie silences around corners of spined, black rock. Sudden rushing of winds and ebbs. All in a high land of shattered rock whose edges were sometimes square, sometimes sharp, always changing as a mole approached them, or passed them by, or flying snow hid them. And strange silences.

Great strength began to surge into Bracken, for he knew that at last he was within reach of Castell y Gwynt. Somewhere in this flat land of waste that was sterile of all life but himself and a few gale-bent tufts of heather, the stones they wrongly called the Stones of Siabod stood. They were beyond Siabod.

And then, off to his right, as he turned away from a great tower of rocks, he heard through the wind the whistling and howling of more wind which came louder

and softer, as varied in its range as only one other thing
he had ever known: the sounds in the Chamber of Roots
beneath the Duncton Stone. The sound of Castell y
Gwynt.

The ground was now pure loose rock, if rocks a hundred thousand times the size of a mole can ever be called
loose. His vision was still obscured by racing, powdered
snow, so he clambered blindly on toward the sound,
awe and fear growing in his heart as it grew louder and
more varied, menacing and sweet. The sound grew louder
and was somewhere in the sky above him, the sound of
wind among rock, twisting and swirling in and out of the
hollows and flutes and rises and falls of rock. Sharp
rocks, talons of rocks, a rock mass that rose from out of
the snow and now was steep and massive before him,
and he stopped in wonder before its great power and
raised a paw as if to touch its great talons with his own,
his mouth open in wonder. Castell y Gwynt.

So much suffering to get here. So much struggle. And
Rebecca, what of my Rebecca? Are these the Stones I've
lost you for? And which of you are the Tryfan Stones?

As his eyes searched among the rising stones, each of
which was four or five times the height of the Duncton
Stone and whose tops were obscured again and again: Is
the Stone here? What must a mole do to reach up to it?
Why so much suffering for *this*? Why so much suffering
at all?

But as he stood doubtful before the Stones, what great
shape rose behind him among the other stones of the
plateau of Gwynt and urged him to trust the Stone? He
thought he heard a mole, a massive mole, the sound
of life, and turned round to see . . . but there was nothing
but the howling of the wind through the rocks behind
him, and those of the Castell y Gwynt above.

Well, he whispered softly to himself, at last, well, what
am I anyway, unless I'm part of it, whatever it may be?
Then Bracken began to pray to the Stone, before the
Stones, and say those words that so long before Mandrake, standing in this very spot, might himself have said
if only he had had the love of Rebecca then, or had
known Boswell, or had been graced to hear the silence
of the Duncton Stone. Bracken prayed for the moles of
Siabod, he gave thanks for the life within himself, he
prayed that the Stone would protect Rebecca wherever

it had taken her. He prayed to the memory of Skeat and in honor of the scribemoles of Uffington. He prayed that Boswell would know these prayers had been made. As he prayed, and the cold wind began to die, and he noticed nothing of himself but his silence in the Stone, he brought the worship of the Stone back to Siabod and the black heights beyond it.

When he thought he had finished, he found he had not. He prayed again for his Rebecca and thanked the Stone for the love that they had seen. And he wondered, curiously, which of the Stones were the Stones of Tryfan.

Then he *was* finished and became suddenly cold, so he turned at last from the Stones to find the winds growing lighter and the snow almost finished. Beneath him, only a few moleyards off, he saw a cliff edge into a steep, snow-filled drop into a cwm that went down and down as far as anymole could sense, and farther. Beyond it, the swirling snow danced in the wind, growing lighter and weaker as it faded away, and there came slowly through it not light but black darkness that rose before him as the snow cleared in a steepness of more rock. It rose higher and higher as his eyes widened in wonder and awe and the snow finally swirled away, revealing a massive, isolated peak on top of which he could sense there stood other Stones he could sense, but not see. The Stones of Tryfan, he thought.

"But it's impossible," he whispered, "impossible for mole—" for though it seemed so close across the void beneath him, almost within a talon's touch, it was impossible to reach. He now gazed at it in wonder as, so long before, Mandrake had gazed at it in fear. And as Mandrake had stepped forward to touch it in contempt, so now Bracken stepped forward, his paw outstretched in wonder, for he saw that a mole *can* touch the Stone, he can, he can; but as he tried, he was falling forward and rolling into steep snow, tumbling over, the peak of Tryfan rising higher and higher above him, rising away from his grasp as he fell down into the nameless cwm that had gaped beneath him and now took him. Snow flurried down as he fell, rolling on into an avalanche, carrying him down and down and farther down, and faster, snow all around him worse than a blizzard, and a sliding avalanche of silence building up about him as the cwm echoed outside the snow that enveloped him and of which he was a tumbling part. Far, far above him the two Stones of Tryfan stood out in a clearing sky.

As Bracken fell into white silence, the wind across on Siabod began to die away and the blizzard to stop. But Rebecca knew it had come too late for her; she might still have struggled alone down the slopes, and she might even have managed a single pup. But she looked at the four that lay against her teats but were now no longer able to get milk from them, felt them grow colder and colder against her encompassing belly and knew she could not leave three to die alone.

Whatever strength it was that had kept her alive for nearly six days through the howling winds was finally failing her now. Her mind had begun to wander, and she found it harder and harder to find the strength to keep the pups from crawling blindly from her protection into the chill that would kill them.

She whispered and mumbled to herself, talking to imaginary moles. She had even laughed in the night and with the dawn: she remembered them all, the moles she had loved. Why, Mekkins was there, out in the snow, calling her to him gruffly; and Rose was there, sweet Rose. And Sarah, and Bracken there, near her, and dear Boswell, sweet mole. And Mandrake up near the rocks that she now saw were nearby, he was there in the shadows, his talons trying to protect her from the wind because he loved her, yes he did.

Only the cold stopped her dreaming, though sometimes it lured her toward sleep—which she fought, and had fought for days, because there is no waking up on a mountain like Moel Siabod, above which the black ravens fly.

Food. She thought of it as a dream, an impossible thing, and it smelled so good. Remember the worms she stole from the elder burrows and Mandrake was angry, yes he was. Silly thing, he was, never seeing what was at the end of his snout.

The smell of food in these cold wastes where nothing lived! And Mandrake, the thought of him had given her such strength. Mandrake. Mandrake. She whispered his name and mixed it with the slidings of dreams of food and her Bracken as tiredness came toward her like darkness at night and even the strength to tend to the pups she had kept alive, and whose bleatings seemed so far away now, was leaving her.

"Difryd difro Mandrake, difryd difro Mandrake." She heard the words from beyond the darkness of sleep into which she was finally sinking, but it was his name that brought her back again, and a strong nuzzling, stronger than the pups could manage, much stronger. As she opened her eyes, she smelled food and saw at her side an ancient mole, female and gray, snouting blindly at her and muttering words she could not understand, except that it meant she was no longer alone up here where poor Mandrake had been born.

Y Wrach had found her. The worms she carried were the ones that Celyn had brought up through the tunnels the day before, the fifth day of the blizzard. He had found her writhing and cursing and shouting out at the storm and saying that Mandrake was near, he was, and didn't Celyn know that addewid ni wrieler ni ddiw? A promise not accomplished is no promise at all!

"He promised," she shouted, "he said he could come back. He's here now, up there, up there." So she took the worms and crawled painfully out into the blizzard to find him, refusing to let Celyn go with her. Hadn't she found Mandrake before with no mole's help?

"But you were young," he said, "you were young," and she laughed bitterly at her twisted hind paws and said "Just you see!"

When he asked if he should pray for her, she told him to wait for her in her tunnels, and pray whatever she liked.

Then she snouted her way blindly out into the storm, almost blown off her paws in the wind, and he waited until the wind began to die and there was no more blizzard. Then he did pray in the old Siabod way, prayers that sounded more like curses than worship. In a hard language. She must be dead.

But he stayed on to honor his promise, and before his stay could turn into a wake, she came back off the Siabod slopes, carrying a pup as pink with health as the stem of starry saxifrage.

Shut up and keep him warm, she cursed before she was gone again, and he did, in wonder he did. And then another, and a third. And she was gone again up to where Rebecca lay eating the food this ancient female had brought who now urged her to her paws with no words she understood but "Mandrake! Mandrake!"

It was darkening toward late afternoon by now, and the wind was freshening again, with touches of sleet in it. Rebecca herself picked up the last pup at the gestured bidding of the old mole and slowly went down the slope, following her clear tracks as the wind grew stronger and stronger behind her and the blizzard began again. Behind her she heard the mole call out the name Mandrake once more, the sound flying in the wind, and she turned with difficulty and saw, or thought she saw, great shadows of moles among the rocks higher up the slopes, that moved and melded into scurrying snow, all white and dark in the evening. And then the old female was gone forever, lost in the blizzard that had first brought her life. Rebecca turned away back down the old mole's tracks and entered into huge, slate-lined tunnels where she heard her young mewing for her, and found a scraggy-faced male who reminded her of no mole so much as Hulver doing his best to keep them in order as they wandered here and there vainly seeking out their mother's teats.

Today, in Siabod, Rebecca is legend. They talk still of how Y Wrach grew old and invoked the ancient powers of the Siabod Stones and went out into the blizzard to return with a litter of her own; of how she changed herself into the form of a female whose fur was soft and glossy gray, like no Siabod female's had ever been, and who claimed her name was Rebecca and said she could not speak Siabod.

They tell of how Rebecca's four male pups grew into four moles whose size made them unassailable in fights and whose courage brought back the pride of Siabod. They warn of the eastern slopes of Siabod where Y Wrach's spirit roams and where, when dusk falls and snow flies thick, her Mandrake may sometimes be seen, his talons raised protectively behind Y Wrach, a smile at last on his great, scarred face.

They tell how Rebecca brought love and joy back to the system after the plague, and how, when the summer came and her pups were beginning to leave the nest, she would tell tales of Rose, a healer she knew, and a mole called Bracken, who must have been as big as Mandrake because he faced Arthur the hound and defeated him.

They love to weave tales on Siabod, and confusing legends that shorten long nights and make the bitter days bearable. They love to sing an old song. But always they tell sadly of how, at last, when her pups were mature and her work was done, she said she must leave before the winter returned.

Then they love to tell the story of Bran, who accompanied her on her journey away from Siabod when she said she was going back to her own system, though all Siabod knew she was really Y Wrach in disguise.

"What happened to Bran?" ask the pups when they hear this last tale.

"Now there's a strange thing," they're told, "because he came back, you see. After moleyears and moleyears it was that he came back, but wouldn't ever speak a word about it. And that was strange, too, because there was never a mole liked to talk so much as Bran—before he left, mind. Journeys change a mole, see, so don't you go journeying off too far, little one . . ."

There's many an older Siabod mole, too, will claim that more than once, when they've been caught in a blizzard Rebecca's come for them out of the storm, sometimes like the beautiful mole she was, sometimes looking like Y Wrach had been, but always with the shadow of a great mole that was Mandrake among the rocks nearby to protect her, and she's shown them the way home to safety.

That's what they say, in Siabod.

V

THE SEVENTH
STILLSTONE

⤥§ 44 §⤥

FEW creatures in the world are so well equipped to survive burial in an avalanche as moles, whose very first action at birth is to burrow their way among their siblings and nesting material to find teats for suckling.

So Bracken burrowed through the depths of snow that finally came to rest in silence far, far beneath the towering cliffs of Tryfan. And he burrowed down, not up, for just as the plants in the cwm into which he had fallen knew that the soil was lime-rich so he knew that he would find food there.

He stayed on there long after the snow had cleared, through April and May, living in an isolation that, at last, he had learned to be at peace with.

Sometimes he would peer back at the cliffs and slopes down which he had fallen and wonder if Celyn and Bran were still in the east beyond them and if they thought him dead. Some days he would pick his way among the tussocks of fescue and scurvy grass down to the clear cwm lake and drink at the dappled water, whose surface reflected the distant peaks that lowered over the cwm.

Often he would think of Rebecca, with whom he had never even mated, and of what the power of their love had been—and still was, since it lived on inside him.

But as the summer advanced into June he grew restless, for this was only a haven, not a home, and he wanted to go back finally to where beech trees soared in sunlight and oak trees rustled and the soil was rich. He wanted to see the white of chalk dust on his talons again.

But perhaps what made him finally make the move to leave the cwm was the thought that Boswell at least might still be alive and might have got back safely to Uffington. In any case, he felt an obligation to return to Uffington and tell them that he had reached the Siabod

Stones and worshiped the Stone and even seen the Stones of Tryfan, which no mole could ever reach.

When he finally left the cwm and made his way down into the valley beneath it, he could not bear to turn north to trek a way back round to Siabod, because he feared the memories there would be too bleak. He had done what he had promised to do and now turned south, to make his way finally back to Uffington through other valleys and by way of other systems.

And so it is that systems south of Siabod to this day tell of his passing—Rhinog, Cader, Mynydd, Faldwyn and back to Caer Caradoc, through which he and Boswell had originally passed. He saw that system after system was beginning to recover from the plague, while they saw in him a strange, wild mole with a terrible loss in his eyes but whose power of spirit was so great that none dared oppose him. As he passed through their tunnels he asked for little and said less, just telling them his name was Bracken of Duncton and that he had been to Siabod and was going to Uffington. While they wondered if he was a scribemole or special in some other way.

They were right to see loss in his eyes, for once he was back to gentler country, where the plants were familiar and trees grew tall again, and the river water no longer froze in a mole's mouth, he missed Rebecca more and more. The sun did not shine but that he thought of her; no shadow fell on him but that he ached for the comfort of her touch. But now that she was gone the only thought that took him through the moleyears it took him to travel back to Uffington was the hope that he would find his beloved Boswell safe and well in the Holy Burrows.

He reached them finally in December, climbing up past the Blowing Stone as he had once before and entering the tunnels at the top of the escarpment like a forgotten shadow.

But they remembered him and clustered about him, chattering with excitement, eager for his news. Tell us! Tell us! they exclaimed, as he was led through the great holy tunnels to where the Holy Mole was. Is Boswell safe? was all he wanted to know, but no mole seemed to hear him.

So, in great excitement and with an unaccustomed

celebration in the Holy Burrows themselves, he found himself facing the Holy Mole himself, who was a mole he knew and remembered with love. It was Medlar, who had been in the silent burrows and who had come out on Skeat's death and been made Holy Mole.

Medlar looked on him in silence and saw, without a word being spoken, how much the mole he had taught to fight had suffered, and learned as well. Not being a scribe-mole, Bracken did not know the traditional greetings and another scribemole there said the words for him:

"Styn rix in thine herte!"

"Staye thee hol and soint," intoned Medlar.

"Me desire wot we none," said Bracken's proxy.

"Blessed be thou and ful of blisse," smiled Medlar into Bracken's eyes.

They brought him food and made him rest before he began his tale, but when he did he told it all quietly and with truth, as a warrior should, and they came to know that he had indeed fulfilled his promise to them. It was Medlar himself who raised the question uppermost in Bracken's heart; "And Boswell, do you know what finally came of him?"

"I don't know," said Bracken, "more than what I've said. I had hoped . . . I thought he might be here."

The scribemoles listening fell silent, one or two muttered a prayer of blessing, and the Holy Burrow in which they crouched grew still.

"He is," said Medlar softly. "He did come back and he told us of your courage in leading him so far. He told us how you must have faced Arthur the Hound after he had been injured. All of us here have prayed for you many times, Bracken, and hoped the day would come when you might return."

"But what happened to Boswell?" whispered Bracken, for there was nothing else that mattered to him any more.

"Come," said Medlar, "I'll show you. For though few moles have ever been where you will go, I know that it is right that you should see. If you were a scribemole I would simply tell you, but you are not, and there are things that some moles such as you had better see and accept than wonder about for the rest of their lives." Then he added very seriously: "But you must promise me, or the Stone itself, that you will say not one single word in the place where I shall take you."

But before Bracken began to nod his head and say of course, Medlar went on: "This may be your hardest trial, Bracken, harder than anything you have yet faced."

So, full of awe and fear, Bracken followed Medlar beyond the Holy Burrows into a tunnel that went west for two molemiles until he was inside the holy place where he had once crept unasked and heard the secret song.

The tunnels led down to a place where the soil was almost white with chalk and there was the deepest silence he had ever heard. There were one or two novice scribemoles there, who moved about with great peace and grace and silence and seemed to protect the tunnels into which Medlar led him. Until, at last, there stretched before him a great chamber, on one side of which were a series of simple burrows, some unoccupied with open entrances and many long since sealed. But there was one whose seal was fresh.

Medlar pointed to this one, and Bracken understood that his Boswell was inside it and had come of his own accord to live in the silent burrows.

Silently Medlar led him into a smaller tunnel at the end of the chamber that led to other smaller burrows running behind the bigger ones, each of which had a tiny entrance, no bigger than a paw, where food was put so that the moles who had chosen to live in absolute silence might stay alive. Griefstricken, Bracken gazed at the little opening that was the only contact that his Boswell now had with life. Never, ever, had he felt so desolate.

He returned to the main chamber and stared at the bleak, sealed walls, aching to dash his talons against them and cry out to Boswell to tell him that he loved him and had wanted to see him, and hear his voice, and feel his gentle touch once more. To tell him that Rebecca was gone from him and there was no mole left now who loved him as she and Boswell had.

Unable to move, unable to talk, unable to tell Boswell that he was there so close, Bracken found that all he could do was to weep and say a bitter prayer that Boswell, at least, might find peace.

"How do you know that he's all right?" asked Bracken when Medlar had led him back to the Holy Burrows.

"He takes his food," said Medlar simply. "He has been there ever since he came back in August. He asked that he might be allowed to go there, for he felt that though he had failed in his quest for the Seventh Stillstone and the Book, he might find something there that would bring him closer to the Stone."

"But why?" cried out Bracken bitterly. "That isn't where life is! Not there in that dead, lost place."

"No," said Medlar, "but to somemoles it may be the place where life is found. Always remember that the trials Boswell is now facing alone are the equal of any you have faced. You can fight another mole or a blizzard and know that you have won; but you should know, Bracken, how hard it is to face yourself in silence and seek out the truth that is inside your heart and soul. So pray for him, and try to bear your loss with compassion for him."

Later Medlar said, "He told me that he knew where the Seventh Stillstone was, and what the subject of the Seventh Book is. Do *you*?"

So Bracken told him what he and Rebecca had seen beneath the Duncton Stone, and how he and Boswell had talked about the Seventh Book.

"It was a long time ago, and though we told him where it is, I don't think he knew *what* the book's subject was. I don't think so . . . but perhaps something has told him since. Will he ever come out of the silent burrows, as you did, Medlar?"

"Only the Stone knows that. No mole—not even I!—can ask him. Many moles never come out, and their burrows are finally sealed. We believe that such moles have found the silence of the Stone. Others know, as I knew, when to come out, for their task may be different. As for Boswell, no mole can know. But trust the Stone if you can, Bracken, as I have learned to do."

Bracken was silent for a long time, and the two moles crouched together, the sacred peace of one bringing peace for a while to the restless heart of the other.

"What shall *I* do, Medlar? What is there left to do?" asked Bracken eventually.

Medlar smiled and touched Bracken's paw. "If I thought you might become a scribemole I would say so. But I do not believe that this is your way. Go back to Duncton, Bracken, and make your home there again."

"But Rebecca is gone, and so much of the wood burned down . . . what is Duncton for me now?"

"I cannot tell you," said Medlar, "but I know it is a

question that does have an answer. Go back to Duncton
and give the moles there your love and wisdom, as you
say Rebecca once did."

To Bracken it seemed bleak advice, but what else was
there to do? He was grateful to Medlar for having the
wisdom to show him the burrows in which Boswell was
now sealed, though their silence seemed to him a terrible
thing and a cold kind of holiness. Oh, Boswell, he murmured as finally, not even waiting to regain his full
strength, he left Uffington and turned east into the restless
November wind toward Duncton.

Rebecca's return to Duncton Wood had been as much
a miracle to the Duncton moles as her departure had
been a mystery. She had come back off the pastures one
autumn day as easy as you please, in the company of a
wiry kind of a mole called Bran who spoke with a harsh
accent and whose laugh, when it came, was as cunning
as a wind in gorse.

He stayed a while, seemed unimpressed by what he
saw, wouldn't say a word about Rebecca's journey or
what she had been up to, and then, when November
came, finally left.

Her return established once and for all time Comfrey's
status as a mole whose eccentric isolation and abstracted
habits seemed to have given him special gifts of wisdom
and foresight. He had always said Rebecca would come
back. Now he found the reverence they held him in embarrassing because there wasn't anything special in what
he did or said: he just listened to the Stone. And anyway,
Rebecca was never going to leave Duncton forever, just
like that: so there seemed no call for any fuss and bother.

He accepted Rebecca back rather as a pup takes it as
a complete matter of course that his mother will return,
even if she's been gone a rather long time. But for most
of the moles her return was just a nine-day wonder. She
was their healer, wasn't she? A mole could always turn to
her. In fact, come to think of it, it was just a little bit
cheeky of her ever to have pushed off like that for so
long. . . .

Longest Night passed, the second since the one with
Bracken, and chill January ran into freezing February.
The cycle of seasons again.

Bit by bit she told Comfrey what had happened, and

on those days when he knew that she was mourning
Bracken, who must have been lost up on the slopes of
Siabod looking for her, he made sure to be close by and
quiet, just so she knew that she was loved.

But always, at the back of his mind, was the fear that
the day would come when she would slide down into that
black despair he had seen once before, and he wondered
if he would have the strength again to see her through.

"If it's going to come, then let it come," he used to
mutter to the Stone as he passed it by on leaving her burrows. And there came a day, at the start of February,
when it did.

There is a way to kill a mole that is so unimaginably
cruel that even an owl might quail before the thought of
it. Moles who live in systems plagued by it call it, quite
simply, the Talon. But most, living in woods and distant
fields as they do, have no name for it, and when, by terrible chance, they happen on it, or it on them, then their
imagination can barely take in its harsh reality.

It is called a harpoon trap. It has long, sharp prongs
set on a spring which are poised above a tunnel in which
a pawplate is set. The tunnel is blocked. The mole re-
opens it, touches the plate and down plunges the unseen
Talon, which pierces and squashes at one and the same
cruel time. A lucky mole dies at once. But through the
paw, or shoulder, or flank, many unlucky ones are impaled, often too shocked even to struggle, and death
comes on them with agonized slowness.

By February, Bracken had reached a system on the
chalk no more than twenty moledays from Duncton.
Drawn as ever by the ancient sarsen stones that follow
the chalk, he came one day to a field that seemed almost too good to be true. Open and flat, used as pasture
for sheep in the summer and rich with worms as a result, and empty of moles. Off to one side of it stood a
great circle of stones, which gave him comfort for he
liked their presence, and since he liked to travel in stages
—resting at a good place when he could find one—he
decided to make the field his own.

It already had a few old tunnels in it but no sign of
mole at all. Perhaps he should have been suspicious; perhaps he was tired, and as he approached nearer and
nearer to Duncton, his mind was excited at approaching

so near his home system after so long away and wondering what he might find.

The field was good and he enjoyed prospecting it and then finally starting his tunnels over near the Stones, where another mole had left off. One day, two days, four days passed, and a heavy hoarfrost came. The ground grew white and hard, and as the worms tunneled down deeper he followed suit, throwing up on the surface great heaps of reddish soil conspicuous against the frost.

He ate well and slept long, putting off renewing his journey as long as he could. Then a day came when he found a tunnel burrowed out the evening before, which was blocked and smelled strange. Badgers? Rabbits? Weasels? He shrugged and sighed and started to build it up again, ignoring the strange smell, for he had scented more dangerous things than that.

A forward step, a shiny, sinking flatness where the floor should have been, a click of steel, and from above came a piercing, lunging shock, so painful that he seemed himself to be the scream he screamed as it entered his right shoulder and impaled him to the floor.

To what does a mole turn when a prong of steel thrusts through his body and sticks him to a tunnel floor, cutting through his veins and arteries and breaking through the joints and bones on which so much of his life depends?

As the agony came piercing into him, Bracken began a cry for help no other mole could ever have understood, for it was distorted with such terrible pain: it was a name, the only name that finally, when he had come right to the edge of life itself, he thought of as protection: *Rebecca, Rebecca, Rebecca, Rebecca, Rebecca*, he screamed. And even though he knew that she was dead, he cried out her name that she might come to him, to help her love; his love, *Rebecca*.

Like the other moles in Duncton, Comfrey heard Rebecca's terrible scream of pain echo down the tunnels of the Ancient System that February day. But while the others quailed before it and ran to their burrows in fear, he turned toward it, running, running to help Rebecca, crying out that he was coming, running into her screams.

He found her out on the surface, running wildly this

way and that among the roots of the leafless trees, crying out and sobbing, no no no no, and writhing in a terrible pain and saying help him help him oh help him, and not seeming to see Comfrey or hear him as he asked what it was, what was wrong, what he could do, what was hurting her, and he tried to hold her still to find out what it was—because he could see nothing.

But she was racked with pain, and ran in sobbing agony here and there as if she was trying to find something, or shake something off, and then screaming Bracken's name over and over and saying help him help him help him, her breath coming out in great gasping sobs of pain, her face contorted with it as if she were possessed by an evil that she could not fight.

"Rebecca, Rebecca," Comfrey shouted at her to try to stop her, but the more he called her name, the worse she seemed to get, until her talons cut and dug into the roots she passed and leaf litter flew from under the crazed scrabbling of her desperate paws.

Then she was into the Stone clearing and running randomly around it, not caring if she hit herself on the great roots by the Stone, dashing her talons on the ground and thrashing them in the air and shouting help him, help my Bracken, help my love, and then dashing against the very Stone itself, her paws and talons scratching and splintering on it as she shouted or screamed I can't help him I can't help you I can't so help him help him—and there were tears of grief and pain down her twisted face and sweat on her flanks, and her breathing seemed to fill the Stone clearing with its pain. And Comfrey watched in horror as she cried oh help him, he's Bracken, he's still alive, so help him.

The turf above Bracken was torn open and white light from the sky added to his agony. A smell of roaring owl thrust down to the steel that impaled him and picked the trap and Bracken up bodily together. It grasped him firmly and then pulled him off the Talon, down a tunnel whose sides were his own exposed nerves, and though he was free of the Talon, the pain became worse as he was held up in the air, limp as death, and bloody. There was the growl of a voice whose language he could not understand.

"Little bastard," he said.

And then he was thrown swinging through the air, arcing up into the sky and down, down into a floating sea of pain, down and down and thumping, bumping against one of the great Stones by the side of the field, and he had a moment's sight of his paw flopping against it, covered in his own red blood, before he felt the pain again.

The smell of the creature went away. Wind rustled the grass by the Stones. Agony filled him. And all he could think of was the absurd thought, so silly, that he must be dying; and yet the Stone was warm against his paw, vibrating with a life and power that frightened him, but which he could not turn away from.

Comfrey stayed on with Rebecca in the clearing but no longer said her name. He stayed by her to protect her if other danger came, watching as her terrible agony gave way to something which, in some ways, was even worse—the sight of her draining herself away into the Stone with continual, almost inaudible, healing words, each one drawn out from all the agony she herself had known and passed in some mysterious way into the Stone of Duncton which now seemed to vibrate with her life. Until darkness began to fall, and then night came, and then it was dark, and only her sobs and whispers to the Stone sounded among the winter trees, my love I'm here my love my love my love my love, the sounds growing weaker and weaker as the night drew on.

Some time after darkness took the light away, Bracken came to again into a sea of pain and found that he was not dead, not dead at all, and that around him the circle of Stones on whose edge he lay was warm and shaking in the night with a power and light that he knew and had seen before. A light of life that was calling him to its center, a light of love that had a being and warmth and the feel of soft fur as he whispered again and again the only thing that made him feel his way beyond the pain, Rebecca Rebecca Rebecca . . . she was there in the center of the circle of Stones and she, and their power, were calling him, stopping him falling asleep, stopping him drowning into the pain, making him crawl, inch by bloody inch, each inch a mile of pain, into the center of Rebecca's healing love that told him she was there alive, waiting

waiting, her healing power a call to him. And feeling her need for him, feeling her love, he crawled through the pain into the healing circle of the Stones and back from the edge of life.

While by the Stone in Duncton Wood, when everything had fallen still and it was nearly midnight, Rebecca finally sighed and took her paws away from the Stone's face. Oh, she sighed, oh my love.

When Comfrey went to her, he was astonished to see that she was smiling. "Bracken is alive," she said. "He is, you know, he really is. He may never come back to Duncton but it no longer matters, for he knows the love is there, our love is there . . ." But it did matter, and Comfrey saw that it mattered, now more than ever.

"C—come on, Rebecca, you'd better go back to your burrows and get some sleep. Come on." And he led her down to her burrow and settled down near her until she slept, and watched over her until her breathing was regular and slow, and peaceful as the Stone.

ᓵ 45 ᕐ

REBECCA ran laughing down the slopes toward the Old Wood, calling out, "Comfrey, Comfrey! See if you can find me!"

Comfrey chased after her, a little clumsily because he was never much good on his paws, but marveling at how Rebecca had changed for the better since that terrible night in February. Since then she had shed moleyears, and behaved more and more like a happy-go-lucky pup each day than the female who had seen four Longest Nights through and was healer to the system.

Healer? Well, no more. It wasn't that she no longer cared for the other moles, or tried to ignore them, or wasn't helpful when they came to her: but everymole seemed to sense that Rebecca had changed and no longer had the desire or will to support them when, it must be said, they could so often find support within themselves. She seemed now to see beyond their troubles and into their very souls, and it troubled them that she did, and so they preferred to leave her alone.

Only a few of the older moles, and one or two of the young ones, came to her—the ones who understood that the greatest healing she could give was the sense of joy and peace she herself now felt in the wood about her.

So Comfrey now became healer, and it was to him that they mostly went with their troubles, which he was able to help them with in his own eccentric way, giving them herbs that might, or might not, be of practical help.

But once in a while he would take time off—or Rebecca would come and make him do so—and today, on a clear, misty spring morning in April, she had him grumblingly playing hide and seek.

Down past the slopes she ran, into the Old Wood where a few trees still stood stark and black to remind them of the fire, but where fresh undergrowth and two seasons of leaf mold had made the gray ashes of the wood a memory. But burrow a little way and a mole could still find the ashes—and they were alive with life now as fronds of the roots of a new spring of anemones grew into them, or young sinewy roots of sapling hazel and the suckers of elm and lime pierced up through them.

She ran instinctively toward Barrow Vale, which she had not found the previous summer but which now, somehow, she knew would be there. The sapling wood was busy and noisy. Birds darted and flitted about the trees, most of which were heavy with bud or catkins.

Still calling "Comfrey! Comfrey!" her laugh following the sound of his name, she ran on faster than he could, stopping only for a moment to sigh with delight at the sight of a cluster of yellow celandine.

As she ran on toward Barrow Vale, it was as if she were herself the plants and trees and every creature, everything, alive with the sunlight that began to clear the mist and the life that the spring always finally brought. Oh! she sighed, just as she had when she had been a pup and had first run with such wonder through the wood. Comfrey! Comfrey! And her laughter filled the wood.

She came to a clearing where the vegetation was lighter because the soil was gravelly, and knew it had been Barrow Vale.

Shall I burrow? she wondered. But though she tried to start, she didn't finish, because she was distracted by the last of the morning mist swirling away and then by the sound of the first bumblebee she had heard that spring. Then by a distant cawing of rooks in the trees on the eastside which had survived the fire. She crouched in the pale sunshine, thinking she should go and find Comfrey or help him to find her, and just a little sad that he couldn't play with her like a sibling or a lover because, she knew deep down, it wasn't quite his way.

But then what mole had ever played with her with the fullness of life that she saw and enjoyed! But her sadness was part of her happiness that there was so much to see and do and enjoy in the wood. So much of the sadness had left her when, on that night by the Stone when she knew with certainty that somewhere her Bracken was alive, even if now he might not come back; and that somehow the love they had known had changed but he was alive, and she had helped him be so. She smiled for the memory of it and laughed aloud again for the distant nervous call of Comfrey, wondering where she was.

She crouched in the sun that grew clearer by the minute, and said aloud, "It's my wood! My wood!"

"That's what you always used to say, Rebecca, remember?" The voice came from the shadows of the roots of a dead oak tree and cast an immediate fearful chill into her heart.

She looked behind to the darkness of the place where the voice came from. His coat was glossy and his smile bland. It was Rune!

"Hullo, Rebecca," he said. She saw that though his face had become lined with the moleyears and his eyes bitter with age, his coat was as unnaturally smooth and glossy as it had always been. His talons were black, there was not a scar on him—face, flank or shoulder—which was unusual in a mole as old as he must be. But then, Rune had a way of avoiding hurt by passing it on to others.

"So you're all living up in the Ancient System now, are you, what's left of you?" he asked. He smiled blandly as he said it, but still his voice seemed to hold a sneer.

She simply stared at him, unable to comprehend that he was there. He had gone off after the fight by the Stone but hadn't he *died* after that, in the plague? Or somewhere else?

"No, no, I didn't die," he said, sensing precisely what she was thinking. "If you survived, why shouldn't I? Perhaps the thought of you kept me alive. You know how much I always admired you, Rebecca."

She shuddered at the way he said it, an old weariness coming over her as she realized he *was* Rune, and he was back in the system he had once nearly destroyed. And she wondered if she had the strength for such things any more.

"Well, you don't have to say anything if you don't want to. You always had a will of your own, Rebecca, I remember." He laughed again, the sound of it like cold gray clouds blocking out the sunshine.

"A good time for an old mole like me to come back, isn't it? Well, you know, the start of the mating season . . . a few fights . . . you know? Now I think I'll go and explore the system you must all have so patiently been creating . . ." And he slipped away with cruel humor in his narrow eyes, his body lithe as a youngster's and cunning as evil.

Rebecca shook for a while in disbelief, then turned away back toward the slopes, toward the sound of Comfrey coming down through the wood toward her.

"Rebecca—Reb–b–becca," he said, beginning to stutter as he saw the tiredness that had suddenly come over her. "There was a m–m–mole I met who said he was l–looking for you. I told him you were down here and that I was tr–trying to find you . . ."

She nodded.

"I d–d–didn't like him, Rebecca."

"No," she said. "His name is Rune. There was a time when he would have killed you if he could."

"I d–don't like him," said Comfrey. But his misery was not for himself, because that never worried him now, but for Rebecca, for whose happiness he cared so much and who had lost the joy that shone from her earlier that day.

It seemed to Bracken that the yellow cowslips that shook and waved in the April wind outside the shallow tunnel in which he had first hidden when he had crawled away from the Stones had sprouted, leaved, and blossomed overnight.

He looked at them puzzled and felt the warm air about them, wondering where he was and how long he had been there. So late into spring already? But surely, there was a hoarfrost only yesterday . . .

Next time he went to admire them, two of the florets were already withering and brown, and there was an unaccustomed blue in the sky, which echoed to the high rise and fall of a skylark's song. On and on it went, all day long it seemed, on into another day. So whole days had passed by, whole weeks had stolen away, most of which he forgot because he was not conscious most of the time. He slept; he pulled himself into the adjacent plowed field whose soil was sparse with flints and chalk subsoil but where he managed to find food. He crawled back to sleep away the pain.

Kestrels and crows had wheeled and dived, suns and moons had come and gone, until, at last, he was all there, and his body ached and throbbed with hurt.

There was not one wound but two—one at the top of his shoulder where the joints had been broken and ripped, one out of his chest, where the fur seemed to have been misplaced and there was a scar. He could move his right paw, thank the Stone, but two of his talons in it were stiff and would no longer respond as well as they did in his left paw.

Then he noticed that another three florets of the cow-slips had died, and he knew that spring was passing. What dreams he had had, what nightmares! All so pointless and comic. He saw himself as he had been, different moles at different times, nervous or brave, serious or sad, in-different and loving. Sometimes one, sometimes another. The mole that left Duncton wasn't the one that arrived in Uffington; and the one that had left Uffington again wasn't the same as the one who went up Cwmoer. Each one searching for something Bracken could only smile about now as he looked at the gray earth of his tunnel, thinking there was nothing more real than that.

One dawn he went back up to the Stone circle, just to see if it was as he remembered it. It wasn't. The stones were smaller and they did not vibrate or become suffused with light. It grew dark in the time he crouched there so he must have been there a long time, since he came at dawn. Strange . . . where had time gone?

Then a day came when he woke up and ran his talons through the soil and saw what magnificent things his paws were, and how wonderful they felt. One sweep and the soil crumbled and broke up before his snout; another and he thrust it behind him. His body ached and yet he had never in his life felt its power so strongly! He played like this for hours before he knew he was playing, and then he stopped and that was the first moment since he had been caught by the Talon that he thought of Re-becca.

He said her name aloud—"Rebecca"—and nothing happened. Rebecca! No reaction at all. That was strange as well. But then later he thought that if a mole said "sunshine" or "earth" or "food," he didn't normally react in any special way. Those things just were. So was Re-becca. She was. She is. And I am, he thought.

He had never been so peaceful in his life.

A few days later he remembered Medlar's advice: re-turn to Duncton, he had said, because that's your home. He wondered if he would be able to find it, and so, when it got dark, he took to the surface and climbed uphill to where it was highest and snouted about to the east. Yes, it was there, he could still feel the pull of its great Stone up on top of the hill where the beeches are. Full of sharp buds by now, he told himself.

He could feel something else, too, as he snouted eastward. Something troublesome and tedious: a job that had to be done. But after that he would play like a pup in love with life because finally what other way was there to be? Rebecca? He felt her to be alive, he felt that the trouble he sensed affected her, but he shook his head and sighed. How could she be alive? But the peace her love had brought him, oh! it was all about him wherever he went. Except for something troublesome and tedious . . .

Without another thought, he set off for it, not even looking back to the tunnel that had been his home since that terrible day in February or wondering about the cowslip that grew by it and that had given him so much pleasure: another mole would enjoy it one day.

Strange to be going home after so long. He should have felt old with all the scars and aches he had, but he had never felt more like a pup in his life. Nor had he ever felt so excited to be alive.

"He's changed, you know, so much nicer than what I remember . . ." So said one of the few moles who remembered Rune from the old days.

He had settled himself down well out of anymole's way, careful not to trespass on anymole's territory, not throwing his weight around at all— "and he used to be pretty important, really he did, but now there's no side to him at all. He's a really good addition to the system . . ."

So, subtly, did Rune re-establish himself in Duncton. He was never abject in his approach—simply quiet, and always smiling and willing to pass the time of day if a mole wanted to talk to him.

Which they did, since he was full of knowledge and always pleased to give advice—very helpful advice—and was quite unstinting in the trouble he took. "Mind you, he's not one to take liberties with—you've got to respect a mole like him, you know. Oh, yes, he's the sort of mole to have on your side in a fight!"

Which was a relevant thing to say since, all of a sudden, there was a lot more fighting in the system than there had been for a long time, and not just mating fights, either. Mole seemed to be set against mole; troubles ap-

peared where no troubles had been; there was grumbling
and chatter behind other moles' backs.

Mind you, Rune was always there to give advice: in
fact, he seemed to be advising all sides at once, trying to
be placatory and stop trouble, only somehow, wherever
he had been, more trouble seemed to come along.

Rebecca knew what the trouble was. It was the power
of evil. Rune was not evil himself but he was the catalyst
for it, whose every action seemed to generate trouble and
suspicion and led finally to a death of spirit, and sometimes a death of body.

For a long time he left her alone. But then the day
came at the end of April when he called by and she
knew what he wanted because she had seen him like that
before—with a kind of cold lust in his eyes and a terrible
desire about his body that made her want to shiver and
groan herself clean of it.

He began to cause trouble for her, though it didn't
seem as if it was him. But somehow other moles seemed
to start saying that she was no longer pulling her weight
and what was the use of a healer who didn't heal and
hadn't some mole or another told Rune that it just wasn't
fair being fobbed off with that half-mad Comfrey all the
time? Though Rune himself stressed how unfair *that* was.
But then, Rune was too fair for his own good sometimes
and not all moles were as thoughtful as he was. . . .

Now Rune began to visit Rebecca frequently, with that
cold glitter in his eyes and sensual insinuations.

He made her so weary, so tired, that she wondered
sometimes if perhaps the best way to combat evil was to
face it with love. Was that it? Or was that obscene? She
tried asking the Stone, but somehow it didn't help her, or
she couldn't hear it, and she did feel weary because tomorrow he would come again, and the next day, and the
next.

46

COMFREY turned away miserably from Rebecca's tunnels. Rune was there, talking. Always talking he was, and getting near Rebecca, which Comfrey didn't like.

But Rebecca seemed tired and when Comfrey asked if she wanted anything, she had looked so sad and lost that he could have killed Rune, if he had known how. But he wasn't a fighter. He didn't want Rune to mate with Rebecca, not him. But Rebecca sort of shook her head and looked down at the burrow floor, and Rune looked triumphant and Comfrey knew he would have to fight or go; so he went because only a potential mate fights.

Why did Rebecca look so sad? And why was there such a feeling of evil in her burrows, which were normally so fresh and alive, or had been until that Rune came back?

From far off down the tunnels came the sound of pups' cries—probably one of the earlier litters whose pups were already getting out of hand. You expect that by the first week of May.

Comfrey couldn't face the tunnels, and anyway, he wasn't popular with the moles there now, so he went slowly onto the surface and looked for a while at the beech branches above him, which were just beginning to leaf at last. Always so late, beech leaves, but what a gentle rustle of a sound when they came!

But it was no use. Comfrey could not shake the misery out of himself, or the thought of Rebecca with Rune in her burrows. He turned without thinking toward the Stone clearing and, as so often before, went to it and crouched by the Stone. Why had he been made so weak and nervous, even when he wasn't afraid? Why did the Stone let moles like Rune live?

He looked up at it above him, light and still against the tiny, shimmering beech leaves. Always so different and always such a mystery.

Then he heard a rustle from the northwest, which was unusual. He smelled mole, but not mole that he knew. Hesitating over whether or not to find cover, he hesitated too long and the mole came out boldly into the clearing and straight toward him.

"What m–m–mole are you, and where are you f–from?" asked Comfrey as firmly as he could.

The mole looked at him calmly for a while and then laughed aloud, not laughing at Comfrey but rather with him, as if the whole world was full of humor and there wasn't a thing to worry about. And despite himself, despite his thoughts about Rune, Comfrey found himself laughing as well.

"I used to live here in this system, you know," said the mole. "My name is Bracken."

Comfrey's laugh froze in his mouth; in fact, the whole of him froze. He looked at the mole, who was scarred and looked quite old, his face lined and his fur straggly. He was big and very powerful now Comfrey looked at him closely, and his paws seemed more solidly on the ground than anymole he had ever known, except Rebecca.

"Bracken?" whispered Comfrey, without a stutter.

Bracken nodded.

"Rebecca's Bracken?" said Comfrey.

Bracken laughed again. "Well, I was when she was alive, by the Stone's grace I was," he said gently.

"B–but—" and now Comfrey did stutter and looked confused, because the whole world seemed to whirl about him and he couldn't catch his breath, and the Stone was towering behind him and he was shaking with a mixture of pride and tears and relief all at once.

"But she is alive," he said, "and she's here, now."

Behind Comfrey the Stone rose into the sky and Bracken gazed up at it, his head tilting higher and higher as the words sank in. She's here now, now where the Stone was, now, now where their love was, now. The trees were the same, the sounds were the same, the scent of the leaf litter was just the same as it had always been, so where had he been for so long? The moleyears began to leave him, though if anything he looked older and more solid for the knowledge that she was here, now.

Slowly he began to hear Comfrey's voice again as he continued to talk, his voice stumbling faster and a mixture of relief and distress running through it.

"She's in the old tunnels you burrowed yourself because that's where she lives, but it's not right any more because Rune came back, who was here before, and he's there now, and I don't like him because it's not right what he wants." And Comfrey began to cry, because though he was an adult and a healer, he knew it didn't matter in front of Bracken because there was no mole in the world stronger than he was, or who could help so much, except Rebecca, and she needed his help now . . .

Bracken touched him gently. "It's all right," he said. Then he turned away from the mole whose sadness he knew so well, and away from the Stone behind him, and without one trace of urgency in his step he made his way toward the nearest entrance to those tunnels he had himself burrowed so long before, thinking it was his home and no mole but Rebecca had the right to be there. No mole.

Rebecca was suffering Rune's snoutings with the thought that surely all moles may be loved finally, all and every one; but that didn't take away the disgust she felt or the obscenity of it and she wondered whether, if she had not been made so weary by so many moleyears of giving, perhaps she might be bringing down her talons upon him instead of crouching here like this.

He was saying something, meaningless words whose real meaning was his triumph and he felt like a solid shadow about her, which made her begin to weep silently, the tears becoming a protective veil beyond which Rune could do what he liked, which he was beginning to do, because she could feel his talons on her now, first at her side and then at her flank as she shuddered and wondered if *any* mole can be loved, or whether there are some who lose the right or for whom she did not have the power, and she felt so weak and in need of forgiveness; just as she had when this same mole had been there with Mandrake, tearing at her litter, and she didn't have the strength to fight them. Cairn had not come. But she needed help and wanted Bracken, who would have helped her had she called out to him. So she did . . . Bracken, Bracken, *Bracken* . . .

Then the burrow was filled with blood: Rune's.

And scrabbling desperate paws: Rune's.

And screams of anger and fear: Rune's.

And Bracken was there.

He was in the center of the burrow with Rebecca behind him and Rune thrown back against one of the walls, his flank bloody where Bracken's talons had swung gently down and sent him sailing through the air.

There was no anger about Bracken at all, just certain
and great power.

"I thought you were dead, Rune," said Bracken matter-
of-factly.

Rune gathered himself up and lunged viciously forward
to where Bracken was and yet wasn't; when Rune got
there, his taloned paw stubbed uselessly into thin air, because Bracken was round to his side and another gentle
blow seemed to send Rune backward against another
wall, his neck savaged with talon cuts.

Rune turned to face Bracken again but never pushed
forward his attack: he found himself looking not just at
Bracken but at Rebecca as well, and they crouched side by
side, not angry or contemptuous or hostile in any way:
their eyes held compassion and pity. It made Rune turn
around in terrible fear, as if he were fleeing from the edge
of a void, and he ran out of the burrow into the tunnel
beyond.

Bracken barely seemed to move and yet, when Rune
looked round to see if he was following, there he was,
right behind him, not angry but compassionate, and that
was something Rune could not face. He turned away again,
running and running away, twisting and turning through
the tunnels and up onto the surface, anything to get away
from Bracken.

But there he was again, or seemed to be. Bracken was
there waiting for him and the great soaring beech trees,
sinewy and light, seemed to twist around Rune and en-
circle him so that he could not bear the simple shimmering of their leaves, which were somehow like Bracken.

Rune began to run across the rustling surface of the
wood, trying to control the fear he felt, to wonder at it and
so control it, but he could hear Bracken pattering along
behind him, a mole who seemed now only to have to raise
his talon and it sent him, Rune, powerful Rune, who knew
how to kill, who could hurt other moles, painfully flying
through the air.

His breath wouldn't come and his body felt twisted and
out of control with pains and wounds, and there was red
blood on his fur, always glossy before but now matted with
blood and sweat. The trees fell away and he was into the
Stone clearing running and turning to see if Bracken was
after him, wh'ch he was, so that Rune fell behind himself,
hurting himself as he twisted and fell among the roots of

the tree and was pressing against the Stone which he hated, turning around with Bracken above him.

Bracken looked down at the withered, trembling, shaking form of Rune, who was trying to pull himself up to face him, and then slowly up at the Stone he had asked so many times, in so many different ways, why a mole like Rune existed.

Bracken raised his paws and extended his talons and mercilessly brought them down toward Rune against the Stone. Bracken's breathing was as gentle as soft wind as his death blow fell on Rune, but his breathing stopped short when, somehow, the Stone seemed to stop his paws, for he hit them against it, he who knew how to fight, and they only scratched squealing down on its face toward Rune, but not into him.

Seeing death stopped above him, Rune twisted and ran from the Stone and behind him heard Bracken, angry at last, and cursing: "Bugger the Stone, I'm going to kill that Rune."

And now Rune was afraid, finally, truly, deeply afraid. He was going to be killed. And he ran on and on into the wood, away from that Stone, faster and faster, as he heard Bracken follow, whose paws sounded so calm in their running, while his scrabbled to get away and wouldn't grip.

On and on Rune ran, his strength failing rapidly, as if he was growing old and ancient all at once. He could no longer think clearly and his breath was coming in pants and gasps. Behind him he could hear Bracken getting nearer, beech leaves and leaf mold scattering in their wakes.

The hill rose to the right toward its final height, while Bracken now veered a little to his left, stopping him turning that way but too close for him to turn back. So he had to go forward toward the void of the chalk escarpment, his heart pounding in pain and each breath harder and harder to grasp hold of.

Bracken watched Rune ahead of him and saw age creep over him, his coat now ugly and matted, his body twisted with fear. Had he once looked so pathetic to Mandrake when he had been chased, as Rune now was, over these leaves and roots, with the beech branches above, and the sky lightening ahead because there were no more trees left, just the straggly line of the sheer cliff edge?

No, he couldn't kill him, it was no longer necessary.
So he would catch him now and stop him, because killing
isn't the way; couldn't Rune see? So he raised his paws
to stop Rune, while behind him came a shout from Rebecca.

"Don't touch him. Don't hurt him, he can't harm
us . . ."

Rune heard it, Rebecca's voice, and hated the love in
it which he could not bear to face, and where Bracken
had turned once to face Mandrake, Rune ran on, the void
of pity behind him far, far worse than the void ahead,
which was full of air with a chalkfall far below, nothing
under his scrabbling paws and a last terrible look back at
moles who pitied him, whose faces and eyes and snouts
rose far, far above him into the sky, as his back arched
under him and his talons tried to hold onto the sky beyond them. Then darkness blotted Rune out.

Rebecca shook like a pup, and stood as weakly as one,
as relief, such a relief, came slowly into her. Bracken was
still peering over the cliff edge and Oh! she was frightened
of him. She was shy of him. He was no mole she knew,
and yet she knew him to his heart's core.

As for Bracken, he was only pretending to look over
the cliff's edge. She was there, behind him, his Rebecca,
her voice still in the wood about them.

As he turned finally with such love to her, she said
"Bracken?" and he could hear, and she knew he could
hear, that she was calling him, calling out to him and he
was coming to her at last.

He could see her, she knew he could see her, and she
whispered to herself I'm Rebecca my name is Rebecca
and I'm not Mandrake's daughter or Cairn's mate or the
healer, but I'm Rebecca and oh! she could hear the whole
wood behind her, rustling and free, and the bird-sounds
from where the slopes were and they were all part of her
and he could see it and it was such relief to be seen like
that because at last that's what she was.

"Rebecca, Rebecca . . ."

"Yes, my love, that's right, my love," she said, looking
at the love and beauty in his eyes that saw the love and
beauty in her own as they lost themselves at last within
it.

THERE is a point at which the gentlest touch becomes the softest caress becomes the sweetest nuzzle becomes the lightest push becomes the most loving romp in the world: but Bracken and Rebecca never found out exactly where it was.

He would look at her in burrow or among dry leaves, and she at him, and they would wonder at the wonder of where they were. And what words they said, or never finished saying, they never knew. Except that when he said I love you I love you I love you it was never, never enough for him, because what words can satisfy the ache to be so wholly with another mole which even bodies cannot satisfy?

Sometimes playful, rompish, silly, she would ask him again, just one more time, do you really love me and he would hesitate and sadly shake his head and she would cry out oh oh oh oh Oh as he said No I don't *think* I do with such love that it was better than him saying that he did.

Or she would talk about a mole who wasn't there, whom she had known, whom she really *did* love, yes she did!

What was he like? Bracken would ask and she would think and nuzzle him and start to say, then stop, then start again that, well (nuzzling close), describe a mole whose paws and snout and fur and scars and very soul were just like Bracken's own and Bracken would say: Strange, I knew a female once, not far from here, who I think I loved . . .

"Oh, what was she like?" asked Rebecca breathlessly. "And *did* you love her?"

But Bracken wouldn't say but only show, by putting his claws among her soft, gray fur and snouting at her soft as wind and strong as roots so that she closed her eyes and smiled and sighed aloud until he did it harder and she held him to her so that the mole he knew was she, Rebecca, and she was moist where he snouted and she wide and he pushing and she snouting him soft and hard so that he was hard to her with haunches so powerful to her, and claws that hurt before exquisite now, running down her back and up it, up it higher, higher, and

higher until they didn't need the preface words, or feel
the ache of being two apart because he was there upon
her, mole of moles and she so proud and he as well, for
his the sound of sighs and calls and cries of the only mole
that held a beauty for his eyes, beneath above upon below.

Theirs was the laughter and theirs the tears of making
love as days passed into night and leaves changed into
stars.

Rebecca knew she was with litter at the very moment
that it happened, because the light about them both, in
the deep darkness of their burrow, was just as it had been
by the Stillstone beneath the Duncton Stone: glimmering
white, a halo over them, as the burrow filled with the
sound of the sighs of wonder.

Bracken knew she was with litter when one dawn he
heard her burrowing nearby, at the end of one of the
tunnels, and singing the kind of song that she must have
sung as a pup, before he had met her. He laughed and
smiled and fell asleep again, the scent and warmth of her
all about him; while she heard his laugh and knowing
why he made it laughed as well as she felt his power and
strength in the tunnels all around her, giving her a kind
of freedom that she'd never had.

It was May, and the nesting leaves she began to take
down to the birth-burrow she was making bore a fresh
Maytime scent, each one seeming to her more and more
special. She took down grass as well, and the fragrant
stems and florets of ground ivy which, because they were
not so brittle as the dry and delicate beech leaves, gave
her litternest the strength she felt it needed.

As the days passed and May grew warmer, she kept
more and more to herself as she steadily extended her
tunnels, which lay adjacent to the ones Bracken had
originally burrowed between the Stone and the pastures.

Bracken had reoccupied his old tunnels, the ones she
had lived in for so long, and she liked the feeling that he
was there in tunnels she had grown to love and where,
he said, he basked in what he called her "delicious scent."
They spent long periods near each other, wallowing in
the pleasure of having to say so little to understand so
much.

Their only visitor was Comfrey who, as the days went
by, grew less and less nervous and awkward and was

able to crouch for long hours near them without even twitching his tail or looking about himself uncomfortably. Their love calmed him.

It was only because of him that they found out about what each of them had done in their long moleyears of separation. By themselves they never talked of it, but Comfrey had always been a mole to ask questions and there was so much he wanted to know. Rebecca would tell him things very simply, almost as if nearly dying in a blizzard or traveling all the way back from Siabod were the sort of things moles did every other day. Although she rarely referred to the Stone or its providence, there was in all she said the sense that behind each incident there was its common power, whose pattern a mole might wonder at but never fully understand.

Bracken's stories were more dramatic, more male, and Comfrey would often shudder at the close escapes he and Boswell had had and wonder what powers the two moles must have possessed to have faced so much and come out of it all alive.

But it was only to Comfrey that Bracken would talk like this—to the other moles in the system he was a mystery: they knew what he had achieved, but none of them could ever make him talk of it, and sometimes they wondered if a mole like him, who didn't seem all that special, could really have done so much.

But more often it was the fact of Bracken and Rebecca being together that they talked about, and there was barely a mole in the system who did not sense the peace and love that surrounded the two most respected moles in Duncton. Their presence together near the Stone began to bring a peace and depth of feeling to the system that contrasted almost magically with the dark dissension created by Rune before Bracken came.

As for Rune being killed, it must be said that the communal opinion in the Ancient System, fickle as ever, now held the consensus "He never was a nice one, that Rune, and I always said it was a bit suspicious the way that he came back like that and pretended to be doin' us all a great big good turn . . ."

"That's wot I thought exactly, only I didn't like to say because, well, you don't like to carp when things seem all right about a particular mole even though you yourself have your own doubts . . ." And so forth.

Comfrey, of course, was their darling again and now

that Rebecca was definitely out of the running, there was no doubt in anymole's mind who the healer was.

It all made Comfrey smile, but he didn't mind because, like Rebecca, he healed and listened and cared for them for no other reason than that he wanted to—it was the Stone he tried to listen to, not the changing words of other moles.

Rebecca's litter came one night two hours before dawn in early June and was the last to be born that summer. Its birth was quick and joyous, all four pups being nudged at and licked to start their tiny scrabble into life almost before a mole could blink.

It was her third litter and the second she had reared, and she did it as simply as eating or breathing.

Bracken heard the births and stayed nearby but did not enter her burrow, much though he wanted to. But a day or two after they came and their bleats and mewing were beginning to carry, she called out for him and he came slowly into her tunnels to look at them.

How big he seemed to her, crouching at the burrow entrance and looking in wonder at the four pups who seemed to be permanently trying to untie the knot into which they had tied themselves as pink, soft paws and questing snouts jostled and pushed at soft, furless bodies and they climbed over each other with innocent indifference.

Rebecca had three of their names already—Rose and Curlew for the two females and Beech for the smaller of the males. This last was a common name and Rebecca knew it had always been his favorite tree to shelter by, so Bracken did not bother to tell her that one of Rue's litter by him had been called the same.

As for the fourth, she hesitated over what name to give it, wondering if she might not choose the name of one of the moles they had both loved—Mekkins or Boswell.

Bracken shook his head. It wouldn't have been right. This mole did not look (if pups can look like anything) like either of them. He was, in fact, the largest of the litter and though not the quickest to fight his way through a scrabble for a suckle (that was Curlew's place), he was always close behind.

Bracken watched indifferently—names didn't mean much to him. In fact, he was thinking of something else, as fathers often do when faced by the wonder of new life they have not borne themselves yet helped to create and before which they may often feel a curious impotence. Can these pups really live to be adult, they think, as they gaze in awe at the weak, blind things that carry life in every single movement they make?

The four rolled and tangled up before him and Bracken's mind took him back to the blizzard on Moel Siabod and he wondered how such tiny things, for Rebecca's Siabod litter can have been no bigger, could ever have survived conditions in which he himself had nearly died. The thought was horrifying. For a moment their paws all piled on top of each other and then splayed out in tiny protracted talons, and he thought of the great rock splinters and fragments near Castell y Gwynt; and the mixing of their mewings seemed like the winds he had heard howling there.

Then suddenly, for a moment, the so-far-unnamed mole scrabbled his way to the top, his snout shooting up above them all, his paws clutching out into thin air and failing to catch onto anything to stop him falling back down again, away from Bracken, and behind the pile formed by the other three.

It seemed to Bracken that he was back beside the desolate Stones near Siabod and slipping and falling as his son had just done, down into the nameless cwm with the great peak of Tryfan which was, for that moment, his son's tiny snout, above him and he falling away from it. He shivered with the memory and yet felt the wonder again of seeing Tryfan.

"Call him Tryfan," said Bracken simply.

"Yes," said Rebecca, not needing to ask the reason. "Tryfan, sweet thing: Tryfan, my love . . ." It was the first of their pups Bracken heard Rebecca talk to by name.

Close though Rebecca's tunnels were to the Stone, the litter seemed too young to go up to it out on the surface a few weeks later, when Bracken was to speak the Midsummer ritual once again.

But they sensed the excitement and knew that the adults were doing something special, for all of them were restless and fractious that day, bleating especially loud and mewing for no reason at all.

In fact, by Midsummer Night they had already started to wander far and wide in Rebecca's tunnels and she of-

ten had to round them up and shoo them back to her
main burrow because she still liked them all to sleep together. Because of this, one of the females from the system agreed to come to watch over them while Rebecca
went up for the ritual itself at midnight, so that she would
know they were safe.

Even so, they must have sensed that she was leaving
them for the surface, because they stumbled bleating after her when she left, despite her smiles and love words
to them, and the female had to quiet them with her own
words. "There, there, she's not going far, you silly things;
she'll come back, so don't you go fearing over that. Shhh,
my darlings, shhh."

What a night it was! Warm and clear, with a moon that
shone as powerfully as a sun, and beech-tree branches
that swayed against it high above the gathering moles,
the shiny sides of the beech leaves shimmering with pale
light in a faint breeze.

What excitement for them all to know they were going
to hear the ritual as it should be spoken, by Bracken who
had traveled off so far—all the way to Uffington and farther, so they said—and who was taught the ritual by as
fine an elder as Duncton Wood has ever seen, name of
Hulver!

Youngsters from early litters were brought up to the
clearing and crouched about in groups or scampered
when they shouldn't, wondering what the fuss was about
until they saw the Stone and were awed by its great size
and the way it seemed to move against the rising moon.

How many mothers whispered "Now don't you forget
what you're going to be seeing and hearing tonight, because this is for you, this is, and Duncton's honored to
have a mole like Bracken here to say those holy words he
learned when he was scarcely older than you are now! So
don't you forget!" And strange to say, although their puppish eyes wandered here and there, and they thought
mainly of play and worms and chasing their siblings
through the tunnels, there was many a youngster who *did*
always remember that special night.

But there was one who was not there—not on the surface, anyway—who would have an even more special reason to remember the Midsummer Night when Bracken
spoke the ritual: Tryfan.

He was not only bigger than his other siblings, he was
also by now far the most adventurous; and even the most

careful females can lose track of a single pup when she's trying to keep track of four of them at once. So, as they scampered round in Rebecca's burrow, the female looking after them did not see Tryfan scramble into the tunnel.

Did he go looking for Rebecca, or was it just the excitement of exploring the tunnels? He himself was never able to say, for all he could remember were snatches of images, moments of places, wondrous and fearful incidents such as any pup remembers of something that happened when he was very young and which made an impression for a lifetime upon him.

He remembered the sound of his siblings' play, suddenly distant, and wondering why he was alone; he remembered the tunnels seeming huge and chalky and looking around behind him and hearing his lonely bleat echo about him, confusing him. He remembered running into tunnels that felt old as time, and curving round and seeing chalk dust on his paws.

He heard the murmur of moles on the surface above where the moles were collecting, carried by some tunnel wind or rootway of vibration, down to where he actually was—the round, circular tunnel that surrounded the Chamber of Echoes, the tunnel from which Bracken had first started his exploration of the central core of the Ancient System. Now Bracken's son, Tryfan, wandered there alone, and tiny, his fur too young to show, snouting this way and that and not knowing where he was.

Moleyears later Tryfan remembered finding himself in the Chamber of Echoes itself, his pawsounds and whimpers echoing around him as if there were a whole lot of youngsters lost like him, but not one of them near enough to give him comfort.

"But then, all of a sudden, even though I was lost and should really have been very frightened, I knew it was all right," he was to recall. "I didn't know what it was then, but I know now, as I know that Midsummer Night is the night for the blessing on the young, when the Stone gives them its protection. That's what it did for me."

As Tryfan was later to remember, there shone in the confusing tunnels around him a light—not all around him but from somewhere ahead, and with its white glimmer on his snout and pale fur he turned toward it and ran toward it without question, knowing he would be quite, quite safe—just as he would have done had he heard Rebecca calling for him: "Tryfan, my love, I'm here!"

So he scampered toward the light, but whenever he thought he had reached it, he found it was ahead of him again, until he was in a great chamber, bigger than the place of echoes, with swaying, sliding tree roots all around, towering high into the darkness above him and plunging into crevices along whose edge he teetered, led forward among them by the light.

How long this took he never knew, but eventually he was beyond the roots and inside the hollow of a great tree from whose heights echoed down the faintest sound of wind among beech leaves and the murmur of adult voices chanting and saying prayers.

Then he followed the light around the side of the tree's deep hollow, the sound of the wind above, so distant that it might have been another world.

The next thing he remembered, and what he remembered most of all and yet most confusedly, was plunging into the ground even deeper, over and among great roots that towered and rolled above him, the light getting stronger and warmer and all around him the massive, tilted underside of the Stone of Duncton.

Right under the buried part of the Stone he went, toward the source of the light itself, which was a stone, a Stillstone, the Seventh Stillstone, whose glimmering lit up his fur and cast his shadow on the roots of stone and chalk walls about him as if he were a huge, strong mole, and adult, with not a single trace of fear in the way he boldly stood, looking into the eternal light of the Stone.

He remembered that as he stood there he heard the deep voice of his father, carried down to where he was by the hollows and convolutions of the ancient beech whose roots encircled the Stone, as he said the final words of the Midsummer ritual. But of course he could not yet understand the words:

> We bathe their paws in showers of dew
> We free their fur with wind from the west.

Then, as the seven blessings began to be spoken, the wonder of the Stillstone became too much for Tryfan, and as any youngster would, he stepped forward and touched it with his left paw. Instead of its light going out, as it had when Bracken had touched it, it seemed to glimmer even more—so brightly, indeed, that had any other mole been watching, he, or she, might have sworn that Tryfan was suddenly completely white with light.

The grace of form
The grace of goodness
The grace of suffering
The grace of wisdom
The grace of true words
The grace of trust
The grace of whole-souled loveliness.

And that, or rather the sounds of the words, was all that Tryfan ever remembered. Except that much later that night, when he was very tired, he heard voices calling "Tryfan! Tryfan!" and scampering, urgent paws running here and there; and it took him a long time to find them until he turned a corner in tunnels he knew again and an adult voice said "There you are! We've been looking for you everywhere!" Then his mother, Rebecca, was there and for a moment he thought she'd be so angry, but all she did was take him into her paws and he could feel her love and it was safe, so safe, like a light he had seen and was beginning to forget he'd seen because he was so tired now and Rebecca's fur was all around him and he was safe again, snuggling into the safety of her love.

But those adult paws searching for Tryfan after the Midsummer ritual was over were not the only paws that scampered and urgently raced that Midsummer Night.

There were some that did the same in Uffington as well. From the silent burrows they ran, down the long tunnels, through the deep night, on and on they ran to find Medlar, the Holy Mole, in the Holy Burrows.

"What is it?" he gently asked the two novice scribe-moles who finally gained an entrance to him. "What is it that makes you run in the Holy Burrows on this happiest of nights?"

"It's Boswell," they gasped out. "He's leaving the silent burrow. He wants to come out."

"Yes?" smiled Medlar.

"But that's not all. He began to scratch at the wall inside the burrow, where the seal is and then, when we heard that, well . . . there was suddenly a light—" began one.

"All around the outside of his burrow," continued the other, "shining and bright."

"Sort of white and glimmering," finished the first.

Medlar could see the awe in their faces. Indeed, he

could see something of the reflection of the light they had seen.

He raised a paw and spoke softly to them: "This is a blessed night, a holy night, and what you have witnessed may be remembered for generations to come. I have felt the peace in the Holy Burrows, felt the silence." He stopped and stared at them, and they saw that awe was on his old face as well. "Come," said Medlar, "come. We will return to the silent burrows and see what we may do."

So back went Medlar and several of the masters, with the novices as well, gathering in a circle around the burrow in which Boswell was sealed. The light the novices had spoken of was gone, but the weak scratching continued sporadically, and as several of the moles went forward to start breaking the seal from the outside, Medlar raised his paw to stop them.

"Let Boswell do it for himself," he said quietly, "for he would wish it to be so."

They crouched in silence, whispering and chanting prayers of thanksgiving as Boswell continued slowly to burrow his way through the seal, his sounds falling silent for long periods as, no doubt, he rested from the effort of it. He had, after all, been sealed in the silent burrows for no less than seven moleyears, nearly eight. He must have been very weak.

But eventually dust began to fall from the outside of the wall, a tiny crack appeared in the seal, crumbling soil fell on the floor at the paws of the waiting moles; and the seal began to break away.

Then, as they caught sight of his paws at the widening hole, while the others continued to pray, two or three of them did step forward to help him tear down the last of the seal and bring Boswell out into the main chamber.

He looked as frail as a pup and almost translucently thin, his fur pale and his snout even paler. Yet from him there came a strength that filled all who saw him with exaltation and wonder. There came from his eyes a brightness, a light, a life and a love that made each one of them feel that they had come home.

They stood in awe about him as he looked slowly about him, and at each of them, and then said softly "Blessed be thou, and ful of blisse," and they had never heard the blessing said with such power. They were blessed to hear it.

He was silent for a long time, as if thinking, and then

he spoke again, with an authority that made each word he spoke seem absolute so that none doubted that what he said would come to pass: "Soon the Seventh Stillstone will come to Uffington from Duncton, in whose ancient tunnels it lies waiting. With the Stone's guidance I shall make a final trek there myself and find it. There, too, I will meet a mole whose life will be a blessing on us all, and those who follow us, and only with his help will the Seventh Stillstone come back here. For he has seen its light and been graced with it, and it is of him that the ancient text that I myself found so long ago is finally about:

> *Find the last Book send the last Stone*
> *Bring them back to Uffington.*
>> *Send a mole in courage living*
>> *And a mole compassionate*
>> *With a third and last to bind them*
>> *By the warmest light to love . . .*

Bracken, Boswell and Rebecca, they were the moles, they were the ones. But as Boswell paused in the middle of the verse and looked at them all with gentle love, he was thinking only of the fourth mole, the mole he would himself guide back to Uffington but whose name he did not yet know. So he continued:

> *Song of silence*
> *Dance of mystery*
> *From their love one more will come . . .*
> *He the Stone holds*
> *He the Book brings*
> *His the silence of the Stone . . .*

There was silence as he finished until one of the moles there whispered, "Will you bring the Seventh Book as well? Will *he* bring it?"

"I do not know," said Boswell softly. "Only the Seventh Stillstone will come. I do not know about the Book," he whispered.

They went to his side, for he was suddenly very weak, and held him until he was steady again, and then they led him slowly back to the Holy Burrows, their prayers changing to songs of exaltation as they went.

By August Rebecca's litter had nearly caught up with litters born in April and was almost ready to leave the home burrow. In some ways they had already, for all of them spent longer and longer away, roaming and exploring about as they began to put out feelers for territory of their own.

Of all, Tryfan was the most independent and yet the most loved. He had grown into as fine a mole as a mole who is not yet adult can be: strong, ready to laugh, well enough able to look after himself not to need to be unnecessarily aggressive; and able to spend long periods alone, as any mole must.

Early on, he had taken to wandering off by himself, spending whole days on the slopes, or exploring bits of the Ancient System that other moles did not bother with —though like everymole in the system, he kept away from its central core, for that was a special place where a mole had best tread carefully.

But for all his disappearances, Tryfan had a way of turning up in the right place at the right time. There had been occasion, for example, when a pack of youngsters from the far side of the system had taken it into their heads one day to intimidate Rose and Curlew—still smaller than other females born that spring. But intimidation sometimes escalates into roughness, and roughness into hurt—so that Rose began to cry and Curlew to try to hit out at the bigger youngsters, who started scratching and lunging at them for real.

Eventually, Rose and Curlew shivered and trembled with fear, not sure what to do except cry, and the other youngsters jeered and hit out at them even harder until Tryfan quietly appeared and crouched looking at them all.

"Leave them alone," he said.

"And what are you going to do about it, mate?" one of the biggest youngsters said, coming aggressively forward. Youngster males liked a good scrap, the rougher the better.

"Yeh, why don't you go and scratch yerself?" said another male, ganging up with the first.

As Tryfan came forward to protect his two sisters, who now stood wide-eyed in alarm and fear, the pack went for him.

"He was wonderful!" Curlew told Rebecca later. "Gosh, he was *amazing*. They all went straight for him and he sort of smiled at them, and calm as you please, he raised one paw and hit the first one, then the second, then the third, and the first one fell back and hit the fourth one and then they were all crying and it was fantastic!"

"Then Rose started crying again," added Curlew disdainfully.

"Why?" asked Rebecca.

"She said because she was so proud of Tryfan but I said she was being stupid. Mind you, he was pretty good!"

There was another occasion, too, more dangerous and more mysterious, when Tryfan appeared when he was needed, but the truth of which neither Bracken nor Rebecca ever got at, and even then they only heard about it from Comfrey, to whom Tryfan went afterward.

It seemed that Beech and Rose had run into a pack of weasels one day on the wood's edge, when they were exploring a tunnel they shouldn't have been in. Perhaps they were not used to weasel scent. What happened wasn't clear, but Beech and Rose came back to Rebecca's tunnels frightened out of their lives and had nightmares for a long time afterward. All they could say was that weasels had attacked them.

"Nearly k–k–killed them, more like," Comfrey told Bracken later, when he reported how Tryfan had come to him with vicious cuts and bites on his shoulder and forehead. "He wouldn't say anything to me, but I'm pretty certain he came just in t–t–time to save them both and must have fought off the weasels single-pawed, b–b–because I doubt if the other two were any good."

But try as they did, they could never get Tryfan to tell them what had happened. He liked to keep his silence.

He grew very close to Comfrey, and the two of them would spend days in silence together, or Tryfan would ask Comfrey to explain things about plants and show him where he got them.

Tryfan took to spending long periods by the Stone, both by day and night, and would ask Bracken and Rebecca to explain things about it to him which the others

never asked. What was it for? Were there others like it?
What was inside it?

He was fascinated by Uffington and by the stories of
scribemoles just as Bracken had been, though Bracken
could never tell him enough about Boswell and the things
he had said. Yet strangely, from Bracken's point of view,
Tryfan never wanted to go down to the Chamber of Dark
Sound, or be shown—or even told—anything about the
chambers of echoes and roots. It was the one thing that
seemed to upset him.

Then, one day in mid-August, he was gone, just like
that, as mole youngsters will. And soon the others left as
well, Rose and Curlew to the slopes and Beech over near
the eastside where he had found friends. But they did not
know where Tryfan went and of them all they missed
him the most.

Yet it would not be true to say that Bracken and Rebecca were sad to see them go. For Rebecca especially,
their departure marked the start of a period of great
quiet and contentment. She had nurtured her young,
cherished them through illness and growing up, and seen
them leave in August as fine a quartet of youngsters as
any mother could wish to have borne.

But she wanted, and no longer felt it wrong to want it,
the peace of long days of solitude and the love that
Bracken, living so nearby, made with her.

As for Bracken, he had watched over the raising of
his young from a distance as male moles always must,
but had taken care to protect Rebecca if she needed it,
showing that he was always there.

It was a time in which he grew closer and closer to
the Stone, as things that Boswell and Hulver and so many
other moles had said to him began to fall into a kind of
pattern, whose shapes were finally as simple as the way
in which he now began to live.

He still loved to explore, only now it was to the Old
Wood he went, where the system had been in his puphood; retracing old tunnels, seeing how the burnt wood
was beginning to grow alive with saplings and birds once
more and wondering about things he had done and not
done.

Yet quiet and nearly anonymous though Bracken and
Rebecca now became it would be wrong to think that
they had no influence on the system. No conscious influence, it is true; but their love, or the sense of it that

pervaded all of the system, now began to work a slow miracle in Duncton Wood. Without knowing it, they created an atmosphere in the Ancient System and in the slopes and beyond, where the wood was beginning to be recolonized, that moles from other nearby systems seemed to sense and came to, as they might to untunneled, worm-full soil.

In the wake of the plagues, whose worst horrors were now beginning to be forgotten (or turned into a tale of the past), litters had been especially large—and a relatively moist summer made it easy for youngsters to burrow and find new territory in the devastated systems, so that survival rates were unusually high. Which made it more curious and more magical that so many youngsters, and some older moles from nearby systems, made the trek over to Duncton, perhaps sensing the great peace that was coming, and about to come, to the Ancient System of Duncton Wood.

The fame of Bracken and Rebecca and their loyalty and love seemed to have spread far and wide, though as August crept into September and then on toward the tail end of autumn, they were seen less and less, as they kept to their tunnels beyond the Stone and to themselves.

It was in December, when a cold and chilly winter had already set in, that Tryfan reappeared. They heard of him first from Comfrey, to whose burrows on the slopes he had gone, and then, one evening a few days later he came to Bracken's burrows. He had been down to what had once been the Marsh End, he told them, and then over to the pastures, living alone and "thinking," as he quietly put it.

He had changed. The last of his puppishness had gone and Bracken saw that he was now large and powerful—larger than Bracken himself—and that his unusually dark coat was full and glossy, while he had about himself a calm that Bracken had never had at his age.

Yet he seemed to have suffered. There was a restlessness in his eyes, and searching, and Bracken knew that he had come back to seek answers to those questions that may be raised in a moment and yet not answered for a lifetime.

"Why do you believe in the Stone?" he asked Bracken after they had greeted each other and eaten food together.

"I can't give you a reason, Tryfan, or reasons, for that matter, and I know it won't be enough to tell you that

I simply do. I remember moles saying that to me once, and not being satisfied. But you know how Rebecca and I love each other . . ."

Tryfan nodded. He knew.

"Well, you know how that 'feels'—you can't give it reasons but you know it's there, as solid as rock. That's how my belief in the Stone feels as well. I know it's there. My belief in the Stone started when I began to see that really I'm nothing at all against the flow of life into which I was born and that will continue after I've gone. Yet I felt its wonder in *me,* not any other mole, and without me the flow of life is nothing, as well. This feeling gave me a sense of wonder which we say comes from the Stone and is part of what the Stone is. Each of us is nothing—and everything—and only believing in the Stone makes sense of it." Bracken sighed with frustration; he had never been much good at talking about it.

"Rebecca might be better than me at telling you about it, though I doubt it. You've missed your chance! She hardly says a thing these days!" Bracken laughed and ran down his tunnels toward Rebecca's, calling out her name. "Look who's here! Come and see!"

Rebecca looked at Tryfan for a long time, almost drinking in the sight of him before she smiled and came forward to touch him. "Where have you been?" she asked, in a way that said "There's no need to tell me, my love, I think I know."

The three of them talked for a long time, over several moledays, and they told him things they only half remembered, or had never spoken of before. Both of them felt it was right to tell him of the Seventh Stillstone and the wonder of what they had seen together, and he listened to them in awe, for as they spoke he felt he had been there before . . . and knew that he would go there again.

He asked about Uffington, and Boswell, and scribe-moles—just as he had when he was a pup. And one day, finally, he told them he wanted to be a scribemole like Boswell had been and that perhaps he should try to make his way to Uffington.

They nodded, though Bracken warned him that winter was not the time to travel so far and that if he was going to go, then there were things about travel, about fighting, about route-finding that perhaps he ought to teach him.

But Tryfan shook his head, and looking at them both where they crouched close together, said: "You've both taught me more than all those things, and surely the Stone will teach me the rest. The Stone will show me the way and it will protect me if I need to fight."

How big he was now, how strong and young, and Rebecca could not help smiling with love at the contrast he made with Bracken, whose face and sides were scarred with the fights he had been in but whose eyes held the clear light of peace Tryfan's did not yet have. But how hard-won had Bracken's peace been, and how much courage a mole needed to hold on to it! Rebecca knew that the times Bracken spent with the Stone were not always easy for him. They weren't for her.

It was at that moment, as Tryfan gazed on their love together, and perhaps with their words during their long conversations about the Stillstone still in his mind, that the first definite memories of the Midsummer Night, when he had got lost, began to stir in his mind.

Soon after, he went up to the Stone and crouched by it in silence as the cold evening darkened about him and wind stirred at the leaf litter, wet from afternoon drizzle, as those memories became clearer and he saw again, in his mind, the glimmer of the Stillstone. Then he began to talk to the Stone, seeking its guidance and help, as so many moles of so many generations had done before him. He trembled to think of Uffington and the difficulties of becoming a scribemole, feeling how unworthy and ignorant he was to crouch here before it and to seek for so much. He thought of Bracken and Rebecca, and of what Comfrey had told him about the wonderful things they had done, and then of the increasing simplicity of their lives so near each other back in the system from which both, at different times, had roamed so far.

"Why does a mole have to travel so far just to find himself back in the same place?" he asked the Stone. "Where should I turn?"

Light spots of rain began to mix in with the chill, blustery wind, pattering weakly here and there. How miserable the wood seemed. How desolate he felt. How much in need of help.

From the shadows around the Stone clearing, the eyes of an old mole watched him gently and smiled. Here he

was in Duncton Wood after all this time and what does
he find but a mole before the Stone, worrying himself as
he had done so many times and by so many different
Stones!

Boswell raised a paw and said a blessing on the mole,
but he did not step forward. There are times, many, many
times, when it is better not to speak or interrupt another
mole but to leave him to work out for himself what questions to ask. It was one of the things these great Stones
were for. But the answers! Ah—so simple, all so simple
at the end!

So Boswell watched Tryfan and blessed him, moving
out into the clearing only when Tryfan left it to make his
way down toward the slopes to find Comfrey.

Boswell crouched beside the Stone for a while. He had
no expectation at all in Duncton Wood—he had, indeed,
been personally reluctant to make the trek, for it was a
long, long way, and he was getting old. And everywhere
he went, moles sensed his holiness and flocked to him to
touch him and to ask his blessing and see him on his way.
It had been all he could do to stop a whole host of them
following him on his way here, but somehow he had managed to make them understand that this was a solitary
journey. Yet now he was here, how different it seemed
and how weak he felt—and how surprised young Tryfan
would have been had he known that moments after he
left the Stone, a mole from Uffington had crouched where
he had and asked himself just the same question he had
asked: "Why does a mole have to travel . . ." But Boswell's answer to himself was a smile and a sort of nod to
the Stone. Then he asked "Why have you sent me back
here, what do you want me to find?" And he smiled at
that, too: for the Stone gave its answers in its own way
and the best thing a mole can do is to trust that it will do
so.

"Now by the Stone's grace, I'll find Bracken and Rebecca and I hope that they've found themselves some
sense at last!" He laughed with pleasure to think of seeing them again, and knew—or suspected—where they
would be.

"Why did Tryfan come back?" Bracken wondered
aloud.

"Perhaps he needs to see and feel, once again, the love that made him," said Rebecca.

"What love?" asked Bracken. And Rebecca nudged him and he mock-fought her, and they giggled like their pups had, rolling about the floor, each feeling that they were playing with the most beautiful pup in the world.

It was Bracken who heard it. Laughter like their own, from down the tunnels toward where the entrance up to the Stone was. Laughter he knew and had heard so many, many times and thought he would never hear again; laughter he loved and that had him still as roots, eyes wide, and reaching a paw out to touch Rebecca to share with her his wonder. Laughter and polite burrowing noises, the kind of noise a courteous mole makes to announce his arrival.

"What mole is it?" asked Rebecca.

Bracken answered, not with a word but with a laugh and a shout, a cry of joy and a bounding forward from his burrow and out into the tunnel and the speaking of a name that made Rebecca gasp and smile at the pleasure she knew it would bring them all.

"Boswell! Boswell!" And so it was. His eyes bright as they had always been, his limping walk just as she remembered but his laughter more gentle, even more full of joy.

"Oh, Boswell," said Rebecca. And what brought tears to Boswell's eyes was not her nuzzling and love so much as the fact that it was him she loved, and always had, and not the fact that he was a scribemole.

"Rebecca!" he said, "Rebecca!" She was as beautiful as love. And then, turning to his old companion, he started "Bracken, Bracken . . ." And it was a long, long time before they stopped talking and touching.

What a time then came to Duncton Wood! What excitement! For when the news that a scribemole had come, and none other than Boswell himself, how they all came flocking to the tunnels of Bracken and Rebecca to see and to touch him!

What excitement there was in the preparations before Longest Night *that* December! How especially thorough were so many of the moles in cleaning out and tidying their burrows! How full of hope that Boswell would go their way in the ancient tunnels and crouch near their

burrows and talk softly to them as he answered their
questions!

Never was there so much song and chatter, laughter
and games, both on the surface and below it, as there
was that Longest Night. Never did moles revel so much
in the old tales, telling and retelling again the stories of
Ballagan and Vervain, the first moles, and Linden, the
first scribemole, and the stories of the Holy Books.

And, of course, it soon got out that there was a possibility, just a possibility, mind, that the Seventh Book,
the lost book, was, of all places, *here,* in Duncton!

"No!"

"Aye, that's what they do say . . . you don't think
somemole as important as Boswell himself, who's one of
the most important moles in the land now, would come
all this way just to say hello to his old friends and touch
the Stone. No! If you ask me, what they say about this
Book is right, and it *is* here."

Once this was established, it was a short step for the
Duncton moles to start debating where the Holy Book
was—and *that* wasn't hard to guess. Under the Stone,
that's where. Beyond that Chamber of Dark Sound where
no mole goes if he's sensible, because there are charms
and spells to protect it, and strange sounds that frighten
the fur off a mole! Oh, yes! You'd be daft to try it!

But being crazy never stops somemoles from trying,
and more than one sneaked his way past the Chamber of
Dark Sound and into the Chamber of Echoes in search of
the Book. Most got no farther than a snout's length before turning back from fear. But one did go farther and
got lost, and he was saved only because he had a friend
with him who had the sense to summon Bracken for help
—for everymole knew *he* knew the system like no other
mole. He had to go in and rescue the explorer, who got a
good many cuffs and curses on his way out—and a pat
or two of encouragement too, for Bracken knew better
than most what courage he must have needed, even if he
did get lost.

Tryfan himself did not meet Boswell until several moledays after Longest Night when Bracken introduced them
with joy—his most loved of friends and his son by
Rebecca. What more could he have asked?

Boswell gazed gently at Tryfan, recognizing him as the
mole he had seen on the night of his arrival by the Stone,

and knowing much about him—and guessing more—from what Rebecca had told him. He saw that Tryfan had about him qualities of both Rebecca and Bracken, and bore within himself a great deal of their love. And perhaps he knew that this was the mole he had come to find.

But if he did, he did not show it. Indeed, Bracken was rather surprised at Boswell's apparent lack of interest and his unusually brief replies to the questions Tryfan asked him.

"There's not something wrong with the lad, is there, Boswell?"

"No," said Boswell, shaking his head. "It's just that I'm afraid for him. You said he wants to be a scribemole. Well, you, of all moles, ought to know how hard that can be. So leave me to find out if he has the character he'll need."

Again and again Boswell avoided, or put off, or refused to answer the questions Tryfan repeatedly asked. "How can I become a scribemole?"

"Pray" was Boswell's succinct answer.

Replies like this made Tryfan upset and uncharacteristically uncertain of himself and led him to go to the Stone even more, or talk for hours to Comfrey, as he wondered what he had done to offend Boswell, who was so pleasant to everymole else.

Yet, for all Boswell's seeming refusal to talk, Tryfan began to see how much light there was in him and to follow him around at a distance, sometimes helping him with finding food if he needed it or showing him somewhere in the system that he wanted for some reason to see.

One day, and a very long day it was, Tryfan came to Boswell very nervously—his paws almost trembling with tension. Boswell pretended not to notice, but went about the tunnels as he often did, talking here, telling a tale there, saying blessings or sitting still.

"Boswell—" began Tryfan several times, but Boswell didn't seem to encourage him, and Tryfan did not quite have the courage to finish his question. It was all so unlike him to be nervous, but there was something so simple about Boswell that he felt unworthy to ask him anything.

But then finally, toward the end of the day, when Boswell was growing tired and Tryfan was afraid he would disappear into his burrow and the opportunity would be gone, he summoned up his courage and started: "Boswell?"

Boswell crouched down and gazed at him. But said nothing.

"Boswell . . . Bracken told me once that you had a master called Skeat. He said he took you to Uffington. He said you admired him more than anymole and that he taught you."

Boswell nodded: "And very hard he made it for me sometimes!" he said, remembering Skeat with an affectionate smile.

"Boswell?" began Tryfan again. "Could I . . . I mean would you . . . teach me? As a master?"

Boswell looked at Tryfan for a very long time, just as once, long ago, Rose had looked at Rebecca when she knew that Rebecca would become a healer and had wished she could take from her shoulders some of the suffering that that would bring.

"Yes," said Boswell simply. "Though always remember that it is not I who will teach you anything at all, but the Stone."

The relief on Tryfan's face was better than seeing the sun rise in the morning or the look on the face of a pup who rediscovers his mother after he thought she had been lost forever.

"Well . . . I mean . . . what must I do?" stumbled Tryfan.

"Learn to hear the silence of the Stone," said Boswell.

They sat in silence for a long time before Tryfan, emboldened by Boswell's agreement, asked another question. "Why have you come to Duncton?"

"I'm not sure," said Boswell. "I thought I knew. I thought it was to find the Seventh Book, and to take it and the Seventh Stillstone back to Uffington. But now I find I'm waiting for something, but I don't know what. The Stone will show us finally, as it always does."

This sense of waiting now began to grow stronger and stronger in Duncton. It was like the buildup to Longest Night, or Midsummer, only much slower and subtler, yet infinitely more powerful.

Winter set in and January grew colder, and then the snows and freezings of February came. The Duncton moles grew used to the presence of Boswell, who would often go among them, Tryfan in close attendance, and tell them tales of the Stone and of many legends which only scribemoles know.

There were only two things he would not do. One was show them how he scribed—"for that is something a mole must prepare himself for and these tunnels are no longer the place: you have far finer things here!" The second was that he refused to tell them about his travels with Bracken, or to talk about Rebecca—about whom he was often asked.

But apart from those things, there was nothing that Boswell would not do for other moles, or tell them—although the winter affected him badly and Tryfan had often to make sure that he rested and did not overexert himself.

Still the system waited, and as February advanced and the very first stirrings of still-distant spring were felt in the restlessness in the tunnels, there was the feeling that something, something, would happen soon in the system. Something.

Only two moles in Duncton seemed utterly unaffected by this strange tension—Bracken and Rebecca. They lived more and more quietly and joyously near each other and there were long periods during the winter when neither was seen. All moles respected their privacy and even Comfrey, always one to pop in and see Rebecca, stopped visiting them. Sometimes, though, Boswell would talk to them, indicating to Tryfan that it was best if he did so alone, and Boswell would be especially still and quiet for days afterward.

All around them the system they had loved, and to which both had contributed so much, seemed to be waiting; but they, who had once been so sensitive to its moods and changes, never seemed to notice.

49

THE bitter weather of February ran on into March until, after several days of more changeable weather, there came one of those dawns that takes a mole by surprise and revives the hope that there *can* be such a thing as spring. Life need not, after all, be permanently damp and cold.

Rebecca knew it even before dawn came and, leaving her burrow only moments after she awoke, went up onto the surface and over toward the Stone clearing. The wood was still dark when she arrived, but it began to lighten as she found a place to settle down as the mauves of the last of night gave way to the first greens and dark pinks of the dawn. On the wood floor, beneath the leafless beeches, the shadows were still black in the deepest root crevices of the trees, but already some of the leaf litter and fallen twigs and branches were catching the new day's light that came from the east.

Behind Rebecca, to the west, the last of the dark in the sky was going, revealing high scatters of cloud, now gray, then cream, finally white. As the sun started to rise and its first rays pierced through the wood, brightly catching the green, damp lichen on the beech trunks, or the warm brown of the few leaves that had never left the branch, or the dark green of a bramble leaf which somehow took no notice of last year's autumn, Rebecca stretched and sighed. The air was clear and fresh.

An early spring day! The kind that lulls some moles into thinking that there will not be any more winter! Rebecca knew days like that and that the best thing to do with them was to enjoy their every single moment and forget tomorrow. That could turn into winter again.

But for now there was some blue at last in the sky, and lovely white clouds to set it off, and sunrays that grew warmer by the second and made a mole feel it time to clear out a tunnel or two, or cast about for a mate.

Bracken stirred and stretched in his burrow. He wondered whether to go and find Rebecca, thinking pleasurably about it for a while before deciding not to, not yet. See what kind of day it is, find some food, groom a bit, listen to the wood. Anyway, these days it took him longer to wake up and he liked to stretch and get the aches out of his body.

Outside on the surface, he headed off toward the slopes as in the distance he heard the sound of carrion crows and pigeons, blackbird and robin, and what might have been a thrush. But it was the crows he heard most of all, for there is something about an early spring day in a leafless wood that makes their call carry. And it *was* a spring day!

Soon Bracken's paws felt as light as a pup's and he wanted to run, so he did. But as he started down the slopes, it occurred to him that it *would* be more fun running with Rebecca, so he went back to get her.

When he found that she wasn't in her burrow, he guessed where she would be and with a laugh, took a route by a tunnel that brought him out on the surface a little below the Stone clearing.

With what sighs and dragging steps did he pretend to pull himself up and into the clearing, with what absurdly mopish snout-lowering and tired weavings here and there did he approach Rebecca, who was crouched in spring sunshine near the Stone! She tried not to laugh, but couldn't help smiling as she first scented him and then heard him. So sad? Not possible, not him, not today.

With a hesitant cough he finally spoke. "I'm lost," he said. "How do I get back into the system?" And when she didn't answer immediately, he added: "I'm a Duncton mole, you know."

She turned to him, eyes alight with her love for him, and came right to him and caressed him on the shoulder, just as she had on the same day she herself had spoken those words near this spot, the first time they ever met. Did he remember them so well?

When her paw left his shoulder, he put his own paw there, breathless—still utterly moved by the way she touched him.

"Do you remember what I replied?" he asked.

"You said 'It's easy' and later you said 'I'll show you.' "

"And did I?" he wanted to know.

She nodded. "And I think I can remember the way you went," she said.

"Show me, Rebecca."

And she did. She ran past him, just as he had once run past her, though neither as fast as they had been then, and then by the ancient mole track down the slopes this way and that, down the hill, until he was quite out of breath following her.

"You stopped by a fallen oak branch because that was where the entrance into the system was, and I asked your name, because I didn't want you to go," remembered Rebecca.

He smiled, caressing her as she had him. The sun caught her fur, which was as thick and silvery-gray as it had ever been, though her face was lined now. But there was not a single line he would want taken away or changed, for she was the most beautiful mole he had ever known, just as she had always been.

"Rebecca?"

"Mmm?"

"I want to look at the wood again, the places where our lives were first made."

"I'm lost, my love, the wood's so changed. You'll have to show me . . ."

"I will," he whispered.

Then he ran past her and led her down on into the Old Wood, hesitating at a turn sometimes, stopping still with his head on one side, sometimes whispering to himself "No, it's not *this* way," until they were back in the heart of the Duncton Wood and she saw they were near clumps of anemones, not yet in full bloom, though one or two white buds were showing.

"Barrow Vale was somewhere here," he said.

He snouted over the surface, which was open and grassy with brambles at its far edges, until he found a spot where he started to burrow. Then he stopped when he was halfway into it and tried a bit farther on, suddenly disappearing.

She peered down after him into the tunnels of Barrow Vale, which no mole had visited since the plague and the fire.

"Do you want to look?" he called.

Most of it was still there, the tunnels and the burrowing just as they had been, though dusty and unkempt. Empty of sound and with a few scatterings of bones and many roof-falls. A dead place where Bracken had once been leader, after Rune and Mandrake.

They looked around it together, staying close to each other, and occasionally one or the other would say "Look!" and point to a place they both remembered, where so many things had happened. But the voices of the past did not come back, just a shimmer of memory that was gone forever almost the moment it returned.

"One day other moles will find this place and recolonize it—they might call it something else, or perhaps somemole will remember being told there was a place called Barrow Vale . . . but I doubt it. Why should moles remember?" wondered Bracken aloud.

They peered into the elder burrows, which were thick with soil dust and partially collapsed from a tree that had fallen onto the surface above, perhaps during the fire.

"It's strange," said Bracken, "but when I first explored the Ancient System it wasn't like this at all. It felt alive there, waiting for something. This all feels dead. It *is* dead."

"It never found the power of the Stone," whispered Rebecca.

"No," said Bracken. The tunnels and the burrows of Barrow Vale fell away from him, for nothing was more real, or ever had been, than this love he was in now.

"I love you," he said softly, and she felt he had never said it before to her: he said it with the wisdom of his whole life.

"If there was a mole you wanted to bring back, just for a moment here in Barrow Vale, who would it be?" he asked.

Image on image came to her as she thought of the question, and remembered the moles she had loved. Rose? Mekkins? Cairn? She hesitated for a moment and then said another name to herself—Mandrake? She shook her head.

"Hulver," she whispered finally.

"Why?" Bracken asked, surprised, for it wasn't a name he would have expected her to say.

"Because it was near here just before a June elder meeting that I met and talked to him and he mentioned your name. It was the first time a mole ever mentioned it to me."

"What did he say?" asked Bracken.

"Nothing much. But . . ." She stopped to think about

it. What *had* he said? It wasn't that he said anything, it
was that he had somehow shown her, without either of
them seeing it, that he loved Bracken. Now how did she
know that?

Suddenly Barrow Vale was over for them. The tunnels were just tunnels, any tunnels, and they had no
more need to see them. Bracken led the way out, back
into the spring sunshine to the surface, where Rebecca
started off toward the Marsh End.

"But it's miles!" said Bracken.

"Oh, listen!" said Rebecca excitedly, for from far away
toward the north they could hear the soft cawings of nesting rooks.

They didn't go into the tunnels at the Marsh End;
there was something too derelict about the place without
a mole like Mekkins to greet them. But they wandered
as far to the east as Curlew's tunnels, which they
couldn't find but whose position they could guess at
roughly. They remembered the fire, the flames, and then
they remembered the plague. They wondered whether
to go back west toward the pastures or perhaps . . . but
there was no need. The memories were falling away
from them. It was Rebecca Bracken wanted, and she
was there in the early spring warmth with him; it was
Bracken Rebecca wanted, and he is here, here with me
now, she thought.

"There'll be bluebells soon and daffodils after the
wood anemones."

"These trees will leaf again," said Bracken, "starting
with the chestnut over by the pastures."

"It's gone," said Rebecca. "Comfrey took me there
last summer."

"It'll come back. They'll all come back."

They crouched down near some tiny shoots of dog's
mercury; they found some food; they dozed in the sun;
morning slid into afternoon, as time started to matter no
more.

They were dancing together in the wood they loved,
but that, they knew, was no longer theirs. Its trees were
blurring, its plants waiting to delight the hearts of other
moles, its scents and sounds, lights and shades, darkness
and night and returning dawns were all one thing, Rebecca; Bracken my love. Were they tired? They didn't

feel it, not when they were so close and the woods and the lovely spring day were fading.

Were they old? Yes, yes, yes, my sweet love, by the Stone's grace; or young as two pups, if you like. Young enough to make love with a touch and caress and nuzzle of familiar paws and claws and fur that feel as exciting as the first spring day, whose light catches a mole's fur if she's in love, or he's in love to see it, Rebecca; Bracken, you came back; we're here now, my love.

There was a tremble of wind among the buds of a sapling sycamore; the sun was lost behind returning cloud. Evening was starting early and the light had the cast of a storm about it.

"Will you show me the way back?" whispered Rebecca.

"Will you help me?" he asked.

Bracken turned to the south toward the top of the hill where the Stone stood. He went slowly and calmly without one moment of hesitation or doubt, climbing steadily upward toward the slopes, and then up them over toward the top of the hill. Sometimes he turned around for a moment to check that his Rebecca was close behind, but really he would have known if she weren't there, for they moved steadily together, like a single mole. Sometimes they rested, and there was no need to hurry.

Up on the slopes they met Comfrey, who began to say a greeting but stopped when he saw them. There was something about them that didn't need words. Below them, in the Old Wood where they must have been, he heard the wind begin to sway what trees there were and scurry at the undergrowth.

"Rebecca?" began Comfrey finally.

But she only looked at him and touched him for a moment as if to say it was all right, he didn't need her now, it was all right, and as they passed him by, he thought how old they looked and how full of joy.

"Rebecca" he whispered, after them. And he trembled, because he knew he would never see her again.

I'll go to the Stone, he told himself, that's the best thing. I'll go there now. But he hesitated, going back down to his tunnels first and tidying up a bit, and sniffing a herb or two. Then, when he felt he was ready, he went.

Bracken and Rebecca climbed on steadily up to where the hill leveled off among the beech trees, the leaf litter between the trees rustling with the strengthening storm wind all about them. As the sky began to darken, brambles that had glowed with the early morning sun now rasped against each other restlessly. They turned toward the Stone clearing without pause, then across it to the great beech whose roots encircled the Stone, among which Bracken had spent his first night near the Stone with Hulver.

Branches had fallen from the tree since then, and some had rotted. Among the gnarled convolutions of the roots he found a pool of rainwater and drank from it. Rebecca looked into it, but didn't drink.

The wild sky seemed suddenly to be below them, in the reflection of the water's surface, with a rising of interlacing dark branches and the twists and turns of the ancient tree trunk.

Bracken looked about them, thinking that apart from Rebecca's words of love there was never, ever any sound he loved more than the sound of the wind in beech leaves. Well, it was too early in the spring for beech leaves, but Rebecca was there near him.

She watched him turn away from the tree roots, his old fur now the color of the lighter parts of their bark, and she followed him back out of the clearing without looking at the Stone. A single rush of wind caught the trees over near the wood's edge and then ran high through the trees and into the branches of the tree by the Stone as they found an entrance to their tunnels and went down it.

But neither paused or hesitated. They turned back toward the ancient tunnels as one, taking the route Bracken himself had burrowed long before and that led, finally, to the circular chamber around the Chamber of Echoes. They were old now, but moved with the grace of tall grass before a full wind and with the simple purpose of two mallards rising over a desolate marsh.

From beyond the Chamber of Echoes they could hear the massive sounds of the beech roots, sliding and trembling with the tensions of the mounting wind over the wood, but they turned without thought toward it, in among the confusing tunnels that were no longer confusing but simple as trust itself. No need to remember a way from the past or a way for the future; they could see a glimmer of light ahead of them, growing brighter as they went toward it, showing them the way forward.

Then, when they were beyond the Echoes and into the Chamber of Roots themselves, it seemed to them both that the terrible sound of the roots began to die away before them and another sound grew in power and strength —the sound of the Stone's silence to where the light was leading them.

They ran on toward it, not even noticing the huge roots above them that pulled and plunged and yet seemed to make way for them.

On through they traveled, the light ever brighter, their fur growing whiter with it, until they were past the roots and into the tunnels that led through the old roots of beech near the Stone, around whose hollow center they pattered, their paws almost dancing, as they got nearer and nearer the glimmering of white light that came from the Seventh Stillstone.

Then it was there and they were back, under the buried part of the Stone which rose above them and tilted down ahead of them as they ran on toward its center to the glimmering whiteness of the Stillstone itself.

Sighing and roaring among the dry grass of Uffington, pulling at tunnel entrances, winding down in scurries into the burrows itself, a wind prefaced a storm. Such a long winter, such a long time, such a long wait since Boswell had left them; so many prayers said, so many whispered hopes.

Below the hill the wind twisted and blew around the Blowing Stone, which began to moan softly with it as the grass at its base swayed back and forth in the lengthening darkness. A light kind of darkness, the kind a mole finds on some stormy nights in March when the days are beginning to lengthen. The wind grew grimmer and stronger, battering now against the Stone, pushing at it, taking it and shaking at it; until the moans ceased, the humming stopped and the Blowing Stone at last let out a great long vibrant note as the wind finally conquered it.

Every scribemole heard it and all stopped to listen. Waiting.

Then a second note came, more powerful than the first, and then a third, clear and strong, vibrating down into the Holy Burrows themselves and shaking chalk dust off some of the walls.

As the third note came, Medlar began moving up

through the tunnels toward the surface, while from all over Uffington moles were moving, trying not to run but starting to all the same, moving up to the surface as the fourth note of the Stone sounded. While the chosen moles who were still alive, those who had sung the secret song before, wondered if theirs was to be the honor, theirs now the moment, as the fifth great note came from the Stone, and moles snouted out in awe onto the grassy surface of Uffington Hill, facing the northeast where the Stone stood, listening through the wind that tore at their fur and the grass around them.

A sixth note came, stronger than any had ever heard, and in Medlar's eyes a look of certainty began to form, a look of joy. He began to say a blessing on his moles, on all moles, his words rising into the wind. As he did so, there came at last a seventh great note from the Stone. As its sound carried about them the winds suddenly died and the grass fell still. Then quietly, here and there, each one of the chosen moles there began to sing the sacred song, its sound faint and disjointed at first, a scatter of song across an ancient hill. Until its rhythm and melody began to become established as other moles began to whisper the words and then to start singing them—young and old, novices and scribes—until they were all singing the ancient song of celebration and exaltation which told that the Seventh Book was coming to Uffington and that the Seventh Stillstone had been found.

Boswell finally and slowly turned in his burrow and looked across it to Tryfan. The angry wind of a storm on the surface sounded about them.

"Go to the Stone now," he said.

Tryfan did not want to leave Boswell, who had been weak and restless all day, refusing to eat his food and saying hardly a word. Tryfan had watched over him troubled, knowing that something was changing and that what they had waited for for so long was here; troubled by not knowing what it was.

"Where are you going?" he asked Boswell. "What are you going to do?"

Boswell went over to him. "Have trust in the Stone, which will tell *you* what to do," he said. "I must go to the center of the Ancient System where the Stillstone lies and to where Bracken and Rebecca have at last found the

silence to return. Pray that the Stone will give me
strength, pray that it will send the help I need. Trust the
Stone."

Tryfan watched Boswell turning down toward the Ancient System to where the Chamber of Echoes was, and
then turned himself up onto the surface, unhappy to let
Boswell out of his sight. He looked so frail as he entered
those great tunnels by himself, as if the wind that was
growing in strength by the minute would blow him away.

Above Tryfan the beeches were now swaying massively in the wind, and the surface of the Ancient System
reverberated to the creakings and knocking of their
branches against each other.

The noise was even louder by the Stone, and the wind
so wild that it was some time before he saw that Comfrey
was crouched before it. He was weeping.

"What is it?" asked Tryfan. "What has happened?"

"I d–don't know," said Comfrey. "I'm sure I saw
Bracken and Rebecca going to the Stone just like Rose
the Healer went to the Stone when I was a pup."

"What do you mean?" asked Tryfan.

"I d–don't know," said Comfrey. "I'm not sure."

Tryfan stared up at the Stone, the only still thing on a
wild and stormy night. He was in awe of it, and afraid
now for Bracken, for Rebecca and for Boswell.

He repeated Boswell's words to him over and over
again—"Trust the Stone, trust it—" and then he began to
pray, his words lost in the wind as Comfrey sat waiting
beside him and the trees began to sway back and forth
and against each other and there were sounds of falling
branches and a whining and howling as the wind was
whipped and cut by the leafless branches in the terrible
darkness about them.

The tree by the Stone pulled and stressed above them,
even its massive trunk beginning to move before the
power of the wind, so that the ground beneath them began to shake and shudder with the stress of the roots pulling through it.

In among the roots of the beech by the Stone, the surface of the pool of rainwater caught among them, where
Bracken had taken a drink earlier that day, began to
shake with the straining of the tree in the mounting storm.

Boswell approached the Chamber of Echoes slowly,

feeling the power of the storm above shaking the tunnel walls all around him. The sounds from the Chamber of Roots were so massive that they drowned out the patter of his paws on the tunnel's floor but he went calmly, now at peace with himself.

When he stood on the threshold of the Chamber of Roots, which was in violent and dangerous motion everywhere, with crashing of chalk subsoil from the roof above and tearing and crunching across the floor as root fissures heaved and widened before him in clouds of dust and soil, he felt nothing but peace.

The light of the Stillstone led him through the roots safely and beyond to the buried part of the Stone itself.

Down into the depths beneath the Stone he went, the roots of the tree now pulling and straining about him, some twisting under windstress off the tunnel floor and then whipping or crashing down again, while others, enwrapped about the Stone, were pulling at it, pushing it under and around so that the very Stone itself was beginning to shake and move, the tilted end now rising higher above Boswell and then sinking ominously down toward him.

Deep under its lowest part crouched Bracken and Rebecca, the light of the Stillstone filling their fur with brightness and turning everything it touched into white.

As he went forward to this most sacred of places, Boswell sought to see what he had looked for for so long: the Seventh Book. The Stillstone was there, but where was the Book, where was it hidden? His eyes cast about into the shadows caused by the Stillstone among the shifting roots and into the recesses of the burrow in which Bracken and Rebecca crouched together.

Rebecca turned to him and looked as if she expected to see him there with them both, as if she could read his thoughts. There was no need for words, even if words could have been heard in the increasing sounds of rootstress and strain as the very world they were in seemed to be swaying and pulling and collapsing, and they were the only still things in it.

She looked at him as he at her and knew he was wondering where the Book was. Don't you know? she seemed to be saying without saying a word. Oh, Boswell, don't you know?

Bracken turned to him, a look of unutterable joy about

him as the Stillstone glimmered and shone brighter about
them and cast its light onto Boswell's fur. The Book's
here, you have it, you have it, Bracken was thinking, and
Boswell had no need to hear the words; he knew them.
You have it, it is yours already.

The light from the Stillstone shone fully now on Boswell, whose fur seemed as white before it as that of
Bracken and Rebecca.

The Stone above them began to move more and more,
pulled and pushed by the roots of the tree that, high
above where Comfrey and Tryfan waited and prayed in
the storm, was caught more and more strongly by the
wind, and its aged roots began a battle through the night
against the storm's might.

Now the Stone moved on the surface. A gap between
its base and surrounding soil appeared that widened and
narrowed to the swaying of the tree above it. The ground
began to tremor and Comfrey began to pray aloud.

Among the roots beneath the great Stone in the silence
created by love, Bracken turned to the Stillstone and took
it up. Its brightness did not fade nor did its glimmering
cease as it had when he had touched it once before. Now
its light traveled into his paw and from there to his body
and over his fur and into his eyes, and where his other
paw touched Rebecca's its light traveled on until both
seemed aflame with the Stillstone's light and there were
no words, they were beyond words as Bracken joyfully
passed the Stillstone to Boswell of Uffington.

As Boswell took the Stillstone he saw that its light
stayed on with Bracken and Rebecca, for it was in them
now and shining from them as their love had done, growing stronger and stronger every moment. Above them, the
Duncton Stone's tilted base began to rise and fall, and
fall farther, and rise and fall farther again, and Boswell
could only see them vaguely now, in the light of their
love where they seemed to be dancing before him, laughing and dancing and singing "You have the Book, you
have the Book" as the Stone was pulled at by the tree
roots out on the surface tilting first toward Uffington and
then away from it up toward the storm-filled sky, back
and forth as the beech tree began to lose its battle with
the wind, its roots growing weaker and weaker as the
Stone swayed and pulled itself more and more upright,
more toward the sky.

But underground Boswell could only see the white light of the Stillstone and feel the joy of holding it as he watched, or felt, the dance in its light of Bracken and Rebecca. Oh, he wanted to join them, to dance with them, to cast off the weight of his old body as they were doing and dance where his crippled paw would not slow him, nor his age, nor the cold, nor the wind that was straightening the Stone and making it fall blissfully upon them.

Did he want any more to find the Seventh Book? Did it matter when the dance in the light was such joy? As he started forward toward them he saw, from the brightness of where Bracken and Rebecca had been crouched together so peacefully, Rebecca's smile coming toward him and love and trust for him in her eyes. He heard her voice with Bracken's as they said, or called, or sang "Not yet, not yet, go back beloved, for yours is the task of the Seventh Stillstone, we give you the Book Boswell beloved, beloved mole who has loved us, we give you the Book that you may inscribe it, the great Book of Silence, the lost and the last Book, for you who have lived it are its author-protector scribe and creator and the Stillstone will give you the strength for the scribing beloved Boswell, White Mole of Uffington."

Boswell reached a paw forward to touch his Rebecca, to feel the fur of Bracken, for he wanted to join them and not take this burden, for who was he before their light or before the Stone? "Help me," he called out. "Help me!"

And the light from the Stillstone traveled into his paw and from there to his body and over his fur until it shone from his eyes so that he had the courage to turn away from their light into the sound of the wind and the cold, and feel again the weight of his frail body. But he knew that their love was within him and that he would scribe the great Book of Silence. The lost and the last Book.

Above him the great mass of the Stone's base began finally to sink down upon him and behind him upon Bracken and Rebecca, roots breaking about him as it crashed down through them, but holding the Stillstone he ran from under the Stone's base as his old limbs raced to escape the cracking roots and shattering soil; he heard the thump of the Stone behind him and he began to turn back up the tunnel to the hollow of the tree, which swayed and shook before him as he picked his way around its edge, limping and hobbling with great difficulty because of the Stillstone, trying to get away as the tree began to pull out its roots beneath the Stone and start to sway and crash and begin to fall.

As the tree began its final descent he called out "Tryfan, Tryfan, help me. Now you can help me. Tryfan, yours is the power."

Mole upon mole had come to the circular chamber around the Chamber of Echoes, from which the fiercest sounds came, drawn by a sense that a great moment of change was taking place in the system, fearful of the sounds and awed by the majesty.

They chattered and stamped their paws with fear, for somemole had said he had seen Bracken and Rebecca go into the chamber and that Boswell was there as well and all moles could sense that danger and great joy were there together.

"Should we go in, should we help, can we do anything?" they whispered and muttered to each other, looking fearfully at the entrances to the chamber, not one there with the courage to enter in. Some braver moles wandered from entrance to entrance, passing by all seven of them still unable to find the strength they needed to risk going in. Most just stared.

But all of them agreed afterward on one strange and mysterious fact. As they watched and trembled they seemed to hear the singing of a sacred song whose words they knew but which they had, until then, forgotten. And all began to sing it, a song of hope and exaltation that spoke of the coming of a White Mole.

Then suddenly, as their song gained strength, Tryfan entered the circular tunnel, the only completely calm and silent one among them. He stared for a moment at one of the entrances into the Chamber of Echoes by which so many of the moles had been crouched hesitating. He was strong and purposeful and, moving without pause or apparent hesitation, he boldly entered into the echoing tunnel from whose darkness the sounds of stressing destruction were coming. He did it so naturally that, seeing him, a mole might have thought he had been that way before. . . .

The strange thing is that afterward each mole in the circular tunnel swore, and would have sworn by the

Stone, that it was the entrance that they were standing near by which Tryfan entered—which is impossible, for how could Tryfan or anymole enter all seven entrances at once?

As he disappeared from sight the song fell away from them and they waited in terrible fear as the root-pulling and stressing reached a climax of destructive sound. Yet although many of them wanted to run away to a place of safety not one moved, for they sensed they were witnessing a moment of profound change, a moment of wonder.

And then back out of the tunnel Tryfan came, half carrying and half pulling old Boswell of Uffington, who was covered in dust and grime and barely conscious from the power of the forces that had so nearly overwhelmed him. And who carried, clasped against his old chest, a small pebble or stone that looked as if it had nothing special about it to make a mole want to carry it out from such destruction.

Up on the surface by the Stone, where he had watched the storm continue into the first light of a wild, gray dawn, Comfrey saw the beech by the Stone finally sway back and back, and back and down, as its crown and branches and trunk crashed through the surrounding trees, and one by one its roots tore themselves from the soil around the Stone, which swayed and rocked on the edge of the crater they had left.

Then, as he watched, the Stone slipped back and down into where the roots had been until it stood firm and upright, no longer tilted by the roots toward Uffington, but upright as it must originally have been, with its great sides and top thrusting straight up into the sky.

But even though the crashing tree thundered and shook through all the tunnels of the Ancient System and the walls of the circular tunnel where the moles had gathered cracked and fissured by the shock, that was not what the moles noticed. What made them gasp in awe, and sing the sacred song that all moles thought they had forgotten, was that they saw that Boswell was changed. In the time he had been caught in the violence of the Chamber of Roots and seen the Stillstone's light pass into Bracken and Rebecca, he had become a Holy Mole surrounded by silent love; and they saw that his fur had turned completely white. The White Mole had come. They sang in exaltation and reached out to touch him.

50

DUNCTON Wood stood quiet, bedraggled by the storm as last drops of rain dripped onto the damp leaf mold and the sky cleared to the west. Every tree, every bush, every plant seemed battered and shaken and there was a silent, almost wounded, air about the wood, as if a great mole were resting after a very long fight.

Boswell crouched with Tryfan and Comfrey by the Stone.

The other moles had finally gone back to their burrows, reluctant to leave the wonder and love they found in the presence of Boswell, beloved Boswell, Blessed Boswell, the White Mole of Uffington. Now only Tryfan and Comfrey remained, one who was in deep awe of Boswell and the other, Comfrey, who accepted him matter-of-factly, just as he had accepted Rebecca's return to the system and her final departure with Bracken into the Stone where all moles must go.

"So you found the Seventh Stillstone but not the Book?" said Comfrey, looking at the smooth, flinty stone that Boswell had placed on the ground before them; it did not look special at all.

Boswell smiled wryly. "No, I know where the Book is, Comfrey," he said simply. "I have to scribe it myself."

"Oh," said Comfrey, "yes, of course." He should have thought of that. Bracken and Rebecca and Boswell had made the book together, so it couldn't have been scribed before. A mole can't scribe a book until it's ready—it's probably just like picking herbs.

Boswell had told them both something of what had happened, and Comfrey had understood that finally Rebecca was safe and so he could stop worrying about her. She was all right now.

He looked at Boswell and thought what a contrast he made to Tryfan—one frail and white, the other strong and black-furred. He smiled, too, because he saw that Tryfan watched with love and care over Boswell's every move, as if he were afraid that a puff of wind would blow Boswell away. Well, one day he would know Boswell better than that.

"I will pray for your safe journey," said Comfrey finally. "But then there's not much harm can come to you, Boswell, with Tryfan by your side."

Tryfan snouted about to size up the hour and the weather and decided that the time had come when they ought to leave. But he did not need to say a word of what he felt to Boswell, because Boswell knew.

"It would be an honor to have your prayers, Comfrey," said Boswell, looking up for one last time at the Stone that now stood upright and towering over the base of the fallen tree. "If a mole could scribe on stone, I would scribe their names on it," he said.

Then, with a last touch and final farewell, they left Comfrey by the Stone and set off across the clearing, out through the wood to the pastures and then off across them to the west toward Uffington. Comfrey whispered a prayer after them and a journey blessing and crouched wondering why he felt such a sense of relief. The air in the wood was so clear after the rain, it smelled so good, and he was at the start of a new spring in a system that had pride and memories and so much hope.

He could teach some of the youngsters the rituals and show them how they should be done. And if he didn't remember all the words, it didn't matter, because true words come from a mole's heart, not his memory.

He looked back into the direction toward Uffington and whispered again "May they return home safeguarded." Then he laughed, a rare thing for Comfrey. He liked its sound so much that he laughed aloud again, with relief and happiness.

Off to the west, on the pastures, Tryfan and Boswell wound their way downhill. The trees of Duncton rose behind them at the top of the hill, the pasture dropped away below, and Tryfan asked "How long will it take?"

"Not too long," said Boswell.

"Will you tell me about the things that happened to you and Bracken, and to Rebecca? All the things they would never talk about? All the stories?"

"Yes, yes," said Boswell, smiling.

"Will I become a scribemole?" asked Tryfan.

Boswell stopped and touched him gently. "You've begun already," he said, "just as I did, without ever knowing it."

But Tryfan found this hard to believe, even though Boswell himself said it.

"Tell me about them," he asked, and Boswell sensed that it was right to start doing so, for surely no mole held more of their joint spirit than Tryfan. And so Boswell began to tell the story, from the beginning, drawing on the memories of what Bracken and Rebecca had told him. Stories that gave him joy as well.

While Tryfan, after taking a final look back to Duncton Wood, which was now almost too far even to scent, moved protectively nearer to Boswell, whom he would see safely home to Uffington whatever dangers or trials they had to face. He felt strong and powerful, with the Stone of Duncton behind him and the White Mole who carried the Seventh Stillstone at his side and who would scribe the Seventh Book, the Book of Silence, telling him stories that he had so long wanted to hear.

As evening fell and they settled down into the first stage of their long journey, Tryfan thought to himself that if he ever did become a scribemole, then perhaps, with the Stone's grace, he might one day record all that Boswell was beginning now to tell him of the story of Bracken and his beloved Rebecca.

AUTHOR'S NOTE

The moles of Duncton Wood are *Talpa europaea*, the most widespread species of the mole family *(Talpidae)*, whose members occur in Europe, Asia and the Americas. *Talpa europaea* is similar to *Scalopus aquaticus* or the Eastern mole, one of the most widely distributed species in North America.

Moles are just under 6 inches long when mature (males are 5¾ inches, females 5¼ inches) and have a long, cylindrical body whose head merges straight into the trunk. They have large spadelike forelegs that are as broad as they are long. Each has five powerful claws or talons which, combined with powerful shoulder muscles, give moles a remarkable ability for rapid burrowing through soil.

Their snouts are pink and hairless and extremely sensitive to both smell and touch and to changes in humidity and temperature. Although some species of moles are blind—their vestigial eyes being covered with skin— *Talpa europaea* has eyes, though they are no more than minute black dots on the facial skin and are normally found only with difficulty beneath the fur. They appear to be of little use except, perhaps, to distinguish between light and dark. But moles' sense of vibration is very acute and this combined with hearing and the ability to smell, equips them to live very successfully in their normal subterranean environment. They also have an erect tail that is almost certainly a sensory organ—maintaining contact with tunnel roofs rather like, as one authority puts it, "the overhead pick-up of an electric train."

Mole fur, once prized for outer garments, is characteristically dark gray. It has no single direction of lay (unlike, for example, a cat's), and this gives a mole the advantage of being able to move in any direction in a narrow tunnel without difficulty.

Although many people associate moles with open grassland—principally because that is where molehills are most easily seen—they live in a very wide range of habitats, from woodland through to marginal coastal areas. The only two conditions in which they are not found is heavy peat and pure sand, where their invertebrate food (mainly worms) is almost impossible to find. One reason they are so rarely observed in woodland is that their molehills are obscured by leaf mold and wood litter, but this is probably their most common habitat.

Their tunnel systems are complex and extensive (about 350 square yards), though the shape is variable and reflects local conditions. They frequently create tunnels at different levels, perhaps using the deeper tunnels (up to 39 inches deep) in colder conditions. The familiar molehills are outcastings of burrowed soil from tunnels.

Moles appear to be strongly territorial: they will attack to kill if confined together. Laboratory conditions are nevertheless not the same as real life and there is now much evidence that, though defensive of their own territory, they will share communal tunnels with other moles. It also seems possible that moles are more willing to share at least some territory in woodland habitats than in pastureland—or, put another way, moles have less defined territories in woodland. Moles are frequently seen on the surface and there are well-confirmed reports of them being seen in amicable company with each other.

Like many other creatures, moles tend to mate and have their young in spring and early summer. A small proportion of females appear to have second litters in summer, and there are isolated reports of pregnant females being found in the autumn. Gestation takes about four weeks and the average litter size is four, the young being born in underground nests carefully lined with leaf litter. They are weaned after another four weeks or so and begin to leave the mother to find their own territory after six or seven weeks. At this period, when the young are still too weak to burrow deeply or find their own territory, mortality from such predators as owls is high.

The vocal range of moles varies from a characteristic

squeaking and soft purring to alarm sounds of shriller twittering.

From this account it will be clear that the moles of Duncton Wood make various departures from the normal lifestyle of "real" moles: they are probably more sociable; the journeys Bracken, Rebecca and Boswell make are abnormal; and the autumn births in the story are probably rare in real life. But then, Duncton Wood is a story and allegory rather than a doctoral thesis, and the realities it is about are different from those that preoccupy a zoologist.

A special problem in the narration relates to the mole's power of vision. The simple fact is that moles cannot see very far and some maintain that they cannot see at all. They "see" with their snouts and through their senses of smell and hearing. Because *we* see through our eyes, our language is richer in its vocabulary of vision. So, while we have a vocabulary of vision, a *mole* ought to be given a rich vocabulary of smell and hearing, the senses they use most of all. But, logical though this is, it would not work to write a book in which characters say such things as "I smell what you mean" when humans would say "I see what you mean." For this reason I have applied the human vocabulary of vision to the moles' senses of smell, vibration and hearing.

Moles live for up to five years and perhaps very occasionally a little longer—though the majority die younger. This makes a single year in the life of a mole equivalent to about fourteen human years. On this basis I have arbitrarily made a moleyear equivalent to a human month.

Which leaves just two issues for the really pernickety: First, how do moles read? The books in the libraries of the Holy Burrows are "written"—*scribed* is the precise word—in molebraille and a mole reads them with his snout.

Ah, but can moles talk? Of course, though the chatterings and twitterings they make in real life are impossible for humans to interpret. But anyone who has had the pleasure of being close to creatures—whether quietly in their own home or in the deep peace of the country when no other sounds are heard—will know that they talk in many different ways. And certainly *moles* talk, just like anymole else.

'About the Author

Formerly a journalist for the *London Daily Mail*, William Horwood grew up in Oxfordshire, England, where the forests resemble those of Duncton Wood. For eighteen months prior to writing his novel, Horwood returned to those forests, living as an ascetic in a one-room shack, immersing himself in the world of animals, wildflowers, and the seasons. To create his characters, however, Horwood relied on human inspiration.

Horwood, 34, is now at work on his second novel. It is set well outside the realm of Duncton Wood.

The national bestseller by
the author of THE WOMEN'S ROOM,
now in paperback.

MARILYN FRENCH

THE
BLEEDING
HEART

A
LOVE STORY
FOR AND ABOUT
ADULTS

28896/$3.50

An extraordinary novel
about the devastating power
of marriage—and the unexpected
possibility of love.

ℬℬ BALLANTINE BOOKS